TARZAN: THE NOVELS

VOLUME II

SECOND EDITION

TARZAN

THE NOVELS

BEING THE ADVENTURES OF
JOHN CLAYTON, LORD GREYSTOKE

AS RECOUNTED BY

EDGAR RICE BURROUGHS

VOLUME II

SECOND EDITION

FOUR NOVELS

TARZAN AND THE JEWELS OF OPAR

TARZAN THE UNTAMED

TARZAN THE TERRIBLE

TARZAN AND THE GOLDEN LION

EX FONTIBUS CO.

The novels reproduced in this volume were published as follows:

Tarzan & the Jewels of Opar. All-Story Cavalier November–Dec. 1916.   Book 1918.
Tarzan the Untamed.   *Redbook*, Mar.–Aug. 1919; *All-Story* Mar.–Apr. 1920.   Book 1920.
Tarzan the Terrible.   *Argosy All-Story* Feb.–Mar. 1921   Book 1921.
Tarzan & The Golden Lion. Argosy All-Story Dec. 1922   Book 1923.

Visit us

EX FONTIBUS
COMPANY

CONTACT@EXFONTIBUS.COM
EXFONTIBUSCOMPANY@GMAIL.COM
HTTP://WWW.EXFONTIBUS.COM
HTTP://WWW.FACEBOOK.COM/EXFONT

CONTENTS

ABOUT THE AUTHOR

EDGAR Rice Burroughs (September 1, 1875–March 19, 1950) was born in Chicago, Illinois, the son of a Civil War veteran Major George Tyler Burroughs (1833–1913). He graduated in 1895 from the Michigan Military Academy after attending the Phillips Academy (Andover, Mass.). After his aspirations to West Point were disappointed when he failed the entrance exam, he enlisted in the Army 7th U.S. Cavalry (Fort Grant, Arizona Territory). These hopes, too, were frustrated by a heart irregularity for which he was discharged in 1897.

Moving from job to job, he took a position at his father's firm in 1899 after spending some time on an Idaho ranch. A year later, he married Emma Hulbert (1876–1944), his childhood sweetheart. He departed from the firm in 1904, and again worked irregularly until 1911 found him as a wholesaler of pencil-sharpeners. Burroughs and Emma now had two children, Joan (1908–1972) and Hulbert (1909–91). (Joan would later marry Tarzan film actor James Pierce). During the periods of inactivity that came with his job, Burroughs began reading many pulp fiction magazines. Of his musings during that time time, he later wrote:

[It came to me that] if people were paid for writing rot such as I read in some of those magazines, that I could write stories just as rotten. As a matter of fact, although I had never written a story, I knew absolutely that I could write stories just as entertaining and probably a whole lot more so than any I chanced to read in those magazines.[*]

Thus it was at this time that he began to write fiction.

Burroughs' first story, "Under the Moons of Mars," was published serially in the February to July 1912 issues of *The All-Story*. His output was so rapid that, he had completed two new novels, including *Tarzan of the Apes*, by the time that "Moons" had completed publication. *Tarzan*, beignning in October of 1912, was his most enduringly famous invention.

Friedrich Nietzsche's book *The Birth of Tragedy* (1872) had introduced into the zeitgeist the notion that the rationally ordered edifice of culture and civilization was often but a veneer thinly covering the elemental and even savage impulses whereby humanity is one with nature. Many late nineteenth and early twentieth century novelists developed the idea of a return to nature and the nobility of uncivlized man. On ground thus prepared, *Tarzan* was a cultural sensation when introduced. Tarzan himself is savage but rarely cruel. He kills for food, for safety, and for revenge, but while he takes pleasure in such activities his pleasure is in struggle and vitality rather than in the infliction of death. Thus where his nobility is not so Nietzschean, it is that of the American frontier, tinged with the Christian inheritance.

Burroughs has been received as a cultural rather than a literary giant. In an interview with the *Paris Review*, Ray Bradbury said that "Edgar Rice Burroughs never would have looked upon himself as a social mover and shaker with social obligations. But as it turns out—and I love to say it because it upsets everyone terribly—Burroughs is probably the most influential writer in the entire history of the world." Bradbury continued that "By giving romance and adventure to a whole generation of boys, Burroughs caused them to go out and decide to become special."[†] While *Tarzan of the Apes* met with some critical success, however, subsequent books in the series received a cooler reception. The characters are often said to be two-dimensional, the dialogue wooden, and the formulaic storytelling devices (such as excessive reliance on coincidence) strain credulity. Rudyard Kipling owned that Burroughs wrote *Tarzan of the Apes* just so that he could "find out how bad a book he could write and get away with it." Gore Vidal, still critical, yet acknowledged a certain admiration for the book when he wrote in *Esquire*:

> [While] Burroughs is innocent of literature and cannot reproduce human speech, he does have a gift very few writers of any kind possess: he can describe action vividly. . . . Because it is so hard, the craftier contemporary novelists usually prefer to tell their stories in the first person, which is simply writing dialogue. In character, as it were, the

---

[*] Burroughs, Edgar Rice (October 27, 1929). "How I Wrote the Tarzan Stories." *The Washington Post*, *The New York World* (Sunday supplement). ERBZine.com.

[†] *The Paris Review*. Accessed May 26, 2015. http://www.theparisreview.org/interviews/6012/the-art-of-fiction-no-203-ray-bradbury

writer settles for an impression of what happened rather than creating the sense of a happening. Tarzan in action is excellent.[‡]

In the present day, Burroughs's depiction of native Africans has come to be seen as problematic. While the honorable Waziri tribe is depicted as intelligent and virtuous, the cannibal tribe of Mbonga in *Tarzan of the Apes* is uniformly cruel, superstitious, and savage—although some of this savagery is explained as owed to their harsh treatment at the hands of whites. Later books in the series depict African characters as distinct individuals without a stereotyped moral character. The only racial group or cultural group that comes in for consistent criticism, ironically, is the white European aristocrat. Burroughs was not above reproach in his own life; the community of Tarzana that grew up around his ranch was a "sundown" town, permitting no blacks as residents. Without at all condoning his views, we can say that Burroughs reflected his times and culture. Perhaps we find him at his best when, in *Tarzan of the Apes*, he has Tarzan declare to some men on safari:

> [E]ach of you are right in your judgment of the characteristics of the lions—[that] you have met. But one might as well judge all blacks by the fellow who ran amuck last week, or decide that all whites are cowards because one has met a cowardly white. There is as much individuality among the lower orders, gentlemen, as there is among ourselves.[§]

Despite his stature in literature of cultural history and criticism, Burroughs is the subject of but few mongraphs. The most scholarly are Erling Holtsmark's two books: *Tarzan and Tradition* and *Edgar Rice Burroughs*; and Stan Galloway's *The Teenage Tarzan: A Literary Analysis of Edgar Rice Burroughs' Jungle Tales of Tarzan*; and Richard Lupoff's two books: *Master of Adventure: Edgar Rice Burroughs* and *Barsoom: Edgar Rice Burroughs and the Martian Vision*. An enjoyable popular contribution is Philip José Farmer's book *Tarzan Alive: A Definitive Biography of Lord Greystoke*, which offers an enchanting "biography" of the ape man as if he were a real person. Among Burroughs's living descendants are the American film director Wes Anderson, a great-grandson; and the American actor Reid Markel, a great-great- grandson. Let us now close this brief introduction, the sooner to journey with Tarzan into the primeval forest.

[‡] "Tarzan Revisited." Accessed May 26, 2015. http://www.esquire.com/news-politics/a4599/tarzan-revisited-1263/
[§] The "lower orders" here mentioned are the animals.

TARZAN AND THE JEWELS OF OPAR

CHAPTER I—BELGIAN AND ARAB

Lieutenant Albert Werper had only the prestige of the name he had dishonored to thank for his narrow escape from being cashiered. At first he had been humbly thankful, too, that they had sent him to this Godforsaken Congo post instead of court-martialing him, as he had so justly deserved; but now six months of the monotony, the frightful isolation and the loneliness had wrought a change. The young man brooded continually over his fate. His days were filled with morbid self-pity, which eventually engendered in his weak and vacillating mind a hatred for those who had sent him here—for the very men he had at first inwardly thanked for saving him from the ignominy of degradation.

He regretted the gay life of Brussels as he never had regretted the sins which had snatched him from that gayest of capitals, and as the days passed he came to center his resentment upon the representative in Congo land of the authority which had exiled him—his captain and immediate superior.

This officer was a cold, taciturn man, inspiring little love in those directly beneath him, yet respected and feared by the black soldiers of his little command.

Werper was accustomed to sit for hours glaring at his superior as the two sat upon the veranda of their common quarters, smoking their evening cigarets in a silence which neither seemed desirous of breaking. The senseless hatred of the lieutenant grew at last into a form of mania. The captain's natural taciturnity he distorted into a studied attempt to insult him because of his past shortcomings. He imagined that his superior held him in contempt, and so he chafed and fumed inwardly until one evening his madness became suddenly homicidal. He fingered the butt of the revolver at his hip, his eyes narrowed and his brows contracted. At last he spoke.

"You have insulted me for the last time!" he cried, springing to his feet. "I am an officer and a gentleman, and I shall put up with it no longer without an accounting from you, you pig."

The captain, an expression of surprise upon his features, turned toward his junior. He had seen men before with the jungle madness upon them—the madness of solitude and unrestrained brooding, and perhaps a touch of fever.

He rose and extended his hand to lay it upon the other's shoulder. Quiet words of counsel were upon his lips; but they were never spoken. Werper construed his superior's action into an attempt to close with him. His revolver was on a level with the captain's heart, and the latter had taken but a step when Werper pulled the trigger. Without a moan the man sank to the rough planking of the veranda, and as he fell the mists that had clouded Werper's brain lifted, so that he saw himself and the deed that he had done in the same light that those who must judge him would see them.

He heard excited exclamations from the quarters of the soldiers and he heard men running in his direction. They would seize him, and if they didn't kill him they would take him down the Congo to a point where a properly ordered military tribunal would do so just as effectively, though in a more regular manner.

Werper had no desire to die. Never before had he so yearned for life as in this moment that he had so effectively forfeited his right to live. The men were nearing him. What was he to do? He glanced about as though searching for the tangible form of a legitimate excuse for his crime; but he could find only the body of the man he had so causelessly shot down.

In despair, he turned and fled from the oncoming soldiery. Across the compound he ran, his revolver still clutched tightly in his hand. At the gates a sentry halted him. Werper did not pause to parley or to exert the influence of his commission—he merely raised his weapon and shot down the innocent black. A moment later the fugitive had torn open the gates and vanished into the blackness of the jungle, but not before he had transferred the rifle and ammunition belts of the dead sentry to his own person.

All that night Werper fled farther and farther into the heart of the wilderness. Now and again the voice of a lion brought him to a listening halt; but with cocked and ready rifle he pushed ahead again, more fearful of the human huntsmen in his rear than of the wild carnivora ahead.

Dawn came at last, but still the man plodded on. All sense of hunger and fatigue were lost in the terrors of contemplated capture. He could think only of escape. He dared not pause to rest or eat until there was no further danger from pursuit, and so he staggered on until at last he fell and could rise no more. How long he had fled he did not know, or try to know. When he could flee no longer the knowledge that he had reached his limit was hidden from him in the unconsciousness of utter exhaustion.

And thus it was that Achmet Zek, the Arab, found him. Achmet's followers were for running a spear through the body of their hereditary enemy; but Achmet would have it otherwise. First he would question the Belgian. It were easier to question a man first and kill him afterward, than kill him first and then question him.

So he had Lieutenant Albert Werper carried to his own tent, and there slaves administered wine and food in small quantities until at last the prisoner regained consciousness. As he opened his eyes he saw the faces of strange black men about him, and just outside the tent the figure of an Arab. Nowhere was the uniform of his soldiers to be seen.

The Arab turned and seeing the open eyes of the prisoner upon him, entered the tent.

"I am Achmet Zek," he announced. "Who are you, and what were you doing in my country? Where are your soldiers?"

Achmet Zek! Werper's eyes went wide, and his heart sank. He was in the clutches of the most notorious of cut-throats—a hater of all Europeans, especially those who wore the uniform of Belgium. For years the military forces of Belgian Congo had waged a fruitless war upon this man and his followers—a war in which quarter had never been asked nor expected by either side.

But presently in the very hatred of the man for Belgians, Werper saw a faint ray of hope for himself. He, too, was an outcast and an outlaw. So far, at least, they possessed a common interest, and Werper decided to play upon it for all that it might yield.

"I have heard of you," he replied, "and was searching for you. My people have turned against me. I hate them. Even now their soldiers are searching for me, to kill me. I knew that you would protect me from them, for you, too, hate them. In return I will take service with you. I am a trained soldier. I can fight, and your enemies are my enemies."

Achmet Zek eyed the European in silence. In his mind he revolved many thoughts, chief among which was that the unbeliever lied. Of course there was the chance that he did not lie, and if he told the truth then his proposition was one well worthy of consideration, since fighting men were never over plentiful—especially white men with the training and knowledge of military matters that a European officer must possess.

Achmet Zek scowled and Werper's heart sank; but Werper did not know Achmet Zek, who was quite apt to scowl where another would smile, and smile where another would scowl.

"And if you have lied to me," said Achmet Zek, "I will kill you at any time. What return, other than your life, do you expect for your services?"

"My keep only, at first," replied Werper. "Later, if I am worth more, we can easily reach an understanding." Werper's only desire at the moment was to preserve his life. And so the agreement was reached and Lieutenant Albert Werper became a member of the ivory and slave raiding band of the notorious Achmet Zek.

For months the renegade Belgian rode with the savage raider. He fought with a savage abandon, and a vicious cruelty fully equal to that of his fellow desperadoes. Achmet Zek watched his recruit with eagle eye, and with a growing satisfaction which finally found expression in a greater confidence in the man, and resulted in an increased independence of action for Werper.

Achmet Zek took the Belgian into his confidence to a great extent, and at last unfolded to him a pet scheme which the Arab had long fostered, but which he never had found an opportunity to effect. With the aid of a European, however, the thing might be easily accomplished. He sounded Werper.

"You have heard of the man men call Tarzan?" he asked.

Werper nodded. "I have heard of him; but I do not know him."

"But for him we might carry on our 'trading' in safety and with great profit," continued the Arab. "For years he has fought us, driving us from the richest part of the country, harassing us, and arming the natives that they may repel us when we come to 'trade.' He is very rich. If we could find some way to make him pay us many pieces of gold we should not only be avenged upon him; but repaid for much that he has prevented us from winning from the natives under his protection."

Werper withdrew a cigaret from a jeweled case and lighted it.

"And you have a plan to make him pay?" he asked.

"He has a wife," replied Achmet Zek, "whom men say is very beautiful. She would bring a great price farther north, if we found it too difficult to collect ransom money from this Tarzan."

Werper bent his head in thought. Achmet Zek stood awaiting his reply. What good remained in Albert Werper revolted at the thought of selling a white woman into the slavery and degradation of a Moslem harem. He looked up at Achmet Zek. He saw the Arab's eyes narrow, and he guessed that the other had sensed his antagonism to the plan. What would it mean to Werper to refuse? His life lay in the hands of this semi-barbarian, who esteemed the life of an unbeliever less highly than that of a dog. Werper loved life. What was this woman to him, anyway?

She was a European, doubtless, a member of organized society. He was an outcast. The hand of every white man was against him. She was his natural enemy, and if he refused to lend himself to her undoing, Achmet Zek would have him killed.

"You hesitate," murmured the Arab.

"I was but weighing the chances of success," lied Werper, "and my reward. As a European I can gain admittance to their home and table. You have no other with you who could do so much. The risk will be great. I should be well paid, Achmet Zek."

A smile of relief passed over the raider's face.

"Well said, Werper," and Achmet Zek slapped his lieutenant upon the shoulder. "You should be well paid and you shall. Now let us sit together and plan how best the thing may be done," and the two men squatted upon a soft rug beneath the faded silks of Achmet's once gorgeous tent, and talked together in low voices well into the night. Both were tall and bearded, and the exposure to sun and wind had given an almost Arab hue to the European's complexion. In every detail of dress, too, he copied the fashions of his chief, so that outwardly he was as much an Arab as the other. It was late when he arose and retired to his own tent.

The following day Werper spent in overhauling his Belgian uniform, removing from it every vestige of evidence that might indicate its military purposes. From a heterogeneous collection of loot, Achmet Zek procured a pith helmet and a European saddle, and from his black slaves and followers a party of porters, askaris and tent boys to make up a modest safari for a big game hunter. At the head of this party Werper set out from camp.

CHAPTER II—ON THE ROAD TO OPAR

It was two weeks later that John Clayton, Lord Greystoke, riding in from a tour of inspection of his vast African estate, glimpsed the head of a column of men crossing the plain that lay between his bungalow and the forest to the north and west.

He reined in his horse and watched the little party as it emerged from a concealing swale. His keen eyes caught the reflection of the sun upon the white helmet of a mounted man, and with the conviction that a wandering European hunter was seeking his hospitality, he wheeled his mount and rode slowly forward to meet the newcomer.

A half hour later he was mounting the steps leading to the veranda of his bungalow, and introducing M. Jules Frecoult to Lady Greystoke.

"I was completely lost," M. Frecoult was explaining. "My head man had never before been in this part of the country and the guides who were to have accompanied me from the last village we passed knew even less of the country than we. They finally deserted us two days since. I am very fortunate indeed to have stumbled so providentially upon succor. I do not know what I should have done, had I not found you."

It was decided that Frecoult and his party should remain several days, or until they were thoroughly rested, when Lord Greystoke would furnish guides to lead them safely back into country with which Frecoult's head man was supposedly familiar.

In his guise of a French gentleman of leisure, Werper found little difficulty in deceiving his host and in ingratiating himself with both Tarzan and Jane Clayton; but the longer he remained the less hopeful he became of an easy accomplishment of his designs.

Lady Greystoke never rode alone at any great distance from the bungalow, and the savage loyalty of the ferocious Waziri warriors who formed a great part of Tarzan's followers seemed to preclude the possibility of a successful attempt at forcible abduction, or of the bribery of the Waziri themselves.

A week passed, and Werper was no nearer the fulfillment of his plan, in so far as he could judge, than upon the day of his arrival, but at that very moment something occurred which gave him renewed hope and set his mind upon an even greater reward than a woman's ransom.

A runner had arrived at the bungalow with the weekly mail, and Lord Greystoke had spent the afternoon in his study reading and answering letters. At dinner he seemed distraught, and early in the evening he excused himself and retired, Lady Greystoke following him very soon after. Werper, sitting upon the veranda, could hear their voices in earnest discussion, and having realized that something of unusual moment was afoot, he quietly rose from his chair, and keeping well in the shadow of the shrubbery growing profusely about the bungalow, made his silent way to a point beneath the window of the room in which his host and hostess slept.

Here he listened, and not without result, for almost the first words he overheard filled him with excitement. Lady Greystoke was speaking as Werper came within hearing.

"I always feared for the stability of the company," she was saying; "but it seems incredible that they should have failed for so enormous a sum—unless there has been some dishonest manipulation."

"That is what I suspect," replied Tarzan; "but whatever the cause, the fact remains that I have lost everything, and there is nothing for it but to return to Opar and get more."

"Oh, John," cried Lady Greystoke, and Werper could feel the shudder through her voice, "is there no other way? I cannot bear to think of you returning to that frightful city. I would rather live in poverty always than to have you risk the hideous dangers of Opar."

"You need have no fear," replied Tarzan, laughing. "I am pretty well able to take care of myself, and were I not, the Waziri who will accompany me will see that no harm befalls me."

"They ran away from Opar once, and left you to your fate," she reminded him.

"They will not do it again," he answered. "They were very much ashamed of themselves, and were coming back when I met them."

"But there must be some other way," insisted the woman.

"There is no other way half so easy to obtain another fortune, as to go to the treasure vaults of Opar and bring it away," he replied. "I shall be very careful, Jane, and the chances are that the inhabitants of Opar will never know that I have been there again and despoiled them of another portion of the treasure, the very existence of which they are as ignorant of as they would be of its value."

The finality in his tone seemed to assure Lady Greystoke that further argument was futile, and so she abandoned the subject.

Werper remained, listening, for a short time, and then, confident that he had overheard all that was necessary and fearing discovery, returned to the veranda, where he smoked numerous cigarets in rapid succession before retiring.

The following morning at breakfast, Werper announced his intention of making an early departure, and asked Tarzan's permission to hunt big game in the Waziri country on his way out—permission which Lord Greystoke readily granted.

The Belgian consumed two days in completing his preparations, but finally got away with his safari, accompanied by a single Waziri guide whom Lord Greystoke had loaned him. The party made but a single short march when Werper simulated illness, and announced his intention of remaining where he was until he had fully recovered. As they had gone but a short distance from the Greystoke bungalow, Werper dismissed the Waziri guide, telling the warrior that he would send for him when he was able to proceed. The Waziri gone, the Belgian summoned one of Achmet Zek's trusted blacks to his tent, and dispatched him to watch for the departure of Tarzan, returning immediately to advise Werper of the event and the direction taken by the Englishman.

The Belgian did not have long to wait, for the following day his emissary returned with word that Tarzan and a party of fifty Waziri warriors had set out toward the southeast early in the morning.

Werper called his head man to him, after writing a long letter to Achmet Zek. This letter he handed to the head man.

"Send a runner at once to Achmet Zek with this," he instructed the head man. "Remain here in camp awaiting further instructions from him or from me. If any come from the bungalow of the Englishman, tell them that I am very ill within my tent and can see no one. Now, give me six porters and six askaris—the strongest and bravest of the safari—and I will march after the Englishman and discover where his gold is hidden."

And so it was that as Tarzan, stripped to the loin cloth and armed after the primitive fashion he best loved, led his loyal Waziri toward the dead city of Opar, Werper, the renegade, haunted his trail through the long, hot days, and camped close behind him by night.

And as they marched, Achmet Zek rode with his entire following southward toward the Greystoke farm.

To Tarzan of the Apes the expedition was in the nature of a holiday outing. His civilization was at best but an outward veneer which he gladly peeled off with his uncomfortable European clothes whenever any reasonable pretext presented itself. It was a woman's love which kept Tarzan even to the semblance of civilization—a condition for which familiarity had bred contempt. He hated the shams and the hypocrisies of it and with the clear vision of an unspoiled mind he had penetrated to the rotten core of the heart of the thing—the cowardly greed for peace and ease and the safe-guarding of property rights. That the fine things of life—art, music and literature—had thriven upon such enervating ideals he strenuously denied, insisting, rather, that they had endured in spite of civilization.

"Show me the fat, opulent coward," he was wont to say, "who ever originated a beautiful ideal. In the clash of arms, in the battle for survival, amid hunger and death and danger, in the face of God as manifested in the display of Nature's most terrific forces, is born all that is finest and best in the human heart and mind."

And so Tarzan always came back to Nature in the spirit of a lover keeping a long deferred tryst after a period behind prison walls. His Waziri, at marrow, were more civilized than he. They cooked their meat before they ate it and they shunned many articles of food as unclean that Tarzan had eaten with gusto all his life and so insidious is the virus of hypocrisy that even the stalwart ape-man hesitated to give rein to his natural longings before them. He ate burnt flesh when he would have preferred it raw and unspoiled, and he brought down game with arrow or spear when he would far rather have leaped upon it from ambush and sunk his strong teeth in its jugular; but at last the call of the milk of the savage mother that had suckled him in infancy rose to an insistent demand—he craved the hot blood of a fresh kill and his muscles yearned to pit themselves against the savage jungle in the battle for existence that had been his sole birthright for the first twenty years of his life.

CHAPTER III—THE CALL OF THE JUNGLE

Moved by these vague yet all-powerful urgings the ape-man lay awake one night in the little thorn boma that protected, in a way, his party from the depredations of the great carnivora of the jungle. A single warrior stood sleepy guard beside the fire that yellow eyes out of the darkness beyond the camp made imperative. The moans and the coughing of the big cats mingled with the myriad noises of the lesser denizens of the jungle to fan the savage flame in the breast of this savage English lord. He tossed upon his bed of grasses, sleepless, for an hour and then he rose, noiseless as a wraith, and while the Waziri's back was turned, vaulted the boma wall in the face of the flaming eyes, swung silently into a great tree and was gone.

For a time in sheer exuberance of animal spirit he raced swiftly through the middle terrace, swinging perilously across wide spans from one jungle giant to the next, and then he clambered upward to the swaying, lesser boughs of the upper terrace where the moon shone full upon him and the air was stirred by little breezes and death lurked ready in each frail branch. Here he paused and raised his face to Goro, the moon. With uplifted arm he stood, the cry of the bull ape quivering upon his lips, yet he remained silent lest he arouse his faithful Waziri who were all too familiar with the hideous challenge of their master.

And then he went on more slowly and with greater stealth and caution, for now Tarzan of the Apes was seeking a kill. Down to the ground he came in the utter blackness of the close-set boles and the overhanging verdure of the jungle. He stooped from time to time and put his nose close to earth. He sought and found a wide game trail and at last his nostrils were rewarded with the scent of the fresh spoor of Bara, the deer. Tarzan's mouth watered and a low growl escaped his patrician lips. Sloughed from him was the last vestige of artificial caste—once again he was the primeval hunter—the first man—the highest caste type of the human race. Up wind he followed the elusive spoor with a sense of perception so transcending that of ordinary man as to be inconceivable to us. Through counter currents of the heavy stench of meat eaters he traced the trail of Bara; the sweet and cloying stink of Horta, the boar, could not drown his quarry's scent—the permeating, mellow musk of the deer's foot.

Presently the body scent of the deer told Tarzan that his prey was close at hand. It sent him into the trees again—into the lower terrace where he could watch the ground below and catch with ears and nose the first intimation of actual contact with his quarry. Nor was it long before the ape-man came upon Bara standing alert at the edge of a moon-bathed clearing. Noiselessly Tarzan crept through the trees until he was directly over the deer. In the ape-man's right hand was the long hunting knife of his father and in his heart the blood lust of the carnivore. Just for an instant he poised above the unsuspecting Bara and then he launched himself downward upon the sleek back. The impact of his weight carried the deer to its knees and before the animal could regain its feet the knife had found its heart. As Tarzan rose upon the body of his kill to scream forth his hideous victory cry into the face of the moon the wind carried to his nostrils something which froze him to statuesque immobility and silence. His savage eyes blazed into the direction from which the wind had borne down the warning to him and a moment later the grasses at one side of the clearing parted and Numa, the lion, strode majestically into view. His yellow-green eyes were fastened upon Tarzan as he halted just within the clearing and glared enviously at the successful hunter, for Numa had had no luck this night.

From the lips of the ape-man broke a rumbling growl of warning. Numa answered but he did not advance. Instead he stood waving his tail gently to and fro, and presently Tarzan squatted upon his kill and cut a generous portion from a hind quarter. Numa eyed him with growing resentment and rage as, between mouthfuls, the ape-man growled out his savage warnings. Now this particular lion had never before come in contact with Tarzan of the Apes and he was much mystified. Here was the appearance and the scent of a man-thing and Numa had tasted of human flesh and learned that though not the most palatable it was certainly by far the easiest to secure, yet there was that in the bestial growls of the strange creature which reminded him of formidable antagonists and gave him pause, while his hunger and the odor of the hot flesh of Bara goaded him almost to madness. Always Tarzan watched him, guessing what was passing in the little brain of the carnivore and well it was that he did watch him, for at last Numa could stand it no longer. His tail shot suddenly erect and at the same instant the wary ape-man, knowing all too well what the signal portended, grasped the remainder of the deer's hind quarter between his teeth and leaped into a nearby tree as Numa charged him with all the speed and a sufficient semblance of the weight of an express train.

Tarzan's retreat was no indication that he felt fear. Jungle life is ordered along different lines than ours and different standards prevail. Had Tarzan been famished he would, doubtless, have stood his ground and met the lion's charge. He had done the thing before upon more than one occasion, just as in the past he had charged lions himself; but tonight he was far from famished and in the hind quarter he had carried off with him was more raw flesh than he could eat; yet it was with no equanimity that he looked down upon Numa rending the flesh of Tarzan's kill. The presumption of this strange Numa must be punished! And forthwith Tarzan set out to make life miserable for the big cat. Close by were many trees bearing large, hard fruits and to one of these the ape-man swung with the agility of a squirrel. Then commenced a bombardment which brought forth earthshaking roars from Numa. One after another as rapidly as he could gather and hurl them, Tarzan pelted the hard fruit down upon the lion. It was impossible for the tawny cat to eat under that hail of missiles—he could but roar and growl and dodge and eventually he was driven away entirely from the carcass of Bara, the deer. He went roaring and resentful; but in the very center of the clearing his voice was suddenly hushed and Tarzan saw the great head lower and flatten out, the body crouch and the long tail quiver, as the beast slunk cautiously toward the trees upon the opposite side.

Immediately Tarzan was alert. He lifted his head and sniffed the slow, jungle breeze. What was it that had attracted Numa's attention and taken him soft-footed and silent away from the scene of his discomfiture? Just as the lion disappeared among the trees beyond the clearing Tarzan caught upon the down-coming wind the explanation of his new interest—the scent spoor of man was wafted strongly to the sensitive nostrils. Caching the remainder of the deer's hind quarter in the crotch of a tree the ape-man wiped his greasy palms upon his naked thighs and swung off in pursuit of Numa. A broad, well-beaten elephant path led into the forest from the clearing.

Parallel to this slunk Numa, while above him Tarzan moved through the trees, the shadow of a wraith. The savage cat and the savage man saw Numa's quarry almost simultaneously, though both had known before it came within the vision of their eyes that it was a black man. Their sensitive nostrils had told them this much and Tarzan's had told him that the scent spoor was that of a stranger—old and a male, for race and sex and age each has its own distinctive scent. It was an old man that made his way alone through the gloomy jungle, a wrinkled, dried up, little old man hideously scarred and tattooed and strangely garbed, with the skin of a hyena about his shoulders and the dried head mounted upon his grey pate. Tarzan recognized the ear-marks of the witch-doctor and awaited Numa's charge with a feeling of pleasurable anticipation, for the ape-man had no love for witch-doctors; but in the instant that Numa did charge, the white man suddenly recalled that the lion had stolen his kill a few minutes before and that revenge is sweet.

The first intimation the black man had that he was in danger was the crash of twigs as Numa charged through the bushes into the game trail not twenty yards behind him. Then he turned to see a huge, black-maned lion racing toward him and even as he turned, Numa seized him. At the same instant the ape-man dropped from an overhanging limb full upon the lion's back and as he alighted he plunged his knife into the tawny side behind the left shoulder, tangled the fingers of his right hand in the long mane, buried his teeth in Numa's neck and wound his powerful legs about the beast's torso. With a roar of pain and rage, Numa reared up and fell backward upon the ape-man; but still the mighty man-thing clung to his hold and repeatedly the long knife plunged rapidly into his side. Over and over rolled Numa, the lion, clawing and biting at the air, roaring and growling horribly in savage attempt to reach the thing upon its back. More than once was Tarzan almost brushed from his hold. He was battered and bruised and covered with blood from Numa and dirt from the trail, yet not for an instant did he lessen the ferocity of his mad attack nor his grim hold upon the back of his antagonist. To have loosened for an instant his grip there, would have been to bring him within reach of those tearing talons or rending fangs, and have ended forever the grim career of this jungle-bred English lord. Where he had fallen beneath the spring of the lion the witch-doctor lay, torn and bleeding, unable to drag himself away and watched the terrific battle between these two lords of the jungle. His sunken eyes glittered and his wrinkled lips moved over toothless gums as he mumbled weird incantations to the demons of his cult.

For a time he felt no doubt as to the outcome—the strange white man must certainly succumb to terrible Simba—whoever heard of a lone man armed only with a knife slaying so mighty a beast! Yet presently the old black man's eyes went wider and he commenced to have his doubts and misgivings. What wonderful sort of creature was this that battled with Simba and held his own despite the mighty muscles of the king of beasts and slowly there dawned in those sunken eyes, gleaming so brightly from the scarred and wrinkled face, the light of a dawning recollection. Gropingly backward into the past reached the fingers of memory, until at last they seized upon a faint picture, faded and yellow with the passing years. It was the picture of a lithe, white-skinned youth swinging through the trees in company with a band of huge apes, and the old eyes blinked and a great fear came into them—the superstitious fear of one who believes in ghosts and spirits and demons.

And came the time once more when the witch-doctor no longer doubted the outcome of the duel, yet his first judgment was reversed, for now he knew that the jungle god would slay Simba and the old black was even more terrified of his own impending fate at the hands of the victor than he had been by the sure and sudden death which the triumphant lion would have meted out to him. He saw the lion weaken from loss of blood. He saw the mighty limbs tremble and stagger and at last he saw the beast sink down to rise no more. He saw the forest god or demon rise from the vanquished foe, and placing a foot upon the still quivering carcass, raise his face to the moon and bay out a hideous cry that froze the ebbing blood in the veins of the witch-doctor.

CHAPTER IV—PROPHECY AND FULFILLMENT

Then Tarzan turned his attention to the man. He had not slain Numa to save the Negro—he had merely done it in revenge upon the lion; but now that he saw the old man lying helpless and dying before him something akin to pity touched his savage heart. In his youth he would have slain the witch-doctor without the slightest compunction; but civilization had had its softening effect upon him even as it does upon the nations and races which it touches, though it had not yet gone far enough with Tarzan to render him either cowardly or effeminate. He saw an old man suffering and dying, and he stooped and felt of his wounds and stanched the flow of blood.

"Who are you?" asked the old man in a trembling voice.

"I am Tarzan—Tarzan of the Apes," replied the ape-man and not without a greater touch of pride than he would have said, "I am John Clayton, Lord Greystoke."

The witch-doctor shook convulsively and closed his eyes. When he opened them again there was in them a resignation to whatever horrible fate awaited him at the hands of this feared demon of the woods. "Why do you not kill me?" he asked.

"Why should I kill you?" inquired Tarzan. "You have not harmed me, and anyway you are already dying. Numa, the lion, has killed you."

"You would not kill me?" Surprise and incredulity were in the tones of the quavering old voice.

"I would save you if I could," replied Tarzan, "but that cannot be done. Why did you think I would kill you?"

For a moment the old man was silent. When he spoke it was evidently after some little effort to muster his courage. "I knew you of old," he said, "when you ranged the jungle in the country of Mbonga, the chief. I was already a witch-doctor when you slew Kulonga and the others, and when you robbed our huts and our poison pot. At first I did not remember you; but at last I did—the white-skinned ape that lived with the hairy apes and made life miserable in the village of Mbonga, the chief—the forest god—the Munango-Keewati for whom we set food outside our gates and who came and ate it. Tell me before I die—are you man or devil?"

Tarzan laughed. "I am a man," he said.

The old fellow sighed and shook his head. "You have tried to save me from Simba," he said. "For that I shall reward you. I am a great witch-doctor. Listen to me, white man! I see bad days ahead of you. It is writ in my own blood which I have smeared upon my palm. A god greater even than you will rise up and strike you down. Turn back, Munango-Keewati! Turn back before it is too late. Danger lies ahead of you and danger lurks behind; but greater is the danger before. I see—" He paused and drew a long, gasping breath. Then he crumpled into a little, wrinkled heap and died. Tarzan wondered what else he had seen.

It was very late when the ape-man re-entered the boma and lay down among his black warriors. None had seen him go and none saw him return. He thought about the warning of the old witch-doctor before he fell asleep and he thought of it again after he awoke; but he did not turn back for he was unafraid, though had he known what lay in store for one he loved most in all the world he would have flown through the trees to her side and allowed the gold of Opar to remain forever hidden in its forgotten storehouse.

Behind him that morning another white man pondered something he had heard during the night and very nearly did he give up his project and turn back upon his trail. It was Werper, the murderer, who in the still of the night had heard far away upon the trail ahead of him a sound that had filled his cowardly soul with terror—a sound such as he never before had heard in all his life, nor dreamed that such a frightful thing could emanate from the lungs of a God-created creature. He had heard the victory cry of the bull ape as Tarzan had screamed it forth into the face of Goro, the moon, and he had trembled then and hidden his face; and now in the broad light of a new day he trembled again as he recalled it, and would have turned back from the nameless danger the echo of that frightful sound seemed to portend, had he not stood in even greater fear of Achmet Zek, his master.

And so Tarzan of the Apes forged steadily ahead toward Opar's ruined ramparts and behind him slunk Werper, jackal-like, and only God knew what lay in store for each.

At the edge of the desolate valley, overlooking the golden domes and minarets of Opar, Tarzan halted. By night he would go alone to the treasure vault, reconnoitering, for he had determined that caution should mark his every move upon this expedition.

With the coming of night he set forth, and Werper, who had scaled the cliffs alone behind the ape-man's party, and hidden through the day among the rough boulders of the mountain top, slunk stealthily after him. The boulder-strewn plain between the valley's edge and the mighty granite kopje, outside the city's walls, where lay the entrance to the passage-way leading to the treasure vault, gave the Belgian ample cover as he followed Tarzan toward Opar.

He saw the giant ape-man swing himself nimbly up the face of the great rock. Werper, clawing fearfully during the perilous ascent, sweating in terror, almost palsied by fear, but spurred on by avarice, following upward, until at last he stood upon the summit of the rocky hill.

Tarzan was nowhere in sight. For a time Werper hid behind one of the lesser boulders that were scattered over the top of the hill, but, seeing or hearing nothing of the Englishman, he crept from his place of concealment to undertake a systematic search of his surroundings, in the hope that he might discover the location of the treasure in ample time to make his escape before Tarzan returned, for it was the Belgian's desire merely to locate the gold, that, after Tarzan had departed, he might come in safety with his followers and carry away as much as he could transport.

He found the narrow cleft leading downward into the heart of the kopje along well-worn, granite steps. He advanced quite to the dark mouth of the tunnel into which the runway disappeared; but here he halted, fearing to enter, lest he meet Tarzan returning.

The ape-man, far ahead of him, groped his way along the rocky passage, until he came to the ancient wooden door. A moment later he stood within the treasure chamber, where, ages since, long-dead hands had ranged the lofty rows of precious ingots for the rulers of that great continent which now lies submerged beneath the waters of the Atlantic.

No sound broke the stillness of the subterranean vault. There was no evidence that another had discovered the forgotten wealth since last the ape-man had visited its hiding place.

Satisfied, Tarzan turned and retraced his steps toward the summit of the kopje. Werper, from the concealment of a jutting, granite shoulder, watched him pass up from the shadows of the stairway and advance toward the edge of the hill which faced the rim of the valley where the Waziri awaited the signal of their master. Then Werper, slipping stealthily from his hiding place, dropped into the somber darkness of the entrance and disappeared.

Tarzan, halting upon the kopje's edge, raised his voice in the thunderous roar of a lion. Twice, at regular intervals, he repeated the call, standing in attentive silence for several minutes after the echoes of the third call had died away. And then, from far across the valley, faintly, came an answering roar—once, twice, thrice. Basuli, the Waziri chieftain, had heard and replied.

Tarzan again made his way toward the treasure vault, knowing that in a few hours his blacks would be with him, ready to bear away another fortune in the strangely shaped, golden ingots of Opar. In the meantime he would carry as much of the precious metal to the summit of the kopje as he could.

Six trips he made in the five hours before Basuli reached the kopje, and at the end of that time he had transported forty-eight ingots to the edge of the great boulder, carrying upon each trip a load which might well have staggered two ordinary men, yet his giant frame showed no evidence of fatigue, as he helped to raise his ebon warriors to the hill top with the rope that had been brought for the purpose.

Six times he had returned to the treasure chamber, and six times Werper, the Belgian, had cowered in the black shadows at the far end of the long vault. Once again came the ape-man, and this time there came with him fifty fighting men, turning porters for love of the only creature in the world who might command of their fierce and haughty natures such menial service. Fifty-two more ingots passed out of the vaults, making the total of one hundred which Tarzan intended taking away with him.

As the last of the Waziri filed from the chamber, Tarzan turned back for a last glimpse of the fabulous wealth upon which his two inroads had made no appreciable impression. Before he extinguished the single candle he had brought with him for the purpose, and the flickering light of which had cast the first alleviating rays into the impenetrable darkness of the buried chamber, that it had known for the countless ages since it had lain forgotten of man, Tarzan's mind reverted to that first occasion upon which he had entered the treasure vault, coming upon it by chance as he fled from the pits beneath the temple, where he had been hidden by La, the High Priestess of the Sun Worshipers.

He recalled the scene within the temple when he had lain stretched upon the sacrificial altar, while La, with high-raised dagger, stood above him, and the rows of priests and priestesses awaited, in the ecstatic hysteria of fanaticism, the first gush of their victim's warm blood, that they might fill their golden goblets and drink to the glory of their Flaming God.

The brutal and bloody interruption by Tha, the mad priest, passed vividly before the ape-man's recollective eyes, the flight of the votaries before the insane blood lust of the hideous creature, the brutal attack upon La, and his own part of the grim tragedy when he had battled with the infuriated Oparian and left him dead at the feet of the priestess he would have profaned.

This and much more passed through Tarzan's memory as he stood gazing at the long tiers of dull-yellow metal. He wondered if La still ruled the temples of the ruined city whose crumbling walls rose upon the very foundations about him. Had she finally been forced into a union with one of her grotesque priests? It seemed a hideous fate, indeed, for one so beautiful. With a shake of his head, Tarzan stepped to the flickering candle, extinguished its feeble rays and turned toward the exit.

Behind him the spy waited for him to be gone. He had learned the secret for which he had come, and now he could return at his leisure to his waiting followers, bring them to the treasure vault and carry away all the gold that they could stagger under.

The Waziri had reached the outer end of the tunnel, and were winding upward toward the fresh air and the welcome starlight of the kopje's summit, before Tarzan shook off the detaining hand of reverie and started slowly after them.

Once again, and, he thought, for the last time, he closed the massive door of the treasure room. In the darkness behind him Werper rose and stretched his cramped muscles. He stretched forth a hand and lovingly caressed a golden ingot on the nearest tier. He raised it from its immemorial resting place and weighed it in his hands. He clutched it to his bosom in an ecstasy of avarice.

Tarzan dreamed of the happy homecoming which lay before him, of dear arms about his neck, and a soft cheek pressed to his; but there rose to dispel that dream the memory of the old witch-doctor and his warning.

And then, in the span of a few brief seconds, the hopes of both these men were shattered. The one forgot even his greed in the panic of terror—the other was plunged into total forgetfulness of the past by a jagged fragment of rock which gashed a deep cut upon his head.

CHAPTER V—THE ALTAR OF THE FLAMING GOD

It was at the moment that Tarzan turned from the closed door to pursue his way to the outer world. The thing came without warning. One instant all was quiet and stability—the next, and the world rocked, the tortured sides of the narrow passageway split and crumbled, great blocks of granite, dislodged from the ceiling, tumbled into the narrow way, choking it, and the walls bent inward upon the wreckage. Beneath the blow of a fragment of the roof, Tarzan staggered back against the door to the treasure room, his weight pushed it open and his body rolled inward upon the floor.

In the great apartment where the treasure lay less damage was wrought by the earthquake. A few ingots toppled from the higher tiers, a single piece of the rocky ceiling splintered off and crashed downward to the floor, and the walls cracked, though they did not collapse.

There was but the single shock, no other followed to complete the damage undertaken by the first. Werper, thrown to his length by the suddenness and violence of the disturbance, staggered to his feet when he found himself unhurt. Groping his way toward the far end of the chamber, he sought the candle which Tarzan had left stuck in its own wax upon the protruding end of an ingot.

By striking numerous matches the Belgian at last found what he sought, and when, a moment later, the sickly rays relieved the Stygian darkness about him, he breathed a nervous sigh of relief, for the impenetrable gloom had accentuated the terrors of his situation.

As they became accustomed to the light the man turned his eyes toward the door—his one thought now was of escape from this frightful tomb—and as he did so he saw the body of the naked giant lying stretched upon the floor just within the doorway. Werper drew back in sudden fear of detection; but a second glance convinced him that the Englishman was dead. From a great gash in the man's head a pool of blood had collected upon the concrete floor.

Quickly, the Belgian leaped over the prostrate form of his erstwhile host, and without a thought of succor for the man in whom, for aught he knew, life still remained, he bolted for the passageway and safety.

But his renewed hopes were soon dashed. Just beyond the doorway he found the passage completely clogged and choked by impenetrable masses of shattered rock. Once more he turned and re-entered the treasure vault. Taking the candle from its place he commenced a systematic search of the apartment, nor had he gone far before he discovered another door in the opposite end of the room, a door which gave upon creaking hinges to the weight of his body. Beyond the door lay another narrow passageway. Along this Werper made his way, ascending a flight of stone steps to another corridor twenty feet above the level of the first. The flickering candle lighted the way before him, and a moment later he was thankful for the possession of this crude and antiquated luminant, which, a few hours before he might have looked upon with contempt, for it showed him, just in time, a yawning pit, apparently terminating the tunnel he was traversing.

Before him was a circular shaft. He held the candle above it and peered downward. Below him, at a great distance, he saw the light reflected back from the surface of a pool of water. He had come upon a well. He raised the candle above his head and peered across the black void, and there upon the opposite side he saw the continuation of the tunnel; but how was he to span the gulf?

As he stood there measuring the distance to the opposite side and wondering if he dared venture so great a leap, there broke suddenly upon his startled ears a piercing scream which diminished gradually until it ended in a series of dismal moans. The voice seemed partly human, yet so hideous that it might well have emanated from the tortured throat of a lost soul, writhing in the fires of hell.

The Belgian shuddered and looked fearfully upward, for the scream had seemed to come from above him. As he looked he saw an opening far overhead, and a patch of sky pinked with brilliant stars.

His half-formed intention to call for help was expunged by the terrifying cry—where such a voice lived, no human creatures could dwell. He dared not reveal himself to whatever inhabitants dwelt in the place above him. He cursed himself for a fool that he had ever embarked upon such a mission. He wished himself safely back in the camp of Achmet Zek, and would almost have embraced an opportunity to give himself up to the military authorities of the Congo if by so doing he might be rescued from the frightful predicament in which he now was.

He listened fearfully, but the cry was not repeated, and at last spurred to desperate means, he gathered himself for the leap across the chasm. Going back twenty paces, he took a running start, and at the edge of the well, leaped upward and outward in an attempt to gain the opposite side.

In his hand he clutched the sputtering candle, and as he took the leap the rush of air extinguished it. In utter darkness he flew through space, clutching outward for a hold should his feet miss the invisible ledge.

He struck the edge of the door of the opposite terminus of the rocky tunnel with his knees, slipped backward, clutched desperately for a moment, and at last hung half within and half without the opening; but he was safe. For several minutes he dared not move; but clung, weak and sweating, where he lay. At last, cautiously, he drew himself well within the tunnel, and again he lay at full length upon the floor, fighting to regain control of his shattered nerves.

When his knees struck the edge of the tunnel he had dropped the candle. Presently, hoping against hope that it had fallen upon the floor of the passageway, rather than back into the depths of the well, he rose upon all fours and commenced a diligent search for the little tallow cylinder, which now seemed infinitely more precious to him than all the fabulous wealth of the hoarded ingots of Opar.

And when, at last, he found it, he clasped it to him and sank back sobbing and exhausted. For many minutes he lay trembling and broken; but finally he drew himself to a sitting posture, and taking a match from his pocket, lighted the stump of the candle which remained to him. With the light he found it easier to regain control of his nerves, and presently he was again making his way along the tunnel in search of an avenue of escape. The horrid cry that had come down to him from above through the ancient well-shaft still haunted him, so that he trembled in terror at even the sounds of his own cautious advance.

He had gone forward but a short distance, when, to his chagrin, a wall of masonry barred his farther progress, closing the tunnel completely from top to bottom and from side to side. What could it mean? Werper was an educated and intelligent man. His military training had taught him to use his mind for the purpose for which it was intended. A blind tunnel such as this was senseless. It must continue beyond the wall. Someone, at some time in the past, had had it blocked for an unknown purpose of his own. The man fell to examining the masonry by the light of his candle. To his delight he discovered that the thin blocks of hewn stone of which it was constructed were fitted in loosely without mortar or cement. He tugged upon one of them, and to his joy found that it was easily removable. One after another he pulled out the blocks until he had opened an aperture large enough to admit his body, then he crawled through into a large, low chamber. Across this another door barred his way; but this, too, gave before his efforts, for it was not barred. A long, dark corridor showed before him, but before he had followed it far, his candle burned down until it scorched his fingers. With an oath he dropped it to the floor, where it sputtered for a moment and went out.

Now he was in total darkness, and again terror rode heavily astride his neck. What further pitfalls and dangers lay ahead he could not guess; but that he was as far as ever from liberty he was quite willing to believe, so depressing is utter absence of light to one in unfamiliar surroundings.

Slowly he groped his way along, feeling with his hands upon the tunnel's walls, and cautiously with his feet ahead of him upon the floor before he could take a single forward step. How long he crept on thus he could not guess; but at last, feeling that the tunnel's length was interminable, and exhausted by his efforts, by terror, and loss of sleep, he determined to lie down and rest before proceeding farther.

When he awoke there was no change in the surrounding blackness. He might have slept a second or a day—he could not know; but that he had slept for some time was attested by the fact that he felt refreshed and hungry.

Again he commenced his groping advance; but this time he had gone but a short distance when he emerged into a room, which was lighted through an opening in the ceiling, from which a flight of concrete steps led downward to the floor of the chamber.

Above him, through the aperture, Werper could see sunlight glancing from massive columns, which were twined about by clinging vines. He listened; but he heard no sound other than the soughing of the wind through leafy branches, the hoarse cries of birds, and the chattering of monkeys.

Boldly he ascended the stairway, to find himself in a circular court. Just before him stood a stone altar, stained with rusty-brown discolorations. At the time Werper gave no thought to an explanation of these stains—later their origin became all too hideously apparent to him.

Beside the opening in the floor, just behind the altar, through which he had entered the court from the subterranean chamber below, the Belgian discovered several doors leading from the enclosure upon the level of the floor. Above, and circling the courtyard, was a series of open balconies. Monkeys scampered about the deserted ruins, and gaily plumaged birds flitted in and out among the columns and the galleries far above; but no sign of human presence was discernible. Werper felt relieved. He sighed, as though a great weight had been lifted from his shoulders. He took a step toward one of the exits, and then he halted, wide-eyed in astonishment and terror, for almost at the same instant a dozen doors opened in the courtyard wall and a horde of frightful men rushed in upon him.

They were the priests of the Flaming God of Opar—the same, shaggy, knotted, hideous little men who had dragged Jane Clayton to the sacrificial altar at this very spot years before. Their long arms, their short and crooked legs, their close-set, evil eyes, and their low, receding foreheads gave them a bestial appearance that sent a qualm of paralyzing fright through the shaken nerves of the Belgian.

With a scream he turned to flee back into the lesser terrors of the gloomy corridors and apartments from which he had just emerged, but the frightful men anticipated his intentions. They blocked the way; they seized him, and though he fell, groveling upon his knees before them, begging for his life, they bound him and hurled him to the floor of the inner temple.

The rest was but a repetition of what Tarzan and Jane Clayton had passed through. The priestesses came, and with them La, the High Priestess. Werper was raised and laid across the altar. Cold sweat exuded from his every pore as La raised the cruel, sacrificial knife above him. The death chant fell upon his tortured ears. His staring eyes wandered to the golden goblets from which the hideous votaries would soon quench their inhuman thirst in his own, warm life-blood.

He wished that he might be granted the brief respite of unconsciousness before the final plunge of the keen blade—and then there was a frightful roar that sounded almost in his ears. The High Priestess lowered her dagger. Her eyes went wide in horror. The priestesses, her votaresses, screamed and fled madly toward the exits. The priests roared out their rage and terror according to the temper of their courage. Werper strained his neck about to catch a sight of the cause of their panic, and when, at last he saw it, he too went cold in dread, for what his eyes beheld was the figure of a huge lion standing in the center of the temple, and already a single victim lay mangled beneath his cruel paws.

Again the lord of the wilderness roared, turning his baleful gaze upon the altar. La staggered forward, reeled, and fell across Werper in a swoon.

CHAPTER VI—THE ARAB RAID

After their first terror had subsided subsequent to the shock of the earthquake, Basuli and his warriors hastened back into the passageway in search of Tarzan and two of their own number who were also missing.

They found the way blocked by jammed and distorted rock. For two days they labored to tear a way through to their imprisoned friends; but when, after Herculean efforts, they had unearthed but a few yards of the choked passage, and discovered the mangled remains of one of their fellows they were forced to the conclusion that Tarzan and the second Waziri also lay dead beneath the rock mass farther in, beyond human aid, and no longer susceptible of it.

Again and again as they labored they called aloud the names of their master and their comrade; but no answering call rewarded their listening ears. At last they gave up the search. Tearfully they cast a last look at the shattered tomb of their master, shouldered the heavy burden of gold that would at least furnish comfort, if not happiness, to their bereaved and beloved mistress, and made their mournful way back across the desolate valley of Opar, and downward through the forests beyond toward the distant bungalow.

And as they marched what sorry fate was already drawing down upon that peaceful, happy home!

From the north came Achmet Zek, riding to the summons of his lieutenant's letter. With him came his horde of renegade Arabs, outlawed marauders, these, and equally degraded blacks, garnered from the more debased and ignorant tribes of savage cannibals through whose countries the raider passed to and fro with perfect impunity.

Mugambi, the ebon Hercules, who had shared the dangers and vicissitudes of his beloved Bwana, from Jungle Island, almost to the headwaters of the Ugambi, was the first to note the bold approach of the sinister caravan.

He it was whom Tarzan had left in charge of the warriors who remained to guard Lady Greystoke, nor could a braver or more loyal guardian have been found in any clime or upon any soil. A giant in stature, a savage, fearless warrior, the huge black possessed also soul and judgment in proportion to his bulk and his ferocity.

Not once since his master had departed had he been beyond sight or sound of the bungalow, except when Lady Greystoke chose to canter across the broad plain, or relieve the monotony of her loneliness by a brief hunting excursion. On such occasions Mugambi, mounted upon a wiry Arab, had ridden close at her horse's heels.

The raiders were still a long way off when the warrior's keen eyes discovered them. For a time he stood scrutinizing the advancing party in silence, then he turned and ran rapidly in the direction of the native huts which lay a few hundred yards below the bungalow.

Here he called out to the lolling warriors. He issued orders rapidly. In compliance with them the men seized upon their weapons and their shields. Some ran to call in the workers from the fields and to warn the tenders of the flocks and herds. The majority followed Mugambi back toward the bungalow.

The dust of the raiders was still a long distance away. Mugambi could not know positively that it hid an enemy; but he had spent a lifetime of savage life in savage Africa, and he had seen parties before come thus unheralded. Sometimes they had come in peace and sometimes they had come in war—one could never tell. It was well to be prepared. Mugambi did not like the haste with which the strangers advanced.

The Greystoke bungalow was not well adapted for defense. No palisade surrounded it, for, situated as it was, in the heart of loyal Waziri, its master had anticipated no possibility of an attack in force by any enemy. Heavy, wooden shutters there were to close the window apertures against hostile arrows, and these Mugambi was engaged in lowering when Lady Greystoke appeared upon the veranda.

"Why, Mugambi!" she exclaimed. "What has happened? Why are you lowering the shutters?"

Mugambi pointed out across the plain to where a white-robed force of mounted men was now distinctly visible.

"Arabs," he explained. "They come for no good purpose in the absence of the Great Bwana."

Beyond the neat lawn and the flowering shrubs, Jane Clayton saw the glistening bodies of her Waziri. The sun glanced from the tips of their metal-shod spears, picked out the gorgeous colors in the feathers of their war bonnets, and reflected the high-lights from the glossy skins of their broad shoulders and high cheek bones.

Jane Clayton surveyed them with unmixed feelings of pride and affection. What harm could befall her with such as these to protect her?

The raiders had halted now, a hundred yards out upon the plain. Mugambi had hastened down to join his warriors. He advanced a few yards before them and raising his voice hailed the strangers. Achmet Zek sat straight in his saddle before his henchmen.

"Arab!" cried Mugambi. "What do you here?"

"We come in peace," Achmet Zek called back.

"Then turn and go in peace," replied Mugambi. "We do not want you here. There can be no peace between Arab and Waziri."

Mugambi, although not born in Waziri, had been adopted into the tribe, which now contained no member more jealous of its traditions and its prowess than he.

Achmet Zek drew to one side of his horde, speaking to his men in a low voice. A moment later, without warning, a ragged volley was poured into the ranks of the Waziri. A couple of warriors fell, the others were for charging the attackers; but Mugambi was a cautious as well as a brave leader. He knew the futility of charging mounted men armed with muskets. He withdrew his force behind the shrubbery of the garden. Some he dispatched to various other parts of the grounds surrounding the bungalow. Half a dozen he sent to the bungalow itself with instructions to keep their mistress within doors, and to protect her with their lives.

Adopting the tactics of the desert fighters from which he had sprung, Achmet Zek led his followers at a gallop in a long, thin line, describing a great circle which drew closer and closer in toward the defenders.

At that part of the circle closest to the Waziri, a constant fusillade of shots was poured into the bushes behind which the black warriors had concealed themselves. The latter, on their part, loosed their slim shafts at the nearest of the enemy.

The Waziri, justly famed for their archery, found no cause to blush for their performance that day. Time and again some swarthy horseman threw hands above his head and toppled from his saddle, pierced by a deadly arrow; but the contest was uneven. The Arabs outnumbered the Waziri; their bullets penetrated the shrubbery and found marks that the Arab riflemen had not even seen; and then Achmet Zek circled inward a half mile above the bungalow, tore down a section of the fence, and led his marauders within the grounds.

Across the fields they charged at a mad run. Not again did they pause to lower fences, instead, they drove their wild mounts straight for them, clearing the obstacles as lightly as winged gulls.

Mugambi saw them coming, and, calling those of his warriors who remained, ran for the bungalow and the last stand. Upon the veranda Lady Greystoke stood, rifle in hand. More than a single raider had accounted to her steady nerves and cool aim for his outlawry; more than a single pony raced, riderless, in the wake of the charging horde.

Mugambi pushed his mistress back into the greater security of the interior, and with his depleted force prepared to make a last stand against the foe.

On came the Arabs, shouting and waving their long guns above their heads. Past the veranda they raced, pouring a deadly fire into the kneeling Waziri who discharged their volley of arrows from behind their long, oval shields—shields well adapted, perhaps, to stop a hostile arrow, or deflect a spear; but futile, quite, before the leaden missiles of the riflemen.

From beneath the half-raised shutters of the bungalow other bowmen did effective service in greater security, and after the first assault, Mugambi withdrew his entire force within the building.

Again and again the Arabs charged, at last forming a stationary circle about the little fortress, and outside the effective range of the defenders' arrows. From their new position they fired at will at the windows. One by one the Waziri fell. Fewer and fewer were the arrows that replied to the guns of the raiders, and at last Achmet Zek felt safe in ordering an assault.

Firing as they ran, the bloodthirsty horde raced for the veranda. A dozen of them fell to the arrows of the defenders; but the majority reached the door. Heavy gun butts fell upon it. The crash of splintered wood mingled with the report of a rifle as Jane Clayton fired through the panels upon the relentless foe.

Upon both sides of the door men fell; but at last the frail barrier gave to the vicious assaults of the maddened attackers; it crumpled inward and a dozen swarthy murderers leaped into the living-room. At the far end stood Jane Clayton surrounded by the remnant of her devoted guardians. The floor was covered by the bodies of those who already had given up their lives in her defense. In the forefront of her protectors stood the giant Mugambi. The Arabs raised their rifles to pour in the last volley that would effectually end all resistance; but Achmet Zek roared out a warning order that stayed their trigger fingers.

"Fire not upon the woman!" he cried. "Who harms her, dies. Take the woman alive!"

The Arabs rushed across the room; the Waziri met them with their heavy spears. Swords flashed, long-barreled pistols roared out their sullen death dooms. Mugambi launched his spear at the nearest of the enemy with a force that drove the heavy shaft completely through the Arab's body, then he seized a pistol from another, and grasping it by the barrel brained all who forced their way too near his mistress.

Emulating his example the few warriors who remained to him fought like demons; but one by one they fell, until only Mugambi remained to defend the life and honor of the ape-man's mate.

From across the room Achmet Zek watched the unequal struggle and urged on his minions. In his hands was a jeweled musket. Slowly he raised it to his shoulder, waiting until another move should place Mugambi at his mercy without endangering the lives of the woman or any of his own followers.

At last the moment came, and Achmet Zek pulled the trigger. Without a sound the brave Mugambi sank to the floor at the feet of Jane Clayton.

An instant later she was surrounded and disarmed. Without a word they dragged her from the bungalow. A giant Negro lifted her to the pommel of his saddle, and while the raiders searched the bungalow and outhouses for plunder he rode with her beyond the gates and waited the coming of his master.

Jane Clayton saw the raiders lead the horses from the corral, and drive the herds in from the fields. She saw her home plundered of all that represented intrinsic worth in the eyes of the Arabs, and then she saw the torch applied, and the flames lick up what remained.

And at last, when the raiders assembled after glutting their fury and their avarice, and rode away with her toward the north, she saw the smoke and the flames rising far into the heavens until the winding of the trail into the thick forests hid the sad view from her eyes.

As the flames ate their way into the living-room, reaching out forked tongues to lick up the bodies of the dead, one of that gruesome company whose bloody welterings had long since been stilled, moved again. It was a huge black who rolled over upon his side and opened blood-shot, suffering eyes. Mugambi, whom the Arabs had left for dead, still lived. The hot flames were almost upon him as he raised himself painfully upon his hands and knees and crawled slowly toward the doorway.

Again and again he sank weakly to the floor; but each time he rose again and continued his pitiful way toward safety. After what seemed to him an interminable time, during which the flames had become a veritable fiery furnace at the far side of the room, the great black managed to reach the veranda, roll down the steps, and crawl off into the cool safety of some nearby shrubbery.

All night he lay there, alternately unconscious and painfully sentient; and in the latter state watching with savage hatred the lurid flames which still rose from burning crib and hay cock. A prowling lion roared close at hand; but the giant black was unafraid. There was place for but a single thought in his savage mind—revenge! revenge! revenge!

CHAPTER VII—THE JEWEL-ROOM OF OPAR

For some time Tarzan lay where he had fallen upon the floor of the treasure chamber beneath the ruined walls of Opar. He lay as one dead; but he was not dead. At length he stirred. His eyes opened upon the utter darkness of the room. He raised his hand to his head and brought it away sticky with clotted blood. He sniffed at his fingers, as a wild beast might sniff at the life-blood upon a wounded paw.

Slowly he rose to a sitting posture—listening. No sound reached to the buried depths of his sepulcher. He staggered to his feet, and groped his way about among the tiers of ingots. What was he? Where was he? His head ached; but otherwise he felt no ill effects from the blow that had felled him. The accident he did not recall, nor did he recall aught of what had led up to it.

He let his hands grope unfamiliarly over his limbs, his torso, and his head. He felt of the quiver at his back, the knife in his loin cloth. Something struggled for recognition within his brain. Ah! he had it. There was something missing. He crawled about upon the floor, feeling with his hands for the thing that instinct warned him was gone. At last he found it—the heavy war spear that in past years had formed so important a feature of his daily life, almost of his very existence, so inseparably had it been connected with his every action since the long-gone day that he had wrested his first spear from the body of a black victim of his savage training.

Tarzan was sure that there was another and more lovely world than that which was confined to the darkness of the four stone walls surrounding him. He continued his search and at last found the doorway leading inward beneath the city and the temple. This he followed, most incautiously. He came to the stone steps leading upward to the higher level. He ascended them and continued onward toward the well.

Nothing spurred his hurt memory to a recollection of past familiarity with his surroundings. He blundered on through the darkness as though he were traversing an open plain under the brilliance of a noonday sun, and suddenly there happened that which had to happen under the circumstances of his rash advance.

He reached the brink of the well, stepped outward into space, lunged forward, and shot downward into the inky depths below. Still clutching his spear, he struck the water, and sank beneath its surface, plumbing the depths.

The fall had not injured him, and when he rose to the surface, he shook the water from his eyes, and found that he could see. Daylight was filtering into the well from the orifice far above his head. It illumined the inner walls faintly. Tarzan gazed about him. On the level with the surface of the water he saw a large opening in the dark and slimy wall. He swam to it, and drew himself out upon the wet floor of a tunnel.

Along this he passed; but now he went warily, for Tarzan of the Apes was learning. The unexpected pit had taught him care in the traversing of dark passageways—he needed no second lesson.

For a long distance the passage went straight as an arrow. The floor was slippery, as though at times the rising waters of the well overflowed and flooded it. This, in itself, retarded Tarzan's pace, for it was with difficulty that he kept his footing.

The foot of a stairway ended the passage. Up this he made his way. It turned back and forth many times, leading, at last, into a small, circular chamber, the gloom of which was relieved by a faint light which found ingress through a tubular shaft several feet in diameter which rose from the center of the room's ceiling, upward to a distance of a hundred feet or more, where it terminated in a stone grating through which Tarzan could see a blue and sun-lit sky.

Curiosity prompted the ape-man to investigate his surroundings. Several metal-bound, copper-studded chests constituted the sole furniture of the round room. Tarzan let his hands run over these. He felt of the copper studs, he pulled upon the hinges, and at last, by chance, he raised the cover of one.

An exclamation of delight broke from his lips at sight of the pretty contents. Gleaming and glistening in the subdued light of the chamber, lay a great tray full of brilliant stones. Tarzan, reverted to the primitive by his accident, had no conception of the fabulous value of his find. To him they were but pretty pebbles. He plunged his hands into them and let the priceless gems filter through his fingers. He went to others of the chests, only to find still further stores of precious stones. Nearly all were cut, and from these he gathered a handful and filled the pouch which dangled at his side—the uncut stones he tossed back into the chests.

Unwittingly, the ape-man had stumbled upon the forgotten jewel-room of Opar. For ages it had lain buried beneath the temple of the Flaming God, midway of one of the many inky passages which the superstitious descendants of the ancient Sun Worshipers had either dared not or cared not to explore.

Tiring at last of this diversion, Tarzan took up his way along the corridor which led upward from the jewel-room by a steep incline. Winding and twisting, but always tending upward, the tunnel led him nearer and nearer to the surface, ending finally in a low-ceiled room, lighter than any that he had as yet discovered.

Above him an opening in the ceiling at the upper end of a flight of concrete steps revealed a brilliant sunlit scene. Tarzan viewed the vine-covered columns in mild wonderment. He puckered his brows in an attempt to recall some recollection of similar things. He was not sure of himself. There was a tantalizing suggestion always present in his mind that something was eluding him— that he should know many things which he did not know.

His earnest cogitation was rudely interrupted by a thunderous roar from the opening above him. Following the roar came the cries and screams of men and women. Tarzan grasped his spear more firmly and ascended the steps. A strange sight met his eyes as he emerged from the semi-darkness of the cellar to the brilliant light of the temple.

The creatures he saw before him he recognized for what they were—men and women, and a huge lion. The men and women were scuttling for the safety of the exits. The lion stood upon the body of one who had been less fortunate than the others. He was in the center of the temple. Directly before Tarzan, a woman stood beside a block of stone. Upon the top of the stone lay stretched a man, and as the ape-man watched the scene, he saw the lion glare terribly at the two who remained within the temple. Another thunderous roar broke from the savage throat, the woman screamed and swooned across the body of the man stretched prostrate upon the stone altar before her.

The lion advanced a few steps and crouched. The tip of his sinuous tail twitched nervously. He was upon the point of charging when his eyes were attracted toward the ape-man.

Werper, helpless upon the altar, saw the great carnivore preparing to leap upon him. He saw the sudden change in the beast's expression as his eyes wandered to something beyond the altar and out of the Belgian's view. He saw the formidable creature rise to a standing position. A figure darted past Werper. He saw a mighty arm upraised, and a stout spear shoot forward toward the lion, to bury itself in the broad chest.

He saw the lion snapping and tearing at the weapon's shaft, and he saw, wonder of wonders, the naked giant who had hurled the missile charging upon the great beast, only a long knife ready to meet those ferocious fangs and talons.

The lion reared up to meet this new enemy. The beast was growling frightfully, and then upon the startled ears of the Belgian, broke a similar savage growl from the lips of the man rushing upon the beast.

By a quick side step, Tarzan eluded the first swinging clutch of the lion's paws. Darting to the beast's side, he leaped upon the tawny back. His arms encircled the maned neck, his teeth sank deep into the brute's flesh. Roaring, leaping, rolling and struggling, the giant cat attempted to dislodge this savage enemy, and all the while one great, brown fist was driving a long keen blade repeatedly into the beast's side.

During the battle, La regained consciousness. Spellbound, she stood above her victim watching the spectacle. It seemed incredible that a human being could best the king of beasts in personal encounter and yet before her very eyes there was taking place just such an improbability.

At last Tarzan's knife found the great heart, and with a final, spasmodic struggle the lion rolled over upon the marble floor, dead. Leaping to his feet the conqueror placed a foot upon the carcass of his kill, raised his face toward the heavens, and gave voice to so hideous a cry that both La and Werper trembled as it reverberated through the temple.

Then the ape-man turned, and Werper recognized him as the man he had left for dead in the treasure room.

CHAPTER VIII—THE ESCAPE FROM OPAR

Werper was astounded. Could this creature be the same dignified Englishman who had entertained him so graciously in his luxurious African home? Could this wild beast, with blazing eyes, and bloody countenance, be at the same time a man? Could the horrid, victory cry he had but just heard have been formed in human throat?

Tarzan was eyeing the man and the woman, a puzzled expression in his eyes, but there was no faintest tinge of recognition. It was as though he had discovered some new species of living creature and was marveling at his find.

La was studying the ape-man's features. Slowly her large eyes opened very wide.

"Tarzan!" she exclaimed, and then, in the vernacular of the great apes which constant association with the anthropoids had rendered the common language of the Oparians: "You have come back to me! La has ignored the mandates of her religion, waiting, always waiting for Tarzan—for her Tarzan. She has taken no mate, for in all the world there was but one with whom La would mate. And now you have come back! Tell me, O Tarzan, that it is for me you have returned."

Werper listened to the unintelligible jargon. He looked from La to Tarzan. Would the latter understand this strange tongue? To the Belgian's surprise, the Englishman answered in a language evidently identical to hers.

"Tarzan," he repeated, musingly. "Tarzan. The name sounds familiar."

"It is your name—you are Tarzan," cried La.

"I am Tarzan?" The ape-man shrugged. "Well, it is a good name—I know no other, so I will keep it; but I do not know you. I did not come hither for you. Why I came, I do not know at all; neither do I know from whence I came. Can you tell me?"

La shook her head. "I never knew," she replied.

Tarzan turned toward Werper and put the same question to him; but in the language of the great apes. The Belgian shook his head.

"I do not understand that language," he said in French.

Without effort, and apparently without realizing that he made the change, Tarzan repeated his question in French. Werper suddenly came to a full realization of the magnitude of the injury of which Tarzan was a victim. The man had lost his memory—no longer could he recollect past events. The Belgian was upon the point of enlightening him, when it suddenly occurred to him that by keeping Tarzan in ignorance, for a time at least, of his true identity, it might be possible to turn the ape-man's misfortune to his own advantage.

"I cannot tell you from whence you came," he said; "but this I can tell you—if we do not get out of this horrible place we shall both be slain upon this bloody altar. The woman was about to plunge her knife into my heart when the lion interrupted the fiendish ritual. Come! Before they recover from their fright and reassemble, let us find a way out of their damnable temple."

Tarzan turned again toward La.

"Why," he asked, "would you have killed this man? Are you hungry?"

The High Priestess cried out in disgust.

"Did he attempt to kill you?" continued Tarzan.

The woman shook her head.

"Then why should you have wished to kill him?" Tarzan was determined to get to the bottom of the thing.

La raised her slender arm and pointed toward the sun.

"We were offering up his soul as a gift to the Flaming God," she said.

Tarzan looked puzzled. He was again an ape, and apes do not understand such matters as souls and Flaming Gods.

"Do you wish to die?" he asked Werper.

The Belgian assured him, with tears in his eyes, that he did not wish to die.

"Very well then, you shall not," said Tarzan. "Come! We will go. This *she* would kill you and keep me for herself. It is no place anyway for a Mangani. I should soon die, shut up behind these stone walls."

He turned toward La. "We are going now," he said.

The woman rushed forward and seized the ape-man's hands in hers.

"Do not leave me!" she cried. "Stay, and you shall be High Priest. La loves you. All Opar shall be yours. Slaves shall wait upon you. Stay, Tarzan of the Apes, and let love reward you."

The ape-man pushed the kneeling woman aside. "Tarzan does not desire you," he said, simply, and stepping to Werper's side he cut the Belgian's bonds and motioned him to follow.

Panting—her face convulsed with rage, La sprang to her feet.

"Stay, you shall!" she screamed. "La will have you—if she cannot have you alive, she will have you dead," and raising her face to the sun she gave voice to the same hideous shriek that Werper had heard once before and Tarzan many times.

In answer to her cry a babel of voices broke from the surrounding chambers and corridors.

"Come, Guardian Priests!" she cried. "The infidels have profaned the holiest of the holies. Come! Strike terror to their hearts; defend La and her altar; wash clean the temple with the blood of the polluters."

Tarzan understood, though Werper did not. The former glanced at the Belgian and saw that he was unarmed. Stepping quickly to La's side the ape-man seized her in his strong arms and though she fought with all the mad savagery of a demon, he soon disarmed her, handing her long, sacrificial knife to Werper.

"You will need this," he said, and then from each doorway a horde of the monstrous, little men of Opar streamed into the temple.

They were armed with bludgeons and knives, and fortified in their courage by fanatical hate and frenzy. Werper was terrified. Tarzan stood eyeing the foe in proud disdain. Slowly he advanced toward the exit he had chosen to utilize in making his way from the temple. A burly priest barred his way. Behind the first was a score of others. Tarzan swung his heavy spear, clublike, down upon the skull of the priest. The fellow collapsed, his head crushed.

Again and again the weapon fell as Tarzan made his way slowly toward the doorway. Werper pressed close behind, casting backward glances toward the shrieking, dancing mob menacing their rear. He held the sacrificial knife ready to strike whoever might come within its reach; but none came. For a time he wondered that they should so bravely battle with the giant ape-man, yet hesitate to rush upon him, who was relatively so weak. Had they done so he knew that he must have fallen at the first charge. Tarzan had reached the doorway over the corpses of all that had stood to dispute his way, before Werper guessed at the reason for his immunity. The priests feared the sacrificial knife! Willingly would they face death and welcome it if it came while they defended their High Priestess and her altar; but evidently there were deaths, and deaths. Some strange superstition must surround that polished blade, that no Oparian cared to chance a death thrust from it, yet gladly rushed to the slaughter of the ape-man's flaying spear.

Once outside the temple court, Werper communicated his discovery to Tarzan. The ape-man grinned, and let Werper go before him, brandishing the jeweled and holy weapon. Like leaves before a gale, the Oparians scattered in all directions and Tarzan and the Belgian found a clear passage through the corridors and chambers of the ancient temple.

The Belgian's eyes went wide as they passed through the room of the seven pillars of solid gold. With ill-concealed avarice he looked upon the age-old, golden tablets set in the walls of nearly every room and down the sides of many of the corridors. To the ape-man all this wealth appeared to mean nothing.

On the two went, chance leading them toward the broad avenue which lay between the stately piles of the half-ruined edifices and the inner wall of the city. Great apes jabbered at them and menaced them; but Tarzan answered them after their own kind, giving back taunt for taunt, insult for insult, challenge for challenge.

Werper saw a hairy bull swing down from a broken column and advance, stiff-legged and bristling, toward the naked giant. The yellow fangs were bared, angry snarls and barkings rumbled threateningly through the thick and hanging lips.

The Belgian watched his companion. To his horror, he saw the man stoop until his closed knuckles rested upon the ground as did those of the anthropoid. He saw him circle, stiff-legged about the circling ape. He heard the same bestial barkings and growlings issue from the human throat that were coming from the mouth of the brute. Had his eyes been closed he could not have known but that two giant apes were bridling for combat.

But there was no battle. It ended as the majority of such jungle encounters end—one of the boasters loses his nerve, and becomes suddenly interested in a blowing leaf, a beetle, or the lice upon his hairy stomach.

In this instance it was the anthropoid that retired in stiff dignity to inspect an unhappy caterpillar, which he presently devoured. For a moment Tarzan seemed inclined to pursue the argument. He swaggered truculently, stuck out his chest, roared and advanced closer to the bull. It was with difficulty that Werper finally persuaded him to leave well enough alone and continue his way from the ancient city of the Sun Worshipers.

The two searched for nearly an hour before they found the narrow exit through the inner wall. From there the well-worn trail led them beyond the outer fortification to the desolate valley of Opar.

Tarzan had no idea, in so far as Werper could discover, as to where he was or whence he came. He wandered aimlessly about, searching for food, which he discovered beneath small rocks, or hiding in the shade of the scant brush which dotted the ground.

The Belgian was horrified by the hideous menu of his companion. Beetles, rodents and caterpillars were devoured with seeming relish. Tarzan was indeed an ape again.

At last Werper succeeded in leading his companion toward the distant hills which mark the northwestern boundary of the valley, and together the two set out in the direction of the Greystoke bungalow.

What purpose prompted the Belgian in leading the victim of his treachery and greed back toward his former home it is difficult to guess, unless it was that without Tarzan there could be no ransom for Tarzan's wife.

That night they camped in the valley beyond the hills, and as they sat before a little fire where cooked a wild pig that had fallen to one of Tarzan's arrows, the latter sat lost in speculation. He seemed continually to be trying to grasp some mental image which as constantly eluded him.

At last he opened the leathern pouch which hung at his side. From it he poured into the palm of his hand a quantity of glittering gems. The firelight playing upon them conjured a multitude of scintillating rays, and as the wide eyes of the Belgian looked on in rapt fascination, the man's expression at last acknowledged a tangible purpose in courting the society of the ape-man.

CHAPTER IX—THE THEFT OF THE JEWELS

For two days Werper sought for the party that had accompanied him from the camp to the barrier cliffs; but not until late in the afternoon of the second day did he find clew to its whereabouts, and then in such gruesome form that he was totally unnerved by the sight.

In an open glade he came upon the bodies of three of the blacks, terribly mutilated, nor did it require considerable deductive power to explain their murder. Of the little party only these three had not been slaves. The others, evidently tempted to hope for freedom from their cruel Arab master, had taken advantage of their separation from the main camp, to slay the three representatives of the hated power which held them in slavery, and vanish into the jungle.

Cold sweat exuded from Werper's forehead as he contemplated the fate which chance had permitted him to escape, for had he been present when the conspiracy bore fruit, he, too, must have been of the garnered.

Tarzan showed not the slightest surprise or interest in the discovery. Inherent in him was a calloused familiarity with violent death. The refinements of his recent civilization expunged by the force of the sad calamity which had befallen him, left only the primitive sensibilities which his childhood's training had imprinted indelibly upon the fabric of his mind.

The training of Kala, the examples and precepts of Kerchak, of Tublat, and of Terkoz now formed the basis of his every thought and action. He retained a mechanical knowledge of French and English speech. Werper had spoken to him in French, and Tarzan had replied in the same tongue without conscious realization that he had departed from the anthropoidal speech in which he had addressed La. Had Werper used English, the result would have been the same.

Again, that night, as the two sat before their camp fire, Tarzan played with his shining baubles. Werper asked him what they were and where he had found them. The ape-man replied that they were gay-colored stones, with which he purposed fashioning a necklace, and that he had found them far beneath the sacrificial court of the temple of the Flaming God.

Werper was relieved to find that Tarzan had no conception of the value of the gems. This would make it easier for the Belgian to obtain possession of them. Possibly the man would give them to him for the asking. Werper reached out his hand toward the little pile that Tarzan had arranged upon a piece of flat wood before him.

"Let me see them," said the Belgian.

Tarzan placed a large palm over his treasure. He bared his fighting fangs, and growled. Werper withdrew his hand more quickly than he had advanced it. Tarzan resumed his playing with the gems, and his conversation with Werper as though nothing unusual had occurred. He had but exhibited the beast's jealous protective instinct for a possession. When he killed he shared the meat with Werper; but had Werper ever, by accident, laid a hand upon Tarzan's share, he would have aroused the same savage, and resentful warning.

From that occurrence dated the beginning of a great fear in the breast of the Belgian for his savage companion. He had never understood the transformation that had been wrought in Tarzan by the blow upon his head, other than to attribute it to a form of amnesia. That Tarzan had once been, in truth, a savage, jungle beast, Werper had not known, and so, of course, he could not guess that the man had reverted to the state in which his childhood and young manhood had been spent.

Now Werper saw in the Englishman a dangerous maniac, whom the slightest untoward accident might turn upon him with rending fangs. Not for a moment did Werper attempt to delude himself into the belief that he could defend himself successfully against an attack by the ape-man. His one hope lay in eluding him, and making for the far distant camp of Achmet Zek as rapidly as he could; but armed only with the sacrificial knife, Werper shrank from attempting the journey through the jungle. Tarzan constituted a protection that was by no means despicable, even in the face of the larger carnivora, as Werper had reason to acknowledge from the evidence he had witnessed in the Oparian temple.

Too, Werper had his covetous soul set upon the pouch of gems, and so he was torn between the various emotions of avarice and fear. But avarice it was that burned most strongly in his breast, to the end that he dared the dangers and suffered the terrors of constant association with him he thought a mad man, rather than give up the hope of obtaining possession of the fortune which the contents of the little pouch represented.

Achmet Zek should know nothing of these—these would be for Werper alone, and so soon as he could encompass his design he would reach the coast and take passage for America, where he could conceal himself beneath the veil of a new identity and enjoy to some measure the fruits of his theft. He had it all planned out, did Lieutenant Albert Werper, living in anticipation the luxurious life of the idle rich. He even found himself regretting that America was so provincial, and that nowhere in the new world was a city that might compare with his beloved Brussels.

It was upon the third day of their progress from Opar that the keen ears of Tarzan caught the sound of men behind them. Werper heard nothing above the humming of the jungle insects, and the chattering life of the lesser monkeys and the birds.

For a time Tarzan stood in statuesque silence, listening, his sensitive nostrils dilating as he assayed each passing breeze. Then he withdrew Werper into the concealment of thick brush, and waited. Presently, along the game trail that Werper and Tarzan had been following, there came in sight a sleek, black warrior, alert and watchful.

In single file behind him, there followed, one after another, near fifty others, each burdened with two dull-yellow ingots lashed upon his back. Werper recognized the party immediately as that which had accompanied Tarzan on his journey to Opar. He glanced at the ape-man; but in the savage, watchful eyes he saw no recognition of Basuli and those other loyal Waziri.

When all had passed, Tarzan rose and emerged from concealment. He looked down the trail in the direction the party had gone. Then he turned to Werper.

"We will follow and slay them," he said.

"Why?" asked the Belgian.

"They are black," explained Tarzan. "It was a black who killed Kala. They are the enemies of the Manganis."

Werper did not relish the idea of engaging in a battle with Basuli and his fierce fighting men. And, again, he had welcomed the sight of them returning toward the Greystoke bungalow, for he had begun to have doubts as to his ability to retrace his steps to the Waziri country. Tarzan, he knew, had not the remotest idea of whither they were going. By keeping at a safe distance behind the laden warriors, they would have no difficulty in following them home. Once at the bungalow, Werper knew the way to the camp of Achmet Zek. There was still another reason why he did not wish to interfere with the Waziri—they were bearing the great burden of treasure in the direction he wished it borne. The farther they took it, the less the distance that he and Achmet Zek would have to transport it.

He argued with the ape-man therefore, against the latter's desire to exterminate the blacks, and at last he prevailed upon Tarzan to follow them in peace, saying that he was sure they would lead them out of the forest into a rich country, teeming with game.

It was many marches from Opar to the Waziri country; but at last came the hour when Tarzan and the Belgian, following the trail of the warriors, topped the last rise, and saw before them the broad Waziri plain, the winding river, and the distant forests to the north and west.

A mile or more ahead of them, the line of warriors was creeping like a giant caterpillar through the tall grasses of the plain. Beyond, grazing herds of zebra, hartebeest, and topi dotted the level landscape, while closer to the river a bull buffalo, his head and shoulders protruding from the reeds watched the advancing blacks for a moment, only to turn at last and disappear into the safety of his dank and gloomy retreat.

Tarzan looked out across the familiar vista with no faintest gleam of recognition in his eyes. He saw the game animals, and his mouth watered; but he did not look in the direction of his bungalow. Werper, however, did. A puzzled expression entered the Belgian's eyes. He shaded them with his palms and gazed long and earnestly toward the spot where the bungalow had stood. He could not credit the testimony of his eyes—there was no bungalow—no barns—no out-houses. The corrals, the hay stacks—all were gone. What could it mean?

And then, slowly there filtered into Werper's consciousness an explanation of the havoc that had been wrought in that peaceful valley since last his eyes had rested upon it—Achmet Zek had been there!

Basuli and his warriors had noted the devastation the moment they had come in sight of the farm. Now they hastened on toward it talking excitedly among themselves in animated speculation upon the cause and meaning of the catastrophe.

When, at last they crossed the trampled garden and stood before the charred ruins of their master's bungalow, their greatest fears became convictions in the light of the evidence about them.

Remnants of human dead, half devoured by prowling hyenas and others of the carnivora which infested the region, lay rotting upon the ground, and among the corpses remained sufficient remnants of their clothing and ornaments to make clear to Basuli the frightful story of the disaster that had befallen his master's house.

"The Arabs," he said, as his men clustered about him.

The Waziri gazed about in mute rage for several minutes. Everywhere they encountered only further evidence of the ruthlessness of the cruel enemy that had come during the Great Bwana's absence and laid waste his property.

"What did they with 'Lady'?" asked one of the blacks.

They had always called Lady Greystoke thus.

"The women they would have taken with them," said Basuli. "Our women and his."

A giant black raised his spear above his head, and gave voice to a savage cry of rage and hate. The others followed his example. Basuli silenced them with a gesture.

"This is no time for useless noises of the mouth," he said. "The Great Bwana has taught us that it is acts by which things are done, not words. Let us save our breath—we shall need it all to follow up the Arabs and slay them. If 'Lady' and our women live the greater the need of haste, and warriors cannot travel fast upon empty lungs."

From the shelter of the reeds along the river, Werper and Tarzan watched the blacks. They saw them dig a trench with their knives and fingers. They saw them lay their yellow burdens in it and scoop the overturned earth back over the tops of the ingots.

Tarzan seemed little interested, after Werper had assured him that that which they buried was not good to eat; but Werper was intensely interested. He would have given much had he had his own followers with him, that he might take away the treasure as soon as the blacks left, for he was sure that they would leave this scene of desolation and death as soon as possible.

The treasure buried, the blacks removed themselves a short distance up wind from the fetid corpses, where they made camp, that they might rest before setting out in pursuit of the Arabs. It was already dusk. Werper and Tarzan sat devouring some pieces of meat they had brought from their last camp. The Belgian was occupied with his plans for the immediate future. He was positive that the Waziri would pursue Achmet Zek, for he knew enough of savage warfare, and of the characteristics of the Arabs and their degraded followers to guess that they had carried the Waziri women off into slavery. This alone would assure immediate pursuit by so warlike a people as the Waziri.

Werper felt that he should find the means and the opportunity to push on ahead, that he might warn Achmet Zek of the coming of Basuli, and also of the location of the buried treasure. What the Arab would now do with Lady Greystoke, in view of the mental affliction of her husband, Werper neither knew nor cared. It was enough that the golden treasure buried upon the site of the burned bungalow was infinitely more valuable than any ransom that would have occurred even to the avaricious mind of the Arab, and if Werper could persuade the raider to share even a portion of it with him he would be well satisfied.

But by far the most important consideration, to Werper, at least, was the incalculably valuable treasure in the little leathern pouch at Tarzan's side. If he could but obtain possession of this! He must! He would!

His eyes wandered to the object of his greed. They measured Tarzan's giant frame, and rested upon the rounded muscles of his arms. It was hopeless. What could he, Werper, hope to accomplish, other than his own death, by an attempt to wrest the gems from their savage owner?

Disconsolate, Werper threw himself upon his side. His head was pillowed on one arm, the other rested across his face in such a way that his eyes were hidden from the ape-man, though one of them was fastened upon him from beneath the shadow of the Belgian's forearm. For a time he lay thus, glowering at Tarzan, and originating schemes for plundering him of his treasure— schemes that were discarded as futile as rapidly as they were born.

Tarzan presently let his own eyes rest upon Werper. The Belgian saw that he was being watched, and lay very still. After a few moments he simulated the regular breathing of deep slumber.

Tarzan had been thinking. He had seen the Waziri bury their belongings. Werper had told him that they were hiding them lest some one find them and take them away. This seemed to Tarzan a splendid plan for safeguarding valuables. Since Werper had evinced a desire to possess his glittering pebbles, Tarzan, with the suspicions of a savage, had guarded the baubles, of whose worth he was entirely ignorant, as zealously as though they spelled life or death to him.

For a long time the ape-man sat watching his companion. At last, convinced that he slept, Tarzan withdrew his hunting knife and commenced to dig a hole in the ground before him. With the blade he loosened up the earth, and with his hands he scooped it out until he had excavated a little cavity a few inches in diameter, and five or six inches in depth. Into this he placed the pouch of jewels. Werper almost forgot to breathe after the fashion of a sleeper as he saw what the ape-man was doing—he scarce repressed an ejaculation of satisfaction.

Tarzan become suddenly rigid as his keen ears noted the cessation of the regular inspirations and expirations of his companion. His narrowed eyes bored straight down upon the Belgian. Werper felt that he was lost—he must risk all on his ability to carry on the deception. He sighed, threw both arms outward, and turned over on his back mumbling as though in the throes of a bad dream. A moment later he resumed the regular breathing.

Now he could not watch Tarzan, but he was sure that the man sat for a long time looking at him. Then, faintly, Werper heard the other's hands scraping dirt, and later patting it down. He knew then that the jewels were buried.

It was an hour before Werper moved again, then he rolled over facing Tarzan and opened his eyes. The ape-man slept. By reaching out his hand Werper could touch the spot where the pouch was buried.

For a long time he lay watching and listening. He moved about, making more noise than necessary, yet Tarzan did not awaken. He drew the sacrificial knife from his belt, and plunged it into the ground. Tarzan did not move. Cautiously the Belgian pushed the blade downward through the loose earth above the pouch. He felt the point touch the soft, tough fabric of the leather. Then he pried down upon the handle. Slowly the little mound of loose earth rose and parted. An instant later a corner of the pouch came into view. Werper pulled it from its hiding place, and tucked it in his shirt. Then he refilled the hole and pressed the dirt carefully down as it had been before.

Greed had prompted him to an act, the discovery of which by his companion could lead only to the most frightful consequences for Werper. Already he could almost feel those strong, white fangs burying themselves in his neck. He shuddered. Far out across the plain a leopard screamed, and in the dense reeds behind him some great beast moved on padded feet.

Werper feared these prowlers of the night; but infinitely more he feared the just wrath of the human beast sleeping at his side. With utmost caution the Belgian arose. Tarzan did not move. Werper took a few steps toward the plain and the distant forest to the northwest, then he paused and fingered the hilt of the long knife in his belt. He turned and looked down upon the sleeper.

"Why not?" he mused. "Then I should be safe."

He returned and bent above the ape-man. Clutched tightly in his hand was the sacrificial knife of the High Priestess of the Flaming God!

CHAPTER X—ACHMET ZEK SEES THE JEWELS

Mugambi, weak and suffering, had dragged his painful way along the trail of the retreating raiders. He could move but slowly, resting often; but savage hatred and an equally savage desire for vengeance kept him to his task. As the days passed his wounds healed and his strength returned, until at last his giant frame had regained all of its former mighty powers. Now he went more rapidly; but the mounted Arabs had covered a great distance while the wounded black had been painfully crawling after them.

They had reached their fortified camp, and there Achmet Zek awaited the return of his lieutenant, Albert Werper. During the long, rough journey, Jane Clayton had suffered more in anticipation of her impending fate than from the hardships of the road.

Achmet Zek had not deigned to acquaint her with his intentions regarding her future. She prayed that she had been captured in the hope of ransom, for if such should prove the case, no great harm would befall her at the hands of the Arabs; but there was the chance, the horrid chance, that another fate awaited her. She had heard of many women, among whom were white women, who had been sold by outlaws such as Achmet Zek into the slavery of black harems, or taken farther north into the almost equally hideous existence of some Turkish seraglio.

Jane Clayton was of sterner stuff than that which bends in spineless terror before danger. Until hope proved futile she would not give it up; nor did she entertain thoughts of self-destruction only as a final escape from dishonor. So long as Tarzan lived there was every reason to expect succor. No man nor beast who roamed the savage continent could boast the cunning and the powers of her lord and master. To her, he was little short of omnipotent in his native world—this world of savage beasts and savage men. Tarzan would come, and she would be rescued and avenged, of that she was certain. She counted the days that must elapse before he would return from Opar and discover what had transpired during his absence. After that it would be but a short time before he had surrounded the Arab stronghold and punished the motley crew of wrongdoers who inhabited it.

That he could find her she had no slightest doubt. No spoor, however faint, could elude the keen vigilance of his senses. To him, the trail of the raiders would be as plain as the printed page of an open book to her.

And while she hoped, there came through the dark jungle another. Terrified by night and by day, came Albert Werper. A dozen times he had escaped the claws and fangs of the giant carnivora only by what seemed a miracle to him. Armed with nothing more than the knife he had brought with him from Opar, he had made his way through as savage a country as yet exists upon the face of the globe.

By night he had slept in trees. By day he had stumbled fearfully on, often taking refuge among the branches when sight or sound of some great cat warned him from danger. But at last he had come within sight of the palisade behind which were his fierce companions.

At almost the same time Mugambi came out of the jungle before the walled village. As he stood in the shadow of a great tree, reconnoitering, he saw a man, ragged and disheveled, emerge from the jungle almost at his elbow. Instantly he recognized the newcomer as he who had been a guest of his master before the latter had departed for Opar.

The black was upon the point of hailing the Belgian when something stayed him. He saw the white man walking confidently across the clearing toward the village gate. No sane man thus approached a village in this part of Africa unless he was sure of a friendly welcome. Mugambi waited. His suspicions were aroused.

He heard Werper halloo; he saw the gates swing open, and he witnessed the surprised and friendly welcome that was accorded the erstwhile guest of Lord and Lady Greystoke. A light broke upon the understanding of Mugambi. This white man had been a traitor and a spy. It was to him they owed the raid during the absence of the Great Bwana. To his hate for the Arabs, Mugambi added a still greater hate for the white spy.

Within the village Werper passed hurriedly toward the silken tent of Achmet Zek. The Arab arose as his lieutenant entered. His face showed surprise as he viewed the tattered apparel of the Belgian.

"What has happened?" he asked.

Werper narrated all, save the little matter of the pouch of gems which were now tightly strapped about his waist, beneath his clothing. The Arab's eyes narrowed greedily as his henchman described the treasure that the Waziri had buried beside the ruins of the Greystoke bungalow.

"It will be a simple matter now to return and get it," said Achmet Zek. "First we will await the coming of the rash Waziri, and after we have slain them we may take our time to the treasure—none will disturb it where it lies, for we shall leave none alive who knows of its existence."

"And the woman?" asked Werper.

"I shall sell her in the north," replied the raider. "It is the only way, now. She should bring a good price."

The Belgian nodded. He was thinking rapidly. If he could persuade Achmet Zek to send him in command of the party which took Lady Greystoke north it would give him the opportunity he craved to make his escape from his chief. He would forego a share of the gold, if he could but get away unscathed with the jewels.

He knew Achmet Zek well enough by this time to know that no member of his band ever was voluntarily released from the service of Achmet Zek. Most of the few who deserted were recaptured. More than once had Werper listened to their agonized screams as they were tortured before being put to death. The Belgian had no wish to take the slightest chance of recapture.

"Who will go north with the woman," he asked, "while we are returning for the gold that the Waziri buried by the bungalow of the Englishman?"

Achmet Zek thought for a moment. The buried gold was of much greater value than the price the woman would bring. It was necessary to rid himself of her as quickly as possible and it was also well to obtain the gold with the least possible delay. Of all his followers, the Belgian was the most logical lieutenant to intrust with the command of one of the parties. An Arab, as familiar with the trails and tribes as Achmet Zek himself, might collect the woman's price and make good his escape into the far north. Werper, on the other hand, could scarce make his escape alone through a country hostile to Europeans while the men he would send with the Belgian could be carefully selected with a view to preventing Werper from persuading any considerable portion of his command to accompany him should he contemplate desertion of his chief.

At last the Arab spoke: "It is not necessary that we both return for the gold. You shall go north with the woman, carrying a letter to a friend of mine who is always in touch with the best markets for such merchandise, while I return for the gold. We can meet again here when our business is concluded."

Werper could scarce disguise the joy with which he received this welcome decision. And that he did entirely disguise it from the keen and suspicious eyes of Achmet Zek is open to question. However, the decision reached, the Arab and his lieutenant discussed the details of their forthcoming ventures for a short time further, when Werper made his excuses and returned to his own tent for the comforts and luxury of a long-desired bath and shave.

Having bathed, the Belgian tied a small hand mirror to a cord sewn to the rear wall of his tent, placed a rude chair beside an equally rude table that stood beside the glass, and proceeded to remove the rough stubble from his face.

In the catalog of masculine pleasures there is scarce one which imparts a feeling of greater comfort and refreshment than follows a clean shave, and now, with weariness temporarily banished, Albert Werper sprawled in his rickety chair to enjoy a final cigaret before retiring. His thumbs, tucked in his belt in lazy support of the weight of his arms, touched the belt which held the jewel pouch about his waist. He tingled with excitement as he let his mind dwell upon the value of the treasure, which, unknown to all save himself, lay hidden beneath his clothing.

What would Achmet Zek say, if he knew? Werper grinned. How the old rascal's eyes would pop could he but have a glimpse of those scintillating beauties! Werper had never yet had an opportunity to feast his eyes for any great length of time upon them. He had not even counted them—only roughly had he guessed at their value.

He unfastened the belt and drew the pouch from its hiding place. He was alone. The balance of the camp, save the sentries, had retired—none would enter the Belgian's tent. He fingered the pouch, feeling out the shapes and sizes of the precious, little nodules within. He hefted the bag, first in one palm, then in the other, and at last he wheeled his chair slowly around before the table, and in the rays of his small lamp let the glittering gems roll out upon the rough wood.

The refulgent rays transformed the interior of the soiled and squalid canvas to the splendor of a palace in the eyes of the dreaming man. He saw the gilded halls of pleasure that would open their portals to the possessor of the wealth which lay scattered upon this stained and dented table top. He dreamed of joys and luxuries and power which always had been beyond his grasp, and as he dreamed his gaze lifted from the table, as the gaze of a dreamer will, to a far distant goal above the mean horizon of terrestrial commonplaceness.

Unseeing, his eyes rested upon the shaving mirror which still hung upon the tent wall above the table; but his sight was focused far beyond. And then a reflection moved within the polished surface of the tiny glass, the man's eyes shot back out of space to the mirror's face, and in it he saw reflected the grim visage of Achmet Zek, framed in the flaps of the tent doorway behind him.

Werper stifled a gasp of dismay. With rare self-possession he let his gaze drop, without appearing to have halted upon the mirror until it rested again upon the gems. Without haste, he replaced them in the pouch, tucked the latter into his shirt, selected a cigaret from his case, lighted it and rose. Yawning, and stretching his arms above his head, he turned slowly toward the opposite end of the tent. The face of Achmet Zek had disappeared from the opening.

To say that Albert Werper was terrified would be putting it mildly. He realized that he not only had sacrificed his treasure; but his life as well. Achmet Zek would never permit the wealth that he had discovered to slip through his fingers, nor would he forgive the duplicity of a lieutenant who had gained possession of such a treasure without offering to share it with his chief.

Slowly the Belgian prepared for bed. If he were being watched, he could not know; but if so the watcher saw no indication of the nervous excitement which the European strove to conceal. When ready for his blankets, the man crossed to the little table and extinguished the light.

It was two hours later that the flaps at the front of the tent separated silently and gave entrance to a dark-robed figure, which passed noiselessly from the darkness without to the darkness within. Cautiously the prowler crossed the interior. In one hand was a long knife. He came at last to the pile of blankets spread upon several rugs close to one of the tent walls.

Lightly, his fingers sought and found the bulk beneath the blankets—the bulk that should be Albert Werper. They traced out the figure of a man, and then an arm shot upward, poised for an instant and descended. Again and again it rose and fell, and each time the long blade of the knife buried itself in the thing beneath the blankets. But there was an initial lifelessness in the silent bulk that gave the assassin momentary wonder. Feverishly he threw back the coverlets, and searched with nervous hands for the pouch of jewels which he expected to find concealed upon his victim's body.

An instant later he rose with a curse upon his lips. It was Achmet Zek, and he cursed because he had discovered beneath the blankets of his lieutenant only a pile of discarded clothing arranged in the form and semblance of a sleeping man—Albert Werper had fled.

Out into the village ran the chief, calling in angry tones to the sleepy Arabs, who tumbled from their tents in answer to his voice. But though they searched the village again and again they found no trace of the Belgian. Foaming with anger, Achmet Zek called his followers to horse, and though the night was pitchy black they set out to scour the adjoining forest for their quarry.

As they galloped from the open gates, Mugambi, hiding in a nearby bush, slipped, unseen, within the palisade. A score of blacks crowded about the entrance to watch the searchers depart, and as the last of them passed out of the village the blacks seized the portals and drew them to, and Mugambi lent a hand in the work as though the best of his life had been spent among the raiders.

In the darkness he passed, unchallenged, as one of their number, and as they returned from the gates to their respective tents and huts, Mugambi melted into the shadows and disappeared.

For an hour he crept about in the rear of the various huts and tents in an effort to locate that in which his master's mate was imprisoned. One there was which he was reasonably assured contained her, for it was the only hut before the door of which a sentry had been posted. Mugambi was crouching in the shadow of this structure, just around the corner from the unsuspecting guard, when another approached to relieve his comrade.

"The prisoner is safe within?" asked the newcomer.

"She is," replied the other, "for none has passed this doorway since I came."

The new sentry squatted beside the door, while he whom he had relieved made his way to his own hut. Mugambi slunk closer to the corner of the building. In one powerful hand he gripped a heavy knob-stick. No sign of elation disturbed his phlegmatic calm, yet inwardly he was aroused to joy by the proof he had just heard that "Lady" really was within.

The sentry's back was toward the corner of the hut which hid the giant black. The fellow did not see the huge form which silently loomed behind him. The knob-stick swung upward in a curve, and downward again. There was the sound of a dull thud, the crushing of heavy bone, and the sentry slumped into a silent, inanimate lump of clay.

A moment later Mugambi was searching the interior of the hut. At first slowly, calling, "Lady!" in a low whisper, and finally with almost frantic haste, until the truth presently dawned upon him—the hut was empty!

CHAPTER XI—TARZAN BECOMES A BEAST AGAIN

For a moment Werper had stood above the sleeping ape-man, his murderous knife poised for the fatal thrust; but fear stayed his hand. What if the first blow should fail to drive the point to his victim's heart? Werper shuddered in contemplation of the disastrous consequences to himself. Awakened, and even with a few moments of life remaining, the giant could literally tear his assailant to pieces should he choose, and the Belgian had no doubt but that Tarzan would so choose.

Again came the soft sound of padded footsteps in the reeds—closer this time. Werper abandoned his design. Before him stretched the wide plain and escape. The jewels were in his possession. To remain longer was to risk death at the hands of Tarzan, or the jaws of the hunter creeping ever nearer. Turning, he slunk away through the night, toward the distant forest.

Tarzan slept on. Where were those uncanny, guardian powers that had formerly rendered him immune from the dangers of surprise? Could this dull sleeper be the alert, sensitive Tarzan of old?

Perhaps the blow upon his head had numbed his senses, temporarily—who may say? Closer crept the stealthy creature through the reeds. The rustling curtain of vegetation parted a few paces from where the sleeper lay, and the massive head of a lion appeared. The beast surveyed the ape-man intently for a moment, then he crouched, his hind feet drawn well beneath him, his tail lashing from side to side.

It was the beating of the beast's tail against the reeds which awakened Tarzan. Jungle folk do not awaken slowly—instantly, full consciousness and full command of their every faculty returns to them from the depth of profound slumber.

Even as Tarzan opened his eyes he was upon his feet, his spear grasped firmly in his hand and ready for attack. Again was he Tarzan of the Apes, sentient, vigilant, ready.

No two lions have identical characteristics, nor does the same lion invariably act similarly under like circumstances. Whether it was surprise, fear or caution which prompted the lion crouching ready to spring upon the man, is immaterial—the fact remains that he did not carry out his original design, he did not spring at the man at all, but, instead, wheeled and sprang back into the reeds as Tarzan arose and confronted him.

The ape-man shrugged his broad shoulders and looked about for his companion. Werper was nowhere to be seen. At first Tarzan suspected that the man had been seized and dragged off by another lion, but upon examination of the ground he soon discovered that the Belgian had gone away alone out into the plain.

For a moment he was puzzled; but presently came to the conclusion that Werper had been frightened by the approach of the lion, and had sneaked off in terror. A sneer touched Tarzan's lips as he pondered the man's act—the desertion of a comrade in time of danger, and without warning. Well, if that was the sort of creature Werper was, Tarzan wished nothing more of him. He had gone, and for all the ape-man cared, he might remain away—Tarzan would not search for him.

A hundred yards from where he stood grew a large tree, alone upon the edge of the reedy jungle. Tarzan made his way to it, clambered into it, and finding a comfortable crotch among its branches, reposed himself for uninterrupted sleep until morning.

And when morning came Tarzan slept on long after the sun had risen. His mind, reverted to the primitive, was untroubled by any more serious obligations than those of providing sustenance, and safeguarding his life. Therefore, there was nothing to awaken for until danger threatened, or the pangs of hunger assailed. It was the latter which eventually aroused him.

Opening his eyes, he stretched his giant thews, yawned, rose and gazed about him through the leafy foliage of his retreat. Across the wasted meadowlands and fields of John Clayton, Lord

Greystoke, Tarzan of the Apes looked, as a stranger, upon the moving figures of Basuli and his braves as they prepared their morning meal and made ready to set out upon the expedition which Basuli had planned after discovering the havoc and disaster which had befallen the estate of his dead master.

The ape-man eyed the blacks with curiosity. In the back of his brain loitered a fleeting sense of familiarity with all that he saw, yet he could not connect any of the various forms of life, animate and inanimate, which had fallen within the range of his vision since he had emerged from the darkness of the pits of Opar, with any particular event of the past.

Hazily he recalled a grim and hideous form, hairy, ferocious. A vague tenderness dominated his savage sentiments as this phantom memory struggled for recognition. His mind had reverted to his childhood days—it was the figure of the giant she-ape, Kala, that he saw; but only half recognized. He saw, too, other grotesque, manlike forms. They were of Terkoz, Tublat, Kerchak, and a smaller, less ferocious figure, that was Neeta, the little playmate of his boyhood.

Slowly, very slowly, as these visions of the past animated his lethargic memory, he came to recognize them. They took definite shape and form, adjusting themselves nicely to the various incidents of his life with which they had been intimately connected. His boyhood among the apes spread itself in a slow panorama before him, and as it unfolded it induced within him a mighty longing for the companionship of the shaggy, low-browed brutes of his past.

He watched the blacks scatter their cook fire and depart; but though the face of each of them had but recently been as familiar to him as his own, they awakened within him no recollections whatsoever.

When they had gone, he descended from the tree and sought food. Out upon the plain grazed numerous herds of wild ruminants. Toward a sleek, fat bunch of zebra he wormed his stealthy way. No intricate process of reasoning caused him to circle widely until he was down wind from his prey—he acted instinctively. He took advantage of every form of cover as he crawled upon all fours and often flat upon his stomach toward them.

A plump young mare and a fat stallion grazed nearest to him as he neared the herd. Again it was instinct which selected the former for his meat. A low bush grew but a few yards from the unsuspecting two. The ape-man reached its shelter. He gathered his spear firmly in his grasp. Cautiously he drew his feet beneath him. In a single swift move he rose and cast his heavy weapon at the mare's side. Nor did he wait to note the effect of his assault, but leaped cat-like after his spear, his hunting knife in his hand.

For an instant the two animals stood motionless. The tearing of the cruel barb into her side brought a sudden scream of pain and fright from the mare, and then they both wheeled and broke for safety; but Tarzan of the Apes, for a distance of a few yards, could equal the speed of even these, and the first stride of the mare found her overhauled, with a savage beast at her shoulder. She turned, biting and kicking at her foe. Her mate hesitated for an instant, as though about to rush to her assistance; but a backward glance revealed to him the flying heels of the balance of the herd, and with a snort and a shake of his head he wheeled and dashed away.

Clinging with one hand to the short mane of his quarry, Tarzan struck again and again with his knife at the unprotected heart. The result had, from the first, been inevitable. The mare fought bravely, but hopelessly, and presently sank to the earth, her heart pierced. The ape-man placed a foot upon her carcass and raised his voice in the victory call of the Mangani. In the distance, Basuli halted as the faint notes of the hideous scream broke upon his ears.

"The great apes," he said to his companion. "It has been long since I have heard them in the country of the Waziri. What could have brought them back?"

Tarzan grasped his kill and dragged it to the partial seclusion of the bush which had hidden his own near approach, and there he squatted upon it, cut a huge hunk of flesh from the loin and proceeded to satisfy his hunger with the warm and dripping meat.

Attracted by the shrill screams of the mare, a pair of hyenas slunk presently into view. They trotted to a point a few yards from the gorging ape-man, and halted. Tarzan looked up, bared his fighting fangs and growled. The hyenas returned the compliment, and withdrew a couple of paces. They made no move to attack; but continued to sit at a respectful distance until Tarzan had concluded his meal. After the ape-man had cut a few strips from the carcass to carry with him, he walked slowly off in the direction of the river to quench his thirst. His way lay directly toward the hyenas, nor did he alter his course because of them.

With all the lordly majesty of Numa, the lion, he strode straight toward the growling beasts. For a moment they held their ground, bristling and defiant; but only for a moment, and then slunk away to one side while the indifferent ape-man passed them on his lordly way. A moment later they were tearing at the remains of the zebra.

Back to the reeds went Tarzan, and through them toward the river. A herd of buffalo, startled by his approach, rose ready to charge or to fly. A great bull pawed the ground and bellowed as his bloodshot eyes discovered the intruder; but the ape-man passed across their front as though ignorant of their existence. The bull's bellowing lessened to a low rumbling, he turned and scraped a horde of flies from his side with his muzzle, cast a final glance at the ape-man and resumed his feeding. His numerous family either followed his example or stood gazing after Tarzan in mild-eyed curiosity, until the opposite reeds swallowed him from view.

At the river, Tarzan drank his fill and bathed. During the heat of the day he lay up under the shade of a tree near the ruins of his burned barns. His eyes wandered out across the plain toward the forest, and a longing for the pleasures of its mysterious depths possessed his thoughts for a considerable time. With the next sun he would cross the open and enter the forest! There was no hurry—there lay before him an endless vista of tomorrows with naught to fill them but the satisfying of the appetites and caprices of the moment.

The ape-man's mind was untroubled by regret for the past, or aspiration for the future. He could lie at full length along a swaying branch, stretching his giant limbs, and luxuriating in the blessed peace of utter thoughtlessness, without an apprehension or a worry to sap his nervous energy and rob him of his peace of mind. Recalling only dimly any other existence, the ape-man was happy. Lord Greystoke had ceased to exist.

For several hours Tarzan lolled upon his swaying, leafy couch until once again hunger and thirst suggested an excursion. Stretching lazily he dropped to the ground and moved slowly toward the river. The game trail down which he walked had become by ages of use a deep, narrow trench, its walls topped on either side by impenetrable thicket and dense-growing trees closely interwoven with thick-stemmed creepers and lesser vines inextricably matted into two solid ramparts of vegetation. Tarzan had almost reached the point where the trail debouched upon the open river bottom when he saw a family of lions approaching along the path from the direction of the river. The ape-man counted seven—a male and two lionesses, full grown, and four young lions as large and quite as formidable as their parents. Tarzan halted, growling, and the lions paused, the great male in the lead baring his fangs and rumbling forth a warning roar. In his hand the ape-man held his heavy spear; but he had no intention of pitting his puny weapon against seven lions; yet he stood there growling and roaring and the lions did likewise. It was purely an exhibition of jungle bluff. Each was trying to frighten off the other. Neither wished to turn back and give way, nor did either at first desire to precipitate an encounter. The lions were fed sufficiently so as not to be goaded by pangs of hunger and as for Tarzan he seldom ate the meat of the carnivores; but a point of ethics was at stake and neither side wished to back down. So they stood there facing one another, making all sorts of hideous noises the while they hurled jungle invective back and forth. How long this bloodless duel would have persisted it is difficult to say, though eventually Tarzan would have been forced to yield to superior numbers.

There came, however, an interruption which put an end to the deadlock and it came from Tarzan's rear. He and the lions had been making so much noise that neither could hear anything above their concerted bedlam, and so it was that Tarzan did not hear the great bulk bearing down upon him from behind until an instant before it was upon him, and then he turned to see Buto, the rhinoceros, his little, pig eyes blazing, charging madly toward him and already so close that escape seemed impossible; yet so perfectly were mind and muscles coordinated in this unspoiled, primitive man that almost simultaneously with the sense perception of the threatened danger he wheeled and hurled his spear at Buto's chest. It was a heavy spear shod with iron, and behind it were the giant muscles of the ape-man, while coming to meet it was the enormous weight of Buto and the momentum of his rapid rush. All that happened in the instant that Tarzan turned to meet the charge of the irascible rhinoceros might take long to tell, and yet would have taxed the swiftest lens to record. As his spear left his hand the ape-man was looking down upon the mighty horn lowered to toss him, so close was Buto to him. The spear entered the rhinoceros' neck at its junction with the left shoulder and passed almost entirely through the beast's body, and at the instant that he launched it, Tarzan leaped straight into the air alighting upon Buto's back but escaping the mighty horn.

Then Buto espied the lions and bore madly down upon them while Tarzan of the Apes leaped nimbly into the tangled creepers at one side of the trail. The first lion met Buto's charge and was tossed high over the back of the maddened brute, torn and dying, and then the six remaining lions were upon the rhinoceros, rending and tearing the while they were being gored or trampled. From the safety of his perch Tarzan watched the royal battle with the keenest interest, for the more intelligent of the jungle folk are interested in such encounters. They are to them what the racetrack and the prize ring, the theater and the movies are to us. They see them often; but always they enjoy them for no two are precisely alike.

For a time it seemed to Tarzan that Buto, the rhinoceros, would prove victor in the gory battle. Already had he accounted for four of the seven lions and badly wounded the three remaining when in a momentary lull in the encounter he sank limply to his knees and rolled over upon his side. Tarzan's spear had done its work. It was the man-made weapon which killed the great beast that might easily have survived the assault of seven mighty lions, for Tarzan's spear had pierced the great lungs, and Buto, with victory almost in sight, succumbed to internal hemorrhage.

Then Tarzan came down from his sanctuary and as the wounded lions, growling, dragged themselves away, the ape-man cut his spear from the body of Buto, hacked off a steak and vanished into the jungle. The episode was over. It had been all in the day's work—something which you and I might talk about for a lifetime Tarzan dismissed from his mind the moment that the scene passed from his sight.

CHAPTER XII—LA SEEKS VENGEANCE

Swinging back through the jungle in a wide circle the ape-man came to the river at another point, drank and took to the trees again and while he hunted, all oblivious of his past and careless of his future, there came through the dark jungles and the open, parklike places and across the wide meadows, where grazed the countless herbivora of the mysterious continent, a weird and terrible caravan in search of him. There were fifty frightful men with hairy bodies and gnarled and crooked legs. They were armed with knives and great bludgeons and at their head marched an almost naked woman, beautiful beyond compare. It was La of Opar, High Priestess of the Flaming God, and fifty of her horrid priests searching for the purloiner of the sacred sacrificial knife.

Never before had La passed beyond the crumbling outer walls of Opar; but never before had need been so insistent. The sacred knife was gone! Handed down through countless ages it had come to her as a heritage and an insignia of her religious office and regal authority from some long-dead progenitor of lost and forgotten Atlantis. The loss of the crown jewels or the Great Seal of England could have brought no greater consternation to a British king than did the pilfering of the sacred knife bring to La, the Oparian, Queen and High Priestess of the degraded remnants of the oldest civilization upon earth. When Atlantis, with all her mighty cities and her cultivated fields and her great commerce and culture and riches sank into the sea long ages since, she took with her all but a handful of her colonists working the vast gold mines of Central Africa. From these and their degraded slaves and a later intermixture of the blood of the anthropoids sprung the gnarled men of Opar; but by some queer freak of fate, aided by natural selection, the old Atlantean strain had remained pure and undegraded in the females descended from a single princess of the royal house of Atlantis who had been in Opar at the time of the great catastrophe. Such was La.

Burning with white-hot anger was the High Priestess, her heart a seething, molten mass of hatred for Tarzan of the Apes. The zeal of the religious fanatic whose altar has been desecrated was triply enhanced by the rage of a woman scorned. Twice had she thrown her heart at the feet of the godlike ape-man and twice had she been repulsed. La knew that she was beautiful—and she was beautiful, not by the standards of prehistoric Atlantis alone, but by those of modern times was La physically a creature of perfection. Before Tarzan came that first time to Opar, La had never seen a human male other than the grotesque and knotted men of her clan. With one of these she must mate sooner or later that the direct line of high priestesses might not be broken, unless Fate should bring other men to Opar. Before Tarzan came upon his first visit, La had had no thought that such men as he existed, for she knew only her hideous little priests and the bulls of the tribe of great anthropoids that had dwelt from time immemorial in and about Opar, until they had come to be looked upon almost as equals by the Oparians. Among the legends of Opar were tales of godlike men of the olden time and of black men who had come more recently; but these latter had been enemies who killed and robbed. And, too, these legends always held forth the hope that some day that nameless continent from which their race had sprung, would rise once more out of the sea and with slaves at the long sweeps would send her carven, gold-picked galleys forth to succor the long-exiled colonists.

The coming of Tarzan had aroused within La's breast the wild hope that at last the fulfillment of this ancient prophecy was at hand; but more strongly still had it aroused the hot fires of love in a heart that never otherwise would have known the meaning of that all-consuming passion, for such a wondrous creature as La could never have felt love for any of the repulsive priests of Opar. Custom, duty and religious zeal might have commanded the union; but there could have been no love on La's part. She had grown to young womanhood a cold and heartless creature, daughter of a thousand other cold, heartless, beautiful women who had never known love. And so when love came to her it liberated all the pent passions of a thousand generations, transforming La into a pulsing, throbbing volcano of desire, and with desire thwarted this great force of love and gentleness and sacrifice was transmuted by its own fires into one of hatred and revenge.

It was in a state of mind superinduced by these conditions that La led forth her jabbering company to retrieve the sacred emblem of her high office and wreak vengeance upon the author of her wrongs. To Werper she gave little thought. The fact that the knife had been in his hand when it departed from Opar brought down no thoughts of vengeance upon his head. Of course, he should be slain when captured; but his death would give La no pleasure—she looked for that in the contemplated death agonies of Tarzan. He should be tortured. His should be a slow and frightful death. His punishment should be adequate to the immensity of his crime. He had wrested the sacred knife from La; he had lain sacrilegious hands upon the High Priestess of the Flaming God; he had desecrated the altar and the temple. For these things he should die; but he had scorned the love of La, the woman, and for this he should die horribly with great anguish.

The march of La and her priests was not without its adventures. Unused were these to the ways of the jungle, since seldom did any venture forth from behind Opar's crumbling walls, yet their very numbers protected them and so they came without fatalities far along the trail of Tarzan and Werper. Three great apes accompanied them and to these was delegated the business of tracking the quarry, a feat beyond the senses of the Oparians. La commanded. She arranged the order of march, she selected the camps, she set the hour for halting and the hour for resuming and though she was inexperienced in such matters, her native intelligence was so far above that of the men or the apes that she did better than they could have done. She was a hard taskmaster, too, for she looked down with loathing and contempt upon the misshapen creatures amongst which cruel Fate had thrown her and to some extent vented upon them her dissatisfaction and her thwarted love. She made them build her a strong protection and shelter each night and keep a great fire burning before it from dusk to dawn. When she tired of walking they were forced to carry her upon an improvised litter, nor did one dare to question her authority or her right to such services. In fact they did not question either. To them she was a goddess and each loved her and each hoped that he would be chosen as her mate, so they slaved for her and bore the stinging lash of her displeasure and the habitually haughty disdain of her manner without a murmur.

For many days they marched, the apes following the trail easily and going a little distance ahead of the body of the caravan that they might warn the others of impending danger. It was during a noonday halt while all were lying resting after a tiresome march that one of the apes rose suddenly and sniffed the breeze. In a low guttural he cautioned the others to silence and a moment later was swinging quietly up wind into the jungle. La and the priests gathered silently together, the hideous little men fingering their knives and bludgeons, and awaited the return of the shaggy anthropoid.

Nor had they long to wait before they saw him emerge from a leafy thicket and approach them. Straight to La he came and in the language of the great apes which was also the language of decadent Opar he addressed her.

"The great Tarmangani lies asleep there," he said, pointing in the direction from which he had just come. "Come and we can kill him."

"Do not kill him," commanded La in cold tones. "Bring the great Tarmangani to me alive and unhurt. The vengeance is La's. Go; but make no sound!" and she waved her hands to include all her followers.

Cautiously the weird party crept through the jungle in the wake of the great ape until at last he halted them with a raised hand and pointed upward and a little ahead. There they saw the giant form of the ape-man stretched along a low bough and even in sleep one hand grasped a stout limb and one strong, brown leg reached out and overlapped another. At ease lay Tarzan of the Apes, sleeping heavily upon a full stomach and dreaming of Numa, the lion, and Horta, the boar, and other creatures of the jungle. No intimation of danger assailed the dormant faculties of the ape-man—he saw no crouching hairy figures upon the ground beneath him nor the three apes that swung quietly into the tree beside him.

The first intimation of danger that came to Tarzan was the impact of three bodies as the three apes leaped upon him and hurled him to the ground, where he alighted half stunned beneath their combined weight and was immediately set upon by the fifty hairy men or as many of them as could swarm upon his person. Instantly the ape-man became the center of a whirling, striking, biting maelstrom of horror. He fought nobly but the odds against him were too great. Slowly they overcame him though there was scarce one of them that did not feel the weight of his mighty fist or the rending of his fangs.

CHAPTER XIII—CONDEMNED TO TORTURE AND DEATH

La had followed her company and when she saw them clawing and biting at Tarzan, she raised her voice and cautioned them not to kill him. She saw that he was weakening and that soon the greater numbers would prevail over him, nor had she long to wait before the mighty jungle creature lay helpless and bound at her feet.

"Bring him to the place at which we stopped," she commanded and they carried Tarzan back to the little clearing and threw him down beneath a tree.

"Build me a shelter!" ordered La. "We shall stop here tonight and tomorrow in the face of the Flaming God, La will offer up the heart of this defiler of the temple. Where is the sacred knife? Who took it from him?"

But no one had seen it and each was positive in his assurance that the sacrificial weapon had not been upon Tarzan's person when they captured him. The ape-man looked upon the menacing creatures which surrounded him and snarled his defiance. He looked upon La and smiled. In the face of death he was unafraid.

"Where is the knife?" La asked him.

"I do not know," replied Tarzan. "The man took it with him when he slipped away during the night. Since you are so desirous for its return I would look for him and get it back for you, did you not hold me prisoner; but now that I am to die I cannot get it back. Of what good was your knife, anyway? You can make another. Did you follow us all this way for nothing more than a knife? Let me go and find him and I will bring it back to you."

La laughed a bitter laugh, for in her heart she knew that Tarzan's sin was greater than the purloining of the sacrificial knife of Opar; yet as she looked at him lying bound and helpless before her, tears rose to her eyes so that she had to turn away to hide them; but she remained inflexible in her determination to make him pay in frightful suffering and in eventual death for daring to spurn the love of La.

When the shelter was completed La had Tarzan transferred to it. "All night I shall torture him," she muttered to her priests, "and at the first streak of dawn you may prepare the flaming altar upon which his heart shall be offered up to the Flaming God. Gather wood well filled with pitch, lay it in the form and size of the altar at Opar in the center of the clearing that the Flaming God may look down upon our handiwork and be pleased."

During the balance of the day the priests of Opar were busy erecting an altar in the center of the clearing, and while they worked they chanted weird hymns in the ancient tongue of that lost continent that lies at the bottom of the Atlantic. They knew not the meanings of the words they mouthed; they but repeated the ritual that had been handed down from preceptor to neophyte since that long-gone day when the ancestors of the Piltdown man still swung by their tails in the humid jungles that are England now.

And in the shelter of the hut, La paced to and fro beside the stoic ape-man. Resigned to his fate was Tarzan. No hope of succor gleamed through the dead black of the death sentence hanging over him. He knew that his giant muscles could not part the many strands that bound his wrists and ankles, for he had strained often, but ineffectually for release. He had no hope of outside help and only enemies surrounded him within the camp, and yet he smiled at La as she paced nervously back and forth the length of the shelter.

And La? She fingered her knife and looked down upon her captive. She glared and muttered but she did not strike. "Tonight!" she thought. "Tonight, when it is dark I will torture him." She looked upon his perfect, godlike figure and upon his handsome, smiling face and then she steeled her heart again by thoughts of her love spurned; by religious thoughts that damned the infidel who had desecrated the holy of holies; who had taken from the blood-stained altar of Opar the offering to the Flaming God—and not once but thrice. Three times had Tarzan cheated the god of her fathers. At the thought La paused and knelt at his side. In her hand was a sharp knife. She placed its point against the ape-man's side and pressed upon the hilt; but Tarzan only smiled and shrugged his shoulders.

How beautiful he was! La bent low over him, looking into his eyes. How perfect was his figure. She compared it with those of the knurled and knotted men from whom she must choose a mate, and La shuddered at the thought. Dusk came and after dusk came night. A great fire blazed within the little thorn boma about the camp. The flames played upon the new altar erected in the center of the clearing, arousing in the mind of the High Priestess of the Flaming God a picture of the event of the coming dawn. She saw this giant and perfect form writhing amid the flames of the burning pyre. She saw those smiling lips, burned and blackened, falling away from the strong, white teeth. She saw the shock of black hair tousled upon Tarzan's well-shaped head disappear in a spurt of flame. She saw these and many other frightful pictures as she stood with closed eyes and clenched fists above the object of her hate—ah! was it hate that La of Opar felt?

The darkness of the jungle night had settled down upon the camp, relieved only by the fitful flarings of the fire that was kept up to warn off the man-eaters. Tarzan lay quietly in his bonds. He suffered from thirst and from the cutting of the tight strands about his wrists and ankles; but he made no complaint. A jungle beast was Tarzan with the stoicism of the beast and the intelligence of man. He knew that his doom was sealed—that no supplications would avail to temper the severity of his end and so he wasted no breath in pleadings; but waited patiently in the firm conviction that his sufferings could not endure forever.

In the darkness La stooped above him. In her hand was a sharp knife and in her mind the determination to initiate his torture without further delay. The knife was pressed against his side and La's face was close to his when a sudden burst of flame from new branches thrown upon the fire without, lighted up the interior of the shelter. Close beneath her lips La saw the perfect features of the forest god and into her woman's heart welled all the great love she had felt for Tarzan since first she had seen him, and all the accumulated passion of the years that she had dreamed of him.

Dagger in hand, La, the High Priestess, towered above the helpless creature that had dared to violate the sanctuary of her deity. There should be no torture—there should be instant death. No longer should the defiler of the temple pollute the sight of the lord god almighty. A single stroke of the heavy blade and then the corpse to the flaming pyre without. The knife arm stiffened ready for the downward plunge, and then La, the woman, collapsed weakly upon the body of the man she loved.

She ran her hands in mute caress over his naked flesh; she covered his forehead, his eyes, his lips with hot kisses; she covered him with her body as though to protect him from the hideous fate she had ordained for him, and in trembling, piteous tones she begged him for his love. For hours the frenzy of her passion possessed the burning hand-maiden of the Flaming God, until at last sleep overpowered her and she lapsed into unconsciousness beside the man she had sworn to torture and to slay. And Tarzan, untroubled by thoughts of the future, slept peacefully in La's embrace.

At the first hint of dawn the chanting of the priests of Opar brought Tarzan to wakefulness. Initiated in low and subdued tones, the sound soon rose in volume to the open diapason of barbaric blood lust. La stirred. Her perfect arm pressed Tarzan closer to her—a smile parted her lips and then she awoke, and slowly the smile faded and her eyes went wide in horror as the significance of the death chant impinged upon her understanding.

"Love me, Tarzan!" she cried. "Love me, and you shall be saved."

Tarzan's bonds hurt him. He was suffering the tortures of long-restricted circulation. With an angry growl he rolled over with his back toward La. That was her answer! The High Priestess leaped to her feet. A hot flush of shame mantled her cheek and then she went dead white and stepped to the shelter's entrance.

"Come, Priests of the Flaming God!" she cried, "and make ready the sacrifice."

The warped things advanced and entered the shelter. They laid hands upon Tarzan and bore him forth, and as they chanted they kept time with their crooked bodies, swaying to and fro to the rhythm of their song of blood and death. Behind them came La, swaying too; but not in unison with the chanted cadence. White and drawn was the face of the High Priestess—white and drawn with unrequited love and hideous terror of the moments to come. Yet stern in her resolve was La. The infidel should die! The scorner of her love should pay the price upon the fiery altar. She saw them lay the perfect body there upon the rough branches. She saw the High Priest, he to whom custom would unite her—bent, crooked, gnarled, stunted, hideous—advance with the flaming torch and stand awaiting her command to apply it to the faggots surrounding the sacrificial pyre. His hairy, bestial face was distorted in a yellow-fanged grin of anticipatory enjoyment. His hands were cupped to receive the life blood of the victim—the red nectar that at Opar would have filled the golden sacrificial goblets.

La approached with upraised knife, her face turned toward the rising sun and upon her lips a prayer to the burning deity of her people. The High Priest looked questioningly toward her—the brand was burning close to his hand and the faggots lay temptingly near. Tarzan closed his eyes and awaited the end. He knew that he would suffer, for he recalled the faint memories of past burns. He knew that he would suffer and die; but he did not flinch. Death is no great adventure to the jungle bred who walk hand-in-hand with the grim specter by day and lie down at his side by night through all the years of their lives. It is doubtful that the ape-man even speculated upon what came after death. As a matter of fact as his end approached, his mind was occupied by thoughts of the pretty pebbles he had lost, yet his every faculty still was open to what passed around him.

He felt La lean over him and he opened his eyes. He saw her white, drawn face and he saw tears blinding her eyes. "Tarzan, my Tarzan!" she moaned, "tell me that you love me—that you will return to Opar with me—and you shall live. Even in the face of the anger of my people I will save you. This last chance I give you. What is your answer?"

At the last moment the woman in La had triumphed over the High Priestess of a cruel cult. She saw upon the altar the only creature that ever had aroused the fires of love within her virgin breast; she saw the beast-faced fanatic who would one day be her mate, unless she found another less repulsive, standing with the burning torch ready to ignite the pyre; yet with all her mad passion for the ape-man she would give the word to apply the flame if Tarzan's final answer was unsatisfactory. With heaving bosom she leaned close above him. "Yes or no?" she whispered.

Through the jungle, out of the distance, came faintly a sound that brought a sudden light of hope to Tarzan's eyes. He raised his voice in a weird scream that sent La back from him a step or two. The impatient priest grumbled and switched the torch from one hand to the other at the same time holding it closer to the tinder at the base of the pyre.

"Your answer!" insisted La. "What is your answer to the love of La of Opar?"

Closer came the sound that had attracted Tarzan's attention and now the others heard it—the shrill trumpeting of an elephant. As La looked wide-eyed into Tarzan's face, there to read her fate for happiness or heartbreak, she saw an expression of concern shadow his features. Now, for the first time, she guessed the meaning of Tarzan's shrill scream—he had summoned Tantor, the elephant, to his rescue! La's brows contracted in a savage scowl. "You refuse La!" she cried. "Then die! The torch!" she commanded, turning toward the priest.

Tarzan looked up into her face. "Tantor is coming," he said. "I thought that he would rescue me; but I know now from his voice that he will slay me and you and all that fall in his path, searching out with the cunning of Sheeta, the panther, those who would hide from him, for Tantor is mad with the madness of love."

La knew only too well the insane ferocity of a bull elephant in *must*. She knew that Tarzan had not exaggerated. She knew that the devil in the cunning, cruel brain of the great beast might send it hither and thither hunting through the forest for those who escaped its first charge, or the beast might pass on without returning—no one might guess which.

"I cannot love you, La," said Tarzan in a low voice. "I do not know why, for you are very beautiful. I could not go back and live in Opar—I who have the whole broad jungle for my range. No, I cannot love you but I cannot see you die beneath the goring tusks of mad Tantor. Cut my bonds before it is too late. Already he is almost upon us. Cut them and I may yet save you."

A little spiral of curling smoke rose from one corner of the pyre—the flames licked upward, crackling. La stood there like a beautiful statue of despair gazing at Tarzan and at the spreading flames. In a moment they would reach out and grasp him. From the tangled forest came the sound of cracking limbs and crashing trunks—Tantor was coming down upon them, a huge Juggernaut of the jungle. The priests were becoming uneasy. They cast apprehensive glances in the direction of the approaching elephant and then back at La.

"Fly!" she commanded them and then she stooped and cut the bonds securing her prisoner's feet and hands. In an instant Tarzan was upon the ground. The priests screamed out their rage and disappointment. He with the torch took a menacing step toward La and the ape-man. "Traitor!" He shrieked at the woman. "For this you too shall die!" Raising his bludgeon he rushed upon the High Priestess; but Tarzan was there before her. Leaping in to close quarters the ape-man seized the upraised weapon and wrenched it from the hands of the frenzied fanatic and then the priest closed upon him with tooth and nail. Seizing the stocky, stunted body in his mighty hands Tarzan raised the creature high above his head, hurling him at his fellows who were now gathered ready to bear down upon their erstwhile captive. La stood proudly with ready knife behind the ape-man. No faint sign of fear marked her perfect brow—only haughty disdain for her priests and admiration for the man she loved so hopelessly filled her thoughts.

Suddenly upon this scene burst the mad bull—a huge tusker, his little eyes inflamed with insane rage. The priests stood for an instant paralyzed with terror; but Tarzan turned and gathering La in his arms raced for the nearest tree. Tantor bore down upon him trumpeting shrilly. La clung with both white arms about the ape-man's neck. She felt him leap into the air and marveled at his strength and his ability as, burdened with her weight, he swung nimbly into the lower branches of a large tree and quickly bore her upward beyond reach of the sinuous trunk of the pachyderm.

Momentarily baffled here, the huge elephant wheeled and bore down upon the hapless priests who had now scattered, terror-stricken, in every direction. The nearest he gored and threw high among the branches of a tree. One he seized in the coils of his trunk and broke upon a huge bole, dropping the mangled pulp to charge, trumpeting, after another. Two he trampled beneath his huge feet and by then the others had disappeared into the jungle. Now Tantor turned his attention once more to Tarzan for one of the symptoms of madness is a revulsion of affection—objects of sane love become the objects of insane hatred. Peculiar in the unwritten annals of the jungle was the proverbial love that had existed between the ape-man and the tribe of Tantor. No elephant in all the jungle would harm the Tarmangani—the white-ape; but with the madness of *must* upon him the great bull sought to destroy his long-time play-fellow.

Back to the tree where La and Tarzan perched came Tantor, the elephant. He reared up with his forefeet against the bole and reached high toward them with his long trunk; but Tarzan had foreseen this and clambered beyond the bull's longest reach. Failure but tended to further enrage the mad creature. He bellowed and trumpeted and screamed until the earth shook to the mighty volume of his noise. He put his head against the tree and pushed and the tree bent before his mighty strength; yet still it held.

The actions of Tarzan were peculiar in the extreme. Had Numa, or Sabor, or Sheeta, or any other beast of the jungle been seeking to destroy him, the ape-man would have danced about hurling missiles and invectives at his assailant. He would have insulted and taunted them, reviling in the jungle Billingsgate he knew so well; but now he sat silent out of Tantor's reach and upon his handsome face was an expression of deep sorrow and pity, for of all the jungle folk Tarzan loved Tantor the best. Could he have slain him he would not have thought of doing so. His one idea was to escape, for he knew that with the passing of the *must* Tantor would be sane again and that once more he might stretch at full length upon that mighty back and make foolish speech into those great, flapping ears.

Finding that the tree would not fall to his pushing, Tantor was but enraged the more. He looked up at the two perched high above him, his red-rimmed eyes blazing with insane hatred, and then he wound his trunk about the bole of the tree, spread his giant feet wide apart and tugged to uproot the jungle giant. A huge creature was Tantor, an enormous bull in the full prime of all his stupendous strength. Mightily he strove until presently, to Tarzan's consternation, the great tree gave slowly at the roots. The ground rose in little mounds and ridges about the base of the bole, the tree tilted—in another moment it would be uprooted and fall.

The ape-man whirled La to his back and just as the tree inclined slowly in its first movement out of the perpendicular, before the sudden rush of its final collapse, he swung to the branches of a lesser neighbor. It was a long and perilous leap. La closed her eyes and shuddered; but when she opened them again she found herself safe and Tarzan whirling onward through the forest. Behind them the uprooted tree crashed heavily to the ground, carrying with it the lesser trees in its path and then Tantor, realizing that his prey had escaped him, set up once more his hideous trumpeting and followed at a rapid charge upon their trail.

CHAPTER XIV—A PRIESTESS BUT YET A WOMAN

At first La closed her eyes and clung to Tarzan in terror, though she made no outcry; but presently she gained sufficient courage to look about her, to look down at the ground beneath and even to keep her eyes open during the wide, perilous swings from tree to tree, and then there came over her a sense of safety because of her confidence in the perfect physical creature in whose strength and nerve and agility her fate lay. Once she raised her eyes to the burning sun and murmured a prayer of thanks to her pagan god that she had not been permitted to destroy this godlike man, and her long lashes were wet with tears. A strange anomaly was La of Opar—a creature of circumstance torn by conflicting emotions. Now the cruel and bloodthirsty creature of a heartless god and again a melting woman filled with compassion and tenderness. Sometimes the incarnation of jealousy and revenge and sometimes a sobbing maiden, generous and forgiving; at once a virgin and a wanton; but always—a woman. Such was La.

She pressed her cheek close to Tarzan's shoulder. Slowly she turned her head until her hot lips were pressed against his flesh. She loved him and would gladly have died for him; yet within an hour she had been ready to plunge a knife into his heart and might again within the coming hour.

A hapless priest seeking shelter in the jungle chanced to show himself to enraged Tantor. The great beast turned to one side, bore down upon the crooked, little man, snuffed him out and then, diverted from his course, blundered away toward the south. In a few minutes even the noise of his trumpeting was lost in the distance.

Tarzan dropped to the ground and La slipped to her feet from his back. "Call your people together," said Tarzan.

"They will kill me," replied La.

"They will not kill you," contradicted the ape-man. "No one will kill you while Tarzan of the Apes is here. Call them and we will talk with them."

La raised her voice in a weird, flutelike call that carried far into the jungle on every side. From near and far came answering shouts in the barking tones of the Oparian priests: "We come! We come!" Again and again, La repeated her summons until singly and in pairs the greater portion of her following approached and halted a short distance away from the High Priestess and her savior. They came with scowling brows and threatening mien. When all had come Tarzan addressed them.

"Your La is safe," said the ape-man. "Had she slain me she would now herself be dead and many more of you; but she spared me that I might save her. Go your way with her back to Opar, and Tarzan will go his way into the jungle. Let there be peace always between Tarzan and La. What is your answer?"

The priests grumbled and shook their heads. They spoke together and La and Tarzan could see that they were not favorably inclined toward the proposition. They did not wish to take La back and they did wish to complete the sacrifice of Tarzan to the Flaming God. At last the ape-man became impatient.

"You will obey the commands of your queen," he said, "and go back to Opar with her or Tarzan of the Apes will call together the other creatures of the jungle and slay you all. La saved me that I might save you and her. I have served you better alive than I could have dead. If you are not all fools you will let me go my way in peace and you will return to Opar with La. I know not where the sacred knife is; but you can fashion another. Had I not taken it from La you would have slain me and now your god must be glad that I took it since I have saved his priestess from love-mad Tantor. Will you go back to Opar with La, promising that no harm shall befall her?"

The priests gathered together in a little knot arguing and discussing. They pounded upon their breasts with their fists; they raised their hands and eyes to their fiery god; they growled and barked among themselves until it became evident to Tarzan that one of their number was preventing the acceptance of his proposal. This was the High Priest whose heart was filled with jealous rage because La openly acknowledged her love for the stranger, when by the worldly customs of their cult she should have belonged to him. Seemingly there was to be no solution of the problem until another priest stepped forth and, raising his hand, addressed La.

"Cadj, the High Priest," he announced, "would sacrifice you both to the Flaming God; but all of us except Cadj would gladly return to Opar with our queen."

"You are many against one," spoke up Tarzan. "Why should you not have your will? Go your way with La to Opar and if Cadj interferes slay him."

The priests of Opar welcomed this suggestion with loud cries of approval. To them it appeared nothing short of divine inspiration. The influence of ages of unquestioning obedience to high priests had made it seem impossible to them to question his authority; but when they realized that they could force him to their will they were as happy as children with new toys.

They rushed forward and seized Cadj. They talked in loud menacing tones into his ear. They threatened him with bludgeon and knife until at last he acquiesced in their demands, though sullenly, and then Tarzan stepped close before Cadj.

"Priest," he said, "La goes back to her temple under the protection of her priests and the threat of Tarzan of the Apes that whoever harms her shall die. Tarzan will go again to Opar before the next rains and if harm has befallen La, woe betide Cadj, the High Priest."

Sullenly Cadj promised not to harm his queen.

"Protect her," cried Tarzan to the other Oparians. "Protect her so that when Tarzan comes again he will find La there to greet him."

"La will be there to greet thee," exclaimed the High Priestess, "and La will wait, longing, always longing, until you come again. Oh, tell me that you will come!"

"Who knows?" asked the ape-man as he swung quickly into the trees and raced off toward the east.

For a moment La stood looking after him, then her head drooped, a sigh escaped her lips and like an old woman she took up the march toward distant Opar.

Through the trees raced Tarzan of the Apes until the darkness of night had settled upon the jungle, then he lay down and slept, with no thought beyond the morrow and with even La but the shadow of a memory within his consciousness.

But a few marches to the north Lady Greystoke looked forward to the day when her mighty lord and master should discover the crime of Achmet Zek, and be speeding to rescue and avenge, and even as she pictured the coming of John Clayton, the object of her thoughts squatted almost naked, beside a fallen log, beneath which he was searching with grimy fingers for a chance beetle or a luscious grub.

Two days elapsed following the theft of the jewels before Tarzan gave them a thought. Then, as they chanced to enter his mind, he conceived a desire to play with them again, and, having nothing better to do than satisfy the first whim which possessed him, he rose and started across the plain from the forest in which he had spent the preceding day.

Though no mark showed where the gems had been buried, and though the spot resembled the balance of an unbroken stretch several miles in length, where the reeds terminated at the edge of the meadowland, yet the ape-man moved with unerring precision directly to the place where he had hid his treasure.

With his hunting knife he upturned the loose earth, beneath which the pouch should be; but, though he excavated to a greater distance than the depth of the original hole there was no sign of pouch or jewels. Tarzan's brow clouded as he discovered that he had been despoiled. Little or no reasoning was required to convince him of the identity of the guilty party, and with the same celerity that had marked his decision to unearth the jewels, he set out upon the trail of the thief.

Though the spoor was two days old, and practically obliterated in many places, Tarzan followed it with comparative ease. A white man could not have followed it twenty paces twelve hours after it had been made, a black man would have lost it within the first mile; but Tarzan of the Apes had been forced in childhood to develop senses that an ordinary mortal scarce ever uses.

We may note the garlic and whisky on the breath of a fellow strap hanger, or the cheap perfume emanating from the person of the wondrous lady sitting in front of us, and deplore the fact of our sensitive noses; but, as a matter of fact, we cannot smell at all, our olfactory organs are practically atrophied, by comparison with the development of the sense among the beasts of the wild.

Where a foot is placed an effluvium remains for a considerable time. It is beyond the range of our sensibilities; but to a creature of the lower orders, especially to the hunters and the hunted, as interesting and ofttimes more lucid than is the printed page to us.

Nor was Tarzan dependent alone upon his sense of smell. Vision and hearing had been brought to a marvelous state of development by the necessities of his early life, where survival itself depended almost daily upon the exercise of the keenest vigilance and the constant use of all his faculties.

And so he followed the old trail of the Belgian through the forest and toward the north; but because of the age of the trail he was constrained to a far from rapid progress. The man he followed was two days ahead of him when Tarzan took up the pursuit, and each day he gained upon the ape-man. The latter, however, felt not the slightest doubt as to the outcome. Some day he would overhaul his quarry—he could bide his time in peace until that day dawned. Doggedly he followed the faint spoor, pausing by day only to kill and eat, and at night only to sleep and refresh himself.

Occasionally he passed parties of savage warriors; but these he gave a wide berth, for he was hunting with a purpose that was not to be distracted by the minor accidents of the trail.

These parties were of the collecting hordes of the Waziri and their allies which Basuli had scattered his messengers broadcast to summon. They were marching to a common rendezvous in preparation for an assault upon the stronghold of Achmet Zek; but to Tarzan they were enemies—he retained no conscious memory of any friendship for the black men.

It was night when he halted outside the palisaded village of the Arab raider. Perched in the branches of a great tree he gazed down upon the life within the enclosure. To this place had the spoor led him. His quarry must be within; but how was he to find him among so many huts? Tarzan, although cognizant of his mighty powers, realized also his limitations. He knew that he could not successfully cope with great numbers in open battle. He must resort to the stealth and trickery of the wild beast, if he were to succeed.

Sitting in the safety of his tree, munching upon the leg bone of Horta, the boar, Tarzan waited a favorable opportunity to enter the village. For awhile he gnawed at the bulging, round ends of the large bone, splintering off small pieces between his strong jaws, and sucking at the delicious marrow within; but all the time he cast repeated glances into the village. He saw white-robed figures, and half-naked blacks; but not once did he see one who resembled the stealer of the gems.

Patiently he waited until the streets were deserted by all save the sentries at the gates, then he dropped lightly to the ground, circled to the opposite side of the village and approached the palisade.

At his side hung a long, rawhide rope—a natural and more dependable evolution from the grass rope of his childhood. Loosening this, he spread the noose upon the ground behind him, and with a quick movement of his wrist tossed the coils over one of the sharpened projections of the summit of the palisade.

Drawing the noose taut, he tested the solidity of its hold. Satisfied, the ape-man ran nimbly up the vertical wall, aided by the rope which he clutched in both hands. Once at the top it required but a moment to gather the dangling rope once more into its coils, make it fast again at his waist, take a quick glance downward within the palisade, and, assured that no one lurked directly beneath him, drop softly to the ground.

Now he was within the village. Before him stretched a series of tents and native huts. The business of exploring each of them would be fraught with danger; but danger was only a natural factor of each day's life—it never appalled Tarzan. The chances appealed to him—the chances of life and death, with his prowess and his faculties pitted against those of a worthy antagonist.

It was not necessary that he enter each habitation—through a door, a window or an open chink, his nose told him whether or not his prey lay within. For some time he found one disappointment following upon the heels of another in quick succession. No spoor of the Belgian was discernible. But at last he came to a tent where the smell of the thief was strong. Tarzan listened, his ear close to the canvas at the rear, but no sound came from within.

At last he cut one of the pin ropes, raised the bottom of the canvas, and intruded his head within the interior. All was quiet and dark. Tarzan crawled cautiously within—the scent of the Belgian was strong; but it was not live scent. Even before he had examined the interior minutely, Tarzan knew that no one was within it.

In one corner he found a pile of blankets and clothing scattered about; but no pouch of pretty pebbles. A careful examination of the balance of the tent revealed nothing more, at least nothing to indicate the presence of the jewels; but at the side where the blankets and clothing lay, the ape-man discovered that the tent wall had been loosened at the bottom, and presently he sensed that the Belgian had recently passed out of the tent by this avenue.

Tarzan was not long in following the way that his prey had fled. The spoor led always in the shadow and at the rear of the huts and tents of the village—it was quite evident to Tarzan that the Belgian had gone alone and secretly upon his mission. Evidently he feared the inhabitants of the village, or at least his work had been of such a nature that he dared not risk detection.

At the back of a native hut the spoor led through a small hole recently cut in the brush wall and into the dark interior beyond. Fearlessly, Tarzan followed the trail. On hands and knees, he crawled through the small aperture. Within the hut his nostrils were assailed by many odors; but clear and distinct among them was one that half aroused a latent memory of the past—it was the faint and delicate odor of a woman. With the cognizance of it there rose in the breast of the ape-man a strange uneasiness—the result of an irresistible force which he was destined to become acquainted with anew—the instinct which draws the male to his mate.

In the same hut was the scent spoor of the Belgian, too, and as both these assailed the nostrils of the ape-man, mingling one with the other, a jealous rage leaped and burned within him, though his memory held before the mirror of recollection no image of the she to which he had attached his desire.

Like the tent he had investigated, the hut, too, was empty, and after satisfying himself that his stolen pouch was secreted nowhere within, he left, as he had entered, by the hole in the rear wall.

Here he took up the spoor of the Belgian, followed it across the clearing, over the palisade, and out into the dark jungle beyond.

CHAPTER XV—THE FLIGHT OF WERPER

After Werper had arranged the dummy in his bed, and sneaked out into the darkness of the village beneath the rear wall of his tent, he had gone directly to the hut in which Jane Clayton was held captive.

Before the doorway squatted a black sentry. Werper approached him boldly, spoke a few words in his ear, handed him a package of tobacco, and passed into the hut. The black grinned and winked as the European disappeared within the darkness of the interior.

The Belgian, being one of Achmet Zek's principal lieutenants, might naturally go where he wished within or without the village, and so the sentry had not questioned his right to enter the hut with the white, woman prisoner.

Within, Werper called in French and in a low whisper: "Lady Greystoke! It is I, M. Frecoult. Where are you?" But there was no response. Hastily the man felt around the interior, groping blindly through the darkness with outstretched hands. There was no one within!

Werper's astonishment surpassed words. He was on the point of stepping without to question the sentry, when his eyes, becoming accustomed to the dark, discovered a blotch of lesser blackness near the base of the rear wall of the hut. Examination revealed the fact that the blotch was an opening cut in the wall. It was large enough to permit the passage of his body, and assured as he was that Lady Greystoke had passed out through the aperture in an attempt to escape the village, he lost no time in availing himself of the same avenue; but neither did he lose time in a fruitless search for Jane Clayton.

His own life depended upon the chance of his eluding, or outdistancing Achmet Zek, when that worthy should have discovered that he had escaped. His original plan had contemplated connivance in the escape of Lady Greystoke for two very good and sufficient reasons. The first was that by saving her he would win the gratitude of the English, and thus lessen the chance of his extradition should his identity and his crime against his superior officer be charged against him.

The second reason was based upon the fact that only one direction of escape was safely open to him. He could not travel to the west because of the Belgian possessions which lay between him and the Atlantic. The south was closed to him by the feared presence of the savage ape-man he had robbed. To the north lay the friends and allies of Achmet Zek. Only toward the east, through British East Africa, lay reasonable assurance of freedom.

Accompanied by a titled Englishwoman whom he had rescued from a frightful fate, and his identity vouched for by her as that of a Frenchman by the name of Frecoult, he had looked forward, and not without reason, to the active assistance of the British from the moment that he came in contact with their first outpost.

But now that Lady Greystoke had disappeared, though he still looked toward the east for hope, his chances were lessened, and another, subsidiary design completely dashed. From the moment that he had first laid eyes upon Jane Clayton he had nursed within his breast a secret passion for the beautiful American wife of the English lord, and when Achmet Zek's discovery of the jewels had necessitated flight, the Belgian had dreamed, in his planning, of a future in which he might convince Lady Greystoke that her husband was dead, and by playing upon her gratitude win her for himself.

At that part of the village farthest from the gates, Werper discovered that two or three long poles, taken from a nearby pile which had been collected for the construction of huts, had been leaned against the top of the palisade, forming a precarious, though not impossible avenue of escape.

Rightly, he inferred that thus had Lady Greystoke found the means to scale the wall, nor did he lose even a moment in following her lead. Once in the jungle he struck out directly eastward.

A few miles south of him, Jane Clayton lay panting among the branches of a tree in which she had taken refuge from a prowling and hungry lioness.

Her escape from the village had been much easier than she had anticipated. The knife which she had used to cut her way through the brush wall of the hut to freedom she had found sticking in the wall of her prison, doubtless left there by accident when a former tenant had vacated the premises.

To cross the rear of the village, keeping always in the densest shadows, had required but a few moments, and the fortunate circumstance of the discovery of the hut poles lying so near the palisade had solved for her the problem of the passage of the high wall.

For an hour she had followed the old game trail toward the south, until there fell upon her trained hearing the stealthy padding of a stalking beast behind her. The nearest tree gave her instant sanctuary, for she was too wise in the ways of the jungle to chance her safety for a moment after discovering that she was being hunted.

Werper, with better success, traveled slowly onward until dawn, when, to his chagrin, he discovered a mounted Arab upon his trail. It was one of Achmet Zek's minions, many of whom were scattered in all directions through the forest, searching for the fugitive Belgian.

Jane Clayton's escape had not yet been discovered when Achmet Zek and his searchers set forth to overhaul Werper. The only man who had seen the Belgian after his departure from his tent was the black sentry before the doorway of Lady Greystoke's prison hut, and he had been silenced by the discovery of the dead body of the man who had relieved him, the sentry that Mugambi had dispatched.

The bribe taker naturally inferred that Werper had slain his fellow and dared not admit that he had permitted him to enter the hut, fearing as he did, the anger of Achmet Zek. So, as chance directed that he should be the one to discover the body of the sentry when the first alarm had been given following Achmet Zek's discovery that Werper had outwitted him, the crafty black had dragged the dead body to the interior of a nearby tent, and himself resumed his station before the doorway of the hut in which he still believed the woman to be.

With the discovery of the Arab close behind him, the Belgian hid in the foliage of a leafy bush. Here the trail ran straight for a considerable distance, and down the shady forest aisle, beneath the overarching branches of the trees, rode the white-robed figure of the pursuer.

Nearer and nearer he came. Werper crouched closer to the ground behind the leaves of his hiding place. Across the trail a vine moved. Werper's eyes instantly centered upon the spot. There was no wind to stir the foliage in the depths of the jungle. Again the vine moved. In the mind of the Belgian only the presence of a sinister and malevolent force could account for the phenomenon.

The man's eyes bored steadily into the screen of leaves upon the opposite side of the trail. Gradually a form took shape beyond them—a tawny form, grim and terrible, with yellow-green eyes glaring fearsomely across the narrow trail straight into his.

Werper could have screamed in fright, but up the trail was coming the messenger of another death, equally sure and no less terrible. He remained silent, almost paralyzed by fear. The Arab approached. Across the trail from Werper the lion crouched for the spring, when suddenly his attention was attracted toward the horseman.

The Belgian saw the massive head turn in the direction of the raider and his heart all but ceased its beating as he awaited the result of this interruption. At a walk the horseman approached. Would the nervous animal he rode take fright at the odor of the carnivore, and, bolting, leave Werper still to the mercies of the king of beasts?

But he seemed unmindful of the near presence of the great cat. On he came, his neck arched, champing at the bit between his teeth. The Belgian turned his eyes again toward the lion. The beast's whole attention now seemed riveted upon the horseman. They were abreast the lion now, and still the brute did not spring. Could he be but waiting for them to pass before returning his attention to the original prey? Werper shuddered and half rose. At the same instant the lion sprang from his place of concealment, full upon the mounted man. The horse, with a shrill neigh of terror, shrank sideways almost upon the Belgian, the lion dragged the helpless Arab from his saddle, and the horse leaped back into the trail and fled away toward the west.

But he did not flee alone. As the frightened beast had pressed in upon him, Werper had not been slow to note the quickly emptied saddle and the opportunity it presented. Scarcely had the lion dragged the Arab down from one side, than the Belgian, seizing the pommel of the saddle and the horse's mane, leaped upon the horse's back from the other.

A half hour later a naked giant, swinging easily through the lower branches of the trees, paused, and with raised head, and dilating nostrils sniffed the morning air. The smell of blood fell strong upon his senses, and mingled with it was the scent of Numa, the lion. The giant cocked his head upon one side and listened.

From a short distance up the trail came the unmistakable noises of the greedy feeding of a lion. The crunching of bones, the gulping of great pieces, the contented growling, all attested the nearness of the king at table.

Tarzan approached the spot, still keeping to the branches of the trees. He made no effort to conceal his approach, and presently he had evidence that Numa had heard him, from the ominous, rumbling warning that broke from a thicket beside the trail.

Halting upon a low branch just above the lion Tarzan looked down upon the grisly scene. Could this unrecognizable thing be the man he had been trailing? The ape-man wondered. From time to time he had descended to the trail and verified his judgment by the evidence of his scent that the Belgian had followed this game trail toward the east.

Now he proceeded beyond the lion and his feast, again descended and examined the ground with his nose. There was no scent spoor here of the man he had been trailing. Tarzan returned to the tree. With keen eyes he searched the ground about the mutilated corpse for a sign of the missing pouch of pretty pebbles; but naught could he see of it.

He scolded Numa and tried to drive the great beast away; but only angry growls rewarded his efforts. He tore small branches from a nearby limb and hurled them at his ancient enemy. Numa looked up with bared fangs, grinning hideously, but he did not rise from his kill.

Then Tarzan fitted an arrow to his bow, and drawing the slim shaft far back let drive with all the force of the tough wood that only he could bend. As the arrow sank deeply into his side, Numa leaped to his feet with a roar of mingled rage and pain. He leaped futilely at the grinning ape-man, tore at the protruding end of the shaft, and then, springing into the trail, paced back and forth beneath his tormentor. Again Tarzan loosed a swift bolt. This time the missile, aimed with care, lodged in the lion's spine. The great creature halted in its tracks, and lurched awkwardly forward upon its face, paralyzed.

Tarzan dropped to the trail, ran quickly to the beast's side, and drove his spear deep into the fierce heart, then after recovering his arrows turned his attention to the mutilated remains of the animal's prey in the nearby thicket.

The face was gone. The Arab garments aroused no doubt as to the man's identity, since he had trailed him into the Arab camp and out again, where he might easily have acquired the apparel. So sure was Tarzan that the body was that of he who had robbed him that he made no effort to verify his deductions by scent among the conglomerate odors of the great carnivore and the fresh blood of the victim.

He confined his attentions to a careful search for the pouch, but nowhere upon or about the corpse was any sign of the missing article or its contents. The ape-man was disappointed— possibly not so much because of the loss of the colored pebbles as with Numa for robbing him of the pleasures of revenge.

Wondering what could have become of his possessions, the ape-man turned slowly back along the trail in the direction from which he had come. In his mind he revolved a plan to enter and search the Arab camp, after darkness had again fallen. Taking to the trees, he moved directly south in search of prey, that he might satisfy his hunger before midday, and then lie up for the afternoon in some spot far from the camp, where he might sleep without fear of discovery until it came time to prosecute his design.

Scarcely had he quitted the trail when a tall, black warrior, moving at a dogged trot, passed toward the east. It was Mugambi, searching for his mistress. He continued along the trail, halting to examine the body of the dead lion. An expression of puzzlement crossed his features as he bent to search for the wounds which had caused the death of the jungle lord. Tarzan had removed his arrows, but to Mugambi the proof of death was as strong as though both the lighter missiles and the spear still protruded from the carcass.

The black looked furtively about him. The body was still warm, and from this fact he reasoned that the killer was close at hand, yet no sign of living man appeared. Mugambi shook his head, and continued along the trail, but with redoubled caution.

All day he traveled, stopping occasionally to call aloud the single word, "Lady," in the hope that at last she might hear and respond; but in the end his loyal devotion brought him to disaster.

From the northeast, for several months, Abdul Mourak, in command of a detachment of Abyssinian soldiers, had been assiduously searching for the Arab raider, Achmet Zek, who, six months previously, had affronted the majesty of Abdul Mourak's emperor by conducting a slave raid within the boundaries of Menelek's domain.

And now it happened that Abdul Mourak had halted for a short rest at noon upon this very day and along the same trail that Werper and Mugambi were following toward the east.

It was shortly after the soldiers had dismounted that the Belgian, unaware of their presence, rode his tired mount almost into their midst, before he had discovered them. Instantly he was surrounded, and a volley of questions hurled at him, as he was pulled from his horse and led toward the presence of the commander.

Falling back upon his European nationality, Werper assured Abdul Mourak that he was a Frenchman, hunting in Africa, and that he had been attacked by strangers, his safari killed or scattered, and himself escaping only by a miracle.

From a chance remark of the Abyssinian, Werper discovered the purpose of the expedition, and when he realized that these men were the enemies of Achmet Zek, he took heart, and immediately blamed his predicament upon the Arab.

Lest, however, he might again fall into the hands of the raider, he discouraged Abdul Mourak in the further prosecution of his pursuit, assuring the Abyssinian that Achmet Zek commanded a large and dangerous force, and also that he was marching rapidly toward the south.

Convinced that it would take a long time to overhaul the raider, and that the chances of engagement made the outcome extremely questionable, Mourak, none too unwillingly, abandoned his plan and gave the necessary orders for his command to pitch camp where they were, preparatory to taking up the return march toward Abyssinia the following morning.

It was late in the afternoon that the attention of the camp was attracted toward the west by the sound of a powerful voice calling a single word, repeated several times: "Lady! Lady! Lady!"

True to their instincts of precaution, a number of Abyssinians, acting under orders from Abdul Mourak, advanced stealthily through the jungle toward the author of the call.

A half hour later they returned, dragging Mugambi among them. The first person the big black's eyes fell upon as he was hustled into the presence of the Abyssinian officer, was M. Jules Frecoult, the Frenchman who had been the guest of his master and whom he last had seen entering the village of Achmet Zek under circumstances which pointed to his familiarity and friendship for the raiders.

Between the disasters that had befallen his master and his master's house, and the Frenchman, Mugambi saw a sinister relationship, which kept him from recalling to Werper's attention the identity which the latter evidently failed to recognize.

Pleading that he was but a harmless hunter from a tribe farther south, Mugambi begged to be allowed to go upon his way; but Abdul Mourak, admiring the warrior's splendid physique, decided to take him back to Adis Abeba and present him to Menelek. A few moments later

Mugambi and Werper were marched away under guard, and the Belgian learned for the first time, that he too was a prisoner rather than a guest. In vain he protested against such treatment, until a strapping soldier struck him across the mouth and threatened to shoot him if he did not desist.

Mugambi took the matter less to heart, for he had not the slightest doubt but that during the course of the journey he would find ample opportunity to elude the vigilance of his guards and make good his escape. With this idea always uppermost in his mind, he courted the good opinion of the Abyssinians, asked them many questions about their emperor and their country, and evinced a growing desire to reach their destination, that he might enjoy all the good things which they assured him the city of Adis Abeba contained. Thus he disarmed their suspicions, and each day found a slight relaxation of their watchfulness over him.

By taking advantage of the fact that he and Werper always were kept together, Mugambi sought to learn what the other knew of the whereabouts of Tarzan, or the authorship of the raid upon the bungalow, as well as the fate of Lady Greystoke; but as he was confined to the accidents of conversation for this information, not daring to acquaint Werper with his true identity, and as Werper was equally anxious to conceal from the world his part in the destruction of his host's home and happiness, Mugambi learned nothing—at least in this way.

But there came a time when he learned a very surprising thing, by accident.

The party had camped early in the afternoon of a sultry day, upon the banks of a clear and beautiful stream. The bottom of the river was gravelly, there was no indication of crocodiles, those menaces to promiscuous bathing in the rivers of certain portions of the dark continent, and so the Abyssinians took advantage of the opportunity to perform long-deferred, and much needed, ablutions.

As Werper, who, with Mugambi, had been given permission to enter the water, removed his clothing, the black noted the care with which he unfastened something which circled his waist, and which he took off with his shirt, keeping the latter always around and concealing the object of his suspicious solicitude.

It was this very carefulness which attracted the black's attention to the thing, arousing a natural curiosity in the warrior's mind, and so it chanced that when the Belgian, in the nervousness of overcaution, fumbled the hidden article and dropped it, Mugambi saw it as it fell upon the ground, spilling a portion of its contents on the sward.

Now Mugambi had been to London with his master. He was not the unsophisticated savage that his apparel proclaimed him. He had mingled with the cosmopolitan hordes of the greatest city in the world; he had visited museums and inspected shop windows; and, besides, he was a shrewd and intelligent man.

The instant that the jewels of Opar rolled, scintillating, before his astonished eyes, he recognized them for what they were; but he recognized something else, too, that interested him far more deeply than the value of the stones. A thousand times he had seen the leathern pouch which dangled at his master's side, when Tarzan of the Apes had, in a spirit of play and adventure, elected to return for a few hours to the primitive manners and customs of his boyhood, and surrounded by his naked warriors hunt the lion and the leopard, the buffalo and the elephant after the manner he loved best.

Werper saw that Mugambi had seen the pouch and the stones. Hastily he gathered up the precious gems and returned them to their container, while Mugambi, assuming an air of indifference, strolled down to the river for his bath.

The following morning Abdul Mourak was enraged and chagrined to discover that his huge, black prisoner had escaped during the night, while Werper was terrified for the same reason, until his trembling fingers discovered the pouch still in its place beneath his shirt, and within it the hard outlines of its contents.

CHAPTER XVI—TARZAN AGAIN LEADS THE MANGANI

Achmet Zek with two of his followers had circled far to the south to intercept the flight of his deserting lieutenant, Werper. Others had spread out in various directions, so that a vast circle had been formed by them during the night, and now they were beating in toward the center.

Achmet and the two with him halted for a short rest just before noon. They squatted beneath the trees upon the southern edge of a clearing. The chief of the raiders was in ill humor. To have been outwitted by an unbeliever was bad enough; but to have, at the same time, lost the jewels upon which he had set his avaricious heart was altogether too much—Allah must, indeed be angry with his servant.

Well, he still had the woman. She would bring a fair price in the north, and there was, too, the buried treasure beside the ruins of the Englishman's house.

A slight noise in the jungle upon the opposite side of the clearing brought Achmet Zek to immediate and alert attention. He gathered his rifle in readiness for instant use, at the same time motioning his followers to silence and concealment. Crouching behind the bushes the three waited, their eyes fastened upon the far side of the open space.

Presently the foliage parted and a woman's face appeared, glancing fearfully from side to side. A moment later, evidently satisfied that no immediate danger lurked before her, she stepped out into the clearing in full view of the Arab.

Achmet Zek caught his breath with a muttered exclamation of incredulity and an imprecation. The woman was the prisoner he had thought safely guarded at his camp!

Apparently she was alone, but Achmet Zek waited that he might make sure of it before seizing her. Slowly Jane Clayton started across the clearing. Twice already since she had quitted the village of the raiders had she barely escaped the fangs of carnivora, and once she had almost stumbled into the path of one of the searchers. Though she was almost despairing of ever reaching safety she still was determined to fight on, until death or success terminated her endeavors.

As the Arabs watched her from the safety of their concealment, and Achmet Zek noted with satisfaction that she was walking directly into his clutches, another pair of eyes looked down upon the entire scene from the foliage of an adjacent tree.

Puzzled, troubled eyes they were, for all their gray and savage glint, for their owner was struggling with an intangible suggestion of the familiarity of the face and figure of the woman below him.

A sudden crashing of the bushes at the point from which Jane Clayton had emerged into the clearing brought her to a sudden stop and attracted the attention of the Arabs and the watcher in the tree to the same point.

The woman wheeled about to see what new danger menaced her from behind, and as she did so a great, anthropoid ape waddled into view. Behind him came another and another; but Lady Greystoke did not wait to learn how many more of the hideous creatures were so close upon her trail.

With a smothered scream she rushed toward the opposite jungle, and as she reached the bushes there, Achmet Zek and his two henchmen rose up and seized her. At the same instant a naked, brown giant dropped from the branches of a tree at the right of the clearing.

Turning toward the astonished apes he gave voice to a short volley of low gutturals, and without waiting to note the effect of his words upon them, wheeled and charged for the Arabs.

Achmet Zek was dragging Jane Clayton toward his tethered horse. His two men were hastily unfastening all three mounts. The woman, struggling to escape the Arab, turned and saw the ape-man running toward her. A glad light of hope illuminated her face.

"John!" she cried. "Thank God that you have come in time."

Behind Tarzan came the great apes, wondering, but obedient to his summons. The Arabs saw that they would not have time to mount and make their escape before the beasts and the man were upon them. Achmet Zek recognized the latter as the redoubtable enemy of such as he, and he saw, too, in the circumstance an opportunity to rid himself forever of the menace of the ape-man's presence.

Calling to his men to follow his example he raised his rifle and leveled it upon the charging giant. His followers, acting with no less alacrity than himself, fired almost simultaneously, and with the reports of the rifles, Tarzan of the Apes and two of his hairy henchmen pitched forward among the jungle grasses.

The noise of the rifle shots brought the balance of the apes to a wondering pause, and, taking advantage of their momentary distraction, Achmet Zek and his fellows leaped to their horses' backs and galloped away with the now hopeless and grief-stricken woman.

Back to the village they rode, and once again Lady Greystoke found herself incarcerated in the filthy, little hut from which she had thought to have escaped for good. But this time she was not only guarded by an additional sentry, but bound as well.

Singly and in twos the searchers who had ridden out with Achmet Zek upon the trail of the Belgian, returned empty handed. With the report of each the raider's rage and chagrin increased, until he was in such a transport of ferocious anger that none dared approach him. Threatening and cursing, Achmet Zek paced up and down the floor of his silken tent; but his temper served him naught—Werper was gone and with him the fortune in scintillating gems which had aroused the cupidity of his chief and placed the sentence of death upon the head of the lieutenant.

With the escape of the Arabs the great apes had turned their attention to their fallen comrades. One was dead, but another and the great white ape still breathed. The hairy monsters gathered about these two, grumbling and muttering after the fashion of their kind.

Tarzan was the first to regain consciousness. Sitting up, he looked about him. Blood was flowing from a wound in his shoulder. The shock had thrown him down and dazed him; but he was far from dead. Rising slowly to his feet he let his eyes wander toward the spot where last he had seen the she, who had aroused within his savage breast such strange emotions.

"Where is she?" he asked.

"The Tarmangani took her away," replied one of the apes. "Who are you who speak the language of the Mangani?"

"I am Tarzan," replied the ape-man; "mighty hunter, greatest of fighters. When I roar, the jungle is silent and trembles with terror. I am Tarzan of the Apes. I have been away; but now I have come back to my people."

"Yes," spoke up an old ape, "he is Tarzan. I know him. It is well that he has come back. Now we shall have good hunting."

The other apes came closer and sniffed at the ape-man. Tarzan stood very still, his fangs half bared, and his muscles tense and ready for action; but there was none there to question his right to be with them, and presently, the inspection satisfactorily concluded, the apes again returned their attention to the other survivor.

He too was but slightly wounded, a bullet, grazing his skull, having stunned him, so that when he regained consciousness he was apparently as fit as ever.

The apes told Tarzan that they had been traveling toward the east when the scent spoor of the she had attracted them and they had stalked her. Now they wished to continue upon their interrupted march; but Tarzan preferred to follow the Arabs and take the woman from them. After a considerable argument it was decided that they should first hunt toward the east for a few days and then return and search for the Arabs, and as time is of little moment to the ape folk, Tarzan acceded to their demands, he, himself, having reverted to a mental state but little superior to their own.

Another circumstance which decided him to postpone pursuit of the Arabs was the painfulness of his wound. It would be better to wait until that had healed before he pitted himself again against the guns of the Tarmangani.

And so, as Jane Clayton was pushed into her prison hut and her hands and feet securely bound, her natural protector roamed off toward the east in company with a score of hairy monsters, with whom he rubbed shoulders as familiarly as a few months before he had mingled with his immaculate fellow-members of one of London's most select and exclusive clubs.

But all the time there lurked in the back of his injured brain a troublesome conviction that he had no business where he was—that he should be, for some unaccountable reason, elsewhere and among another sort of creature. Also, there was the compelling urge to be upon the scent of the Arabs, undertaking the rescue of the woman who had appealed so strongly to his savage sentiments; though the thought-word which naturally occurred to him in the contemplation of the venture, was "capture," rather than "rescue."

To him she was as any other jungle she, and he had set his heart upon her as his mate. For an instant, as he had approached closer to her in the clearing where the Arabs had seized her, the subtle aroma which had first aroused his desires in the hut that had imprisoned her had fallen upon his nostrils, and told him that he had found the creature for whom he had developed so sudden and inexplicable a passion.

The matter of the pouch of jewels also occupied his thoughts to some extent, so that he found a double urge for his return to the camp of the raiders. He would obtain possession of both his pretty pebbles and the she. Then he would return to the great apes with his new mate and his baubles, and leading his hairy companions into a far wilderness beyond the ken of man, live out his life, hunting and battling among the lower orders after the only manner which he now recollected.

He spoke to his fellow-apes upon the matter, in an attempt to persuade them to accompany him; but all except Taglat and Chulk refused. The latter was young and strong, endowed with a greater intelligence than his fellows, and therefore the possessor of better developed powers of imagination. To him the expedition savored of adventure, and so appealed, strongly. With Taglat there was another incentive—a secret and sinister incentive, which, had Tarzan of the Apes had knowledge of it, would have sent him at the other's throat in jealous rage.

Taglat was no longer young; but he was still a formidable beast, mightily muscled, cruel, and, because of his greater experience, crafty and cunning. Too, he was of giant proportions, the very weight of his huge bulk serving ofttimes to discount in his favor the superior agility of a younger antagonist.

He was of a morose and sullen disposition that marked him even among his frowning fellows, where such characteristics are the rule rather than the exception, and, though Tarzan did not guess it, he hated the ape-man with a ferocity that he was able to hide only because the dominant spirit of the nobler creature had inspired within him a species of dread which was as powerful as it was inexplicable to him.

These two, then, were to be Tarzan's companions upon his return to the village of Achmet Zek. As they set off, the balance of the tribe vouchsafed them but a parting stare, and then resumed the serious business of feeding.

Tarzan found difficulty in keeping the minds of his fellows set upon the purpose of their adventure, for the mind of an ape lacks the power of long-sustained concentration. To set out upon a long journey, with a definite destination in view, is one thing, to remember that purpose and keep it uppermost in one's mind continually is quite another. There are so many things to distract one's attention along the way.

Chulk was, at first, for rushing rapidly ahead as though the village of the raiders lay but an hour's march before them instead of several days; but within a few minutes a fallen tree attracted his attention with its suggestion of rich and succulent forage beneath, and when Tarzan, missing him, returned in search, he found Chulk squatting beside the rotting bole, from beneath which he was assiduously engaged in digging out the grubs and beetles, whose kind form a considerable proportion of the diet of the apes.

Unless Tarzan desired to fight there was nothing to do but wait until Chulk had exhausted the storehouse, and this he did, only to discover that Taglat was now missing. After a considerable search, he found that worthy gentleman contemplating the sufferings of an injured rodent he had pounced upon. He would sit in apparent indifference, gazing in another direction, while the crippled creature wriggled slowly and painfully away from him, and then, just as his victim felt assured of escape, he would reach out a giant palm and slam it down upon the fugitive. Again and again he repeated this operation, until, tiring of the sport, he ended the sufferings of his plaything by devouring it.

Such were the exasperating causes of delay which retarded Tarzan's return journey toward the village of Achmet Zek; but the ape-man was patient, for in his mind was a plan which necessitated the presence of Chulk and Taglat when he should have arrived at his destination.

It was not always an easy thing to maintain in the vacillating minds of the anthropoids a sustained interest in their venture. Chulk was wearying of the continued marching and the infrequency and short duration of the rests. He would gladly have abandoned this search for adventure had not Tarzan continually filled his mind with alluring pictures of the great stores of food which were to be found in the village of Tarmangani.

Taglat nursed his secret purpose to better advantage than might have been expected of an ape, yet there were times when he, too, would have abandoned the adventure had not Tarzan cajoled him on.

It was mid-afternoon of a sultry, tropical day when the keen senses of the three warned them of the proximity of the Arab camp. Stealthily they approached, keeping to the dense tangle of growing things which made concealment easy to their uncanny jungle craft.

First came the giant ape-man, his smooth, brown skin glistening with the sweat of exertion in the close, hot confines of the jungle. Behind him crept Chulk and Taglat, grotesque and shaggy caricatures of their godlike leader.

Silently they made their way to the edge of the clearing which surrounded the palisade, and here they clambered into the lower branches of a large tree overlooking the village occupied by the enemy, the better to spy upon his goings and comings.

A horseman, white burnoosed, rode out through the gateway of the village. Tarzan, whispering to Chulk and Taglat to remain where they were, swung, monkey-like, through the trees in the direction of the trail the Arab was riding. From one jungle giant to the next he sped with the rapidity of a squirrel and the silence of a ghost.

The Arab rode slowly onward, unconscious of the danger hovering in the trees behind him. The ape-man made a slight detour and increased his speed until he had reached a point upon the trail in advance of the horseman. Here he halted upon a leafy bough which overhung the narrow, jungle trail. On came the victim, humming a wild air of the great desert land of the north. Above him poised the savage brute that was today bent upon the destruction of a human life—the same creature who a few months before, had occupied his seat in the House of Lords at London, a respected and distinguished member of that august body.

The Arab passed beneath the overhanging bough, there was a slight rustling of the leaves above, the horse snorted and plunged as a brown-skinned creature dropped upon its rump. A pair of mighty arms encircled the Arab and he was dragged from his saddle to the trail.

Ten minutes later the ape-man, carrying the outer garments of an Arab bundled beneath an arm, rejoined his companions. He exhibited his trophies to them, explaining in low gutturals the details of his exploit. Chulk and Taglat fingered the fabrics, smelled of them, and, placing them to their ears, tried to listen to them.

Then Tarzan led them back through the jungle to the trail, where the three hid themselves and waited. Nor had they long to wait before two of Achmet Zek's blacks, clothed in habiliments similar to their master's, came down the trail on foot, returning to the camp.

One moment they were laughing and talking together—the next they lay stretched in death upon the trail, three mighty engines of destruction bending over them. Tarzan removed their outer garments as he had removed those of his first victim, and again retired with Chulk and Taglat to the greater seclusion of the tree they had first selected.

Here the ape-man arranged the garments upon his shaggy fellows and himself, until, at a distance, it might have appeared that three white-robed Arabs squatted silently among the branches of the forest.

Until dark they remained where they were, for from his point of vantage, Tarzan could view the enclosure within the palisade. He marked the position of the hut in which he had first discovered the scent spoor of the she he sought. He saw the two sentries standing before its doorway, and he located the habitation of Achmet Zek, where something told him he would most likely find the missing pouch and pebbles.

Chulk and Taglat were, at first, greatly interested in their wonderful raiment. They fingered the fabric, smelled of it, and regarded each other intently with every mark of satisfaction and pride. Chulk, a humorist in his way, stretched forth a long and hairy arm, and grasping the hood of Taglat's burnoose pulled it down over the latter's eyes, extinguishing him, snuffer-like, as it were.

The older ape, pessimistic by nature, recognized no such thing as humor. Creatures laid their paws upon him for but two things—to search for fleas and to attack. The pulling of the Tarmangani-scented thing about his head and eyes could not be for the performance of the former act; therefore it must be the latter. He was attacked! Chulk had attacked him.

With a snarl he was at the other's throat, not even waiting to lift the woolen veil which obscured his vision. Tarzan leaped upon the two, and swaying and toppling upon their insecure perch the three great beasts tussled and snapped at one another until the ape-man finally succeeded in separating the enraged anthropoids.

As apology is unknown to these savage progenitors of man, and explanation a laborious and usually futile process, Tarzan bridged the dangerous gulf by distracting their attention from their altercation to a consideration of their plans for the immediate future. Accustomed to frequent arguments in which more hair than blood is wasted, the apes speedily forget such trivial encounters, and presently Chulk and Taglat were again squatting in close proximity to each other and peaceful repose, awaiting the moment when the ape-man should lead them into the village of the Tarmangani.

It was long after darkness had fallen, that Tarzan led his companions from their hiding place in the tree to the ground and around the palisade to the far side of the village.

Gathering the skirts of his burnoose, beneath one arm, that his legs might have free action, the ape-man took a short running start, and scrambled to the top of the barrier. Fearing lest the apes should rend their garments to shreds in a similar attempt, he had directed them to wait below for him, and himself securely perched upon the summit of the palisade he unslung his spear and lowered one end of it to Chulk.

The ape seized it, and while Tarzan held tightly to the upper end, the anthropoid climbed quickly up the shaft until with one paw he grasped the top of the wall. To scramble then to Tarzan's side was the work of but an instant. In like manner Taglat was conducted to their sides, and a moment later the three dropped silently within the enclosure.

Tarzan led them first to the rear of the hut in which Jane Clayton was confined, where, through the roughly repaired aperture in the wall, he sought with his sensitive nostrils for proof that the she he had come for was within.

Chulk and Taglat, their hairy faces pressed close to that of the patrician, sniffed with him. Each caught the scent spoor of the woman within, and each reacted according to his temperament and his habits of thought.

It left Chulk indifferent. The she was for Tarzan—all that he desired was to bury his snout in the foodstuffs of the Tarmangani. He had come to eat his fill without labor—Tarzan had told him that that should be his reward, and he was satisfied.

But Taglat's wicked, bloodshot eyes, narrowed to the realization of the nearing fulfillment of his carefully nursed plan. It is true that sometimes during the several days that had elapsed since they had set out upon their expedition it had been difficult for Taglat to hold his idea uppermost in his mind, and on several occasions he had completely forgotten it, until Tarzan, by a chance word, had recalled it to him, but, for an ape, Taglat had done well.

Now, he licked his chops, and he made a sickening, sucking noise with his flabby lips as he drew in his breath.

Satisfied that the she was where he had hoped to find her, Tarzan led his apes toward the tent of Achmet Zek. A passing Arab and two slaves saw them, but the night was dark and the white burnooses hid the hairy limbs of the apes and the giant figure of their leader, so that the three, by squatting down as though in conversation, were passed by, unsuspected. To the rear of the tent they made their way. Within, Achmet Zek conversed with several of his lieutenants. Without, Tarzan listened.

CHAPTER XVII—THE DEADLY PERIL OF JANE CLAYTON

Lieutenant Albert Werper, terrified by contemplation of the fate which might await him at Adis Abeba, cast about for some scheme of escape, but after the black Mugambi had eluded their vigilance the Abyssinians redoubled their precautions to prevent Werper following the lead of the Negro.

For some time Werper entertained the idea of bribing Abdul Mourak with a portion of the contents of the pouch; but fearing that the man would demand all the gems as the price of liberty, the Belgian, influenced by avarice, sought another avenue from his dilemma.

It was then that there dawned upon him the possibility of the success of a different course which would still leave him in possession of the jewels, while at the same time satisfying the greed of the Abyssinian with the conviction that he had obtained all that Werper had to offer.

And so it was that a day or so after Mugambi had disappeared, Werper asked for an audience with Abdul Mourak. As the Belgian entered the presence of his captor the scowl upon the features of the latter boded ill for any hope which Werper might entertain, still he fortified himself by recalling the common weakness of mankind, which permits the most inflexible of natures to bend to the consuming desire for wealth.

Abdul Mourak eyed him, frowningly. "What do you want now?" he asked.

"My liberty," replied Werper.

The Abyssinian sneered. "And you disturbed me thus to tell me what any fool might know," he said.

"I can pay for it," said Werper.

Abdul Mourak laughed loudly. "Pay for it?" he cried. "What with—the rags that you have upon your back? Or, perhaps you are concealing beneath your coat a thousand pounds of ivory. Get out! You are a fool. Do not bother me again or I shall have you whipped."

But Werper persisted. His liberty and perhaps his life depended upon his success.

"Listen to me," he pleaded. "If I can give you as much gold as ten men may carry will you promise that I shall be conducted in safety to the nearest English commissioner?"

"As much gold as ten men may carry!" repeated Abdul Mourak. "You are crazy. Where have you so much gold as that?"

"I know where it is hid," said Werper. "Promise, and I will lead you to it—if ten loads is enough?"

Abdul Mourak had ceased to laugh. He was eyeing the Belgian intently. The fellow seemed sane enough—yet ten loads of gold! It was preposterous. The Abyssinian thought in silence for a moment.

"Well, and if I promise," he said. "How far is this gold?"

"A long week's march to the south," replied Werper.

"And if we do not find it where you say it is, do you realize what your punishment will be?"

"If it is not there I will forfeit my life," replied the Belgian. "I know it is there, for I saw it buried with my own eyes. And more—there are not only ten loads, but as many as fifty men may carry. It is all yours if you will promise to see me safely delivered into the protection of the English."

"You will stake your life against the finding of the gold?" asked Abdul.

Werper assented with a nod.

"Very well," said the Abyssinian, "I promise, and even if there be but five loads you shall have your freedom; but until the gold is in my possession you remain a prisoner."

"I am satisfied," said Werper. "Tomorrow we start?"

Abdul Mourak nodded, and the Belgian returned to his guards. The following day the Abyssinian soldiers were surprised to receive an order which turned their faces from the northeast to the south. And so it happened that upon the very night that Tarzan and the two apes entered the village of the raiders, the Abyssinians camped but a few miles to the east of the same spot.

While Werper dreamed of freedom and the unmolested enjoyment of the fortune in his stolen pouch, and Abdul Mourak lay awake in greedy contemplation of the fifty loads of gold which lay but a few days farther to the south of him, Achmet Zek gave orders to his lieutenants that they should prepare a force of fighting men and carriers to proceed to the ruins of the Englishman's *douar* on the morrow and bring back the fabulous fortune which his renegade lieutenant had told him was buried there.

And as he delivered his instructions to those within, a silent listener crouched without his tent, waiting for the time when he might enter in safety and prosecute his search for the missing pouch and the pretty pebbles that had caught his fancy.

At last the swarthy companions of Achmet Zek quitted his tent, and the leader went with them to smoke a pipe with one of their number, leaving his own silken habitation unguarded. Scarcely had they left the interior when a knife blade was thrust through the fabric of the rear wall, some six feet above the ground, and a swift downward stroke opened an entrance to those who waited beyond.

Through the opening stepped the ape-man, and close behind him came the huge Chulk; but Taglat did not follow them. Instead he turned and slunk through the darkness toward the hut where the she who had arrested his brutish interest lay securely bound. Before the doorway the sentries sat upon their haunches, conversing in monotones. Within, the young woman lay upon a filthy sleeping mat, resigned, through utter hopelessness to whatever fate lay in store for her until the opportunity arrived which would permit her to free herself by the only means which now seemed even remotely possible—the hitherto detested act of self-destruction.

Creeping silently toward the sentries, a white-burnoosed figure approached the shadows at one end of the hut. The meager intellect of the creature denied it the advantage it might have taken of its disguise. Where it could have walked boldly to the very sides of the sentries, it chose rather to sneak upon them, unseen, from the rear.

It came to the corner of the hut and peered around. The sentries were but a few paces away; but the ape did not dare expose himself, even for an instant, to those feared and hated thunder-sticks which the Tarmangani knew so well how to use, if there were another and safer method of attack.

Taglat wished that there was a tree nearby from the over-hanging branches of which he might spring upon his unsuspecting prey; but, though there was no tree, the idea gave birth to a plan. The eaves of the hut were just above the heads of the sentries—from them he could leap upon the Tarmangani, unseen. A quick snap of those mighty jaws would dispose of one of them before the other realized that they were attacked, and the second would fall an easy prey to the strength, agility and ferocity of a second quick charge.

Taglat withdrew a few paces to the rear of the hut, gathered himself for the effort, ran quickly forward and leaped high into the air. He struck the roof directly above the rear wall of the hut, and the structure, reinforced by the wall beneath, held his enormous weight for an instant, then he moved forward a step, the roof sagged, the thatching parted and the great anthropoid shot through into the interior.

The sentries, hearing the crashing of the roof poles, leaped to their feet and rushed into the hut. Jane Clayton tried to roll aside as the great form lit upon the floor so close to her that one foot pinned her clothing to the ground.

The ape, feeling the movement beside him, reached down and gathered the girl in the hollow of one mighty arm. The burnoose covered the hairy body so that Jane Clayton believed that a human arm supported her, and from the extremity of hopelessness a great hope sprang into her breast that at last she was in the keeping of a rescuer.

The two sentries were now within the hut, but hesitating because of doubt as to the nature of the cause of the disturbance. Their eyes, not yet accustomed to the darkness of the interior, told them nothing, nor did they hear any sound, for the ape stood silently awaiting their attack.

Seeing that they stood without advancing, and realizing that, handicapped as he was by the weight of the she, he could put up but a poor battle, Taglat elected to risk a sudden break for liberty. Lowering his head, he charged straight for the two sentries who blocked the doorway. The impact of his mighty shoulders bowled them over upon their backs, and before they could scramble to their feet, the ape was gone, darting in the shadows of the huts toward the palisade at the far end of the village.

The speed and strength of her rescuer filled Jane Clayton with wonder. Could it be that Tarzan had survived the bullet of the Arab? Who else in all the jungle could bear the weight of a grown woman as lightly as he who held her? She spoke his name; but there was no response. Still she did not give up hope.

At the palisade the beast did not even hesitate. A single mighty leap carried it to the top, where it poised but for an instant before dropping to the ground upon the opposite side. Now the girl was almost positive that she was safe in the arms of her husband, and when the ape took to the trees and bore her swiftly into the jungle, as Tarzan had done at other times in the past, belief became conviction.

In a little moonlit glade, a mile or so from the camp of the raiders, her rescuer halted and dropped her to the ground. His roughness surprised her, but still she had no doubts. Again she called him by name, and at the same instant the ape, fretting under the restraints of the unaccustomed garments of the Tarmangani, tore the burnoose from him, revealing to the eyes of the horror-struck woman the hideous face and hairy form of a giant anthropoid.

With a piteous wail of terror, Jane Clayton swooned, while, from the concealment of a nearby bush, Numa, the lion, eyed the pair hungrily and licked his chops.

Tarzan, entering the tent of Achmet Zek, searched the interior thoroughly. He tore the bed to pieces and scattered the contents of box and bag about the floor. He investigated whatever his eyes discovered, nor did those keen organs overlook a single article within the habitation of the raider chief; but no pouch or pretty pebbles rewarded his thoroughness.

Satisfied at last that his belongings were not in the possession of Achmet Zek, unless they were on the person of the chief himself, Tarzan decided to secure the person of the she before further prosecuting his search for the pouch.

Motioning for Chulk to follow him, he passed out of the tent by the same way that he had entered it, and walking boldly through the village, made directly for the hut where Jane Clayton had been imprisoned.

He noted with surprise the absence of Taglat, whom he had expected to find awaiting him outside the tent of Achmet Zek; but, accustomed as he was to the unreliability of apes, he gave no serious attention to the present defection of his surly companion. So long as Taglat did not cause interference with his plans, Tarzan was indifferent to his absence.

As he approached the hut, the ape-man noticed that a crowd had collected about the entrance. He could see that the men who composed it were much excited, and fearing lest Chulk's disguise should prove inadequate to the concealment of his true identity in the face of so many observers, he commanded the ape to betake himself to the far end of the village, and there await him.

As Chulk waddled off, keeping to the shadows, Tarzan advanced boldly toward the excited group before the doorway of the hut. He mingled with the blacks and the Arabs in an endeavor to learn the cause of the commotion, in his interest forgetting that he alone of the assemblage carried a spear, a bow and arrows, and thus might become an object of suspicious attention.

Shouldering his way through the crowd he approached the doorway, and had almost reached it when one of the Arabs laid a hand upon his shoulder, crying: "Who is this?" at the same time snatching back the hood from the ape-man's face.

Tarzan of the Apes in all his savage life had never been accustomed to pause in argument with an antagonist. The primitive instinct of self-preservation acknowledges many arts and wiles; but argument is not one of them, nor did he now waste precious time in an attempt to convince the raiders that he was not a wolf in sheep's clothing. Instead he had his unmasker by the throat ere the man's words had scarce quitted his lips, and hurling him from side to side brushed away those who would have swarmed upon him.

Using the Arab as a weapon, Tarzan forced his way quickly to the doorway, and a moment later was within the hut. A hasty examination revealed the fact that it was empty, and his sense of smell discovered, too, the scent spoor of Taglat, the ape. Tarzan uttered a low, ominous growl. Those who were pressing forward at the doorway to seize him, fell back as the savage notes of the bestial challenge smote upon their ears. They looked at one another in surprise and consternation. A man had entered the hut alone, and yet with their own ears they had heard the voice of a wild beast within. What could it mean? Had a lion or a leopard sought sanctuary in the interior, unbeknown to the sentries?

Tarzan's quick eyes discovered the opening in the roof, through which Taglat had fallen. He guessed that the ape had either come or gone by way of the break, and while the Arabs hesitated without, he sprang, catlike, for the opening, grasped the top of the wall and clambered out upon the roof, dropping instantly to the ground at the rear of the hut.

When the Arabs finally mustered courage to enter the hut, after firing several volleys through the walls, they found the interior deserted. At the same time Tarzan, at the far end of the village, sought for Chulk; but the ape was nowhere to be found.

Robbed of his she, deserted by his companions, and as much in ignorance as ever as to the whereabouts of his pouch and pebbles, it was an angry Tarzan who climbed the palisade and vanished into the darkness of the jungle.

For the present he must give up the search for his pouch, since it would be paramount to self-destruction to enter the Arab camp now while all its inhabitants were aroused and upon the alert.

In his escape from the village, the ape-man had lost the spoor of the fleeing Taglat, and now he circled widely through the forest in an endeavor to again pick it up.

Chulk had remained at his post until the cries and shots of the Arabs had filled his simple soul with terror, for above all things the ape folk fear the thunder-sticks of the Tarmangani; then he had clambered nimbly over the palisade, tearing his burnoose in the effort, and fled into the depths of the jungle, grumbling and scolding as he went.

Tarzan, roaming the jungle in search of the trail of Taglat and the she, traveled swiftly. In a little moonlit glade ahead of him the great ape was bending over the prostrate form of the woman Tarzan sought. The beast was tearing at the bonds that confined her ankles and wrists, pulling and gnawing upon the cords.

The course the ape-man was taking would carry him but a short distance to the right of them, and though he could not have seen them the wind was bearing down from them to him, carrying their scent spoor strongly toward him.

A moment more and Jane Clayton's safety might have been assured, even though Numa, the lion, was already gathering himself in preparation for a charge; but Fate, already all too cruel, now outdid herself—the wind veered suddenly for a few moments, the scent spoor that would have led the ape-man to the girl's side was wafted in the opposite direction; Tarzan passed within fifty yards of the tragedy that was being enacted in the glade, and the opportunity was gone beyond recall.

CHAPTER XVIII—THE FIGHT FOR THE TREASURE

It was morning before Tarzan could bring himself to a realization of the possibility of failure of his quest, and even then he would only admit that success was but delayed. He would eat and sleep, and then set forth again. The jungle was wide; but wide too were the experience and cunning of Tarzan. Taglat might travel far; but Tarzan would find him in the end, though he had to search every tree in the mighty forest.

Soliloquizing thus, the ape-man followed the spoor of Bara, the deer, the unfortunate upon which he had decided to satisfy his hunger. For half an hour the trail led the ape-man toward the east along a well-marked game path, when suddenly, to the stalker's astonishment, the quarry broke into sight, racing madly back along the narrow way straight toward the hunter.

Tarzan, who had been following along the trail, leaped so quickly to the concealing verdure at the side that the deer was still unaware of the presence of an enemy in this direction, and while the animal was still some distance away, the ape-man swung into the lower branches of the tree which overhung the trail. There he crouched, a savage beast of prey, awaiting the coming of its victim.

What had frightened the deer into so frantic a retreat, Tarzan did not know—Numa, the lion, perhaps, or Sheeta, the panther; but whatsoever it was mattered little to Tarzan of the Apes—he was ready and willing to defend his kill against any other denizen of the jungle. If he were unable to do it by means of physical prowess, he had at his command another and a greater power—his shrewd intelligence.

And so, on came the running deer, straight into the jaws of death. The ape-man turned so that his back was toward the approaching animal. He poised with bent knees upon the gently swaying limb above the trail, timing with keen ears the nearing hoof beats of frightened Bara.

In a moment the victim flashed beneath the limb and at the same instant the ape-man above sprang out and down upon its back. The weight of the man's body carried the deer to the ground. It stumbled forward once in a futile effort to rise, and then mighty muscles dragged its head far back, gave the neck a vicious wrench, and Bara was dead.

Quick had been the killing, and equally quick were the ape-man's subsequent actions, for who might know what manner of killer pursued Bara, or how close at hand he might be? Scarce had the neck of the victim snapped than the carcass was hanging over one of Tarzan's broad shoulders, and an instant later the ape-man was perched once more among the lower branches of a tree above the trail, his keen, gray eyes scanning the pathway down which the deer had fled.

Nor was it long before the cause of Bara's fright became evident to Tarzan, for presently came the unmistakable sounds of approaching horsemen. Dragging his kill after him the ape-man ascended to the middle terrace, and settling himself comfortably in the crotch of a tree where he could still view the trail beneath, cut a juicy steak from the deer's loin, and burying his strong, white teeth in the hot flesh proceeded to enjoy the fruits of his prowess and his cunning.

Nor did he neglect the trail beneath while he satisfied his hunger. His sharp eyes saw the muzzle of the leading horse as it came into view around a bend in the tortuous trail, and one by one they scrutinized the riders as they passed beneath him in single file.

Among them came one whom Tarzan recognized, but so schooled was the ape-man in the control of his emotions that no slightest change of expression, much less any hysterical demonstration that might have revealed his presence, betrayed the fact of his inward excitement.

Beneath him, as unconscious of his presence as were the Abyssinians before and behind him, rode Albert Werper, while the ape-man scrutinized the Belgian for some sign of the pouch which he had stolen.

As the Abyssinians rode toward the south, a giant figure hovered ever upon their trail—a huge, almost naked white man, who carried the bloody carcass of a deer upon his shoulders, for Tarzan knew that he might not have another opportunity to hunt for some time if he were to follow the Belgian.

To endeavor to snatch him from the midst of the armed horsemen, not even Tarzan would attempt other than in the last extremity, for the way of the wild is the way of caution and cunning, unless they be aroused to rashness by pain or anger.

So the Abyssinians and the Belgian marched southward and Tarzan of the Apes swung silently after them through the swaying branches of the middle terrace.

A two days' march brought them to a level plain beyond which lay mountains—a plain which Tarzan remembered and which aroused within him vague half memories and strange longings. Out upon the plain the horsemen rode, and at a safe distance behind them crept the ape-man, taking advantage of such cover as the ground afforded.

Beside a charred pile of timbers the Abyssinians halted, and Tarzan, sneaking close and concealing himself in nearby shrubbery, watched them in wonderment. He saw them digging up the earth, and he wondered if they had hidden meat there in the past and now had come for it. Then he recalled how he had buried his pretty pebbles, and the suggestion that had caused him to do it. They were digging for the things the blacks had buried here!

Presently he saw them uncover a dirty, yellow object, and he witnessed the joy of Werper and of Abdul Mourak as the grimy object was exposed to view. One by one they unearthed many similar pieces, all of the same uniform, dirty yellow, until a pile of them lay upon the ground, a pile which Abdul Mourak fondled and petted in an ecstasy of greed.

Something stirred in the ape-man's mind as he looked long upon the golden ingots. Where had he seen such before? What were they? Why did these Tarmangani covet them so greatly? To whom did they belong?

He recalled the black men who had buried them. The things must be theirs. Werper was stealing them as he had stolen Tarzan's pouch of pebbles. The ape-man's eyes blazed in anger. He would like to find the black men and lead them against these thieves. He wondered where their village might be.

As all these things ran through the active mind, a party of men moved out of the forest at the edge of the plain and advanced toward the ruins of the burned bungalow.

Abdul Mourak, always watchful, was the first to see them, but already they were halfway across the open. He called to his men to mount and hold themselves in readiness, for in the heart of Africa who may know whether a strange host be friend or foe?

Werper, swinging into his saddle, fastened his eyes upon the newcomers, then, white and trembling he turned toward Abdul Mourak.

"It is Achmet Zek and his raiders," he whispered. "They are come for the gold."

It must have been at about the same instant that Achmet Zek discovered the pile of yellow ingots and realized the actuality of what he had already feared since first his eyes had alighted upon the party beside the ruins of the Englishman's bungalow. Someone had forestalled him—another had come for the treasure ahead of him.

The Arab was crazed by rage. Recently everything had gone against him. He had lost the jewels, the Belgian, and for the second time he had lost the Englishwoman. Now some one had come to rob him of this treasure which he had thought as safe from disturbance here as though it never had been mined.

He cared not whom the thieves might be. They would not give up the gold without a battle, of that he was certain, and with a wild whoop and a command to his followers, Achmet Zek put spurs to his horse and dashed down upon the Abyssinians, and after him, waving their long guns above their heads, yelling and cursing, came his motley horde of cut-throat followers.

The men of Abdul Mourak met them with a volley which emptied a few saddles, and then the raiders were among them, and sword, pistol and musket, each was doing its most hideous and bloody work.

Achmet Zek, spying Werper at the first charge, bore down upon the Belgian, and the latter, terrified by contemplation of the fate he deserved, turned his horse's head and dashed madly away in an effort to escape. Shouting to a lieutenant to take command, and urging him upon pain of death to dispatch the Abyssinians and bring the gold back to his camp, Achmet Zek set off across the plain in pursuit of the Belgian, his wicked nature unable to forego the pleasures of revenge, even at the risk of sacrificing the treasure.

As the pursued and the pursuer raced madly toward the distant forest the battle behind them raged with bloody savageness. No quarter was asked or given by either the ferocious Abyssinians or the murderous cut-throats of Achmet Zek.

From the concealment of the shrubbery Tarzan watched the sanguinary conflict which so effectually surrounded him that he found no loop-hole through which he might escape to follow Werper and the Arab chief.

The Abyssinians were formed in a circle which included Tarzan's position, and around and into them galloped the yelling raiders, now darting away, now charging in to deliver thrusts and cuts with their curved swords.

Numerically the men of Achmet Zek were superior, and slowly but surely the soldiers of Menelek were being exterminated. To Tarzan the result was immaterial. He watched with but a single purpose—to escape the ring of blood-mad fighters and be away after the Belgian and his pouch.

When he had first discovered Werper upon the trail where he had slain Bara, he had thought that his eyes must be playing him false, so certain had he been that the thief had been slain and devoured by Numa; but after following the detachment for two days, with his keen eyes always upon the Belgian, he no longer doubted the identity of the man, though he was put to it to explain the identity of the mutilated corpse he had supposed was the man he sought.

As he crouched in hiding among the unkempt shrubbery which so short a while since had been the delight and pride of the wife he no longer recalled, an Arab and an Abyssinian wheeled their mounts close to his position as they slashed at each other with their swords.

Step by step the Arab beat back his adversary until the latter's horse all but trod upon the ape-man, and then a vicious cut clove the black warrior's skull, and the corpse toppled backward almost upon Tarzan.

As the Abyssinian tumbled from his saddle the possibility of escape which was represented by the riderless horse electrified the ape-man to instant action. Before the frightened beast could gather himself for flight a naked giant was astride his back. A strong hand had grasped his bridle rein, and the surprised Arab discovered a new foe in the saddle of him, whom he had slain.

But this enemy wielded no sword, and his spear and bow remained upon his back. The Arab, recovered from his first surprise, dashed in with raised sword to annihilate this presumptuous stranger. He aimed a mighty blow at the ape-man's head, a blow which swung harmlessly through thin air as Tarzan ducked from its path, and then the Arab felt the other's horse brushing his leg, a great arm shot out and encircled his waist, and before he could recover himself he was dragged from his saddle, and forming a shield for his antagonist was borne at a mad run straight through the encircling ranks of his fellows.

Just beyond them he was tossed aside upon the ground, and the last he saw of his strange foeman the latter was galloping off across the plain in the direction of the forest at its farther edge.

For another hour the battle raged nor did it cease until the last of the Abyssinians lay dead upon the ground, or had galloped off toward the north in flight. But a handful of men escaped, among them Abdul Mourak.

The victorious raiders collected about the pile of golden ingots which the Abyssinians had uncovered, and there awaited the return of their leader. Their exultation was slightly tempered by the glimpse they had had of the strange apparition of the naked white man galloping away upon the horse of one of their foemen and carrying a companion who was now among them expatiating upon the superhuman strength of the ape-man. None of them there but was familiar with the name and fame of Tarzan of the Apes, and the fact that they had recognized the white giant as the ferocious enemy of the wrongdoers of the jungle, added to their terror, for they had been assured that Tarzan was dead.

Naturally superstitious, they fully believed that they had seen the disembodied spirit of the dead man, and now they cast fearful glances about them in expectation of the ghost's early return to the scene of the ruin they had inflicted upon him during their recent raid upon his home, and discussed in affrighted whispers the probable nature of the vengeance which the spirit would inflict upon them should he return to find them in possession of his gold.

As they conversed their terror grew, while from the concealment of the reeds along the river below them a small party of naked, black warriors watched their every move. From the heights beyond the river these black men had heard the noise of the conflict, and creeping warily down to the stream had forded it and advanced through the reeds until they were in a position to watch every move of the combatants.

For a half hour the raiders awaited Achmet Zek's return, their fear of the earlier return of the ghost of Tarzan constantly undermining their loyalty to and fear of their chief. Finally one among them voiced the desires of all when he announced that he intended riding forth toward the forest in search of Achmet Zek. Instantly every man of them sprang to his mount.

"The gold will be safe here," cried one. "We have killed the Abyssinians and there are no others to carry it away. Let us ride in search of Achmet Zek!"

And a moment later, amidst a cloud of dust, the raiders were galloping madly across the plain, and out from the concealment of the reeds along the river, crept a party of black warriors toward the spot where the golden ingots of Opar lay piled on the ground.

Werper had still been in advance of Achmet Zek when he reached the forest; but the latter, better mounted, was gaining upon him. Riding with the reckless courage of desperation the Belgian urged his mount to greater speed even within the narrow confines of the winding, game trail that the beast was following.

Behind him he could hear the voice of Achmet Zek crying to him to halt; but Werper only dug the spurs deeper into the bleeding sides of his panting mount. Two hundred yards within the forest a broken branch lay across the trail. It was a small thing that a horse might ordinarily take in his natural stride without noticing its presence; but Werper's horse was jaded, his feet were heavy with weariness, and as the branch caught between his front legs he stumbled, was unable to recover himself, and went down, sprawling in the trail.

Werper, going over his head, rolled a few yards farther on, scrambled to his feet and ran back. Seizing the reins he tugged to drag the beast to his feet; but the animal would not or could not rise, and as the Belgian cursed and struck at him, Achmet Zek appeared in view.

Instantly the Belgian ceased his efforts with the dying animal at his feet, and seizing his rifle, dropped behind the horse and fired at the oncoming Arab.

His bullet, going low, struck Achmet Zek's horse in the breast, bringing him down a hundred yards from where Werper lay preparing to fire a second shot.

The Arab, who had gone down with his mount, was standing astride him, and seeing the Belgian's strategic position behind his fallen horse, lost no time in taking up a similar one behind his own.

And there the two lay, alternately firing at and cursing each other, while from behind the Arab, Tarzan of the Apes approached to the edge of the forest. Here he heard the occasional shots of the duelists, and choosing the safer and swifter avenue of the forest branches to the uncertain transportation afforded by a half-broken Abyssinian pony, took to the trees.

Keeping to one side of the trail, the ape-man came presently to a point where he could look down in comparative safety upon the fighters. First one and then the other would partially raise himself above his breastwork of horseflesh, fire his weapon and immediately drop flat behind his shelter, where he would reload and repeat the act a moment later.

Werper had but little ammunition, having been hastily armed by Abdul Mourak from the body of one of the first of the Abyssinians who had fallen in the fight about the pile of ingots, and now he realized that soon he would have used his last bullet, and be at the mercy of the Arab—a mercy with which he was well acquainted.

Facing both death and despoilment of his treasure, the Belgian cast about for some plan of escape, and the only one that appealed to him as containing even a remote possibility of success hinged upon the chance of bribing Achmet Zek.

Werper had fired all but a single cartridge, when, during a lull in the fighting, he called aloud to his opponent.

"Achmet Zek," he cried, "Allah alone knows which one of us may leave our bones to rot where he lies upon this trail today if we keep up our foolish battle. You wish the contents of the pouch I wear about my waist, and I wish my life and my liberty even more than I do the jewels. Let us each, then, take that which he most desires and go our separate ways in peace. I will lay the pouch upon the carcass of my horse, where you may see it, and you, in turn, will lay your gun upon your horse, with butt toward me. Then I will go away, leaving the pouch to you, and you will let me go in safety. I want only my life, and my freedom."

The Arab thought in silence for a moment. Then he spoke. His reply was influenced by the fact that he had expended his last shot.

"Go your way, then," he growled, "leaving the pouch in plain sight behind you. See, I lay my gun thus, with the butt toward you. Go."

Werper removed the pouch from about his waist. Sorrowfully and affectionately he let his fingers press the hard outlines of the contents. Ah, if he could extract a little handful of the precious stones! But Achmet Zek was standing now, his eagle eyes commanding a plain view of the Belgian and his every act.

Regretfully Werper laid the pouch, its contents undisturbed, upon the body of his horse, rose, and taking his rifle with him, backed slowly down the trail until a turn hid him from the view of the watchful Arab.

Even then Achmet Zek did not advance, fearful as he was of some such treachery as he himself might have been guilty of under like circumstances; nor were his suspicions groundless, for the Belgian, no sooner had he passed out of the range of the Arab's vision, halted behind the bole of a tree, where he still commanded an unobstructed view of his dead horse and the pouch, and raising his rifle covered the spot where the other's body must appear when he came forward to seize the treasure.

But Achmet Zek was no fool to expose himself to the blackened honor of a thief and a murderer. Taking his long gun with him, he left the trail, entering the rank and tangled vegetation which walled it, and crawling slowly forward on hands and knees he paralleled the trail; but never for an instant was his body exposed to the rifle of the hidden assassin.

Thus Achmet Zek advanced until he had come opposite the dead horse of his enemy. The pouch lay there in full view, while a short distance along the trail, Werper waited in growing impatience and nervousness, wondering why the Arab did not come to claim his reward.

Presently he saw the muzzle of a rifle appear suddenly and mysteriously a few inches above the pouch, and before he could realize the cunning trick that the Arab had played upon him the sight of the weapon was adroitly hooked into the rawhide thong which formed the carrying strap of the pouch, and the latter was drawn quickly from his view into the dense foliage at the trail's side.

Not for an instant had the raider exposed a square inch of his body, and Werper dared not fire his one remaining shot unless every chance of a successful hit was in his favor.

Chuckling to himself, Achmet Zek withdrew a few paces farther into the jungle, for he was as positive that Werper was waiting nearby for a chance to pot him as though his eyes had penetrated the jungle trees to the figure of the hiding Belgian, fingering his rifle behind the bole of the buttressed giant.

Werper did not dare advance—his cupidity would not permit him to depart, and so he stood there, his rifle ready in his hands, his eyes watching the trail before him with catlike intensity.

But there was another who had seen the pouch and recognized it, who did advance with Achmet Zek, hovering above him, as silent and as sure as death itself, and as the Arab, finding a little spot less overgrown with bushes than he had yet encountered, prepared to gloat his eyes upon the contents of the pouch, Tarzan paused directly above him, intent upon the same object.

Wetting his thin lips with his tongue, Achmet Zek loosened the tie strings which closed the mouth of the pouch, and cupping one claw-like hand poured forth a portion of the contents into his palm.

A single look he took at the stones lying in his hand. His eyes narrowed, a curse broke from his lips, and he hurled the small objects upon the ground, disdainfully. Quickly he emptied the balance of the contents until he had scanned each separate stone, and as he dumped them all upon the ground and stamped upon them his rage grew until the muscles of his face worked in demon-like fury, and his fingers clenched until his nails bit into the flesh.

Above, Tarzan watched in wonderment. He had been curious to discover what all the pow-wow about his pouch had meant. He wanted to see what the Arab would do after the other had gone away, leaving the pouch behind him, and, having satisfied his curiosity, he would then have pounced upon Achmet Zek and taken the pouch and his pretty pebbles away from him, for did they not belong to Tarzan?

He saw the Arab now throw aside the empty pouch, and grasping his long gun by the barrel, clublike, sneak stealthily through the jungle beside the trail along which Werper had gone.

As the man disappeared from his view, Tarzan dropped to the ground and commenced gathering up the spilled contents of the pouch, and the moment that he obtained his first near view of the scattered pebbles he understood the rage of the Arab, for instead of the glittering and scintillating gems which had first caught and held the attention of the ape-man, the pouch now contained but a collection of ordinary river pebbles.

CHAPTER XIX—JANE CLAYTON AND THE BEASTS OF THE JUNGLE

Mugambi, after his successful break for liberty, had fallen upon hard times. His way had led him through a country with which he was unfamiliar, a jungle country in which he could find no water, and but little food, so that after several days of wandering he found himself so reduced in strength that he could barely drag himself along.

It was with growing difficulty that he found the strength necessary to construct a shelter by night wherein he might be reasonably safe from the large carnivora, and by day he still further exhausted his strength in digging for edible roots, and searching for water.

A few stagnant pools at considerable distances apart saved him from death by thirst; but his was a pitiable state when finally he stumbled by accident upon a large river in a country where fruit was abundant, and small game which he might bag by means of a combination of stealth, cunning, and a crude knob-stick which he had fashioned from a fallen limb.

Realizing that he still had a long march ahead of him before he could reach even the outskirts of the Waziri country, Mugambi wisely decided to remain where he was until he had recuperated his strength and health. A few days' rest would accomplish wonders for him, he knew, and he could ill afford to sacrifice his chances for a safe return by setting forth handicapped by weakness.

And so it was that he constructed a substantial thorn boma, and rigged a thatched shelter within it, where he might sleep by night in security, and from which he sallied forth by day to hunt the flesh which alone could return to his giant thews their normal prowess.

One day, as he hunted, a pair of savage eyes discovered him from the concealment of the branches of a great tree beneath which the black warrior passed. Bloodshot, wicked eyes they were, set in a fierce and hairy face.

They watched Mugambi make his little kill of a small rodent, and they followed him as he returned to his hut, their owner moving quietly through the trees upon the trail of the Negro.

The creature was Chulk, and he looked down upon the unconscious man more in curiosity than in hate. The wearing of the Arab burnoose which Tarzan had placed upon his person had aroused in the mind of the anthropoid a desire for similar mimicry of the Tarmangani. The burnoose, though, had obstructed his movements and proven such a nuisance that the ape had long since torn it from him and thrown it away.

Now, however, he saw a Gomangani arrayed in less cumbersome apparel—a loin cloth, a few copper ornaments and a feather headdress. These were more in line with Chulk's desires than a flowing robe which was constantly getting between one's legs, and catching upon every limb and bush along the leafy trail.

Chulk eyed the pouch, which, suspended over Mugambi's shoulder, swung beside his black hip. This took his fancy, for it was ornamented with feathers and a fringe, and so the ape hung about Mugambi's boma, waiting an opportunity to seize either by stealth or might some object of the black's apparel.

Nor was it long before the opportunity came. Feeling safe within his thorny enclosure, Mugambi was wont to stretch himself in the shade of his shelter during the heat of the day, and sleep in peaceful security until the declining sun carried with it the enervating temperature of midday.

Watching from above, Chulk saw the black warrior stretched thus in the unconsciousness of sleep one sultry afternoon. Creeping out upon an overhanging branch the anthropoid dropped to the ground within the boma. He approached the sleeper upon padded feet which gave forth no sound, and with an uncanny woodcraft that rustled not a leaf or a grass blade.

Pausing beside the man, the ape bent over and examined his belongings. Great as was the strength of Chulk there lay in the back of his little brain a something which deterred him from arousing the man to combat—a sense that is inherent in all the lower orders, a strange fear of man, that rules even the most powerful of the jungle creatures at times.

To remove Mugambi's loin cloth without awakening him would be impossible, and the only detachable things were the knob-stick and the pouch, which had fallen from the black's shoulder as he rolled in sleep.

Seizing these two articles, as better than nothing at all, Chulk retreated with haste, and every indication of nervous terror, to the safety of the tree from which he had dropped, and, still haunted by that indefinable terror which the close proximity of man awakened in his breast, fled precipitately through the jungle. Aroused by attack, or supported by the presence of another of his kind, Chulk could have braved the presence of a score of human beings, but alone—ah, that was a different matter—alone, and unenraged.

It was some time after Mugambi awoke that he missed the pouch. Instantly he was all excitement. What could have become of it? It had been at his side when he lay down to sleep—of that he was certain, for had he not pushed it from beneath him when its bulging bulk, pressing against his ribs, caused him discomfort? Yes, it had been there when he lay down to sleep. How then had it vanished?

Mugambi's savage imagination was filled with visions of the spirits of departed friends and enemies, for only to the machinations of such as these could he attribute the disappearance of his pouch and knob-stick in the first excitement of the discovery of their loss; but later and more careful investigation, such as his woodcraft made possible, revealed indisputable evidence of a more material explanation than his excited fancy and superstition had at first led him to accept.

In the trampled turf beside him was the faint impress of huge, manlike feet. Mugambi raised his brows as the truth dawned upon him. Hastily leaving the boma he searched in all directions about the enclosure for some further sign of the tell-tale spoor. He climbed trees and sought for evidence of the direction of the thief's flight; but the faint signs left by a wary ape who elects to travel through the trees eluded the woodcraft of Mugambi. Tarzan might have followed them; but no ordinary mortal could perceive them, or perceiving, translate.

The black, now strengthened and refreshed by his rest, felt ready to set out again for Waziri, and finding himself another knob-stick, turned his back upon the river and plunged into the mazes of the jungle.

As Taglat struggled with the bonds which secured the ankles and wrists of his captive, the great lion that eyed the two from behind a nearby clump of bushes wormed closer to his intended prey.

The ape's back was toward the lion. He did not see the broad head, fringed by its rough mane, protruding through the leafy wall. He could not know that the powerful hind paws were gathering close beneath the tawny belly preparatory to a sudden spring, and his first intimation of impending danger was the thunderous and triumphant roar which the charging lion could no longer suppress.

Scarce pausing for a backward glance, Taglat abandoned the unconscious woman and fled in the opposite direction from the horrid sound which had broken in so unexpected and terrifying a manner upon his startled ears; but the warning had come too late to save him, and the lion, in his second bound, alighted full upon the broad shoulders of the anthropoid.

As the great bull went down there was awakened in him to the full all the cunning, all the ferocity, all the physical prowess which obey the mightiest of the fundamental laws of nature, the law of self-preservation, and turning upon his back he closed with the carnivore in a death struggle so fearless and abandoned, that for a moment the great Numa himself may have trembled for the outcome.

Seizing the lion by the mane, Taglat buried his yellowed fangs deep in the monster's throat, growling hideously through the muffled gag of blood and hair. Mixed with the ape's voice the lion's roars of rage and pain reverberated through the jungle, till the lesser creatures of the wild, startled from their peaceful pursuits, scurried fearfully away.

Rolling over and over upon the turf the two battled with demoniac fury, until the colossal cat, by doubling his hind paws far up beneath his belly sank his talons deep into Taglat's chest, then, ripping downward with all his strength, Numa accomplished his design, and the disemboweled anthropoid, with a last spasmodic struggle, relaxed in limp and bloody dissolution beneath his titanic adversary.

Scrambling to his feet, Numa looked about quickly in all directions, as though seeking to detect the possible presence of other foes; but only the still and unconscious form of the girl, lying a few paces from him met his gaze, and with an angry growl he placed a forepaw upon the body of his kill and raising his head gave voice to his savage victory cry.

For another moment he stood with fierce eyes roving to and fro about the clearing. At last they halted for a second time upon the girl. A low growl rumbled from the lion's throat. His lower jaw rose and fell, and the slaver drooled and dripped upon the dead face of Taglat.

Like two yellow-green augurs, wide and unblinking, the terrible eyes remained fixed upon Jane Clayton. The erect and majestic pose of the great frame shrank suddenly into a sinister crouch as, slowly and gently as one who treads on eggs, the devil-faced cat crept forward toward the girl.

Beneficent Fate maintained her in happy unconsciousness of the dread presence sneaking stealthily upon her. She did not know when the lion paused at her side. She did not hear the sniffing of his nostrils as he smelled about her. She did not feel the heat of the fetid breath upon her face, nor the dripping of the saliva from the frightful jaws half opened so close above her.

Finally the lion lifted a forepaw and turned the body of the girl half over, then he stood again eyeing her as though still undetermined whether life was extinct or not. Some noise or odor from the nearby jungle attracted his attention for a moment. His eyes did not again return to Jane Clayton, and presently he left her, walked over to the remains of Taglat, and crouching down upon his kill with his back toward the girl, proceeded to devour the ape.

It was upon this scene that Jane Clayton at last opened her eyes. Inured to danger, she maintained her self-possession in the face of the startling surprise which her new-found consciousness revealed to her. She neither cried out nor moved a muscle, until she had taken in every detail of the scene which lay within the range of her vision.

She saw that the lion had killed the ape, and that he was devouring his prey less than fifty feet from where she lay; but what could she do? Her hands and feet were bound. She must wait then, in what patience she could command, until Numa had eaten and digested the ape, when, without doubt, he would return to feast upon her, unless, in the meantime, the dread hyenas should discover her, or some other of the numerous prowling carnivora of the jungle.

As she lay tormented by these frightful thoughts, she suddenly became conscious that the bonds at her wrists and ankles no longer hurt her, and then of the fact that her hands were separated, one lying upon either side of her, instead of both being confined at her back.

Wonderingly she moved a hand. What miracle had been performed? It was not bound! Stealthily and noiselessly she moved her other limbs, only to discover that she was free. She could not know how the thing had happened, that Taglat, gnawing upon them for sinister purposes of his own, had cut them through but an instant before Numa had frightened him from his victim.

For a moment Jane Clayton was overwhelmed with joy and thanksgiving; but only for a moment. What good was her new-found liberty in the face of the frightful beast crouching so close beside her? If she could have had this chance under different conditions, how happily she would have taken advantage of it; but now it was given to her when escape was practically impossible.

The nearest tree was a hundred feet away, the lion less than fifty. To rise and attempt to reach the safety of those tantalizing branches would be but to invite instant destruction, for Numa would doubtless be too jealous of this future meal to permit it to escape with ease. And yet, too, there was another possibility—a chance which hinged entirely upon the unknown temper of the great beast.

His belly already partially filled, he might watch with indifference the departure of the girl; yet could she afford to chance so improbable a contingency? She doubted it. Upon the other hand she was no more minded to allow this frail opportunity for life to entirely elude her without taking or attempting to take some advantage from it.

She watched the lion narrowly. He could not see her without turning his head more than halfway around. She would attempt a ruse. Silently she rolled over in the direction of the nearest tree, and away from the lion, until she lay again in the same position in which Numa had left her, but a few feet farther from him.

Here she lay breathless watching the lion; but the beast gave no indication that he had heard aught to arouse his suspicions. Again she rolled over, gaining a few more feet and again she lay in rigid contemplation of the beast's back.

During what seemed hours to her tense nerves, Jane Clayton continued these tactics, and still the lion fed on in apparent unconsciousness that his second prey was escaping him. Already the girl was but a few paces from the tree—a moment more and she would be close enough to chance springing to her feet, throwing caution aside and making a sudden, bold dash for safety. She was halfway over in her turn, her face away from the lion, when he suddenly turned his great head and fastened his eyes upon her. He saw her roll over upon her side away from him, and then her eyes were turned again toward him, and the cold sweat broke from the girl's every pore as she realized that with life almost within her grasp, death had found her out.

For a long time neither the girl nor the lion moved. The beast lay motionless, his head turned upon his shoulders and his glaring eyes fixed upon the rigid victim, now nearly fifty yards away. The girl stared back straight into those cruel orbs, daring not to move even a muscle.

The strain upon her nerves was becoming so unbearable that she could scarcely restrain a growing desire to scream, when Numa deliberately turned back to the business of feeding; but his back-layed ears attested a sinister regard for the actions of the girl behind him.

Realizing that she could not again turn without attracting his immediate and perhaps fatal attention, Jane Clayton resolved to risk all in one last attempt to reach the tree and clamber to the lower branches.

Gathering herself stealthily for the effort, she leaped suddenly to her feet, but almost simultaneously the lion sprang up, wheeled and with wide-distended jaws and terrific roars, charged swiftly down upon her.

Those who have spent lifetimes hunting the big game of Africa will tell you that scarcely any other creature in the world attains the speed of a charging lion. For the short distance that the great cat can maintain it, it resembles nothing more closely than the onrushing of a giant locomotive under full speed, and so, though the distance that Jane Clayton must cover was relatively small, the terrific speed of the lion rendered her hopes of escape almost negligible.

Yet fear can work wonders, and though the upward spring of the lion as he neared the tree into which she was scrambling brought his talons in contact with her boots she eluded his raking grasp, and as he hurtled against the bole of her sanctuary, the girl drew herself into the safety of the branches above his reach.

For some time the lion paced, growling and moaning, beneath the tree in which Jane Clayton crouched, panting and trembling. The girl was a prey to the nervous reaction from the frightful ordeal through which she had so recently passed, and in her overwrought state it seemed that never again should she dare descend to the ground among the fearsome dangers which infested the broad stretch of jungle that she knew must lie between herself and the nearest village of her faithful Waziri.

It was almost dark before the lion finally quit the clearing, and even had his place beside the remnants of the mangled ape not been immediately usurped by a pack of hyenas, Jane Clayton would scarcely have dared venture from her refuge in the face of impending night, and so she composed herself as best she could for the long and tiresome wait, until daylight might offer some means of escape from the dread vicinity in which she had witnessed such terrifying adventures.

Tired nature at last overcame even her fears, and she dropped into a deep slumber, cradled in a comparatively safe, though rather uncomfortable, position against the bole of the tree, and supported by two large branches which grew outward, almost horizontally, but a few inches apart.

The sun was high in the heavens when she at last awoke, and beneath her was no sign either of Numa or the hyenas. Only the clean-picked bones of the ape, scattered about the ground, attested the fact of what had transpired in this seemingly peaceful spot but a few hours before.

Both hunger and thirst assailed her now, and realizing that she must descend or die of starvation, she at last summoned courage to undertake the ordeal of continuing her journey through the jungle.

Descending from the tree, she set out in a southerly direction, toward the point where she believed the plains of Waziri lay, and though she knew that only ruin and desolation marked the spot where once her happy home had stood, she hoped that by coming to the broad plain she might eventually reach one of the numerous Waziri villages that were scattered over the surrounding country, or chance upon a roving band of these indefatigable huntsmen.

The day was half spent when there broke unexpectedly upon her startled ears the sound of a rifle shot not far ahead of her. As she paused to listen, this first shot was followed by another and another and another. What could it mean? The first explanation which sprung to her mind attributed the firing to an encounter between the Arab raiders and a party of Waziri; but as she did not know upon which side victory might rest, or whether she were behind friend or foe, she dared not advance nearer on the chance of revealing herself to an enemy.

After listening for several minutes she became convinced that no more than two or three rifles were engaged in the fight, since nothing approximating the sound of a volley reached her ears; but still she hesitated to approach, and at last, determining to take no chance, she climbed into the concealing foliage of a tree beside the trail she had been following and there fearfully awaited whatever might reveal itself.

As the firing became less rapid she caught the sound of men's voices, though she could distinguish no words, and at last the reports of the guns ceased, and she heard two men calling to each other in loud tones. Then there was a long silence which was finally broken by the stealthy padding of footfalls on the trail ahead of her, and in another moment a man appeared in view backing toward her, a rifle ready in his hands, and his eyes directed in careful watchfulness along the way that he had come.

Almost instantly Jane Clayton recognized the man as M. Jules Frecoult, who so recently had been a guest in her home. She was upon the point of calling to him in glad relief when she saw him leap quickly to one side and hide himself in the thick verdure at the trail's side. It was evident that he was being followed by an enemy, and so Jane Clayton kept silent, lest she distract Frecoult's attention, or guide his foe to his hiding place.

Scarcely had Frecoult hidden himself than the figure of a white-robed Arab crept silently along the trail in pursuit. From her hiding place, Jane Clayton could see both men plainly. She recognized Achmet Zek as the leader of the band of ruffians who had raided her home and made her a prisoner, and as she saw Frecoult, the supposed friend and ally, raise his gun and take careful aim at the Arab, her heart stood still and every power of her soul was directed upon a fervent prayer for the accuracy of his aim.

Achmet Zek paused in the middle of the trail. His keen eyes scanned every bush and tree within the radius of his vision. His tall figure presented a perfect target to the perfidious assassin. There was a sharp report, and a little puff of smoke arose from the bush that hid the Belgian, as Achmet Zek stumbled forward and pitched, face down, upon the trail.

As Werper stepped back into the trail, he was startled by the sound of a glad cry from above him, and as he wheeled about to discover the author of this unexpected interruption, he saw Jane Clayton drop lightly from a nearby tree and run forward with outstretched hands to congratulate him upon his victory.

CHAPTER XX—JANE CLAYTON AGAIN A PRISONER

Though her clothes were torn and her hair disheveled, Albert Werper realized that he never before had looked upon such a vision of loveliness as that which Lady Greystoke presented in the relief and joy which she felt in coming so unexpectedly upon a friend and rescuer when hope had seemed so far away.

If the Belgian had entertained any doubts as to the woman's knowledge of his part in the perfidious attack upon her home and herself, it was quickly dissipated by the genuine friendliness of her greeting. She told him quickly of all that had befallen her since he had departed from her home, and as she spoke of the death of her husband her eyes were veiled by the tears which she could not repress.

"I am shocked," said Werper, in well-simulated sympathy; "but I am not surprised. That devil there," and he pointed toward the body of Achmet Zek, "has terrorized the entire country. Your Waziri are either exterminated, or have been driven out of their country, far to the south. The men of Achmet Zek occupy the plain about your former home—there is neither sanctuary nor escape in that direction. Our only hope lies in traveling northward as rapidly as we may, of coming to the camp of the raiders before the knowledge of Achmet Zek's death reaches those who were left there, and of obtaining, through some ruse, an escort toward the north.

"I think that the thing can be accomplished, for I was a guest of the raider's before I knew the nature of the man, and those at the camp are not aware that I turned against him when I discovered his villainy.

"Come! We will make all possible haste to reach the camp before those who accompanied Achmet Zek upon his last raid have found his body and carried the news of his death to the cut-throats who remained behind. It is our only hope, Lady Greystoke, and you must place your entire faith in me if I am to succeed. Wait for me here a moment while I take from the Arab's body the wallet that he stole from me," and Werper stepped quickly to the dead man's side, and, kneeling, sought with quick fingers the pouch of jewels. To his consternation, there was no sign of them in the garments of Achmet Zek. Rising, he walked back along the trail, searching for some trace of the missing pouch or its contents; but he found nothing, even though he searched carefully the vicinity of his dead horse, and for a few paces into the jungle on either side. Puzzled, disappointed and angry, he at last returned to the girl. "The wallet is gone," he explained, crisply, "and I dare not delay longer in search of it. We must reach the camp before the returning raiders."

Unsuspicious of the man's true character, Jane Clayton saw nothing peculiar in his plans, or in his specious explanation of his former friendship for the raider, and so she grasped with alacrity the seeming hope for safety which he proffered her, and turning about she set out with Albert Werper toward the hostile camp in which she so lately had been a prisoner.

It was late in the afternoon of the second day before they reached their destination, and as they paused upon the edge of the clearing before the gates of the walled village, Werper cautioned the girl to accede to whatever he might suggest by his conversation with the raiders.

"I shall tell them," he said, "that I apprehended you after you escaped from the camp, that I took you to Achmet Zek, and that as he was engaged in a stubborn battle with the Waziri, he directed me to return to camp with you, to obtain here a sufficient guard, and to ride north with you as rapidly as possible and dispose of you at the most advantageous terms to a certain slave broker whose name he gave me."

Again the girl was deceived by the apparent frankness of the Belgian. She realized that desperate situations required desperate handling, and though she trembled inwardly at the thought of again entering the vile and hideous village of the raiders she saw no better course than that which her companion had suggested.

Calling aloud to those who tended the gates, Werper, grasping Jane Clayton by the arm, walked boldly across the clearing. Those who opened the gates to him permitted their surprise to show clearly in their expressions. That the discredited and hunted lieutenant should be thus returning fearlessly of his own volition, seemed to disarm them quite as effectually as his manner toward Lady Greystoke had deceived her.

The sentries at the gate returned Werper's salutations, and viewed with astonishment the prisoner whom he brought into the village with him.

Immediately the Belgian sought the Arab who had been left in charge of the camp during Achmet Zek's absence, and again his boldness disarmed suspicion and won the acceptance of his false explanation of his return. The fact that he had brought back with him the woman prisoner who had escaped, added strength to his claims, and Mohammed Beyd soon found himself fraternizing good-naturedly with the very man whom he would have slain without compunction had he discovered him alone in the jungle a half hour before.

Jane Clayton was again confined to the prison hut she had formerly occupied, but as she realized that this was but a part of the deception which she and Frecoult were playing upon the credulous raiders, it was with quite a different sensation that she again entered the vile and filthy interior, from that which she had previously experienced, when hope was so far away.

Once more she was bound and sentries placed before the door of her prison; but before Werper left her he whispered words of cheer into her ear. Then he left, and made his way back to the tent of Mohammed Beyd. He had been wondering how long it would be before the raiders who had ridden out with Achmet Zek would return with the murdered body of their chief, and the more he thought upon the matter the greater his fears became, that without accomplices his plan would fail.

What, even, if he got away from the camp in safety before any returned with the true story of his guilt—of what value would this advantage be other than to protract for a few days his mental torture and his life? These hard riders, familiar with every trail and bypath, would get him long before he could hope to reach the coast.

As these thoughts passed through his mind he entered the tent where Mohammed Beyd sat cross-legged upon a rug, smoking. The Arab looked up as the European came into his presence.

"Greetings, O Brother!" he said.

"Greetings!" replied Werper.

For a while neither spoke further. The Arab was the first to break the silence.

"And my master, Achmet Zek, was well when last you saw him?" he asked.

"Never was he safer from the sins and dangers of mortality," replied the Belgian.

"It is well," said Mohammed Beyd, blowing a little puff of blue smoke straight out before him.

Again there was silence for several minutes.

"And if he were dead?" asked the Belgian, determined to lead up to the truth, and attempt to bribe Mohammed Beyd into his service.

The Arab's eyes narrowed and he leaned forward, his gaze boring straight into the eyes of the Belgian.

"I have been thinking much, Werper, since you returned so unexpectedly to the camp of the man whom you had deceived, and who sought you with death in his heart. I have been with Achmet Zek for many years—his own mother never knew him so well as I. He never forgives— much less would he again trust a man who had once betrayed him; that I know.

"I have thought much, as I said, and the result of my thinking has assured me that Achmet Zek is dead—for otherwise you would never have dared return to his camp, unless you be either a braver man or a bigger fool than I have imagined. And, if this evidence of my judgment is not sufficient, I have but just now received from your own lips even more confirmatory witness—for did you not say that Achmet Zek was never more safe from the sins and dangers of mortality?

"Achmet Zek is dead—you need not deny it. I was not his mother, or his mistress, so do not fear that my wailings shall disturb you. Tell me why you have come back here. Tell me what you want, and, Werper, if you still possess the jewels of which Achmet Zek told me, there is no reason why you and I should not ride north together and divide the ransom of the white woman and the contents of the pouch you wear about your person. Eh?"

The evil eyes narrowed, a vicious, thin-lipped smile tortured the villainous face, as Mohammed Beyd grinned knowingly into the face of the Belgian.

Werper was both relieved and disturbed by the Arab's attitude. The complacency with which he accepted the death of his chief lifted a considerable burden of apprehension from the shoulders of Achmet Zek's assassin; but his demand for a share of the jewels boded ill for Werper when Mohammed Beyd should have learned that the precious stones were no longer in the Belgian's possession.

To acknowledge that he had lost the jewels might be to arouse the wrath or suspicion of the Arab to such an extent as would jeopardize his new-found chances of escape. His one hope seemed, then, to lie in fostering Mohammed Beyd's belief that the jewels were still in his possession, and depend upon the accidents of the future to open an avenue of escape.

Could he contrive to tent with the Arab upon the march north, he might find opportunity in plenty to remove this menace to his life and liberty—it was worth trying, and, further, there seemed no other way out of his difficulty.

"Yes," he said, "Achmet Zek is dead. He fell in battle with a company of Abyssinian cavalry that held me captive. During the fighting I escaped; but I doubt if any of Achmet Zek's men live, and the gold they sought is in the possession of the Abyssinians. Even now they are doubtless marching on this camp, for they were sent by Menelek to punish Achmet Zek and his followers for a raid upon an Abyssinian village. There are many of them, and if we do not make haste to escape we shall all suffer the same fate as Achmet Zek."

Mohammed Beyd listened in silence. How much of the unbeliever's story he might safely believe he did not know; but as it afforded him an excuse for deserting the village and making for the north he was not inclined to cross-question the Belgian too minutely.

"And if I ride north with you," he asked, "half the jewels and half the ransom of the woman shall be mine?"

"Yes," replied Werper.

"Good," said Mohammed Beyd. "I go now to give the order for the breaking of camp early on the morrow," and he rose to leave the tent.

Werper laid a detaining hand upon his arm.

"Wait," he said, "let us determine how many shall accompany us. It is not well that we be burdened by the women and children, for then indeed we might be overtaken by the Abyssinians. It would be far better to select a small guard of your bravest men, and leave word behind that we are riding *west*. Then, when the Abyssinians come they will be put upon the wrong trail should they have it in their hearts to pursue us, and if they do not they will at least ride north with less rapidity than as though they thought that we were ahead of them."

"The serpent is less wise than thou, Werper," said Mohammed Beyd with a smile. "It shall be done as you say. Twenty men shall accompany us, and we shall ride *west*—when we leave the village."

"Good," cried the Belgian, and so it was arranged.

Early the next morning Jane Clayton, after an almost sleepless night, was aroused by the sound of voices outside her prison, and a moment later, M. Frecoult, and two Arabs entered. The latter unbound her ankles and lifted her to her feet. Then her wrists were loosed, she was given a handful of dry bread, and led out into the faint light of dawn.

She looked questioningly at Frecoult, and at a moment that the Arab's attention was attracted in another direction the man leaned toward her and whispered that all was working out as he had planned. Thus assured, the young woman felt a renewal of the hope which the long and miserable night of bondage had almost expunged.

Shortly after, she was lifted to the back of a horse, and surrounded by Arabs, was escorted through the gateway of the village and off into the jungle toward the west. Half an hour later the party turned north, and northerly was their direction for the balance of the march.

M. Frecoult spoke with her but seldom, and she understood that in carrying out his deception he must maintain the semblance of her captor, rather than protector, and so she suspected nothing though she saw the friendly relations which seemed to exist between the European and the Arab leader of the band.

If Werper succeeded in keeping himself from conversation with the young woman, he failed signally to expel her from his thoughts. A hundred times a day he found his eyes wandering in her direction and feasting themselves upon her charms of face and figure. Each hour his infatuation for her grew, until his desire to possess her gained almost the proportions of madness.

If either the girl or Mohammed Beyd could have guessed what passed in the mind of the man which each thought a friend and ally, the apparent harmony of the little company would have been rudely disturbed.

Werper had not succeeded in arranging to tent with Mohammed Beyd, and so he revolved many plans for the assassination of the Arab that would have been greatly simplified had he been permitted to share the other's nightly shelter.

Upon the second day out Mohammed Beyd reined his horse to the side of the animal on which the captive was mounted. It was, apparently, the first notice which the Arab had taken of the girl; but many times during these two days had his cunning eyes peered greedily from beneath the hood of his burnoose to gloat upon the beauties of the prisoner.

Nor was this hidden infatuation of any recent origin. He had conceived it when first the wife of the Englishman had fallen into the hands of Achmet Zek; but while that austere chieftain lived, Mohammed Beyd had not even dared hope for a realization of his imaginings.

Now, though, it was different—only a despised dog of a Christian stood between himself and possession of the girl. How easy it would be to slay the unbeliever, and take unto himself both the woman and the jewels! With the latter in his possession, the ransom which might be obtained for the captive would form no great inducement to her relinquishment in the face of the pleasures of sole ownership of her. Yes, he would kill Werper, retain all the jewels and keep the Englishwoman.

He turned his eyes upon her as she rode along at his side. How beautiful she was! His fingers opened and closed—skinny, brown talons itching to feel the soft flesh of the victim in their remorseless clutch.

"Do you know," he asked leaning toward her, "where this man would take you?"

Jane Clayton nodded affirmatively.

"And you are willing to become the plaything of a black sultan?"

The girl drew herself up to her full height, and turned her head away; but she did not reply. She feared lest her knowledge of the ruse that M. Frecoult was playing upon the Arab might cause her to betray herself through an insufficient display of terror and aversion.

"You can escape this fate," continued the Arab; "Mohammed Beyd will save you," and he reached out a brown hand and seized the fingers of her right hand in a grasp so sudden and so fierce that his brutal passion was revealed as clearly in the act as though his lips had confessed it in words. Jane Clayton wrenched herself from his grasp.

"You beast!" she cried. "Leave me or I shall call M. Frecoult."

Mohammed Beyd drew back with a scowl. His thin, upper lip curled upward, revealing his smooth, white teeth.

"M. Frecoult?" he jeered. "There is no such person. The man's name is Werper. He is a liar, a thief, and a murderer. He killed his captain in the Congo country and fled to the protection of Achmet Zek. He led Achmet Zek to the plunder of your home. He followed your husband, and planned to steal his gold from him. He has told me that you think him your protector, and he has played upon this to win your confidence that it might be easier to carry you north and sell you into some black sultan's harem. Mohammed Beyd is your only hope," and with this assertion to provide the captive with food for thought, the Arab spurred forward toward the head of the column.

Jane Clayton could not know how much of Mohammed Beyd's indictment might be true, or how much false; but at least it had the effect of dampening her hopes and causing her to review with suspicion every past act of the man upon whom she had been looking as her sole protector in the midst of a world of enemies and dangers.

On the march a separate tent had been provided for the captive, and at night it was pitched between those of Mohammed Beyd and Werper. A sentry was posted at the front and another at the back, and with these precautions it had not been thought necessary to confine the prisoner to bonds. The evening following her interview with Mohammed Beyd, Jane Clayton sat for some time at the opening of her tent watching the rough activities of the camp. She had eaten the meal that had been brought her by Mohammed Beyd's Negro slave—a meal of cassava cakes and a nondescript stew in which a new-killed monkey, a couple of squirrels and the remains of a zebra, slain the previous day, were impartially and unsavorily combined; but the one-time Baltimore belle had long since submerged in the stern battle for existence, an estheticism which formerly revolted at much slighter provocation.

As the girl's eyes wandered across the trampled jungle clearing, already squalid from the presence of man, she no longer apprehended either the nearer objects of the foreground, the uncouth men laughing or quarreling among themselves, or the jungle beyond, which circumscribed the extreme range of her material vision. Her gaze passed through all these, unseeing, to center itself upon a distant bungalow and scenes of happy security which brought to her eyes tears of mingled joy and sorrow. She saw a tall, broad-shouldered man riding in from distant fields; she saw herself waiting to greet him with an armful of fresh-cut roses from the bushes which flanked the little rustic gate before her. All this was gone, vanished into the past, wiped out by the torches and bullets and hatred of these hideous and degenerate men. With a stifled sob, and a little shudder, Jane Clayton turned back into her tent and sought the pile of unclean blankets which were her bed. Throwing herself face downward upon them she sobbed forth her misery until kindly sleep brought her, at least temporary, relief.

And while she slept a figure stole from the tent that stood to the right of hers. It approached the sentry before the doorway and whispered a few words in the man's ear. The latter nodded, and strode off through the darkness in the direction of his own blankets. The figure passed to the rear of Jane Clayton's tent and spoke again to the sentry there, and this man also left, following in the trail of the first.

Then he who had sent them away stole silently to the tent flap and untying the fastenings entered with the noiselessness of a disembodied spirit.

CHAPTER XXI—THE FLIGHT TO THE JUNGLE

Sleepless upon his blankets, Albert Werper let his evil mind dwell upon the charms of the woman in the nearby tent. He had noted Mohammed Beyd's sudden interest in the girl, and judging the man by his own standards, had guessed at the basis of the Arab's sudden change of attitude toward the prisoner.

And as he let his imaginings run riot they aroused within him a bestial jealousy of Mohammed Beyd, and a great fear that the other might encompass his base designs upon the defenseless girl. By a strange process of reasoning, Werper, whose designs were identical with the Arab's, pictured himself as Jane Clayton's protector, and presently convinced himself that the attentions which might seem hideous to her if proffered by Mohammed Beyd, would be welcomed from Albert Werper.

Her husband was dead, and Werper fancied that he could replace in the girl's heart the position which had been vacated by the act of the grim reaper. He could offer Jane Clayton marriage—a thing which Mohammed Beyd would not offer, and which the girl would spurn from him with as deep disgust as she would his unholy lust.

It was not long before the Belgian had succeeded in convincing himself that the captive not only had every reason for having conceived sentiments of love for him; but that she had by various feminine methods acknowledged her new-born affection.

And then a sudden resolution possessed him. He threw the blankets from him and rose to his feet. Pulling on his boots and buckling his cartridge belt and revolver about his hips he stepped to the flap of his tent and looked out. There was no sentry before the entrance to the prisoner's tent! What could it mean? Fate was indeed playing into his hands.

Stepping outside he passed to the rear of the girl's tent. There was no sentry there, either! And now, boldly, he walked to the entrance and stepped within.

Dimly the moonlight illumined the interior. Across the tent a figure bent above the blankets of a bed. There was a whispered word, and another figure rose from the blankets to a sitting position. Slowly Albert Werper's eyes were becoming accustomed to the half darkness of the tent.

He saw that the figure leaning over the bed was that of a man, and he guessed at the truth of the nocturnal visitor's identity.

A sullen, jealous rage enveloped him. He took a step in the direction of the two. He heard a frightened cry break from the girl's lips as she recognized the features of the man above her, and he saw Mohammed Beyd seize her by the throat and bear her back upon the blankets.

Cheated passion cast a red blur before the eyes of the Belgian. No! The man should not have her. She was for him and him alone. He would not be robbed of his rights.

Quickly he ran across the tent and threw himself upon the back of Mohammed Beyd. The latter, though surprised by this sudden and unexpected attack, was not one to give up without a battle. The Belgian's fingers were feeling for his throat, but the Arab tore them away, and rising wheeled upon his adversary. As they faced each other Werper struck the Arab a heavy blow in the face, sending him staggering backward. If he had followed up his advantage he would have had Mohammed Beyd at his mercy in another moment; but instead he tugged at his revolver to draw it from its holster, and Fate ordained that at that particular moment the weapon should stick in its leather scabbard.

Before he could disengage it, Mohammed Beyd had recovered himself and was dashing upon him. Again Werper struck the other in the face, and the Arab returned the blow. Striking at each other and ceaselessly attempting to clinch, the two battled about the small interior of the tent, while the girl, wide-eyed in terror and astonishment, watched the duel in frozen silence.

Again and again Werper struggled to draw his weapon. Mohammed Beyd, anticipating no such opposition to his base desires, had come to the tent unarmed, except for a long knife which he now drew as he stood panting during the first brief rest of the encounter.

"Dog of a Christian," he whispered, "look upon this knife in the hands of Mohammed Beyd! Look well, unbeliever, for it is the last thing in life that you shall see or feel. With it Mohammed Beyd will cut out your black heart. If you have a God pray to him now—in a minute more you shall be dead," and with that he rushed viciously upon the Belgian, his knife raised high above his head.

Werper was still dragging futilely at his weapon. The Arab was almost upon him. In desperation the European waited until Mohammed Beyd was all but against him, then he threw himself to one side to the floor of the tent, leaving a leg extended in the path of the Arab.

The trick succeeded. Mohammed Beyd, carried on by the momentum of his charge, stumbled over the projecting obstacle and crashed to the ground. Instantly he was up again and wheeling to renew the battle; but Werper was on foot ahead of him, and now his revolver, loosened from its holster, flashed in his hand.

The Arab dove headfirst to grapple with him, there was a sharp report, a lurid gleam of flame in the darkness, and Mohammed Beyd rolled over and over upon the floor to come to a final rest beside the bed of the woman he had sought to dishonor.

Almost immediately following the report came the sound of excited voices in the camp without. Men were calling back and forth to one another asking the meaning of the shot. Werper could hear them running hither and thither, investigating.

Jane Clayton had risen to her feet as the Arab died, and now she came forward with outstretched hands toward Werper.

"How can I ever thank you, my friend?" she asked. "And to think that only today I had almost believed the infamous story which this beast told me of your perfidy and of your past. Forgive me, M. Frecoult. I might have known that a white man and a gentleman could be naught else than the protector of a woman of his own race amid the dangers of this savage land."

Werper's hands dropped limply at his sides. He stood looking at the girl; but he could find no words to reply to her. Her innocent arraignment of his true purposes was unanswerable.

Outside, the Arabs were searching for the author of the disturbing shot. The two sentries who had been relieved and sent to their blankets by Mohammed Beyd were the first to suggest going to the tent of the prisoner. It occurred to them that possibly the woman had successfully defended herself against their leader.

Werper heard the men approaching. To be apprehended as the slayer of Mohammed Beyd would be equivalent to a sentence of immediate death. The fierce and brutal raiders would tear to pieces a Christian who had dared spill the blood of their leader. He must find some excuse to delay the finding of Mohammed Beyd's dead body.

Returning his revolver to its holster, he walked quickly to the entrance of the tent. Parting the flaps he stepped out and confronted the men, who were rapidly approaching. Somehow he found within him the necessary bravado to force a smile to his lips, as he held up his hand to bar their farther progress.

"The woman resisted," he said, "and Mohammed Beyd was forced to shoot her. She is not dead—only slightly wounded. You may go back to your blankets. Mohammed Beyd and I will look after the prisoner;" then he turned and re-entered the tent, and the raiders, satisfied by this explanation, gladly returned to their broken slumbers.

As he again faced Jane Clayton, Werper found himself animated by quite different intentions than those which had lured him from his blankets but a few minutes before. The excitement of his encounter with Mohammed Beyd, as well as the dangers which he now faced at the hands of the raiders when morning must inevitably reveal the truth of what had occurred in the tent of the prisoner that night, had naturally cooled the hot passion which had dominated him when he entered the tent.

But another and stronger force was exerting itself in the girl's favor. However low a man may sink, honor and chivalry, has he ever possessed them, are never entirely eradicated from his character, and though Albert Werper had long since ceased to evidence the slightest claim to either the one or the other, the spontaneous acknowledgment of them which the girl's speech had presumed had reawakened them both within him.

For the first time he realized the almost hopeless and frightful position of the fair captive, and the depths of ignominy to which he had sunk, that had made it possible for him, a well-born, European gentleman, to have entertained even for a moment the part that he had taken in the ruin of her home, happiness, and herself.

Too much of baseness already lay at the threshold of his conscience for him ever to hope entirely to redeem himself; but in the first, sudden burst of contrition the man conceived an honest intention to undo, in so far as lay within his power, the evil that his criminal avarice had brought upon this sweet and unoffending woman.

As he stood apparently listening to the retreating footsteps—Jane Clayton approached him.

"What are we to do now?" she asked. "Morning will bring discovery of this," and she pointed to the still body of Mohammed Beyd. "They will kill you when they find him."

For a time Werper did not reply, then he turned suddenly toward the woman.

"I have a plan," he cried. "It will require nerve and courage on your part; but you have already shown that you possess both. Can you endure still more?"

"I can endure anything," she replied with a brave smile, "that may offer us even a slight chance for escape."

"You must simulate death," he explained, "while I carry you from the camp. I will explain to the sentries that Mohammed Beyd has ordered me to take your body into the jungle. This seemingly unnecessary act I shall explain upon the grounds that Mohammed Beyd had conceived a violent passion for you and that he so regretted the act by which he had become your slayer that he could not endure the silent reproach of your lifeless body."

The girl held up her hand to stop. A smile touched her lips.

"Are you quite mad?" she asked. "Do you imagine that the sentries will credit any such ridiculous tale?"

"You do not know them," he replied. "Beneath their rough exteriors, despite their calloused and criminal natures, there exists in each a well-defined strain of romantic emotionalism—you will find it among such as these throughout the world. It is romance which lures men to lead wild lives of outlawry and crime. The ruse will succeed—never fear."

Jane Clayton shrugged. "We can but try it—and then what?"

"I shall hide you in the jungle," continued the Belgian, "coming for you alone and with two horses in the morning."

"But how will you explain Mohammed Beyd's death?" she asked. "It will be discovered before ever you can escape the camp in the morning."

"I shall not explain it," replied Werper. "Mohammed Beyd shall explain it himself—we must leave that to him. Are you ready for the venture?"

"Yes."

"But wait, I must get you a weapon and ammunition," and Werper walked quickly from the tent.

Very shortly he returned with an extra revolver and ammunition belt strapped about his waist.

"Are you ready?" he asked.

"Quite ready," replied the girl.

"Then come and throw yourself limply across my left shoulder," and Werper knelt to receive her.

"There," he said, as he rose to his feet. "Now, let your arms, your legs and your head hang limply. Remember that you are dead."

A moment later the man walked out into the camp, the body of the woman across his shoulder.

A thorn boma had been thrown up about the camp, to discourage the bolder of the hungry carnivora. A couple of sentries paced to and fro in the light of a fire which they kept burning brightly. The nearer of these looked up in surprise as he saw Werper approaching.

"Who are you?" he cried. "What have you there?"

Werper raised the hood of his burnoose that the fellow might see his face.

"This is the body of the woman," he explained. "Mohammed Beyd has asked me to take it into the jungle, for he cannot bear to look upon the face of her whom he loved, and whom necessity compelled him to slay. He suffers greatly—he is inconsolable. It was with difficulty that I prevented him taking his own life."

Across the speaker's shoulder, limp and frightened, the girl waited for the Arab's reply. He would laugh at this preposterous story; of that she was sure. In an instant he would unmask the deception that M. Frecoult was attempting to practice upon him, and they would both be lost. She tried to plan how best she might aid her would-be rescuer in the fight which must most certainly follow within a moment or two.

Then she heard the voice of the Arab as he replied to M. Frecoult.

"Are you going alone, or do you wish me to awaken someone to accompany you?" he asked, and his tone denoted not the least surprise that Mohammed Beyd had suddenly discovered such remarkably sensitive characteristics.

"I shall go alone," replied Werper, and he passed on and out through the narrow opening in the boma, by which the sentry stood.

A moment later he had entered among the boles of the trees with his burden, and when safely hidden from the sentry's view lowered the girl to her feet, with a low, "sh-sh," when she would have spoken.

Then he led her a little farther into the forest, halted beneath a large tree with spreading branches, buckled a cartridge belt and revolver about her waist, and assisted her to clamber into the lower branches.

"Tomorrow," he whispered, "as soon as I can elude them, I will return for you. Be brave, Lady Greystoke—we may yet escape."

"Thank you," she replied in a low tone. "You have been very kind, and very brave."

Werper did not reply, and the darkness of the night hid the scarlet flush of shame which swept upward across his face. Quickly he turned and made his way back to camp. The sentry, from his post, saw him enter his own tent; but he did not see him crawl under the canvas at the rear and sneak cautiously to the tent which the prisoner had occupied, where now lay the dead body of Mohammed Beyd.

Raising the lower edge of the rear wall, Werper crept within and approached the corpse. Without an instant's hesitation he seized the dead wrists and dragged the body upon its back to the point where he had just entered. On hands and knees he backed out as he had come in, drawing the corpse after him. Once outside the Belgian crept to the side of the tent and surveyed as much of the camp as lay within his vision—no one was watching.

Returning to the body, he lifted it to his shoulder, and risking all on a quick sally, ran swiftly across the narrow opening which separated the prisoner's tent from that of the dead man. Behind the silken wall he halted and lowered his burden to the ground, and there he remained motionless for several minutes, listening.

Satisfied, at last, that no one had seen him, he stooped and raised the bottom of the tent wall, backed in and dragged the thing that had been Mohammed Beyd after him. To the sleeping rugs of the dead raider he drew the corpse, then he fumbled about in the darkness until he had found Mohammed Beyd's revolver. With the weapon in his hand he returned to the side of the dead man, kneeled beside the bedding, and inserted his right hand with the weapon beneath the rugs, piled a number of thicknesses of the closely woven fabric over and about the revolver with his left hand. Then he pulled the trigger, and at the same time he coughed.

The muffled report could not have been heard above the sound of his cough by one directly outside the tent. Werper was satisfied. A grim smile touched his lips as he withdrew the weapon from the rugs and placed it carefully in the right hand of the dead man, fixing three of the fingers around the grip and the index finger inside the trigger guard.

A moment longer he tarried to rearrange the disordered rugs, and then he left as he had entered, fastening down the rear wall of the tent as it had been before he had raised it.

Going to the tent of the prisoner he removed there also the evidence that someone might have come or gone beneath the rear wall. Then he returned to his own tent, entered, fastened down the canvas, and crawled into his blankets.

The following morning he was awakened by the excited voice of Mohammed Beyd's slave calling to him at the entrance of his tent.

"Quick! Quick!" cried the black in a frightened tone. "Come! Mohammed Beyd is dead in his tent—dead by his own hand."

Werper sat up quickly in his blankets at the first alarm, a startled expression upon his countenance; but at the last words of the black a sigh of relief escaped his lips and a slight smile replaced the tense lines upon his face.

"I come," he called to the slave, and drawing on his boots, rose and went out of his tent.

Excited Arabs and blacks were running from all parts of the camp toward the silken tent of Mohammed Beyd, and when Werper entered he found a number of the raiders crowded about the corpse, now cold and stiff.

Shouldering his way among them, the Belgian halted beside the dead body of the raider. He looked down in silence for a moment upon the still face, then he wheeled upon the Arabs.

"Who has done this thing?" he cried. His tone was both menacing and accusing. "Who has murdered Mohammed Beyd?"

A sudden chorus of voices arose in tumultuous protest.

"Mohammed Beyd was not murdered," they cried. "He died by his own hand. This, and Allah, are our witnesses," and they pointed to a revolver in the dead man's hand.

For a time Werper pretended to be skeptical; but at last permitted himself to be convinced that Mohammed Beyd had indeed killed himself in remorse for the death of the white woman he had, all unknown to his followers, loved so devotedly.

Werper himself wrapped the blankets of the dead man about the corpse, taking care to fold inward the scorched and bullet-torn fabric that had muffled the report of the weapon he had fired the night before. Then six husky blacks carried the body out into the clearing where the camp stood, and deposited it in a shallow grave. As the loose earth fell upon the silent form beneath the tell-tale blankets, Albert Werper heaved another sigh of relief—his plan had worked out even better than he had dared hope.

With Achmet Zek and Mohammed Beyd both dead, the raiders were without a leader, and after a brief conference they decided to return into the north on visits to the various tribes to which they belonged. Werper, after learning the direction they intended taking, announced that for his part, he was going east to the coast, and as they knew of nothing he possessed which any of them coveted, they signified their willingness that he should go his way.

As they rode off, he sat his horse in the center of the clearing watching them disappear one by one into the jungle, and thanked his God that he had at last escaped their villainous clutches.

When he could no longer hear any sound of them, he turned to the right and rode into the forest toward the tree where he had hidden Lady Greystoke, and drawing rein beneath it, called up in a gay and hopeful voice a pleasant, "Good morning!"

There was no reply, and though his eyes searched the thick foliage above him, he could see no sign of the girl. Dismounting, he quickly climbed into the tree, where he could obtain a view of all its branches. The tree was empty—Jane Clayton had vanished during the silent watches of the jungle night.

CHAPTER XX—TARZAN RECOVERS HIS REASON

As Tarzan let the pebbles from the recovered pouch run through his fingers, his thoughts returned to the pile of yellow ingots about which the Arabs and the Abyssinians had waged their relentless battle.

What was there in common between that pile of dirty metal and the beautiful, sparkling pebbles that had formerly been in his pouch? What was the metal? From whence had it come? What was that tantalizing half-conviction which seemed to demand the recognition of his memory that the yellow pile for which these men had fought and died had been intimately connected with his past—that it had been his?

What had been his past? He shook his head. Vaguely the memory of his apish childhood passed slowly in review—then came a strangely tangled mass of faces, figures and events which seemed to have no relation to Tarzan of the Apes, and yet which were, even in their fragmentary form, familiar.

Slowly and painfully, recollection was attempting to reassert itself, the hurt brain was mending, as the cause of its recent failure to function was being slowly absorbed or removed by the healing processes of perfect circulation.

The people who now passed before his mind's eye for the first time in weeks wore familiar faces; but yet he could neither place them in the niches they had once filled in his past life, nor call them by name. One was a fair she, and it was her face which most often moved through the tangled recollections of his convalescing brain. Who was she? What had she been to Tarzan of the Apes? He seemed to see her about the very spot upon which the pile of gold had been unearthed by the Abyssinians; but the surroundings were vastly different from those which now obtained.

There was a building—there were many buildings—and there were hedges, fences, and flowers. Tarzan puckered his brow in puzzled study of the wonderful problem. For an instant he seemed to grasp the whole of a true explanation, and then, just as success was within his grasp, the picture faded into a jungle scene where a naked, white youth danced in company with a band of hairy, primordial ape-things.

Tarzan shook his head and sighed. Why was it that he could not recollect? At least he was sure that in some way the pile of gold, the place where it lay, the subtle aroma of the elusive she he had been pursuing, the memory figure of the white woman, and he himself, were inextricably connected by the ties of a forgotten past.

If the woman belonged there, what better place to search or await her than the very spot which his broken recollections seemed to assign to her? It was worth trying. Tarzan slipped the thong of the empty pouch over his shoulder and started off through the trees in the direction of the plain.

At the outskirts of the forest he met the Arabs returning in search of Achmet Zek. Hiding, he let them pass, and then resumed his way toward the charred ruins of the home he had been almost upon the point of recalling to his memory.

His journey across the plain was interrupted by the discovery of a small herd of antelope in a little swale, where the cover and the wind were well combined to make stalking easy. A fat yearling rewarded a half hour of stealthy creeping and a sudden, savage rush, and it was late in the afternoon when the ape-man settled himself upon his haunches beside his kill to enjoy the fruits of his skill, his cunning, and his prowess.

His hunger satisfied, thirst next claimed his attention. The river lured him by the shortest path toward its refreshing waters, and when he had drunk, night already had fallen and he was some half mile or more down stream from the point where he had seen the pile of yellow ingots, and where he hoped to meet the memory woman, or find some clew to her whereabouts or her identity.

To the jungle bred, time is usually a matter of small moment, and haste, except when engendered by terror, by rage, or by hunger, is distasteful. Today was gone. Therefore tomorrow, of which there was an infinite procession, would answer admirably for Tarzan's further quest. And, besides, the ape-man was tired and would sleep.

A tree afforded him the safety, seclusion and comforts of a well-appointed bedchamber, and to the chorus of the hunters and the hunted of the wild river bank he soon dropped off into deep slumber.

Morning found him both hungry and thirsty again, and dropping from his tree he made his way to the drinking place at the river's edge. There he found Numa, the lion, ahead of him. The big fellow was lapping the water greedily, and at the approach of Tarzan along the trail in his rear, he raised his head, and turning his gaze backward across his maned shoulders glared at the intruder. A low growl of warning rumbled from his throat; but Tarzan, guessing that the beast had but just quitted his kill and was well filled, merely made a slight detour and continued to the river, where he stopped a few yards above the tawny cat, and dropping upon his hands and knees plunged his face into the cool water. For a moment the lion continued to eye the man; then he resumed his drinking, and man and beast quenched their thirst side by side each apparently oblivious of the other's presence.

Numa was the first to finish. Raising his head, he gazed across the river for a few minutes with that stony fixity of attention which is a characteristic of his kind. But for the ruffling of his black mane to the touch of the passing breeze he might have been wrought from golden bronze, so motionless, so statuesque his pose.

A deep sigh from the cavernous lungs dispelled the illusion. The mighty head swung slowly around until the yellow eyes rested upon the man. The bristled lip curved upward, exposing yellow fangs. Another warning growl vibrated the heavy jowls, and the king of beasts turned majestically about and paced slowly up the trail into the dense reeds.

Tarzan of the Apes drank on, but from the corners of his gray eyes he watched the great brute's every move until he had disappeared from view, and, after, his keen ears marked the movements of the carnivore.

A plunge in the river was followed by a scant breakfast of eggs which chance discovered to him, and then he set off up river toward the ruins of the bungalow where the golden ingots had marked the center of yesterday's battle.

And when he came upon the spot, great was his surprise and consternation, for the yellow metal had disappeared. The earth, trampled by the feet of horses and men, gave no clew. It was as though the ingots had evaporated into thin air.

The ape-man was at a loss to know where to turn or what next to do. There was no sign of any spoor which might denote that the she had been here. The metal was gone, and if there was any connection between the she and the metal it seemed useless to wait for her now that the latter had been removed elsewhere.

Everything seemed to elude him—the pretty pebbles, the yellow metal, the she, his memory. Tarzan was disgusted. He would go back into the jungle and look for Chulk, and so he turned his steps once more toward the forest. He moved rapidly, swinging across the plain in a long, easy trot, and at the edge of the forest, taking to the trees with the agility and speed of a small monkey.

His direction was aimless—he merely raced on and on through the jungle, the joy of unfettered action his principal urge, with the hope of stumbling upon some clew to Chulk or the she, a secondary incentive.

For two days he roamed about, killing, eating, drinking and sleeping wherever inclination and the means to indulge it occurred simultaneously. It was upon the morning of the third day that the scent spoor of horse and man were wafted faintly to his nostrils. Instantly he altered his course to glide silently through the branches in the direction from which the scent came.

It was not long before he came upon a solitary horseman riding toward the east. Instantly his eyes confirmed what his nose had previously suspected—the rider was he who had stolen his pretty pebbles. The light of rage flared suddenly in the gray eyes as the ape-man dropped lower among the branches until he moved almost directly above the unconscious Werper.

There was a quick leap, and the Belgian felt a heavy body hurtle onto the rump of his terror-stricken mount. The horse, snorting, leaped forward. Giant arms encircled the rider, and in the twinkling of an eye he was dragged from his saddle to find himself lying in the narrow trail with a naked, white giant kneeling upon his breast.

Recognition came to Werper with the first glance at his captor's face, and a pallor of fear overspread his features. Strong fingers were at his throat, fingers of steel. He tried to cry out, to plead for his life; but the cruel fingers denied him speech, as they were as surely denying him life.

"The pretty pebbles?" cried the man upon his breast. "What did you with the pretty pebbles—with Tarzan's pretty pebbles?"

The fingers relaxed to permit a reply. For some time Werper could only choke and cough—at last he regained the powers of speech.

"Achmet Zek, the Arab, stole them from me," he cried; "he made me give up the pouch and the pebbles."

"I saw all that," replied Tarzan; "but the pebbles in the pouch were not the pebbles of Tarzan—they were only such pebbles as fill the bottoms of the rivers, and the shelving banks beside them. Even the Arab would not have them, for he threw them away in anger when he had looked upon them. It is my pretty pebbles that I want—where are they?"

"I do not know, I do not know," cried Werper. "I gave them to Achmet Zek or he would have killed me. A few minutes later he followed me along the trail to slay me, although he had promised to molest me no further, and I shot and killed him; but the pouch was not upon his person and though I searched about the jungle for some time I could not find it."

"I found it, I tell you," growled Tarzan, "and I also found the pebbles which Achmet Zek had thrown away in disgust. They were not Tarzan's pebbles. You have hidden them! Tell me where they are or I will kill you," and the brown fingers of the ape-man closed a little tighter upon the throat of his victim.

Werper struggled to free himself. "My God, Lord Greystoke," he managed to scream, "would you commit murder for a handful of stones?"

The fingers at his throat relaxed, a puzzled, far-away expression softened the gray eyes.

"Lord Greystoke!" repeated the ape-man. "Lord Greystoke! Who is Lord Greystoke? Where have I heard that name before?"

"Why man, you are Lord Greystoke," cried the Belgian. "You were injured by a falling rock when the earthquake shattered the passage to the underground chamber to which you and your black Waziri had come to fetch golden ingots back to your bungalow. The blow shattered your memory. You are John Clayton, Lord Greystoke—don't you remember?"

"John Clayton, Lord Greystoke!" repeated Tarzan. Then for a moment he was silent. Presently his hand went falteringly to his forehead, an expression of wonderment filled his eyes—of wonderment and sudden understanding. The forgotten name had reawakened the returning memory that had been struggling to reassert itself. The ape-man relinquished his grasp upon the throat of the Belgian, and leaped to his feet.

"God!" he cried, and then, "Jane!" Suddenly he turned toward Werper. "My wife?" he asked. "What has become of her? The farm is in ruins. You know. You have had something to do with all this. You followed me to Opar, you stole the jewels which I thought but pretty pebbles. You are a crook! Do not try to tell me that you are not."

"He is worse than a crook," said a quiet voice close behind them.

Tarzan turned in astonishment to see a tall man in uniform standing in the trail a few paces from him. Back of the man were a number of black soldiers in the uniform of the Congo Free State.

"He is a murderer, Monsieur," continued the officer. "I have followed him for a long time to take him back to stand trial for the killing of his superior officer."

Werper was upon his feet now, gazing, white and trembling, at the fate which had overtaken him even in the fastness of the labyrinthine jungle. Instinctively he turned to flee; but Tarzan of the Apes reached out a strong hand and grasped him by the shoulder.

"Wait!" said the ape-man to his captive. "This gentleman wishes you, and so do I. When I am through with you, he may have you. Tell me what has become of my wife."

The Belgian officer eyed the almost naked, white giant with curiosity. He noted the strange contrast of primitive weapons and apparel, and the easy, fluent French which the man spoke. The former denoted the lowest, the latter the highest type of culture. He could not quite determine the social status of this strange creature; but he knew that he did not relish the easy assurance with which the fellow presumed to dictate when he might take possession of the prisoner.

"Pardon me," he said, stepping forward and placing his hand on Werper's other shoulder; "but this gentleman is my prisoner. He must come with me."

"When I am through with him," replied Tarzan, quietly.

The officer turned and beckoned to the soldiers standing in the trail behind him. A company of uniformed blacks stepped quickly forward and pushing past the three, surrounded the ape-man and his captive.

"Both the law and the power to enforce it are upon my side," announced the officer. "Let us have no trouble. If you have a grievance against this man you may return with me and enter your charge regularly before an authorized tribunal."

"Your legal rights are not above suspicion, my friend," replied Tarzan, "and your power to enforce your commands are only apparent—not real. You have presumed to enter British territory with an armed force. Where is your authority for this invasion? Where are the extradition papers which warrant the arrest of this man? And what assurance have you that I cannot bring an armed force about you that will prevent your return to the Congo Free State?"

The Belgian lost his temper. "I have no disposition to argue with a naked savage," he cried. "Unless you wish to be hurt you will not interfere with me. Take the prisoner, Sergeant!"

Werper raised his lips close to Tarzan's ear. "Keep me from them, and I can show you the very spot where I saw your wife last night," he whispered. "She cannot be far from here at this very minute."

The soldiers, following the signal from their sergeant, closed in to seize Werper. Tarzan grabbed the Belgian about the waist, and bearing him beneath his arm as he might have borne a sack of flour, leaped forward in an attempt to break through the cordon. His right fist caught the nearest soldier upon the jaw and sent him hurtling backward upon his fellows. Clubbed rifles were torn from the hands of those who barred his way, and right and left the black soldiers stumbled aside in the face of the ape-man's savage break for liberty.

So completely did the blacks surround the two that they dared not fire for fear of hitting one of their own number, and Tarzan was already through them and upon the point of dodging into the concealing mazes of the jungle when one who had sneaked upon him from behind struck him a heavy blow upon the head with a rifle.

In an instant the ape-man was down and a dozen black soldiers were upon his back. When he regained consciousness he found himself securely bound, as was Werper also. The Belgian officer, success having crowned his efforts, was in good humor, and inclined to chaff his prisoners about the ease with which they had been captured; but from Tarzan of the Apes he elicited no response. Werper, however, was voluble in his protests. He explained that Tarzan was an English lord; but the officer only laughed at the assertion, and advised his prisoner to save his breath for his defense in court.

As soon as Tarzan regained his senses and it was found that he was not seriously injured, the prisoners were hastened into line and the return march toward the Congo Free State boundary commenced.

Toward evening the column halted beside a stream, made camp and prepared the evening meal. From the thick foliage of the nearby jungle a pair of fierce eyes watched the activities of the uniformed blacks with silent intensity and curiosity. From beneath beetling brows the creature saw the boma constructed, the fires built, and the supper prepared.

Tarzan and Werper had been lying bound behind a small pile of knapsacks from the time that the company had halted; but with the preparation of the meal completed, their guard ordered them to rise and come forward to one of the fires where their hands would be unfettered that they might eat.

As the giant ape-man rose, a startled expression of recognition entered the eyes of the watcher in the jungle, and a low guttural broke from the savage lips. Instantly Tarzan was alert, but the answering growl died upon his lips, suppressed by the fear that it might arouse the suspicions of the soldiers.

Suddenly an inspiration came to him. He turned toward Werper.

"I am going to speak to you in a loud voice and in a tongue which you do not understand. Appear to listen intently to what I say, and occasionally mumble something as though replying in the same language—our escape may hinge upon the success of your efforts."

Werper nodded in assent and understanding, and immediately there broke from the lips of his companion a strange jargon which might have been compared with equal propriety to the barking and growling of a dog and the chattering of monkeys.

The nearer soldiers looked in surprise at the ape-man. Some of them laughed, while others drew away in evident superstitious fear. The officer approached the prisoners while Tarzan was still jabbering, and halted behind them, listening in perplexed interest. When Werper mumbled some ridiculous jargon in reply his curiosity broke bounds, and he stepped forward, demanding to know what language it was that they spoke.

Tarzan had gauged the measure of the man's culture from the nature and quality of his conversation during the march, and he rested the success of his reply upon the estimate he had made.

"Greek," he explained.

"Oh, I thought it was Greek," replied the officer; "but it has been so many years since I studied it that I was not sure. In future, however, I will thank you to speak in a language which I am more familiar with."

Werper turned his head to hide a grin, whispering to Tarzan: "It was Greek to him all right—and to me, too."

But one of the black soldiers mumbled in a low voice to a companion: "I have heard those sounds before—once at night when I was lost in the jungle, I heard the hairy men of the trees talking among themselves, and their words were like the words of this white man. I wish that we had not found him. He is not a man at all—he is a bad spirit, and we shall have bad luck if we do not let him go," and the fellow rolled his eyes fearfully toward the jungle.

His companion laughed nervously, and moved away, to repeat the conversation, with variations and exaggerations, to others of the black soldiery, so that it was not long before a frightful tale of black magic and sudden death was woven about the giant prisoner, and had gone the rounds of the camp.

And deep in the gloomy jungle amidst the darkening shadows of the falling night a hairy, manlike creature swung swiftly southward upon some secret mission of his own.

CHAPTER XXIII—A NIGHT OF TERROR

To Jane Clayton, waiting in the tree where Werper had placed her, it seemed that the long night would never end, yet end it did at last, and within an hour of the coming of dawn her spirits leaped with renewed hope at sight of a solitary horseman approaching along the trail.

The flowing burnoose, with its loose hood, hid both the face and the figure of the rider; but that it was M. Frecoult the girl well knew, since he had been garbed as an Arab, and he alone might be expected to seek her hiding place.

That which she saw relieved the strain of the long night vigil; but there was much that she did not see. She did not see the black face beneath the white hood, nor the file of ebon horsemen beyond the trail's bend riding slowly in the wake of their leader. These things she did not see at first, and so she leaned downward toward the approaching rider, a cry of welcome forming in her throat.

At the first word the man looked up, reining in in surprise, and as she saw the black face of Abdul Mourak, the Abyssinian, she shrank back in terror among the branches; but it was too late. The man had seen her, and now he called to her to descend. At first she refused; but when a dozen black cavalrymen drew up behind their leader, and at Abdul Mourak's command one of them started to climb the tree after her she realized that resistance was futile, and came slowly down to stand upon the ground before this new captor and plead her cause in the name of justice and humanity.

Angered by recent defeat, and by the loss of the gold, the jewels, and his prisoners, Abdul Mourak was in no mood to be influenced by any appeal to those softer sentiments to which, as a matter of fact, he was almost a stranger even under the most favourable conditions.

He looked for degradation and possible death in punishment for his failures and his misfortunes when he should have returned to his native land and made his report to Menelek; but an acceptable gift might temper the wrath of the emperor, and surely this fair flower of another race should be gratefully received by the black ruler!

When Jane Clayton had concluded her appeal, Abdul Mourak replied briefly that he would promise her protection; but that he must take her to his emperor. The girl did not need ask him why, and once again hope died within her breast. Resignedly she permitted herself to be lifted to a seat behind one of the troopers, and again, under new masters, her journey was resumed toward what she now began to believe was her inevitable fate.

Abdul Mourak, bereft of his guides by the battle he had waged against the raiders, and himself unfamiliar with the country, had wandered far from the trail he should have followed, and as a result had made but little progress toward the north since the beginning of his flight. Today he was beating toward the west in the hope of coming upon a village where he might obtain guides; but night found him still as far from a realization of his hopes as had the rising sun.

It was a dispirited company which went into camp, waterless and hungry, in the dense jungle. Attracted by the horses, lions roared about the boma, and to their hideous din was added the shrill neighs of the terror-stricken beasts they hunted. There was little sleep for man or beast, and the sentries were doubled that there might be enough on duty both to guard against the sudden charge of an overbold, or overhungry lion, and to keep the fire blazing which was an even more effectual barrier against them than the thorny boma.

It was well past midnight, and as yet Jane Clayton, notwithstanding that she had passed a sleepless night the night before, had scarcely more than dozed. A sense of impending danger seemed to hang like a black pall over the camp. The veteran troopers of the black emperor were nervous and ill at ease. Abdul Mourak left his blankets a dozen times to pace restlessly back and forth between the tethered horses and the crackling fire. The girl could see his great frame silhouetted against the lurid glare of the flames, and she guessed from the quick, nervous movements of the man that he was afraid.

The roaring of the lions rose in sudden fury until the earth trembled to the hideous chorus. The horses shrilled their neighs of terror as they lay back upon their halter ropes in their mad endeavors to break loose. A trooper, braver than his fellows, leaped among the kicking, plunging, fear-maddened beasts in a futile attempt to quiet them. A lion, large, and fierce, and courageous, leaped almost to the boma, full in the bright light from the fire. A sentry raised his piece and fired, and the little leaden pellet unstoppered the vials of hell upon the terror-stricken camp.

The shot ploughed a deep and painful furrow in the lion's side, arousing all the bestial fury of the little brain; but abating not a whit the power and vigor of the great body.

Unwounded, the boma and the flames might have turned him back; but now the pain and the rage wiped caution from his mind, and with a loud, and angry roar he topped the barrier with an easy leap and was among the horses.

What had been pandemonium before became now an indescribable tumult of hideous sound. The stricken horse upon which the lion leaped shrieked out its terror and its agony. Several about it broke their tethers and plunged madly about the camp. Men leaped from their blankets and with guns ready ran toward the picket line, and then from the jungle beyond the boma a dozen lions, emboldened by the example of their fellow charged fearlessly upon the camp.

Singly and in twos and threes they leaped the boma, until the little enclosure was filled with cursing men and screaming horses battling for their lives with the green-eyed devils of the jungle.

With the charge of the first lion, Jane Clayton had scrambled to her feet, and now she stood horror-struck at the scene of savage slaughter that swirled and eddied about her. Once a bolting horse knocked her down, and a moment later a lion, leaping in pursuit of another terror-stricken animal, brushed her so closely that she was again thrown from her feet.

Amidst the cracking of the rifles and the growls of the carnivora rose the death screams of stricken men and horses as they were dragged down by the blood-mad cats. The leaping carnivora and the plunging horses, prevented any concerted action by the Abyssinians—it was every man for himself—and in the melee, the defenseless woman was either forgotten or ignored by her black captors. A score of times was her life menaced by charging lions, by plunging horses, or by the wildly fired bullets of the frightened troopers, yet there was no chance of escape, for now with the fiendish cunning of their kind, the tawny hunters commenced to circle about their prey, hemming them within a ring of mighty, yellow fangs, and sharp, long talons. Again and again an individual lion would dash suddenly among the frightened men and horses, and occasionally a horse, goaded to frenzy by pain or terror, succeeded in racing safely through the circling lions, leaping the boma, and escaping into the jungle; but for the men and the woman no such escape was possible.

A horse, struck by a stray bullet, fell beside Jane Clayton, a lion leaped across the expiring beast full upon the breast of a black trooper just beyond. The man clubbed his rifle and struck futilely at the broad head, and then he was down and the carnivore was standing above him.

Shrieking out his terror, the soldier clawed with puny fingers at the shaggy breast in vain endeavor to push away the grinning jaws. The lion lowered his head, the gaping fangs closed with a single sickening crunch upon the fear-distorted face, and turning strode back across the body of the dead horse dragging his limp and bloody burden with him.

Wide-eyed the girl stood watching. She saw the carnivore step upon the corpse, stumblingly, as the grisly thing swung between its forepaws, and her eyes remained fixed in fascination while the beast passed within a few paces of her.

The interference of the body seemed to enrage the lion. He shook the inanimate clay venomously. He growled and roared hideously at the dead, insensate thing, and then he dropped it and raised his head to look about in search of some living victim upon which to wreak his ill temper. His yellow eyes fastened themselves balefully upon the figure of the girl, the bristling lips raised, disclosing the grinning fangs. A terrific roar broke from the savage throat, and the great beast crouched to spring upon this new and helpless victim.

Quiet had fallen early upon the camp where Tarzan and Werper lay securely bound. Two nervous sentries paced their beats, their eyes rolling often toward the impenetrable shadows of the gloomy jungle. The others slept or tried to sleep—all but the ape-man. Silently and powerfully he strained at the bonds which fettered his wrists.

The muscles knotted beneath the smooth, brown skin of his arms and shoulders, the veins stood out upon his temples from the force of his exertions—a strand parted, another and another, and one hand was free. Then from the jungle came a low guttural, and the ape-man became suddenly a silent, rigid statue, with ears and nostrils straining to span the black void where his eyesight could not reach.

Again came the uncanny sound from the thick verdure beyond the camp. A sentry halted abruptly, straining his eyes into the gloom. The kinky wool upon his head stiffened and raised. He called to his comrade in a hoarse whisper.

"Did you hear it?" he asked.

The other came closer, trembling.

"Hear what?"

Again was the weird sound repeated, followed almost immediately by a similar and answering sound from the camp. The sentries drew close together, watching the black spot from which the voice seemed to come.

Trees overhung the boma at this point which was upon the opposite side of the camp from them. They dared not approach. Their terror even prevented them from arousing their fellows— they could only stand in frozen fear and watch for the fearsome apparition they momentarily expected to see leap from the jungle.

Nor had they long to wait. A dim, bulky form dropped lightly from the branches of a tree into the camp. At sight of it one of the sentries recovered command of his muscles and his voice. Screaming loudly to awaken the sleeping camp, he leaped toward the flickering watch fire and threw a mass of brush upon it.

The white officer and the black soldiers sprang from their blankets. The flames leaped high upon the rejuvenated fire, lighting the entire camp, and the awakened men shrank back in superstitious terror from the sight that met their frightened and astonished vision.

A dozen huge and hairy forms loomed large beneath the trees at the far side of the enclosure. The white giant, one hand freed, had struggled to his knees and was calling to the frightful, nocturnal visitors in a hideous medley of bestial gutturals, barkings and growlings.

Werper had managed to sit up. He, too, saw the savage faces of the approaching anthropoids and scarcely knew whether to be relieved or terror-stricken.

Growling, the great apes leaped forward toward Tarzan and Werper. Chulk led them. The Belgian officer called to his men to fire upon the intruders; but the Negroes held back, filled as they were with superstitious terror of the hairy treemen, and with the conviction that the white giant who could thus summon the beasts of the jungle to his aid was more than human.

Drawing his own weapon, the officer fired, and Tarzan fearing the effect of the noise upon his really timid friends called to them to hasten and fulfill his commands.

A couple of the apes turned and fled at the sound of the firearm; but Chulk and a half dozen others waddled rapidly forward, and, following the ape-man's directions, seized both him and Werper and bore them off toward the jungle.

By dint of threats, reproaches and profanity the Belgian officer succeeded in persuading his trembling command to fire a volley after the retreating apes. A ragged, straggling volley it was, but at least one of its bullets found a mark, for as the jungle closed about the hairy rescuers, Chulk, who bore Werper across one broad shoulder, staggered and fell.

In an instant he was up again; but the Belgian guessed from his unsteady gait that he was hard hit. He lagged far behind the others, and it was several minutes after they had halted at Tarzan's command before he came slowly up to them, reeling from side to side, and at last falling again beneath the weight of his burden and the shock of his wound.

As Chulk went down he dropped Werper, so that the latter fell face downward with the body of the ape lying half across him. In this position the Belgian felt something resting against his hands, which were still bound at his back—something that was not a part of the hairy body of the ape.

Mechanically the man's fingers felt of the object resting almost in their grasp—it was a soft pouch, filled with small, hard particles. Werper gasped in wonderment as recognition filtered through the incredulity of his mind. It was impossible, and yet—it was true!

Feverishly he strove to remove the pouch from the ape and transfer it to his own possession; but the restricted radius to which his bonds held his hands prevented this, though he did succeed in tucking the pouch with its precious contents inside the waist band of his trousers.

Tarzan, sitting at a short distance, was busy with the remaining knots of the cords which bound him. Presently he flung aside the last of them and rose to his feet. Approaching Werper he knelt beside him. For a moment he examined the ape.

"Quite dead," he announced. "It is too bad—he was a splendid creature," and then he turned to the work of liberating the Belgian.

He freed his hands first, and then commenced upon the knots at his ankles.

"I can do the rest," said the Belgian. "I have a small pocketknife which they overlooked when they searched me," and in this way he succeeded in ridding himself of the ape-man's attentions that he might find and open his little knife and cut the thong which fastened the pouch about Chulk's shoulder, and transfer it from his waist band to the breast of his shirt. Then he rose and approached Tarzan.

Once again had avarice claimed him. Forgotten were the good intentions which the confidence of Jane Clayton in his honor had awakened. What she had done, the little pouch had undone. How it had come upon the person of the great ape, Werper could not imagine, unless it had been that the anthropoid had witnessed his fight with Achmet Zek, seen the Arab with the pouch and taken it away from him; but that this pouch contained the jewels of Opar, Werper was positive, and that was all that interested him greatly.

"Now," said the ape-man, "keep your promise to me. Lead me to the spot where you last saw my wife."

It was slow work pushing through the jungle in the dead of night behind the slow-moving Belgian. The ape-man chafed at the delay, but the European could not swing through the trees as could his more agile and muscular companions, and so the speed of all was limited to that of the slowest.

The apes trailed out behind the two white men for a matter of a few miles; but presently their interest lagged, the foremost of them halted in a little glade and the others stopped at his side. There they sat peering from beneath their shaggy brows at the figures of the two men forging steadily ahead, until the latter disappeared in the leafy trail beyond the clearing. Then an ape sought a comfortable couch beneath a tree, and one by one the others followed his example, so that Werper and Tarzan continued their journey alone; nor was the latter either surprised or concerned.

The two had gone but a short distance beyond the glade where the apes had deserted them, when the roaring of distant lions fell upon their ears. The ape-man paid no attention to the familiar sounds until the crack of a rifle came faintly from the same direction, and when this was followed by the shrill neighing of horses, and an almost continuous fusillade of shots intermingled with increased and savage roaring of a large troop of lions, he became immediately concerned.

"Someone is having trouble over there," he said, turning toward Werper. "I'll have to go to them—they may be friends."

"Your wife might be among them," suggested the Belgian, for since he had again come into possession of the pouch he had become fearful and suspicious of the ape-man, and in his mind had constantly revolved many plans for eluding this giant Englishman, who was at once his savior and his captor.

At the suggestion Tarzan started as though struck with a whip.

"God!" he cried, "she might be, and the lions are attacking them—they are in the camp. I can tell from the screams of the horses—and there! that was the cry of a man in his death agonies. Stay here man—I will come back for you. I must go first to them," and swinging into a tree the lithe figure swung rapidly off into the night with the speed and silence of a disembodied spirit.

For a moment Werper stood where the ape-man had left him. Then a cunning smile crossed his lips. "Stay here?" he asked himself. "Stay here and wait until you return to find and take these jewels from me? Not I, my friend, not I," and turning abruptly eastward Albert Werper passed through the foliage of a hanging vine and out of the sight of his fellow-man—forever.

CHAPTER XXIV—HOME

As Tarzan of the Apes hurtled through the trees the discordant sounds of the battle between the Abyssinians and the lions smote more and more distinctly upon his sensitive ears, redoubling his assurance that the plight of the human element of the conflict was critical indeed.

At last the glare of the camp fire shone plainly through the intervening trees, and a moment later the giant figure of the ape-man paused upon an overhanging bough to look down upon the bloody scene of carnage below.

His quick eye took in the whole scene with a single comprehending glance and stopped upon the figure of a woman standing facing a great lion across the carcass of a horse.

The carnivore was crouching to spring as Tarzan discovered the tragic tableau. Numa was almost beneath the branch upon which the ape-man stood, naked and unarmed. There was not even an instant's hesitation upon the part of the latter—it was as though he had not even paused in his swift progress through the trees, so lightning-like his survey and comprehension of the scene below him—so instantaneous his consequent action.

So hopeless had seemed her situation to her that Jane Clayton but stood in lethargic apathy awaiting the impact of the huge body that would hurl her to the ground—awaiting the momentary agony that cruel talons and grisly fangs may inflict before the coming of the merciful oblivion which would end her sorrow and her suffering.

What use to attempt escape? As well face the hideous end as to be dragged down from behind in futile flight. She did not even close her eyes to shut out the frightful aspect of that snarling face, and so it was that as she saw the lion preparing to charge she saw, too, a bronzed and mighty figure leap from an overhanging tree at the instant that Numa rose in his spring.

Wide went her eyes in wonder and incredulity, as she beheld this seeming apparition risen from the dead. The lion was forgotten—her own peril—everything save the wondrous miracle of this strange recrudescence. With parted lips, with palms tight pressed against her heaving bosom, the girl leaned forward, large-eyed, enthralled by the vision of her dead mate.

She saw the sinewy form leap to the shoulder of the lion, hurtling against the leaping beast like a huge, animate battering ram. She saw the carnivore brushed aside as he was almost upon her, and in the instant she realized that no substanceless wraith could thus turn the charge of a maddened lion with brute force greater than the brute's.

Tarzan, her Tarzan, lived! A cry of unspeakable gladness broke from her lips, only to die in terror as she saw the utter defenselessness of her mate, and realized that the lion had recovered himself and was turning upon Tarzan in mad lust for vengeance.

At the ape-man's feet lay the discarded rifle of the dead Abyssinian whose mutilated corpse sprawled where Numa had abandoned it. The quick glance which had swept the ground for some weapon of defense discovered it, and as the lion reared upon his hind legs to seize the rash man-thing who had dared interpose its puny strength between Numa and his prey, the heavy stock whirred through the air and splintered upon the broad forehead.

Not as an ordinary mortal might strike a blow did Tarzan of the Apes strike; but with the maddened frenzy of a wild beast backed by the steel thews which his wild, arboreal boyhood had bequeathed him. When the blow ended the splintered stock was driven through the splintered skull into the savage brain, and the heavy iron barrel was bent into a rude V.

In the instant that the lion sank, lifeless, to the ground, Jane Clayton threw herself into the eager arms of her husband. For a brief instant he strained her dear form to his breast, and then a glance about him awakened the ape-man to the dangers which still surrounded them.

Upon every hand the lions were still leaping upon new victims. Fear-maddened horses still menaced them with their erratic bolting from one side of the enclosure to the other. Bullets from the guns of the defenders who remained alive but added to the perils of their situation.

To remain was to court death. Tarzan seized Jane Clayton and lifted her to a broad shoulder. The blacks who had witnessed his advent looked on in amazement as they saw the naked giant leap easily into the branches of the tree from whence he had dropped so uncannily upon the scene, and vanish as he had come, bearing away their prisoner with him.

They were too well occupied in self-defense to attempt to halt him, nor could they have done so other than by the wasting of a precious bullet which might be needed the next instant to turn the charge of a savage foe.

And so, unmolested, Tarzan passed from the camp of the Abyssinians, from which the din of conflict followed him deep into the jungle until distance gradually obliterated it entirely.

Back to the spot where he had left Werper went the ape-man, joy in his heart now, where fear and sorrow had so recently reigned; and in his mind a determination to forgive the Belgian and aid him in making good his escape. But when he came to the place, Werper was gone, and though Tarzan called aloud many times he received no reply. Convinced that the man had purposely eluded him for reasons of his own, John Clayton felt that he was under no obligations to expose his wife to further danger and discomfort in the prosecution of a more thorough search for the missing Belgian.

"He has acknowledged his guilt by his flight, Jane," he said. "We will let him go to lie in the bed that he has made for himself."

Straight as homing pigeons, the two made their way toward the ruin and desolation that had once been the center of their happy lives, and which was soon to be restored by the willing black hands of laughing laborers, made happy again by the return of the master and mistress whom they had mourned as dead.

Past the village of Achmet Zek their way led them, and there they found but the charred remains of the palisade and the native huts, still smoking, as mute evidence of the wrath and vengeance of a powerful enemy.

"The Waziri," commented Tarzan with a grim smile.

"God bless them!" cried Jane Clayton.

"They cannot be far ahead of us," said Tarzan, "Basuli and the others. The gold is gone and the jewels of Opar, Jane; but we have each other and the Waziri—and we have love and loyalty and friendship. And what are gold and jewels to these?"

"If only poor Mugambi lived," she replied, "and those other brave fellows who sacrificed their lives in vain endeavor to protect me!"

In the silence of mingled joy and sorrow they passed along through the familiar jungle, and as the afternoon was waning there came faintly to the ears of the ape-man the murmuring cadence of distant voices.

"We are nearing the Waziri, Jane," he said. "I can hear them ahead of us. They are going into camp for the night, I imagine."

A half hour later the two came upon a horde of ebon warriors which Basuli had collected for his war of vengeance upon the raiders. With them were the captured women of the tribe whom they had found in the village of Achmet Zek, and tall, even among the giant Waziri, loomed a familiar black form at the side of Basuli. It was Mugambi, whom Jane had thought dead amidst the charred ruins of the bungalow.

Ah, such a reunion! Long into the night the dancing and the singing and the laughter awoke the echoes of the somber wood. Again and again were the stories of their various adventures retold. Again and once again they fought their battles with savage beast and savage man, and dawn was already breaking when Basuli, for the fortieth time, narrated how he and a handful of his warriors had watched the battle for the golden ingots which the Abyssinians of Abdul Mourak had waged against the Arab raiders of Achmet Zek, and how, when the victors had ridden away they had sneaked out of the river reeds and stolen away with the precious ingots to hide them where no robber eye ever could discover them.

Pieced out from the fragments of their various experiences with the Belgian the truth concerning the malign activities of Albert Werper became apparent. Only Lady Greystoke found aught to praise in the conduct of the man, and it was difficult even for her to reconcile his many heinous acts with this one evidence of chivalry and honor.

"Deep in the soul of every man," said Tarzan, "must lurk the germ of righteousness. It was your own virtue, Jane, rather even than your helplessness which awakened for an instant the latent decency of this degraded man. In that one act he retrieved himself, and when he is called to face his Maker may it outweigh in the balance, all the sins he has committed."

And Jane Clayton breathed a fervent, "Amen!"

Months had passed. The labor of the Waziri and the gold of Opar had rebuilt and refurnished the wasted homestead of the Greystokes. Once more the simple life of the great African farm went on as it had before the coming of the Belgian and the Arab. Forgotten were the sorrows and dangers of yesterday.

For the first time in months Lord Greystoke felt that he might indulge in a holiday, and so a great hunt was organized that the faithful laborers might feast in celebration of the completion of their work.

In itself the hunt was a success, and ten days after its inauguration, a well-laden safari took up its return march toward the Waziri plain. Lord and Lady Greystoke with Basuli and Mugambi rode together at the head of the column, laughing and talking together in that easy familiarity which common interests and mutual respect breed between honest and intelligent men of any races.

Jane Clayton's horse shied suddenly at an object half hidden in the long grasses of an open space in the jungle. Tarzan's keen eyes sought quickly for an explanation of the animal's action.

"What have we here?" he cried, swinging from his saddle, and a moment later the four were grouped about a human skull and a little litter of whitened human bones.

Tarzan stooped and lifted a leathern pouch from the grisly relics of a man. The hard outlines of the contents brought an exclamation of surprise to his lips.

"The jewels of Opar!" he cried, holding the pouch aloft, "and," pointing to the bones at his feet, "all that remains of Werper, the Belgian."

Mugambi laughed. "Look within, Bwana," he cried, "and you will see what are the jewels of Opar—you will see what the Belgian gave his life for," and the black laughed aloud.

"Why do you laugh?" asked Tarzan.

"Because," replied Mugambi, "I filled the Belgian's pouch with river gravel before I escaped the camp of the Abyssinians whose prisoners we were. I left the Belgian only worthless stones, while I brought away with me the jewels he had stolen from you. That they were afterward stolen from me while I slept in the jungle is my shame and my disgrace; but at least the Belgian lost them—open his pouch and you will see."

Tarzan untied the thong which held the mouth of the leathern bag closed, and permitted the contents to trickle slowly forth into his open palm. Mugambi's eyes went wide at the sight, and the others uttered exclamations of surprise and incredulity, for from the rusty and weatherworn pouch ran a stream of brilliant, scintillating gems.

"The jewels of Opar!" cried Tarzan. "But how did Werper come by them again?"

None could answer, for both Chulk and Werper were dead, and no other knew.

"Poor devil!" said the ape-man, as he swung back into his saddle. "Even in death he has made restitution—let his sins lie with his bones."

TARZAN THE UNTAMED

CHAPTER I—MURDER AND PILLAGE

Hauptmann Fritz Schneider trudged wearily through the somber aisles of the dark forest. Sweat rolled down his bullet head and stood upon his heavy jowls and bull neck. His lieutenant marched beside him while Underlieutenant von Goss brought up the rear, following with a handful of askaris the tired and all but exhausted porters whom the black soldiers, following the example of their white officer, encouraged with the sharp points of bayonets and the metal-shod butts of rifles.

There were no porters within reach of Hauptmann Schneider so he vented his Prussian spleen upon the askaris nearest at hand, yet with greater circumspection since these men bore loaded rifles—and the three white men were alone with them in the heart of Africa.

Ahead of the hauptmann marched half his company, behind him the other half—thus were the dangers of the savage jungle minimized for the German captain. At the forefront of the column staggered two naked savages fastened to each other by a neck chain. These were the native guides impressed into the service of Kultur and upon their poor, bruised bodies Kultur's brand was revealed in divers cruel wounds and bruises.

Thus even in darkest Africa was the light of German civilization commencing to reflect itself upon the undeserving natives just as at the same period, the fall of 1914, it was shedding its glorious effulgence upon benighted Belgium.

It is true that the guides had led the party astray; but this is the way of most African guides. Nor did it matter that ignorance rather than evil intent had been the cause of their failure. It was enough for Hauptmann Fritz Schneider to know that he was lost in the African wilderness and that he had at hand human beings less powerful than he who could be made to suffer by torture. That he did not kill them outright was partially due to a faint hope that they might eventually prove the means of extricating him from his difficulties and partially that so long as they lived they might still be made to suffer.

The poor creatures, hoping that chance might lead them at last upon the right trail, insisted that they knew the way and so led on through a dismal forest along a winding game trail trodden deep by the feet of countless generations of the savage denizens of the jungle.

Here Tantor, the elephant, took his long way from dust wallow to water. Here Buto, the rhinoceros, blundered blindly in his solitary majesty, while by night the great cats paced silently upon their padded feet beneath the dense canopy of overreaching trees toward the broad plain beyond, where they found their best hunting.

It was at the edge of this plain which came suddenly and unexpectedly before the eyes of the guides that their sad hearts beat with renewed hope. Here the hauptmann drew a deep sigh of relief, for after days of hopeless wandering through almost impenetrable jungle the broad vista of waving grasses dotted here and there with open park like woods and in the far distance the winding line of green shrubbery that denoted a river appeared to the European a veritable heaven.

The Hun smiled in his relief, passed a cheery word with his lieutenant, and then scanned the broad plain with his field glasses. Back and forth they swept across the rolling land until at last they came to rest upon a point near the center of the landscape and close to the green-fringed contours of the river.

"We are in luck," said Schneider to his companions. "Do you see it?"

The lieutenant, who was also gazing through his own glasses, finally brought them to rest upon the same spot that had held the attention of his superior.

"Yes," he said, "an English farm. It must be Greystoke's, for there is none other in this part of British East Africa. God is with us, Herr Captain."

"We have come upon the English schweinhund long before he can have learned that his country is at war with ours," replied Schneider. "Let him be the first to feel the iron hand of Germany."

"Let us hope that he is at home," said the lieutenant, "that we may take him with us when we report to Kraut at Nairobi. It will go well indeed with Herr Hauptmann Fritz Schneider if he brings in the famous Tarzan of the Apes as a prisoner of war."

Schneider smiled and puffed out his chest. "You are right, my friend," he said, "it will go well with both of us; but I shall have to travel far to catch General Kraut before he reaches Mombasa. These English pigs with their contemptible army will make good time to the Indian Ocean."

It was in a better frame of mind that the small force set out across the open country toward the trim and well-kept farm buildings of John Clayton, Lord Greystoke; but disappointment was to be their lot since neither Tarzan of the Apes nor his son was at home.

Lady Jane, ignorant of the fact that a state of war existed between Great Britain and Germany, welcomed the officers most hospitably and gave orders through her trusted Waziri to prepare a feast for the black soldiers of the enemy.

Far to the east, Tarzan of the Apes was traveling rapidly from Nairobi toward the farm. At Nairobi he had received news of the World War that had already started, and, anticipating an immediate invasion of British East Africa by the Germans, was hurrying homeward to fetch his wife to a place of greater security. With him were a score of his ebon warriors, but far too slow for the ape-man was the progress of these trained and hardened woodsmen.

When necessity demanded, Tarzan of the Apes sloughed the thin veneer of his civilization and with it the hampering apparel that was its badge. In a moment the polished English gentleman reverted to the naked ape man.

His mate was in danger. For the time, that single thought dominated. He did not think of her as Lady Jane Greystoke, but rather as the she he had won by the might of his steel thews, and that he must hold and protect by virtue of the same offensive armament.

It was no member of the House of Lords who swung swiftly and grimly through the tangled forest or trod with untiring muscles the wide stretches of open plain—it was a great he ape filled with a single purpose that excluded all thoughts of fatigue or danger.

Little Manu, the monkey, scolding and chattering in the upper terraces of the forest, saw him pass. Long had it been since he had thus beheld the great Tarmangani naked and alone hurtling through the jungle. Bearded and gray was Manu, the monkey, and to his dim old eyes came the fire of recollection of those days when Tarzan of the Apes had ruled supreme, Lord of the Jungle, over all the myriad life that trod the matted vegetation between the boles of the great trees, or flew or swung or climbed in the leafy fastness upward to the very apex of the loftiest terraces.

And Numa, the lion, lying up for the day close beside last night's successful kill, blinked his yellow-green eyes and twitched his tawny tail as he caught the scent spoor of his ancient enemy.

Nor was Tarzan senseless to the presence of Numa or Manu or any of the many jungle beasts he passed in his rapid flight towards the west. No particle had his shallow probing of English society dulled his marvelous sense faculties. His nose had picked out the presence of Numa, the lion, even before the majestic king of beasts was aware of his passing.

He had heard noisy little Manu, and even the soft rustling of the parting shrubbery where Sheeta passed before either of these alert animals sensed his presence.

But however keen the senses of the ape-man, however swift his progress through the wild country of his adoption, however mighty the muscles that bore him, he was still mortal. Time and space placed their inexorable limits upon him; nor was there another who realized this truth more keenly than Tarzan. He chafed and fretted that he could not travel with the swiftness of thought and that the long tedious miles stretching far ahead of him must require hours and hours of tireless effort upon his part before he would swing at last from the final bough of the fringing forest into the open plain and in sight of his goal.

Days it took, even though he lay up at night for but a few hours and left to chance the finding of meat directly on his trail. If Wappi, the antelope, or Horta, the boar, chanced in his way when he was hungry, he ate, pausing but long enough to make the kill and cut himself a steak.

Then at last the long journey drew to its close and he was passing through the last stretch of heavy forest that bounded his estate upon the east, and then this was traversed and he stood upon the plain's edge looking out across his broad lands towards his home.

At the first glance his eyes narrowed and his muscles tensed. Even at that distance he could see that something was amiss. A thin spiral of smoke arose at the right of the bungalow where the barns had stood, but there were no barns there now, and from the bungalow chimney from which smoke should have arisen, there arose nothing.

Once again Tarzan of the Apes was speeding onward, this time even more swiftly than before, for he was goaded now by a nameless fear, more product of intuition than of reason. Even as the beasts, Tarzan of the Apes seemed to possess a sixth sense. Long before he reached the bungalow, he had almost pictured the scene that finally broke upon his view.

Silent and deserted was the vine-covered cottage. Smoldering embers marked the site of his great barns. Gone were the thatched huts of his sturdy retainers, empty the fields, the pastures, and corrals. Here and there vultures rose and circled above the carcasses of men and beasts.

It was with a feeling as nearly akin to terror as he ever had experienced that the ape-man finally forced himself to enter his home. The first sight that met his eyes set the red haze of hate and bloodlust across his vision, for there, crucified against the wall of the living-room, was Wasimbu, giant son of the faithful Muviro and for over a year the personal bodyguard of Lady Jane.

The overturned and shattered furniture of the room, the brown pools of dried blood upon the floor, and prints of bloody hands on walls and woodwork evidenced something of the frightfulness of the battle that had been waged within the narrow confines of the apartment. Across the baby grand piano lay the corpse of another black warrior, while before the door of Lady Jane's boudoir were the dead bodies of three more of the faithful Greystoke servants.

The door of this room was closed. With drooping shoulders and dull eyes Tarzan stood gazing dumbly at the insensate panel which hid from him what horrid secret he dared not even guess.

Slowly, with leaden feet, he moved toward the door. Gropingly his hand reached for the knob. Thus he stood for another long minute, and then with a sudden gesture he straightened his giant frame, threw back his mighty shoulders and, with fearless head held high, swung back the door and stepped across the threshold into the room which held for him the dearest memories and associations of his life. No change of expression crossed his grim and stern-set features as he strode across the room and stood beside the little couch and the inanimate form which lay face downward upon it; the still, silent thing that had pulsed with life and youth and love.

No tear dimmed the eye of the ape-man, but the God who made him alone could know the thoughts that passed through that still half-savage brain. For a long time he stood there just looking down upon the dead body, charred beyond recognition, and then he stooped and lifted it in his arms. As he turned the body over and saw how horribly death had been meted he plumbed, in that instant, the uttermost depths of grief and horror and hatred.

Nor did he require the evidence of the broken German rifle in the outer room, or the torn and blood-stained service cap upon the floor, to tell him who had been the perpetrators of this horrid and useless crime.

For a moment he had hoped against hope that the blackened corpse was not that of his mate, but when his eyes discovered and recognized the rings upon her fingers the last faint ray of hope forsook him.

In silence, in love, and in reverence he buried, in the little rose garden that had been Jane Clayton's pride and love, the poor, charred form and beside it the great black warriors who had given their lives so futilely in their mistress' protection.

At one side of the house Tarzan found other newly made graves and in these he sought final evidence of the identity of the real perpetrators of the atrocities that had been committed there in his absence.

Here he disinterred the bodies of a dozen German askaris and found upon their uniforms the insignia of the company and regiment to which they had belonged. This was enough for the ape-man. White officers had commanded these men, nor would it be a difficult task to discover who they were.

Returning to the rose garden, he stood among the Hun trampled blooms and bushes above the grave of his dead—with bowed head he stood there in a last mute farewell. As the sun sank slowly behind the towering forests of the west, he turned slowly away upon the still-distinct trail of Hauptmann Fritz Schneider and his blood-stained company.

His was the suffering of the dumb brute—mute; but though voiceless no less poignant. At first his vast sorrow numbed his other faculties of thought—his brain was overwhelmed by the calamity to such an extent that it reacted to but a single objective suggestion: She is dead! She is dead! She is dead! Again and again this phrase beat monotonously upon his brain—a dull, throbbing pain, yet mechanically his feet followed the trail of her slayer while, subconsciously, his every sense was upon the alert for the ever-present perils of the jungle.

Gradually the labor of his great grief brought forth another emotion so real, so tangible, that it seemed a companion walking at his side. It was Hate—and it brought to him a measure of solace and of comfort, for it was a sublime hate that ennobled him as it has ennobled countless thousands since—hatred for Germany and Germans. It centered about the slayer of his mate, of course; but it included everything German, animate or inanimate. As the thought took firm hold upon him he paused and raising his face to Goro, the moon, cursed with upraised hand the authors of the hideous crime that had been perpetrated in that once peaceful bungalow behind him; and he cursed their progenitors, their progeny, and all their kind the while he took silent oath to war upon them relentlessly until death overtook him.

There followed almost immediately a feeling of content, for, where before his future at best seemed but a void, now it was filled with possibilities the contemplation of which brought him, if not happiness, at least a surcease of absolute grief, for before him lay a great work that would occupy his time.

Stripped not only of all the outward symbols of civilization, Tarzan had also reverted morally and mentally to the status of the savage beast he had been reared. Never had his civilization been more than a veneer put on for the sake of her he loved because he thought it made her happier to see him thus. In reality he had always held the outward evidences of so-called culture in deep contempt. Civilization meant to Tarzan of the Apes a curtailment of freedom in all its aspects—freedom of action, freedom of thought, freedom of love, freedom of hate. Clothes he abhorred—uncomfortable, hideous, confining things that reminded him somehow of bonds securing him to the life he had seen the poor creatures of London and Paris living. Clothes were the emblems of that hypocrisy for which civilization stood—a pretense that the wearers were ashamed of what the clothes covered, of the human form made in the semblance of God. Tarzan knew how silly and pathetic the lower orders of animals appeared in the clothing of civilization, for he had seen several poor creatures thus appareled in various traveling shows in Europe, and he knew, too, how silly and pathetic man appears in them since the only men he had seen in the first twenty years of his life had been, like himself, naked savages. The ape-man had a keen admiration for a well-muscled, well-proportioned body, whether lion, or antelope, or man, and it had ever been beyond him to understand how clothes could be considered more beautiful than a clear, firm, healthy skin, or coat and trousers more graceful than the gentle curves of rounded muscles playing beneath a flexible hide.

In civilization Tarzan had found greed and selfishness and cruelty far beyond that which he had known in his familiar, savage jungle, and though civilization had given him his mate and several friends whom he loved and admired, he never had come to accept it as you and I who have known little or nothing else; so it was with a sense of relief that he now definitely abandoned it and all that it stood for, and went forth into the jungle once again stripped to his loin cloth and weapons.

The hunting knife of his father hung at his left hip, his bow and his quiver of arrows were slung across his shoulders, while around his chest over one shoulder and beneath the opposite arm was coiled the long grass rope without which Tarzan would have felt quite as naked as would you should you be suddenly thrust upon a busy highway clad only in a union suit. A heavy war spear which he sometimes carried in one hand and again slung by a thong about his neck so that it hung down his back completed his armament and his apparel. The diamond-studded locket with the pictures of his mother and father that he had worn always until he had given it as a token of his highest devotion to Jane Clayton before their marriage was missing. She always had worn it since, but it had not been upon her body when he found her slain in her boudoir, so that now his quest for vengeance included also a quest for the stolen trinket.

Toward midnight Tarzan commenced to feel the physical strain of his long hours of travel and to realize that even muscles such as his had their limitations. His pursuit of the murderers had not been characterized by excessive speed; but rather more in keeping with his mental attitude, which was marked by a dogged determination to require from the Germans more than an eye for an eye and more than a tooth for a tooth, the element of time entering but slightly into his calculations.

Inwardly as well as outwardly Tarzan had reverted to beast and in the lives of beasts, time, as a measurable aspect of duration, has no meaning. The beast is actively interested only in *now*, and as it is always *now* and always shall be, there is an eternity of time for the accomplishment of objects. The ape-man, naturally, had a slightly more comprehensive realization of the limitations of time; but, like the beasts, he moved with majestic deliberation when no emergency prompted him to swift action.

Having dedicated his life to vengeance, vengeance became his natural state and, therefore, no emergency, so he took his time in pursuit. That he had not rested earlier was due to the fact that he had felt no fatigue, his mind being occupied by thoughts of sorrow and revenge; but now he realized that he was tired, and so he sought a jungle giant that had harbored him upon more than a single other jungle night.

Dark clouds moving swiftly across the heavens now and again eclipsed the bright face of Goro, the moon, and forewarned the ape-man of impending storm. In the depth of the jungle the cloud shadows produced a thick blackness that might almost be felt—a blackness that to you and me might have proven terrifying with its accompaniment of rustling leaves and cracking twigs, and its even more suggestive intervals of utter silence in which the crudest of imaginations might have conjured crouching beasts of prey tensed for the fatal charge; but through it Tarzan passed unconcerned, yet always alert. Now he swung lightly to the lower terraces of the overarching trees when some subtle sense warned him that Numa lay upon a kill directly in his path, or again he sprang lightly to one side as Buto, the rhinoceros, lumbered toward him along the narrow, deep-worn trail, for the ape-man, ready to fight upon necessity's slightest pretext, avoided unnecessary quarrels.

When he swung himself at last into the tree he sought, the moon was obscured by a heavy cloud, and the tree tops were waving wildly in a steadily increasing wind whose soughing drowned the lesser noises of the jungle. Upward went Tarzan toward a sturdy crotch across which he long since had laid and secured a little platform of branches. It was very dark now, darker even than it had been before, for almost the entire sky was overcast by thick, black clouds.

Presently the man-beast paused, his sensitive nostrils dilating as he sniffed the air about him. Then, with the swiftness and agility of a cat, he leaped far outward upon a swaying branch, sprang upward through the darkness, caught another, swung himself upon it and then to one still higher. What could have so suddenly transformed his matter-of-fact ascent of the giant bole to the swift and wary action of his detour among the branches? You or I could have seen nothing—not even the little platform that an instant before had been just above him and which now was immediately below—but as he swung above it we should have heard an ominous growl; and then as the moon was momentarily uncovered, we should have seen both the platform, dimly, and a dark mass that lay stretched upon it—a dark mass that presently, as our eyes became accustomed to the lesser darkness, would take the form of Sheeta, the panther.

In answer to the cat's growl, a low and equally ferocious growl rumbled upward from the ape-man's deep chest—a growl of warning that told the panther he was trespassing upon the other's lair; but Sheeta was in no mood to be dispossessed. With upturned, snarling face he glared at the brown-skinned Tarmangani above him. Very slowly the ape-man moved inward along the branch until he was directly above the panther. In the man's hand was the hunting knife of his long-dead father—the weapon that had first given him his real ascendancy over the beasts of the jungle; but he hoped not to be forced to use it, knowing as he did that more jungle battles were settled by hideous growling than by actual combat, the law of bluff holding quite as good in the jungle as elsewhere—only in matters of love and food did the great beasts ordinarily close with fangs and talons.

Tarzan braced himself against the bole of the tree and leaned closer toward Sheeta.

"Stealer of balus!" he cried. The panther rose to a sitting position, his bared fangs but a few feet from the ape-man's taunting face. Tarzan growled hideously and struck at the cat's face with his knife. "I am Tarzan of the Apes," he roared. "This is Tarzan's lair. Go, or I will kill you."

Though he spoke in the language of the great apes of the jungle, it is doubtful that Sheeta understood the words, though he knew well enough that the hairless ape wished to frighten him from his well-chosen station past which edible creatures might be expected to wander sometime during the watches of the night.

Like lightning the cat reared and struck a vicious blow at his tormentor with great, bared talons that might well have torn away the ape-man's face had the blow landed; but it did not land—Tarzan was even quicker than Sheeta. As the panther came to all fours again upon the little platform, Tarzan un-slung his heavy spear and prodded at the snarling face, and as Sheeta warded off the blows, the two continued their horrid duet of blood-curdling roars and growls.

Goaded to frenzy the cat presently determined to come up after this disturber of his peace; but when he essayed to leap to the branch that held Tarzan he found the sharp spear point always in his face, and each time as he dropped back he was prodded viciously in some tender part; but at length, rage having conquered his better judgment, he leaped up the rough bole to the very branch upon which Tarzan stood. Now the two faced each other upon even footing and Sheeta saw a quick revenge and a supper all in one. The hairless ape-thing with the tiny fangs and the puny talons would be helpless before him.

The heavy limb bent beneath the weight of the two beasts as Sheeta crept cautiously out upon it and Tarzan backed slowly away, growling. The wind had risen to the proportions of a gale so that even the greatest giants of the forest swayed, groaning, to its force and the branch upon which the two faced each other rose and fell like the deck of a storm-tossed ship. Goro was now entirely obscured, but vivid flashes of lightning lit up the jungle at brief intervals, revealing the grim tableau of primitive passion upon the swaying limb.

Tarzan backed away, drawing Sheeta farther from the stem of the tree and out upon the tapering branch, where his footing became ever more precarious. The cat, infuriated by the pain of spear wounds, was overstepping the bounds of caution. Already he had reached a point where he could do little more than maintain a secure footing, and it was this moment that Tarzan chose to charge. With a roar that mingled with the booming thunder from above he leaped toward the panther, who could only claw futilely with one huge paw while he clung to the branch with the other; but the ape-man did not come within that parabola of destruction. Instead he leaped above menacing claws and snapping fangs, turning in mid-air and alighting upon Sheeta's back, and at the instant of impact his knife struck deep into the tawny side. Then Sheeta, impelled by pain and hate and rage and the first law of Nature, went mad. Screaming and clawing he attempted to turn upon the ape-thing clinging to his back. For an instant he toppled upon the now wildly gyrating limb, clutched frantically to save himself, and then plunged downward into the darkness with Tarzan still clinging to him. Crashing through splintering branches the two fell. Not for an instant did the ape-man consider relinquishing his death-hold upon his adversary. He had entered the lists in mortal combat and true to the primitive instincts of the wild—the unwritten law of the jungle—one or both must die before the battle ended.

Sheeta, catlike, alighted upon four out-sprawled feet, the weight of the ape-man crushing him to earth, the long knife again imbedded in his side. Once the panther struggled to rise; but only to sink to earth again. Tarzan felt the giant muscles relax beneath him. Sheeta was dead. Rising, the ape-man placed a foot upon the body of his vanquished foe, raised his face toward the thundering heavens, and as the lightning flashed and the torrential rain broke upon him, screamed forth the wild victory cry of the bull ape.

Having accomplished his aim and driven the enemy from his lair, Tarzan gathered an armful of large fronds and climbed to his dripping couch. Laying a few of the fronds upon the poles he lay down and covered himself against the rain with the others, and despite the wailing of the wind and the crashing of the thunder, immediately fell asleep.

CHAPTER II—THE LION'S CAVE

The rain lasted for twenty-four hours and much of the time it fell in torrents so that when it ceased, the trail he had been following was entirely obliterated. Cold and uncomfortable—it was a savage Tarzan who threaded the mazes of the soggy jungle. Manu, the monkey, shivering and chattering in the dank trees, scolded and fled at his approach. Even the panthers and the lions let the growling Tarmangani pass unmolested.

When the sun shone again upon the second day and a wide, open plain let the full heat of Kudu flood the chilled, brown body, Tarzan's spirits rose; but it was still a sullen, surly brute that moved steadily onward into the south where he hoped again to pick up the trail of the Germans. He was now in German East Africa and it was his intention to skirt the mountains west of Kilimanjaro, whose rugged peaks he was quite willing to give a wide berth, and then swing eastward along the south side of the range to the railway that led to Tanga, for his experience among men suggested that it was toward this railroad that German troops would be likely to converge.

Two days later, from the southern slopes of Kilimanjaro, he heard the boom of cannon far away to the east. The afternoon had been dull and cloudy and now as he was passing through a narrow gorge a few great drops of rain began to splatter upon his naked shoulders. Tarzan shook his head and growled his disapproval; then he cast his eyes about for shelter, for he had had quite enough of the cold and drenching. He wanted to hasten on in the direction of the booming noise, for he knew that there would be Germans fighting against the English. For an instant his bosom swelled with pride at the thought that he was English and then he shook his head again viciously. "No!" he muttered, "Tarzan of the Apes is not English, for the English are men and Tarzan is Tarmangani;" but he could not hide even from his sorrow or from his sullen hatred of mankind in general that his heart warmed at the thought it was Englishmen who fought the Germans. His regret was that the English were human and not great white apes as he again considered himself.

"Tomorrow," he thought, "I will travel that way and find the Germans," and then he set himself to the immediate task of discovering some shelter from the storm. Presently he espied the low and narrow entrance to what appeared to be a cave at the base of the cliffs which formed the northern side of the gorge. With drawn knife he approached the spot warily, for he knew that if it were a cave it was doubtless the lair of some other beast. Before the entrance lay many large fragments of rock of different sizes, similar to others scattered along the entire base of the cliff, and it was in Tarzan's mind that if he found the cave unoccupied he would barricade the door and insure himself a quiet and peaceful night's repose within the sheltered interior. Let the storm rage without—Tarzan would remain within until it ceased, comfortable and dry. A tiny rivulet of cold water trickled outward from the opening.

Close to the cave Tarzan kneeled and sniffed the ground. A low growl escaped him and his upper lip curved to expose his fighting fangs. "Numa!" he muttered; but he did not stop. Numa might not be at home—he would investigate. The entrance was so low that the ape-man was compelled to drop to all fours before he could poke his head within the aperture; but first he looked, listened, and sniffed in each direction at his rear—he would not be taken by surprise from that quarter.

His first glance within the cave revealed a narrow tunnel with daylight at its farther end. The interior of the tunnel was not so dark but that the ape-man could readily see that it was untenanted at present. Advancing cautiously he crawled toward the opposite end imbued with a full realization of what it would mean if Numa should suddenly enter the tunnel in front of him; but Numa did not appear and the ape-man emerged at length into the open and stood erect, finding himself in a rocky cleft whose precipitous walls rose almost sheer on every hand, the tunnel from the gorge passing through the cliff and forming a passageway from the outer world into a large pocket or gulch entirely enclosed by steep walls of rock. Except for the small passageway from the gorge, there was no other entrance to the gulch which was some hundred feet in length and about fifty in width and appeared to have been worn from the rocky cliff by the falling of water during long ages. A tiny stream from Kilimanjaro's eternal snow cap still trickled over the edge of the rocky wall at the upper end of the gulch, forming a little pool at the bottom of the cliff from which a small rivulet wound downward to the tunnel through which it passed to the gorge beyond. A single great tree flourished near the center of the gulch, while tufts of wiry grass were scattered here and there among the rocks of the gravelly floor.

The bones of many large animals lay about and among them were several human skulls. Tarzan raised his eyebrows. "A man-eater," he murmured, "and from appearances he has held sway here for a long time. Tonight Tarzan will take the lair of the man-eater and Numa may roar and grumble upon the outside."

The ape-man had advanced well into the gulch as he investigated his surroundings and now as he stood near the tree, satisfied that the tunnel would prove a dry and quiet retreat for the night, he turned to retrace his way to the outer end of the entrance that he might block it with boulders against Numa's return, but even with the thought there came something to his sensitive ears that froze him into statuesque immobility with eyes glued upon the tunnel's mouth. A moment later the head of a huge lion framed in a great black mane appeared in the opening. The yellow-green eyes glared, round and unblinking, straight at the trespassing Tarmangani, a low growl rumbled from the deep chest, and lips curled back to expose the mighty fangs.

"Brother of Dango!" shouted Tarzan, angered that Numa's return should have been so timed as to frustrate his plans for a comfortable night's repose. "I am Tarzan of the Apes, Lord of the Jungle. Tonight I lair here—go!"

But Numa did not go. Instead he rumbled forth a menacing roar and took a few steps in Tarzan's direction. The ape-man picked up a rock and hurled it at the snarling face. One can never be sure of a lion. This one might turn tail and run at the first intimation of attack—Tarzan had bluffed many in his time—but not now. The missile struck Numa full upon the snout—a tender part of a cat's anatomy—and instead of causing him to flee it transformed him into an infuriated engine of wrath and destruction.

Up went his tail, stiff and erect, and with a series of frightful roars he bore down upon the Tarmangani at the speed of an express train. Not an instant too soon did Tarzan reach the tree and swing himself into its branches and there he squatted, hurling insults at the king of beasts while Numa paced a circle beneath him, growling and roaring in rage.

It was raining now in earnest adding to the ape-man's discomfort and disappointment. He was very angry; but as only direct necessity had ever led him to close in mortal combat with a lion, knowing as he did that he had only luck and agility to pit against the frightful odds of muscle, weight, fangs, and talons, he did not now even consider descending and engaging in so unequal and useless a duel for the mere reward of a little added creature comfort. And so he sat perched in the tree while the rain fell steadily and the lion padded round and round beneath, casting a baleful eye upward after every few steps.

Tarzan scanned the precipitous walls for an avenue of escape. They would have baffled an ordinary man; but the ape-man, accustomed to climbing, saw several places where he might gain a foothold, precarious possibly; but enough to give him reasonable assurance of escape if Numa would but betake himself to the far end of the gulch for a moment. Numa, however, notwithstanding the rain, gave no evidence of quitting his post so that at last Tarzan really began to consider seriously if it might not be as well to take the chance of a battle with him rather than remain longer cold and wet and humiliated in the tree.

But even as he turned the matter over in his mind Numa turned suddenly and walked majestically toward the tunnel without even a backward glance. The instant that he disappeared, Tarzan dropped lightly to the ground upon the far side of the tree and was away at top speed for the cliff. The lion had no sooner entered the tunnel than he backed immediately out again and, pivoting like a flash, was off across the gulch in full charge after the flying ape-man; but Tarzan's lead was too great—if he could find finger or foothold upon the sheer wall he would be safe; but should he slip from the wet rocks his doom was already sealed as he would fall directly into Numa's clutches where even the Great Tarmangani would be helpless.

With the agility of a cat Tarzan ran up the cliff for thirty feet before he paused, and there finding a secure foothold, he stopped and looked down upon Numa who was leaping upward in a wild and futile attempt to scale the rocky wall to his prey. Fifteen or twenty feet from the ground the lion would scramble only to fall backward again defeated. Tarzan eyed him for a moment and then commenced a slow and cautious ascent toward the summit. Several times he had difficulty in finding holds but at last he drew himself over the edge, rose, picked up a bit of loose rock, hurled it at Numa and strode away.

Finding an easy descent to the gorge, he was about to pursue his journey in the direction of the still-booming guns when a sudden thought caused him to halt and a half-smile to play about his lips. Turning, he trotted quickly back to the outer opening of Numa's tunnel. Close beside it he listened for a moment and then rapidly began to gather large rocks and pile them within the entrance. He had almost closed the aperture when the lion appeared upon the inside—a very ferocious and angry lion that pawed and clawed at the rocks and uttered mighty roars that caused the earth to tremble; but roars did not frighten Tarzan of the Apes. At Kala's shaggy breast he had closed his infant eyes in sleep upon countless nights in years gone by to the savage chorus of similar roars. Scarcely a day or night of his jungle life—and practically all his life had been spent in the jungle—had he not heard the roaring of hungry lions, or angry lions, or love-sick lions. Such sounds affected Tarzan as the tooting of an automobile horn may affect you—if you are in front of the automobile it warns you out of the way, if you are not in front of it you scarcely notice it. Figuratively Tarzan was not in front of the automobile—Numa could not reach him and Tarzan knew it, so he continued deliberately to choke the entrance until there was no possibility of Numa's getting out again. When he was quite through he made a grimace at the hidden lion beyond the barrier and resumed his way toward the east. "A man-eater who will eat no more men," he soliloquized.

That night Tarzan lay up under an overhanging shelf of rock. The next morning he resumed his journey, stopping only long enough to make a kill and satisfy his hunger. The other beasts of the wild eat and lie up; but Tarzan never let his belly interfere with his plans. In this lay one of the greatest differences between the ape-man and his fellows of the jungles and forests. The firing ahead rose and fell during the day. He had noticed that it was highest at dawn and immediately after dusk and that during the night it almost ceased. In the middle of the afternoon of the second day he came upon troops moving up toward the front. They appeared to be raiding parties, for they drove goats and cows along with them and there were native porters laden with grain and other foodstuffs. He saw that these natives were all secured by neck chains and he also saw that the troops were composed of native soldiers in German uniforms. The officers were white men. No one saw Tarzan, yet he was here and there about and among them for two hours. He inspected the insignia upon their uniforms and saw that they were not the same as that which he had taken from one of the dead soldiers at the bungalow and then he passed on ahead of them, unseen in the dense bush. He had come upon Germans and had not killed them; but it was because the killing of Germans at large was not yet the prime motive of his existence—now it was to discover the individual who slew his mate.

After he had accounted for him he would take up the little matter of slaying *all* Germans who crossed his path, and he meant that many should cross it, for he would hunt them precisely as professional hunters hunt the man-eaters.

As he neared the front lines the troops became more numerous. There were motor trucks and ox teams and all the impedimenta of a small army and always there were wounded men walking or being carried toward the rear. He had crossed the railroad some distance back and judged that the wounded were being taken to it for transportation to a base hospital and possibly as far away as Tanga on the coast.

It was dusk when he reached a large camp hidden in the foothills of the Pare Mountains. As he was approaching from the rear he found it but lightly guarded and what sentinels there were, were not upon the alert, and so it was an easy thing for him to enter after darkness had fallen and prowl about listening at the backs of tents, searching for some clew to the slayer of his mate.

As he paused at the side of a tent before which sat a number of native soldiers he caught a few words spoken in native dialect that riveted his attention instantly: "The Waziri fought like devils; but we are greater fighters and we killed them all. When we were through the captain came and killed the woman. He stayed outside and yelled in a very loud voice until all the men were killed. Underlieutenant von Goss is braver—he came in and stood beside the door shouting at us, also in a very loud voice, and bade us nail one of the Waziri who was wounded to the wall, and then he laughed loudly because the man suffered. We all laughed. It was very funny."

Like a beast of prey, grim and terrible, Tarzan crouched in the shadows beside the tent. What thoughts passed through that savage mind? Who may say? No outward sign of passion was revealed by the expression of the handsome face; the cold, gray eyes denoted only intense watchfulness. Presently the soldier Tarzan had heard first rose and with a parting word turned away. He passed within ten feet of the ape-man and continued on toward the rear of the camp. Tarzan followed and in the shadows of a clump of bushes overtook his quarry. There was no sound as the man beast sprang upon the back of his prey and bore it to the ground for steel fingers closed simultaneously upon the soldier's throat, effectually stifling any outcry. By the neck Tarzan dragged his victim well into the concealment of the bushes.

"Make no sound," he cautioned in the man's own tribal dialect as he released his hold upon the other's throat.

The fellow gasped for breath, rolling frightened eyes upward to see what manner of creature it might be in whose power he was. In the darkness he saw only a naked brown body bending above him; but he still remembered the terrific strength of the mighty muscles that had closed upon his wind and dragged him into the bushes as though he had been but a little child. If any thought of resistance had crossed his mind he must have discarded it at once, as he made no move to escape.

"What is the name of the officer who killed the woman at the bungalow where you fought with the Waziri?" asked Tarzan.

"Hauptmann Schneider," replied the black when he could again command his voice.

"Where is he?" demanded the ape-man.

"He is here. It may be that he is at headquarters. Many of the officers go there in the evening to receive orders."

"Lead me there," commanded Tarzan, "and if I am discovered I will kill you immediately. Get up!"

The black rose and led the way by a roundabout route back through the camp. Several times they were forced to hide while soldiers passed; but at last they reached a great pile of baled hay from about the corner of which the black pointed out a two-story building in the distance.

"Headquarters," he said. "You can go no farther unseen. There are many soldiers about."

Tarzan realized that he could not proceed farther in company with the black. He turned and looked at the fellow for a moment as though pondering what disposition to make of him.

"You helped to crucify Wasimbu, the Waziri," he accused in a low yet none the less terrible tone.

The black trembled, his knees giving beneath him. "He ordered us to do it," he plead.

"Who ordered it done?" demanded Tarzan.

"Underlieutenant von Goss," replied the soldier. "He, too, is here."

"I shall find him," returned Tarzan, grimly. "You helped to crucify Wasimbu, the Waziri, and, while he suffered, you laughed."

The fellow reeled. It was as though in the accusation he read also his death sentence. With no other word Tarzan seized the man again by the neck. As before there was no outcry. The giant muscles tensed. The arms swung quickly upward and with them the body of the black soldier who had helped to crucify Wasimbu, the Waziri, described a circle in the air—once, twice, three times, and then it was flung aside and the ape-man turned in the direction of General Kraut's headquarters.

A single sentinel in the rear of the building barred the way. Tarzan crawled, belly to the ground, toward him, taking advantage of cover as only the jungle-bred beast of prey can do. When the sentinel's eyes were toward him, Tarzan hugged the ground, motionless as stone; when they were turned away, he moved swiftly forward. Presently he was within charging distance. He waited until the man had turned his back once more and then he rose and sped noiselessly down upon him. Again there was no sound as he carried the dead body with him toward the building.

The lower floor was lighted, the upper dark. Through the windows Tarzan saw a large front room and a smaller room in rear of it. In the former were many officers. Some moved about talking to one another, others sat at field tables writing. The windows were open and Tarzan could hear much of the conversation; but nothing that interested him. It was mostly about the German successes in Africa and conjectures as to when the German army in Europe would reach Paris. Some said the Kaiser was doubtlessly already there, and there was a great deal of damning Belgium.

In the smaller back room a large, red-faced man sat behind a table. Some other officers were also sitting a little in rear of him, while two stood at attention before the general, who was questioning them. As he talked, the general toyed with an oil lamp that stood upon the table before him. Presently there came a knock upon the door and an aide entered the room. He saluted and reported: "Fräulein Kircher has arrived, sir."

"Bid her enter," commanded the general, and then nodded to the two officers before him in sign of dismissal.

The Fräulein, entering, passed them at the door. The officers in the little room rose and saluted, the Fräulein acknowledging the courtesy with a bow and a slight smile. She was a very pretty girl. Even the rough, soiled riding habit and the caked dust upon her face could not conceal the fact, and she was young. She could not have been over nineteen.

She advanced to the table behind which the general stood and, taking a folded paper from an inside pocket of her coat, handed it to him.

"Be seated, Fräulein," he said, and another officer brought her a chair. No one spoke while the general read the contents of the paper.

Tarzan appraised the various people in the room. He wondered if one might not be Hauptmann Schneider, for two of them were captains. The girl he judged to be of the intelligence department—a spy. Her beauty held no appeal for him—without a glimmer of compunction he could have wrung that fair, young neck. She was German and that was enough; but he had other and more important work before him. He wanted Hauptmann Schneider.

Finally the general looked up from the paper.

"Good," he said to the girl, and then to one of his aides, "Send for Major Schneider."

Major Schneider! Tarzan felt the short hairs at the back of his neck rise. Already they had promoted the beast who had murdered his mate—doubtless they had promoted him for that very crime.

The aide left the room and the others fell into a general conversation from which it became apparent to Tarzan that the German East African forces greatly outnumbered the British and that the latter were suffering heavily. The ape-man stood so concealed in a clump of bushes that he could watch the interior of the room without being seen from within, while he was at the same time hidden from the view of anyone who might chance to pass along the post of the sentinel he had slain. Momentarily he was expecting a patrol or a relief to appear and discover that the sentinel was missing, when he knew an immediate and thorough search would be made.

Impatiently he awaited the coming of the man he sought and at last he was rewarded by the reappearance of the aide who had been dispatched to fetch him accompanied by an officer of medium size with fierce, upstanding mustaches. The newcomer strode to the table, halted and saluted, reporting. The general acknowledged the salute and turned toward the girl.

"Fräulein Kircher," he said, "allow me to present Major Schneider—"

Tarzan waited to hear no more. Placing a palm upon the sill of the window he vaulted into the room into the midst of an astounded company of the Kaiser's officers. With a stride he was at the table and with a sweep of his hand sent the lamp crashing into the fat belly of the general who, in his mad effort to escape cremation, fell over backward, chair and all, upon the floor. Two of the aides sprang for the ape-man who picked up the first and flung him in the face of the other. The girl had leaped from her chair and stood flattened against the wall. The other officers were calling aloud for the guard and for help. Tarzan's purpose centered upon but a single individual and him he never lost sight of. Freed from attack for an instant he seized Major Schneider, threw him over his shoulder and was out of the window so quickly that the astonished assemblage could scarce realize what had occurred.

A single glance showed him that the sentinel's post was still vacant and a moment later he and his burden were in the shadows of the hay dump. Major Schneider had made no outcry for the very excellent reason that his wind was shut off. Now Tarzan released his grasp enough to permit the man to breathe.

"If you make a sound you will be choked again," he said.

Cautiously and after infinite patience Tarzan passed the final outpost. Forcing his captive to walk before him he pushed on toward the west until, late into the night, he re-crossed the railway where he felt reasonably safe from discovery. The German had cursed and grumbled and threatened and asked questions; but his only reply was another prod from Tarzan's sharp war spear. The ape-man herded him along as he would have driven a hog with the difference that he would have had more respect and therefore more consideration for a hog.

Until now Tarzan had given little thought to the details of revenge. Now he pondered what form the punishment should take. Of only one thing was he certain—it must end in death. Like all brave men and courageous beasts Tarzan had little natural inclination to torture—none, in fact; but this case was unique in his experience. An inherent sense of justice called for an eye for an eye and his recent oath demanded even more. Yes, the creature must suffer even as he had caused Jane Clayton to suffer. Tarzan could not hope to make the man suffer as he had suffered, since physical pain may never approach the exquisiteness of mental torture.

All through the long night the ape-man goaded on the exhausted and now terrified Hun. The awful silence of his captor wrought upon the German's nerves. If he would only speak! Again and again Schneider tried to force or coax a word from him; but always the result was the same—continued silence and a vicious and painful prod from the spear point. Schneider was bleeding and sore. He was so exhausted that he staggered at every step, and often he fell only to be prodded to his feet again by that terrifying and remorseless spear.

It was not until morning that Tarzan reached a decision and it came to him then like an inspiration from above. A slow smile touched his lips and he immediately sought a place to lie up and rest—he wished his prisoner to be fit now for what lay in store for him. Ahead was a stream which Tarzan had crossed the day before. He knew the ford for a drinking place and a likely spot to make an easy kill. Cautioning the German to utter silence with a gesture the two approached the stream quietly. Down the game trail Tarzan saw some deer about to leave the water. He shoved Schneider into the brush at one side and, squatting next him, waited. The German watched the silent giant with puzzled, frightened eyes. In the new dawn he, for the first time, was able to obtain a good look at his captor, and, if he had been puzzled and frightened before, those sensations were nothing to what he experienced now.

Who and what could this almost naked, white savage be? He had heard him speak but once—when he had cautioned him to silence—and then in excellent German and the well-modulated tones of culture. He watched him now as the fascinated toad watches the snake that is about to devour it. He saw the graceful limbs and symmetrical body motionless as a marble statue as the creature crouched in the concealment of the leafy foliage. Not a muscle, not a nerve moved. He saw the deer coming slowly along the trail, down wind and unsuspecting. He saw a buck pass—an old buck—and then a young and plump one came opposite the giant in ambush, and Schneider's eyes went wide and a scream of terror almost broke from his lips as he saw the agile beast at his side spring straight for the throat of the young buck and heard from those human lips the hunting roar of a wild beast. Down went the buck and Tarzan and his captive had meat. The ape-man ate his raw, but he permitted the German to build a fire and cook his portion.

The two lay up until late in the afternoon and then took up the journey once again—a journey that was so frightful to Schneider because of his ignorance of its destination that he at times groveled at Tarzan's feet begging for an explanation and for mercy; but on and on in silence the ape-man went, prodding the failing Hun whenever the latter faltered.

It was noon of the third day before they reached their destination. After a steep climb and a short walk they halted at the edge of a precipitous cliff and Schneider looked down into a narrow gulch where a single tree grew beside a tiny rivulet and sparse grass broke from a rock-strewn soil. Tarzan motioned him over the edge; but the German drew back in terror. The Ape-man seized him and pushed him roughly toward the brink. "Descend," he said. It was the second time he had spoken in three days and perhaps his very silence, ominous in itself, had done more to arouse terror in the breast of the Boche than even the spear point, ever ready as it always was.

Schneider looked fearfully over the edge; but was about to essay the attempt when Tarzan halted him. "I am Lord Greystoke," he said. "It was my wife you murdered in the Waziri country. You will understand now why I came for you. Descend."

The German fell upon his knees. "I did not murder your wife," he cried. "Have mercy! I did not murder your wife. I do not know anything about—"

"Descend!" snapped Tarzan, raising the point of his spear. He knew that the man lied and was not surprised that he did. A man who would murder for no cause would lie for less. Schneider still hesitated and pled. The ape-man jabbed him with the spear and Schneider slid fearfully over the top and began the perilous descent. Tarzan accompanied and assisted him over the worst places until at last they were within a few feet of the bottom.

"Be quiet now," cautioned the ape-man. He pointed at the entrance to what appeared to be a cave at the far end of the gulch. "There is a hungry lion in there. If you can reach that tree before he discovers you, you will have several days longer in which to enjoy life and then—when you are too weak to cling longer to the branches of the tree Numa, the man-eater, will feed again for the last time." He pushed Schneider from his foothold to the ground below. "Now run," he said.

The German trembling in terror started for the tree. He had almost reached it when a horrid roar broke from the mouth of the cave and almost simultaneously a gaunt, hunger mad lion leaped into the daylight of the gulch. Schneider had but a few yards to cover; but the lion flew over the ground to circumvent him while Tarzan watched the race with a slight smile upon his lips.

Schneider won by a slender margin, and as Tarzan scaled the cliff to the summit, he heard behind him mingled with the roaring of the baffled cat, the gibbering of a human voice that was at the same time more bestial than the beast's.

Upon the brink of the cliff the ape-man turned and looked back into the gulch. High in the tree the German clung frantically to a branch across which his body lay. Beneath him was Numa—waiting.

The ape-man raised his face to Kudu, the sun, and from his mighty chest rose the savage victory cry of the bull ape.

CHAPTER III—IN THE GERMAN LINES

Tarzan was not yet fully revenged. There were many millions of Germans yet alive—enough to keep Tarzan pleasantly occupied the balance of his life, and yet not enough, should he kill them all, to recompense him for the great loss he had suffered—nor could the death of all those million Germans bring back his loved one.

While in the German camp in the Pare Mountains, which lie just east of the boundary line between German and British East Africa, Tarzan had overheard enough to suggest that the British were getting the worst of the fighting in Africa. At first he had given the matter but little thought, since, after the death of his wife, the one strong tie that had held him to civilization, he had renounced all mankind, considering himself no longer man, but ape.

After accounting for Schneider as satisfactorily as lay within his power he circled Kilimanjaro and hunted in the foothills to the north of that mightiest of mountains as he had discovered that in the neighborhood of the armies there was no hunting at all. Some pleasure he derived through conjuring mental pictures from time to time of the German he had left in the branches of the lone tree at the bottom of the high-walled gulch in which was penned the starving lion. He could imagine the man's mental anguish as he became weakened from hunger and maddened by thirst, knowing that sooner or later he must slip exhausted to the ground where waited the gaunt man-eater. Tarzan wondered if Schneider would have the courage to descend to the little rivulet for water should Numa leave the gulch and enter the cave, and then he pictured the mad race for the tree again when the lion charged out to seize his prey as he was certain to do, since the clumsy German could not descend to the rivulet without making at least some slight noise that would attract Numa's attention.

But even this pleasure palled, and more and more the ape-man found himself thinking of the English soldiers fighting against heavy odds and especially of the fact that it was Germans who were beating them. The thought made him lower his head and growl and it worried him not a little—a bit, perhaps, because he was finding it difficult to forget that he was an Englishman when he wanted only to be an ape. And at last the time came when he could not longer endure the thought of Germans killing Englishmen while he hunted in safety a bare march away.

His decision made, he set out in the direction of the German camp, no well-defined plan formulated; but with the general idea that once near the field of operations he might find an opportunity to harass the German command as he so well knew how to do. His way took him along the gorge close to the gulch in which he had left Schneider, and, yielding to a natural curiosity, he scaled the cliffs and made his way to the edge of the gulch. The tree was empty, nor was there sign of Numa, the lion. Picking up a rock he hurled it into the gulch, where it rolled to the very entrance to the cave. Instantly the lion appeared in the aperture; but such a different-looking lion from the great sleek brute that Tarzan had trapped there two weeks before. Now he was gaunt and emaciated, and when he walked he staggered.

"Where is the German?" shouted Tarzan. "Was he good eating, or only a bag of bones when he slipped and fell from the tree?"

Numa growled. "You look hungry, Numa," continued the ape-man. "You must have been very hungry to eat all the grass from your lair and even the bark from the tree as far up as you can reach. Would you like another German?" and smiling he turned away.

A few minutes later he came suddenly upon Bara, the deer, asleep beneath a tree, and as Tarzan was hungry he made a quick kill, and squatting beside his prey proceeded to eat his fill. As he was gnawing the last morsel from a bone his quick ears caught the padding of stealthy feet behind him, and turning he confronted Dango, the hyena, sneaking upon him. With a growl the ape-man picked up a fallen branch and hurled it at the skulking brute. "Go away, eater of carrion!" he cried; but Dango was hungry and being large and powerful he only snarled and circled slowly about as though watching for an opportunity to charge. Tarzan of the Apes knew Dango even better than Dango knew himself. He knew that the brute, made savage by hunger, was mustering its courage for an attack, that it was probably accustomed to man and therefore more or less fearless of him and so he un-slung his heavy spear and laid it ready at his side while he continued his meal, all the time keeping a watchful eye upon the hyena.

He felt no fear, for long familiarity with the dangers of his wild world had so accustomed him to them that he took whatever came as a part of each day's existence as you accept the homely though no less real dangers of the farm, the range, or the crowded metropolis. Being jungle bred he was ready to protect his kill from all comers within ordinary limitations of caution. Under favorable conditions Tarzan would face even Numa himself and, if forced to seek safety by flight, he could do so without any feeling of shame. There was no braver creature roamed those savage wilds and at the same time there was none more wise—the two factors that had permitted him to survive.

Dango might have charged sooner but for the savage growls of the ape-man—growls which, coming from human lips, raised a question and a fear in the hyena's heart. He had attacked women and children in the native fields and he had frightened their men about their fires at night; but he never had seen a man-thing who made this sound that reminded him more of Numa angry than of a man afraid.

When Tarzan had completed his repast he was about to rise and hurl a clean-picked bone at the beast before he went his way, leaving the remains of his kill to Dango; but a sudden thought stayed him and instead he picked up the carcass of the deer, threw it over his shoulder, and set off in the direction of the gulch. For a few yards Dango followed, growling, and then realizing that he was being robbed of even a taste of the luscious flesh he cast discretion to the winds and charged. Instantly, as though Nature had given him eyes in the back of his head, Tarzan sensed the impending danger and, dropping Bara to the ground, turned with raised spear. Far back went the brown, right hand and then forward, lightning-like, backed by the power of giant muscles and the weight of his brawn and bone. The spear, released at the right instant, drove straight for Dango, caught him in the neck where it joined the shoulders and passed through the body.

When he had withdrawn the shaft from the hyena Tarzan shouldered both carcasses and continued on toward the gulch. Below lay Numa beneath the shade of the lone tree and at the ape-man's call he staggered slowly to his feet, yet weak as he was, he still growled savagely, even essaying a roar at the sight of his enemy. Tarzan let the two bodies slide over the rim of the cliff. "Eat, Numa!" he cried. "It may be that I shall need you again." He saw the lion, quickened to new life at the sight of food, spring upon the body of the deer and then he left him rending and tearing the flesh as he bolted great pieces into his empty maw.

The following day Tarzan came within sight of the German lines. From a wooded spur of the hills he looked down upon the enemy's left flank and beyond to the British lines. His position gave him a bird's-eye view of the field of battle, and his keen eyesight picked out many details that would not have been apparent to a man whose every sense was not trained to the highest point of perfection as were the ape-man's. He noted machine-gun emplacements cunningly hidden from the view of the British and listening posts placed well out in No Man's Land.

As his interested gaze moved hither and thither from one point of interest to another he heard from a point upon the hillside below him, above the roar of cannon and the crack of rifle fire, a single rifle spit. Immediately his attention was centered upon the spot where he knew a sniper must be hid. Patiently he awaited the next shot that would tell him more surely the exact location of the rifleman, and when it came he moved down the steep hillside with the stealth and quietness of a panther. Apparently he took no cognizance of where he stepped, yet never a loose stone was disturbed nor a twig broken—it was as though his feet saw.

Presently, as he passed through a clump of bushes, he came to the edge of a low cliff and saw upon a ledge some fifteen feet below him a German soldier prone behind an embankment of loose rock and leafy boughs that hid him from the view of the British lines. The man must have been an excellent shot, for he was well back of the German lines, firing over the heads of his fellows. His high-powered rifle was equipped with telescope sights and he also carried binoculars which he was in the act of using as Tarzan discovered him, either to note the effect of his last shot or to discover a new target. Tarzan let his eye move quickly toward that part of the British line the German seemed to be scanning, his keen sight revealing many excellent targets for a rifle placed so high above the trenches.

The Hun, evidently satisfied with his observations, laid aside his binoculars and again took up his rifle, placed its butt in the hollow of his shoulder and took careful aim. At the same instant a brown body sprang outward from the cliff above him. There was no sound and it is doubtful that the German ever knew what manner of creature it was that alighted heavily upon his back, for at the instant of impact the sinewy fingers of the ape-man circled the hairy throat of the Boche. There was a moment of futile struggling followed by the sudden realization of dissolution—the sniper was dead.

Lying behind the rampart of rocks and boughs, Tarzan looked down upon the scene below. Near at hand were the trenches of the Germans. He could see officers and men moving about in them and almost in front of him a well-hidden machine gun was traversing No Man's Land in an oblique direction, striking the British at such an angle as to make it difficult for them to locate it.

Tarzan watched, toying idly with the rifle of the dead German. Presently he fell to examining the mechanism of the piece. He glanced again toward the German trenches and changed the adjustment of the sights, then he placed the rifle to his shoulder and took aim. Tarzan was an excellent shot. With his civilized friends he had hunted big game with the weapons of civilization and though he never had killed except for food or in self-defense he had amused himself firing at inanimate targets thrown into the air and had perfected himself in the use of firearms without realizing that he had done so. Now indeed would he hunt big game. A slow smile touched his lips as his finger closed gradually upon the trigger. The rifle spoke and a German machine gunner collapsed behind his weapon. In three minutes Tarzan picked off the crew of that gun. Then he spotted a German officer emerging from a dugout and the three men in the bay with him. Tarzan was careful to leave no one in the immediate vicinity to question how Germans could be shot in German trenches when they were entirely concealed from enemy view.

Again adjusting his sights he took a long-range shot at a distant machine-gun crew to his right. With calm deliberation he wiped them out to a man. Two guns were silenced. He saw men running through the trenches and he picked off several of them. By this time the Germans were aware that something was amiss—that an uncanny sniper had discovered a point of vantage from which this sector of the trenches was plainly visible to him. At first they sought to discover his location in No Man's Land; but when an officer looking over the parapet through a periscope was struck full in the back of the head with a rifle bullet which passed through his skull and fell to the bottom of the trench they realized that it was beyond the parados rather than the parapet that they should search.

One of the soldiers picked up the bullet that had killed his officer, and then it was that real excitement prevailed in that particular bay, for the bullet was obviously of German make. Hugging the parados, messengers carried the word in both directions and presently periscopes were leveled above the parados and keen eyes were searching out the traitor. It did not take them long to locate the position of the hidden sniper and then Tarzan saw a machine gun being trained upon him. Before it had gotten into action its crew lay dead about it; but there were other men to take their places, reluctantly perhaps; but driven on by their officers they were forced to it and at the same time two other machine guns were swung around toward the ape-man and put into operation.

Realizing that the game was about up Tarzan with a farewell shot laid aside the rifle and melted into the hills behind him. For many minutes he could hear the sputter of machinegun fire concentrated upon the spot he had just quit and smiled as he contemplated the waste of German ammunition.

"They have paid heavily for Wasimbu, the Waziri, whom they crucified, and for his slain fellows," he mused; "but for Jane they can never pay—no, not if I killed them all."

After dark that night he circled the flanks of both armies and passed through the British out-guards and into the British lines. No man saw him come. No man knew that he was there.

Headquarters of the Second Rhodesians occupied a sheltered position far enough back of the lines to be comparatively safe from enemy observation. Even lights were permitted, and Colonel Capell sat before a field table, on which was spread a military map, talking with several of his officers. A large tree spread above them, a lantern sputtered dimly upon the table, while a small fire burned upon the ground close at hand. The enemy had no planes and no other observers could have seen the lights from the German lines.

The officers were discussing the advantage in numbers possessed by the enemy and the inability of the British to more than hold their present position. They could not advance. Already they had sustained severe losses in every attack and had always been driven back by overwhelming numbers. There were hidden machine guns, too, that bothered the colonel considerably. It was evidenced by the fact that he often reverted to them during the conversation.

"Something silenced them for a while this afternoon," said one of the younger officers. "I was observing at the time and I couldn't make out what the fuss was about; but they seemed to be having a devil of a time in a section of trench on their left. At one time I could have sworn they were attacked in the rear—I reported it to you at the time, sir, you'll recall—for the blighters were pepperin' away at the side of that bluff behind them. I could see the dirt fly. I don't know what it could have been."

There was a slight rustling among the branches of the tree above them and simultaneously a lithe, brown body dropped in their midst. Hands moved quickly to the butts of pistols; but otherwise there was no movement among the officers. First they looked wonderingly at the almost naked white man standing there with the firelight playing upon rounded muscles, took in the primitive attire and the equally primitive armament and then all eyes turned toward the colonel.

"Who the devil are you, sir?" snapped that officer.

"Tarzan of the Apes," replied the newcomer.

"Oh, Greystoke!" cried a major, and stepped forward with outstretched hand.

"Preswick," acknowledged Tarzan as he took the proffered hand.

"I didn't recognize you at first," apologized the major. "The last time I saw you you were in London in evening dress. Quite a difference—'pon my word, man, you'll have to admit it."

Tarzan smiled and turned toward the colonel. "I overheard your conversation," he said. "I have just come from behind the German lines. Possibly I can help you."

The colonel looked questioningly toward Major Preswick who quickly rose to the occasion and presented the ape-man to his commanding officer and fellows. Briefly Tarzan told them what it was that brought him out alone in pursuit of the Germans.

"And now you have come to join us?" asked the colonel.

Tarzan shook his head. "Not regularly," he replied. "I must fight in my own way; but I can help you. Whenever I wish I can enter the German lines."

Capell smiled and shook his head. "It's not so easy as you think," he said; "I've lost two good officers in the last week trying it—and they were experienced men; none better in the Intelligence Department."

"Is it more difficult than entering the British lines?" asked Tarzan.

The colonel was about to reply when a new thought appeared to occur to him and he looked quizzically at the ape-man. "Who brought you here?" he asked. "Who passed you through our out-guards?"

"I have just come through the German lines and yours and passed through your camp," he replied. "Send word to ascertain if anyone saw me."

"But who accompanied you?" insisted Capell.

"I came alone," replied Tarzan and then, drawing himself to his full height, "You men of civilization, when you come into the jungle, are as dead among the quick. Manu, the monkey, is a sage by comparison. I marvel that you exist at all—only your numbers, your weapons, and your power of reasoning save you. Had I a few hundred great apes with your reasoning power I could drive the Germans into the ocean as quickly as the remnant of them could reach the coast. Fortunate it is for you that the dumb brutes cannot combine. Could they, Africa would remain forever free of men. But come, can I help you? Would you like to know where several machinegun emplacements are hidden?"

The colonel assured him that they would, and a moment later Tarzan had traced upon the map the location of three that had been bothering the English. "There is a weak spot here," he said, placing a finger upon the map. "It is held by blacks; but the machine guns out in front are manned by whites. If—wait! I have a plan. You can fill that trench with your own men and enfilade the trenches to its right with their own machine guns."

Colonel Capell smiled and shook his head. "It sounds very easy," he said.

"It *is* easy—for me," replied the ape-man. "I can empty that section of trench without a shot. I was raised in the jungle—I know the jungle folk—the Gomangani as well as the others. Look for me again on the second night," and he turned to leave.

"Wait," said the colonel. "I will send an officer to pass you through the lines."

Tarzan smiled and moved away. As he was leaving the little group about headquarters he passed a small figure wrapped in an officer's heavy overcoat. The collar was turned up and the visor of the military cap pulled well down over the eyes; but, as the ape-man passed, the light from the fire illuminated the features of the newcomer for an instant, revealing to Tarzan a vaguely familiar face. Some officer he had known in London, doubtless, he surmised, and went his way through the British camp and the British lines all unknown to the watchful sentinels of the out-guard.

Nearly all night he moved across Kilimanjaro's foothills, tracking by instinct an unknown way, for he guessed that what he sought would be found on some wooded slope higher up than he had come upon his other recent journeys in this, to him, little known country. Three hours before dawn his keen nostrils apprised him that somewhere in the vicinity he would find what he wanted, and so he climbed into a tall tree and settled himself for a few hours' sleep.

CHAPTER IV—WHEN THE LION FED

Kudu, the sun, was well up in the heavens when Tarzan awoke. The ape-man stretched his giant limbs, ran his fingers through his thick hair, and swung lightly down to earth. Immediately he took up the trail he had come in search of, following it by scent down into a deep ravine. Cautiously he went now, for his nose told him that the quarry was close at hand, and presently from an overhanging bough he looked down upon Horta, the boar, and many of his kinsmen. Unslinging his bow and selecting an arrow, Tarzan fitted the shaft and, drawing it far back, took careful aim at the largest of the great pigs. In the ape-man's teeth were other arrows, and no sooner had the first one sped, than he had fitted and shot another bolt. Instantly the pigs were in turmoil, not knowing from whence the danger threatened. They stood stupidly at first and then commenced milling around until six of their number lay dead or dying about them; then with a chorus of grunts and squeals they started off at a wild run, disappearing quickly in the dense underbrush.

Tarzan then descended from the tree, dispatched those that were not already dead and proceeded to skin the carcasses. As he worked, rapidly and with great skill, he neither hummed nor whistled as does the average man of civilization. It was in numerous little ways such as these that he differed from other men, due, probably, to his early jungle training. The beasts of the jungle that he had been reared among were playful to maturity but seldom thereafter. His fellow-apes, especially the bulls, became fierce and surly as they grew older. Life was a serious matter during lean seasons—one had to fight to secure one's share of food then, and the habit once formed became lifelong. Hunting for food was the life labor of the jungle bred, and a life labor is a thing not to be approached with levity nor prosecuted lightly. So all work found Tarzan serious, though he still retained what the other beasts lost as they grew older—a sense of humor, which he gave play to when the mood suited him. It was a grim humor and sometimes ghastly; but it satisfied Tarzan.

Then, too, were one to sing and whistle while working on the ground, concentration would be impossible. Tarzan possessed the ability to concentrate each of his five senses upon its particular business. Now he worked at skinning the six pigs and his eyes and his fingers worked as though there was naught else in all the world than these six carcasses; but his ears and his nose were as busily engaged elsewhere—the former ranging the forest all about and the latter assaying each passing zephyr. It was his nose that first discovered the approach of Sabor, the lioness, when the wind shifted for a moment.

As clearly as though he had seen her with his eyes, Tarzan knew that the lioness had caught the scent of the freshly killed pigs and immediately had moved down wind in their direction. He knew from the strength of the scent spoor and the rate of the wind about how far away she was and that she was approaching from behind him. He was finishing the last pig and he did not hurry. The five pelts lay close at hand—he had been careful to keep them thus together and near him— an ample tree waved its low branches above him.

He did not even turn his head for he knew she was not yet in sight; but he bent his ears just a bit more sharply for the first sound of her nearer approach. When the final skin had been removed he rose. Now he heard Sabor in the bushes to his rear, but not yet too close. Leisurely he gathered up the six pelts and one of the carcasses, and as the lioness appeared between the boles of two trees he swung upward into the branches above him. Here he hung the hides over a limb, seated himself comfortably upon another with his back against the bole of the tree, cut a hind quarter from the carcass he had carried with him and proceeded to satisfy his hunger. Sabor slunk, growling, from the brush, cast a wary eye upward toward the ape-man and then fell upon the nearest carcass.

Tarzan looked down upon her and grinned, recalling an argument he had once had with a famous big-game hunter who had declared that the king of beasts ate only what he himself had killed. Tarzan knew better for he had seen Numa and Sabor stoop even to carrion.

Having filled his belly, the ape-man fell to work upon the hides—all large and strong. First he cut strips from them about half an inch wide. When he had sufficient number of these strips he sewed two of the hides together, afterwards piercing holes every three or four inches around the edges. Running another strip through these holes gave him a large bag with a drawstring. In similar fashion he produced four other like bags, but smaller, from the four remaining hides and had several strips left over.

All this done he threw a large, juicy fruit at Sabor, cached the remainder of the pig in a crotch of the tree and swung off toward the southwest through the middle terraces of the forest, carrying his five bags with him. Straight he went to the rim of the gulch where he had imprisoned Numa, the lion. Very stealthily he approached the edge and peered over. Numa was not in sight. Tarzan sniffed and listened. He could hear nothing, yet he knew that Numa must be within the cave. He hoped that he slept—much depended upon Numa not discovering him.

Cautiously he lowered himself over the edge of the cliff, and with utter noiselessness commenced the descent toward the bottom of the gulch. He stopped often and turned his keen eyes and ears in the direction of the cave's mouth at the far end of the gulch, some hundred feet away. As he neared the foot of the cliff his danger increased greatly. If he could reach the bottom and cover half the distance to the tree that stood in the center of the gulch he would feel comparatively safe for then, even if Numa appeared, he felt that he could beat him either to the cliff or to the tree, but to scale the first thirty feet of the cliff rapidly enough to elude the leaping beast would require a running start of at least twenty feet as there were no very good hand- or footholds close to the bottom—he had had to run up the first twenty feet like a squirrel running up a tree that other time he had beaten an infuriated Numa to it. He had no desire to attempt it again unless the conditions were equally favorable at least, for he had escaped Numa's raking talons by only a matter of inches on the former occasion.

At last he stood upon the floor of the gulch. Silent as a disembodied spirit he advanced toward the tree. He was half way there and no sign of Numa. He reached the scarred bole from which the famished lion had devoured the bark and even torn pieces of the wood itself and yet Numa had not appeared. As he drew himself up to the lower branches he commenced to wonder if Numa were in the cave after all. Could it be possible that he had forced the barrier of rocks with which Tarzan had plugged the other end of the passage where it opened into the outer world of freedom? Or was Numa dead? The ape-man doubted the verity of the latter suggestion as he had fed the lion the entire carcasses of a deer and a hyena only a few days since—he could not have starved in so short a time, while the little rivulet running across the gulch furnished him with water a-plenty.

Tarzan started to descend and investigate the cavern when it occurred to him that it would save effort were he to lure Numa out instead. Acting upon the thought he uttered a low growl. Immediately he was rewarded by the sound of a movement within the cave and an instant later a wild-eyed, haggard lion rushed forth ready to face the devil himself were he edible. When Numa saw Tarzan, fat and sleek, perched in the tree he became suddenly the embodiment of frightful rage. His eyes and his nose told him that this was the creature responsible for his predicament and also that this creature was good to eat. Frantically the lion sought to scramble up the bole of the tree. Twice he leaped high enough to catch the lowest branches with his paws, but both times he fell backward to the earth. Each time he became more furious. His growls and roars were incessant and horrible and all the time Tarzan sat grinning down upon him, taunting him in jungle billingsgate for his inability to reach him and mentally exulting that always Numa was wasting his already waning strength.

Finally the ape-man rose and un-slung his rope. He arranged the coils carefully in his left hand and the noose in his right, and then he took a position with each foot on one of two branches that lay in about the same horizontal plane and with his back pressed firmly against the stem of the tree. There he stood hurling insults at Numa until the beast was again goaded into leaping upward at him, and as Numa rose the noose dropped quickly over his head and about his neck. A quick movement of Tarzan's rope hand tightened the coil and when Numa slipped backward to the ground only his hind feet touched, for the ape-man held him swinging by the neck.

Moving slowly outward upon the two branches Tarzan swung Numa out so that he could not reach the bole of the tree with his raking talons, then he made the rope fast after drawing the lion clear of the ground, dropped his five pigskin sacks to earth and leaped down himself. Numa was striking frantically at the grass rope with his fore claws. At any moment he might sever it and Tarzan must, therefore, work rapidly.

First he drew the larger bag over Numa's head and secured it about his neck with the draw string, then he managed, after considerable effort, during which he barely escaped being torn to ribbons by the mighty talons, to hog-tie Numa—drawing his four legs together and securing them in that position with the strips trimmed from the pigskins.

By this time the lion's efforts had almost ceased—it was evident that he was being rapidly strangled and as that did not at all suit the purpose of the Tarmangani the latter swung again into the tree, unfastened the rope from above and lowered the lion to the ground where he immediately followed it and loosed the noose about Numa's neck. Then he drew his hunting knife and cut two round holes in the front of the head bag opposite the lion's eyes for the double purpose of permitting him to see and giving him sufficient air to breathe.

This done Tarzan busied himself fitting the other bags, one over each of Numa's formidably armed paws. Those on the hind feet he secured not only by tightening the draw strings but also rigged garters that fastened tightly around the legs above the hocks. He secured the front-feet bags in place similarly above the great knees. Now, indeed, was Numa, the lion, reduced to the harmlessness of Bara, the deer.

By now Numa was showing signs of returning life. He gasped for breath and struggled; but the strips of pigskin that held his four legs together were numerous and tough. Tarzan watched and was sure that they would hold, yet Numa is mightily muscled and there was the chance, always, that he might struggle free of his bonds after which all would depend upon the efficacy of Tarzan's bags and draw strings.

After Numa had again breathed normally and was able to roar out his protests and his rage, his struggles increased to Titanic proportions for a short time; but as a lion's powers of endurance are in no way proportionate to his size and strength he soon tired and lay quietly. Amid renewed growling and another futile attempt to free himself, Numa was finally forced to submit to the further indignity of having a rope secured about his neck; but this time it was no noose that might tighten and strangle him; but a bowline knot, which does not tighten or slip under strain.

The other end of the rope Tarzan fastened to the stem of the tree, then he quickly cut the bonds securing Numa's legs and leaped aside as the beast sprang to his feet. For a moment the lion stood with legs far outspread, then he raised first one paw and then another, shaking them energetically in an effort to dislodge the strange footgear that Tarzan had fastened upon them. Finally he began to paw at the bag upon his head. The ape-man, standing with ready spear, watched Numa's efforts intently. Would the bags hold? He sincerely hoped so. Or would all his labor prove fruitless?

As the clinging things upon his feet and face resisted his every effort to dislodge them, Numa became frantic. He rolled upon the ground, fighting, biting, scratching, and roaring; he leaped to his feet and sprang into the air; he charged Tarzan, only to be brought to a sudden stop as the rope securing him to the tree tautened. Then Tarzan stepped in and rapped him smartly on the head with the shaft of his spear. Numa reared upon his hind feet and struck at the ape-man and in return received a cuff on one ear that sent him reeling sideways. When he returned to the attack he was again sent sprawling. After the fourth effort it appeared to dawn upon the king of beasts that he had met his master, his head and tail dropped and when Tarzan advanced upon him he backed away, though still growling.

Leaving Numa tied to the tree Tarzan entered the tunnel and removed the barricade from the opposite end, after which he returned to the gulch and strode straight for the tree. Numa lay in his path and as Tarzan approached growled menacingly. The ape-man cuffed him aside and unfastened the rope from the tree. Then ensued a half-hour of stubbornly fought battle while Tarzan endeavored to drive Numa through the tunnel ahead of him and Numa persistently refused to be driven. At last, however, by dint of the unrestricted use of his spear point, the ape-man succeeded in forcing the lion to move ahead of him and eventually guided him into the passageway. Once inside, the problem became simpler since Tarzan followed closely in the rear with his sharp spear point, an unremitting incentive to forward movement on the part of the lion. If Numa hesitated he was prodded. If he backed up the result was extremely painful and so, being a wise lion who was learning rapidly, he decided to keep on going and at the end of the tunnel, emerging into the outer world, he sensed freedom, raised his head and tail and started off at a run.

Tarzan, still on his hands and knees just inside the entrance, was taken unaware with the result that he was sprawled forward upon his face and dragged a hundred yards across the rocky ground before Numa was brought to a stand. It was a scratched and angry Tarzan who scrambled to his feet. At first he was tempted to chastise Numa; but, as the ape-man seldom permitted his temper to guide him in any direction not countenanced by reason, he quickly abandoned the idea.

Having taught Numa the rudiments of being driven, he now urged him forward and there commenced as strange a journey as the unrecorded history of the jungle contains. The balance of that day was eventful both for Tarzan and for Numa. From open rebellion at first the lion passed through stages of stubborn resistance and grudging obedience to final surrender. He was a very tired, hungry, and thirsty lion when night overtook them; but there was to be no food for him that day or the next—Tarzan did not dare risk removing the head bag, though he did cut another hole which permitted Numa to quench his thirst shortly after dark. Then he tied him to a tree, sought food for himself, and stretched out among the branches above his captive for a few hours' sleep.

Early the following morning they resumed their journey, winding over the low foothills south of Kilimanjaro, toward the east. The beasts of the jungle who saw them took one look and fled. The scent spoor of Numa, alone, might have been enough to have provoked flight in many of the lesser animals, but the sight of this strange apparition that smelled like a lion, but looked like nothing they ever had seen before, being led through the jungles by a giant Tarmangani was too much for even the more formidable denizens of the wild.

Sabor, the lioness, recognizing from a distance the scent of her lord and master intermingled with that of a Tarmangani and the hide of Horta, the boar, trotted through the aisles of the forest to investigate. Tarzan and Numa heard her coming, for she voiced a plaintive and questioning whine as the baffling mixture of odors aroused her curiosity and her fears, for lions, however terrible they may appear, are often timid animals and Sabor, being of the gentler sex, was, naturally, habitually inquisitive as well.

Tarzan un-slung his spear for he knew that he might now easily have to fight to retain his prize. Numa halted and turned his outraged head in the direction of the coming she. He voiced a throaty growl that was almost a purr. Tarzan was upon the point of prodding him on again when

Sabor broke into view, and behind her the ape-man saw that which gave him instant pause—four full-grown lions trailing the lioness.

To have goaded Numa then into active resistance might have brought the whole herd down upon him and so Tarzan waited to learn first what their attitude would be. He had no idea of relinquishing his lion without a battle; but knowing lions as he did, he knew that there was no assurance as to just what the newcomers would do.

The lioness was young and sleek, and the four males were in their prime—as handsome lions as he ever had seen. Three of the males were scantily maned but one, the foremost, carried a splendid, black mane that rippled in the breeze as he trotted majestically forward. The lioness halted a hundred feet from Tarzan, while the lions came on past her and stopped a few feet nearer. Their ears were upstanding and their eyes filled with curiosity. Tarzan could not even guess what they might do. The lion at his side faced them fully, standing silent now and watchful.

Suddenly the lioness gave vent to another little whine, at which Tarzan's lion voiced a terrific roar and leaped forward straight toward the beast of the black mane. The sight of this awesome creature with the strange face was too much for the lion toward which he leaped, dragging Tarzan after him, and with a growl the lion turned and fled, followed by his companions and the she.

Numa attempted to follow them; Tarzan held him in leash and when he turned upon him in rage, beat him unmercifully across the head with his spear. Shaking his head and growling, the lion at last moved off again in the direction they had been traveling; but it was an hour before he ceased to sulk. He was very hungry—half famished in fact—and consequently of an ugly temper, yet so thoroughly subdued by Tarzan's heroic methods of lion taming that he was presently pacing along at the ape-man's side like some huge St. Bernard.

It was dark when the two approached the British right, after a slight delay farther back because of a German patrol it had been necessary to elude. A short distance from the British line of out-guard sentinels Tarzan tied Numa to a tree and continued on alone. He evaded a sentinel, passed the out-guard and support, and by devious ways came again to Colonel Capell's headquarters, where he appeared before the officers gathered there as a disembodied spirit materializing out of thin air.

When they saw who it was that came thus unannounced they smiled and the colonel scratched his head in perplexity.

"Someone should be shot for this," he said. "I might just as well not establish an out-post if a man can filter through whenever he pleases."

Tarzan smiled. "Do not blame them," he said, "for I am not a man. I am Tarmangani. Any Mangani who wished to, could enter your camp almost at will; but if you have them for sentinels no one could enter without their knowledge."

"What are the Mangani?" asked the colonel. "Perhaps we might enlist a bunch of the beggars."

Tarzan shook his head. "They are the great apes," he explained; "my people; but you could not use them. They cannot concentrate long enough upon a single idea. If I told them of this they would be much interested for a short time—I might even hold the interest of a few long enough to get them here and explain their duties to them; but soon they would lose interest and when you needed them most they might be off in the forest searching for beetles instead of watching their posts. They have the minds of little children—that is why they remain what they are."

"You call them Mangani and yourself Tarmangani—what is the difference?" asked Major Preswick.

"Tar means white," replied Tarzan, "and Mangani, great ape. My name—the name they gave me in the tribe of Kerchak—means White-skin. When I was a little balu my skin, I presume, looked very white indeed against the beautiful, black coat of Kala, my foster mother and so they called me Tarzan, the Tarmangani. They call you, too, Tarmangani," he concluded, smiling.

Capell smiled. "It is no reproach, Greystoke," he said; "and, by Jove, it would be a mark of distinction if a fellow could act the part. And now how about your plan? Do you still think you can empty the trench opposite our sector?"

"Is it still held by Gomangani?" asked Tarzan.

"What are Gomangani?" inquired the colonel. "It is still held by native troops, if that is what you mean."

"Yes," replied the ape-man, "the Gomangani are the great black apes—the Negroes."

"What do you intend doing and what do you want us to do?" asked Capell.

Tarzan approached the table and placed a finger on the map. "Here is a listening post," he said; "they have a machine gun in it. A tunnel connects it with this trench at this point." His finger moved from place to place on the map as he talked. "Give me a bomb and when you hear it burst in this listening post let your men start across No Man's Land slowly. Presently they will hear a commotion in the enemy trench; but they need not hurry, and, whatever they do, have them come quietly. You might also warn them that I may be in the trench and that I do not care to be shot or bayoneted."

"And that is all?" queried Capell, after directing an officer to give Tarzan a hand grenade; "you will empty the trench alone?"

"Not exactly alone," replied Tarzan with a grim smile; "but I shall empty it, and, by the way, your men may come in through the tunnel from the listening post if you prefer. In about half an hour, Colonel," and he turned and left them.

As he passed through the camp there flashed suddenly upon the screen of recollection, conjured there by some reminder of his previous visit to headquarters, doubtless, the image of the officer he had passed as he quit the colonel that other time and simultaneously recognition of the face that had been revealed by the light from the fire. He shook his head dubiously. No, it could not be and yet the features of the young officer were identical with those of Fräulein Kircher, the German spy he had seen at German headquarters the night he took Major Schneider from under the nose of the Hun general and his staff.

Beyond the last line of sentinels Tarzan moved quickly in the direction of Numa, the lion. The beast was lying down as Tarzan approached, but he rose as the ape-man reached his side. A low whine escaped his muzzled lips. Tarzan smiled for he recognized in the new note almost a supplication—it was more like the whine of a hungry dog begging for food than the voice of the proud king of beasts.

"Soon you will kill—and feed," he murmured in the vernacular of the great apes.

He unfastened the rope from about the tree and, with Numa close at his side, slunk into No Man's Land. There was little rifle fire and only an occasional shell vouched for the presence of artillery behind the opposing lines. As the shells from both sides were falling well back of the trenches, they constituted no menace to Tarzan; but the noise of them and that of the rifle fire had a marked effect upon Numa who crouched, trembling, close to the Tarmangani as though seeking protection.

Cautiously the two beasts moved forward toward the listening post of the Germans. In one hand Tarzan carried the bomb the English had given him, in the other was the coiled rope attached to the lion. At last Tarzan could see the position a few yards ahead. His keen eyes picked out the head and shoulders of the sentinel on watch. The ape-man grasped the bomb firmly in his right hand. He measured the distance with his eye and gathered his feet beneath him, then in a single motion he rose and threw the missile, immediately flattening himself prone upon the ground.

Five seconds later there was a terrific explosion in the center of the listening post. Numa gave a nervous start and attempted to break away; but Tarzan held him and, leaping to his feet, ran forward, dragging Numa after him. At the edge of the post he saw below him but slight evidence that the position had been occupied at all, for only a few shreds of torn flesh remained. About the only thing that had not been demolished was a machine gun which had been protected by sand bags.

There was not an instant to lose. Already a relief might be crawling through the communication tunnel, for it must have been evident to the sentinels in the Hun trenches that the listening post had been demolished. Numa hesitated to follow Tarzan into the excavation; but the ape-man, who was in no mood to temporize, jerked him roughly to the bottom. Before them lay the mouth of the tunnel that led back from No Man's Land to the German trenches. Tarzan pushed Numa forward until his head was almost in the aperture, then as though it were an afterthought, he turned quickly and, taking the machine gun from the parapet, placed it in the bottom of the hole close at hand, after which he turned again to Numa, and with his knife quickly cut the garters that held the bags upon his front paws. Before the lion could know that a part of his formidable armament was again released for action, Tarzan had cut the rope from his neck and the head bag from his face, and grabbing the lion from the rear had thrust him partially into the mouth of the tunnel.

Then Numa balked, only to feel the sharp prick of Tarzan's knife point in his hind quarters. Goading him on the ape-man finally succeeded in getting the lion sufficiently far into the tunnel so that there was no chance of his escaping other than by going forward or deliberately backing into the sharp blade at his rear. Then Tarzan cut the bags from the great hind feet, placed his shoulder and his knife point against Numa's seat, dug his toes into the loose earth that had been broken up by the explosion of the bomb, and shoved.

Inch by inch at first Numa advanced. He was growling now and presently he commenced to roar. Suddenly he leaped forward and Tarzan knew that he had caught the scent of meat ahead. Dragging the machine gun beside him the ape-man followed quickly after the lion whose roars he could plainly hear ahead mingled with the unmistakable screams of frightened men. Once again a grim smile touched the lips of this man-beast.

"They murdered my Waziri," he muttered; "they crucified Wasimbu, son of Muviro."

When Tarzan reached the trench and emerged into it there was no one in sight in that particular bay, nor in the next, nor the next as he hurried forward in the direction of the German center; but in the fourth bay he saw a dozen men jammed in the angle of the traverse at the end while leaping upon them and rending with talons and fangs was Numa, a terrific incarnation of ferocity and ravenous hunger.

Whatever held the men at last gave way as they fought madly with one another in their efforts to escape this dread creature that from their infancy had filled them with terror, and again they were retreating. Some clambered over the parados and some even over the parapet preferring the dangers of No Man's Land to this other soul-searing menace.

As the British advanced slowly toward the German trenches, they first met terrified blacks who ran into their arms only too willing to surrender. That pandemonium had broken loose in the Hun trench was apparent to the Rhodesians not only from the appearance of the deserters, but from the sounds of screaming, cursing men which came clearly to their ears; but there was one that baffled them for it resembled nothing more closely than the infuriated growling of an angry lion.

And when at last they reached the trench, those farthest on the left of the advancing Britishers heard a machine gun sputter suddenly before them and saw a huge lion leap over the German parados with the body of a screaming Hun soldier between his jaws and vanish into the shadows of the night, while squatting upon a traverse to their left was Tarzan of the Apes with a machine gun before him with which he was raking the length of the German trenches.

The foremost Rhodesians saw something else—they saw a huge German officer emerge from a dugout just in rear of the ape-man. They saw him snatch up a discarded rifle with bayonet fixed and creep upon the apparently unconscious Tarzan. They ran forward, shouting warnings; but above the pandemonium of the trenches and the machine gun their voices could not reach him. The German leaped upon the parapet behind him—the fat hands raised the rifle butt aloft for the cowardly downward thrust into the naked back and then, as moves Ara, the lightning, moved Tarzan of the Apes.

It was no man who leaped forward upon that Boche officer, striking aside the sharp bayonet as one might strike aside a straw in a baby's hand—it was a wild beast and the roar of a wild beast was upon those savage lips, for as that strange sense that Tarzan owned in common with the other jungle-bred creatures of his wild domain warned him of the presence behind him and he had whirled to meet the attack, his eyes had seen the corps and regimental insignia upon the other's blouse—it was the same as that worn by the murderers of his wife and his people, by the despoilers of his home and his happiness.

It was a wild beast whose teeth fastened upon the shoulder of the Hun—it was a wild beast whose talons sought that fat neck. And then the boys of the Second Rhodesian Regiment saw that which will live forever in their memories. They saw the giant ape-man pick the heavy German from the ground and shake him as a terrier might shake a rat—as Sabor, the lioness, sometimes shakes her prey. They saw the eyes of the Hun bulge in horror as he vainly struck with his futile hands against the massive chest and head of his assailant. They saw Tarzan suddenly spin the man about and placing a knee in the middle of his back and an arm about his neck bend his shoulders slowly backward. The German's knees gave and he sank upon them, but still that irresistible force bent him further and further. He screamed in agony for a moment—then something snapped and Tarzan cast him aside, a limp and lifeless thing.

The Rhodesians started forward, a cheer upon their lips—a cheer that never was uttered—a cheer that froze in their throats, for at that moment Tarzan placed a foot upon the carcass of his kill and, raising his face to the heavens, gave voice to the weird and terrifying victory cry of the bull ape.

Underlieutenant von Goss was dead.

Without a backward glance at the awe-struck soldiers Tarzan leaped the trench and was gone.

CHAPTER V—THE GOLDEN LOCKET

The little British army in East Africa, after suffering severe reverses at the hands of a numerically much superior force, was at last coming into its own. The German offensive had been broken and the Huns were now slowly and doggedly retreating along the railway to Tanga. The break in the German lines had followed the clearing of a section of their left-flank trenches of native soldiers by Tarzan and Numa, the lion, upon that memorable night that the ape-man had loosed a famishing man-eater among the superstitious and terror-stricken blacks. The Second Rhodesian Regiment had immediately taken possession of the abandoned trench and from this position their flanking fire had raked contiguous sections of the German line, the diversion rendering possible a successful night attack on the part of the balance of the British forces.

Weeks had elapsed. The Germans were contesting stubbornly every mile of waterless, thorn-covered ground and clinging desperately to their positions along the railway. The officers of the Second Rhodesians had seen nothing more of Tarzan of the Apes since he had slain Underlieutenant von Goss and disappeared toward the very heart of the German position, and there were those among them who believed that he had been killed within the enemy lines.

"They may have killed him," assented Colonel Capell; "but I fancy they never captured the beggar alive."

Nor had they, nor killed him either. Tarzan had spent those intervening weeks pleasantly and profitably. He had amassed a considerable fund of knowledge concerning the disposition and strength of German troops, their methods of warfare, and the various ways in which a lone Tarmangani might annoy an army and lower its morale.

At present he was prompted by a specific desire. There was a certain German spy whom he wished to capture alive and take back to the British. When he had made his first visit to German headquarters, he had seen a young woman deliver a paper to the German general, and later he had seen that same young woman within the British lines in the uniform of a British officer. The conclusions were obvious—she was a spy.

And so Tarzan haunted German headquarters upon many nights hoping to see her again or to pick up some clew as to her whereabouts, and at the same time he utilized many an artifice whereby he might bring terror to the hearts of the Germans. That he was successful was often demonstrated by the snatches of conversation he overheard as he prowled through the German camps. One night as he lay concealed in the bushes close beside a regimental headquarters he listened to the conversation of several Boche officers. One of the men reverted to the stories told by the native troops in connection with their rout by a lion several weeks before and the simultaneous appearance in their trenches of a naked, white giant whom they were perfectly assured was some demon of the jungle.

"The fellow must have been the same as he who leaped into the general's headquarters and carried off Schneider," asserted one. "I wonder how he happened to single out the poor major.

They say the creature seemed interested in no one but Schneider. He had von Kelter in his grasp, and he might easily have taken the general himself; but he ignored them all except Schneider. Him he pursued about the room, seized and carried off into the night. Gott knows what his fate was."

"Captain Fritz Schneider has some sort of theory," said another. "He told me only a week or two ago that he thinks he knows why his brother was taken—that it was a case of mistaken identity. He was not so sure about it until von Goss was killed, apparently by the same creature, the night the lion entered the trenches. Von Goss was attached to Schneider's company. One of Schneider's men was found with his neck wrung the same night that the major was carried off and Schneider thinks that this devil is after him and his command—that it came for him that night and got his brother by mistake. He says Kraut told him that in presenting the major to Fräulein Kircher the former's name was no sooner spoken than this wild man leaped through the window and made for him."

Suddenly the little group became rigid—listening. "What was that?" snapped one, eyeing the bushes from which a smothered snarl had issued as Tarzan of the Apes realized that through his mistake the perpetrator of the horrid crime at his bungalow still lived—that the murderer of his wife went yet unpunished.

For a long minute the officers stood with tensed nerves, every eye riveted upon the bushes from whence the ominous sound had issued. Each recalled recent mysterious disappearances from the heart of camps as well as from lonely out-guards. Each thought of the silent dead he had seen, slain almost within sight of their fellows by some unseen creature. They thought of the marks upon dead throats—made by talons or by giant fingers, they could not tell which—and those upon shoulders and jugulars where powerful teeth had fastened and they waited with drawn pistols.

Once the bushes moved almost imperceptibly and an instant later one of the officers, without warning, fired into them; but Tarzan of the Apes was not there. In the interval between the moving of the bushes and the firing of the shot he had melted into the night. Ten minutes later he was hovering on the outskirts of that part of camp where were bivouacked for the night the black soldiers of a native company commanded by one Hauptmann Fritz Schneider. The men were stretched upon the ground without tents; but there were tents pitched for the officers. Toward these Tarzan crept. It was slow and perilous work, as the Germans were now upon the alert for the uncanny foe that crept into their camps to take his toll by night, yet the ape-man passed their sentinels, eluded the vigilance of the interior guard, and crept at last to the rear of the officers' line.

Here he flattened himself against the ground close behind the nearest tent and listened. From within came the regular breathing of a sleeping man—one only. Tarzan was satisfied. With his knife he cut the tie strings of the rear flap and entered. He made no noise. The shadow of a falling leaf, floating gently to earth upon a still day, could have been no more soundless. He moved to the side of the sleeping man and bent low over him. He could not know, of course, whether it was Schneider or another, as he had never seen Schneider; but he meant to know and to know even more. Gently he shook the man by the shoulder. The fellow turned heavily and grunted in a thick guttural.

"Silence!" admonished the ape-man in a low whisper. "Silence—I kill."

The Hun opened his eyes. In the dim light he saw a giant figure bending over him. Now a mighty hand grasped his shoulder and another closed lightly about his throat.

"Make no outcry," commanded Tarzan; "but answer in a whisper my questions. What is your name?"

"Luberg," replied the officer. He was trembling. The weird presence of this naked giant filled him with dread. He, too, recalled the men mysteriously murdered in the still watches of the night camps. "What do you want?"

"Where is Hauptmann Fritz Schneider?" asked Tarzan, "Which is his tent?"

"He is not here," replied Luberg. "He was sent to Wilhelmstal yesterday."

"I shall not kill you—now," said the ape-man. "First I shall go and learn if you have lied to me and if you have your death shall be the more terrible. Do you know how Major Schneider died?"

Luberg shook his head negatively.

"I do," continued Tarzan, "and it was not a nice way to die—even for an accursed German. Turn over with your face down and cover your eyes. Do not move or make any sound."

The man did as he was bid and the instant that his eyes were turned away, Tarzan slipped from the tent. An hour later he was outside the German camp and headed for the little hill town of Wilhelmstal, the summer seat of government of German East Africa.

Fräulein Bertha Kircher was lost. She was humiliated and angry—it was long before she would admit it, that she, who prided herself upon her woodcraft, was lost in this little patch of country between the Pangani and the Tanga railway. She knew that Wilhelmstal lay southeast of her about fifty miles; but, through a combination of untoward circumstances, she found herself unable to determine which was southeast.

In the first place she had set out from German headquarters on a well-marked road that was being traveled by troops and with every reason to believe that she would follow that road to Wilhelmstal. Later she had been warned from this road by word that a strong British patrol had come down the west bank of the Pangani, effected a crossing south of her, and was even then marching on the railway at Tonda.

After leaving the road she found herself in thick bush and as the sky was heavily overcast she presently had recourse to her compass and it was not until then that she discovered to her dismay that she did not have it with her. So sure was she of her woodcraft, however, that she continued on in the direction she thought west until she had covered sufficient distance to warrant her in feeling assured that, by now turning south, she could pass safely in rear of the British patrol.

Nor did she commence to feel any doubts until long after she had again turned toward the east well south, as she thought, of the patrol. It was late afternoon—she should long since have struck the road again south of Tonda; but she had found no road and now she began to feel real anxiety.

Her horse had traveled all day without food or water, night was approaching and with it a realization that she was hopelessly lost in a wild and trackless country notorious principally for its tsetse flies and savage beasts. It was maddening to know that she had absolutely no knowledge of the direction she was traveling—that she might be forging steadily further from the railway, deeper into the gloomy and forbidding country toward the Pangani; yet it was impossible to stop—she must go on.

Bertha Kircher was no coward, whatever else she may have been, but as night began to close down around her she could not shut out from her mind entirely contemplation of the terrors of the long hours ahead before the rising sun should dissipate the Stygian gloom—the horrid jungle night—that lures forth all the prowling, preying creatures of destruction.

She found, just before dark, an open meadow-like break in the almost interminable bush. There was a small clump of trees near the center and here she decided to camp. The grass was high and thick, affording feed for her horse and a bed for herself, and there was more than enough dead wood lying about the trees to furnish a good fire well through the night. Removing the saddle and bridle from her mount she placed them at the foot of a tree and then picketed the animal close by. Then she busied herself collecting firewood and by the time darkness had fallen she had a good fire and enough wood to last until morning.

From her saddlebags she took cold food and from her canteen a swallow of water. She could not afford more than a small swallow for she could not know how long a time it might be before she should find more. It filled her with sorrow that her poor horse must go waterless, for even German spies may have hearts and this one was very young and very feminine.

It was now dark. There was neither moon nor stars and the light from her fire only accentuated the blackness beyond. She could see the grass about her and the boles of the trees which stood out in brilliant relief against the solid background of impenetrable night, and beyond the firelight there was nothing.

The jungle seemed ominously quiet. Far away in the distance she heard faintly the boom of big guns; but she could not locate their direction. She strained her ears until her nerves were on the point of breaking; but she could not tell from whence the sound came. And it meant so much to her to know, for the battle-lines were north of her and if she could but locate the direction of the firing she would know which way to go in the morning.

In the morning! Would she live to see another morning? She squared her shoulders and shook herself together. Such thoughts must be banished—they would never do. Bravely she hummed an air as she arranged her saddle near the fire and pulled a quantity of long grass to make a comfortable seat over which she spread her saddle blanket. Then she un-strapped a heavy, military coat from the cantle of her saddle and donned it, for the air was already chill.

Seating herself where she could lean against the saddle she prepared to maintain a sleepless vigil throughout the night. For an hour the silence was broken only by the distant booming of the guns and the low noises of the feeding horse and then, from possibly a mile away, came the rumbling thunder of a lion's roar. The girl started and laid her hand upon the rifle at her side. A little shudder ran through her slight frame and she could feel the goose flesh rise upon her body.

Again and again was the awful sound repeated and each time she was certain that it came nearer. She could locate the direction of this sound although she could not that of the guns, for the origin of the former was much closer. The lion was up wind and so could not have caught her scent as yet, though he might be approaching to investigate the light of the fire which could doubtless be seen for a considerable distance.

For another fear-filled hour the girl sat straining her eyes and ears out into the black void beyond her little island of light. During all that time the lion did not roar again; but there was constantly the sensation that it was creeping upon her. Again and again she would start and turn to peer into the blackness beyond the trees behind her as her overwrought nerves conjured the stealthy fall of padded feet. She held the rifle across her knees at the ready now and she was trembling from head to foot.

Suddenly her horse raised his head and snorted, and with a little cry of terror the girl sprang to her feet. The animal turned and trotted back toward her until the picket rope brought him to a stand, and then he wheeled about and with ears up-pricked gazed out into the night; but the girl could neither see nor hear aught.

Still another hour of terror passed during which the horse often raised his head to peer long and searchingly into the dark. The girl replenished the fire from time to time. She found herself becoming very sleepy. Her heavy lids persisted in drooping; but she dared not sleep. Fearful lest she might be overcome by the drowsiness that was stealing through her she rose and walked briskly to and fro, then she threw some more wood on the fire, walked over and stroked her horse's muzzle and returned to her seat.

Leaning against the saddle she tried to occupy her mind with plans for the morrow; but she must have dozed. With a start she awoke. It was broad daylight. The hideous night with its indescribable terrors was gone.

She could scarce believe the testimony of her senses. She had slept for hours, the fire was out and yet she and the horse were safe and alive, nor was there sign of savage beast about. And, best of all, the sun was shining, pointing the straight road to the east. Hastily she ate a few mouthfuls of her precious rations, which with a swallow of water constituted her breakfast. Then she saddled her horse and mounted. Already she felt that she was as good as safe in Wilhelmstal.

Possibly, however, she might have revised her conclusions could she have seen the two pairs of eyes watching her every move intently from different points in the bush.

Light-hearted and unsuspecting, the girl rode across the clearing toward the bush while directly before her two yellow-green eyes glared round and terrible, a tawny tail twitched nervously and great, padded paws gathered beneath a sleek barrel for a mighty spring. The horse was almost at the edge of the bush when Numa, the lion, launched himself through the air. He struck the animal's right shoulder at the instant that it reared, terrified, to wheel in flight. The force of the impact hurled the horse backward to the ground and so quickly that the girl had no opportunity to extricate herself; but fell to the earth with her mount, her left leg pinned beneath its body.

Horror-stricken, she saw the king of beasts open his mighty jaws and seize the screaming creature by the back of its neck. The great jaws closed, there was an instant's struggle as Numa shook his prey. She could hear the vertebrae crack as the mighty fangs crunched through them, and then the muscles of her faithful friend relaxed in death.

Numa crouched upon his kill. His terrifying eyes riveted themselves upon the girl's face— she could feel his hot breath upon her cheek and the odor of the fetid vapor nauseated her. For what seemed an eternity to the girl the two lay staring at each other and then the lion uttered a menacing growl.

Never before had Bertha Kircher been so terrified—never before had she had such cause for terror. At her hip was a pistol—a formidable weapon with which to face a man; but a puny thing indeed with which to menace the great beast before her. She knew that at best it could but enrage him and yet she meant to sell her life dearly, for she felt that she must die. No human succor could have availed her even had it been there to offer itself. For a moment she tore her gaze from the hypnotic fascination of that awful face and breathed a last prayer to her God. She did not ask for aid, for she felt that she was beyond even divine succor—she only asked that the end might come quickly and with as little pain as possible.

No one can prophesy what a lion will do in any given emergency. This one glared and growled at the girl for a moment and then fell to feeding upon the dead horse. Fräulein Kircher wondered for an instant and then attempted to draw her leg cautiously from beneath the body of her mount; but she could not budge it. She increased the force of her efforts and Numa looked up from his feeding to growl again. The girl desisted. She hoped that he might satisfy his hunger and then depart to lie up, but she could not believe that he would leave her there alive. Doubtless he would drag the remains of his kill into the bush for hiding and, as there could be no doubt that he considered her part of his prey, he would certainly come back for her, or possibly drag her in first and kill her.

Again Numa fell to feeding. The girl's nerves were at the breaking point. She wondered that she had not fainted under the strain of terror and shock. She recalled that she often had wished she might see a lion, close to, make a kill and feed upon it. God! how realistically her wish had been granted.

Again she bethought herself of her pistol. As she had fallen, the holster had slipped around so that the weapon now lay beneath her. Very slowly she reached for it; but in so doing she was forced to raise her body from the ground. Instantly the lion was aroused. With the swiftness of a cat he reached across the carcass of the horse and placed a heavy, taloned paw upon her breast, crushing her back to earth, and all the time he growled and snarled horribly. His face was a picture of frightful rage incarnate. For a moment neither moved and then from behind her the girl heard a human voice uttering bestial sounds.

Numa suddenly looked up from the girl's face at the thing beyond her. His growls increased to roars as he drew back, ripping the front of the girl's waist almost from her body with his long talons, exposing her white bosom, which through some miracle of chance the great claws did not touch.

Tarzan of the Apes had witnessed the entire encounter from the moment that Numa had leaped upon his prey. For some time before, he had been watching the girl, and after the lion attacked her he had at first been minded to let Numa have his way with her. What was she but a hated German and a spy besides? He had seen her at General Kraut's headquarters, in conference with the German staff and again he had seen her within the British lines masquerading as a British officer. It was the latter thought that prompted him to interfere. Doubtless General Jan Smuts would be glad to meet and question her. She might be forced to divulge information of value to the British commander before Smuts had her shot.

Tarzan had recognized not only the girl, but the lion as well. All lions may look alike to you and me; but not so to their intimates of the jungle. Each has his individual characteristics of face and form and gait as well defined as those that differentiate members of the human family, and besides these the creatures of the jungle have a still more positive test—that of scent. Each of us, man or beast, has his own peculiar odor, and it is mostly by this that the beasts of the jungle, endowed with miraculous powers of scent, recognize individuals.

It is the final proof. You have seen it demonstrated a thousand times—a dog recognizes your voice and looks at you. He knows your face and figure. Good, there can be no doubt in his mind but that it is you; but is he satisfied? No, sir—he must come up and smell of you. All his other senses may be fallible, but not his sense of smell, and so he makes assurance positive by the final test.

Tarzan recognized Numa as he whom he had muzzled with the hide of Horta, the boar—as he whom he handled by a rope for two days and finally loosed in a German front-line trench, and he knew that Numa would recognize him—that he would remember the sharp spear that had goaded him into submission and obedience and Tarzan hoped that the lesson he had learned still remained with the lion.

Now he came forward calling to Numa in the language of the great apes—warning him away from the girl. It is open to question that Numa, the lion, understood him; but he did understand the menace of the heavy spear that the Tarmangani carried so ready in his brown, right hand, and so he drew back, growling, trying to decide in his little brain whether to charge or flee.

On came the ape-man with never a pause, straight for the lion. "Go away, Numa," he cried, "or Tarzan will tie you up again and lead you through the jungle without food. See Arad, my spear! Do you recall how his point stuck into you and how with his haft I beat you over the head? Go, Numa! I am Tarzan of the Apes!"

Numa wrinkled the skin of his face into great folds, until his eyes almost disappeared and he growled and roared and snarled and growled again, and when the spear point came at last quite close to him he struck at it viciously with his armed paw; but he drew back. Tarzan stepped over the dead horse and the girl lying behind him gazed in wide-eyed astonishment at the handsome figure driving an angry lion deliberately from its kill.

When Numa had retreated a few yards, the ape-man called back to the girl in perfect German, "Are you badly hurt?"

"I think not," she replied; "but I cannot extricate my foot from beneath my horse."

"Try again," commanded Tarzan. "I do not know how long I can hold Numa thus."

The girl struggled frantically; but at last she sank back upon an elbow.

"It is impossible," she called to him.

He backed slowly until he was again beside the horse, when he reached down and grasped the cinch, which was still intact. Then with one hand he raised the carcass from the ground. The girl freed herself and rose to her feet.

"You can walk?" asked Tarzan.

"Yes," she said; "my leg is numb; but it does not seem to be injured."

"Good," commented the ape-man. "Back slowly away behind me—make no sudden movements. I think he will not charge."

With utmost deliberation the two backed toward the bush. Numa stood for a moment, growling, then he followed them, slowly. Tarzan wondered if he would come beyond his kill or if he would stop there. If he followed them beyond, then they could look for a charge, and if Numa charged it was very likely that he would get one of them. When the lion reached the carcass of the horse Tarzan stopped and so did Numa, as Tarzan had thought that he would and the ape-man waited to see what the lion would do next. He eyed them for a moment, snarled angrily and then looked down at the tempting meat. Presently he crouched upon his kill and resumed feeding.

The girl breathed a deep sigh of relief as she and the ape-man resumed their slow retreat with only an occasional glance from the lion, and when at last they reached the bush and had turned and entered it, she felt a sudden giddiness overwhelm her so that she staggered and would have fallen had Tarzan not caught her. It was only a moment before she regained control of herself.

"I could not help it," she said, in half apology. "I was so close to death—such a horrible death—it unnerved me for an instant; but I am all right now. How can I ever thank you? It was so wonderful—you did not seem to fear the frightful creature in the least; yet he was afraid of you. Who are you?"

"He knows me," replied Tarzan, grimly—"that is why he fears me."

He was standing facing the girl now and for the first time he had a chance to look at her squarely and closely. She was very beautiful—that was undeniable; but Tarzan realized her beauty only in a subconscious way. It was superficial—it did not color her soul which must be black as sin. She was German—a German spy. He hated her and desired only to compass her destruction; but he would choose the manner so that it would work most grievously against the enemy cause.

He saw her naked breasts where Numa had torn her clothing from her and dangling there against the soft, white flesh he saw that which brought a sudden scowl of surprise and anger to his face—the diamond-studded, golden locket of his youth—the love token that had been stolen from the breast of his mate by Schneider, the Hun. The girl saw the scowl but did not interpret it correctly. Tarzan grasped her roughly by the arm.

"Where did you get this?" he demanded, as he tore the bauble from her.

The girl drew herself to her full height. "Take your hand from me," she demanded, but the ape-man paid no attention to her words, only seizing her more forcibly.

"Answer me!" he snapped. "Where did you get this?"

"What is it to you?" she countered.

"It is mine," he replied. "Tell me who gave it to you or I will throw you back to Numa."

"You would do that?" she asked.

"Why not?" he queried. "You are a spy and spies must die if they are caught."

"You were going to kill me, then?"

"I was going to take you to headquarters. They would dispose of you there; but Numa can do it quite as effectively. Which do you prefer?"

"Hauptmann Fritz Schneider gave it to me," she said.

"Headquarters it will be then," said Tarzan. "Come!" The girl moved at his side through the bush and all the time her mind worked quickly. They were moving east, which suited her, and as long as they continued to move east she was glad to have the protection of the great, white savage. She speculated much upon the fact that her pistol still swung at her hip. The man must be mad not to take it from her.

"What makes you think I am a spy?" she asked after a long silence.

"I saw you at German headquarters," he replied, "and then again inside the British lines."

She could not let him take her back to them. She must reach Wilhelmstal at once and she was determined to do so even if she must have recourse to her pistol. She cast a side glance at the tall figure. What a magnificent creature! But yet he was a brute who would kill her or have her killed if she did not slay him. And the locket! She must have that back—it must not fail to reach Wilhelmstal. Tarzan was now a foot or two ahead of her as the path was very narrow. Cautiously she drew her pistol. A single shot would suffice and he was so close that she could not miss. As she figured it all out her eyes rested on the brown skin with the graceful muscles rolling beneath it and the perfect limbs and head and the carriage that a proud king of old might have envied. A wave of revulsion for her contemplated act surged through her. No, she could not do it—yet, she must be free and she must regain possession of the locket. And then, almost blindly, she swung the weapon up and struck Tarzan heavily upon the back of the head with its butt. Like a felled ox he dropped in his tracks.

CHAPTER VI—VENGEANCE AND MERCY

It was an hour later that Sheeta, the panther, hunting, chanced to glance upward into the blue sky where his attention was attracted by Ska, the vulture, circling slowly above the bush a mile away and downwind. For a long minute the yellow eyes stared intently at the gruesome bird. They saw Ska dive and rise again to continue his ominous circling and in these movements their woodcraft read that which, while obvious to Sheeta, would doubtless have meant nothing to you or me.

The hunting cat guessed that on the ground beneath Ska was some living thing of flesh—either a beast feeding upon its kill or a dying animal that Ska did not yet dare attack. In either event it might prove meat for Sheeta, and so the wary feline stalked by a circuitous route, upon soft, padded feet that gave forth no sound, until the circling aasvogel and his intended prey were upwind. Then, sniffing each vagrant zephyr, Sheeta, the panther, crept cautiously forward, nor had he advanced any considerable distance before his keen nostrils were rewarded with the scent of man—a Tarmangani.

Sheeta paused. He was not a hunter of men. He was young and in his prime; but always before he had avoided this hated presence. Of late he had become more accustomed to it with the passing of many soldiers through his ancient hunting ground, and as the soldiers had frightened away a great part of the game Sheeta had been wont to feed upon, the days had been lean, and Sheeta was hungry.

The circling Ska suggested that this Tarmangani might be helpless and upon the point of dying, else Ska would not have been interested in him, and so easy prey for Sheeta. With this thought in mind the cat resumed his stalking. Presently he pushed through the thick bush and his yellow-green eyes rested gloatingly upon the body of an almost naked Tarmangani lying face down in a narrow game trail.

Numa, sated, rose from the carcass of Bertha Kircher's horse and seized the partially devoured body by the neck and dragged it into the bush; then he started east toward the lair where he had left his mate. Being uncomfortably full he was inclined to be sleepy and far from belligerent. He moved slowly and majestically with no effort at silence or concealment. The king walked abroad, unafraid.

With an occasional regal glance to right or left he moved along a narrow game trail until at a turn he came to a sudden stop at what lay revealed before him—Sheeta, the panther, creeping stealthily upon the almost naked body of a Tarmangani lying face down in the deep dust of the pathway. Numa glared intently at the quiet body in the dust. Recognition came. It was his Tarmangani. A low growl of warning rumbled from his throat and Sheeta halted with one paw upon Tarzan's back and turned suddenly to eye the intruder.

What passed within those savage brains? Who may say? The panther seemed debating the wisdom of defending his find, for he growled horribly as though warning Numa away from the prey. And Numa? Was the idea of property rights dominating his thoughts? The Tarmangani was his, or he was the Tarmangani's. Had not the Great White Ape mastered and subdued him and, too, had he not fed him? Numa recalled the fear that he had felt of this man-thing and his cruel spear; but in savage brains fear is more likely to engender respect than hatred and so Numa found that he respected the creature who had subdued and mastered him. He saw Sheeta, upon whom he looked with contempt, daring to molest the master of the lion. Jealousy and greed alone might have been sufficient to prompt Numa to drive Sheeta away, even though the lion was not sufficiently hungry to devour the flesh that he thus wrested from the lesser cat; but then, too, there was in the little brain within the massive head a sense of loyalty, and perhaps this it was that sent Numa quickly forward, growling, toward the spitting Sheeta.

For a moment the latter stood his ground with arched back and snarling face, for all the world like a great, spotted tabby.

Numa had not felt like fighting; but the sight of Sheeta daring to dispute his rights kindled his ferocious brain to sudden fire. His rounded eyes glared with rage, his undulating tail snapped to stiff erectness as, with a frightful roar, he charged this presuming vassal.

It came so suddenly and from so short a distance that Sheeta had no chance to turn and flee the rush, and so he met it with raking talons and snapping jaws; but the odds were all against him. To the larger fangs and the more powerful jaws of his adversary were added huge talons and the preponderance of the lion's great weight. At the first clash Sheeta was crushed and, though he deliberately fell upon his back and drew up his powerful hind legs beneath Numa with the intention of disemboweling him, the lion forestalled him and at the same time closed his awful jaws upon Sheeta's throat.

It was soon over. Numa rose, shaking himself, and stood above the torn and mutilated body of his foe. His own sleek coat was cut and the red blood trickled down his flank; though it was but a minor injury, it angered him. He glared down at the dead panther and then, in a fit of rage, he seized and mauled the body only to drop it in a moment, lower his head, voice a single terrific roar, and turn toward the ape-man.

Approaching the still form he sniffed it over from head to foot. Then he placed a huge paw upon it and turned it over with its face up. Again he smelled about the body and at last with his rough tongue licked Tarzan's face. It was then that Tarzan opened his eyes.

Above him towered the huge lion, its hot breath upon his face, its rough tongue upon his cheek. The ape-man had often been close to death; but never before so close as this, he thought, for he was convinced that death was but a matter of seconds. His brain was still numb from the effects of the blow that had felled him, and so he did not, for a moment, recognize the lion that stood over him as the one he had so recently encountered.

Presently, however, recognition dawned upon him and with it a realization of the astounding fact that Numa did not seem bent on devouring him—at least not immediately. His position was a delicate one. The lion stood astraddle Tarzan with his front paws. The ape-man could not rise, therefore, without pushing the lion away and whether Numa would tolerate being pushed was an open question. Too, the beast might consider him already dead and any movement that indicated the contrary was true would, in all likelihood, arouse the killing instinct of the man-eater.

But Tarzan was tiring of the situation. He was in no mood to lie there forever, especially when he contemplated the fact that the girl spy who had tried to brain him was undoubtedly escaping as rapidly as possible.

Numa was looking right into his eyes now evidently aware that he was alive. Presently the lion cocked his head on one side and whined. Tarzan knew the note, and he knew that it spelled neither rage nor hunger, and then he risked all on a single throw, encouraged by that low whine.

"Move, Numa!" he commanded and placing a palm against the tawny shoulder he pushed the lion aside. Then he rose and with a hand on his hunting knife awaited that which might follow. It was then that his eyes fell for the first time on the torn body of Sheeta. He looked from the dead cat to the live one and saw the marks of conflict upon the latter, too, and in an instant realized something of what had happened—Numa had saved him from the panther!

It seemed incredible and yet the evidence pointed clearly to the fact. He turned toward the lion and without fear approached and examined his wounds which he found superficial, and as Tarzan knelt beside him Numa rubbed an itching ear against the naked, brown shoulder. Then the ape-man stroked the great head, picked up his spear, and looked about for the trail of the girl. This he soon found leading toward the east, and as he set out upon it something prompted him to feel for the locket he had hung about his neck. It was gone!

No trace of anger was apparent upon the ape-man's face unless it was a slight tightening of the jaws; but he put his hand ruefully to the back of his head where a bump marked the place where the girl had struck him and a moment later a half-smile played across his lips. He could not help but admit that she had tricked him neatly, and that it must have taken nerve to do the thing she did and to set out armed only with a pistol through the trackless waste that lay between them and the railway and beyond into the hills where Wilhelmstal lies.

Tarzan admired courage. He was big enough to admit it and admire it even in a German spy, but he saw that in this case it only added to her resourcefulness and made her all the more dangerous and the necessity for putting her out of the way paramount. He hoped to overtake her before she reached Wilhelmstal and so he set out at the swinging trot that he could hold for hours at a stretch without apparent fatigue.

That the girl could hope to reach the town on foot in less than two days seemed improbable, for it was a good thirty miles and part of it hilly. Even as the thought crossed his mind he heard the whistle of a locomotive to the east and knew that the railway was in operation again after a shutdown of several days. If the train was going south the girl would signal it if she had reached the right of way. His keen ears caught the whining of brake shoes on wheels and a few minutes later the signal blast for brakes off. The train had stopped and started again and, as it gained headway and greater distance, Tarzan could tell from the direction of the sound that it was moving south.

The ape-man followed the trail to the railway where it ended abruptly on the west side of the track, showing that the girl had boarded the train, just as he thought. There was nothing now but to follow on to Wilhelmstal, where he hoped to find Captain Fritz Schneider, as well as the girl, and to recover his diamond-studded locket.

It was dark when Tarzan reached the little hill town of Wilhelmstal. He loitered on the outskirts, getting his bearings and trying to determine how an almost naked white man might explore the village without arousing suspicion. There were many soldiers about and the town was under guard, for he could see a lone sentinel walking his post scarce a hundred yards from him. To elude this one would not be difficult; but to enter the village and search it would be practically impossible, garbed, or un-garbed, as he was.

Creeping forward, taking advantage of every cover, lying flat and motionless when the sentry's face was toward him, the ape-man at last reached the sheltering shadows of an outhouse just inside the lines. From there he moved stealthily from building to building until at last he was discovered by a large dog in the rear of one of the bungalows. The brute came slowly toward him, growling. Tarzan stood motionless beside a tree. He could see a light in the bungalow and uniformed men moving about and he hoped that the dog would not bark. He did not; but he growled more savagely and, just at the moment that the rear door of the bungalow opened and a man stepped out, the animal charged.

He was a large dog, as large as Dango, the hyena, and he charged with all the vicious impetuosity of Numa, the lion. As he came Tarzan knelt and the dog shot through the air for his throat; but he was dealing with no man now and he found his quickness more than matched by the quickness of the Tarmangani. His teeth never reached the soft flesh—strong fingers, fingers of steel, seized his neck. He voiced a single startled yelp and clawed at the naked breast before him with his talons; but he was powerless. The mighty fingers closed upon his throat; the man rose, snapped the clawing body once, and cast it aside. At the same time a voice from the open bungalow door called: "Simba!"

There was no response. Repeating the call the man descended the steps and advanced toward the tree. In the light from the doorway Tarzan could see that he was a tall, broad-shouldered man in the uniform of a German officer. The ape-man withdrew into the shadow of the tree's stem. The man came closer, still calling the dog—he did not see the savage beast, crouching now in the shadow, awaiting him. When he had approached within ten feet of the Tarmangani, Tarzan leaped upon him—as Sabor springs to the kill, so sprang the ape-man. The momentum and weight of his body hurled the German to the ground, powerful fingers prevented an outcry and, though the officer struggled, he had no chance and a moment later lay dead beside the body of the dog.

As Tarzan stood for a moment looking down upon his kill and regretting that he could not risk voicing his beloved victory cry, the sight of the uniform suggested a means whereby he might pass to and fro through Wilhelmstal with the minimum chance of detection. Ten minutes later a tall, broad-shouldered officer stepped from the yard of the bungalow leaving behind him the corpses of a dog and a naked man.

He walked boldly along the little street and those who passed him could not guess that beneath Imperial Germany's uniform beat a savage heart that pulsed with implacable hatred for the Hun. Tarzan's first concern was to locate the hotel, for here he guessed he would find the girl, and where the girl was doubtless would be Hauptmann Fritz Schneider, who was either her confederate, her sweetheart, or both, and there, too, would be Tarzan's precious locket.

He found the hotel at last, a low, two-storied building with a veranda. There were lights on both floors and people, mostly officers, could be seen within. The ape-man considered entering and inquiring for those he sought; but his better judgment finally prompted him to reconnoiter first. Passing around the building he looked into all the lighted rooms on the first floor and, seeing neither of those for whom he had come, he swung lightly to the roof of the veranda and continued his investigations through windows of the second story.

At one corner of the hotel in a rear room the blinds were drawn; but he heard voices within and once he saw a figure silhouetted momentarily against the blind. It appeared to be the figure of a woman; but it was gone so quickly that he could not be sure. Tarzan crept close to the window and listened. Yes, there was a woman there and a man—he heard distinctly the tones of their voices although he could overhear no words, as they seemed to be whispering.

The adjoining room was dark. Tarzan tried the window and found it unlatched. All was quiet within. He raised the sash and listened again—still silence. Placing a leg over the sill he slipped within and hurriedly glanced about. The room was vacant. Crossing to the door he opened it and looked out into the hall. There was no one there, either, and he stepped out and approached the door of the adjoining room where the man and woman were.

Pressing close to the door he listened. Now he distinguished words, for the two had raised their voices as though in argument. The woman was speaking.

"I have brought the locket," she said, "as was agreed upon between you and General Kraut, as my identification. I carry no other credentials. This was to be enough. You have nothing to do but give me the papers and let me go."

The man replied in so low a tone that Tarzan could not catch the words and then the woman spoke again—a note of scorn and perhaps a little of fear in her voice.

"You would not dare, Hauptmann Schneider," she said, and then: "Do not touch me! Take your hands from me!"

It was then that Tarzan of the Apes opened the door and stepped into the room. What he saw was a huge, bull-necked German officer with one arm about the waist of Fräulein Bertha Kircher and a hand upon her forehead pushing her head back as he tried to kiss her on the mouth. The girl was struggling against the great brute; but her efforts were futile. Slowly the man's lips were coming closer to hers and slowly, step by step, she was being carried backward.

Schneider heard the noise of the opening and closing door behind him and turned. At sight of this strange officer he dropped the girl and straightened up.

"What is the meaning of this intrusion, Lieutenant?" he demanded, noting the other's epaulettes. "Leave the room at once."

Tarzan made no articulate reply; but the two there with him heard a low growl break from those firm lips—a growl that sent a shudder through the frame of the girl and brought a pallor to the red face of the Hun and his hand to his pistol but even as he drew his weapon it was wrested from him and hurled through the blind and window to the yard beyond. Then Tarzan backed against the door and slowly removed the uniform coat.

"You are Hauptmann Schneider," he said to the German.

"What of it?" growled the latter.

"I am Tarzan of the Apes," replied the ape-man. "Now you know why I intrude."

The two before him saw that he was naked beneath the coat which he threw upon the floor and then he slipped quickly from the trousers and stood there clothed only in his loin cloth. The girl had recognized him by this time, too.

"Take your hand off that pistol," Tarzan admonished her. Her hand dropped at her side. "Now come here!"

She approached and Tarzan removed the weapon and hurled it after the other. At the mention of his name Tarzan had noted the sickly pallor that overspread the features of the Hun. At last he had found the right man. At last his mate would be partially avenged—never could she be entirely avenged. Life was too short and there were too many Germans.

"What do you want of me?" demanded Schneider.

"You are going to pay the price for the thing you did at the little bungalow in the Waziri country," replied the ape-man.

Schneider commenced to bluster and threaten. Tarzan turned the key in the lock of the door and hurled the former through the window after the pistols. Then he turned to the girl. "Keep out of the way," he said in a low voice. "Tarzan of the Apes is going to kill."

The Hun ceased blustering and began to plead. "I have a wife and children at home," he cried. "I have done nothing, I—"

"You are going to die as befits your kind," said Tarzan, "with blood on your hands and a lie on your lips." He started across the room toward the burly Hauptmann. Schneider was a large and powerful man—about the height of the ape-man but much heavier. He saw that neither threats nor pleas would avail him and so he prepared to fight as a cornered rat fights for its life with all the maniacal rage, cunning, and ferocity that the first law of nature imparts to many beasts.

Lowering his bull head he charged for the ape-man and in the center of the floor the two clinched. There they stood locked and swaying for a moment until Tarzan succeeded in forcing his antagonist backward over a table which crashed to the floor, splintered by the weight of the two heavy bodies.

The girl stood watching the battle with wide eyes. She saw the two men rolling hither and thither across the floor and she heard with horror the low growls that came from the lips of the naked giant. Schneider was trying to reach his foe's throat with his fingers while, horror of horrors, Bertha Kircher could see that the other was searching for the German's jugular with his teeth!

Schneider seemed to realize this too, for he redoubled his efforts to escape and finally succeeded in rolling over on top of the ape-man and breaking away. Leaping to his feet he ran for the window; but the ape-man was too quick for him and before he could leap through the sash a heavy hand fell upon his shoulder and he was jerked back and hurled across the room to the opposite wall. There Tarzan followed him, and once again they locked, dealing each other terrific blows, until Schneider in a piercing voice screamed, "Kamerad! Kamerad!"

Tarzan grasped the man by the throat and drew his hunting knife. Schneider's back was against the wall so that though his knees wobbled he was held erect by the ape-man. Tarzan brought the sharp point to the lower part of the German's abdomen.

"Thus you slew my mate," he hissed in a terrible voice. "Thus shall you die!"

The girl staggered forward. "Oh, God, no!" she cried. "Not that. You are too brave—you cannot be such a beast as that!"

Tarzan turned at her. "No," he said, "you are right, I cannot do it—I am no German," and he raised the point of his blade and sunk it deep into the putrid heart of Hauptmann Fritz Schneider, putting a bloody period to the Hun's last gasping cry: "I did not do it! She is not—"

Then Tarzan turned toward the girl and held out his hand. "Give me my locket," he said.

She pointed toward the dead officer. "He has it." Tarzan searched him and found the trinket. "Now you may give me the papers," he said to the girl, and without a word she handed him a folded document.

For a long time he stood looking at her before ho spoke again.

"I came for you, too," he said. "It would be difficult to take you back from here and so I was going to kill you, as I have sworn to kill all your kind; but you were right when you said that I was not such a beast as that slayer of women. I could not slay him as he slew mine, nor can I slay you, who are a woman."

He crossed to the window, raised the sash and an instant later he had stepped out and disappeared into the night. And then Fräulein Bertha Kircher stepped quickly to the corpse upon the floor, slipped her hand inside the blouse and drew forth a little sheaf of papers which she tucked into her waist before she went to the window and called for help.

CHAPTER VII—WHEN BLOOD TOLD

Tarzan of the Apes was disgusted. He had had the German spy, Bertha Kircher, in his power and had left her unscathed. It is true that he had slain Hauptmann Fritz Schneider, that Underlieutenant von Goss had died at his hands, and that he had otherwise wreaked vengeance upon the men of the German company who had murdered, pillaged, and raped at Tarzan's bungalow in the Waziri country. There was still another officer to be accounted for, but him he could not find. It was Lieutenant Obergatz he still sought, though vainly, for at last he learned that the man had been sent upon some special mission, whether in Africa or back to Europe Tarzan's informant either did not know or would not divulge.

But the fact that he had permitted sentiment to stay his hand when he might so easily have put Bertha Kircher out of the way in the hotel at Wilhelmstal that night rankled in the ape-man's bosom. He was shamed by his weakness, and when he had handed the paper she had given him to the British chief of staff, even though the information it contained permitted the British to frustrate a German flank attack, he was still much dissatisfied with himself. And possibly the root of this dissatisfaction lay in the fact that he realized that were he again to have the same opportunity he would still find it as impossible to slay a woman as it had been in Wilhelmstal that night.

Tarzan blamed this weakness, as he considered it, upon his association with the effeminizing influences of civilization, for in the bottom of his savage heart he held in contempt both civilization and its representatives—the men and women of the civilized countries of the world. Always was he comparing their weaknesses, their vices, their hypocrisies, and their little vanities with the open, primitive ways of his ferocious jungle mates, and all the while there battled in that same big heart with these forces another mighty force—Tarzan's love and loyalty for his friends of the civilized world.

The ape-man, reared as he had been by savage beasts amid savage beasts, was slow to make friends. Acquaintances he numbered by the hundreds; but of friends he had few. These few he would have died for as, doubtless, they would have died for him; but there were none of these fighting with the British forces in East Africa, and so, sickened and disgusted by the sight of man waging his cruel and inhuman warfare, Tarzan determined to heed the insistent call of the remote jungle of his youth, for the Germans were now on the run and the war in East Africa was so nearly over that he realized that his further services would be of negligible value.

Never regularly sworn into the service of the King, he was under no obligation to remain now that the moral obligation had been removed, and so it was that he disappeared from the British camp as mysteriously as he had appeared a few months before.

More than once had Tarzan reverted to the primitive only to return again to civilization through love for his mate; but now that she was gone he felt that this time he had definitely departed forever from the haunts of man, and that he should live and die a beast among beasts even as he had been from infancy to maturity.

Between him and his destination lay a trackless wilderness of untouched primeval savagery where, doubtless in many spots, his would be the first human foot to touch the virgin turf. Nor did this prospect dismay the Tarmangani—rather was it an urge and an inducement, for rich in his veins flowed that noble strain of blood that has made most of the earth's surface habitable for man.

The question of food and water that would have risen paramount in the mind of an ordinary man contemplating such an excursion gave Tarzan little concern. The wilderness was his natural habitat and woodcraft as inherent to him as breathing. Like other jungle animals he could scent water from a great distance and, where you or I might die of thirst, the ape-man would unerringly select the exact spot at which to dig and find water.

For several days Tarzan traversed a country rich in game and watercourses. He moved slowly, hunting and fishing, or again fraternizing or quarreling with the other savage denizens of the jungle. Now it was little Manu, the monkey, who chattered and scolded at the mighty Tarmangani and in the next breath warned him that Histah, the snake, lay coiled in the long grass just ahead. Of Manu Tarzan inquired concerning the great apes—the Mangani—and was told that few inhabited this part of the jungle, and that even these were hunting farther to the north this season of the year.

"But there is Bolgani," said Manu. "Would you like to see Bolgani?"

Manu's tone was sneering, and Tarzan knew that it was because little Manu thought all creatures feared mighty Bolgani, the gorilla. Tarzan arched his great chest and struck it with a clinched fist. "I am Tarzan," he cried. "While Tarzan was yet a balu he slew a Bolgani. Tarzan seeks the Mangani, who are his brothers, but Bolgani he does not seek, so let Bolgani keep from the path of Tarzan."

Little Manu, the monkey, was much impressed, for the way of the jungle is to boast and to believe. It was then that he condescended to tell Tarzan more of the Mangani.

"They go there and there and there," he said, making a wide sweep with a brown hand first toward the north, then west, and then south again. "For there," and he pointed due west, "is much hunting; but between lies a great place where there is no food and no water, so they must go that way," and again he swung his hand through the half-circle that explained to Tarzan the great detour the apes made to come to their hunting ground to the west.

That was all right for the Mangani, who are lazy and do not care to move rapidly; but for Tarzan the straight road would be the best. He would cross the dry country and come to the good hunting in a third of the time that it would take to go far to the north and circle back again. And so it was that he continued on toward the west, and crossing a range of low mountains came in sight of a broad plateau, rock strewn and desolate. Far in the distance he saw another range of mountains beyond which he felt must lie the hunting ground of the Mangani. There he would join them and remain for a while before continuing on toward the coast and the little cabin that his father had built beside the land-locked harbor at the jungle's edge.

Tarzan was full of plans. He would rebuild and enlarge the cabin of his birth, constructing storage houses where he would make the apes lay away food when it was plenty against the times that were lean—a thing no ape ever had dreamed of doing. And the tribe would remain always in the locality and he would be king again as he had in the past. He would try to teach them some of the better things that he had learned from man, yet knowing the ape-mind as only Tarzan could, he feared that his labors would be for naught.

The ape-man found the country he was crossing rough in the extreme, the roughest he ever had encountered. The plateau was cut by frequent canyons the passage of which often entailed hours of wearing effort. The vegetation was sparse and of a faded brown color that lent to the whole landscape a most depressing aspect. Great rocks were strewn in every direction as far as the eye could see, lying partially embedded in an impalpable dust that rose in clouds about him at every step. The sun beat down mercilessly out of a cloudless sky.

For a day Tarzan toiled across this now hateful land and at the going down of the sun the distant mountains to the west seemed no nearer than at morn. Never a sign of living thing had the ape-man seen, other than Ska, that bird of ill omen, that had followed him tirelessly since he had entered this parched waste.

No littlest beetle that he might eat had given evidence that life of any sort existed here, and it was a hungry and thirsty Tarzan who lay down to rest in the evening. He decided now to push on during the cool of the night, for he realized that even mighty Tarzan had his limitations and that where there was no food one could not eat and where there was no water the greatest woodcraft in the world could find none. It was a totally new experience to Tarzan to find so barren and terrible a country in his beloved Africa. Even the Sahara had its oases; but this frightful world gave no indication of containing a square foot of hospitable ground.

However, he had no misgivings but that he would fare forth into the wonder country of which little Manu had told him, though it was certain that he would do it with a dry skin and an empty belly. And so he fought on until daylight, when he again felt the need of rest. He was at the edge of another of those terrible canyons, the eighth he had crossed, whose precipitous sides would have taxed to the uttermost the strength of an untired man well fortified by food and water, and for the first time, as he looked down into the abyss and then at the opposite side that he must scale, misgivings began to assail his mind.

He did not fear death—with the memory of his murdered mate still fresh in his mind he almost courted it, yet strong within him was that primal instinct of self-preservation—the battling force of life that would keep him an active contender against the Great Reaper until, fighting to the very last, he should be overcome by a superior power.

A shadow swung slowly across the ground beside him, and looking up, the ape-man saw Ska, the vulture, wheeling a wide circle above him. The grim and persistent harbinger of evil aroused the man to renewed determination. He arose and approached the edge of the canyon, and then, wheeling, with his face turned upward toward the circling bird of prey, he bellowed forth the challenge of the bull ape.

"I am Tarzan," he shouted, "Lord of the Jungle. Tarzan of the Apes is not for Ska, eater of carrion. Go back to the lair of Dango and feed off the leavings of the hyenas, for Tarzan will leave no bones for Ska to pick in this empty wilderness of death."

But before he reached the bottom of the canyon he again was forced to the realization that his great strength was waning, and when he dropped exhausted at the foot of the cliff and saw before him the opposite wall that must be scaled, he bared his fighting fangs and growled. For an hour he lay resting in the cool shade at the foot of the cliff. All about him reigned utter silence—the silence of the tomb. No fluttering birds, no humming insects, no scurrying reptiles relieved the deathlike stillness. This indeed was the valley of death. He felt the depressing influence of the horrible place settling down upon him; but he staggered to his feet, shaking himself like a great lion, for was he not still Tarzan, mighty Tarzan of the Apes? Yes, and Tarzan the mighty he would be until the last throb of that savage heart!

As he crossed the floor of the canyon he saw something lying close to the base of the side wall he was approaching—something that stood out in startling contrast to all the surroundings and yet seemed so much a part and parcel of the somber scene as to suggest an actor amid the settings of a well-appointed stage, and, as though to carry out the allegory, the pitiless rays of flaming Kudu topped the eastern cliff, picking out the thing lying at the foot of the western wall like a giant spotlight.

And as Tarzan came nearer he saw the bleached skull and bones of a human being about which were remnants of clothing and articles of equipment that, as he examined them, filled the ape-man with curiosity to such an extent that for a time he forgot his own predicament in contemplation of the remarkable story suggested by these mute evidences of a tragedy of a time long past.

The bones were in a fair state of preservation and indicated by their intactness that the flesh had probably been picked from them by vultures as none was broken; but the pieces of equipment bore out the suggestion of their great age. In this protected spot where there were no frosts and evidently but little rainfall, the bones might have lain for ages without disintegrating, for there were here no other forces to scatter or disturb them.

Near the skeleton lay a helmet of hammered brass and a corroded breastplate of steel while at one side was a long, straight sword in its scabbard and an ancient harquebus. The bones were those of a large man—a man of wondrous strength and vitality Tarzan knew he must have been to have penetrated thus far through the dangers of Africa with such a ponderous yet at the same time futile armament.

The ape-man felt a sense of deep admiration for this nameless adventurer of a bygone day. What a brute of a man he must have been and what a glorious tale of battle and kaleidoscopic vicissitudes of fortune must once have been locked within that whitened skull! Tarzan stooped to examine the shreds of clothing that still lay about the bones. Every particle of leather had disappeared, doubtless eaten by Ska. No boots remained, if the man had worn boots, but there were several buckles scattered about suggesting that a great part of his trappings had been of leather, while just beneath the bones of one hand lay a metal cylinder about eight inches long and two inches in diameter. As Tarzan picked it up he saw that it had been heavily lacquered and had withstood the slight ravages of time so well as to be in as perfect a state of preservation today as it had been when its owner dropped into his last, long sleep perhaps centuries ago.

As he examined it he discovered that one end was closed with a friction cover which a little twisting force soon loosened and removed, revealing within a roll of parchment which the ape-man removed and opened, disclosing a number of age-yellowed sheets closely written upon in a fine hand in a language which he guessed to be Spanish but which he could not decipher. Upon the last sheet was a roughly drawn map with numerous reference points marked upon it, all unintelligible to Tarzan, who, after a brief examination of the papers, returned them to their metal case, replaced the top and was about to toss the little cylinder to the ground beside the mute remains of its former possessor when some whim of curiosity unsatisfied prompted him to slip it into the quiver with his arrows, though as he did so it was with the grim thought that possibly centuries hence it might again come to the sight of man beside his own bleached bones.

And then, with a parting glance at the ancient skeleton, he turned to the task of ascending the western wall of the canyon. Slowly and with many rests he dragged his weakening body upwards. Again and again he slipped back from sheer exhaustion and would have fallen to the floor of the canyon but for merest chance. How long it took him to scale that frightful wall he could not have told, and when at last he dragged himself over the top it was to lie weak and gasping, too spent to rise or even to move a few inches farther from the perilous edge of the chasm.

At last he arose, very slowly and with evident effort gaining his knees first and then staggering to his feet, yet his indomitable will was evidenced by a sudden straightening of his shoulders and a determined shake of his head as he lurched forward on unsteady legs to take up his valiant fight for survival. Ahead he scanned the rough landscape for sign of another canyon which he knew would spell inevitable doom. The western hills rose closer now though weirdly unreal as they seemed to dance in the sunlight as though mocking him with their nearness at the moment that exhaustion was about to render them forever unattainable.

Beyond them he knew must be the fertile hunting grounds of which Manu had told. Even if no canyon intervened, his chances of surmounting even low hills seemed remote should he have the fortune to reach their base; but with another canyon hope was dead. Above them Ska still circled, and it seemed to the ape-man that the ill-omened bird hovered ever lower and lower as though reading in that failing gait the nearing of the end, and through cracked lips Tarzan growled out his defiance.

Mile after mile Tarzan of the Apes put slowly behind him, borne up by sheer force of will where a lesser man would have lain down to die and rest forever tired muscles whose every move was an agony of effort; but at last his progress became practically mechanical—he staggered on with a dazed mind that reacted numbly to a single urge—on, on, on! The hills were now but a dim, ill-defined blur ahead. Sometimes he forgot that they were hills, and again he wondered vaguely why he must go on forever through all this torture endeavoring to overtake them—the fleeing, elusive hills. Presently he began to hate them and there formed within his half-delirious brain the hallucination that the hills were German hills, that they had slain someone dear to him, whom he could never quite recall, and that he was pursuing to slay them.

This idea, growing, appeared to give him strength—a new and revivifying purpose—so that for a time he no longer staggered; but went forward steadily with head erect. Once he stumbled and fell, and when he tried to rise he found that he could not—that his strength was so far gone that he could only crawl forward on his hands and knees for a few yards and then sink down again to rest.

It was during one of these frequent periods of utter exhaustion that he heard the flap of dismal wings close above him. With his remaining strength he turned himself over on his back to see Ska wheel quickly upward. With the sight Tarzan's mind cleared for a while.

"Is the end so near as that?" he thought. "Does Ska know that I am so near gone that he dares come down and perch upon my carcass?" And even then a grim smile touched those swollen lips as into the savage mind came a sudden thought—the cunning of the wild beast at bay. Closing his eyes he threw a forearm across them to protect them from Ska's powerful beak and then he lay very still and waited.

It was restful lying there, for the sun was now obscured by clouds and Tarzan was very tired. He feared that he might sleep and something told him that if he did he would never awaken, and so he concentrated all his remaining powers upon the one thought of remaining awake. Not a muscle moved—to Ska, circling above, it became evident that the end had come—that at last he should be rewarded for his long vigil.

Circling slowly he dropped closer and closer to the dying man. Why did not Tarzan move? Had he indeed been overcome by the sleep of exhaustion, or was Ska right—had death at last claimed that mighty body? Was that great, savage heart stilled forever? It is unthinkable.

Ska, filled with suspicions, circled warily. Twice he almost alighted upon the great, naked breast only to wheel suddenly away; but the third time his talons touched the brown skin. It was as though the contact closed an electric circuit that instantaneously vitalized the quiet clod that had lain motionless so long. A brown hand swept downward from the brown forehead and before Ska could raise a wing in flight he was in the clutches of his intended victim.

Ska fought, but he was no match for even a dying Tarzan, and a moment later the ape-man's teeth closed upon the carrion-eater. The flesh was coarse and tough and gave off an unpleasant odor and a worse taste; but it was food and the blood was drink and Tarzan only an ape at heart and a dying ape into the bargain—dying of starvation and thirst.

Even mentally weakened as he was the ape-man was still master of his appetite and so he ate but sparingly, saving the rest, and then, feeling that he now could do so safely, he turned upon his side and slept.

Rain, beating heavily upon his body, awakened him and sitting up he cupped his hands and caught the precious drops which he transferred to his parched throat. Only a little he got at a time; but that was best. The few mouthfuls of Ska that he had eaten, together with the blood and rain water and the sleep had refreshed him greatly and put new strength into his tired muscles.

Now he could see the hills again and they were close and, though there was no sun, the world looked bright and cheerful, for Tarzan knew that he was saved. The bird that would have devoured him, and the providential rain, had saved him at the very moment that death seemed inevitable.

Again partaking of a few mouthfuls of the unsavory flesh of Ska, the vulture, the ape-man arose with something of his old force and set out with steady gait toward the hills of promise rising alluringly ahead. Darkness fell before he reached them; but he kept on until he felt the steeply rising ground that proclaimed his arrival at the base of the hills proper, and then he lay down and waited until morning should reveal the easiest passage to the land beyond. The rain had ceased, but the sky still was overcast so that even his keen eyes could not penetrate the darkness farther than a few feet. And there he slept, after eating again of what remained of Ska, until the morning sun awakened him with a new sense of strength and well-being.

And so at last he came through the hills out of the valley of death into a land of park-like beauty, rich in game. Below him lay a deep valley through the center of which dense jungle vegetation marked the course of a river beyond which a primeval forest extended for miles to terminate at last at the foot of lofty, snow-capped mountains. It was a land that Tarzan never had looked upon before, nor was it likely that the foot of another white man ever had touched it unless, possibly, in some long-gone day the adventurer whose skeleton he had found bleaching in the canyon had traversed it.

CHAPTER VIII—TARZAN AND THE GREAT APES

Three days the ape-man spent in resting and recuperating, eating fruits and nuts and the smaller animals that were most easily bagged, and upon the fourth he set out to explore the valley and search for the great apes. Time was a negligible factor in the equation of life—it was all the same to Tarzan if he reached the west coast in a month or a year or three years. All time was his and all Africa. His was absolute freedom—the last tie that had bound him to civilization and custom had been severed. He was alone but he was not exactly lonely. The greater part of his life had been spent thus, and though there was no other of his kind, he was at all times surrounded by the jungle peoples for whom familiarity had bred no contempt within his breast. The least of them interested him, and, too, there were those with whom he always made friends easily, and there were his hereditary enemies whose presence gave a spice to life that might otherwise have become humdrum and monotonous.

And so it was that on the fourth day he set out to explore the valley and search for his fellow-apes. He had proceeded southward for a short distance when his nostrils were assailed by the scent of man, of Gomangani, the black man. There were many of them, and mixed with their scent was another-that of a she Tarmangani.

Swinging through the trees Tarzan approached the authors of these disturbing scents. He came warily from the flank, but paying no attention to the wind, for he knew that man with his dull senses could apprehend him only through his eyes or ears and then only when comparatively close. Had he been stalking Numa or Sheeta he would have circled about until his quarry was upwind from him, thus taking practically all the advantage up to the very moment that he came within sight or hearing; but in the stalking of the dull clod, man, he approached with almost contemptuous indifference, so that all the jungle about him knew that he was passing—all but the men he stalked.

From the dense foliage of a great tree he watched them pass—a disreputable mob of blacks, some garbed in the uniform of German East African native troops, others wearing a single garment of the same uniform, while many had reverted to the simple dress of their forbears—approximating nudity. There were many black women with them, laughing and talking as they kept pace with the men, all of whom were armed with German rifles and equipped with German belts and ammunition.

There were no white officers there, but it was none the less apparent to Tarzan that these men were from some German native command, and he guessed that they had slain their officers and taken to the jungle with their women, or had stolen some from native villages through which they must have passed. It was evident that they were putting as much ground between themselves and the coast as possible and doubtless were seeking some impenetrable fastness of the vast interior where they might inaugurate a reign of terror among the primitively armed inhabitants and by raiding, looting, and rape grow rich in goods and women at the expense of the district upon which they settled themselves.

Between two of the black women marched a slender white girl. She was hatless and with torn and disheveled clothing that had evidently once been a trim riding habit. Her coat was gone and her waist half torn from her body. Occasionally and without apparent provocation one or the other of the Negresses struck or pushed her roughly. Tarzan watched through half-closed eyes. His first impulse was to leap among them and bear the girl from their cruel clutches. He had recognized her immediately and it was because of this fact that he hesitated.

What was it to Tarzan of the Apes what fate befell this enemy spy? He had been unable to kill her himself because of an inherent weakness that would not permit him to lay hands upon a woman, all of which of course had no bearing upon what others might do to her. That her fate would now be infinitely more horrible than the quick and painless death that the ape-man would have meted to her only interested Tarzan to the extent that the more frightful the end of a German the more in keeping it would be with what they all deserved.

And so he let the blacks pass with Fräulein Bertha Kircher in their midst, or at least until the last straggling warrior suggested to his mind the pleasures of black-baiting—an amusement and a sport in which he had grown ever more proficient since that long-gone day when Kulonga, the son of Mbonga, the chief, had cast his unfortunate spear at Kala, the ape-man's foster mother.

The last man, who must have stopped for some purpose, was fully a quarter of a mile in rear of the party. He was hurrying to catch up when Tarzan saw him, and as he passed beneath the tree in which the ape-man perched above the trail, a silent noose dropped deftly about his neck. The main body still was in plain sight, and as the frightened man voiced a piercing shriek of terror, they looked back to see his body rise as though by magic straight into the air and disappear amidst the leafy foliage above.

For a moment the blacks stood paralyzed by astonishment and fear; but presently the burly sergeant, Usanga, who led them, started back along the trail at a run, calling to the others to follow him. Loading their guns as they came the blacks ran to succor their fellow, and at Usanga's command they spread into a thin line that presently entirely surrounded the tree into which their comrade had vanished.

Usanga called but received no reply; then he advanced slowly with rifle at the ready, peering up into the tree. He could see no one—nothing. The circle closed in until fifty blacks were searching among the branches with their keen eyes. What had become of their fellow? They had seen him rise into the tree and since then many eyes had been fastened upon the spot, yet there was no sign of him. One, more venturesome than his fellows, volunteered to climb into the tree and investigate. He was gone but a minute or two and when he dropped to earth again he swore that there was no sign of a creature there.

Perplexed, and by this time a bit awed, the blacks drew slowly away from the spot and with many backward glances and less laughing continued upon their journey until, when about a mile beyond the spot at which their fellow had disappeared, those in the lead saw him peering from behind a tree at one side of the trail just in front of them. With shouts to their companions that he had been found they ran forwards; but those who were first to reach the tree stopped suddenly and shrank back, their eyes rolling fearfully first in one direction and then in another as though they expected some nameless horror to leap out upon them.

Nor was their terror without foundation. Impaled upon the end of a broken branch the head of their companion was propped behind the tree so that it appeared to be looking out at them from the opposite side of the bole.

It was then that many wished to turn back, arguing that they had offended some demon of the wood upon whose preserve they had trespassed; but Usanga refused to listen to them, assuring them that inevitable torture and death awaited them should they return and fall again into the hands of their cruel German masters. At last his reasoning prevailed to the end that a much-subdued and terrified band moved in a compact mass, like a drove of sheep, forward through the valley and there were no stragglers.

It is a happy characteristic of the Negro race, which they hold in common with little children, that their spirits seldom remain depressed for a considerable length of time after the immediate cause of depression is removed, and so it was that in half an hour Usanga's band was again beginning to take on to some extent its former appearance of carefree lightheartedness. Thus were the heavy clouds of fear slowly dissipating when a turn in the trail brought them suddenly upon the headless body of their erstwhile companion lying directly in their path, and they were again plunged into the depth of fear and gloomy forebodings.

So utterly inexplicable and uncanny had the entire occurrence been that there was not a one of them who could find a ray of comfort penetrating the dead blackness of its ominous portent. What had happened to one of their number each conceived as being a wholly possible fate for himself—in fact quite his probable fate. If such a thing could happen in broad daylight what frightful thing might not fall to their lot when night had enshrouded them in her mantle of darkness. They trembled in anticipation.

The white girl in their midst was no less mystified than they; but far less moved, since sudden death was the most merciful fate to which she might now look forward. So far she had been subjected to nothing worse than the petty cruelties of the women, while, on the other hand, it had alone been the presence of the women that had saved her from worse treatment at the hands of some of the men—notably the brutal, black sergeant, Usanga. His own woman was of the party—a veritable giantess, a virago of the first magnitude—and she was evidently the only thing in the world of which Usanga stood in awe. Even though she was particularly cruel to the young woman, the latter believed that she was her sole protection from the degraded black tyrant.

Late in the afternoon the band came upon a small palisaded village of thatched huts set in a clearing in the jungle close beside a placid river. At their approach the villagers came pouring out, and Usanga advanced with two of his warriors to palaver with the chief. The experiences of the day had so shaken the nerves of the black sergeant that he was ready to treat with these people rather than take their village by force of arms, as would ordinarily have been his preference; but now a vague conviction influenced him that there watched over this part of the jungle a powerful demon who wielded miraculous power for evil against those who offended him. First Usanga would learn how these villagers stood with this savage god and if they had his good will Usanga would be most careful to treat them with kindness and respect.

At the palaver it developed that the village chief had food, goats, and fowl which he would be glad to dispose of for a proper consideration; but as the consideration would have meant parting with precious rifles and ammunition, or the very clothing from their backs, Usanga began to see that after all it might be forced upon him to wage war to obtain food.

A happy solution was arrived at by a suggestion of one of his men—that the soldiers go forth the following day and hunt for the villagers, bringing them in so much fresh meat in return for their hospitality. This the chief agreed to, stipulating the kind and quantity of game to be paid in return for flour, goats, and fowl, and a certain number of huts that were to be turned over to the visitors. The details having been settled after an hour or more of that bickering argument of which the native African is so fond, the newcomers entered the village where they were assigned to huts.

Bertha Kircher found herself alone in a small hut close to the palisade at the far end of the village street, and though she was neither bound nor guarded, she was assured by Usanga that she could not escape the village without running into almost certain death in the jungle, which the villagers assured them was infested by lions of great size and ferocity. "Be good to Usanga," he concluded, "and no harm will befall you. I will come again to see you after the others are asleep. Let us be friends."

As the brute left her the girl's frame was racked by a convulsive shudder as she sank to the floor of the hut and covered her face with her hands. She realized now why the women had not been left to guard her. It was the work of the cunning Usanga, but would not his woman suspect something of his intentions? She was no fool and, further, being imbued with insane jealousy she was ever looking for some overt act upon the part of her ebon lord. Bertha Kircher felt that only she might save her and that she would save her if word could be but gotten to her. But how?

Left alone and away from the eyes of her captors for the first time since the previous night, the girl immediately took advantage of the opportunity to assure herself that the papers she had taken from the body of Hauptmann Fritz Schneider were still safely sewn inside one of her undergarments.

Alas! Of what value could they now ever be to her beloved country? But habit and loyalty were so strong within her that she still clung to the determined hope of eventually delivering the little packet to her chief.

The natives seemed to have forgotten her existence—no one came near the hut, not even to bring her food. She could hear them at the other end of the village laughing and yelling and knew that they were celebrating with food and native beer—knowledge which only increased her apprehension. To be prisoner in a native village in the very heart of an unexplored region of Central Africa—the only white woman among a band of drunken Negroes! The very thought appalled her. Yet there was a slight promise in the fact that she had so far been unmolested—the promise that they might, indeed, have forgotten her and that soon they might become so hopelessly drunk as to be harmless.

Darkness had fallen and still no one came. The girl wondered if she dared venture forth in search of Naratu, Usanga's woman, for Usanga might not forget that he had promised to return. No one was near as she stepped out of the hut and made her way toward the part of the village where the revelers were making merry about a fire. As she approached she saw the villagers and their guests squatting in a large circle about the blaze before which a half-dozen naked warriors leaped and bent and stamped in some grotesque dance. Pots of food and gourds of drink were being passed about among the audience. Dirty hands were plunged into the food pots and the captured portions devoured so greedily that one might have thought the entire community had been upon the point of starvation. The gourds they held to their lips until the beer ran down their chins and the vessels were wrested from them by greedy neighbors. The drink had now begun to take noticeable effect upon most of them, with the result that they were beginning to give themselves up to utter and licentious abandon.

As the girl came nearer, keeping in the shadow of the huts, looking for Naratu she was suddenly discovered by one upon the edge of the crowd—a huge woman, who rose, shrieking, and came toward her. From her aspect the white girl thought that the woman meant literally to tear her to pieces. So utterly wanton and uncalled-for was the attack that it found the girl entirely unprepared, and what would have happened had not a warrior interfered may only be guessed. And then Usanga, noting the interruption, came lurching forward to question her.

"What do you want," he cried, "food and drink? Come with me!" and he threw an arm about her and dragged her toward the circle.

"No!" she cried, "I want Naratu. Where is Naratu?"

This seemed to sober the black for a moment as though he had temporarily forgotten his better half. He cast quick, fearful glances about, and then, evidently assured that Naratu had noticed nothing, he ordered the warrior who was still holding the infuriated black woman from the white girl to take the latter back to her hut and to remain there on guard over her.

First appropriating a gourd of beer for himself the warrior motioned the girl to precede him, and thus guarded she returned to her hut, the fellow squatting down just outside the doorway, where he confined his attentions for some time to the gourd.

Bertha Kircher sat down at the far side of the hut awaiting she knew not what impending fate. She could not sleep so filled was her mind with wild schemes of escape though each new one must always be discarded as impractical. Half an hour after the warrior had returned her to her prison he rose and entered the hut, where he tried to engage in conversation with her. Groping across the interior he leaned his short spear against the wall and sat down beside her, and as he talked he edged closer and closer until at last he could reach out and touch her. Shrinking, she drew away.

"Do not touch me!" she cried. "I will tell Usanga if you do not leave me alone, and you know what he will do to you."

The man only laughed drunkenly, and, reaching out his hand, grabbed her arm and dragged her toward him. She fought and cried aloud for Usanga and at the same instant the entrance to the hut was darkened by the form of a man.

"What is the matter?" shouted the newcomer in the deep tones that the girl recognized as belonging to the black sergeant. He had come, but would she be any better off? She knew that she would not unless she could play upon Usanga's fear of his woman.

When Usanga found what had happened he kicked the warrior out of the hut and bade him begone, and when the fellow had disappeared, muttering and grumbling, the sergeant approached the white girl. He was very drunk, so drunk that several times she succeeded in eluding him and twice she pushed him so violently away that he stumbled and fell.

Finally he became enraged and rushing upon her, seized her in his long, apelike arms. Striking at his face with clenched fists she tried to protect herself and drive him away. She threatened him with the wrath of Naratu, and at that he changed his tactics and began to plead, and as he argued with her, promising her safety and eventual freedom, the warrior he had kicked out of the hut made his staggering way to the hut occupied by Naratu.

Usanga finding that pleas and promises were as unavailing as threats, at last lost both his patience and his head, seizing the girl roughly, and simultaneously there burst into the hut a raging demon of jealousy. Naratu had come. Kicking, scratching, striking, biting, she routed the terrified Usanga in short order, and so obsessed was she by her desire to inflict punishment upon her unfaithful lord and master that she quite forgot the object of his infatuation.

Bertha Kircher heard her screaming down the village street at Usanga's heels and trembled at the thought of what lay in store for her at the hands of these two, for she knew that tomorrow at the latest Naratu would take out upon her the full measure of her jealous hatred after she had spent her first wrath upon Usanga.

The two had departed but a few minutes when the warrior guard returned. He looked into the hut and then entered. "No one will stop me now, white woman," he growled as he stepped quickly across the hut toward her.

Tarzan of the Apes, feasting well upon a juicy haunch from Bara, the deer, was vaguely conscious of a troubled mind. He should have been at peace with himself and all the world, for was he not in his native element surrounded by game in plenty and rapidly filling his belly with the flesh he loved best? But Tarzan of the Apes was haunted by the picture of a slight, young girl being shoved and struck by brutal Negresses, and in imagination could see her now camped in this savage country a prisoner among degraded blacks.

Why was it so difficult to remember that she was only a hated German and a spy? Why would the fact that she was a woman and white always obtrude itself upon his consciousness? He hated her as he hated all her kind, and the fate that was sure to be hers was no more terrible than she in common with all her people deserved. The matter was settled and Tarzan composed himself to think of other things, yet the picture would not die—it rose in all its details and annoyed him. He began to wonder what they were doing to her and where they were taking her. He was very much ashamed of himself as he had been after the episode in Wilhelmstal when his weakness had permitted him to spare this spy's life. Was he to be thus weak again? No!

Night came and he settled himself in an ample tree to rest until morning; but sleep would not come. Instead came the vision of a white girl being beaten by black women, and again of the same girl at the mercy of the warriors somewhere in that dark and forbidding jungle.

With a growl of anger and self-contempt Tarzan arose, shook himself, and swung from his tree to that adjoining, and thus, through the lower terraces, he followed the trail that Usanga's party had taken earlier in the afternoon. He had little difficulty as the band had followed a well-beaten path and when toward midnight the stench of a native village assailed his delicate nostrils he guessed that his goal was near and that presently he should find her whom he sought.

Prowling stealthily as prowls Numa, the lion, stalking a wary prey, Tarzan moved noiselessly about the palisade, listening and sniffing. At the rear of the village he discovered a tree whose branches extended over the top of the palisade and a moment later he had dropped quietly into the village.

From hut to hut he went searching with keen ears and nostrils some confirming evidence of the presence of the girl, and at last, faint and almost obliterated by the odor of the Gomangani, he found it hanging like a delicate vapor about a small hut. The village was quiet now, for the last of the beer and the food had been disposed of and the blacks lay in their huts overcome by stupor, yet Tarzan made no noise that even a sober man keenly alert might have heard.

He passed around to the entrance of the hut and listened. From within came no sound, not even the low breathing of one awake; yet he was sure that the girl had been here and perhaps was even now, and so he entered, slipping in as silently as a disembodied spirit. For a moment he stood motionless just within the entranceway, listening. No, there was no one here, of that he was sure, but he would investigate. As his eyes became accustomed to the greater darkness within the hut an object began to take form that presently outlined itself in a human form supine upon the floor.

Tarzan stepped closer and leaned over to examine it—it was the dead body of a naked warrior from whose chest protruded a short spear. Then he searched carefully every square foot of the remaining floor space and at last returned to the body again where he stooped and smelled of the haft of the weapon that had slain the black. A slow smile touched his lips—that and a slight movement of his head betokened that he understood.

A rapid search of the balance of the village assured him that the girl had escaped and a feeling of relief came over him that no harm had befallen her. That her life was equally in jeopardy in the savage jungle to which she must have flown did not impress him as it would have you or me, since to Tarzan the jungle was not a dangerous place—he considered one safer there than in Paris or London by night.

He had entered the trees again and was outside the palisade when there came faintly to his ears from far beyond the village an old, familiar sound. Balancing lightly upon a swaying branch he stood, a graceful statue of a forest god, listening intently. For a minute he stood thus and then there broke from his lips the long, weird cry of ape calling to ape and he was away through the jungle toward the sound of the booming drum of the anthropoids leaving behind him an awakened and terrified village of cringing blacks, who would forever after connect that eerie cry with the disappearance of their white prisoner and the death of their fellow-warrior.

Bertha Kircher, hurrying through the jungle along a well-beaten game trail, thought only of putting as much distance as possible between herself and the village before daylight could permit pursuit of her. Whither she was going she did not know, nor was it a matter of great moment since death must be her lot sooner or later.

Fortune favored her that night, for she passed unscathed through as savage and lion-ridden an area as there is in all Africa—a natural hunting ground which the white man has not yet discovered, where deer and antelope and zebra, giraffe and elephant, buffalo, rhinoceros, and the other herbivorous animals of central Africa abound unmolested by none but their natural enemies, the great cats which, lured here by easy prey and immunity from the rifles of big-game hunters, swarm the district.

She had fled for an hour or two, perhaps, when her attention was arrested by the sound of animals moving about, muttering and growling close ahead. Assured that she had covered a sufficient distance to insure her a good start in the morning before the blacks could take to her trail, and fearful of what the creatures might be, she climbed into a large tree with the intention of spending the balance of the night there.

She had no sooner reached a safe and comfortable branch when she discovered that the tree stood upon the edge of a small clearing that had been hidden from her by the heavy undergrowth upon the ground below, and simultaneously she discovered the identity of the beasts she had heard.

In the center of the clearing below her, clearly visible in the bright moonlight, she saw fully twenty huge, manlike apes—great, shaggy fellows who went upon their hind feet with only slight assistance from the knuckles of their hands. The moonlight glanced from their glossy coats, the numerous gray-tipped hairs imparting a sheen that made the hideous creatures almost magnificent in their appearance.

The girl had watched them but a minute or two when the little band was joined by others, coming singly and in groups until there were fully fifty of the great brutes gathered there in the moonlight. Among them were young apes and several little ones clinging tightly to their mothers' shaggy shoulders. Presently the group parted to form a circle about what appeared to be a small, flat-topped mound of earth in the center of the clearing. Squatting close about this mound were three old females armed with short, heavy clubs with which they presently began to pound upon the flat top of the earth mound which gave forth a dull, booming sound, and almost immediately the other apes commenced to move about restlessly, weaving in and out aimlessly until they carried the impression of a moving mass of great, black maggots.

The beating of the drum was in a slow, ponderous cadence, at first without time but presently settling into a heavy rhythm to which the apes kept time with measured tread and swaying bodies. Slowly the mass separated into two rings, the outer of which was composed of shes and the very young, the inner of mature bulls. The former ceased to move and squatted upon their haunches, while the bulls now moved slowly about in a circle the center of which was the drum and all now in the same direction.

It was then that there came faintly to the ears of the girl from the direction of the village she had recently quitted a weird and high-pitched cry. The effect upon the apes was electrical—they stopped their movements and stood in attitudes of intent listening for a moment, and then one fellow, huger than his companions, raised his face to the heavens and in a voice that sent the cold shudders through the girl's slight frame answered the far-off cry.

Once again the beaters took up their drumming and the slow dance went on. There was a certain fascination in the savage ceremony that held the girl spellbound, and as there seemed little likelihood of her being discovered, she felt that she might as well remain the balance of the night in her tree and resume her flight by the comparatively greater safety of daylight.

Assuring herself that her packet of papers was safe she sought as comfortable a position as possible among the branches, and settled herself to watch the weird proceedings in the clearing below her.

A half-hour passed, during which the cadence of the drum increased gradually. Now the great bull that had replied to the distant call leaped from the inner circle to dance alone between the drummers and the other bulls. He leaped and crouched and leaped again, now growling and barking, again stopping to raise his hideous face to Goro, the moon, and, beating upon his shaggy breast, uttered a piercing scream-the challenge of the bull ape, had the girl but known it.

He stood thus in the full glare of the great moon, motionless after screaming forth his weird challenge, in the setting of the primeval jungle and the circling apes a picture of primitive savagery and power—a mightily muscled Hercules out of the dawn of life—when from close behind her the girl heard an answering scream, and an instant later saw an almost naked white man drop from a near-by tree into the clearing.

Instantly the apes became a roaring, snarling pack of angry beasts. Bertha Kircher held her breath. What maniac was this who dared approach these frightful creatures in their own haunts, alone against fifty? She saw the brown-skinned figure bathed in moonlight walk straight toward the snarling pack. She saw the symmetry and the beauty of that perfect body—its grace, its strength, its wondrous proportioning, and then she recognized him. It was the same creature whom she had seen carry Major Schneider from General Kraut's headquarters, the same who had rescued her from Numa, the lion; the same whom she had struck down with the butt of her pistol and escaped when he would have returned her to her enemies, the same who had slain Hauptmann Fritz Schneider and spared her life that night in Wilhelmstal.

Fear-filled and fascinated she watched him as he neared the apes. She heard sounds issue from his throat—sounds identical with those uttered by the apes—and though she could scarce believe the testimony of her own ears, she knew that this godlike creature was conversing with the brutes in their own tongue.

Tarzan halted just before he reached the shes of the outer circle. "I am Tarzan of the Apes!" he cried. "You do not know me because I am of another tribe, but Tarzan comes in peace or he comes to fight—which shall it be? Tarzan will talk with your king," and so saying he pushed straight forward through the shes and the young who now gave way before him, making a narrow lane through which he passed toward the inner circle.

Shes and balus growled and bristled as he passed closer, but none hindered him and thus he came to the inner circle of bulls. Here bared fangs menaced him and growling faces hideously contorted. "I am Tarzan," he repeated. "Tarzan comes to dance the Dum-Dum with his brothers. Where is your king?" Again he pressed forward and the girl in the tree clapped her palms to her cheeks as she watched, wide-eyed, this madman going to a frightful death. In another instant they would be upon him, rending and tearing until that perfect form had been ripped to shreds; but again the ring parted, and though the apes roared and menaced him they did not attack, and at last he stood in the inner circle close to the drum and faced the great king ape.

Again he spoke. "I am Tarzan of the Apes," he cried. "Tarzan comes to live with his brothers. He will come in peace and live in peace or he will kill; but he has come and he will stay. Which—shall Tarzan dance the Dum-Dum in peace with his brothers, or shall Tarzan kill first?"

"I am Go-lat, King of the Apes," screamed the great bull. "I kill! I kill! I kill!" and with a sullen roar he charged the Tarmangani.

The ape-man, as the girl watched him, seemed entirely unprepared for the charge and she looked to see him borne down and slain at the first rush. The great bull was almost upon him with huge hands outstretched to seize him before Tarzan made a move, but when he did move his quickness would have put Ara, the lightning, to shame. As darts forward the head of Histah, the snake, so darted forward the left hand of the man-beast as he seized the left wrist of his antagonist. A quick turn and the bull's right arm was locked beneath the right arm of his foe in a jujutsu hold that Tarzan had learned among civilized men—a hold with which he might easily break the great bones, a hold that left the ape helpless.

"I am Tarzan of the Apes!" screamed the ape-man. "Shall Tarzan dance in peace or shall Tarzan kill?"

"I kill! I kill! I kill!" shrieked Go-lat.

With the quickness of a cat Tarzan swung the king ape over one hip and sent him sprawling to the ground. "I am Tarzan, King of all the Apes!" he shouted. "Shall it be peace?"

Go-lat, infuriated, leaped to his feet and charged again, shouting his war cry: "I kill! I kill! I kill!" and again Tarzan met him with a sudden hold that the stupid bull, being ignorant of, could not possibly avert—a hold and a throw that brought a scream of delight from the interested audience and suddenly filled the girl with doubts as to the man's madness—evidently he was quite safe among the apes, for she saw him swing Go-lat to his back and then catapult him over his shoulder. The king ape fell upon his head and lay very still.

"I am Tarzan of the Apes!" cried the ape-man. "I come to dance the Dum-Dum with my brothers," and he made a motion to the drummers, who immediately took up the cadence of the dance where they had dropped it to watch their king slay the foolish Tarmangani.

It was then that Go-lat raised his head and slowly crawled to his feet. Tarzan approached him. "I am Tarzan of the Apes," he cried. "Shall Tarzan dance the Dum-Dum with his brothers now, or shall he kill first?"

Go-lat raised his bloodshot eyes to the face of the Tarmangani. "Kagoda!" he cried. "Tarzan of the Apes will dance the Dum-Dum with his brothers and Go-lat will dance with him!"

And then the girl in the tree saw the savage man leaping, bending, and stamping with the savage apes in the ancient rite of the Dum-Dum. His roars and growls were more beastly than the beasts. His handsome face was distorted with savage ferocity. He beat upon his great breast and screamed forth his challenge as his smooth, brown hide brushed the shaggy coats of his fellows. It was weird; it was wonderful; and in its primitive savagery it was not without beauty—the strange scene she looked upon, such a scene as no other human being, probably, ever had witnessed—and yet, withal, it was horrible.

As she gazed, spell-bound, a stealthy movement in the tree behind her caused her to turn her head, and there, back of her, blazing in the reflected moonlight, shone two great, yellow-green eyes. Sheeta, the panther, had found her out.

The beast was so close that it might have reached out and touched her with a great, taloned paw. There was no time to think, no time to weigh chances or to choose alternatives. Terror-inspired impulse was her guide as, with a loud scream, she leaped from the tree into the clearing.

Instantly the apes, now maddened by the effects of the dancing and the moonlight, turned to note the cause of the interruption. They saw this she Tarmangani, helpless and alone and they started for her. Sheeta, the panther, knowing that not even Numa, the lion, unless maddened by starvation, dares meddle with the great apes at their Dum-Dum, had silently vanished into the night, seeking his supper elsewhere.

Tarzan, turning with the other apes toward the cause of the interruption, saw the girl, recognized her and also her peril. Here again might she die at the hands of others; but why consider it! He knew that he could not permit it, and though the acknowledgment shamed him, it had to be admitted.

The leading shes were almost upon the girl when Tarzan leaped among them, and with heavy blows scattered them to right and left; and then as the bulls came to share in the kill they thought this new ape-thing was about to make that he might steal all the flesh for himself, they found him facing them with an arm thrown about the creature as though to protect her.

"This is Tarzan's she," he said. "Do not harm her." It was the only way he could make them understand that they must not slay her. He was glad that she could not interpret the words. It was humiliating enough to make such a statement to wild apes about this hated enemy.

So once again Tarzan of the Apes was forced to protect a Hun. Growling, he muttered to himself in extenuation:

"She is a woman and I am not a German, so it could not be otherwise!"

CHAPTER IX—DROPPED FROM THE SKY

Lieutenant Harold Percy Smith-Oldwick, Royal Air Service, was on reconnaissance. A report, or it would be better to say a rumor, had come to the British headquarters in German East Africa that the enemy had landed in force on the west coast and was marching across the dark continent to reinforce their colonial troops. In fact the new army was supposed to be no more than ten or twelve days' march to the west. Of course the thing was ridiculous—preposterous—but preposterous things often happen in war; and anyway no good general permits the least rumor of enemy activity to go uninvestigated.

Therefore Lieutenant Harold Percy Smith-Oldwick flew low toward the west, searching with keen eyes for signs of a Hun army. Vast forests unrolled beneath him in which a German army corps might have lain concealed, so dense was the overhanging foliage of the great trees. Mountain, meadowland, and desert passed in lovely panorama; but never a sight of man had the young lieutenant.

Always hoping that he might discover some sign of their passage—a discarded lorry, a broken limber, or an old camp site—he continued farther and farther into the west until well into the afternoon. Above a tree-dotted plain through the center of which flowed a winding river he determined to turn about and start for camp. It would take straight flying at top speed to cover the distance before dark; but as he had ample gasoline and a trustworthy machine there was no doubt in his mind but that he could accomplish his aim. It was then that his engine stalled.

He was too low to do anything but land, and that immediately, while he had the more open country accessible, for directly east of him was a vast forest into which a stalled engine could only have plunged him to certain injury and probable death; and so he came down in the meadowland near the winding river and there started to tinker with his motor.

As he worked he hummed a tune, some music-hall air that had been popular in London the year before, so that one might have thought him working in the security of an English flying field surrounded by innumerable comrades rather than alone in the heart of an unexplored African wilderness. It was typical of the man that he should be wholly indifferent to his surroundings, although his looks entirely belied any assumption that he was of particularly heroic strain.

Lieutenant Harold Percy Smith-Oldwick was fair-haired, blue-eyed, and slender, with a rosy, boyish face that might have been molded more by an environment of luxury, indolence, and ease than the more strenuous exigencies of life's sterner requirements.

And not only was the young lieutenant outwardly careless of the immediate future and of his surroundings, but actually so. That the district might be infested by countless enemies seemed not to have occurred to him in the remotest degree. He bent assiduously to the work of correcting the adjustment that had caused his motor to stall without so much as an upward glance at the surrounding country. The forest to the east of him, and the more distant jungle that bordered the winding river, might have harbored an army of bloodthirsty savages, but neither could elicit even a passing show of interest on the part of Lieutenant Smith-Oldwick.

And even had he looked, it is doubtful if he would have seen the score of figures crouching in the concealment of the undergrowth at the forest's edge. There are those who are reputed to be endowed with that which is sometimes, for want of a better appellation, known as the sixth sense—a species of intuition which apprises them of the presence of an unseen danger. The concentrated gaze of a hidden observer provokes a warning sensation of nervous unrest in such as these, but though twenty pairs of savage eyes were gazing fixedly at Lieutenant Harold Percy Smith-Oldwick, the fact aroused no responsive sensation of impending danger in his placid breast. He hummed peacefully and, his adjustment completed, tried out his motor for a minute or two, then shut it off and descended to the ground with the intention of stretching his legs and taking a smoke before continuing his return flight to camp. Now for the first time he took note of his surroundings, to be immediately impressed by both the wildness and the beauty of the scene. In some respects the tree-dotted meadowland reminded him of a park-like English forest, and that wild beasts and savage men could ever be a part of so quiet a scene seemed the remotest of contingencies.

Some gorgeous blooms upon a flowering shrub at a little distance from his machine caught the attention of his aesthetic eye, and as he puffed upon his cigarette, he walked over to examine the flowers more closely. As he bent above them he was probably some hundred yards from his plane and it was at this instant that Numabo, chief of the Wamabo, chose to leap from his ambush and lead his warriors in a sudden rush upon the white man.

The young Englishman's first intimation of danger was a chorus of savage yells from the forest behind him. Turning, he saw a score of naked, black warriors advancing rapidly toward him. They moved in a compact mass and as they approached more closely their rate of speed noticeably diminished. Lieutenant Smith-Oldwick realized in a quick glance that the direction of their approach and their proximity had cut off all chances of retreating to his plane, and he also understood that their attitude was entirely warlike and menacing. He saw that they were armed with spears and with bows and arrows, and he felt quite confident that notwithstanding the fact that he was armed with a pistol they could overcome him with the first rush. What he did not know about their tactics was that at any show of resistance they would fall back, which is the nature of the native Negroes, but that after numerous advances and retreats, during which they would work themselves into a frenzy of rage by much shrieking, leaping, and dancing, they would eventually come to the point of a determined and final assault.

Numabo was in the forefront, a fact which taken in connection with his considerably greater size and more warlike appearance, indicated him as the natural target and it was at Numabo that the Englishman aimed his first shot. Unfortunately for him it missed its target, as the killing of the chief might have permanently dispersed the others. The bullet passed Numabo to lodge in the breast of a warrior behind him and as the fellow lunged forward with a scream the others turned and retreated, but to the lieutenant's chagrin they ran in the direction of the plane instead of back toward the forest so that he was still cut off from reaching his machine.

Presently they stopped and faced him again. They were talking loudly and gesticulating, and after a moment one of them leaped into the air, brandishing his spear and uttering savage war cries, which soon had their effect upon his fellows so that it was not long ere all of them were taking part in the wild show of savagery, which would bolster their waning courage and presently spur them on to another attack.

The second charge brought them closer to the Englishman, and though he dropped another with his pistol, it was not before two or three spears had been launched at him. He now had five shots remaining and there were still eighteen warriors to be accounted for, so that unless he could frighten them off, it was evident that his fate was sealed.

That they must pay the price of one life for every attempt to take his had its effect upon them and they were longer now in initiating a new rush and when they did so it was more skillfully ordered than those that had preceded it, for they scattered into three bands which, partially surrounding him, came simultaneously toward him from different directions, and though he emptied his pistol with good effect, they reached him at last. They seemed to know that his ammunition was exhausted, for they circled close about him now with the evident intention of taking him alive, since they might easily have riddled him with their sharp spears with perfect safety to themselves.

For two or three minutes they circled about him until, at a word from Numabo, they closed in simultaneously, and though the slender young lieutenant struck out to right and left, he was soon overwhelmed by superior numbers and beaten down by the hafts of spears in brawny hands.

He was all but unconscious when they finally dragged him to his feet, and after securing his hands behind his back, pushed him roughly along ahead of them toward the jungle.

As the guard prodded him along the narrow trail, Lieutenant Smith-Oldwick could not but wonder why they had wished to take him alive. He knew that he was too far inland for his uniform to have any significance to this native tribe to whom no inkling of the World War probably ever had come, and he could only assume that he had fallen into the hands of the warriors of some savage potentate upon whose royal caprice his fate would hinge.

They had marched for perhaps half an hour when the Englishman saw ahead of them, in a little clearing upon the bank of the river, the thatched roofs of native huts showing above a crude but strong palisade; and presently he was ushered into a village street where he was immediately surrounded by a throng of women and children and warriors. Here he was soon the center of an excited mob whose intent seemed to be to dispatch him as quickly as possible. The women were more venomous than the men, striking and scratching him whenever they could reach him, until at last Numabo, the chief, was obliged to interfere to save his prisoner for whatever purpose he was destined.

As the warriors pushed the crowd back, opening a space through which the white man was led toward a hut, Lieutenant Smith-Oldwick saw coming from the opposite end of the village a number of Negroes wearing odds and ends of German uniforms. He was not a little surprised at this, and his first thought was that he had at last come in contact with some portion of the army which was rumored to be crossing from the west coast and for signs of which he had been searching.

A rueful smile touched his lips as he contemplated the unhappy circumstances which surrounded the accession of this knowledge for though he was far from being without hope, he realized that only by the merest chance could he escape these people and regain his machine.

Among the partially uniformed blacks was a huge fellow in the tunic of a sergeant and as this man's eyes fell upon the British officer, a loud cry of exultation broke from his lips, and immediately his followers took up the cry and pressed forward to bait the prisoner.

"Where did you get the Englishman?" asked Usanga, the black sergeant, of the chief Numabo. "Are there many more with him?"

"He came down from the sky," replied the native chief, "in a strange thing which flies like a bird and which frightened us very much at first; but we watched for a long time and saw that it did not seem to be alive, and when this white man left it we attacked him and though he killed some of my warriors, we took him, for we Wamabos are brave men and great warriors."

Usanga's eyes went wide. "He flew here through the sky?" he asked.

"Yes," said Numabo. "In a great thing which resembled a bird he flew down out of the sky. The thing is still there where it came down close to the four trees near the second bend in the river. We left it there because, not knowing what it was, we were afraid to touch it and it is still there if it has not flown away again."

"It cannot fly," said Usanga, "without this man in it. It is a terrible thing which filled the hearts of our soldiers with terror, for it flew over our camps at night and dropped bombs upon us. It is well that you captured this white man, Numabo, for with his great bird he would have flown over your village tonight and killed all your people. These Englishmen are very wicked white men."

"He will fly no more," said Numabo. "It is not intended that a man should fly through the air; only wicked demons do such things as that and Numabo, the chief, will see that this white man does not do it again," and with the words he pushed the young officer roughly toward a hut in the center of the village, where he was left under guard of two stalwart warriors.

For an hour or more the prisoner was left to his own devices, which consisted in vain and unremitting attempts to loosen the strands which fettered his wrists, and then he was interrupted by the appearance of the black sergeant Usanga, who entered his hut and approached him.

"What are they going to do with me?" asked the Englishman. "My country is not at war with these people. You speak their language. Tell them that I am not an enemy, that my people are the friends of the black people and that they must let me go in peace."

Usanga laughed. "They do not know an Englishman from a German," he replied. "It is nothing to them what you are, except that you are a white man and an enemy."

"Then why did they take me alive?" asked the lieutenant.

"Come," said Usanga and he led the Englishman to the doorway of the hut. "Look," he said, and pointed a black forefinger toward the end of the village street where a wider space between the huts left a sort of plaza.

Here Lieutenant Harold Percy Smith-Oldwick saw a number of Negresses engaged in laying fagots around a stake and in preparing fires beneath a number of large cooking vessels. The sinister suggestion was only too obvious.

Usanga was eyeing the white man closely, but if he expected to be rewarded by any signs of fear, he was doomed to disappointment and the young lieutenant merely turned toward him with a shrug: "Really now, do you beggars intend eating me?"

"Not my people," replied Usanga. "We do not eat human flesh, but the Wamabos do. It is they who will eat you, but we will kill you for the feast, Englishman."

The Englishman remained standing in the doorway of the hut, an interested spectator of the preparations for the coming orgy that was so horribly to terminate his earthly existence. It can hardly be assumed that he felt no fear; yet, if he did, he hid it perfectly beneath an imperturbable mask of coolness. Even the brutal Usanga must have been impressed by the bravery of his victim since, though he had come to abuse and possibly to torture the helpless prisoner, he now did neither, contenting himself merely with berating whites as a race and Englishmen especially, because of the terror the British aviators had caused Germany's native troops in East Africa.

"No more," he concluded, "will your great bird fly over our people dropping death among them from the skies—Usanga will see to that," and he walked abruptly away toward a group of his own fighting men who were congregated near the stake where they were laughing and joking with the women.

A few minutes later the Englishman saw them pass out of the village gate, and once again his thoughts reverted to various futile plans for escape.

Several miles north of the village on a little rise of ground close to the river where the jungle, halting at the base of a knoll, had left a few acres of grassy land sparsely wooded, a man and a girl were busily engaged in constructing a small boma, in the center of which a thatched hut already had been erected.

They worked almost in silence with only an occasional word of direction or interrogation between them.

Except for a loin cloth, the man was naked, his smooth skin tanned to a deep brown by the action of sun and wind. He moved with the graceful ease of a jungle cat and when he lifted heavy weights, the action seemed as effortless as the raising of empty hands.

When he was not looking at her, and it was seldom that he did, the girl found her eyes wandering toward him, and at such times there was always a puzzled expression upon her face as though she found in him an enigma which she could not solve. As a matter of fact, her feelings toward him were not un-tinged with awe, since in the brief period of their association she had discovered in this handsome, godlike giant the attributes of the superman and the savage beast closely intermingled. At first she had felt only that unreasoning feminine terror which her unhappy position naturally induced.

To be alone in the heart of an unexplored wilderness of Central Africa with a savage wild man was in itself sufficiently appalling, but to feel also that this man was a blood enemy, that he hated her and her kind and that in addition thereto he owed her a personal grudge for an attack she had made upon him in the past, left no loophole for any hope that he might accord her even the minutest measure of consideration.

She had seen him first months since when he had entered the headquarters of the German high command in East Africa and carried off the luckless Major Schneider, of whose fate no hint had ever reached the German officers; and she had seen him again upon that occasion when he had rescued her from the clutches of the lion and, after explaining to her that he had recognized her in the British camp, had made her prisoner. It was then that she had struck him down with the butt of her pistol and escaped. That he might seek no personal revenge for her act had been evidenced in Wilhelmstal the night that he had killed Hauptmann Fritz Schneider and left without molesting her.

No, she could not fathom him. He hated her and at the same time he had protected her as had been evidenced again when he had kept the great apes from tearing her to pieces after she had escaped from the Wamabo village to which Usanga, the black sergeant, had brought her a captive; but why was he saving her? For what sinister purpose could this savage enemy be protecting her from the other denizens of his cruel jungle? She tried to put from her mind the probable fate which awaited her, yet it persisted in obtruding itself upon her thoughts, though always she was forced to admit that there was nothing in the demeanor of the man to indicate that her fears were well grounded. She judged him perhaps by the standards other men had taught her and because she looked upon him as a savage creature, she felt that she could not expect more of chivalry from him than was to be found in the breasts of the civilized men of her acquaintance.

Fräulein Bertha Kircher was by nature a companionable and cheerful character. She was not given to morbid forebodings, and above all things she craved the society of her kind and that interchange of thought which is one of the marked distinctions between man and the lower animals. Tarzan, on the other hand, was sufficient unto himself. Long years of semi-solitude among creatures whose powers of oral expression are extremely limited had thrown him almost entirely upon his own resources for entertainment.

His active mind was never idle, but because his jungle mates could neither follow nor grasp the vivid train of imaginings that his man-mind wrought, he had long since learned to keep them to himself; and so now he found no need for confiding them in others. This fact, linked with that of his dislike for the girl, was sufficient to seal his lips for other than necessary conversation, and so they worked on together in comparative silence. Bertha Kircher, however, was nothing if not feminine and she soon found that having someone to talk to who would not talk was extremely irksome. Her fear of the man was gradually departing, and she was full of a thousand unsatisfied curiosities as to his plans for the future in so far as they related to her, as well as more personal questions regarding himself, since she could not but wonder as to his antecedents and his strange and solitary life in the jungle, as well as his friendly intercourse with the savage apes among which she had found him.

With the waning of her fears she became sufficiently emboldened to question him, and so she asked him what he intended doing after the hut and boma were completed.

"I am going to the west coast where I was born," replied Tarzan. "I do not know when. I have all my life before me and in the jungle there is no reason for haste. We are not forever running as fast as we can from one place to another as are you of the outer world. When I have been here long enough I will go on toward the west, but first I must see that you have a safe place in which to sleep, and that you have learned how to provide yourself with necessaries. That will take time."

"You are going to leave me here alone?" cried the girl; her tones marked the fear which the prospect induced. "You are going to leave me here alone in this terrible jungle, a prey to wild beasts and savage men, hundreds of miles from a white settlement and in a country which gives every evidence of never having been touched by the foot of civilized men?"

"Why not?" asked Tarzan. "I did not bring you here. Would one of your men accord any better treatment to an enemy woman?"

"Yes," she exclaimed. "They certainly would. No man of my race would leave a defenseless white woman alone in this horrible place."

Tarzan shrugged his broad shoulders. The conversation seemed profitless and it was further distasteful to him for the reason that it was carried on in German, a tongue which he detested as much as he did the people who spoke it. He wished that the girl spoke English and then it occurred to him that as he had seen her in disguise in the British camp carrying on her nefarious work as a German spy, she probably did speak English and so he asked her.

"Of course I speak English," she exclaimed, "but I did not know that you did."

Tarzan looked his wonderment but made no comment. He only wondered why the girl should have any doubts as to the ability of an Englishman to speak English, and then suddenly it occurred to him that she probably looked upon him merely as a beast of the jungle who by accident had learned to speak German through frequenting the district which Germany had colonized. It was there only that she had seen him and so she might not know that he was an Englishman by birth, and that he had had a home in British East Africa. It was as well, he thought, that she knew little of him, as the less she knew the more he might learn from her as to her activities in behalf of the Germans and of the German spy system of which she was a representative; and so it occurred to him to let her continue to think that he was only what he appeared to be—a savage denizen of his savage jungle, a man of no race and no country, hating all white men impartially; and this in truth, was what she did think of him. It explained perfectly his attacks upon Major Schneider and the Major's brother, Hauptmann Fritz.

Again they worked on in silence upon the boma which was now nearly completed, the girl helping the man to the best of her small ability. Tarzan could not but note with grudging approval the spirit of helpfulness she manifested in the oft-times painful labor of gathering and arranging the thorn bushes which constituted the temporary protection against roaming carnivores. Her hands and arms gave bloody token of the sharpness of the numerous points that had lacerated her soft flesh, and even though she were an enemy Tarzan could not but feel compunction that he had permitted her to do this work, and at last he bade her stop.

"Why?" she asked. "It is no more painful to me than it must be to you, and, as it is solely for my protection that you are building this boma, there is no reason why I should not do my share."

"You are a woman," replied Tarzan. "This is not a woman's work. If you wish to do something, take those gourds I brought this morning and fill them with water at the river. You may need it while I am away."

"While you are away—" she said. "You are going away?"

"When the boma is built I am going out after meat," he replied. "Tomorrow I will go again and take you and show you how you may make your own kills after I am gone."

Without a word she took the gourds and walked toward the river. As she filled them, her mind was occupied with painful forebodings of the future. She knew that Tarzan had passed a death sentence upon her, and that the moment that he left her, her doom was sealed, for it could be but a question of time—a very short time—before the grim jungle would claim her, for how could a lone woman hope successfully to combat the savage forces of destruction which constituted so large a part of existence in the jungle?

So occupied was she with the gloomy prophecies that she had neither ears nor eyes for what went on about her. Mechanically she filled the gourds and, taking them up, turned slowly to retrace her steps to the boma only to voice immediately a half-stifled scream and shrink back from the menacing figure looming before her and blocking her way to the hut.

Go-lat, the king ape, hunting a little apart from his tribe, had seen the woman go to the river for water, and it was he who confronted her when she turned back with her filled gourds. Go-lat was not a pretty creature when judged by standards of civilized humanity, though the shes of his tribe and even Go-lat himself, considered his glossy black coat shot with silver, his huge arms dangling to his knees, his bullet head sunk between his mighty shoulders, marks of great personal beauty. His wicked, bloodshot eyes and broad nose, his ample mouth and great fighting fangs only enhanced the claim of this Adonis of the forest upon the affections of his shes.

Doubtless in the little, savage brain there was a well-formed conviction that this strange she belonging to the Tarmangani must look with admiration upon so handsome a creature as Go-lat, for there could be no doubt in the mind of any that his beauty entirely eclipsed such as the hairless white ape might lay claim to.

But Bertha Kircher saw only a hideous beast, a fierce and terrible caricature of man. Could Go-lat have known what passed through her mind, he must have been terribly chagrined, though the chances are that he would have attributed it to a lack of discernment on her part. Tarzan heard the girl's cry and looking up saw at a glance the cause of her terror. Leaping lightly over the boma, he ran swiftly toward her as Go-lat lumbered closer to the girl the while he voiced his emotions in low gutturals which, while in reality the most amicable of advances, sounded to the girl like the growling of an enraged beast. As Tarzan drew nearer he called aloud to the ape and the girl heard from the human lips the same sounds that had fallen from those of the anthropoid.

"I will not harm your she," Go-lat called to Tarzan.

"I know it," replied the ape-man, "but she does not. She is like Numa and Sheeta, who do not understand our talk. She thinks you come to harm her."

By this time Tarzan was beside the girl. "He will not harm you," he said to her. "You need not be afraid. This ape has learned his lesson. He has learned that Tarzan is lord of the jungle. He will not harm that which is Tarzan's."

The girl cast a quick glance at the man's face. It was evident to her that the words he had spoken meant nothing to him and that the assumed proprietorship over her was, like the boma, only another means for her protection.

"But I am afraid of him," she said.

"You must not show your fear. You will be often surrounded by these apes. At such times you will be safest. Before I leave you I will give you the means of protecting yourself against them should one of them chance to turn upon you. If I were you I would seek their society. Few are the animals of the jungle that dare attack the great apes when there are several of them together. If you let them know that you are afraid of them, they will take advantage of it and your life will be constantly menaced. The shes especially would attack you. I will let them know that you have the means of protecting yourself and of killing them. If necessary, I will show you how and then they will respect and fear you."

"I will try," said the girl, "but I am afraid that it will be difficult. He is the most frightful creature I ever have seen." Tarzan smiled. "Doubtless he thinks the same of you," he said.

By this time other apes had entered the clearing and they were now the center of a considerable group, among which were several bulls, some young shes, and some older ones with their little balus clinging to their backs or frolicking around at their feet. Though they had seen the girl the night of the Dum-Dum when Sheeta had forced her to leap from her concealment into the arena where the apes were dancing, they still evinced a great curiosity regarding her. Some of the shes came very close and plucked at her garments, commenting upon them to one another in their strange tongue. The girl, by the exercise of all the will power she could command, succeeded in passing through the ordeal without evincing any of the terror and revulsion that she felt. Tarzan watched her closely, a half-smile upon his face. He was not so far removed from recent contact with civilized people that he could not realize the torture that she was undergoing, but he felt no pity for this woman of a cruel enemy who doubtless deserved the worst suffering that could be meted to her. Yet, notwithstanding his sentiments toward her, he was forced to admire her fine display of courage. Suddenly he turned to the apes.

"Tarzan goes to hunt for himself and his she," he said. "The she will remain there," and he pointed toward the hut. "See that no member of the tribe harms her. Do you understand?"

The apes nodded. "We will not harm her," said Go-lat.

"No," said Tarzan. "You will not. For if you do, Tarzan will kill you," and then turning to the girl, "Come," he said, "I am going to hunt now. You had better remain at the hut. The apes have promised not to harm you. I will leave my spear with you. It will be the best weapon you could have in case you should need to protect yourself, but I doubt if you will be in any danger for the short time that I am away."

He walked with her as far as the boma and when she had entered he closed the gap with thorn bushes and turned away toward the forest. She watched him moving across the clearing, noting the easy, catlike tread and the grace of every movement that harmonized so well with the symmetry and perfection of his figure. At the forest's edge she saw him swing lightly into a tree and disappear from view, and then, being a woman, she entered the hut and, throwing herself upon the ground, burst into tears.

CHAPTER X—IN THE HANDS OF SAVAGES

Tarzan sought Bara, the deer, or Horta, the boar, for of all the jungle animals he doubted if any would prove more palatable to the white woman, but though his keen nostrils were ever on the alert, he traveled far without being rewarded with even the faintest scent spoor of the game he sought. Keeping close to the river where he hoped to find Bara or Horta approaching or leaving a drinking place he came at last upon the strong odor of the Wamabo village and being ever ready to pay his hereditary enemies, the Gomangani, an undesired visit, he swung into a detour and came up in the rear of the village. From a tree which overhung the palisade he looked down into the street where he saw the preparations going on which his experience told him indicated the approach of one of those frightful feasts the piece de resistance of which is human flesh.

One of Tarzan's chief divertissements was the baiting of the blacks. He realized more keen enjoyment through annoying and terrifying them than from any other source of amusement the grim jungle offered. To rob them of their feast in some way that would strike terror to their hearts would give him the keenest of pleasure, and so he searched the village with his eyes for some indication of the whereabouts of the prisoner. His view was circumscribed by the dense foliage of the tree in which he sat, and, so that he might obtain a better view, he climbed further aloft and moved cautiously out upon a slender branch.

Tarzan of the Apes possessed a woodcraft scarcely short of the marvelous but even Tarzan's wondrous senses were not infallible. The branch upon which he made his way outward from the bole was no smaller than many that had borne his weight upon countless other occasions. Outwardly it appeared strong and healthy and was in full foliage, nor could Tarzan know that close to the stem a burrowing insect had eaten away half the heart of the solid wood beneath the bark.

And so when he reached a point far out upon the limb, it snapped close to the bole of the tree without warning. Below him were no larger branches that he might clutch and as he lunged downward his foot caught in a looped creeper so that he turned completely over and alighted on the flat of his back in the center of the village street.

At the sound of the breaking limb and the crashing body falling through the branches the startled blacks scurried to their huts for weapons, and when the braver of them emerged, they saw the still form of an almost naked white man lying where he had fallen. Emboldened by the fact that he did not move they approached more closely, and when their eyes discovered no signs of others of his kind in the tree, they rushed forward until a dozen warriors stood about him with ready spears. At first they thought that the falling had killed him, but upon closer examination they discovered that the man was only stunned. One of the warriors was for thrusting a spear through his heart, but Numabo, the chief, would not permit it.

"Bind him," he said. "We will feed well tonight."

And so they bound his hands and feet with thongs of gut and carried him into the hut where Lieutenant Harold Percy Smith-Oldwick awaited his fate. The Englishman had also been bound hand and foot by this time for fear that at the last moment he might escape and rob them of their feast. A great crowd of natives were gathered about the hut attempting to get a glimpse of the new prisoner, but Numabo doubled the guard before the entrance for fear that some of his people, in the exuberance of their savage joy, might rob the others of the pleasures of the death dance which would precede the killing of the victims.

The young Englishman had heard the sound of Tarzan's body crashing through the tree to the ground and the commotion in the village which immediately followed, and now, as he stood with his back against the wall of the hut, he looked upon the fellow-prisoner that the blacks carried in and laid upon the floor with mixed feelings of surprise and compassion. He realized that he never had seen a more perfect specimen of manhood than that of the unconscious figure before him, and he wondered to what sad circumstances the man owed his capture. It was evident that the new prisoner was himself as much a savage as his captors if apparel and weapons were any criterion by which to judge; yet it was also equally evident that he was a white man and from his well-shaped head and clean-cut features that he was not one of those unhappy halfwits who so often revert to savagery even in the heart of civilized communities.

As he watched the man, he presently noticed that his eyelids were moving. Slowly they opened and a pair of gray eyes looked blankly about. With returning consciousness the eyes assumed their natural expression of keen intelligence, and a moment later, with an effort, the prisoner rolled over upon his side and drew himself to a sitting position. He was facing the Englishman, and as his eyes took in the bound ankles and the arms drawn tightly behind the other's back, a slow smile lighted his features.

"They will fill their bellies tonight," he said.

The Englishman grinned. "From the fuss they made," he said, "the beggars must be awfully hungry. They like to have eaten me alive when they brought me in. How did they get you?"

Tarzan shrugged his head ruefully. "It was my own fault," he replied. "I deserve to be eaten. I crawled out upon a branch that would not bear my weight and when it broke, instead of alighting on my feet, I caught my foot in a trailer and came down on my head. Otherwise they would not have taken me—alive."

"Is there no escape?" asked the Englishman.

"I have escaped them before," replied Tarzan, "and I have seen others escape them. I have seen a man taken away from the stake after a dozen spear thrusts had pierced his body and the fire had been lighted about his feet."

Lieutenant Smith-Oldwick shuddered. "God!" he exclaimed, "I hope I don't have to face that. I believe I could stand anything but the thought of the fire. I should hate like the devil to go into a funk before the devils at the last moment."

"Don't worry," said Tarzan. "It doesn't last long and you won't funk. It is really not half as bad as it sounds. There is only a brief period of pain before you lose consciousness. I have seen it many times before. It is as good a way to go as another. We must die sometime. What difference whether it be tonight, tomorrow night, or a year hence, just so that we have lived—and I have lived!"

"Your philosophy may be all right, old top," said the young lieutenant, "but I can't say that it is exactly satisfying."

Tarzan laughed. "Roll over here," he said, "where I can get at your bonds with my teeth." The Englishman did as he was bid and presently Tarzan was working at the thongs with his strong white teeth. He felt them giving slowly beneath his efforts. In another moment they would part, and then it would be a comparatively simple thing for the Englishman to remove the remaining bonds from Tarzan and himself.

It was then that one of the guards entered the hut. In an instant he saw what the new prisoner was doing and raising his spear, struck the ape-man a vicious blow across the head with its shaft. Then he called in the other guards and together they fell upon the luckless men, kicking and beating them unmercifully, after which they bound the Englishman more securely than before and tied both men fast on opposite sides of the hut. When they had gone Tarzan looked across at his companion in misery.

"While there is life," he said, "there is hope," but he grinned as he voiced the ancient truism.

Lieutenant Harold Percy Smith-Oldwick returned the other's smile. "I fancy," he said, "that we are getting short on both. It must be close to supper time now."

Zu-tag hunted alone far from the balance of the tribe of Go-lat, the great ape. Zu-tag (Big-neck) was a young bull but recently arrived at maturity. He was large, powerful, and ferocious and at the same time far above the average of his kind in intelligence as was denoted by a fuller and less receding forehead. Already Go-lat saw in this young ape a possible contender for the laurels of his kingship and consequently the old bull looked upon Zu-tag with jealousy and disfavor. It was for this reason, possibly, as much as another that Zu-tag hunted so often alone; but it was his utter fearlessness that permitted him to wander far afield away from the protection which numbers gave the great apes. One of the results of this habit was a greatly increased resourcefulness which found him constantly growing in intelligence and powers of observation.

Today he had been hunting toward the south and was returning along the river upon a path he often followed because it led by the village of the Gomangani whose strange and almost apelike actions and peculiar manners of living had aroused his interest and curiosity. As he had done upon other occasions he took up his position in a tree from which he could overlook the interior of the village and watch the blacks at their vocations in the street below.

Zu-tag had scarcely more than established himself in his tree when, with the blacks, he was startled by the crashing of Tarzan's body from the branches of another jungle giant to the ground within the palisade. He saw the Negroes gather about the prostrate form and later carry it into the hut; and once he rose to his full height upon the limb where he had been squatting and raised his face to the heavens to scream out a savage protest and a challenge, for he had recognized in the brown-skinned Tarmangani the strange white ape who had come among them a night or two before in the midst of their Dum-Dum, and who by so easily mastering the greatest among them, had won the savage respect and admiration of this fierce young bull.

But Zu-tag's ferocity was tempered by a certain native cunning and caution. Before he had voiced his protest there formed in his mind the thought that he would like to save this wonderful white ape from the common enemy, the Gomangani, and so he screamed forth no challenge, wisely determining that more could be accomplished by secrecy and stealth than by force of muscle and fang.

At first he thought to enter the village alone and carry off the Tarmangani; but when he saw how numerous were the warriors and that several sat directly before the entrance to the lair into which the prisoner had been carried, it occurred to him that this was work for many rather than one, and so, as silently as he had come, he slipped away through the foliage toward the north.

The tribe was still loitering about the clearing where stood the hut that Tarzan and Bertha Kircher had built. Some were idly searching for food just within the forest's edge, while others squatted beneath the shade of trees within the clearing.

The girl had emerged from the hut, her tears dried and was gazing anxiously toward the south into the jungle where Tarzan had disappeared. Occasionally she cast suspicious glances in the direction of the huge shaggy anthropoids about her. How easy it would be for one of those great beasts to enter the boma and slay her. How helpless she was, even with the spear that the white man had left her, she realized as she noted for the thousandth time the massive shoulders, the bull necks, and the great muscles gliding so easily beneath the glossy coats. Never, she thought, had she seen such personifications of brute power as were represented by these mighty bulls. Those huge hands would snap her futile spear as she might snap a match in two, while their lightest blow could crush her into insensibility and death.

It was while she was occupied with these depressing thoughts that there dropped suddenly into the clearing from the trees upon the south the figure of a mighty young bull. At that time all of the apes looked much alike to Bertha Kircher, nor was it until some time later that she realized that each differed from the others in individual characteristics of face and figure as do individuals of the human races. Yet even then she could not help but note the wondrous strength and agility of this great beast, and as he approached she even found herself admiring the sheen of his heavy, black, silvershot coat.

It was evident that the newcomer was filled with suppressed excitement. His demeanor and bearing proclaimed this even from afar, nor was the girl the only one to note it. For as they saw him coming many of the apes arose and advanced to meet him, bristling and growling as is their way. Go-lat was among these latter, and he advanced stiffly with the hairs upon his neck and down his spine erect, uttering low growls and baring his fighting fangs, for who might say whether Zu-tag came in peace or otherwise? The old king had seen other young apes come thus in his day filled with a sudden resolution to wrest the kingship from their chief. He had seen bulls about to run amuck burst thus suddenly from the jungle upon the members of the tribe, and so Go-lat took no chances.

Had Zu-tag come indolently, feeding as he came, he might have entered the tribe without arousing notice or suspicion, but when one comes thus precipitately, evidently bursting with some emotion out of the ordinary, let all apes beware. There was a certain amount of preliminary circling, growling, and sniffing, stiff-legged and stiff-haired, before each side discovered that the other had no intention of initiating an attack and then Zu-tag told Go-lat what he had seen among the lairs of the Gomangani.

Go-lat grunted in disgust and turned away. "Let the white ape take care of himself," he said.

"He is a great ape," said Zu-tag. "He came to live in peace with the tribe of Go-lat. Let us save him from the Gomangani."

Go-lat grunted again and continued to move away.

"Zu-tag will go alone and get him," cried the young ape, "if Go-lat is afraid of the Gomangani."

The king ape wheeled in anger, growling loudly and beating upon his breast. "Go-lat is not afraid," he screamed, "but he will not go, for the white ape is not of his tribe. Go yourself and take the Tarmangani's she with you if you wish so much to save the white ape."

"Zu-tag will go," replied the younger bull, "and he will take the Tarmangani's she and all the bulls of Go-lat who are not cowards," and so saying he cast his eyes inquiringly about at the other apes. "Who will go with Zu-tag to fight the Gomangani and bring away our brother," he demanded.

Eight young bulls in the full prime of their vigor pressed forward to Zu-tag's side, but the old bulls with the conservatism and caution of many years upon their gray shoulders, shook their heads and waddled away after Go-lat.

"Good," cried Zu-tag. "We want no old shes to go with us to fight the Gomangani for that is work for the fighters of the tribe."

The old bulls paid no attention to his boastful words, but the eight who had volunteered to accompany him were filled with self-pride so that they stood around vaingloriously beating upon their breasts, baring their fangs and screaming their hideous challenge until the jungle reverberated to the horrid sound.

All this time Bertha Kircher was a wide-eyed and terrified spectator to what, as she thought, could end only in a terrific battle between these frightful beasts, and when Zu-tag and his followers began screaming forth their fearsome challenge, the girl found herself trembling in terror, for of all the sounds of the jungle there is none more awe inspiring than that of the great bull ape when he issues his challenge or shrieks forth his victory cry.

If she had been terrified before she was almost paralyzed with fear now as she saw Zu-tag and his apes turn toward the boma and approach her. With the agility of a cat Zu-tag leaped completely over the protecting wall and stood before her. Valiantly she held her spear before her, pointing it at his breast. He commenced to jabber and gesticulate, and even with her scant acquaintance with the ways of the anthropoids, she realized that he was not menacing her, for there was little or no baring of fighting fangs and his whole expression and attitude was of one attempting to explain a knotty problem or plead a worthy cause. At last he became evidently impatient, for with a sweep of one great paw he struck the spear from her hand and coming close, seized her by the arm, but not roughly. She shrank away in terror and yet some sense within her seemed to be trying to assure her that she was in no danger from this great beast. Zu-tag jabbered loudly, ever and again pointing into the jungle toward the south and moving toward the boma, pulling the girl with him. He seemed almost frantic in his efforts to explain something to her. He pointed toward the boma, herself, and then to the forest, and then, at last, as though by a sudden inspiration, he reached down and, seizing the spear, repeatedly touched it with his forefinger and again pointed toward the south. Suddenly it dawned upon the girl that what the ape was trying to explain to her was related in some way to the white man whose property they thought she was. Possibly her grim protector was in trouble and with this thought firmly established, she no longer held back, but started forward as though to accompany the young bull. At the point in the boma where Tarzan had blocked the entrance, she started to pull away the thorn bushes, and, when Zu-tag saw what she was doing, he fell to and assisted her so that presently they had an opening through the boma through which she passed with the great ape.

Immediately Zu-tag and his eight apes started off rapidly toward the jungle, so rapidly that Bertha Kircher would have had to run at top speed to keep up with them. This she realized she could not do, and so she was forced to lag behind, much to the chagrin of Zu-tag, who constantly kept running back and urging her to greater speed. Once he took her by the arm and tried to draw her along. Her protests were of no avail since the beast could not know that they were protests, nor did he desist until she caught her foot in some tangled grass and fell to the ground. Then indeed was Zu-tag furious and growled hideously. His apes were waiting at the edge of the forest for him to lead them. He suddenly realized that this poor weak she could not keep up with them and that if they traveled at her slow rate they might be too late to render assistance to the Tarmangani, and so without more ado, the giant anthropoid picked Bertha Kircher bodily from the ground and swung her to his back. Her arms were about his neck and in this position he seized her wrists in one great paw so that she could not fall off and started at a rapid rate to join his companions.

Dressed as she was in riding breeches with no entangling skirts to hinder or catch upon passing shrubbery, she soon found that she could cling tightly to the back of the mighty bull and when a moment later he took to the lower branches of the trees, she closed her eyes and clung to him in terror lest she be precipitated to the ground below.

That journey through the primeval forest with the nine great apes will live in the memory of Bertha Kircher for the balance of her life, as clearly delineated as at the moment of its enactment.

The first overwhelming wave of fear having passed, she was at last able to open her eyes and view her surroundings with increased interest and presently the sensation of terror slowly left her to be replaced by one of comparative security when she saw the ease and surety with which these great beasts traveled through the trees; and later her admiration for the young bull increased as it became evident that even burdened with her additional weight, he moved more rapidly and with no greater signs of fatigue than his unburdened fellows.

Not once did Zu-tag pause until he came to a stop among the branches of a tree no great distance from the native village. They could hear the noises of the life within the palisade, the laughing and shouting of the Negroes, and the barking of dogs, and through the foliage the girl caught glimpses of the village from which she had so recently escaped. She shuddered to think of the possibility of having to return to it and of possible recapture, and she wondered why Zu-tag had brought her here.

Now the apes advanced slowly once more and with great caution, moving as noiselessly through the trees as the squirrels themselves until they had reached a point where they could easily overlook the palisade and the village street below.

Zu-tag squatted upon a great branch close to the bole of the tree and by loosening the girl's arms from about his neck, indicated that she was to find a footing for herself and when she had done so, he turned toward her and pointed repeatedly at the open doorway of a hut upon the opposite side of the street below them. By various gestures he seemed to be trying to explain something to her and at last she caught at the germ of his idea—that her white man was a prisoner there.

Beneath them was the roof of a hut onto which she saw that she could easily drop, but what she could do after she had entered the village was beyond her.

Darkness was already falling and the fires beneath the cooking pots had been lighted. The girl saw the stake in the village street and the piles of fagots about it and in terror she suddenly realized the portent of these grisly preparations. Oh, if she but only had some sort of a weapon that might give her even a faint hope, some slight advantage against the blacks. Then she would not hesitate to venture into the village in an attempt to save the man who had upon three different occasions saved her. She knew that he hated her and yet strong within her breast burned the sense of her obligation to him. She could not fathom him. Never in her life had she seen a man at once so paradoxical and dependable. In many of his ways he was more savage than the beasts with which he associated and yet, on the other hand, he was as chivalrous as a knight of old. For several days she had been lost with him in the jungle absolutely at his mercy, yet she had come to trust so implicitly in his honor that any fear she had had of him was rapidly disappearing.

On the other hand, that he might be hideously cruel was evidenced to her by the fact that he was planning to leave her alone in the midst of the frightful dangers which menaced her by night and by day.

Zu-tag was evidently waiting for darkness to fall before carrying out whatever plans had matured in his savage little brain, for he and his fellows sat quietly in the tree about her, watching the preparations of the blacks. Presently it became apparent that some altercation had arisen among the Negroes, for a score or more of them were gathered around one who appeared to be their chief, and all were talking and gesticulating heatedly. The argument lasted for some five or ten minutes when suddenly the little knot broke and two warriors ran to the opposite side of the village from whence they presently returned with a large stake which they soon set up beside the one already in place. The girl wondered what the purpose of the second stake might be, nor did she have long to wait for an explanation.

It was quite dark by this time, the village being lighted by the fitful glare of many fires, and now she saw a number of warriors approach and enter the hut Zu-tag had been watching. A moment later they reappeared, dragging between them two captives, one of whom the girl immediately recognized as her protector and the other as an Englishman in the uniform of an aviator. This, then, was the reason for the two stakes.

Arising quickly she placed a hand upon Zu-tag's shoulder and pointed down into the village. "Come," she said, as if she had been talking to one of her own kind, and with the word she swung lightly to the roof of the hut below. From there to the ground was but a short drop and a moment later she was circling the hut upon the side farthest from the fires, keeping in the dense shadows where there was little likelihood of being discovered. She turned once to see that Zu-tag was directly behind her and could see his huge bulk looming up in the dark, while beyond was another one of his eight. Doubtless they had all followed her and this fact gave her a greater sense of security and hope than she had before experienced.

Pausing beside the hut next to the street, she peered cautiously about the corner. A few inches from her was the open doorway of the structure, and beyond, farther down the village street, the blacks were congregating about the prisoners, who were already being bound to the stakes. All eyes were centered upon the victims, and there was only the remotest chance that she and her companions would be discovered until they were close upon the blacks. She wished, however, that she might have some sort of a weapon with which to lead the attack, for she could not know, of course, for a certainty whether the great apes would follow her or not. Hoping that she might find something within the hut, she slipped quickly around the corner and into the doorway and after her, one by one, came the nine bulls. Searching quickly about the interior, she presently discovered a spear, and, armed with this, she again approached the entrance.

Tarzan of the Apes and Lieutenant Harold Percy Smith-Oldwick were bound securely to their respective stakes. Neither had spoken for some time. The Englishman turned his head so that he could see his companion in misery. Tarzan stood straight against his stake. His face was entirely expressionless in so far as either fear or anger were concerned. His countenance portrayed bored indifference though both men knew that they were about to be tortured.

"Good-bye, old top," whispered the young lieutenant.

Tarzan turned his eyes in the direction of the other and smiled. "Good-bye," he said. "If you want to get it over in a hurry, inhale the smoke and flames as rapidly as you can."

"Thanks," replied the aviator and though he made a wry face, he drew himself up very straight and squared his shoulders.

The women and children had seated themselves in a wide circle about the victims while the warriors, hideously painted, were forming slowly to commence the dance of death. Again Tarzan turned to his companion. "If you'd like to spoil their fun," he said, "don't make any fuss no matter how much you suffer. If you can carry on to the end without changing the expression upon your face or uttering a single word, you will deprive them of all the pleasures of this part of the entertainment. Good-bye again and good luck."

The young Englishman made no reply but it was evident from the set of his jaws that the Negroes would get little enjoyment out of him.

The warriors were circling now. Presently Numabo would draw first blood with his sharp spear which would be the signal for the beginning of the torture after a little of which the fagots would be lighted around the feet of the victims.

Closer and closer danced the hideous chief, his yellow, sharp-filed teeth showing in the firelight between his thick, red lips. Now bending double, now stamping furiously upon the ground, now leaping into the air, he danced step by step in the narrowing circle that would presently bring him within spear reach of the intended feast.

At last the spear reached out and touched the ape-man on the breast and when it came away, a little trickle of blood ran down the smooth, brown hide and almost simultaneously there broke from the outer periphery of the expectant audience a woman's shriek which seemed a signal for a series of hideous screamings, growlings and barkings, and a great commotion upon that side of the circle. The victims could not see the cause of the disturbance, but Tarzan did not have to see, for he knew by the voices of the apes the identity of the disturbers. He only wondered what had brought them and what the purpose of the attack, for he could not believe that they had come to rescue him.

Numabo and his warriors broke quickly from the circle of their dance to see pushing toward them through the ranks of their screaming and terrified people the very white girl who had escaped them a few nights before, and at her back what appeared to their surprised eyes a veritable horde of the huge and hairy forest men upon whom they looked with considerable fear and awe.

Striking to right and left with his heavy fists, tearing with his great fangs, came Zu-tag, the young bull, while at his heels, emulating his example, surged his hideous apes. Quickly they came through the old men and the women and children, for straight toward Numabo and his warriors the girl led them. It was then that they came within range of Tarzan's vision and he saw with unmixed surprise who it was that led the apes to his rescue.

To Zu-tag he shouted: "Go for the big bulls while the she unbinds me," and to Bertha Kircher: "Quick! Cut these bonds. The apes will take care of the blacks."

Turning from her advance the girl ran to his side. She had no knife and the bonds were tied tightly but she worked quickly and coolly and as Zu-tag and his apes closed with the warriors, she succeeded in loosening Tarzan's bonds sufficiently to permit him to extricate his own hands so that in another minute he had freed himself.

"Now unbind the Englishman," he cried, and, leaping forward, ran to join Zu-tag and his fellows in their battle against the blacks. Numabo and his warriors, realizing now the relatively small numbers of the apes against them, had made a determined stand and with spears and other weapons were endeavoring to overcome the invaders. Three of the apes were already down, killed or mortally wounded, when Tarzan, realizing that the battle must eventually go against the apes unless some means could be found to break the morale of the Negroes, cast about him for some means of bringing about the desired end. And suddenly his eye lighted upon a number of weapons which he knew would accomplish the result. A grim smile touched his lips as he snatched a vessel of boiling water from one of the fires and hurled it full in the faces of the warriors. Screaming with terror and pain they fell back though Numabo urged them to rush forward.

Scarcely had the first cauldron of boiling water spilled its contents upon them ere Tarzan deluged them with a second, nor was there any third needed to send them shrieking in every direction to the security of their huts.

By the time Tarzan had recovered his own weapons the girl had released the young Englishman, and, with the six remaining apes, the three Europeans moved slowly toward the village gate, the aviator arming himself with a spear discarded by one of the scalded warriors, as they eagerly advanced toward the outer darkness.

Numabo was unable to rally the now thoroughly terrified and painfully burned warriors so that rescued and rescuers passed out of the village into the blackness of the jungle without further interference.

Tarzan strode through the jungle in silence. Beside him walked Zu-tag, the great ape, and behind them strung the surviving anthropoids followed by Fräulein Bertha Kircher and Lieutenant Harold Percy Smith-Oldwick, the latter a thoroughly astonished and mystified Englishman.

In all his life Tarzan of the Apes had been obliged to acknowledge but few obligations. He won his way through his savage world by the might of his own muscle, the superior keenness of his five senses and his God-given power to reason. Tonight the greatest of all obligations had been placed upon him—his life had been saved by another and Tarzan shook his head and growled, for it had been saved by one whom he hated above all others.

CHAPTER XI—FINDING THE AIRPLANE

Tarzan of the Apes, returning from a successful hunt, with the body of Bara, the deer, across one sleek, brown shoulder, paused in the branches of a great tree at the edge of a clearing and gazed ruefully at two figures walking from the river to the boma-encircled hut a short distance away.

The ape-man shook his tousled head and sighed. His eyes wandered toward the west and his thoughts to the far-away cabin by the land-locked harbor of the great water that washed the beach of his boyhood home—to the cabin of his long-dead father to which the memories and treasures of a happy childhood lured him. Since the loss of his mate, a great longing had possessed him to return to the haunts of his youth—to the untracked jungle wilderness where he had lived the life he loved best long before man had invaded the precincts of his wild stamping grounds. There he hoped in a renewal of the old life under the old conditions to win surcease from sorrow and perhaps some measure of forgetfulness.

But the little cabin and the land-locked harbor were many long, weary marches away, and he was handicapped by the duty which he felt he owed to the two figures walking in the clearing before him. One was a young man in a worn and ragged uniform of the British Royal Air Forces, the other, a young woman in the even more disreputable remnants of what once had been trim riding togs.

A freak of fate had thrown these three radically different types together. One was a savage, almost naked beast-man, one an English army officer, and the woman, she whom the ape-man knew and hated as a German spy.

How he was to get rid of them Tarzan could not imagine unless he accompanied them upon the weary march back to the east coast, a march that would necessitate his once more retracing the long, weary way he already had covered towards his goal, yet what else could be done? These two had neither the strength, endurance, nor jungle-craft to accompany him through the unknown country to the west, nor did he wish them with him. The man he might have tolerated, but he could not even consider the presence of the girl in the far-off cabin, which had in a way become sacred to him through its memories, without a growl or anger rising to his lips. There remained, then, but the one way, since he could not desert them. He must move by slow and irksome marches back to the east coast, or at least to the first white settlement in that direction.

He had, it is true, contemplated leaving the girl to her fate but that was before she had been instrumental in saving him from torture and death at the hands of the black Wamabos. He chafed under the obligation she had put upon him, but no less did he acknowledge it and as he watched the two, the rueful expression upon his face was lightened by a smile as he thought of the helplessness of them. What a puny thing, indeed, was man! How ill equipped to combat the savage forces of nature and of nature's jungle. Why, even the tiny balu of the tribe of Go-lat, the great ape, was better fitted to survive than these, for a balu could at least escape the numerous creatures that menaced its existence, while with the possible exception of Kota, the tortoise, none moved so slowly as did helpless and feeble man.

Without him these two doubtless would starve in the midst of plenty, should they by some miracle escape the other forces of destruction which constantly threatened them. That morning Tarzan had brought them fruit, nuts, and plantain, and now he was bringing them the flesh of his kill, while the best that they might do was to fetch water from the river. Even now, as they walked across the clearing toward the boma, they were in utter ignorance of the presence of Tarzan near them. They did not know that his sharp eyes were watching them, nor that other eyes less friendly were glaring at them from a clump of bushes close beside the boma entrance. They did not know these things, but Tarzan did. No more than they could he see the creature crouching in the concealment of the foliage, yet he knew that it was there and what it was and what its intentions, precisely as well as though it had been lying in the open.

A slight movement of the leaves at the top of a single stem had apprised him of the presence of a creature there, for the movement was not that imparted by the wind. It came from pressure at the bottom of the stem which communicates a different movement to the leaves than does the wind passing among them, as anyone who has lived his lifetime in the jungle well knows, and the same wind that passed through the foliage of the bush brought to the ape-man's sensitive nostrils indisputable evidence of the fact that Sheeta, the panther, waited there for the two returning from the river.

They had covered half the distance to the boma entrance when Tarzan called to them to stop. They looked in surprise in the direction from which his voice had come to see him drop lightly to the ground and advance toward them.

"Come slowly toward me," he called to them. "Do not run for if you run Sheeta will charge."

They did as he bid, their faces filled with questioning wonderment.

"What do you mean?" asked the young Englishman. "Who is Sheeta?" but for answer the ape-man suddenly hurled the carcass of Bara, the deer, to the ground and leaped quickly toward them, his eyes upon something in their rear; and then it was that the two turned and learned the identity of Sheeta, for behind them was a devil-faced cat charging rapidly toward them.

Sheeta with rising anger and suspicion had seen the ape-man leap from the tree and approach the quarry. His life's experiences backed by instinct told him that the Tarmangani was about to rob him of his prey and as Sheeta was hungry, he had no intention of being thus easily deprived of the flesh he already considered his own.

The girl stifled an involuntary scream as she saw the proximity of the fanged fury bearing down upon them. She shrank close to the man and clung to him and all unarmed and defenseless as he was, the Englishman pushed her behind him and shielding her with his body, stood squarely in the face of the panther's charge. Tarzan noted the act, and though accustomed as he was to acts of courage, he experienced a thrill from the hopeless and futile bravery of the man.

The charging panther moved rapidly, and the distance which separated the bush in which he had concealed himself from the objects of his desire was not great. In the time that one might understandingly read a dozen words the strong-limbed cat could have covered the entire distance and made his kill, yet if Sheeta was quick, quick too was Tarzan. The English lieutenant saw the ape-man flash by him like the wind. He saw the great cat veer in his charge as though to elude the naked savage rushing to meet him, as it was evidently Sheeta's intention to make good his kill before attempting to protect it from Tarzan.

Lieutenant Smith-Oldwick saw these things and then with increasing wonder he saw the ape-man swerve, too, and leap for the spotted cat as a football player leaps for a runner. He saw the strong, brown arms encircling the body of the carnivore, the left arm in front of the beast's left shoulder and the right arm behind his right foreleg, and with the impact the two together rolling over and over upon the turf. He heard the snarls and growls of bestial combat, and it was with a feeling of no little horror that he realized that the sounds coming from the human throat of the battling man could scarce be distinguished from those of the panther.

The first momentary shock of terror over, the girl released her grasp upon the Englishman's arm. "Cannot we do something?" she asked. "Cannot we help him before the beast kills him?"

The Englishman looked upon the ground for some missile with which to attack the panther and then the girl uttered an exclamation and started at a run toward the hut. "Wait there," she called over her shoulder. "I will fetch the spear that he left me."

Smith-Oldwick saw the raking talons of the panther searching for the flesh of the man and the man on his part straining every muscle and using every artifice to keep his body out of range of them. The muscles of his arms knotted under the brown hide. The veins stood out upon his neck and forehead as with ever-increasing power he strove to crush the life from the great cat. The ape-man's teeth were fastened in the back of Sheeta's neck and now he succeeded in encircling the beast's torso with his legs which he crossed and locked beneath the cat's belly. Leaping and snarling, Sheeta sought to dislodge the ape-man's hold upon him. He hurled himself upon the ground and rolled over and over. He reared upon his hind legs and threw himself backwards but always the savage creature upon his back clung tenaciously to him, and always the mighty brown arms crushed tighter and tighter about his chest.

And then the girl, panting from her quick run, returned with the short spear Tarzan had left her as her sole weapon of protection. She did not wait to hand it to the Englishman who ran forward to receive it, but brushed past him and leaped into close quarters beside the growling, tumbling mass of yellow fur and smooth brown hide. Several times she attempted to press the point home into the cat's body, but on both occasions the fear of endangering the ape-man caused her to desist, but at last the two lay motionless for a moment as the carnivore sought a moment's rest from the strenuous exertions of battle, and then it was that Bertha Kircher pressed the point of the spear to the tawny side and drove it deep into the savage heart.

Tarzan rose from the dead body of Sheeta and shook himself after the manner of beasts that are entirely clothed with hair. Like many other of his traits and mannerisms this was the result of environment rather than heredity or reversion, and even though he was outwardly a man, the Englishman and the girl were both impressed with the naturalness of the act. It was as though Numa, emerging from a fight, had shaken himself to straighten his rumpled mane and coat, and yet, too, there was something uncanny about it as there had been when the savage growls and hideous snarls issued from those clean-cut lips.

Tarzan looked at the girl, a quizzical expression upon his face. Again had she placed him under obligations to her, and Tarzan of the Apes did not wish to be obligated to a German spy; yet in his honest heart he could not but admit a certain admiration for her courage, a trait which always greatly impressed the ape-man, he himself the personification of courage.

"Here is the kill," he said, picking the carcass of Bara from the ground. "You will want to cook your portion, I presume, but Tarzan does not spoil his meat with fire."

They followed him to the boma where he cut several pieces of meat from the carcass for them, retaining a joint for himself. The young lieutenant prepared a fire, and the girl presided over the primitive culinary rights of their simple meal. As she worked some little way apart from them, the lieutenant and the ape-man watched her.

"She is wonderful. Is she not?" murmured Smith-Oldwick.

"She is a German and a spy," replied Tarzan.

The Englishman turned quickly upon him. "What do you mean?" he cried.

"I mean what I say," replied the ape-man. "She is a German and a spy."

"I do not believe it!" exclaimed the aviator.

"You do not have to," Tarzan assured him. "It is nothing to me what you believe. I saw her in conference with the Boche general and his staff at the camp near Taveta. They all knew her and called her by name and she handed him a paper. The next time I saw her she was inside the British lines in disguise, and again I saw her bearing word to a German officer at Wilhelmstal. She is a German and a spy, but she is a woman and therefore I cannot destroy her."

"You really believe that what you say is true?" asked the young lieutenant. "My God! I cannot believe it. She is so sweet and brave and good."

The ape-man shrugged his shoulders. "She is brave," he said, "but even Pamba, the rat, must have some good quality, but she is what I have told you and therefore I hate her and you should hate her."

Lieutenant Harold Percy Smith-Oldwick buried his face in his hands. "God forgive me," he said at last. "I cannot hate her."

The ape-man cast a contemptuous look at his companion and arose. "Tarzan goes again to hunt," he said. "You have enough food for two days. By that time he will return."

The two watched him until he had disappeared in the foliage of the trees at the further side of the clearing.

When he had gone the girl felt a vague sense of apprehension that she never experienced when Tarzan was present. The invisible menaces lurking in the grim jungle seemed more real and much more imminent now that the ape-man was no longer near. While he had been there talking with them, the little thatched hut and its surrounding thorn boma had seemed as safe a place as the world might afford. She wished that he had remained—two days seemed an eternity in contemplation—two days of constant fear, two days, every moment of which would be fraught with danger. She turned toward her companion.

"I wish that he had remained," she said. "I always feel so much safer when he is near. He is very grim and very terrible, and yet I feel safer with him than with any man I ever have known. He seems to dislike me and yet I know that he would let no harm befall me. I cannot understand him."

"Neither do I understand him," replied the Englishman; "but I know this much—our presence here is interfering with his plans. He would like to be rid of us, and I half imagine that he rather hopes to find when he returns that we have succumbed to one of the dangers which must always confront us in this savage land.

"I think that we should try to return to the white settlements. This man does not want us here, nor is it reasonable to assume that we could long survive in such a savage wilderness. I have traveled and hunted in several parts of Africa, but never have I seen or heard of any single locality so overrun with savage beasts and dangerous natives. If we set out for the east coast at once we would be in but little more danger than we are here, and if we could survive a day's march, I believe that we will find the means of reaching the coast in a few hours, for my plane must still be in the same place that I landed just before the blacks captured me. Of course there is no one here who could operate it nor is there any reason why they should have destroyed it. As a matter of fact, the natives would be so fearful and suspicious of so strange and incomprehensible a thing that the chances are they would not dare approach it. Yes, it must be where I left it and all ready to carry us safely to the settlements."

"But we cannot leave," said the girl, "until he returns. We could not go away like that without thanking him or bidding him farewell. We are under too great obligations to him."

The man looked at her in silence for a moment. He wondered if she knew how Tarzan felt toward her and then he himself began to speculate upon the truth of the ape-man's charges. The longer he looked at the girl, the less easy was it to entertain the thought that she was an enemy spy. He was upon the point of asking her point-blank but he could not bring himself to do so, finally determining to wait until time and longer acquaintance should reveal the truth or falsity of the accusation.

"I believe," he said as though there had been no pause in their conversation, "that the man would be more than glad to find us gone when he returns. It is not necessary to jeopardize our lives for two more days in order that we may thank him, however much we may appreciate his services to us. You have more than balanced your obligations to him and from what he told me I feel that you especially should not remain here longer."

The girl looked up at him in astonishment. "What do you mean?" she asked.

"I do not like to tell," said the Englishman, digging nervously at the turf with the point of a stick, "but you have my word that he would rather you were not here."

"Tell me what he said," she insisted, "I have a right to know."

Lieutenant Smith-Oldwick squared his shoulders and raised his eyes to those of the girl. "He said that he hated you," he blurted. "He has only aided you at all from a sense of duty because you are a woman."

The girl paled and then flushed. "I will be ready to go," she said, "in just a moment. We had better take some of this meat with us. There is no telling when we will be able to get more."

And so the two set out down the river toward the south. The man carried the short spear that Tarzan had left with the girl, while she was entirely unarmed except for a stick she had picked up from among those left after the building of the hut. Before departing she had insisted that the man leave a note for Tarzan thanking him for his care of them and bidding him goodbye. This they left pinned to the inside wall of the hut with a little sliver of wood.

It was necessary that they be constantly on the alert since they never knew what might confront them at the next turn of the winding jungle trail or what might lie concealed in the tangled bushes at either side. There was also the ever-present danger of meeting some of Numabo's black warriors and as the village lay directly in their line of march, there was the necessity for making a wide detour before they reached it in order to pass around it without being discovered.

"I am not so much afraid of the native blacks," said the girl, "as I am of Usanga and his people. He and his men were all attached to a German native regiment. They brought me along with them when they deserted, either with the intention of holding me ransom or selling me into the harem of one of the black sultans of the north. Usanga is much more to be feared than Numabo for he has had the advantage of European military training and is armed with more or less modern weapons and ammunition."

"It is lucky for me," remarked the Englishman, "that it was the ignorant Numabo who discovered and captured me rather than the worldly wise Usanga. He would have felt less fear of the giant flying machine and would have known only too well how to wreck it."

"Let us pray that the black sergeant has not discovered it," said the girl.

They made their way to a point which they guessed was about a mile above the village, then they turned into the trackless tangle of undergrowth to the east. So dense was the verdure at many points that it was with the utmost difficulty they wormed their way through, sometimes on hands and knees and again by clambering over numerous fallen tree trunks. Interwoven with dead limbs and living branches were the tough and ropelike creepers which formed a tangled network across their path.

South of them in an open meadowland a number of black warriors were gathered about an object which elicited much wondering comment. The blacks were clothed in fragments of what had once been uniforms of a native German command. They were a most unlovely band and chief among them in authority and repulsiveness was the black sergeant Usanga. The object of their interest was a British aeroplane.

Immediately after the Englishman had been brought to Numabo's village Usanga had gone out in search of the plane, prompted partially by curiosity and partially by an intention to destroy it, but when he had found it, some new thought had deterred him from carrying out his design. The thing represented considerable value as he well knew and it had occurred to him that in some way he might turn his prize to profit. Every day he had returned to it, and while at first it had filled him with considerable awe, he eventually came to look upon it with the accustomed eye of a proprietor, so that he now clambered into the fuselage and even advanced so far as to wish that he might learn to operate it.

What a feat it would be indeed to fly like a bird far above the highest tree top! How it would fill his less favored companions with awe and admiration! If Usanga could but fly, so great would be the respect of all the tribesmen throughout the scattered villages of the great interior, they would look upon him as little less than a god.

Usanga rubbed his palms together and smacked his thick lips. Then indeed, would he be very rich, for all the villages would pay tribute to him and he could even have as many as a dozen wives. With that thought, however, came a mental picture of Naratu, the black termagant, who ruled him with an iron hand. Usanga made a wry face and tried to forget the extra dozen wives, but the lure of the idea remained and appealed so strongly to him that he presently found himself reasoning most logically that a god would not be much of a god with less than twenty-four wives.

He fingered the instruments and the control, half hoping and half fearing that he would alight upon the combination that would put the machine in flight. Often had he watched the British air-men soaring above the German lines and it looked so simple he was quite sure that he could do it himself if there was somebody who could but once show him how. There was, of course, always the hope that the white man who came in the machine and who had escaped from Numabo's village might fall into Usanga's hands and then indeed would he be able to learn how to fly. It was in this hope that Usanga spent so much time in the vicinity of the plane, reasoning as he did that eventually the white man would return in search of it.

And at last he was rewarded, for upon this very day after he had quit the machine and entered the jungle with his warriors, he heard voices to the north and when he and his men had hidden in the dense foliage upon either side of the trail, Usanga was presently filled with elation by the appearance of the British officer and the white girl whom the black sergeant had coveted and who had escaped him.

The Negro could scarce restrain a shout of elation, for he had not hoped that fate would be so kind as to throw these two whom he most desired into his power at the same time.

As the two came down the trail all unconscious of impending danger, the man was explaining that they must be very close to the point at which the plane had landed. Their entire attention was centered on the trail directly ahead of them, as they momentarily expected it to break into the meadowland where they were sure they would see the plane that would spell life and liberty for them.

The trail was broad, and they were walking side by side so that at a sharp turn the park-like clearing was revealed to them simultaneously with the outlines of the machine they sought.

Exclamations of relief and delight broke from their lips, and at the same instant Usanga and his black warriors rose from the bushes all about them.

CHAPTER XII—THE BLACK FLIER

The girl was almost crushed by terror and disappointment. To have been thus close to safety and then to have all hope snatched away by a cruel stroke of fate seemed unendurable. The man was disappointed, too, but more was he angry. He noted the remnants of the uniforms upon the blacks and immediately he demanded to know where were their officers.

"They cannot understand you," said the girl and so in the bastard tongue that is the medium of communication between the Germans and the blacks of their colony, she repeated the white man's question.

Usanga grinned. "You know where they are, white woman," he replied. "They are dead, and if this white man does not do as I tell him, he, too, will be dead."

"What do you want of him?" asked the girl.

"I want him to teach me how to fly like a bird," replied Usanga.

Bertha Kircher looked her astonishment, but repeated the demand to the lieutenant.

The Englishman meditated for a moment. "He wants to learn to fly, does he?" he repeated. "Ask him if he will give us our freedom if I teach him to fly."

The girl put the question to Usanga, who, degraded, cunning, and entirely unprincipled, was always perfectly willing to promise anything whether he had any intentions of fulfilling his promises or not, and so immediately assented to the proposition.

"Let the white man teach me to fly," he said, "and I will take you back close to the settlements of your people, but in return for this I shall keep the great bird," and he waved a black hand in the direction of the aeroplane.

When Bertha Kircher had repeated Usanga's proposition to the aviator, the latter shrugged his shoulders and with a wry face finally agreed. "I fancy there is no other way out of it," he said. "In any event the plane is lost to the British government. If I refuse the black scoundrel's request, there is no doubt but what he will make short work of me with the result that the machine will lie here until it rots. If I accept his offer it will at least be the means of assuring your safe return to civilization and that" he added, "is worth more to me than all the planes in the British Air Service."

The girl cast a quick glance at him. These were the first words he had addressed to her that might indicate that his sentiments toward her were more than those of a companion in distress. She regretted that he had spoken as he had and he, too, regretted it almost instantly as he saw the shadow cross her face and realized that he had unwittingly added to the difficulties of her already almost unbearable situation.

"Forgive me," he said quickly. "Please forget what that remark implied. I promise you that I will not offend again, if it does offend you, until after we are both safely out of this mess."

She smiled and thanked him, but the thing had been said and could never be unsaid, and Bertha Kircher knew even more surely than as though he had fallen upon his knees and protested undying devotion that the young English officer loved her.

Usanga was for taking his first lesson in aviation immediately. The Englishman attempted to dissuade him, but immediately the black became threatening and abusive, since, like all those who are ignorant, he was suspicious that the intentions of others were always ulterior unless they perfectly coincided with his wishes.

"All right, old top," muttered the Englishman, "I will give you the lesson of your life," and then turning to the girl: "Persuade him to let you accompany us. I shall be afraid to leave you here with these devilish scoundrels." But when she put the suggestion to Usanga the black immediately suspected some plan to thwart him—possibly to carry him against his will back to the German masters he had traitorously deserted, and glowering at her savagely, he obstinately refused to entertain the suggestion.

"The white woman will remain here with my people," he said. "They will not harm her unless you fail to bring me back safely."

"Tell him," said the Englishman, "that if you are not standing in plain sight in this meadow when I return, I will not land, but will carry Usanga back to the British camp and have him hanged."

Usanga promised that the girl would be in evidence upon their return, and took immediate steps to impress upon his warriors that under penalty of death they must not harm her. Then, followed by the other members of his party, he crossed the clearing toward the plane with the Englishman. Once seated within what he already considered his new possession, the black's courage began to wane and when the motor was started and the great propeller commenced to whir, he screamed to the Englishman to stop the thing and permit him to alight, but the aviator could neither hear nor understand the black above the noise of the propeller and exhaust. By this time the plane was moving along the ground and even then Usanga was upon the verge of leaping out, and would have done so had he been able to unfasten the strap from about his waist. Then the plane rose from the ground and in a moment soared gracefully in a wide circle until it topped the trees. The black sergeant was in a veritable collapse of terror. He saw the earth dropping rapidly from beneath him. He saw the trees and river and at a distance the little clearing with the thatched huts of Numabo's village. He tried hard not to think of the results of a sudden fall to the rapidly receding ground below. He attempted to concentrate his mind upon the twenty-four wives which this great bird most assuredly would permit him to command. Higher and higher rose the plane, swinging in a wide circle above the forest, river, and meadowland and presently, much to his surprise, Usanga discovered that his terror was rapidly waning, so that it was not long before there was forced upon him a consciousness of utter security, and then it was that he began to take notice of the manner in which the white man guided and manipulated the plane.

After half an hour of skillful maneuvering, the Englishman rose rapidly to a considerable altitude, and then, suddenly, without warning, he looped and flew with the plane inverted for a few seconds.

"I said I'd give this beggar the lesson of his life," he murmured as he heard, even above the whir of the propeller, the shriek of the terrified Negro. A moment later Smith-Oldwick had righted the machine and was dropping rapidly toward the earth. He circled slowly a few times above the meadow until he had assured himself that Bertha Kircher was there and apparently unharmed, then he dropped gently to the ground so that the machine came to a stop a short distance from where the girl and the warriors awaited them.

It was a trembling and ashen-hued Usanga who tumbled out of the fuselage, for his nerves were still on edge as a result of the harrowing experience of the loop, yet with terra firma once more under foot, he quickly regained his composure. Strutting about with great show and braggadocio, he strove to impress his followers with the mere nothingness of so trivial a feat as flying birdlike thousands of yards above the jungle, though it was long until he had thoroughly convinced himself by the force of autosuggestion that he had enjoyed every instant of the flight and was already far advanced in the art of aviation.

So jealous was the black of his new-found toy that he would not return to the village of Numabo, but insisted on making camp close beside the plane, lest in some inconceivable fashion it should be stolen from him. For two days they camped there, and constantly during daylight hours Usanga compelled the Englishman to instruct him in the art of flying.

Smith-Oldwick, in recalling the long months of arduous training he had undergone himself before he had been considered sufficiently adept to be considered a finished flier, smiled at the conceit of the ignorant African who was already demanding that he be permitted to make a flight alone.

"If it was not for losing the machine," the Englishman explained to the girl, "I'd let the bounder take it up and break his fool neck as he would do inside of two minutes."

However, he finally persuaded Usanga to bide his time for a few more days of instruction, but in the suspicious mind of the Negro there was a growing conviction that the white man's advice was prompted by some ulterior motive; that it was in the hope of escaping with the machine himself by night that he refused to admit that Usanga was entirely capable of handling it alone and therefore in no further need of help or instruction, and so in the mind of the black there formed a determination to outwit the white man. The lure of the twenty-four seductive wives proved in itself a sufficient incentive and there, too, was added his desire for the white girl whom he had long since determined to possess.

It was with these thoughts in mind that Usanga lay down to sleep in the evening of the second day. Constantly, however, the thought of Naratu and her temper arose to take the keen edge from his pleasant imaginings. If he could but rid himself of her! The thought having taken form persisted, but always it was more than outweighed by the fact that the black sergeant was actually afraid of his woman, so much afraid of her in fact that he would not have dared to attempt to put her out of the way unless he could do so secretly while she slept. However, as one plan after another was conjured by the strength of his desires, he at last hit upon one which came to him almost with the force of a blow and brought him sitting upright among his sleeping companions.

When morning dawned Usanga could scarce wait for an opportunity to put his scheme into execution, and the moment that he had eaten, he called several of his warriors aside and talked with them for some moments.

The Englishman, who usually kept an eye upon his black captor, saw now that the latter was explaining something in detail to his warriors, and from his gestures and his manner it was apparent that he was persuading them to some new plan as well as giving them instructions as to what they were to do. Several times, too, he saw the eyes of the Negroes turned upon him and once they flashed simultaneously toward the white girl.

Everything about the occurrence, which in itself seemed trivial enough, aroused in the mind of the Englishman a well-defined apprehension that something was afoot that boded ill for him and for the girl. He could not free himself of the idea and so he kept a still closer watch over the black although, as he was forced to admit to himself, he was quite powerless to avert any fate that lay in store for them. Even the spear that he had had when captured had been taken away from him, so that now he was unarmed and absolutely at the mercy of the black sergeant and his followers.

Lieutenant Harold Percy Smith-Oldwick did not have long to wait before discovering something of Usanga's plan, for almost immediately after the sergeant finished giving his instructions, a number of warriors approached the Englishman, while three went directly to the girl.

Without a word of explanation the warriors seized the young officer and threw him to the ground upon his face. For a moment he struggled to free himself and succeeded in landing a few heavy blows among his assailants, but he was too greatly outnumbered to hope to more than delay them in the accomplishment of their object which he soon discovered was to bind him securely hand and foot. When they had finally secured him to their satisfaction, they rolled him over on his side and then it was he saw Bertha Kircher had been similarly trussed.

Smith-Oldwick lay in such a position that he could see nearly the entire expanse of meadow and the aeroplane a short distance away. Usanga was talking to the girl who was shaking her head in vehement negatives.

"What is he saying?" called the Englishman.

"He is going to take me away in the plane," the girl called back. "He is going to take me farther inland to another country where he says that he will be king and I am to be one of his wives," and then to the Englishman's surprise she turned a smiling face toward him, "but there is no danger," she continued, "for we shall both be dead within a few minutes—just give him time enough to get the machine under way, and if he can rise a hundred feet from the ground I shall never need fear him more."

"God!" cried the man. "Is there no way that you can dissuade him? Promise him anything. Anything that you want. I have money, more money than that poor fool could imagine there was in the whole world. With it he can buy anything that money will purchase, fine clothes and food and women, all the women he wants. Tell him this and tell him that if he will spare you I give him my word that I will fetch it all to him."

The girl shook her head. "It is useless," she said. "He would not understand and if he did understand, he would not trust you. The blacks are so unprincipled themselves that they can imagine no such thing as principle or honor in others, and especially do these blacks distrust an Englishman whom the Germans have taught them to believe are the most treacherous and degraded of people. No, it is better thus. I am sorry that you cannot go with us, for if he goes high enough my death will be much easier than that which probably awaits you."

Usanga had been continually interrupting their brief conversation in an attempt to compel the girl to translate it to him, for he feared that they were concocting some plan to thwart him, and to quiet and appease him, she told him that the Englishman was merely bidding her farewell and wishing her good luck. Suddenly she turned to the black. "Will you do something for me?" she asked. "If I go willingly with you?"

"What is it you want?" he inquired.

"Tell your men to free the white man after we are gone. He can never catch us. That is all I ask of you. If you will grant him his freedom and his life, I will go willingly with you."

"You will go with me anyway," growled Usanga. "It is nothing to me whether you go willingly or not. I am going to be a great king and you will do whatever I tell you to do."

He had in mind that he would start properly with this woman. There should be no repetition of his harrowing experience with Naratu. This wife and the twenty-four others should be carefully selected and well trained. Hereafter Usanga would be master in his own house.

Bertha Kircher saw that it was useless to appeal to the brute and so she held her peace though she was filled with sorrow in contemplating the fate that awaited the young officer, scarce more than a boy, who had impulsively revealed his love for her.

At Usanga's order one of the blacks lifted her from the ground and carried her to the machine, and after Usanga had clambered aboard, they lifted her up and he reached down and drew her into the fuselage where he removed the thongs from her wrists and strapped her into her seat and then took his own directly ahead of her.

The girl turned her eyes toward the Englishman. She was very pale but her lips smiled bravely.

"Good-bye!" she cried.

"Good-bye, and God bless you!" he called back—his voice the least bit husky—and then: "The thing I wanted to say—may I say it now, we are so very near the end?"

Her lips moved but whether they voiced consent or refusal he did not know, for the words were drowned in the whir of the propeller.

The black had learned his lesson sufficiently well so that the motor was started without bungling and the machine was soon under way across the meadowland. A groan escaped the lips of the distracted Englishman as he watched the woman he loved being carried to almost certain death. He saw the plane tilt and the machine rise from the ground. It was a good take-off—as good as Lieutenant Harold Percy Smith-Oldwick could make himself but he realized that it was only so by chance. At any instant the machine might plunge to earth and even if, by some miracle of chance, the black could succeed in rising above the tree tops and make a successful flight, there was not one chance in one hundred thousand that he could ever land again without killing his fair captive and himself.

But what was that? His heart stood still.

CHAPTER XIII—USANGA'S REWARD

For two days Tarzan of the Apes had been hunting leisurely to the north, and swinging in a wide circle, he had returned to within a short distance of the clearing where he had left Bertha Kircher and the young lieutenant. He had spent the night in a large tree that overhung the river only a short distance from the clearing, and now in the early morning hours he was crouching at the water's edge waiting for an opportunity to capture Pisah, the fish, thinking that he would take it back with him to the hut where the girl could cook it for herself and her companion.

Motionless as a bronze statue was the wily ape-man, for well he knew how wary is Pisah, the fish. The slightest movement would frighten him away and only by infinite patience might he be captured at all. Tarzan depended upon his own quickness and the suddenness of his attack, for he had no bait or hook. His knowledge of the ways of the denizens of the water told him where to wait for Pisah. It might be a minute or it might be an hour before the fish would swim into the little pool above which he crouched, but sooner or later one would come. That the ape-man knew, so with the patience of the beast of prey he waited for his quarry.

At last there was a glint of shiny scales. Pisah was coming. In a moment he would be within reach and then with the swiftness of light two strong, brown hands would plunge into the pool and seize him, but, just at the moment that the fish was about to come within reach, there was a great crashing in the underbrush behind the ape-man. Instantly Pisah was gone and Tarzan, growling, had wheeled about to face whatever creature might be menacing him. The moment that he turned he saw that the author of the disturbance was Zu-tag.

"What does Zu-tag want?" asked the ape-man.

"Zu-tag comes to the water to drink," replied the ape.

"Where is the tribe?" asked Tarzan.

"They are hunting for pisangs and scimatines farther back in the forest," replied Zu-tag.

"And the Tarmangani she and bull——" asked Tarzan, "are they safe?"

"They have gone away," replied Zu-tag. "Kudu has come out of his lair twice since they left."

"Did the tribe chase them away?" asked Tarzan.

"No," replied the ape. "We did not see them go. We do not know why they left."

Tarzan swung quickly through the trees toward the clearing. The hut and boma were as he had left them, but there was no sign of either the man or the woman. Crossing the clearing, he entered the boma and then the hut. Both were empty, and his trained nostrils told him that they had been gone for at least two days. As he was about to leave the hut he saw a paper pinned upon the wall with a sliver of wood and taking it down, he read:

> *After what you told me about Miss Kircher, and knowing that you dislike her, I feel that it is not fair to her and to you that we should impose longer upon you. I know that our presence is keeping you from continuing your journey to the west coast, and so I have decided that it is better for us to try and reach the white settlements immediately without imposing further upon you. We both thank you for your kindness and protection. If there was any way that I might repay the obligation I feel, I should be only too glad to do so.*

It was signed by Lieutenant Harold Percy Smith-Oldwick.

Tarzan shrugged his shoulders, crumpled the note in his hand and tossed it aside. He felt a certain sense of relief from responsibility and was glad that they had taken the matter out of his hands. They were gone and would forget, but somehow he could not forget. He walked out across the boma and into the clearing. He felt uneasy and restless. Once he started toward the north in response to a sudden determination to continue his way to the west coast. He would follow the winding river toward the north a few miles where its course turned to the west and then on toward its source across a wooded plateau and up into the foothills and the mountains. Upon the other side of the range he would search for a stream running downward toward the west coast, and thus following the rivers he would be sure of game and water in plenty.

But he did not go far. A dozen steps, perhaps, and he came to a sudden stop. "He is an Englishman," he muttered, "and the other is a woman. They can never reach the settlements without my help. I could not kill her with my own hands when I tried, and if I let them go on alone, I will have killed her just as surely as though I had run my knife into her heart. No," and again he shook his head. "Tarzan of the Apes is a fool and a weak, old woman," and he turned back toward the south.

Manu, the monkey, had seen the two Tarmangani pass two days before. Chattering and scolding, he told Tarzan all about it. They had gone in the direction of the village of the Gomangani, that much had Manu seen with his own eyes, so the ape-man swung on through the jungle in a southerly direction and though with no concentrated effort to follow the spoor of those he trailed, he passed numerous evidences that they had gone this way—faint suggestions of their scent spoor clung lightly to leaf or branch or bole that one or the other had touched, or in the earth of the trail their feet had trod, and where the way wound through the gloomy depth of dank forest, the impress of their shoes still showed occasionally in the damp mass of decaying vegetation that floored the way.

An inexplicable urge spurred Tarzan to increasing, speed. The same still, small voice that chided him for having neglected them seemed constantly whispering that they were in dire need of him now. Tarzan's conscience was troubling him, which accounted for the fact that he compared himself to a weak, old woman, for the ape-man, reared in savagery and inured to hardships and cruelty, disliked to admit any of the gentler traits that in reality were his birthright.

The trail made a detour to the east of the village of the Wamabos, and then returned to the wide elephant path nearer to the river, where it continued in a southerly direction for several miles. At last there came to the ears of the ape-man a peculiar whirring, throbbing sound. For an instant he paused, listening intently, "An aeroplane!" he muttered, and hastened forward at greatly increased speed.

When Tarzan of the Apes finally reached the edge of the meadowland where Smith-Oldwick's plane had landed, he took in the entire scene in one quick glance and grasped the situation, although he could scarce give credence to the things he saw. Bound and helpless, the English officer lay upon the ground at one side of the meadow, while around him stood a number of the black deserters from the German command. Tarzan had seen these men before and knew who they were. Coming toward him down the meadow was an aeroplane piloted by the black Usanga and in the seat behind the pilot was the white girl, Bertha Kircher. How it befell that the ignorant savage could operate the plane, Tarzan could not guess nor had he time in which to speculate upon the subject. His knowledge of Usanga, together with the position of the white man, told him that the black sergeant was attempting to carry off the white girl. Why he should be doing this when he had her in his power and had also captured and secured the only creature in the jungle who might wish to defend her in so far as the black could know, Tarzan could not guess, for he knew nothing of Usanga's twenty-four dream wives nor of the black's fear of the horrid temper of Naratu, his present mate. He did not know, then, that Usanga had determined to fly away with the white girl never to return, and to put so great a distance between himself and Naratu that the latter never could find him again; but it was this very thing that was in the black's mind although not even his own warriors guessed it. He had told them that he would take the captive to a sultan of the north and there obtain a great price for her and that when he returned they should have some of the spoils.

These things Tarzan did not know. All he knew was what he saw—a Negro attempting to fly away with a white girl. Already the machine was slowly leaving the ground. In a moment more it would rise swiftly out of reach. At first Tarzan thought of fitting an arrow to his bow and slaying Usanga, but as quickly he abandoned the idea because he knew that the moment the pilot was slain the machine, running wild, would dash the girl to death among the trees.

There was but one way in which he might hope to succor her—a way which if it failed must send him to instant death and yet he did not hesitate in an attempt to put it into execution.

Usanga did not see him, being too intent upon the unaccustomed duties of a pilot, but the blacks across the meadow saw him and they ran forward with loud and savage cries and menacing rifles to intercept him. They saw a giant white man leap from the branches of a tree to the turf and race rapidly toward the plane. They saw him take a long grass rope from about his shoulders as he ran. They saw the noose swinging in an undulating circle above his head. They saw the white girl in the machine glance down and discover him.

Twenty feet above the running ape-man soared the huge plane. The open noose shot up to meet it, and the girl, half guessing the ape-man's intentions, reached out and caught the noose and, bracing herself, clung tightly to it with both hands. Simultaneously Tarzan was dragged from his feet and the plane lurched sideways in response to the new strain. Usanga clutched wildly at the control and the machine shot upward at a steep angle. Dangling at the end of the rope the ape-man swung pendulum-like in space. The Englishman, lying bound upon the ground, had been a witness of all these happenings. His heart stood still as he saw Tarzan's body hurtling through the air toward the tree tops among which it seemed he must inevitably crash; but the plane was rising rapidly, so that the beast-man cleared the top-most branches. Then slowly, hand over hand, he climbed toward the fuselage. The girl, clinging desperately to the noose, strained every muscle to hold the great weight dangling at the lower end of the rope.

Usanga, all unconscious of what was going on behind him, drove the plane higher and higher into the air.

Tarzan glanced downward. Below him the tree tops and the river passed rapidly to the rear and only a slender grass rope and the muscles of a frail girl stood between him and the death yawning there thousands of feet below.

It seemed to Bertha Kircher that the fingers of her hands were dead. The numbness was running up her arms to her elbows. How much longer she could cling to the straining strands she could not guess. It seemed to her that those lifeless fingers must relax at any instant and then, when she had about given up hope, she saw a strong brown hand reach up and grasp the side of the fuselage. Instantly the weight upon the rope was removed and a moment later Tarzan of the Apes raised his body above the side and threw a leg over the edge. He glanced forward at Usanga and then, placing his mouth close to the girl's ear he cried: "Have you ever piloted a plane?" The girl nodded a quick affirmative.

"Have you the courage to climb up there beside the black and seize the control while I take care of him?"

The girl looked toward Usanga and shuddered. "Yes," she replied, "but my feet are bound."

Tarzan drew his hunting knife from its sheath and reaching down, severed the thongs that bound her ankles. Then the girl unsnapped the strap that held her to her seat. With one hand Tarzan grasped the girl's arm and steadied her as the two crawled slowly across the few feet which intervened between the two seats. A single slight tip of the plane would have cast them both into eternity. Tarzan realized that only through a miracle of chance could they reach Usanga and effect the change in pilots and yet he knew that that chance must be taken, for in the brief moments since he had first seen the plane, he had realized that the black was almost without experience as a pilot and that death surely awaited them in any event should the black sergeant remain at the control.

The first intimation Usanga had that all was not well with him was when the girl slipped suddenly to his side and grasped the control and at the same instant steel-like fingers seized his throat. A brown hand shot down with a keen blade and severed the strap about his waist and giant muscles lifted him bodily from his seat. Usanga clawed the air and shrieked but he was helpless as a babe. Far below the watchers in the meadow could see the aeroplane careening in the sky, for with the change of control it had taken a sudden dive. They saw it right itself and, turning in a short circle, return in their direction, but it was so far above them and the light of the sun so strong that they could see nothing of what was going on within the fuselage; but presently Lieutenant Smith-Oldwick gave a gasp of dismay as he saw a human body plunge downward from the plane. Turning and twisting in mid-air it fell with ever-increasing velocity and the Englishman held his breath as the thing hurtled toward them.

With a muffled thud it flattened upon the turf near the center of the meadow, and when at last the Englishman could gain the courage to again turn his eyes upon it, he breathed a fervent prayer of thanks, for the shapeless mass that lay upon the blood-stained turf was covered with an ebon hide. Usanga had reaped his reward.

Again and again the plane circled above the meadow. The blacks, at first dismayed at the death of their leader, were now worked to a frenzy of rage and a determination to be avenged. The girl and the ape-man saw them gather in a knot about the body of their fallen chief. They saw as they circled above the meadow the black fists shaken at them, and the rifles brandishing a menace toward them. Tarzan still clung to the fuselage directly behind the pilot's seat. His face was close beside Bertha Kircher's, and at the top of his voice, above the noise of propeller, engine and exhaust, he screamed a few words of instruction into her ear.

As the girl grasped the significance of his words she paled, but her lips set in a hard line and her eyes shone with a sudden fire of determination as she dropped the plane to within a few feet of the ground and at the opposite end of the meadow from the blacks and then at full speed bore down upon the savages. So quickly the plane came that Usanga's men had no time to escape it after they realized its menace. It touched the ground just as it struck among them and mowed through them, a veritable juggernaut of destruction. When it came to rest at the edge of the forest the ape-man leaped quickly to the ground and ran toward the young lieutenant, and as he went he glanced at the spot where the warriors had stood, ready to defend himself if necessary, but there was none there to oppose him. Dead and dying they lay strewn for fifty feet along the turf.

By the time Tarzan had freed the Englishman the girl joined them. She tried to voice her thanks to the ape-man but he silenced her with a gesture.

"You saved yourself," he insisted, "for had you been unable to pilot the plane, I could not have helped you, and now," he said, "you two have the means of returning to the settlements. The day is still young. You can easily cover the distance in a few hours if you have sufficient petrol." He looked inquiringly toward the aviator.

Smith-Oldwick nodded his head affirmatively. "I have plenty," he replied.

"Then go at once," said the ape-man. "Neither of you belong in the jungle." A slight smile touched his lips as he spoke.

The girl and the Englishman smiled too. "This jungle is no place for us at least," said Smith-Oldwick, "and it is no place for any other white man. Why don't you come back to civilization with us?"

Tarzan shook his head. "I prefer the jungle," he said.

The aviator dug his toe into the ground and still looking down, blurted something which he evidently hated to say. "If it is a matter of living, old top," he said, "er—money, er—you know—"

Tarzan laughed. "No," he said. "I know what you are trying to say. It is not that. I was born in the jungle. I have lived all my life in the jungle, and I shall die in the jungle. I do not wish to live or die elsewhere."

The others shook their heads. They could not understand him.

"Go," said the ape-man. "The quicker you go, the quicker you will reach safety."

They walked to the plane together. Smith-Oldwick pressed the ape-man's hand and clambered into the pilot's seat. "Good-bye," said the girl as she extended her hand to Tarzan. "Before I go won't you tell me you don't hate me any more?" Tarzan's face clouded. Without a word he picked her up and lifted her to her place behind the Englishman. An expression of pain crossed Bertha Kircher's face. The motor started and a moment later the two were being borne rapidly toward the east.

In the center of the meadow stood the ape-man watching them. "It is too bad that she is a German and a spy," he said, "for she is very hard to hate."

CHAPTER XIV—THE BLACK LION

Numa, the lion, was hungry. He had come out of the desert country to the east into a land of plenty but though he was young and strong, the wary grass-eaters had managed to elude his mighty talons each time he had thought to make a kill.

Numa, the lion, was hungry and very savage. For two days he had not eaten and now he hunted in the ugliest of humors. No more did Numa roar forth a rumbling challenge to the world but rather he moved silent and grim, stepping softly that no cracking twig might betray his presence to the keen-eared quarry he sought.

Fresh was the spoor of Bara, the deer, that Numa picked up in the well-beaten game trail he was following. No hour had passed since Bara had come this way; the time could be measured in minutes and so the great lion redoubled the cautiousness of his advance as he crept stealthily in pursuit of his quarry.

A light wind was moving through the jungle aisles, and it wafted down now to the nostrils of the eager carnivore the strong scent spoor of the deer, exciting his already avid appetite to a point where it became a gnawing pain. Yet Numa did not permit himself to be carried away by his desires into any premature charge such as had recently lost him the juicy meat of Pacco, the zebra. Increasing his gait but slightly he followed the tortuous windings of the trail until suddenly just before him, where the trail wound about the bole of a huge tree, he saw a young buck moving slowly ahead of him.

Numa judged the distance with his keen eyes, glowing now like two terrible spots of yellow fire in his wrinkled, snarling face. He could do it—this time he was sure. One terrific roar that would paralyze the poor creature ahead of him into momentary inaction, and a simultaneous charge of lightning-like rapidity and Numa, the lion, would feed. The sinuous tail, undulating slowly at its tufted extremity, whipped suddenly erect. It was the signal for the charge and the vocal organs were shaped for the thunderous roar when, as lightning out of a clear sky, Sheeta, the panther, leaped suddenly into the trail between Numa and the deer.

A blundering charge made Sheeta, for with the first crash of his spotted body through the foliage verging the trail, Bara gave a single startled backward glance and was gone.

The roar that was intended to paralyze the deer broke horribly from the deep throat of the great cat—an angry roar of rage against the meddling Sheeta who had robbed him of his kill, and the charge that was intended for Bara was launched against the panther; but here too Numa was doomed to disappointment, for with the first notes of his fearsome roar Sheeta, considering well the better part of valor, leaped into a near-by tree.

A half-hour later it was a thoroughly furious Numa who came unexpectedly upon the scent of man. Heretofore the lord of the jungle had disdained the unpalatable flesh of the despised man-thing. Such meat was only for the old, the toothless, and the decrepit who no longer could make their kills among the fleet-footed grass-eaters. Bara, the deer, Horta, the boar, and, best and wariest, Pacco, the zebra, were for the young, the strong, and the agile, but Numa was hungry—hungrier than he ever had been in the five short years of his life.

What if he was a young, powerful, cunning, and ferocious beast? In the face of hunger, the great leveler, he was as the old, the toothless, and the decrepit. His belly cried aloud in anguish and his jowls slavered for flesh. Zebra or deer or man, what mattered it so that it was warm flesh, red with the hot juices of life? Even Dango, the hyena, eater of offal, would, at the moment, have seemed a tidbit to Numa.

The great lion knew the habits and frailties of man, though he never before had hunted man for food. He knew the despised Gomangani as the slowest, the most stupid, and the most defenseless of creatures. No woodcraft, no cunning, no stealth was necessary in the hunting of man, nor had Numa any stomach for either delay or silence.

His rage had become an almost equally consuming passion with his hunger, so that now, as his delicate nostrils apprised him of the recent passage of man, he lowered his head and rumbled forth a thunderous roar, and at a swift walk, careless of the noise he made, set forth upon the trail of his intended quarry.

Majestic and terrible, regally careless of his surroundings, the king of beasts strode down the beaten trail. The natural caution that is inherent to all creatures of the wild had deserted him. What had he, lord of the jungle, to fear and, with only man to hunt, what need of caution? And so he did not see or scent what a more wary Numa might readily have discovered until, with the cracking of twigs and a tumbling of earth, he was precipitated into a cunningly devised pit that the wily Wamabos had excavated for just this purpose in the center of the game trail.

Tarzan of the Apes stood in the center of the clearing watching the plane shrinking to diminutive toy-like proportions in the eastern sky. He had breathed a sigh of relief as he saw it rise safely with the British flier and Fräulein Bertha Kircher. For weeks he had felt the hampering responsibility of their welfare in this savage wilderness where their utter helplessness would have rendered them easy prey for the savage carnivores or the cruel Wamabos. Tarzan of the Apes loved unfettered freedom, and now that these two were safely off his hands, he felt that he could continue upon his journey toward the west coast and the long-untenanted cabin of his dead father.

And yet, as he stood there watching the tiny speck in the east, another sigh heaved his broad chest, nor was it a sigh of relief, but rather a sensation which Tarzan had never expected to feel again and which he now disliked to admit even to himself. It could not be possible that he, the jungle bred, who had renounced forever the society of man to return to his beloved beasts of the wilds, could be feeling anything akin to regret at the departure of these two, or any slightest loneliness now that they were gone. Lieutenant Harold Percy Smith-Oldwick Tarzan had liked, but the woman whom he had known as a German spy he had hated, though he never had found it in his heart to slay her as he had sworn to slay all Huns. He had attributed this weakness to the fact that she was a woman, although he had been rather troubled by the apparent inconsistency of his hatred for her and his repeated protection of her when danger threatened.

With an irritable toss of his head he wheeled suddenly toward the west as though by turning his back upon the fast disappearing plane he might expunge thoughts of its passengers from his memory. At the edge of the clearing he paused; a giant tree loomed directly ahead of him and, as though actuated by sudden and irresistible impulse, he leaped into the branches and swung himself with apelike agility to the topmost limbs that would sustain his weight. There, balancing lightly upon a swaying bough, he sought in the direction of the eastern horizon for the tiny speck that would be the British plane bearing away from him the last of his own race and kind that he expected ever again to see.

At last his keen eyes picked up the ship flying at a considerable altitude far in the east. For a few seconds he watched it speeding evenly eastward, when, to his horror, he saw the speck dive suddenly downward. The fall seemed interminable to the watcher and he realized how great must have been the altitude of the plane before the drop commenced. Just before it disappeared from sight its downward momentum appeared to abate suddenly, but it was still moving rapidly at a steep angle when it finally disappeared from view behind the far hills.

For half a minute the ape-man stood noting distant landmarks that he judged might be in the vicinity of the fallen plane, for no sooner had he realized that these people were again in trouble than his inherent sense of duty to his own kind impelled him once more to forego his plans and seek to aid them.

The ape-man feared from what he judged of the location of the machine that it had fallen among the almost impassable gorges of the arid country just beyond the fertile basin that was bounded by the hills to the east of him. He had crossed that parched and desolate country of the dead himself and he knew from his own experience and the narrow escape he had had from succumbing to its relentless cruelty no lesser man could hope to win his way to safety from any considerable distance within its borders. Vividly he recalled the bleached bones of the long-dead warrior in the bottom of the precipitous gorge that had all but proved a trap for him as well. He saw the helmet of hammered brass and the corroded breastplate of steel and the long straight sword in its scabbard and the ancient harquebus—mute testimonials to the mighty physique and the warlike spirit of him who had somehow won, thus illy caparisoned and pitifully armed, to the center of savage, ancient Africa; and he saw the slender English youth and the slight figure of the girl cast into the same fateful trap from which this giant of old had been unable to escape—cast there wounded and broken perhaps, if not killed.

His judgment told him that the latter possibility was probably the fact, and yet there was a chance that they might have landed without fatal injuries, and so upon this slim chance he started out upon what he knew would be an arduous journey, fraught with many hardships and unspeakable peril, that he might attempt to save them if they still lived.

He had covered a mile perhaps when his quick ears caught the sound of rapid movement along the game trail ahead of him. The sound, increasing in volume, proclaimed the fact that whatever caused it was moving in his direction and moving rapidly. Nor was it long before his trained senses convinced him that the footfalls were those of Bara, the deer, in rapid flight. Inextricably confused in Tarzan's character were the attributes of man and of beasts. Long experience had taught him that he fights best or travels fastest who is best nourished, and so, with few exceptions, Tarzan could delay his most urgent business to take advantage of an opportunity to kill and feed. This perhaps was the predominant beast trait in him. The transformation from an English gentleman, impelled by the most humanitarian motives, to that of a wild beast crouching in the concealment of a dense bush ready to spring upon its approaching prey, was instantaneous.

And so, when Bara came, escaping the clutches of Numa and Sheeta, his terror and his haste precluded the possibility of his sensing that other equally formidable foe lying in ambush for him. Abreast of the ape-man came the deer; a light-brown body shot from the concealing verdure of the bush, strong arms encircled the sleek neck of the young buck and powerful teeth fastened themselves in the soft flesh. Together the two rolled over in the trail and a moment later the ape-man rose, and, with one foot upon the carcass of his kill, raised his voice in the victory cry of the bull ape.

Like an answering challenge came suddenly to the ears of the ape-man the thunderous roar of a lion, a hideous angry roar in which Tarzan thought that he discerned a note of surprise and terror. In the breast of the wild things of the jungle, as in the breasts of their more enlightened brothers and sisters of the human race, the characteristic of curiosity is well developed. Nor was Tarzan far from innocent of it. The peculiar note in the roar of his hereditary enemy aroused a desire to investigate, and so, throwing the carcass of Bara, the deer, across his shoulder, the ape-man took to the lower terraces of the forest and moved quickly in the direction from which the sound had come, which was in line with the trail he had set out upon.

As the distance lessened, the sounds increased in volume, which indicated that he was approaching a very angry lion and presently, where a jungle giant overspread the broad game trail that countless thousands of hoofed and padded feet had worn and trampled into a deep furrow during perhaps countless ages, he saw beneath him the lion pit of the Wamabos and in it, leaping futilely for freedom such a lion as even Tarzan of the Apes never before had beheld. A mighty beast it was that glared up at the ape-man—large, powerful and young, with a huge black mane and a coat so much darker than any Tarzan ever had seen that in the depths of the pit it looked almost black—a black lion!

Tarzan who had been upon the point of taunting and reviling his captive foe was suddenly turned to open admiration for the beauty of the splendid beast. What a creature! How by comparison the ordinary forest lion was dwarfed into insignificance! Here indeed was one worthy to be called king of beasts. With his first sight of the great cat the ape-man knew that he had heard no note of terror in that initial roar; surprise doubtless, but the vocal chords of that mighty throat never had reacted to fear.

With growing admiration came a feeling of quick pity for the hapless situation of the great brute rendered futile and helpless by the wiles of the Gomangani. Enemy though the beast was, he was less an enemy to the ape-man than those blacks who had trapped him, for though Tarzan of the Apes claimed many fast and loyal friends among certain tribes of African natives, there were others of degraded character and bestial habits that he looked upon with utter loathing, and of such were the human flesh-eaters of Numabo the chief. For a moment Numa, the lion, glared ferociously at the naked man-thing upon the tree limb above him. Steadily those yellow-green eyes bored into the clear eyes of the ape-man, and then the sensitive nostrils caught the scent of the fresh blood of Bara and the eyes moved to the carcass lying across the brown shoulder, and there came from the cavernous depths of the savage throat a low whine.

Tarzan of the Apes smiled. As unmistakably as though a human voice had spoken, the lion had said to him "I am hungry, even more than hungry. I am starving," and the ape-man looked down upon the lion beneath him and smiled, a slow quizzical smile, and then he shifted the carcass from his shoulder to the branch before him and, drawing the long blade that had been his father's, deftly cut off a hind quarter and, wiping the bloody blade upon Bara's smooth coat, he returned it to its scabbard. Numa, with watering jaws, looked up at the tempting meat and whined again and the ape-man smiled down upon him his slow smile and, raising the hind quarter in his strong brown hands buried his teeth in the tender, juicy flesh.

For the third time Numa, the lion, uttered that low pleading whine and then, with a rueful and disgusted shake of his head, Tarzan of the Apes raised the balance of the carcass of Bara, the deer, and hurled it to the famished beast below.

"Old woman," muttered the ape-man. "Tarzan has become a weak old woman. Presently he would shed tears because he has killed Bara, the deer. He cannot see Numa, his enemy, go hungry, because Tarzan's heart is turning to water by contact with the soft, weak creatures of civilization." But yet he smiled, nor was he sorry that he had given way to the dictates of a kindly impulse.

As Tarzan tore the flesh from that portion of the kill he had retained for himself his eyes were taking in each detail of the scene below. He saw the avidity with which Numa devoured the carcass; he noted with growing admiration the finer points of the beast, and also the cunning construction of the trap. The ordinary lion pit with which Tarzan was familiar had stakes imbedded in the bottom, upon whose sharpened points the hapless lion would be impaled, but this pit was not so made. Here the short stakes were set at intervals of about a foot around the walls near the top, their sharpened points inclining downward so that the lion had fallen unhurt into the trap but could not leap out because each time he essayed it his head came in contact with the sharp end of a stake above him.

Evidently, then, the purpose of the Wamabos was to capture a lion alive. As this tribe had no contact whatsoever with white men in so far as Tarzan knew, their motive was doubtless due to a desire to torture the beast to death that they might enjoy to the utmost his dying agonies.

Having fed the lion, it presently occurred to Tarzan that his act would be futile were he to leave the beast to the mercies of the blacks, and then too it occurred to him that he could derive more pleasure through causing the blacks discomfiture than by leaving Numa to his fate. But how was he to release him? By removing two stakes there would be left plenty of room for the lion to leap from the pit, which was not of any great depth. However, what assurance had Tarzan that

Numa would not leap out instantly the way to freedom was open, and before the ape-man could gain the safety of the trees? Regardless of the fact that Tarzan felt no such fear of the lion as you and I might experience under like circumstances, he yet was imbued with the sense of caution that is necessary to all creatures of the wild if they are to survive. Should necessity require, Tarzan could face Numa in battle, although he was not so egotistical as to think that he could best a full-grown lion in mortal combat other than through accident or the utilization of the cunning of his superior man-mind. To lay himself liable to death futilely, he would have considered as reprehensible as to have shunned danger in time of necessity; but when Tarzan elected to do a thing he usually found the means to accomplish it.

He had now fully determined to liberate Numa, and having so determined, he would accomplish it even though it entailed considerable personal risk. He knew that the lion would be occupied with his feeding for some time, but he also knew that while feeding he would be doubly resentful of any fancied interference. Therefore Tarzan must work with caution.

Coming to the ground at the side of the pit, he examined the stakes and as he did so was rather surprised to note that Numa gave no evidence of anger at his approach. Once he turned a searching gaze upon the ape-man for a moment and then returned to the flesh of Bara. Tarzan felt of the stakes and tested them with his weight. He pulled upon them with the muscles of his strong arms, presently discovering that by working them back and forth he could loosen them: and then a new plan was suggested to him so that he fell to work excavating with his knife at a point above where one of the stakes was imbedded. The loam was soft and easily removed, and it was not long until Tarzan had exposed that part of one of the stakes which was imbedded in the wall of the pit to almost its entire length, leaving only enough imbedded to prevent the stake from falling into the excavation. Then he turned his attention to an adjoining stake and soon had it similarly exposed, after which he threw the noose of his grass rope over the two and swung quickly to the branch of the tree above. Here he gathered in the slack of the rope and, bracing himself against the bole of the tree, pulled steadily upward. Slowly the stakes rose from the trench in which they were imbedded and with them rose Numa's suspicion and growling.

Was this some new encroachment upon his rights and his liberties? He was puzzled and, like all lions, being short of temper, he was irritated. He had not minded it when the Tarmangani squatted upon the verge of the pit and looked down upon him, for had not this Tarmangani fed him? But now something else was afoot and the suspicion of the wild beast was aroused. As he watched, however, Numa saw the stakes rise slowly to an erect position, tumble against each other and then fall backwards out of his sight upon the surface of the ground above. Instantly the lion grasped the possibilities of the situation, and, too, perhaps he sensed the fact that the man-thing had deliberately opened a way for his escape. Seizing the remains of Bara in his great jaws, Numa, the lion, leaped agilely from the pit of the Wamabos and Tarzan of the Apes melted into the jungles to the east.

On the surface of the ground or through the swaying branches of the trees the spoor of man or beast was an open book to the ape-man, but even his acute senses were baffled by the spoorless trail of the airship. Of what good were eyes, or ears, or the sense of smell in following a thing whose path had lain through the shifting air thousands of feet above the tree tops? Only upon his sense of direction could Tarzan depend in his search for the fallen plane. He could not even judge accurately as to the distance it might lie from him, and he knew that from the moment that it disappeared beyond the hills it might have traveled a considerable distance at right angles to its original course before it crashed to earth. If its occupants were killed or badly injured the ape-man might search futilely in their immediate vicinity for some time before finding them.

There was but one thing to do and that was to travel to a point as close as possible to where he judged the plane had landed, and then to follow in ever-widening circles until he picked up their scent spoor. And this he did.

Before he left the valley of plenty he made several kills and carried the choicest cuts of meat with him, leaving all the dead weight of bones behind. The dense vegetation of the jungle terminated at the foot of the western slope, growing less and less abundant as he neared the summit beyond which was a sparse growth of sickly scrub and sunburned grasses, with here and there a gnarled and hardy tree that had withstood the vicissitudes of an almost waterless existence.

From the summit of the hills Tarzan's keen eyes searched the arid landscape before him. In the distance he discerned the ragged tortuous lines that marked the winding course of the hideous gorges which scored the broad plain at intervals—the terrible gorges that had so nearly claimed his life in punishment for his temerity in attempting to invade the sanctity of their ancient solitude.

For two days Tarzan sought futilely for some clew to the whereabouts of the machine or its occupants. He cached portions of his kills at different points, building cairns of rock to mark their locations. He crossed the first deep gorge and circled far beyond it. Occasionally he stopped and called aloud, listening for some response but only silence rewarded him—a sinister silence that his cries only accentuated.

Late in the evening of the second day he came to the well-remembered gorge in which lay the clean-picked bones of the ancient adventurer, and here, for the first time, Ska, the vulture, picked up his trail. "Not this time, Ska," cried the ape-man in a taunting voice, "for now indeed is Tarzan Tarzan. Before, you stalked the grim skeleton of a Tarmangani and even then you lost. Waste not your time upon Tarzan of the Apes in the full of his strength." But still Ska, the vulture, circled and soared above him, and the ape-man, notwithstanding his boasts, felt a shudder of apprehension. Through his brain ran a persistent and doleful chant to which he involuntarily set two words, repeated over and over again in horrible monotony: "Ska knows! Ska knows!" until, shaking himself in anger, he picked up a rock and hurled it at the grim scavenger.

Lowering himself over the precipitous side of the gorge Tarzan half clambered and half slid to the sandy floor beneath. He had come upon the rift at almost the exact spot at which he had clambered from it weeks before, and there he saw, just as he had left it, just, doubtless, as it had lain for centuries, the mighty skeleton and its mighty armor.

As he stood looking down upon this grim reminder that another man of might had succumbed to the cruel powers of the desert, he was brought to startled attention by the report of a firearm, the sound of which came from the depths of the gorge to the south of him, and reverberated along the steep walls of the narrow rift.

CHAPTER XV—MYSTERIOUS FOOTPRINTS

As the British plane piloted by Lieutenant Harold Percy Smith-Oldwick rose above the jungle wilderness where Bertha Kircher's life had so often been upon the point of extinction, and sped toward the east, the girl felt a sudden contraction of the muscles of her throat. She tried very hard to swallow something that was not there. It seemed strange to her that she should feel regret in leaving behind her such hideous perils, and yet it was plain to her that such was the fact, for she was also leaving behind something beside the dangers that had menaced her—a unique figure that had entered her life, and for which she felt an unaccountable attraction.

Before her in the pilot's seat sat an English officer and gentleman whom, she knew, loved her, and yet she dared to feel regret in his company at leaving the stamping ground of a wild beast!

Lieutenant Smith-Oldwick, on his part, was in the seventh heaven of elation. He was in possession again of his beloved ship, he was flying swiftly in the direction of his comrades and his duty, and with him was the woman he loved. The fly in the ointment, however, was the accusation Tarzan had made against this woman. He had said that she was a German, and a spy, and from the heights of bliss the English officer was occasionally plunged to the depths of despair in contemplation of the inevitable, were the ape-man's charges to prove true. He found himself torn between sentiments of love and honor. On the one hand he could not surrender the woman he loved to the certain fate that must be meted out to her if she were in truth an enemy spy, while on the other it would be equally impossible for him as an Englishman and an officer to give her aid or protection.

The young man contented himself therefore with repeated mental denials of her guilt. He tried to convince himself that Tarzan was mistaken, and when he conjured upon the screen of recollection the face of the girl behind him, he was doubly reassured that those lines of sweet femininity and character, those clear and honest eyes, could not belong to one of the hated alien race.

And so they sped toward the east, each wrapped in his own thoughts. Below them they saw the dense vegetation of the jungle give place to the scantier growth upon the hillside, and then before them there spread the wide expanse of arid wastelands marked by the deep scarring of the narrow gorges that long-gone rivers had cut there in some forgotten age.

Shortly after they passed the summit of the ridge which formed the boundary between the desert and the fertile country, Ska, the vulture, winging his way at a high altitude toward his aerie, caught sight of a strange new bird of gigantic proportions encroaching upon the preserves of his aerial domain. Whether with intent to give battle to the interloper or merely impelled by curiosity, Ska rose suddenly upward to meet the plane. Doubtless he misjudged the speed of the newcomer, but be that as it may, the tip of the propeller blade touched him and simultaneously many things happened. The lifeless body of Ska, torn and bleeding, dropped plummet-like toward the ground; a bit of splintered spruce drove backward to strike the pilot on the forehead; the plane shuddered and trembled and as Lieutenant Harold Percy Smith-Oldwick sank forward in momentary unconsciousness the ship dived headlong toward the earth.

Only for an instant was the pilot unconscious, but that instant almost proved their undoing. When he awoke to a realization of their peril it was also to discover that his motor had stalled. The plane had attained frightful momentum, and the ground seemed too close for him to hope to flatten out in time to make a safe landing. Directly beneath him was a deep rift in the plateau, a narrow gorge, the bottom of which appeared comparatively level and sand covered.

In the brief instant in which he must reach a decision, the safest plan seemed to attempt a landing in the gorge, and this he did, but not without considerable damage to the plane and a severe shaking-up for himself and his passenger.

Fortunately neither of them was injured but their condition seemed indeed a hopeless one. It was a grave question as to whether the man could repair his plane and continue the journey, and it seemed equally questionable as to their ability either to proceed on foot to the coast or retrace their way to the country they had just left. The man was confident that they could not hope to cross the desert country to the east in the face of thirst and hunger, while behind them in the valley of plenty lay almost equal danger in the form of carnivores and the warlike natives.

After the plane came to its sudden and disastrous stop, Smith-Oldwick turned quickly to see what the effect of the accident had been on the girl. He found her pale but smiling, and for several seconds the two sat looking at each other in silence.

"This is the end?" the girl asked.

The Englishman shook his head. "It is the end of the first leg, anyway," he replied.

"But you can't hope to make repairs here," she said dubiously.

"No," he said, "not if they amount to anything, but I may be able to patch it up. I will have to look her over a bit first. Let us hope there is nothing serious. It's a long, long way to the Tanga railway."

"We would not get far," said the girl, a slight note of hopelessness in her tone. "Entirely unarmed as we are, it would be little less than a miracle if we covered even a small fraction of the distance."

"But we are not unarmed," replied the man. "I have an extra pistol here, that the beggars didn't discover," and, removing the cover of a compartment, he drew forth an automatic.

Bertha Kircher leaned back in her seat and laughed aloud, a mirthless, half-hysterical laugh. "That popgun!" she exclaimed. "What earthly good would it do other than to infuriate any beast of prey you might happen to hit with it?"

Smith-Oldwick looked rather crestfallen. "But it is a weapon," he said. "You will have to admit that, and certainly I could kill a man with it."

"You could if you happened to hit him," said the girl, "or the thing didn't jam. Really, I haven't much faith in an automatic. I have used them myself."

"Oh, of course," he said ironically, "an express rifle would be better, for who knows but we might meet an elephant here in the desert."

The girl saw that he was hurt, and she was sorry, for she realized that there was nothing he would not do in her service or protection, and that it was through no fault of his that he was so illy armed. Doubtless, too, he realized as well as she the futility of his weapon, and that he had only called attention to it in the hope of reassuring her and lessening her anxiety.

"Forgive me," she said. "I did not mean to be nasty, but this accident is the proverbial last straw. It seems to me that I have borne all that I can. Though I was willing to give my life in the service of my country, I did not imagine that my death agonies would be so long drawn out, for I realize now that I have been dying for many weeks."

"What do you mean!" he exclaimed; "what do you mean by that! You are not dying. There is nothing the matter with you."

"Oh, not that," she said, "I did not mean that. What I mean is that at the moment the black sergeant, Usanga, and his renegade German native troops captured me and brought me inland, my death warrant was signed. Sometimes I have imagined that a reprieve has been granted. Sometimes I have hoped that I might be upon the verge of winning a full pardon, but really in the depths of my heart I have known that I should never live to regain civilization. I have done my bit for my country, and though it was not much I can at least go with the realization that it was the best I was able to offer. All that I can hope for now, all that I ask for, is a speedy fulfillment of the death sentence. I do not wish to linger any more to face constant terror and apprehension. Even physical torture would be preferable to what I have passed through. I have no doubt that you consider me a brave woman, but really my terror has been boundless. The cries of the carnivores at night fill me with a dread so tangible that I am in actual pain. I feel the rending talons in my flesh and the cruel fangs munching upon my bones—it is as real to me as though I were actually enduring the horrors of such a death. I doubt if you can understand it—men are so different."

"Yes," he said, "I think I can understand it, and because I understand I can appreciate more than you imagine the heroism you have shown in your endurance of all that you have passed through. There can be no bravery where there is no fear. A child might walk into a lion's den, but it would take a very brave man to go to its rescue."

"Thank you," she said, "but I am not brave at all, and now I am very much ashamed of my thoughtlessness for your own feelings. I will try and take a new grip upon myself and we will both hope for the best. I will help you all I can if you will tell me what I may do."

"The first thing," he replied, "is to find out just how serious our damage is, and then to see what we can do in the way of repairs."

For two days Smith-Oldwick worked upon the damaged plane—worked in the face of the fact that from the first he realized the case was hopeless. And at last he told her.

"I knew it," she said, "but I believe that I felt much as you must have; that however futile our efforts here might be, it would be infinitely as fatal to attempt to retrace our way to the jungle we just left or to go on toward the coast. You know and I know that we could not reach the Tanga railway on foot. We should die of thirst and starvation before we had covered half the distance, and if we return to the jungle, even were we able to reach it, it would be but to court an equally certain, though different, fate."

"So we might as well sit here and wait for death as to uselessly waste our energies in what we know would be a futile attempt at escape?" he asked.

"No," she replied, "I shall never give up like that. What I meant was that it was useless to attempt to reach either of the places where we know that there is food and water in abundance, so we must strike out in a new direction. Somewhere there may be water in this wilderness and if there is, the best chance of our finding it would be to follow this gorge downward. We have enough food and water left, if we are careful of it, for a couple of days and in that time we might stumble upon a spring or possibly even reach the fertile country which I know lies to the south. When Usanga brought me to the Wamabo country from the coast he took a southerly route along which there was usually water and game in plenty. It was not until we neared our destination that the country became overrun with carnivores. So there is hope if we can reach the fertile country south of us that we can manage to pull through to the coast."

The man shook his head dubiously. "We can try it," he said. "Personally, I do not fancy sitting here waiting for death."

Smith-Oldwick was leaning against the ship, his dejected gaze directed upon the ground at his feet. The girl was looking south down the gorge in the direction of their one slender chance of life. Suddenly she touched him on the arm.

"Look," she whispered.

The man raised his eyes quickly in the direction of her gaze to see the massive head of a great lion who was regarding them from beyond a rocky projection at the first turning of the gorge.

"Phew!" he exclaimed, "the beggars are everywhere."

"They do not go far from water do they," asked the girl hopefully.

"I should imagine not," he replied; "a lion is not particularly strong on endurance."

"Then he is a harbinger of hope," she exclaimed.

The man laughed. "Cute little harbinger of hope!" he said. "Reminds me of Cock Robin heralding spring."

The girl cast a quick glance at him. "Don't be silly, and I don't care if you do laugh. He fills me with hope."

"It is probably mutual," replied Smith-Oldwick, "as we doubtless fill him with hope."

The lion evidently having satisfied himself as to the nature of the creatures before him advanced slowly now in their direction.

"Come," said the man, "let's climb aboard," and he helped the girl over the side of the ship.

"Can't he get in here?" she asked.

"I think he can," said the man.

"You are reassuring," she returned.

"I don't feel so." He drew his pistol.

"For heaven's sake," she cried, "don't shoot at him with that thing. You might hit him."

"I don't intend to shoot at him but I might succeed in frightening him away if he attempts to reach us here. Haven't you ever seen a trainer work with lions? He carries a silly little pop-gun loaded with blank cartridges. With that and a kitchen chair he subdues the most ferocious of beasts."

"But you haven't a kitchen chair," she reminded him.

"No," he said, "Government is always muddling things. I have always maintained that airplanes should be equipped with kitchen chairs."

Bertha Kircher laughed as evenly and with as little hysteria as though she were moved by the small talk of an afternoon tea.

Numa, the lion, came steadily toward them; his attitude seemed more that of curiosity than of belligerency. Close to the side of the ship he stopped and stood gazing up at them.

"Magnificent, isn't he?" exclaimed the man.

"I never saw a more beautiful creature," she replied, "nor one with such a dark coat. Why, he is almost black."

The sound of their voices seemed not to please the lord of the jungle, for he suddenly wrinkled his great face into deep furrows as he bared his fangs beneath snarling lips and gave vent to an angry growl. Almost simultaneously he crouched for a spring and immediately Smith-Oldwick discharged his pistol into the ground in front of the lion. The effect of the noise upon Numa seemed but to enrage him further, and with a horrid roar he sprang for the author of the new and disquieting sound that had outraged his ears.

Simultaneously Lieutenant Harold Percy Smith-Oldwick vaulted nimbly out of the cockpit on the opposite side of his plane, calling to the girl to follow his example. The girl, realizing the futility of leaping to the ground, chose the remaining alternative and clambered to the top of the upper plane.

Numa, unaccustomed to the idiosyncrasies of construction of an airship and having gained the forward cockpit, watched the girl clamber out of his reach without at first endeavoring to prevent her. Having taken possession of the plane his anger seemed suddenly to leave him and he made no immediate move toward following Smith-Oldwick. The girl, realizing the comparative safety of her position, had crawled to the outer edge of the wing and was calling to the man to try and reach the opposite end of the upper plane.

It was this scene upon which Tarzan of the Apes looked as he rounded the bend of the gorge above the plane after the pistol shot had attracted his attention. The girl was so intent upon watching the efforts of the Englishman to reach a place of safety, and the latter was so busily occupied in attempting to do so that neither at once noticed the silent approach of the ape-man.

It was Numa who first noticed the intruder. The lion immediately evinced his displeasure by directing toward him a snarling countenance and a series of warning growls. His action called the attention of the two upon the upper plane to the newcomer, eliciting a stifled "Thank God!" from the girl, even though she could scarce credit the evidence of her own eyes that it was indeed the savage man, whose presence always assured her safety, who had come so providentially in the nick of time.

Almost immediately both were horrified to see Numa leap from the cockpit and advance upon Tarzan. The ape-man, carrying his stout spear in readiness, moved deliberately onward to meet the carnivore, which he had recognized as the lion of the Wamabos' pit. He knew from the manner of Numa's approach what neither Bertha Kircher nor Smith-Oldwick knew—that there was more of curiosity than belligerency in it, and he wondered if in that great head there might not be a semblance of gratitude for the kindness that Tarzan had done him.

There was no question in Tarzan's mind but that Numa recognized him, for he knew his fellows of the jungle well enough to know that while they oft-times forgot certain sensations more quickly than man there are others which remain in their memories for years. A well-defined scent spoor might never be forgotten by a beast if it had first been sensed under unusual circumstances, and so Tarzan was confident that Numa's nose had already reminded him of all the circumstances of their brief connection.

Love of the sporting chance is inherent in the Anglo-Saxon race and it was not now Tarzan of the Apes but rather John Clayton, Lord Greystoke, who smilingly welcomed the sporting chance which he must take to discover how far-reaching was Numa's gratitude.

Smith-Oldwick and the girl saw the two nearing each other. The former swore softly beneath his breath while he nervously fingered the pitiful weapon at his hip. The girl pressed her open palms to her cheeks as she leaned forward in stony-eyed, horror-stricken silence. While she had every confidence in the prowess of the godlike creature who thus dared brazenly to face the king of beasts, she had no false conception of what must certainly happen when they met. She had seen Tarzan battle with Sheeta, the panther, and she had realized then that powerful as the man was, it was only agility, cunning, and chance that placed him upon anywhere near an equal footing with his savage adversary, and that of the three factors upon his side chance was the greatest.

She saw the man and the lion stop simultaneously, not more than a yard apart. She saw the beast's tail whipping from side to side and she could hear his deep-throated growls rumbling from his cavernous breast, but she could read correctly neither the movement of the lashing tail nor the notes of the growl.

To her they seemed to indicate nothing but bestial rage while to Tarzan of the Apes they were conciliatory and reassuring in the extreme. And then she saw Numa move forward again until his nose touched the man's naked leg and she closed her eyes and covered them with her palms. For what seemed an eternity she waited for the horrid sound of the conflict which she knew must come, but all she heard was an explosive sigh of relief from Smith-Oldwick and a half-hysterical "By Jove! Just fancy it!"

She looked up to see the great lion rubbing his shaggy head against the man's hip, and Tarzan's free hand entangled in the black mane as he scratched Numa, the lion, behind a back-laid ear.

Strange friendships are often formed between the lower animals of different species, but less often between man and the savage felidae, because of the former's inherent fear of the great cats. And so after all, therefore, the friendship so suddenly developed between the savage lion and the savage man was not inexplicable.

As Tarzan approached the plane Numa walked at his side, and when Tarzan stopped and looked up at the girl and the man Numa stopped also.

"I had about given up hope of finding you," said the ape-man, "and it is evident that I found you just in time."

"But how did you know we were in trouble?" asked the English officer.

"I saw your plane fall," replied Tarzan. "I was watching you from a tree beside the clearing where you took off. I didn't have much to locate you by other than the general direction, but it seems that you volplaned a considerable distance toward the south after you disappeared from my view behind the hills. I have been looking for you further toward the north. I was just about to turn back when I heard your pistol shot. Is your ship beyond repair?"

"Yes," replied Smith-Oldwick, "it is hopeless."

"What are your plans, then? What do you wish to do?" Tarzan directed his question to the girl.

"We want to reach the coast," she said, "but it seems impossible now."

"I should have thought so a little while ago," replied the ape-man, "but if Numa is here there must be water within a reasonable distance. I ran across this lion two days ago in the Wamabo country. I liberated him from one of their pits. To have reached this spot he must have come by some trail unknown to me—at least I crossed no game trail and no spoor of any animal after I came over the hills out of the fertile country. From which direction did he come upon you?"

"It was from the south," replied the girl. "We thought, too, that there must be water in that direction."

"Let's find out then," said Tarzan.

"But how about the lion?" asked Smith-Oldwick.

"That we will have to discover," replied the ape-man, "and we can only do so if you will come down from your perch."

The officer shrugged his shoulders. The girl turned her gaze upon him to note the effect of Tarzan's proposal. The Englishman grew suddenly very white, but there was a smile upon his lips as without a word he slipped over the edge of the plane and clambered to the ground behind Tarzan.

Bertha Kircher realized that the man was afraid nor did she blame him, and she also realized the remarkable courage that he had shown in thus facing a danger that was very real to him.

Numa standing close to Tarzan's side raised his head and glared at the young Englishman, growled once, and looked up at the ape-man. Tarzan retained a hold upon the beast's mane and spoke to him in the language of the great apes. To the girl and Smith-Oldwick the growling gutturals falling from human lips sounded uncanny in the extreme, but whether Numa understood them or not they appeared to have the desired effect upon him, as he ceased growling, and as Tarzan walked to Smith-Oldwick's side Numa accompanied him, nor did he offer to molest the officer.

"What did you say to him?" asked the girl.

Tarzan smiled. "I told him," he replied, "that I am Tarzan of the Apes, mighty hunter, killer of beasts, lord of the jungle, and that you are my friends. I have never been sure that all of the other beasts understand the language of the Mangani. I know that Manu, the monkey, speaks nearly the same tongue and I am sure that Tantor, the elephant, understands all that I say to him. We of the jungle are great boasters. In our speech, in our carriage, in every detail of our demeanor we must impress others with our physical power and our ferocity. That is why we growl at our enemies. We are telling them to beware or we shall fall upon them and tear them to pieces. Perhaps Numa does not understand the words that I use but I believe that my tones and my manner carry the impression that I wish them to convey. Now you may come down and be introduced."

It required all the courage that Bertha Kircher possessed to lower herself to the ground within reach of the talons and fangs of this untamed forest beast, but she did it. Nor did Numa do more than bare his teeth and growl a little as she came close to the ape-man.

"I think you are safe from him as long as I am present," said the ape-man. "The best thing to do is simply to ignore him. Make no advances, but be sure to give no indication of fear and, if possible always keep me between you and him. He will go away presently I am sure and the chances are that we shall not see him again."

At Tarzan's suggestion Smith-Oldwick removed the remaining water and provisions from the plane and, distributing the burden among them, they set off toward the south. Numa did not follow them, but stood by the plane watching until they finally disappeared from view around a bend in the gorge.

Tarzan had picked up Numa's trail with the intention of following it southward in the belief that it would lead to water. In the sand that floored the bottom of the gorge tracks were plain and easily followed. At first only the fresh tracks of Numa were visible, but later in the day the ape-man discovered the older tracks of other lions and just before dark he stopped suddenly in evident surprise. His two companions looked at him questioningly, and in answer to their implied interrogations he pointed at the ground directly in front of him.

"Look at those," he exclaimed.

At first neither Smith-Oldwick nor the girl saw anything but a confusion of intermingled prints of padded feet in the sand, but presently the girl discovered what Tarzan had seen, and an exclamation of surprise broke from her lips.

"The imprint of human feet!" she cried.

Tarzan nodded.

"But there are no toes," the girl pointed out.

"The feet were shod with a soft sandal," explained Tarzan.

"Then there must be a native village somewhere in the vicinity," said Smith-Oldwick.

"Yes," replied the ape-man, "but not the sort of natives which we would expect to find here in this part of Africa where others all go unshod with the exception of a few of Usanga's renegade German native troops who wear German army shoes. I don't know that you can notice it, but it is evident to me that the foot inside the sandal that made these imprints were not the foot of a Negro. If you will examine them carefully you will notice that the impression of the heel and ball of the foot are well marked even through the sole of the sandal. The weight comes more nearly in the center of a Negro's footprint."

"Then you think these were made by a white person?"

"It looks that way," replied Tarzan, and suddenly, to the surprise of both the girl and Smith-Oldwick, he dropped to his hands and knees and sniffed at the tracks—again a beast utilizing the senses and woodcraft of a beast. Over an area of several square yards his keen nostrils sought the identity of the makers of the tracks. At length he rose to his feet.

"It is not the spoor of the Gomangani," he said, "nor is it exactly like that of white men. There were three who came this way. They were men, but of what race I do not know."

There was no apparent change in the nature of the gorge except that it had steadily grown deeper as they followed it downward until now the rocky and precipitous sides rose far above them. At different points natural caves, which appeared to have been eroded by the action of water in some forgotten age, pitted the side walls at various heights. Near them was such a cavity at the ground's level—an arched cavern floored with white sand. Tarzan indicated it with a gesture of his hand.

"We will lair here tonight," he said, and then with one of his rare, slow smiles: "We will *camp* here tonight."

Having eaten their meager supper Tarzan bade the girl enter the cavern.

"You will sleep inside," he said. "The lieutenant and I will lie outside at the entrance."

CHAPTER XVI—THE NIGHT ATTACK

As the girl turned to bid them good night, she thought that she saw a shadowy form moving in the darkness beyond them, and almost simultaneously she was sure that she heard the sounds of stealthy movement in the same direction.

"What is that?" she whispered. "There is something out there in the darkness."

"Yes," replied Tarzan, "it is a lion. It has been there for some time. Hadn't you noticed it before?"

"Oh!" cried the girl, breathing a sigh of relief, "is it our lion?"

"No," said Tarzan, "it is not our lion; it is another lion and he is hunting."

"He is stalking us?" asked the girl.

"He is," replied the ape-man. Smith-Oldwick fingered the grip of his pistol.

Tarzan saw the involuntary movement and shook his head.

"Leave that thing where it is, Lieutenant," he said.

The officer laughed nervously. "I couldn't help it, you know, old man," he said; "instinct of self-preservation and all that."

"It would prove an instinct of self-destruction," said Tarzan. "There are at least three hunting lions out there watching us. If we had a fire or the moon were up you would see their eyes plainly. Presently they may come after us but the chances are that they will not. If you are very anxious that they should, fire your pistol and hit one of them."

"What if they do charge?" asked the girl; "there is no means of escape."

"Why, we should have to fight them," replied Tarzan.

"What chance would we three have against them?" asked the girl.

The ape-man shrugged his shoulders. "One must die sometime," he said. "To you doubtless it may seem terrible—such a death; but Tarzan of the Apes has always expected to go out in some such way. Few of us die of old age in the jungle, nor should I care to die thus. Some day Numa will get me, or Sheeta, or a black warrior. These or some of the others. What difference does it make which it is, or whether it comes tonight or next year or in ten years? After it is over it will be all the same."

The girl shuddered. "Yes," she said in a dull, hopeless voice, "after it is over it will be all the same."

Then she went into the cavern and lay down upon the sand. Smith-Oldwick sat in the entrance and leaned against the cliff. Tarzan squatted on the opposite side.

"May I smoke?" questioned the officer of Tarzan. "I have been hoarding a few cigarettes and if it won't attract those bouncers out there I would like to have one last smoke before I cash in. Will you join me?" and he proffered the ape-man a cigarette.

"No, thanks," said Tarzan, "but it will be all right if you smoke. No wild animal is particularly fond of the fumes of tobacco so it certainly won't entice them any closer."

Smith-Oldwick lighted his cigarette and sat puffing slowly upon it. He had proffered one to the girl but she had refused, and thus they sat in silence for some time, the silence of the night ruffled occasionally by the faint crunching of padded feet upon the soft sands of the gorge's floor.

It was Smith-Oldwick who broke the silence. "Aren't they unusually quiet for lions?" he asked.

"No," replied the ape-man; "the lion that goes roaring around the jungle does not do it to attract prey. They are very quiet when they are stalking their quarry."

"I wish they would roar," said the officer. "I wish they would do anything, even charge. Just knowing that they are there and occasionally seeing something like a shadow in the darkness and the faint sounds that come to us from them are getting on my nerves. But I hope," he said, "that all three don't charge at once."

"Three?" said Tarzan. "There are seven of them out there now."

"Good Lord! exclaimed Smith-Oldwick.

"Couldn't we build a fire," asked the girl, "and frighten them away?"

"I don't know that it would do any good," said Tarzan, "as I have an idea that these lions are a little different from any that we are familiar with and possibly for the same reason which at first puzzled me a little—I refer to the apparent docility in the presence of a man of the lion who was with us today. A man is out there now with those lions."

"It is impossible!" exclaimed Smith-Oldwick. "They would tear him to pieces."

"What makes you think there is a man there?" asked the girl.

Tarzan smiled and shook his head. "I am afraid you would not understand," he replied. "It is difficult for us to understand anything that is beyond our own powers."

"What do you mean by that?" asked the officer.

"Well," said Tarzan, "if you had been born without eyes you could not understand sense impressions that the eyes of others transmit to their brains, and as you have both been born without any sense of smell I am afraid you cannot understand how I can know that there is a man there."

"You mean that you scent a man?" asked the girl.

Tarzan nodded affirmatively.

"And in the same way you know the number of lions?" asked the man.

"Yes," said Tarzan. "No two lions look alike, no two have the same scent."

The young Englishman shook his head. "No," he said, "I cannot understand."

"I doubt if the lions or the man are here necessarily for the purpose of harming us," said Tarzan, "because there has been nothing to prevent their doing so long before had they wished to. I have a theory, but it is utterly preposterous."

"What is it?" asked the girl.

"I think they are here," replied Tarzan, "to prevent us from going some place that they do not wish us to go; in other words we are under surveillance, and possibly as long as we don't go where we are not wanted we shall not be bothered."

"But how are we to know where they don't want us to go?" asked Smith-Oldwick.

"We can't know," replied Tarzan, "and the chances are that the very place we are seeking is the place they don't wish us to trespass on."

"You mean the water?" asked the girl.

"Yes," replied Tarzan.

For some time they sat in silence which was broken only by an occasional sound of movement from the outer darkness. It must have been an hour later that the ape-man rose quietly and drew his long blade from its sheath. Smith-Oldwick was dozing against the rocky wall of the cavern entrance, while the girl, exhausted by the excitement and fatigue of the day, had fallen into deep slumber. An instant after Tarzan arose, Smith-Oldwick and the girl were aroused by a volley of thunderous roars and the noise of many padded feet rushing toward them.

Tarzan of the Apes stood directly before the entrance to the cavern, his knife in his hand, awaiting the charge. The ape-man had not expected any such concerted action as he now realized had been taken by those watching them. He had known for some time that other men had joined those who were with the lions earlier in the evening, and when he arose to his feet it was because he knew that the lions and the men were moving cautiously closer to him and his party. He might easily have eluded them, for he had seen that the face of the cliff rising above the mouth of the cavern might be scaled by as good a climber as himself. It might have been wiser had he tried to escape, for he knew that in the face of such odds even he was helpless, but he stood his ground though I doubt if he could have told why.

He owed nothing either of duty or friendship to the girl sleeping in the cavern, nor could he longer be of any protection to her or her companion. Yet something held him there in futile self-sacrifice.

The great Tarmangani had not even the satisfaction of striking a blow in self-defense. A veritable avalanche of savage beasts rolled over him and threw him heavily to the ground. In falling his head struck the rocky surface of the cliff, stunning him.

It was daylight when he regained consciousness. The first dim impression borne to his awakening mind was a confusion of savage sounds which gradually resolved themselves into the growling of lions, and then, little by little, there came back to him the recollections of what had preceded the blow that had felled him.

Strong in his nostrils was the scent of Numa, the lion, and against one naked leg he could feel the coat of some animal. Slowly Tarzan opened his eyes. He was lying on his side and as he looked down his body, he saw that a great lion stood straddling him—a great lion who growled hideously at something which Tarzan could not see.

With the full return of his senses Tarzan's nose told him that the beast above him was Numa of the Wamabo pit.

Thus reassured, the ape-man spoke to the lion and at the same time made a motion as though he would arise. Immediately Numa stepped from above him. As Tarzan raised his head, he saw that he still lay where he had fallen before the opening of the cliff where the girl had been sleeping and that Numa, backed against the cliffside, was apparently defending him from two other lions who paced to and fro a short distance from their intended victim.

And then Tarzan turned his eyes into the cave and saw that the girl and Smith-Oldwick were gone.

His efforts had been for naught. With an angry toss of his head, the ape-man turned upon the two lions who had continued to pace back and forth a few yards from him. Numa of the lion pit turned a friendly glance in Tarzan's direction, rubbed his head against the ape-man's side, and then directed his snarling countenance toward the two hunters.

"I think," said Tarzan to Numa, "that you and I together can make these beasts very unhappy." He spoke in English, which, of course, Numa did not understand at all, but there must have been something reassuring in the tone, for Numa whined pleadingly and moved impatiently to and fro parallel with their antagonists.

"Come," said Tarzan suddenly and grasping the lion's mane with his left hand he moved toward the other lions, his companion pacing at his side. As the two advanced the others drew slowly back and, finally separating, moved off to either side. Tarzan and Numa passed between them but neither the great black-maned lion nor the man failed to keep an eye upon the beast nearer him so that they were not caught unawares when, as though at some preconcerted signal, the two cats charged simultaneously from opposite directions.

The ape-man met the charge of his antagonist after the same fashion of fighting that he had been accustomed to employing in previous encounters with Numa and Sheeta. To have attempted to meet the full shock of a lion's charge would have been suicidal even for the giant Tarmangani.

Instead he resorted to methods of agility and cunning, for quick as are the great cats, even quicker is Tarzan of the Apes.

With outspread, raking talons and bared fangs Numa sprang for the naked chest of the ape-man. Throwing up his left arm as a boxer might ward off a blow, Tarzan struck upward beneath the left forearm of the lion, at the same time rushing in with his shoulder beneath the animal's body and simultaneously drove his blade into the tawny hide behind the shoulder. With a roar of pain Numa wheeled again, the personification of bestial rage. Now indeed would he exterminate this presumptuous man-thing who dared even to think that he could thwart the king of beasts in his desires. But as he wheeled, his intended quarry wheeled with him, brown fingers locked in the heavy mane on the powerful neck and again the blade struck deep into the lion's side.

Then it was that Numa went mad with hate and pain and at the same instant the ape-man leaped full upon his back. Easily before had Tarzan locked his legs beneath the belly of a lion while he clung to its long mane and stabbed it until his point reached its heart. So easy it had seemed before that he experienced a sharp feeling of resentment that he was unable to do so now, for the quick movements of the lion prevented him, and presently, to his dismay, as the lion leaped and threw him about, the ape-man realized that he was swinging inevitably beneath those frightful talons.

With a final effort he threw himself from Numa's back and sought, by his quickness, to elude the frenzied beast for the fraction of an instant that would permit him to regain his feet and meet the animal again upon a more even footing. But this time Numa was too quick for him and he was but partially up when a great paw struck him on the side of the head and bowled him over.

As he fell he saw a black streak shoot above him and another lion close upon his antagonist. Rolling from beneath the two battling lions Tarzan regained his feet, though he was half dazed and staggering from the impact of the terrible blow he had received. Behind him he saw a lifeless lion lying torn and bleeding upon the sand, and before him Numa of the pit was savagely mauling the second lion.

He of the black coat tremendously outclassed his adversary in point of size and strength as well as in ferocity. The battling beasts made a few feints and passes at each other before the larger succeeded in fastening his fangs in the other's throat, and then, as a cat shakes a mouse, the larger lion shook the lesser, and when his dying foe sought to roll beneath and rake his conqueror with his hind claws, the other met him halfway at his own game, and as the great talons buried themselves in the lower part of the other's chest and then were raked downward with all the terrific strength of the mighty hind legs, the battle was ended.

As Numa rose from his second victim and shook himself, Tarzan could not but again note the wondrous proportions and symmetry of the beast. The lions they had bested were splendid specimens themselves and in their coats Tarzan noted a suggestion of the black which was such a strongly marked characteristic of Numa of the pit. Their manes were just a trifle darker than an ordinary black-maned lion but the tawny shade on the balance of their coats predominated. However, the ape-man realized that they were a distinct species from any he had seen as though they had sprung originally from a cross between the forest lion of his acquaintance and a breed of which Numa of the pit might be typical.

The immediate obstruction in his way having been removed, Tarzan was for setting out in search of the spoor of the girl and Smith-Oldwick, that he might discover their fate. He suddenly found himself tremendously hungry and as he circled about over the sandy bottom searching among the tangled network of innumerable tracks for those of his proteges, there broke from his lips involuntarily the whine of a hungry beast. Immediately Numa of the pit pricked up his ears and, regarding the ape-man steadily for a moment, he answered the call of hunger and started briskly off toward the south, stopping occasionally to see if Tarzan was following.

The ape-man realized that the beast was leading him to food, and so he followed and as he followed his keen eyes and sensitive nostrils sought for some indication of the direction taken by the man and the girl. Presently out of the mass of lion tracks, Tarzan picked up those of many sandaled feet and the scent spoor of the members of the strange race such as had been with the lions the night before, and then faintly he caught the scent spoor of the girl and a little later that of Smith-Oldwick. Presently the tracks thinned and here those of the girl and the Englishman became well marked.

They had been walking side by side and there had been men and lions to the right and left of them, and men and lions in front and behind. The ape-man was puzzled by the possibilities suggested by the tracks, but in the light of any previous experience he could not explain satisfactorily to himself what his perceptions indicated.

There was little change in the formation of the gorge; it still wound its erratic course between precipitous cliffs. In places it widened out and again it became very narrow and always deeper the further south they traveled. Presently the bottom of the gorge began to slope more rapidly. Here and there were indications of ancient rapids and waterfalls. The trail became more difficult but was well marked and showed indications of great antiquity, and, in places, the handiwork of man. They had proceeded for a half or three-quarters of a mile when, at a turning of the gorge, Tarzan saw before him a narrow valley cut deep into the living rock of the earth's crust, with lofty mountain ranges bounding it upon the south. How far it extended east and west he could not see, but apparently it was no more than three or four miles across from north to south.

That it was a well-watered valley was indicated by the wealth of vegetation that carpeted its floor from the rocky cliffs upon the north to the mountains on the south.

Over the edge of the cliffs from which the ape-man viewed the valley a trail had been hewn that led downward to the base. Preceded by the lion Tarzan descended into the valley, which, at this point, was forested with large trees. Before him the trail wound onward toward the center of the valley. Raucous-voiced birds of brilliant plumage screamed among the branches while innumerable monkeys chattered and scolded above him.

The forest teemed with life, and yet there was borne in upon the ape-man a sense of unutterable loneliness, a sensation that he never before had felt in his beloved jungles. There was unreality in everything about him—in the valley itself, lying hidden and forgotten in what was supposed to be an arid waste. The birds and the monkeys, while similar in type to many with which he was familiar, were identical with none, nor was the vegetation without its idiosyncrasies. It was as though he had been suddenly transported to another world and he felt a strange restlessness that might easily have been a premonition of danger.

Fruits were growing among the trees and some of these he saw that Manu, the monkey, ate. Being hungry he swung to the lower branches and, amidst a great chattering of the monkeys, proceeded to eat such of the fruit as he saw the monkeys ate in safety. When he had partially satisfied his hunger, for meat alone could fully do so, he looked about him for Numa of the pit to discover that the lion had gone.

CHAPTER XVII—THE WALLED CITY

Dropping to the ground once more he picked up the trail of the girl and her captors, which he followed easily along what appeared to be a well-beaten trail. It was not long before he came to a small stream, where he quenched his thirst, and thereafter he saw that the trail followed in the general direction of the stream, which ran southwesterly. Here and there were cross trails and others which joined the main avenue, and always upon each of them were the tracks and scent of the great cats, of Numa, the lion, and Sheeta, the panther.

With the exception of a few small rodents there appeared to be no other wild life on the surface of the valley. There was no indication of Bara, the deer, or Horta, the boar, or of Gorgo, the buffalo, Buto, Tantor, or Duro. Histah, the snake, was there. He saw him in the trees in greater numbers than he ever had seen Histah before; and once beside a reedy pool he caught a scent that could have belonged to none other than Gimla the crocodile, but upon none of these did the Tarmangani care to feed.

And so, as he craved meat, he turned his attention to the birds above him. His assailants of the night before had not disarmed him. Either in the darkness and the rush of the charging lions the human foe had overlooked him or else they had considered him dead; but whatever the reason he still retained his weapons—his spear and his long knife, his bow and arrows, and his grass rope.

Fitting a shaft to his bow Tarzan awaited an opportunity to bring down one of the larger birds, and when the opportunity finally presented itself he drove the arrow straight to its mark. As the gaily plumaged creature fluttered to earth its companions and the little monkeys set up a most terrific chorus of wails and screaming protests. The whole forest became suddenly a babel of hoarse screams and shrill shrieks.

Tarzan would not have been surprised had one or two birds in the immediate vicinity given voice to terror as they fled, but that the whole life of the jungle should set up so weird a protest filled him with disgust. It was an angry face that he turned up toward the monkeys and the birds as there suddenly stirred within him a savage inclination to voice his displeasure and his answer to what he considered their challenge. And so it was that there broke upon this jungle for the first time Tarzan's hideous scream of victory and challenge.

The effect upon the creatures above him was instantaneous. Where before the air had trembled to the din of their voices, now utter silence reigned and a moment later the ape-man was alone with his puny kill.

The silence following so closely the previous tumult carried a sinister impression to the ape-man, which still further aroused his anger. Picking the bird from where it had fallen he withdrew his arrow from the body and returned it to his quiver. Then with his knife he quickly and deftly removed the skin and feathers together. He ate angrily, growling as though actually menaced by a near-by foe, and perhaps, too, his growls were partially induced by the fact that he did not care for the flesh of birds. Better this, however, than nothing and from what his senses had told him there was no flesh in the vicinity such as he was accustomed to and cared most for. How he would have enjoyed a juicy haunch from Pacco, the zebra, or a steak from the loin of Gorgo, the buffalo! The very thought made his mouth water and increased his resentment against this unnatural forest that harbored no such delicious quarry.

He had but partially consumed his kill when he suddenly became aware of a movement in the brush at no great distance from him and downwind, and a moment later his nostrils picked up the scent of Numa from the opposite direction, and then upon either side he caught the fall of padded feet and the brushing of bodies against leafy branches. The ape-man smiled. What stupid creature did they think him, to be surprised by such clumsy stalkers? Gradually the sounds and scents indicated that lions were moving upon him from all directions, that he was in the center of a steadily converging circle of beasts. Evidently they were so sure of their prey that they were making no effort toward stealth, for he heard twigs crack beneath their feet, and the brushing of their bodies against the vegetation through which they forced their way.

He wondered what could have brought them. It seemed unreasonable to believe that the cries of the birds and the monkeys should have summoned them, and yet, if not, it was indeed a remarkable coincidence. His judgment told him that the death of a single bird in this forest which teemed with birds could scarce be of sufficient moment to warrant that which followed. Yet even in the face of reason and past experience he found that the whole affair perplexed him.

He stood in the center of the trail awaiting the coming of the lions and wondering what would be the method of their attack or if they would indeed attack. Presently a maned lion came into view along the trail below him. At sight of him the lion halted. The beast was similar to those that had attacked him earlier in the day, a trifle larger and a trifle darker than the lions of his native jungles, but neither so large nor so black as Numa of the pit.

Presently he distinguished the outlines of other lions in the surrounding brush and among the trees. Each of them halted as it came within sight of the ape-man and there they stood regarding him in silence. Tarzan wondered how long it would be before they charged and while he waited he resumed his feeding, though with every sense constantly alert.

One by one the lions lay down, but always their faces were toward him and their eyes upon him. There had been no growling and no roaring—just the quiet drawing of the silent circle about him. It was all so entirely foreign to anything that Tarzan ever before had seen lions do that it irritated him so that presently, having finished his repast, he fell to making insulting remarks to first one and then another of the lions, after the habit he had learned from the apes of his childhood.

"Dango, eater of carrion," he called them, and he compared them most unfavorably with Histah, the snake, the most loathed and repulsive creature of the jungle. Finally he threw handfuls of earth at them and bits of broken twigs, and then the lions growled and bared their fangs, but none of them advanced.

"Cowards," Tarzan taunted them. "Numa with a heart of Bara, the deer." He told them who he was, and after the manner of the jungle folk he boasted as to the horrible things he would do to them, but the lions only lay and watched him.

It must have been a half hour after their coming that Tarzan caught in the distance along the trail the sound of footsteps approaching. They were the footsteps of a creature who walked upon two legs, and though Tarzan could catch no scent spoor from that direction he knew that a man was approaching. Nor had he long to wait before his judgment was confirmed by the appearance of a man who halted in the trail directly behind the first lion that Tarzan had seen.

At sight of the newcomer the ape-man realized that here was one similar to those who had given off the unfamiliar scent spoor that he had detected the previous night, and he saw that not only in the matter of scent did the man differ from other human beings with whom Tarzan was familiar.

The fellow was strongly built with skin of a leathery appearance, like parchment yellowed with age. His hair, which was coal black and three or four inches in length, grew out stiffly at right angles to his scalp. His eyes were close set and the irises densely black and very small, so that the white of the eyeball showed around them. The man's face was smooth except for a few straggly hairs on his chin and upper lip. The nose was aquiline and fine, but the hair grew so far down on the forehead as to suggest a very low and brutal type. The upper lip was short and fine while the lower lip was rather heavy and inclined to be pendulous, the chin being equally weak. Altogether the face carried the suggestion of a once strong and handsome countenance entirely altered by physical violence or by degraded habits and thoughts. The man's arms were long, though not abnormally so, while his legs were short, though straight.

He was clothed in tight-fitting nether garments and a loose, sleeveless tunic that fell just below his hips, while his feet were shod in soft-soled sandals, the wrappings of which extended halfway to his knees, closely resembling a modern spiral military legging. He carried a short, heavy spear, and at his side swung a weapon that at first so astonished the ape-man that he could scarcely believe the evidence of his senses—a heavy saber in a leather-covered scabbard. The man's tunic appeared to have been fabricated upon a loom—it was certainly not made of skins, while the garments that covered his legs were quite as evidently made from the hides of rodents.

Tarzan noted the utter unconcern with which the man approached the lions, and the equal indifference of Numa to him. The fellow paused for a moment as though appraising the ape-man and then pushed on past the lions, brushing against the tawny hide as he passed him in the trail.

About twenty feet from Tarzan the man stopped, addressing the former in a strange jargon, no syllable of which was intelligible to the Tarmangani. His gestures indicated numerous references to the lions surrounding them, and once he touched his spear with the forefinger of his left hand and twice he struck the saber at his hip.

While he spoke Tarzan studied the fellow closely, with the result that there fastened itself upon his mind a strange conviction—that the man who addressed him was what might only be described as a rational maniac. As the thought came to the ape-man he could not but smile, so paradoxical the description seemed. Yet a closer study of the man's features, carriage, and the contour of his head carried almost incontrovertibly the assurance that he was insane, while the tones of his voice and his gestures resembled those of a sane and intelligent mortal.

Presently the man had concluded his speech and appeared to be waiting questioningly Tarzan's reply. The ape-man spoke to the other first in the language of the great apes, but he soon saw that the words carried no conviction to his listener. Then with equal futility he tried several native dialects but to none of these did the man respond.

By this time Tarzan began to lose patience. He had wasted sufficient time by the road, and as he had never depended much upon speech in the accomplishment of his ends, he now raised his spear and advanced toward the other. This, evidently, was a language common to both, for instantly the fellow raised his own weapon and at the same time a low call broke from his lips, a call which instantly brought to action every lion in the hitherto silent circle. A volley of roars shattered the silence of the forest and simultaneously lions sprang into view upon all sides as they closed in rapidly upon their quarry. The man who had called them stepped back, his teeth bared in a mirthless grin.

It was then that Tarzan first noticed that the fellow's upper canines were unusually long and exceedingly sharp. It was just a flashing glimpse he got of them as he leaped agilely from the ground and, to the consternation of both the lions and their master, disappeared in the foliage of the lower terrace, flinging back over his shoulder as he swung rapidly away: "I am Tarzan of the Apes; mighty hunter; mighty fighter! None in the jungle more powerful, none more cunning than Tarzan!"

A short distance beyond the point at which they had surrounded him, Tarzan came to the trail again and sought for the spoor of Bertha Kircher and Lieutenant Smith-Oldwick. He found them quickly and continued upon his search for the two. The spoor lay directly along the trail for another half-mile when the way suddenly debouched from the forest into open land and there broke upon the astonished view of the ape-man the domes and minarets of a walled city.

Directly before him in the wall nearest him Tarzan saw a low-arched gateway to which a well-beaten trail led from that which he had been following. In the open space between the forest and the city walls, quantities of garden stuff was growing, while before him at his feet, in an open man-made ditch, ran a stream of water! The plants in the garden were laid out in well-spaced, symmetrical rows and appeared to have been given excellent attention and cultivation. Tiny streams were trickling between the rows from the main ditch before him and at some distance to his right he could see people at work among the plants.

The city wall appeared to be about thirty feet in height, its plastered expanse unbroken except by occasional embrasures. Beyond the wall rose the domes of several structures and numerous minarets dotted the sky line of the city. The largest and central dome appeared to be gilded, while others were red, or blue, or yellow. The architecture of the wall itself was of uncompromising simplicity. It was of a cream shade and appeared to be plastered and painted. At its base was a line of well-tended shrubs and at some distance towards its eastern extremity it was vine covered to the top.

As he stood in the shadow of the trail, his keen eyes taking in every detail of the picture before him, he became aware of the approach of a party in his rear and there was borne to him the scent of the man and the lions whom he had so readily escaped. Taking to the trees Tarzan moved a short distance to the west and, finding a comfortable crotch at the edge of the forest where he could watch the trail leading through the gardens to the city gate, he awaited the return of his would-be captors. And soon they came—the strange man followed by the pack of great lions. Like dogs they moved along behind him down the trail among the gardens to the gate.

Here the man struck upon the panels of the door with the butt of his spear, and when it opened in response to his signal he passed in with his lions. Beyond the open door Tarzan, from his distant perch, caught but a fleeting glimpse of life within the city, just enough to indicate that there were other human creatures who abode there, and then the door closed.

Through that door he knew that the girl and the man whom he sought to succor had been taken into the city. What fate lay in store for them or whether already it had been meted out to them he could not even guess, nor where, within that forbidding wall, they were incarcerated he could not know. But of one thing he was assured: that if he were to aid them he could not do it from outside the wall. He must gain entrance to the city first, nor did he doubt, that once within, his keen senses would eventually reveal the whereabouts of those whom he sought.

The low sun was casting long shadows across the gardens when Tarzan saw the workers returning from the eastern field. A man came first, and as he came he lowered little gates along the large ditch of running water, shutting off the streams that had run between the rows of growing plants; and behind him came other men carrying burdens of fresh vegetables in great woven baskets upon their shoulders. Tarzan had not realized that there had been so many men working in the field, but now as he sat there at the close of the day he saw a procession filing in from the east, bearing the tools and the produce back into the city.

And then, to gain a better view, the ape-man ascended to the topmost branches of a tall tree where he overlooked the nearer wall. From this point of vantage he saw that the city was long and narrow, and that while the outer walls formed a perfect rectangle, the streets within were winding. Toward the center of the city there appeared to be a low, white building around which the larger edifices of the city had been built, and here, in the fast-waning light, Tarzan thought that between two buildings he caught the glint of water, but of that he was not sure. His experience of the centers of civilization naturally inclined him to believe that this central area was a plaza about which the larger buildings were grouped and that there would be the most logical place to search first for Bertha Kircher and her companion.

And then the sun went down and darkness quickly enveloped the city—a darkness that was accentuated for the ape-man rather than relieved by the artificial lights which immediately appeared in many of the windows visible to him.

Tarzan had noticed that the roofs of most of the buildings were flat, the few exceptions being those of what he imagined to be the more pretentious public structures. How this city had come to exist in this forgotten part of unexplored Africa the ape-man could not conceive. Better than another, he realized something of the unsolved secrets of the Great Dark Continent, enormous areas of which have as yet been untouched by the foot of civilized man. Yet he could scarce believe that a city of this size and apparently thus well constructed could have existed for the generations that it must have been there, without intercourse with the outer world. Even though it was surrounded by a trackless desert waste, as he knew it to be, he could not conceive that generation after generation of men could be born and die there without attempting to solve the mysteries of the world beyond the confines of their little valley.

And yet, here was the city surrounded by tilled land and filled with people!

With the coming of night there arose throughout the jungle the cries of the great cats, the voice of Numa blended with that of Sheeta, and the thunderous roars of the great males reverberated through the forest until the earth trembled, and from within the city came the answering roars of other lions.

A simple plan for gaining entrance to the city had occurred to Tarzan, and now that darkness had fallen he set about to put it into effect. Its success hinged entirely upon the strength of the vines he had seen surmounting the wall toward the east. In this direction he made his way, while from out of the forest about him the cries of the flesh-eaters increased in volume and ferocity. A quarter of a mile intervened between the forest and the city wall—a quarter of a mile of cultivated land unrelieved by a single tree. Tarzan of the Apes realized his limitations and so he knew that it would undoubtedly spell death for him to be caught in the open space by one of the great black lions of the forest if, as he had already surmised, Numa of the pit was a specimen of the forest lion of the valley.

He must, therefore, depend entirely upon his cunning and his speed, and upon the chance that the vine would sustain his weight.

He moved through the middle terrace, where the way is always easiest, until he reached a point opposite the vine-clad portion of the wall, and there he waited, listening and scenting, until he might assure himself that there was no Numa within his immediate vicinity, or, at least, none that sought him. And when he was quite sure that there was no lion close by in the forest, and none in the clearing between himself and the wall, he dropped lightly to the ground and moved stealthily out into the open.

The rising moon, just topping the eastern cliffs, cast its bright rays upon the long stretch of open garden beneath the wall. And, too, it picked out in clear relief for any curious eyes that chanced to be cast in that direction, the figure of the giant ape-man moving across the clearing. It was only chance, of course, that a great lion hunting at the edge of the forest saw the figure of the man halfway between the forest and the wall. Suddenly there broke upon Tarzan's ears a menacing sound. It was not the roar of a hungry lion, but the roar of a lion in rage, and, as he glanced back in the direction from which the sound came, he saw a huge beast moving out from the shadow of the forest toward him.

Even in the moonlight and at a distance Tarzan saw that the lion was huge; that it was indeed another of the black-maned monsters similar to Numa of the pit. For an instant he was impelled to turn and fight, but at the same time the thought of the helpless girl imprisoned in the city flashed through his brain and, without an instant's hesitation, Tarzan of the Apes wheeled and ran for the wall. Then it was that Numa charged.

Numa, the lion, can run swiftly for a short distance, but he lacks endurance. For the period of an ordinary charge he can cover the ground with greater rapidity possibly than any other creature in the world. Tarzan, on the other hand, could run at great speed for long distances, though never as rapidly as Numa when the latter charged.

The question of his fate, then, rested upon whether, with his start he could elude Numa for a few seconds; and, if so, if the lion would then have sufficient stamina remaining to pursue him at a reduced gait for the balance of the distance to the wall.

Never before, perhaps, was staged a more thrilling race, and yet it was run with only the moon and stars to see. Alone and in silence the two beasts sped across the moonlit clearing. Numa gained with appalling rapidity upon the fleeing man, yet at every bound Tarzan was nearer to the vine-clad wall. Once the ape-man glanced back. Numa was so close upon him that it seemed inevitable that at the next bound he should drag him down; so close was he that the ape-man drew his knife as he ran, that he might at least give a good account of himself in the last moments of his life.

But Numa had reached the limit of his speed and endurance. Gradually he dropped behind but he did not give up the pursuit, and now Tarzan realized how much hinged upon the strength of the untested vines.

If, at the inception of the race, only Goro and the stars had looked down upon the contestants, such was not the case at its finish, since from an embrasure near the summit of the wall two close-set black eyes peered down upon the two. Tarzan was a dozen yards ahead of Numa when he reached the wall. There was no time to stop and institute a search for sturdy stems and safe handholds. His fate was in the hands of chance and with the realization he gave a final spurt and running catlike up the side of the wall among the vines, sought with his hands for something that would sustain his weight. Below him Numa leaped also.

CHAPTER XVIII—AMONG THE MANIACS

As the lions swarmed over her protectors, Bertha Kircher shrank back in the cave in a momentary paralysis of fright super-induced, perhaps, by the long days of terrific nerve strain which she had undergone.

Mingled with the roars of the lions had been the voices of men, and presently out of the confusion and turmoil she felt the near presence of a human being, and then hands reached forth and seized her. It was dark and she could see but little, nor any sign of the English officer or the ape-man. The man who seized her kept the lions from her with what appeared to be a stout spear, the haft of which he used to beat off the beasts. The fellow dragged her from the cavern the while he shouted what appeared to be commands and warnings to the lions.

Once out upon the light sands of the bottom of the gorge objects became more distinguishable, and then she saw that there were other men in the party and that two half led and half carried the stumbling figure of a third, whom she guessed must be Smith-Oldwick.

For a time the lions made frenzied efforts to reach the two captives but always the men with them succeeded in beating them off. The fellows seemed utterly unafraid of the great beasts leaping and snarling about them, handling them much the same as one might handle a pack of obstreperous dogs. Along the bed of the old watercourse that once ran through the gorge they made their way, and as the first faint lightening of the eastern horizon presaged the coming dawn, they paused for a moment upon the edge of a declivity, which appeared to the girl in the strange light of the waning night as a vast, bottomless pit; but, as their captors resumed their way and the light of the new day became stronger, she saw that they were moving downward toward a dense forest.

Once beneath the over-arching trees all was again Cimmerian darkness, nor was the gloom relieved until the sun finally arose beyond the eastern cliffs, when she saw that they were following what appeared to be a broad and well-beaten game trail through a forest of great trees. The ground was unusually dry for an African forest and the underbrush, while heavily foliaged, was not nearly so rank and impenetrable as that which she had been accustomed to find in similar woods. It was as though the trees and the bushes grew in a waterless country, nor was there the musty odor of decaying vegetation or the myriads of tiny insects such as are bred in damp places.

As they proceeded and the sun rose higher, the voices of the arboreal jungle life rose in discordant notes and loud chattering about them. Innumerable monkeys scolded and screamed in the branches overhead, while harsh-voiced birds of brilliant plumage darted hither and thither. She noticed presently that their captors often cast apprehensive glances in the direction of the birds and on numerous occasions seemed to be addressing the winged denizens of the forest.

One incident made a marked impression on her. The man who immediately preceded her was a fellow of powerful build, yet, when a brilliantly colored parrot swooped downward toward him, he dropped upon his knees and covering his face with his arms bent forward until his head touched the ground. Some of the others looked at him and laughed nervously. Presently the man glanced upward and seeing that the bird had gone, rose to his feet and continued along the trail.

It was at this brief halt that Smith-Oldwick was brought to her side by the men who had been supporting him. He had been rather badly mauled by one of the lions; but was now able to walk alone, though he was extremely weak from shock and loss of blood.

"Pretty mess, what?" he remarked with a wry smile, indicating his bloody and disheveled state.

"It is terrible," said the girl. "I hope you are not suffering."

"Not as much as I should have expected," he replied, "but I feel as weak as a fool. What sort of creatures are these beggars, anyway?"

"I don't know," she replied, "there is something terribly uncanny about their appearance."

The man regarded one of their captors closely for a moment and then, turning to the girl asked, "Did you ever visit a madhouse?"

She looked up at him in quick understanding and with a horrified expression in her eyes. "That's it!" she cried.

"They have all the earmarks," he said. "Whites of the eyes showing all around the irises, hair growing stiffly erect from the scalp and low down upon the forehead—even their mannerisms and their carriage are those of maniacs."

The girl shuddered.

"Another thing about them," continued the Englishman, "that doesn't appear normal is that they are afraid of parrots and utterly fearless of lions."

"Yes," said the girl; "and did you notice that the birds seem utterly fearless of them—really seem to hold them in contempt? Have you any idea what language they speak?"

"No," said the man, "I have been trying to figure that out. It's not like any of the few native dialects of which I have any knowledge."

"It doesn't sound at all like the native language," said the girl, "but there is something familiar about it. You know, every now and then I feel that I am just on the verge of understanding what they are saying, or at least that somewhere I have heard their tongue before, but final recognition always eludes me."

"I doubt if you ever heard their language spoken," said the man. "These people must have lived in this out-of-the-way valley for ages and even if they had retained the original language of their ancestors without change, which is doubtful, it must be some tongue that is no longer spoken in the outer world."

At one point where a stream of water crossed the trail the party halted while the lions and the men drank. They motioned to their captives to drink too, and as Bertha Kircher and Smith-Oldwick, lying prone upon the ground drank from the clear, cool water of the rivulet, they were suddenly startled by the thunderous roar of a lion a short distance ahead of them. Instantly the lions with them set up a hideous response, moving restlessly to and fro with their eyes always either turned in the direction from which the roar had come or toward their masters, against whom the tawny beasts slunk. The men loosened the sabers in their scabbards, the weapons that had aroused Smith-Oldwick's curiosity as they had Tarzan's, and grasped their spears more firmly.

Evidently there were lions and lions, and while they evinced no fear of the beasts which accompanied them, it was quite evident that the voice of the newcomer had an entirely different effect upon them, although the men seemed less terrified than the lions. Neither, however, showed any indication of an inclination to flee; on the contrary the entire party advanced along the trail in the direction of the menacing roars, and presently there appeared in the center of the path a black lion of gigantic proportions. To Smith-Oldwick and the girl he appeared to be the same lion that they had encountered at the plane and from which Tarzan had rescued them. But it was not Numa of the pit, although he resembled him closely.

The black beast stood directly in the center of the trail lashing his tail and growling menacingly at the advancing party. The men urged on their own beasts, who growled and whined but hesitated to charge. Evidently becoming impatient, and in full consciousness of his might the intruder raised his tail stiffly erect and shot forward. Several of the defending lions made a half-hearted attempt to obstruct his passage, but they might as well have placed themselves in the path of an express train, as hurling them aside the great beast leaped straight for one of the men. A dozen spears were launched at him and a dozen sabers leaped from their scabbards; gleaming, razor-edged weapons they were, but for the instant rendered futile by the terrific speed of the charging beast.

Two of the spears entering his body but served to further enrage him as, with demoniacal roars, he sprang upon the hapless man he had singled out for his prey. Scarcely pausing in his charge he seized the fellow by the shoulder and, turning quickly at right angles, leaped into the concealing foliage that flanked the trail, and was gone, bearing his victim with him.

So quickly had the whole occurrence transpired that the formation of the little party was scarcely altered. There had been no opportunity for flight, even if it had been contemplated; and now that the lion was gone with his prey the men made no move to pursue him. They paused only long enough to recall the two or three of their lions that had scattered and then resumed the march along the trail.

"Might be an everyday occurrence from all the effect it has on them," remarked Smith-Oldwick to the girl.

"Yes," she said. "They seem to be neither surprised nor disconcerted, and evidently they are quite sure that the lion, having got what he came for, will not molest them further."

"I had thought," said the Englishman, "that the lions of the Wamabo country were about the most ferocious in existence, but they are regular tabby cats by comparison with these big black fellows. Did you ever see anything more utterly fearless or more terribly irresistible than that charge?"

For a while, as they walked side by side, their thoughts and conversation centered upon this latest experience, until the trail emerging from the forest opened to their view a walled city and an area of cultivated land. Neither could suppress an exclamation of surprise.

"Why, that wall is a regular engineering job," exclaimed Smith-Oldwick.

"And look at the domes and minarets of the city beyond," cried the girl. "There must be a civilized people beyond that wall. Possibly we are fortunate to have fallen into their hands."

Smith-Oldwick shrugged his shoulders. "I hope so," he said, "though I am not at all sure about people who travel about with lions and are afraid of parrots. There must be something wrong with them."

The party followed the trail across the field to an arched gateway which opened at the summons of one of their captors, who beat upon the heavy wooden panels with his spear. Beyond, the gate opened into a narrow street which seemed but a continuation of the jungle trail leading from the forest. Buildings on either hand adjoined the wall and fronted the narrow, winding street, which was only visible for a short distance ahead. The houses were practically all two-storied structures, the upper stories flush with the street while the walls of the first story were set back some ten feet, a series of simple columns and arches supporting the front of the second story and forming an arcade on either side of the narrow thoroughfare.

The pathway in the center of the street was unpaved, but the floors of the arcades were cut stone of various shapes and sizes but all carefully fitted and laid without mortar. These floors gave evidence of great antiquity, there being a distinct depression down the center as though the stone had been worn away by the passage of countless sandaled feet during the ages that it had lain there.

There were few people astir at this early hour, and these were of the same type as their captors. At first those whom they saw were only men, but as they went deeper into the city they came upon a few naked children playing in the soft dust of the roadway. Many they passed showed the greatest surprise and curiosity in the prisoners, and often made inquiries of the guards, which the two assumed must have been in relation to themselves, while others appeared not to notice them at all.

"I wish we could understand their bally language," exclaimed Smith-Oldwick.

"Yes," said the girl, "I would like to ask them what they are going to do with us."

"That would be interesting," said the man. "I have been doing considerable wondering along that line myself."

"I don't like the way their canine teeth are filed," said the girl. "It's too suggestive of some of the cannibals I have seen."

"You don't really believe they are cannibals, do you?" asked the man. "You don't think white people are ever cannibals, do you?"

"Are these people white?" asked the girl.

"They're not Negroes, that's certain," rejoined the man. "Their skin is yellow, but yet it doesn't resemble the Chinese exactly, nor are any of their features Chinese."

It was at this juncture that they caught their first glimpse of a native woman. She was similar in most respects to the men though her stature was smaller and her figure more symmetrical. Her face was more repulsive than that of the men, possibly because of the fact that she was a woman, which rather accentuated the idiosyncrasies of eyes, pendulous lip, pointed tusks and stiff, low-growing hair. The latter was longer than that of the men and much heavier. It hung about her shoulders and was confined by a colored bit of some lacy fabric. Her single garment appeared to be nothing more than a filmy scarf which was wound tightly around her body from below her naked breasts, being caught up some way at the bottom near her ankles. Bits of shiny metal resembling gold, ornamented both the headdress and the skirt. Otherwise the woman was entirely without jewelry. Her bare arms were slender and shapely and her hands and feet well proportioned and symmetrical.

She came close to the party as they passed her, jabbering to the guards who paid no attention to her. The prisoners had an opportunity to observe her closely as she followed at their side for a short distance.

"The figure of a houri," remarked Smith-Oldwick, "with the face of an imbecile."

The street they followed was intersected at irregular intervals by crossroads which, as they glanced down them, proved to be equally as tortuous as that through which they were being conducted. The houses varied but little in design. Occasionally there were bits of color, or some attempt at other architectural ornamentation. Through open windows and doors they could see that the walls of the houses were very thick and that all apertures were quite small, as though the people had built against extreme heat, which they realized must have been necessary in this valley buried deep in an African desert.

Ahead they occasionally caught glimpses of larger structures, and as they approached them, came upon what was evidently a part of the business section of the city. There were numerous small shops and bazaars interspersed among the residences, and over the doors of these were signs painted in characters strongly suggesting Greek origin and yet it was not Greek as both the Englishman and the girl knew.

Smith-Oldwick was by this time beginning to feel more acutely the pain of his wounds and the consequent weakness that was greatly aggravated by loss of blood. He staggered now occasionally and the girl, seeing his plight, offered him her arm.

"No," he expostulated, "you have passed through too much yourself to have any extra burden imposed upon you." But though he made a valiant effort to keep up with their captors he occasionally lagged, and upon one such occasion the guards for the first time showed any disposition toward brutality.

It was a big fellow who walked at Smith-Oldwick's left. Several times he took hold of the Englishman's arm and pushed him forward not ungently, but when the captive lagged again and again the fellow suddenly, and certainly with no just provocation, flew into a perfect frenzy of rage. He leaped upon the wounded man, striking him viciously with his fists and, bearing him to the ground, grasped his throat in his left hand while with his right he drew his long sharp saber. Screaming terribly he waved the blade above his head.

The others stopped and turned to look upon the encounter with no particular show of interest. It was as though one of the party had paused to readjust a sandal and the others merely waited until he was ready to march on again.

But if their captors were indifferent, Bertha Kircher was not. The close-set blazing eyes, the snarling fanged face, and the frightful screams filled her with horror, while the brutal and wanton attack upon the wounded man aroused within her the spirit of protection for the weak that is inherent in all women. Forgetful of everything other than that a weak and defenseless man was being brutally murdered before her eyes, the girl cast aside discretion and, rushing to Smith-Oldwick's assistance, seized the uplifted sword arm of the shrieking creature upon the prostrate Englishman.

Clinging desperately to the fellow she surged backward with all her weight and strength with the result that she overbalanced him and sent him sprawling to the pavement upon his back. In his efforts to save himself he relaxed his grasp upon the grip of his saber which had no sooner fallen to the ground than it was seized upon by the girl. Standing erect beside the prostrate form of the English officer Bertha Kircher, the razor-edged weapon grasped firmly in her hand, faced their captors.

She was a brave figure; even her soiled and torn riding togs and disheveled hair detracted nothing from her appearance. The creature she had felled scrambled quickly to his feet and in the instant his whole demeanor changed. From demoniacal rage he became suddenly convulsed with hysterical laughter although it was a question in the girl's mind as to which was the more terrifying. His companions stood looking on with vacuous grins upon their countenances, while he from whom the girl had wrested the weapon leaped up and down shrieking with laughter. If Bertha Kircher had needed further evidence to assure her that they were in the hands of a mentally deranged people the man's present actions would have been sufficient to convince her. The sudden uncontrolled rage and now the equally uncontrolled and mirthless laughter but emphasized the facial attributes of idiocy.

Suddenly realizing how helpless she was in the event any one of the men should seek to overpower her, and moved by a sudden revulsion of feeling that brought on almost a nausea of disgust, the girl hurled the weapon upon the ground at the feet of the laughing maniac and, turning, kneeled beside the Englishman.

"It was wonderful of you," he said, "but you shouldn't have done it. Don't antagonize them: I believe that they are all mad and you know they say that one should always humor a madman."

She shook her head. "I couldn't see him kill you," she said.

A sudden light sprang to the man's eyes as he reached out a hand and grasped the girl's fingers. "Do you care a little now?" he asked. "Can't you tell me that you do—just a bit?"

She did not withdraw her hand from his but she shook her head sadly. "Please don't," she said. "I am sorry that I can only like you very much."

The light died from his eyes and his fingers relaxed their grasp on hers. "Please forgive me," he murmured. "I intended waiting until we got out of this mess and you were safe among your own people. It must have been the shock or something like that, and seeing you defending me as you did. Anyway, I couldn't help it and really it doesn't make much difference what I say now, does it?"

"What do you mean?" she asked quickly.

He shrugged and smiled ruefully. "I will never leave this city alive," he said. "I wouldn't mention it except that I realize that you must know it as well as I. I was pretty badly torn up by the lion and this fellow here has about finished me. There might be some hope if we were among civilized people, but here with these frightful creatures what care could we get even if they were friendly?"

Bertha Kircher knew that he spoke the truth, and yet she could not bring herself to an admission that Smith-Oldwick would die. She was very fond of him, in fact her great regret was that she did not love him, but she knew that she did not.

It seemed to her that it could be such an easy thing for any girl to love Lieutenant Harold Percy Smith-Oldwick—an English officer and a gentleman, the scion of an old family and himself a man of ample means, young, good-looking and affable. What more could a girl ask for than to have such a man love her and that she possessed Smith-Oldwick's love there was no doubt in Bertha Kircher's mind.

She sighed, and then, laying her hand impulsively on his forehead, she whispered, "Do not give up hope, though. Try to live for my sake and for your sake I will try to love you."

It was as though new life had suddenly been injected into the man's veins. His face lightened instantly and with strength that he himself did not know he possessed he rose slowly to his feet, albeit somewhat unsteadily. The girl helped him and supported him after he had arisen.

For the moment they had been entirely unconscious of their surroundings and now as she looked at their captors she saw that they had fallen again into their almost habitual manner of stolid indifference, and at a gesture from one of them the march was resumed as though no untoward incident had occurred.

Bertha Kircher experienced a sudden reaction from the momentary exaltation of her recent promise to the Englishman. She knew that she had spoken more for him than for herself but now that it was over she realized, as she had realized the moment before she had spoken, that it was unlikely she would ever care for him the way he wished. But what had she promised? Only that she would try to love him. "And now?" she asked herself.

She realized that there might be little hope of their ever returning to civilization. Even if these people should prove friendly and willing to let them depart in peace, how were they to find their way back to the coast? With Tarzan dead, as she fully believed him after having seen his body lying lifeless at the mouth of the cave when she had been dragged forth by her captor, there seemed no power at their command which could guide them safely.

The two had scarcely mentioned the ape-man since their capture, for each realized fully what his loss meant to them. They had compared notes relative to those few exciting moments of the final attack and capture and had found that they agreed perfectly upon all that had occurred. Smith-Oldwick had even seen the lion leap upon Tarzan at the instant that the former was awakened by the roars of the charging beasts, and though the night had been dark, he had been able to see that the body of the savage ape-man had never moved from the instant that it had come down beneath the beast.

And so, if at other times within the past few weeks Bertha Kircher had felt that her situation was particularly hopeless, she was now ready to admit that hope was absolutely extinct.

The streets were beginning to fill with the strange men and women of this strange city. Sometimes individuals would notice them and seem to take a great interest in them, and again others would pass with vacant stares, seemingly unconscious of their immediate surroundings and paying no attention whatsoever to the prisoners. Once they heard hideous screams up a side street, and looking they saw a man in the throes of a demoniacal outburst of rage, similar to that which they had witnessed in the recent attack upon Smith-Oldwick. This creature was venting his insane rage upon a child which he repeatedly struck and bit, pausing only long enough to shriek at frequent intervals. Finally, just before they passed out of sight the creature raised the limp body of the child high above his head and cast it down with all his strength upon the pavement, and then, wheeling and screaming madly at the top of his lungs, he dashed headlong up the winding street.

Two women and several men had stood looking on at the cruel attack. They were at too great a distance for the Europeans to know whether their facial expressions portrayed pity or rage, but be that as it may, none offered to interfere.

A few yards farther on a hideous hag leaned from a second story window where she laughed and jibbered and made horrid grimaces at all who passed her. Others went their ways apparently attending to whatever duties called them, as soberly as the inhabitants of any civilized community.

"God," muttered Smith-Oldwick, "what an awful place!"

The girl turned suddenly toward him. "You still have your pistol?" she asked him.

"Yes," he replied. "I tucked it inside my shirt. They did not search me and it was too dark for them to see whether I carried any weapons or not. So I hid it in the hope that I might get through with it."

She moved closer to him and took hold of his hand. "Save one cartridge for me, please?" she begged.

Smith-Oldwick looked down at her and blinked his eyes very rapidly. An unfamiliar and disconcerting moisture had come into them. He had realized, of course, how bad a plight was theirs but somehow it had seemed to affect him only: it did not seem possible that anyone could harm this sweet and beautiful girl.

And that she should have to be destroyed—destroyed by him! It was too hideous: it was unbelievable, unthinkable! If he had been filled with apprehension before, he was doubly perturbed now.

"I don't believe I could do it, Bertha," he said.

"Not even to save me from something worse?" she asked.

He shook his head dismally. "I could never do it," he replied.

The street that they were following suddenly opened upon a wide avenue, and before them spread a broad and beautiful lagoon, the quiet surface of which mirrored the clear cerulean of the sky. Here the aspect of all their surroundings changed. The buildings were higher and much more pretentious in design and ornamentation. The street itself was paved in mosaics of barbaric but stunningly beautiful design. In the ornamentation of the buildings there was considerable color and a great deal of what appeared to be gold leaf. In all the decorations there was utilized in various ways the conventional figure of the parrot, and, to a lesser extent, that of the lion and the monkey.

Their captors led them along the pavement beside the lagoon for a short distance and then through an arched doorway into one of the buildings facing the avenue. Here, directly within the entrance was a large room furnished with massive benches and tables, many of which were elaborately hand carved with the figures of the inevitable parrot, the lion, or the monkey, the parrot always predominating.

Behind one of the tables sat a man who differed in no way that the captives could discover from those who accompanied them. Before this person the party halted, and one of the men who had brought them made what seemed to be an oral report. Whether they were before a judge, a military officer, or a civil dignitary they could not know, but evidently he was a man of authority, for, after listening to whatever recital was being made to him the while he closely scrutinized the two captives, he made a single futile attempt to converse with them and then issued some curt orders to him who had made the report.

Almost immediately two of the men approached Bertha Kircher and signaled her to accompany them. Smith-Oldwick started to follow her but was intercepted by one of their guards. The girl stopped then and turned back, at the same time looking at the man at the table and making signs with her hands, indicating, as best she could, that she wished Smith-Oldwick to remain with her, but the fellow only shook his head negatively and motioned to the guards to remove her. The Englishman again attempted to follow but was restrained. He was too weak and helpless even to make an attempt to enforce his wishes. He thought of the pistol inside his shirt and then of the futility of attempting to overcome an entire city with the few rounds of ammunition left to him.

So far, with the single exception of the attack made upon him, they had no reason to believe that they might not receive fair treatment from their captors, and so he reasoned that it might be wiser to avoid antagonizing them until such a time as he became thoroughly convinced that their intentions were entirely hostile. He saw the girl led from the building and just before she disappeared from his view she turned and waved her hand to him:

"Good luck!" she cried, and was gone.

The lions that had entered the building with the party had, during their examination by the man at the table, been driven from the apartment through a doorway behind him. Toward this same doorway two of the men now led Smith-Oldwick. He found himself in a long corridor from the sides of which other doorways opened, presumably into other apartments of the building. At the far end of the corridor he saw a heavy grating beyond which appeared an open courtyard. Into this courtyard the prisoner was conducted, and as he entered it with the two guards he found himself in an opening which was bounded by the inner walls of the building. It was in the nature of a garden in which a number of trees and flowering shrubs grew. Beneath several of the trees were benches and there was a bench along the south wall, but what aroused his most immediate attention was the fact that the lions who had assisted in their capture and who had accompanied them upon the return to the city, lay sprawled about upon the ground or wandered restlessly to and fro.

Just inside the gate his guard halted. The two men exchanged a few words and then turned and reentered the corridor. The Englishman was horror-stricken as the full realization of his terrible plight forced itself upon his tired brain. He turned and seized the grating in an attempt to open it and gain the safety of the corridor, but he found it securely locked against his every effort, and then he called aloud to the retreating figure of the men within. The only reply he received was a high-pitched, mirthless laugh, and then the two passed through the doorway at the far end of the corridor and he was alone with the lions.

CHAPTER XIX—THE QUEEN'S STORY

In the meantime Bertha Kircher was conducted the length of the plaza toward the largest and most pretentious of the buildings surrounding it. This edifice covered the entire width of one end of the plaza. It was several stories in height, the main entrance being approached by a wide flight of stone steps, the bottom of which was guarded by enormous stone lions, while at the top there were two pedestals flanking the entrance and of the same height, upon each of which was the stone image of a large parrot. As the girl neared these latter images she saw that the capital of each column was hewn into the semblance of a human skull upon which the parrots perched. Above the arched doorway and upon the walls of the building were the figures of other parrots, of lions, and of monkeys. Some of these were carved in bas-relief; others were delineated in mosaics, while still others appeared to have been painted upon the surface of the wall.

The colorings of the last were apparently much subdued by age with the result that the general effect was soft and beautiful. The sculpturing and mosaic work were both finely executed, giving evidence of a high degree of artistic skill. Unlike the first building into which she had been conducted, the entrance to which had been doorless, massive doors closed the entrance which she now approached. In the niches formed by the columns which supported the door's arch, and about the base of the pedestals of the stone parrots, as well as in various other places on the broad stairway, lolled some score of armed men. The tunics of these were all of a vivid yellow and upon the breast and back of each was embroidered the figure of a parrot.

As she was conducted up the stairway one of these yellow-coated warriors approached and halted her guides at the top of the steps. Here they exchanged a few words and while they were talking the girl noticed that he who had halted them, as well as those whom she could see of his companions, appeared to be, if possible, of a lower mentality than her original captors.

Their coarse, bristling hair grew so low upon their foreheads as, in some instances, to almost join their eyebrows, while the irises were smaller, exposing more of the white of the eyeball.

After a short parley the man in charge of the doorway, for such he seemed to be, turned and struck upon one of the panels with the butt of his spear, at the same time calling to several of his companions, who rose and came forward at his command. Soon the great doors commenced slowly to swing creakingly open, and presently, as they separated, the girl saw behind them the motive force which operated the massive doors—to each door a half-dozen naked Negroes.

At the doorway her two guards were turned back and their places taken by a half dozen of the yellow-coated soldiery. These conducted her through the doorway which the blacks, pulling upon heavy chains, closed behind them. And as the girl watched them she noted with horror that the poor creatures were chained by the neck to the doors.

Before her led a broad hallway in the center of which was a little pool of clear water. Here again in floor and walls was repeated in new and ever-changing combinations and designs, the parrots, the monkeys, and the lions, but now many of the figures were of what the girl was convinced must be gold. The walls of the corridor consisted of a series of open archways through which, upon either side, other spacious apartments were visible. The hallway was entirely unfurnished, but the rooms on either side contained benches and tables. Glimpses of some of the walls revealed the fact that they were covered with hangings of some colored fabric, while upon the floors were thick rugs of barbaric design and the skins of black lions and beautifully marked leopards.

The room directly to the right of the entrance was filled with men wearing the yellow tunics of her new guard while the walls were hung with numerous spears and sabers. At the far end of the corridor a low flight of steps led to another closed doorway. Here the guard was again halted. One of the guards at this doorway, after receiving the report of one of those who accompanied her, passed through the door, leaving them standing outside. It was fully fifteen minutes before he returned, when the guard was again changed and the girl conducted into the chamber beyond.

Through three other chambers and past three more massive doors, at each of which her guard was changed, the girl was conducted before she was ushered into a comparatively small room, back and forth across the floor of which paced a man in a scarlet tunic, upon the front and back of which was embroidered an enormous parrot and upon whose head was a barbaric headdress surmounted by a stuffed parrot.

The walls of this room were entirely hidden by hangings upon which hundreds, even thousands, of parrots were embroidered. Inlaid in the floor were golden parrots, while, as thickly as they could be painted, upon the ceiling were brilliant-hued parrots with wings outspread as though in the act of flying.

The man himself was larger of stature than any she had yet seen within the city. His parchment-like skin was wrinkled with age and he was much fatter than any other of his kind that she had seen. His bared arms, however, gave evidence of great strength and his gait was not that of an old man. His facial expression denoted almost utter imbecility and he was quite the most repulsive creature that ever Bertha Kircher had looked upon.

For several minutes after she was conducted into his presence he appeared not to be aware that she was there but continued his restless pacing to and fro. Suddenly, without the slightest warning, and while he was at the far end of the room from her with his back toward her, he wheeled and rushed madly at her. Involuntarily the girl shrank back, extending her open palms toward the frightful creature as though to hold him aloof but a man upon either side of her, the two who had conducted her into the apartment, seized and held her.

Although he rushed violently toward her the man stopped without touching her. For a moment his horrid white-rimmed eyes glared searchingly into her face, immediately following which he burst into maniacal laughter. For two or three minutes the creature gave himself over to merriment and then, stopping as suddenly as he had commenced to laugh, he fell to examining the prisoner. He felt of her hair, her skin, the texture of the garment she wore and by means of signs made her understand she was to open her mouth. In the latter he seemed much interested, calling the attention of one of the guards to her canine teeth and then baring his own sharp fangs for the prisoner to see.

Presently he resumed pacing to and fro across the floor, and it was fully fifteen minutes before he again noticed the prisoner, and then it was to issue a curt order to her guards, who immediately conducted her from the apartment.

The guards now led the girl through a series of corridors and apartments to a narrow stone stairway which led to the floor above, finally stopping before a small door where stood a naked Negro armed with a spear. At a word from one of her guards the Negro opened the door and the party passed into a low-ceiled apartment, the windows of which immediately caught the girl's attention through the fact that they were heavily barred. The room was furnished similarly to those that she had seen in other parts of the building, the same carved tables and benches, the rugs upon the floor, the decorations upon the walls, although in every respect it was simpler than anything she had seen on the floor below. In one corner was a low couch covered with a rug similar to those on the floor except that it was of a lighter texture, and upon this sat a woman.

As Bertha Kircher's eyes alighted upon the occupant of the room the girl gave a little gasp of astonishment, for she recognized immediately that here was a creature more nearly of her own kind than any she had seen within the city's walls. An old woman it was who looked at her through faded blue eyes, sunken deep in a wrinkled and toothless face. But the eyes were those of a sane and intelligent creature, and the wrinkled face was the face of a white woman.

At sight of the girl the woman rose and came forward, her gait so feeble and unsteady that she was forced to support herself with a long staff which she grasped in both her hands. One of the guards spoke a few words to her and then the men turned and left the apartment. The girl stood just within the door waiting in silence for what might next befall her.

The old woman crossed the room and stopped before her, raising her weak and watery eyes to the fresh young face of the newcomer. Then she scanned her from head to foot and once again the old eyes returned to the girl's face. Bertha Kircher on her part was not less frank in her survey of the little old woman. It was the latter who spoke first. In a thin, cracked voice she spoke, hesitatingly, falteringly, as though she were using unfamiliar words and speaking a strange tongue.

"You are from the outer world?" she asked in English. "God grant that you may speak and understand this tongue."

"English?" the girl exclaimed, "Yes, of course, I speak English."

"Thank God!" cried the little old woman. "I did not know whether I myself might speak it so that another could understand. For sixty years I have spoken only their accursed gibberish. For sixty years I have not heard a word in my native language. Poor creature! Poor creature!" she mumbled. "What accursed misfortune threw you into their hands?"

"You are an English woman?" asked Bertha Kircher. "Did I understand you aright that you are an English woman and have been here for sixty years?"

The old woman nodded her head affirmatively. "For sixty years I have never been outside of this palace. Come," she said, stretching forth a bony hand. "I am very old and cannot stand long. Come and sit with me on my couch."

The girl took the proffered hand and assisted the old lady back to the opposite side of the room and when she was seated the girl sat down beside her.

"Poor child! Poor child!" moaned the old woman. "Far better to have died than to have let them bring you here. At first I might have destroyed myself but there was always the hope that someone would come who would take me away, but none ever comes. Tell me how they got you."

Very briefly the girl narrated the principal incidents which led up to her capture by some of the creatures of the city.

"Then there is a man with you in the city?" asked the old woman.

"Yes," said the girl, "but I do not know where he is nor what are their intentions in regard to him. In fact, I do not know what their intentions toward me are."

"No one might even guess," said the old woman. "They do not know themselves from one minute to the next what their intentions are, but I think you can rest assured, my poor child, that you will never see your friend again."

"But they haven't slain you," the girl reminded her, "and you have been their prisoner, you say, for sixty years."

"No," replied her companion, "they have not killed me, nor will they kill you, though God knows before you have lived long in this horrible place you will beg them to kill you."

"Who are they—" asked Bertha Kircher, "what kind of people? They differ from any that I ever have seen. And tell me, too, how you came here."

"It was long ago," said the old woman, rocking back and forth on the couch. "It was long ago. Oh, how long it was! I was only twenty then. Think of it, child! Look at me. I have no mirror other than my bath, I cannot see what I look like for my eyes are old, but with my fingers I can feel my old and wrinkled face, my sunken eyes, and these flabby lips drawn in over toothless gums. I am old and bent and hideous, but then I was young and they said that I was beautiful. No, I will not be a hypocrite; I was beautiful. My glass told me that.

"My father was a missionary in the interior and one day there came a band of Arabian slave raiders. They took the men and women of the little native village where my father labored, and they took me, too. They did not know much about our part of the country so they were compelled to rely upon the men of our village whom they had captured to guide them. They told me that they never before had been so far south and that they had heard there was a country rich in ivory and slaves west of us. They wanted to go there and from there they would take us north, where I was to be sold into the harem of some black sultan.

"They often discussed the price I would bring, and that that price might not lessen, they guarded me jealously from one another so the journeys were made as little fatiguing for me as possible. I was given the best food at their command and I was not harmed.

"But after a short time, when we had reached the confines of the country with which the men of our village were familiar and had entered upon a desolate and arid desert waste, the Arabs realized at last that we were lost. But they still kept on, ever toward the west, crossing hideous gorges and marching across the face of a burning land beneath the pitiless sun. The poor slaves they had captured were, of course, compelled to carry all the camp equipage and loot and thus heavily burdened, half starved and without water, they soon commenced to die like flies.

"We had not been in the desert land long before the Arabs were forced to kill their horses for food, and when we reached the first gorge, across which it would have been impossible to transport the animals, the balance of them were slaughtered and the meat loaded upon the poor staggering blacks who still survived.

"Thus we continued for two more days and now all but a handful of blacks were dead, and the Arabs themselves had commenced to succumb to hunger and thirst and the intense heat of the desert. As far as the eye could reach back toward the land of plenty from whence we had come, our route was marked by circling vultures in the sky and by the bodies of the dead who lay down in the trackless waste for the last time. The ivory had been abandoned tusk by tusk as the blacks gave out, and along the trail of death was strewn the camp equipage and the horse trappings of a hundred men.

"For some reason the Arab chief favored me to the last, possibly with the idea that of all his other treasures I could be most easily transported, for I was young and strong and after the horses were killed I had walked and kept up with the best of the men. We English, you know, are great walkers, while these Arabians had never walked since they were old enough to ride a horse.

"I cannot tell you how much longer we kept on but at last, with our strength almost gone, a handful of us reached the bottom of a deep gorge. To scale the opposite side was out of the question and so we kept on down along the sands of what must have been the bed of an ancient river, until finally we came to a point where we looked out upon what appeared to be a beautiful valley in which we felt assured that we would find game in plenty.

"By then there were only two of us left—the chief and myself. I do not need to tell you what the valley was, for you found it in much the same way as I did. So quickly were we captured that it seemed they must have been waiting for us, and I learned later that such was the case, just as they were waiting for you.

"As you came through the forest you must have seen the monkeys and parrots and since you have entered the palace, how constantly these animals, and the lions, are used in the decorations. At home we were all familiar with talking parrots who repeated the things that they were taught to say, but these parrots are different in that they all talk in the same language that the people of the city use, and they say that the monkeys talk to the parrots and the parrots fly to the city and tell the people what the monkeys say. And, although it is hard to believe, I have learned that this is so, for I have lived here among them for sixty years in the palace of their king.

"They brought me, as they brought you, directly to the palace. The Arabian chief was taken elsewhere. I never knew what became of him. Ago XXV was king then. I have seen many kings since that day. He was a terrible man; but then, they are all terrible."

"What is the matter with them?" asked the girl.

"They are a race of maniacs," replied the old woman. "Had you not guessed it? Among them are excellent craftsmen and good farmers and a certain amount of law and order, such as it is.

"They reverence all birds, but the parrot is their chief deity. There is one who is held here in the palace in a very beautiful apartment. He is their god of gods. He is a very old bird. If what Ago told me when I came is true, he must be nearly three hundred years old by now. Their religious rites are revolting in the extreme, and I believe that it may be the practice of these rites through ages that has brought the race to its present condition of imbecility.

"And yet, as I said, they are not without some redeeming qualities. If legend may be credited, their forebears—a little handful of men and women who came from somewhere out of the north and became lost in the wilderness of central Africa—found here only a barren desert valley. To my own knowledge rain seldom, if ever, falls here, and yet you have seen a great forest and luxuriant vegetation outside of the city as well as within. This miracle is accomplished by the utilization of natural springs which their ancestors developed, and upon which they have improved to such an extent that the entire valley receives an adequate amount of moisture at all times.

"Ago told me that many generations before his time the forest was irrigated by changing the course of the streams which carried the spring water to the city but that when the trees had sent their roots down to the natural moisture of the soil and required no further irrigation, the course of the stream was changed and other trees were planted. And so the forest grew until today it covers almost the entire floor of the valley except for the open space where the city stands. I do not know that this is true. It may be that the forest has always been here, but it is one of their legends and it is borne out by the fact that there is not sufficient rainfall here to support vegetation.

"They are peculiar people in many respects, not only in their form of worship and religious rites but also in that they breed lions as other people breed cattle. You have seen how they use some of these lions but the majority of them they fatten and eat. At first, I imagine, they ate lion meat as a part of their religious ceremony but after many generations they came to crave it so that now it is practically the only flesh they eat. They would, of course, rather die than eat the flesh of a bird, nor will they eat monkey's meat, while the herbivorous animals they raise only for milk, hides, and flesh for the lions. Upon the south side of the city are the corrals and pastures where the herbivorous animals are raised. Boar, deer, and antelope are used principally for the lions, while goats are kept for milk for the human inhabitants of the city."

"And you have lived here all these years," exclaimed the girl, "without ever seeing one of your own kind?"

The old woman nodded affirmatively.

"For sixty years you have lived here," continued Bertha Kircher, "and they have not harmed you!"

"I did not say they had not harmed me," said the old woman, "they did not kill me, that is all."

"What"—the girl hesitated—"what," she continued at last, "was your position among them? Pardon me," she added quickly, "I think I know but I should like to hear from your own lips, for whatever your position was, mine will doubtless be the same."

The old woman nodded. "Yes," she said, "doubtless; if they can keep you away from the women."

"What do you mean?" asked the girl.

"For sixty years I have never been allowed near a woman. They would kill me, even now, if they could reach me. The men are frightful, God knows they are frightful! But heaven keep you from the women!"

"You mean," asked the girl, "that the men will not harm me?"

"Ago XXV made me his queen," said the old woman. "But he had many other queens, nor were they all human. He was not murdered for ten years after I came here. Then the next king took me, and so it has been always. I am the oldest queen now. Very few of their women live to a great age. Not only are they constantly liable to assassination but, owing to their subnormal mentalities, they are subject to periods of depression during which they are very likely to destroy themselves."

She turned suddenly and pointed to the barred windows. "You see this room," she said, "with the black eunuch outside? Wherever you see these you will know that there are women, for with very few exceptions they are never allowed out of captivity. They are considered and really are more violent than the men."

For several minutes the two sat in silence, and then the younger woman turned to the older.

"Is there no way to escape?" she asked.

The old woman pointed again to the barred windows and then to the door, saying: "And there is the armed eunuch. And if you should pass him, how could you reach the street? And if you reached the street, how could you pass through the city to the outer wall? And even if, by some miracle, you should gain the outer wall, and, by another miracle, you should be permitted to pass through the gate, could you ever hope to traverse the forest where the great black lions roam and feed upon men? No!" she exclaimed, answering her own question, "there is no escape, for after one had escaped from the palace and the city and the forest it would be but to invite death in the frightful desert land beyond.

"In sixty years you are the first to find this buried city. In a thousand no denizen of this valley has ever left it, and within the memory of man, or even in their legends, none had found them prior to my coming other than a single warlike giant, the story of whom has been handed down from father to son.

"I think from the description that he must have been a Spaniard, a giant of a man in buckler and helmet, who fought his way through the terrible forest to the city gate, who fell upon those who were sent out to capture him and slew them with his mighty sword. And when he had eaten of the vegetables from the gardens, and the fruit from the trees and drank of the water from the stream, he turned about and fought his way back through the forest to the mouth of the gorge. But though he escaped the city and the forest he did not escape the desert. For a legend runs that the king, fearful that he would bring others to attack them, sent a party after him to slay him.

"For three weeks they did not find him, for they went in the wrong direction, but at last they came upon his bones picked clean by the vultures, lying a day's march up the same gorge through which you and I entered the valley. I do not know," continued the old woman, "that this is true. It is just one of their many legends."

"Yes," said the girl, "it is true. I am sure it is true, for I have seen the skeleton and the corroded armor of this great giant."

At this juncture the door was thrown open without ceremony and a Negro entered bearing two flat vessels in which were several smaller ones. These he set down on one of the tables near the women, and, without a word, turned and left. With the entrance of the man with the vessels, a delightful odor of cooked food had aroused the realization in the girl's mind that she was very hungry, and at a word from the old woman she walked to the table to examine the viands. The larger vessels which contained the smaller ones were of pottery while those within them were quite evidently of hammered gold. To her intense surprise she found lying between the smaller vessels a spoon and a fork, which, while of quaint design, were quite as serviceable as any she had seen in more civilized communities. The tines of the fork were quite evidently of iron or steel, the girl did not know which, while the handle and the spoon were of the same material as the smaller vessels.

There was a highly seasoned stew with meat and vegetables, a dish of fresh fruit, and a bowl of milk beside which was a little jug containing something which resembled marmalade. So ravenous was she that she did not even wait for her companion to reach the table, and as she ate she could have sworn that never before had she tasted more palatable food. The old woman came slowly and sat down on one of the benches opposite her.

As she removed the smaller vessels from the larger and arranged them before her on the table a crooked smile twisted her lips as she watched the younger woman eat.

"Hunger is a great leveler," she said with a laugh.

"What do you mean?" asked the girl.

"I venture to say that a few weeks ago you would have been nauseated at the idea of eating cat."

"Cat?" exclaimed the girl.

"Yes," said the old woman. "What is the difference—a lion is a cat."

"You mean I am eating lion now?"

"Yes," said the old woman, "and as they prepare it, it is very palatable. You will grow very fond of it."

Bertha Kircher smiled a trifle dubiously. "I could not tell it," she said, "from lamb or veal."

"No," said the woman, "it tastes as good to me. But these lions are very carefully kept and very carefully fed and their flesh is so seasoned and prepared that it might be anything so far as taste is concerned."

And so Bertha Kircher broke her long fast upon strange fruits, lion meat, and goat's milk.

Scarcely had she finished when again the door opened and there entered a yellow-coated soldier. He spoke to the old woman.

"The king," she said, "has commanded that you be prepared and brought to him. You are to share these apartments with me. The king knows that I am not like his other women. He never would have dared to put you with them. Herog XVI has occasional lucid intervals. You must have been brought to him during one of these. Like the rest of them he thinks that he alone of all the community is sane, but more than once I have thought that the various men with whom I have come in contact here, including the kings themselves, looked upon me as, at least, less mad than the others. Yet how I have retained my senses all these years is beyond me."

"What do you mean by prepare?" asked Bertha Kircher. "You said that the king had commanded I be prepared and brought to him."

"You will be bathed and furnished with a robe similar to that which I wear."

"Is there no escape?" asked the girl. "Is there no way even in which I can kill myself?"

The woman handed her the fork. "This is the only way," she said, "and you will notice that the tines are very short and blunt."

The girl shuddered and the old woman laid a hand gently upon her shoulder. "He may only look at you and send you away," she said. "Ago XXV sent for me once, tried to talk with me, discovered that I could not understand him and that he could not understand me, ordered that I be taught the language of his people, and then apparently forgot me for a year. Sometimes I do not see the king for a long period. There was one king who ruled for five years whom I never saw. There is always hope; even I whose very memory has doubtless been forgotten beyond these palace walls still hope, though none knows better how futilely."

The old woman led Bertha Kircher to an adjoining apartment in the floor of which was a pool of water. Here the girl bathed and afterward her companion brought her one of the clinging garments of the native women and adjusted it about her figure. The material of the robe was of a gauzy fabric which accentuated the rounded beauty of the girlish form.

"There," said the old woman, as she gave a final pat to one of the folds of the garment, "you are a queen indeed!"

The girl looked down at her naked breasts and but half-concealed limbs in horror. "They are going to lead me into the presence of men in this half-nude condition!" she exclaimed.

The old woman smiled her crooked smile. "It is nothing," she said. "You will become accustomed to it as did I who was brought up in the home of a minister of the gospel, where it was considered little short of a crime for a woman to expose her stockinged ankle. By comparison with what you will doubtless see and the things that you may be called upon to undergo, this is but a trifle."

For what seemed hours to the distraught girl she paced the floor of her apartment, awaiting the final summons to the presence of the mad king. Darkness had fallen and the oil flares within the palace had been lighted long before two messengers appeared with instructions that Herog demanded her immediate presence and that the old woman, whom they called Xanila, was to accompany her. The girl felt some slight relief when she discovered that she was to have at least one friend with her, however powerless to assist her the old woman might be.

The messengers conducted the two to a small apartment on the floor below. Xanila explained that this was one of the anterooms off the main throneroom in which the king was accustomed to hold court with his entire retinue. A number of yellow-tunicked warriors sat about upon the benches within the room. For the most part their eyes were bent upon the floor and their attitudes that of moody dejection. As the two women entered several glanced indifferently at them, but for the most part no attention was paid to them.

While they were waiting in the anteroom there entered from another apartment a young man uniformed similarly to the others with the exception that upon his head was a fillet of gold, in the front of which a single parrot feather rose erectly above his forehead. As he entered, the other soldiers in the room rose to their feet.

"That is Metak, one of the king's sons," Xanila whispered to the girl.

The prince was crossing the room toward the audience chamber when his glance happened to fall upon Bertha Kircher. He halted in his tracks and stood looking at her for a full minute without speaking. The girl, embarrassed by his bold stare and her scant attire, flushed and, dropping her gaze to the floor, turned away. Metak suddenly commenced to tremble from head to foot and then, without warning other than a loud, hoarse scream he sprang forward and seized the girl in his arms.

Instantly pandemonium ensued. The two messengers who had been charged with the duty of conducting the girl to the king's presence danced, shrieking, about the prince, waving their arms and gesticulating wildly as though they would force him to relinquish her, the while they dared not lay hands upon royalty. The other guardsmen, as though suffering in sympathy the madness of their prince, ran forward screaming and brandishing their sabers.

The girl fought to release herself from the horrid embrace of the maniac, but with his left arm about her he held her as easily as though she had been but a babe, while with his free hand he drew his saber and struck viciously at those nearest him.

One of the messengers was the first to feel the keen edge of Metak's blade. With a single fierce cut the prince drove through the fellow's collar bone and downward to the center of his chest. With a shrill shriek that rose above the screaming of the other guardsmen the man dropped to the floor, and as the blood gushed from the frightful wound he struggled to rise once more to his feet and then sank back again and died in a great pool of his own blood.

In the meantime Metak, still clinging desperately to the girl, had backed toward the opposite door. At the sight of the blood two of the guardsmen, as though suddenly aroused to maniacal frenzy, dropped their sabers to the floor and fell upon each other with nails and teeth, while some sought to reach the prince and some to defend him. In a corner of the room sat one of the guardsmen laughing uproariously and just as Metak succeeded in reaching the door and taking the girl through, she thought that she saw another of the men spring upon the corpse of the dead messenger and bury his teeth in its flesh.

During the orgy of madness Xanila had kept closely at the girl's side but at the door of the room Metak had seen her and, wheeling suddenly, cut viciously at her. Fortunately for Xanila she was halfway through the door at the time, so that Metak's blade but dented itself upon the stone arch of the portal, and then Xanila, guided doubtless by the wisdom of sixty years of similar experiences, fled down the corridor as fast as her old and tottering legs would carry her.

Metak, once outside the door, returned his saber to its scabbard and lifting the girl bodily from the ground carried her off in the opposite direction from that taken by Xanila.

CHAPTER XX—CAME TARZAN

Just before dark that evening, an almost exhausted flier entered the headquarters of Colonel Capell of the Second Rhodesians and saluted.

"Well, Thompson," asked the superior, "what luck? The others have all returned. Never saw a thing of Oldwick or his plane. I guess we shall have to give it up unless you were more successful."

"I was," replied the young officer. "I found the plane."

"No!" ejaculated Colonel Capell. "Where was it? Any sign of Oldwick?"

"It is in the rottenest hole in the ground you ever saw, quite a bit inland. Narrow gorge. Saw the plane all right but can't reach it. There was a regular devil of a lion wandering around it. I landed near the edge of the cliff and was going to climb down and take a look at the plane. But this fellow hung around for an hour or more and I finally had to give it up."

"Do you think the lions got Oldwick?" asked the colonel.

"I doubt it," replied Lieutenant Thompson, "from the fact that there was no indication that the lion had fed anywhere about the plane. I arose after I found it was impossible to get down around the plane and reconnoitered up and down the gorge. Several miles to the south I found a small, wooded valley in the center of which—please don't think me crazy, sir—is a regular city— streets, buildings, a central plaza with a lagoon, good-sized buildings with domes and minarets and all that sort of stuff."

The elder officer looked at the younger compassionately. "You're all wrought up, Thompson," he said. "Go and take a good sleep. You have been on this job now for a long while and it must have gotten on your nerves."

The young man shook his head a bit irritably. "Pardon me, sir," he said, "but I am telling you the truth. I am not mistaken. I circled over the place several times. It may be that Oldwick has found his way there—or has been captured by these people."

"Were there people in the city?" asked the colonel.

"Yes, I saw them in the streets."

"Do you think cavalry could reach the valley?" asked the colonel.

"No," replied Thompson, "the country is all cut up with these deep gorges. Even infantry would have a devil of a time of it, and there is absolutely no water that I could discover for at least a two days' march."

It was at this juncture that a big Vauxhall drew up in front of the headquarters of the Second Rhodesians and a moment later General Smuts alighted and entered. Colonel Capell arose from his chair and saluted his superior, and the young lieutenant saluted and stood at attention.

"I was passing," said the general, "and I thought I would stop for a chat. By the way, how is the search for Lieutenant Smith-Oldwick progressing? I see Thompson here and I believe he was one of those detailed to the search."

"Yes," said Capell, "he was. He is the last to come in. He found the lieutenant's ship," and then he repeated what Lieutenant Thompson had reported to him. The general sat down at the table with Colonel Capell, and together the two officers, with the assistance of the flier, marked the approximate location of the city which Thompson had reported he'd discovered.

"It's a mighty rough country," remarked Smuts, "but we can't leave a stone unturned until we have exhausted every resource to find that boy. We will send out a small force; a small one will be more likely to succeed than a large one. About one company, Colonel, or say two, with sufficient motor lorries for transport of rations and water. Put a good man in command and let him establish a base as far to the west as the motors can travel. You can leave one company there and send the other forward. I am inclined to believe you can establish your base within a day's march of the city and if such is the case the force you send ahead should have no trouble on the score of lack of water as there certainly must be water in the valley where the city lies. Detail a couple of planes for reconnaissance and messenger service so that the base can keep in touch at all times with the advance party. When can your force move out?"

"We can load the lorries tonight," replied Capell, "and march about one o'clock tomorrow morning."

"Good," said the general, "keep me advised," and returning the others' salutes he departed.

As Tarzan leaped for the vines he realized that the lion was close upon him and that his life depended upon the strength of the creepers clinging to the city walls; but to his intense relief he found the stems as large around as a man's arm, and the tendrils which had fastened themselves to the wall so firmly fixed, that his weight upon the stem appeared to have no appreciable effect upon them.

He heard Numa's baffled roar as the lion slipped downward clawing futilely at the leafy creepers, and then with the agility of the apes who had reared him, Tarzan bounded nimbly aloft to the summit of the wall.

A few feet below him was the flat roof of the adjoining building and as he dropped to it his back was toward the niche from which an embrasure looked out upon the gardens and the forest beyond, so that he did not see the figure crouching there in the dark shadow. But if he did not see he was not long in ignorance of the fact that he was not alone, for scarcely had his feet touched the roof when a heavy body leaped upon him from behind and brawny arms encircled him about the waist.

Taken at a disadvantage and lifted from his feet, the ape-man was, for the time being, helpless. Whatever the creature was that had seized him, it apparently had a well-defined purpose in mind, for it walked directly toward the edge of the roof so that it was soon apparent to Tarzan that he was to be hurled to the pavement below—a most efficacious manner of disposing of an intruder. That he would be either maimed or killed the ape-man was confident; but he had no intention of permitting his assailant to carry out the plan.

Tarzan's arms and legs were free but he was in such a disadvantageous position that he could not use them to any good effect. His only hope lay in throwing the creature off its balance, and to this end Tarzan straightened his body and leaned as far back against his captor as he could, and then suddenly lunged forward. The result was as satisfactory as he could possibly have hoped. The great weight of the ape-man thrown suddenly out from an erect position caused the other also to lunge violently forward with the result that to save himself he involuntarily released his grasp. Catlike in his movements, the ape-man had no sooner touched the roof than he was upon his feet again, facing his adversary, a man almost as large as himself and armed with a saber which he now whipped from its scabbard. Tarzan, however, had no mind to allow the use of this formidable weapon and so he dove for the other's legs beneath the vicious cut that was directed at him from the side, and as a football player tackles an opposing runner, Tarzan tackled his antagonist, carrying him backward several yards and throwing him heavily to the roof upon his back.

No sooner had the man touched the roof than the ape-man was upon his chest, one brawny hand sought and found the sword wrist and the other the throat of the yellow-tunicked guardsman. Until then the fellow had fought in silence but just as Tarzan's fingers touched his throat he emitted a single piercing shriek that the brown fingers cut off almost instantly. The fellow struggled to escape the clutch of the naked creature upon his breast but equally as well might he have fought to escape the talons of Numa, the lion.

Gradually his struggles lessened, his pin-point eyes popped from their sockets, rolling horribly upward, while from his foam-flecked lips his swollen tongue protruded. As his struggles ceased Tarzan arose, and placing a foot upon the carcass of his kill, was upon the point of screaming forth his victory cry when the thought that the work before him required the utmost caution sealed his lips.

Walking to the edge of the roof he looked down into the narrow, winding street below. At intervals, apparently at each street intersection, an oil flare sputtered dimly from brackets set in the walls a trifle higher than a man's head. For the most part the winding alleys were in dense shadow and even in the immediate vicinity of the flares the illumination was far from brilliant. In the restricted area of his vision he could see that there were still a few of the strange inhabitants moving about the narrow thoroughfares.

To prosecute his search for the young officer and the girl he must be able to move about the city as freely as possible, but to pass beneath one of the corner flares, naked as he was except for a loin cloth, and in every other respect markedly different from the inhabitants of the city, would be but to court almost immediate discovery. As these thoughts flashed through his mind and he cast about for some feasible plan of action, his eyes fell upon the corpse upon the roof near him, and immediately there occurred to him the possibility of disguising himself in the raiment of his conquered adversary.

It required but a few moments for the ape-man to clothe himself in the tights, sandals, and parrot emblazoned yellow tunic of the dead soldier. Around his waist he buckled the saber belt but beneath the tunic he retained the hunting knife of his dead father. His other weapons he could not lightly discard, and so, in the hope that he might eventually recover them, he carried them to the edge of the wall and dropped them among the foliage at its base. At the last moment he found it difficult to part with his rope, which, with his knife, was his most accustomed weapon, and one which he had used for the greatest length of time. He found that by removing the saber belt he could wind the rope about his waist beneath his tunic, and then replacing the belt still retain it entirely concealed from chance observation.

At last, satisfactorily disguised, and with even his shock of black hair adding to the verisimilitude of his likeness to the natives of the city, he sought for some means of reaching the street below. While he might have risked a drop from the eaves of the roof he feared to do so lest he attract the attention of passers-by, and probable discovery. The roofs of the buildings varied in height but as the ceilings were all low he found that he could easily travel along the roof tops and this he did for some little distance, until he suddenly discovered just ahead of him several figures reclining upon the roof of a near-by building.

He had noticed openings in each roof, evidently giving ingress to the apartments below, and now, his advance cut off by those ahead of him, he decided to risk the chance of reaching the street through the interior of one of the buildings. Approaching one of the openings he leaned over the black hole, and listened for sounds of life in the apartment below. Neither his ears nor his nose registered evidence of the presence of any living creature in the immediate vicinity, and so without further hesitation the ape-man lowered his body through the aperture and was about to drop when his foot came in contact with the rung of a ladder, which he immediately took advantage of to descend to the floor of the room below.

Here, all was almost total darkness until his eyes became accustomed to the interior, the darkness of which was slightly alleviated by the reflected light from a distant street flare which shone intermittently through the narrow windows fronting the thoroughfare. Finally, assured that the apartment was unoccupied, Tarzan sought for a stairway to the ground floor. This he found in a dark hallway upon which the room opened—a flight of narrow stone steps leading downward toward the street. Chance favored him so that he reached the shadows of the arcade without encountering any of the inmates of the house.

Once on the street he was not at a loss as to the direction in which he wished to go, for he had tracked the two Europeans practically to the gate, which he felt assured must have given them entry to the city. His keen sense of direction and location made it possible for him to judge with considerable accuracy the point within the city where he might hope to pick up the spoor of those whom he sought.

The first need, however, was to discover a street paralleling the northern wall along which he could make his way in the direction of the gate he had seen from the forest. Realizing that his greatest hope of success lay in the boldness of his operations he moved off in the direction of the nearest street flare without making any other attempt at concealment than keeping in the shadows of the arcade, which he judged would draw no particular attention to him in that he saw other pedestrians doing likewise. The few he passed gave him no heed, and he had almost reached the nearest intersection when he saw several men wearing yellow tunics identical to that which he had taken from his prisoner.

They were coming directly toward him and the ape-man saw that should he continue on he would meet them directly at the intersection of the two streets in the full light of the flare. His first inclination was to go steadily on, for personally he had no objection to chancing a scrimmage with them; but a sudden recollection of the girl, possibly a helpless prisoner in the hands of these people, caused him to seek some other and less hazardous plan of action.

He had almost emerged from the shadow of the arcade into the full light of the flare and the approaching men were but a few yards from him, when he suddenly kneeled and pretended to adjust the wrappings of his sandals—wrappings, which, by the way, he was not at all sure that he had adjusted as their makers had intended them to be adjusted. He was still kneeling when the soldiers came abreast of him. Like the others he had passed they paid no attention to him and the moment they were behind him he continued upon his way, turning to the right at the intersection of the two streets.

The street he now took was, at this point, so extremely winding that, for the most part, it received no benefit from the flares at either corner, so that he was forced practically to grope his way in the dense shadows of the arcade. The street became a little straighter just before he reached the next flare, and as he came within sight of it he saw silhouetted against a patch of light the figure of a lion. The beast was coming slowly down the street in Tarzan's direction.

A woman crossed the way directly in front of it and the lion paid no attention to her, nor she to the lion. An instant later a little child ran after the woman and so close did he run before the lion that the beast was forced to turn out of its way a step to avoid colliding with the little one. The ape-man grinned and crossed quickly to the opposite side of the street, for his delicate senses indicated that at this point the breeze stirring through the city streets and deflected by the opposite wall would now blow from the lion toward him as the beast passed, whereas if he remained upon the side of the street upon which he had been walking when he discovered the carnivore, his scent would have been borne to the nostrils of the animal, and Tarzan was sufficiently jungle-wise to realize that while he might deceive the eyes of man and beast he could not so easily disguise from the nostrils of one of the great cats that he was a creature of a different species from the inhabitants of the city, the only human beings, possibly, that Numa was familiar with. In him the cat would recognize a stranger, and, therefore, an enemy, and Tarzan had no desire to be delayed by an encounter with a savage lion. His ruse worked successfully, the lion passing him with not more than a side glance in his direction.

He had proceeded for some little distance and had about reached a point where he judged he would find the street which led up from the city gate when, at an intersection of two streets, his nostrils caught the scent spoor of the girl. Out of a maze of other scent spoors the ape-man picked the familiar odor of the girl and, a second later, that of Smith-Oldwick. He had been forced to accomplish it, however, by bending very low at each street intersection in repeated attention to his sandal wrappings, bringing his nostrils as close to the pavement as possible.

As he advanced along the street through which the two had been conducted earlier in the day he noted, as had they, the change in the type of buildings as he passed from a residence district into that portion occupied by shops and bazaars. Here the number of flares was increased so that they appeared not only at street intersections but midway between as well, and there were many more people abroad. The shops were open and lighted, for with the setting of the sun the intense heat of the day had given place to a pleasant coolness. Here also the number of lions, roaming loose through the thoroughfares, increased, and also for the first time Tarzan noted the idiosyncrasies of the people.

Once he was nearly upset by a naked man running rapidly through the street screaming at the top of his voice. And again he nearly stumbled over a woman who was making her way in the shadows of one of the arcades upon all fours. At first the ape-man thought she was hunting for something she had dropped, but as he drew to one side to watch her, he saw that she was doing nothing of the kind—that she had merely elected to walk upon her hands and knees rather than erect upon her feet. In another block he saw two creatures struggling upon the roof of an adjacent building until finally one of them, wrenching himself free from the grasp of the other, gave his adversary a mighty push which hurled him to the pavement below, where he lay motionless upon the dusty road. For an instant a wild shriek re-echoed through the city from the lungs of the victor and then, without an instant's hesitation, the fellow leaped headfirst to the street beside the body of his victim. A lion moved out from the dense shadows of a doorway and approached the two bloody and lifeless things before him. Tarzan wondered what effect the odor of blood would have upon the beast and was surprised to see that the animal only sniffed at the corpses and the hot red blood and then lay down beside the two dead men.

He had passed the lion but a short distance when his attention was called to the figure of a man lowering himself laboriously from the roof of a building upon the east side of the thoroughfare. Tarzan's curiosity was aroused.

CHAPTER XXI—IN THE ALCOVE

As Smith-Oldwick realized that he was alone and practically defenseless in an enclosure filled with great lions he was, in his weakened condition, almost in a state verging upon hysterical terror. Clinging to the grating for support he dared not turn his head in the direction of the beasts behind him. He felt his knees giving weakly beneath him. Something within his head spun rapidly around. He became very dizzy and nauseated and then suddenly all went black before his eyes as his limp body collapsed at the foot of the grating.

How long he lay there unconscious he never knew; but as reason slowly reasserted itself in his semi-conscious state he was aware that he lay in a cool bed upon the whitest of linen in a bright and cheery room, and that upon one side close to him was an open window, the delicate hangings of which were fluttering in a soft summer breeze which blew in from a sun-kissed orchard of ripening fruit which he could see without—an old orchard in which soft, green grass grew between the laden trees, and where the sun filtered through the foliage; and upon the dappled greensward a little child was playing with a frolicsome puppy.

"God," thought the man, "what a horrible nightmare I have passed through!" and then he felt a hand stroking his brow and cheek—a cool and gentle hand that smoothed away his troubled recollections. For a long minute Smith-Oldwick lay in utter peace and content until gradually there was forced upon his sensibilities the fact that the hand had become rough, and that it was no longer cool but hot and moist; and suddenly he opened his eyes and looked up into the face of a huge lion.

Lieutenant Harold Percy Smith-Oldwick was not only an English gentleman and an officer in name, he was also what these implied—a brave man; but when he realized that the sweet picture he had looked upon was but the figment of a dream, and that in reality he still lay where he had fallen at the foot of the grating with a lion standing over him licking his face, the tears sprang to his eyes and ran down his cheeks. Never, he thought, had an unkind fate played so cruel a joke upon a human being.

For some time he lay feigning death while the lion, having ceased to lick him, sniffed about his body. There are some things than which death is to be preferred; and there came at last to the Englishman the realization that it would be better to die swiftly than to lie in this horrible predicament until his mind broke beneath the strain and he went mad.

And so, deliberately and without haste, he rose, clinging to the grating for support. At his first move the lion growled, but after that he paid no further attention to the man, and when at last Smith-Oldwick had regained his feet the lion moved indifferently away. Then it was that the man turned and looked about the enclosure.

Sprawled beneath the shade of the trees and lying upon the long bench beside the south wall the great beasts rested, with the exception of two or three who moved restlessly about. It was these that the man feared and yet when two more of them had passed him by he began to feel reassured, recalling the fact that they were accustomed to the presence of man.

And yet he dared not move from the grating. As the man examined his surroundings he noted that the branches of one of the trees near the further wall spread close beneath an open window. If he could reach that tree and had strength to do so, he could easily climb out upon the branch and escape, at least, from the enclosure of the lions. But in order to reach the tree he must pass the full length of the enclosure, and at the very bole of the tree itself two lions lay sprawled out in slumber.

For half an hour the man stood gazing longingly at this seeming avenue of escape, and at last, with a muttered oath, he straightened up and throwing back his shoulders in a gesture of defiance, he walked slowly and deliberately down the center of the courtyard. One of the prowling lions turned from the side wall and moved toward the center directly in the man's path, but Smith-Oldwick was committed to what he considered his one chance, for even temporary safety, and so he kept on, ignoring the presence of the beast. The lion slouched to his side and sniffed him and then, growling, he bared his teeth.

Smith-Oldwick drew the pistol from his shirt. "If he has made up his mind to kill me," he thought. "I can't see that it will make any difference in the long run whether I infuriate him or not. The beggar can't kill me any deader in one mood than another."

But with the man's movement in withdrawing the weapon from his shirt the lion's attitude suddenly altered and though he still growled he turned and sprang away, and then at last the Englishman stood almost at the foot of the tree that was his goal, and between him and safety sprawled a sleeping lion.

Above him was a limb that ordinarily he could have leaped for and reached with ease; but weak from his wounds and loss of blood he doubted his ability to do so now. There was even a question as to whether he would be able to ascend the tree at all. There was just one chance: the lowest branch left the bole within easy reach of a man standing on the ground close to the tree's stem, but to reach a position where the branch would be accessible he must step over the body of a lion. Taking a deep breath he placed one foot between the sprawled legs of the beast and gingerly raised the other to plant it upon the opposite side of the tawny body. "What," he thought, "if the beggar should happen to wake now?" The suggestion sent a shudder through his frame but he did not hesitate or withdraw his foot. Gingerly he planted it beyond the lion, threw his weight forward upon it and cautiously brought his other foot to the side of the first. He had passed and the lion had not awakened.

Smith-Oldwick was weak from loss of blood and the hardships he had undergone, but the realization of his situation impelled him to a show of agility and energy which he probably could scarcely have equaled when in possession of his normal strength. With his life depending upon the success of his efforts, he swung himself quickly to the lower branches of the tree and scrambled upward out of reach of possible harm from the lions below—though the sudden movement in the branches above them awakened both the sleeping beasts. The animals raised their heads and looked questioningly up for a moment and then lay back again to resume their broken slumber.

So easily had the Englishman succeeded thus far that he suddenly began to question as to whether he had at any time been in real danger. The lions, as he knew, were accustomed to the presence of men, but yet they were still lions and he was free to admit that he breathed more easily now that he was safe above their clutches.

Before him lay the open window he had seen from the ground. He was now on a level with it and could see an apparently unoccupied chamber beyond, and toward this he made his way along a stout branch that swung beneath the opening. It was not a difficult feat to reach the window, and a moment later he drew himself over the sill and dropped into the room.

He found himself in a rather spacious apartment, the floor of which was covered with rugs of barbaric design, while the few pieces of furniture were of a similar type to that which he had seen in the room on the first floor into which he and Bertha Kircher had been ushered at the conclusion of their journey. At one end of the room was what appeared to be a curtained alcove, the heavy hangings of which completely hid the interior. In the wall opposite the window and near the alcove was a closed door, apparently the only exit from the room.

He could see, in the waning light without, that the close of the day was fast approaching, and he hesitated while he deliberated the advisability of waiting until darkness had fallen, or of immediately searching for some means of escape from the building and the city. He at last decided that it would do no harm to investigate beyond the room, that he might have some idea as how best to plan his escape after dark. To this end he crossed the room toward the door but he had taken only a few steps when the hangings before the alcove separated and the figure of a woman appeared in the opening.

She was young and beautifully formed; the single drapery wound around her body from below her breasts left no detail of her symmetrical proportions unrevealed, but her face was the face of an imbecile. At sight of her Smith-Oldwick halted, momentarily expecting that his presence would elicit screams for help from her. On the contrary she came toward him smiling, and when she was close her slender, shapely fingers touched the sleeve of his torn blouse as a curious child might handle a new toy, and still with the same smile she examined him from head to foot, taking in, in childish wonderment, every detail of his apparel.

Presently she spoke to him in a soft, well-modulated voice which contrasted sharply with her facial appearance. The voice and the girlish figure harmonized perfectly and seemed to belong to each other, while the head and face were those of another creature. Smith-Oldwick could understand no word of what she said, but nevertheless he spoke to her in his own cultured tone, the effect of which upon her was evidently most gratifying, for before he realized her intentions or could prevent her she had thrown both arms about his neck and was kissing him with the utmost abandon.

The man tried to free himself from her rather surprising attentions, but she only clung more tightly to him, and suddenly, as he recalled that he had always heard that one must humor the mentally deficient, and at the same time seeing in her a possible agency of escape, he closed his eyes and returned her embraces.

It was at this juncture that the door opened and a man entered. With the sound from the first movement of the latch, Smith-Oldwick opened his eyes, but though he endeavored to disengage himself from the girl he realized that the newcomer had seen their rather compromising position. The girl, whose back was toward the door, seemed at first not to realize that someone had entered, but when she did she turned quickly and as her eyes fell upon the man whose terrible face was now distorted with an expression of hideous rage she turned, screaming, and fled toward the alcove. The Englishman, flushed and embarrassed, stood where she had left him. With the sudden realization of the futility of attempting an explanation, came that of the menacing appearance of the man, whom he now recognized as the official who had received them in the room below. The fellow's face, livid with insane rage and, possibly, jealousy, was twitching violently, accentuating the maniacal expression that it habitually wore.

For a moment he seemed paralyzed by anger, and then with a loud shriek that rose into an uncanny wail, he drew his curved saber and sprang toward the Englishman. To Smith-Oldwick there seemed no possible hope of escaping the keen-edged weapon in the hands of the infuriated man, and though he felt assured that it would draw down upon him an equally sudden and possibly more terrible death, he did the only thing that remained for him to do—drew his pistol and fired straight for the heart of the oncoming man. Without even so much as a groan the fellow lunged forward upon the floor at Smith-Oldwick's feet—killed instantly with a bullet through the heart. For several seconds the silence of the tomb reigned in the apartment.

The Englishman, standing over the prostrate figure of the dead man, watched the door with drawn weapon, expecting momentarily to hear the rush of feet of those whom he was sure would immediately investigate the report of the pistol. But no sounds came from below to indicate that anyone there had heard the explosion, and presently the man's attention was distracted from the door to the alcove, between the hangings of which the face of the girl appeared. The eyes were widely dilated and the lower jaw dropped in an expression of surprise and awe.

The girl's gaze was riveted upon the figure upon the floor, and presently she crept stealthily into the room and tiptoed toward the corpse. She appeared as though constantly poised for flight, and when she had come to within two or three feet of the body she stopped and, looking up at Smith-Oldwick, voiced some interrogation which he could not, of course, understand. Then she came close to the side of the dead man and kneeling upon the floor felt gingerly of the body.

Presently she shook the corpse by the shoulder, and then with a show of strength which her tenderly girlish form belied, she turned the body over on its back. If she had been in doubt before, one glance at the hideous features set in death must have convinced her that life was extinct, and with the realization there broke from her lips peal after peal of mad, maniacal laughter as with her little hands she beat upon the upturned face and breast of the dead man. It was a gruesome sight from which the Englishman involuntarily drew back—a gruesome, disgusting sight such as, he realized, might never be witnessed outside a madhouse or this frightful city.

In the midst of her frenzied rejoicing at the death of the man, and Smith-Oldwick could attribute her actions to no other cause, she suddenly desisted from her futile attacks upon the insensate flesh and, leaping to her feet, ran quickly to the door, where she shot a wooden bolt into its socket, thus securing them from interference from without. Then she returned to the center of the room and spoke rapidly to the Englishman, gesturing occasionally toward the body of the slain man. When he could not understand, she presently became provoked and in a sudden hysteria of madness she rushed forward as though to strike the Englishman. Smith-Oldwick dropped back a few steps and leveled his pistol upon her. Mad though she must have been, she evidently was not so mad but what she had connected the loud report, the diminutive weapon, and the sudden death of the man in whose house she dwelt, for she instantly desisted and quite as suddenly as it had come upon her, her homicidal mood departed.

Again the vacuous, imbecile smile took possession of her features, and her voice, dropping its harshness, resumed the soft, well-modulated tones with which she had first addressed him. Now she attempted by signs to indicate her wishes, and motioning Smith-Oldwick to follow her she went to the hangings and opening them disclosed the alcove. It was rather more than an alcove, being a fair-sized room heavy with rugs and hangings and soft, pillowed couches. Turning at the entrance she pointed to the corpse upon the floor of the outer room, and then crossing the alcove she raised some draperies which covered a couch and fell to the floor upon all sides, disclosing an opening beneath the furniture.

To this opening she pointed and then again to the corpse, indicating plainly to the Englishman that it was her desire that the body be hidden here. But if he had been in doubt, she essayed to dispel it by grasping his sleeve and urging him in the direction of the body which the two of them then lifted and half carried and half dragged into the alcove. At first they encountered some difficulty when they endeavored to force the body of the man into the small space she had selected for it, but eventually they succeeded in doing so. Smith-Oldwick was again impressed by the fiendish brutality of the girl. In the center of the room lay a blood-stained rug which the girl quickly gathered up and draped over a piece of furniture in such a way that the stain was hidden. By rearranging the other rugs and by bringing one from the alcove she restored the room to order so no outward indication of the tragedy so recently enacted there was apparent.

These things attended to, and the hangings draped once more about the couch that they might hide the gruesome thing beneath, the girl once more threw her arms about the Englishman's neck and dragged him toward the soft and luxurious pillows above the dead man. Acutely conscious of the horror of his position, filled with loathing, disgust, and an outraged sense of decency, Smith-Oldwick was also acutely alive to the demands of self-preservation. He felt that he was warranted in buying his life at almost any price; but there was a point at which his finer nature rebelled.

It was at this juncture that a loud knock sounded upon the door of the outer room. Springing from the couch, the girl seized the man by the arm and dragged him after her to the wall close by the head of the couch. Here she drew back one of the hangings, revealing a little niche behind, into which she shoved the Englishman and dropped the hangings before him, effectually hiding him from observation from the rooms beyond.

He heard her cross the alcove to the door of the outer room, and heard the bolt withdrawn followed by the voice of a man mingled with that of the girl. The tones of both seemed rational so that he might have been listening to an ordinary conversation in some foreign tongue. Yet with the gruesome experiences of the day behind him, he could not but momentarily expect some insane outbreak from beyond the hangings.

He was aware from the sounds that the two had entered the alcove, and, prompted by a desire to know what manner of man he might next have to contend with, he slightly parted the heavy folds that hid the two from his view and looking out saw them sitting on the couch with their arms about each other, the girl with the same expressionless smile upon her face that she had vouchsafed him. He found he could so arrange the hangings that a very narrow slit between two of them permitted him to watch the actions of those in the alcove without revealing himself or increasing his liability of detection.

He saw the girl lavishing her kisses upon the newcomer, a much younger man than he whom Smith-Oldwick had dispatched. Presently the girl disengaged herself from the embrace of her lover as though struck by a sudden memory. Her brows puckered as in labored thought and then with a startled expression, she threw a glance backward toward the hidden niche where the Englishman stood, after which she whispered rapidly to her companion, occasionally jerking her head in the direction of the niche and on several occasions making a move with one hand and forefinger, which Smith-Oldwick could not mistake as other than an attempt to describe his pistol and its use.

It was evident then to him that she was betraying him, and without further loss of time he turned his back toward the hangings and commenced a rapid examination of his hiding place. In the alcove the man and the girl whispered, and then cautiously and with great stealth, the man rose and drew his curved saber. On tiptoe he approached the hangings, the girl creeping at his side. Neither spoke now, nor was there any sound in the room as the girl sprang forward and with outstretched arm and pointing finger indicated a point upon the curtain at the height of a man's breast. Then she stepped to one side, and her companion, raising his blade to a horizontal position, lunged suddenly forward and with the full weight of his body and his right arm, drove the sharp point through the hangings and into the niche behind for its full length.

Bertha Kircher, finding her struggles futile and realizing that she must conserve her strength for some chance opportunity of escape, desisted from her efforts to break from the grasp of Prince Metak as the fellow fled with her through the dimly lighted corridors of the palace. Through many chambers the prince fled, bearing his prize. It was evident to the girl that, though her captor was the king's son, he was not above capture and punishment for his deeds, as otherwise he would not have shown such evident anxiety to escape with her, as well as from the results of his act.

From the fact that he was constantly turning affrighted eyes behind them, and glancing suspiciously into every nook and corner that they passed, she guessed that the prince's punishment might be both speedy and terrible were he caught.

She knew from their route that they must have doubled back several times although she had quite lost all sense of direction; but she did not know that the prince was as equally confused as she, and that really he was running in an aimless, erratic manner, hoping that he might stumble eventually upon a place of refuge.

Nor is it to be wondered at that this offspring of maniacs should have difficulty in orienting himself in the winding mazes of a palace designed by maniacs for a maniac king. Now a corridor turned gradually and almost imperceptibly in a new direction, again one doubled back upon and crossed itself; here the floor rose gradually to the level of another story, or again there might be a spiral stairway down which the mad prince rushed dizzily with his burden. Upon what floor they were or in what part of the palace even Metak had no idea until, halting abruptly at a closed door, he pushed it open to step into a brilliantly lighted chamber filled with warriors, at one end of which sat the king upon a great throne; beside this, to the girl's surprise, she saw another throne where was seated a huge lioness, recalling to her the words of Xanila which, at the time, had made no impression on her: "But he had many other queens, nor were they all human."

At sight of Metak and the girl, the king rose from his throne and started across the chamber, all semblance of royalty vanishing in the maniac's uncontrollable passion. And as he came he shrieked orders and commands at the top of his voice. No sooner had Metak so unwarily opened the door to this hornets' nest than he immediately withdrew and, turning, fled again in a new direction. But now a hundred men were close upon his heels, laughing, shrieking, and possibly cursing. He dodged hither and thither, distancing them for several minutes until, at the bottom of a long runway that inclined steeply downward from a higher level, he burst into a subterranean apartment lighted by many flares.

In the center of the room was a pool of considerable size, the level of the water being but a few inches below the floor. Those behind the fleeing prince and his captive entered the chamber in time to see Metak leap into the water with the girl and disappear beneath the surface taking his captive with him, nor, though they waited excitedly around the rim of the pool, did either of the two again emerge.

When Smith-Oldwick turned to investigate his hiding place, his hands, groping upon the rear wall, immediately came in contact with the wooden panels of a door and a bolt such as that which secured the door of the outer room. Cautiously and silently drawing the wooden bar he pushed gently against the panel to find that the door swung easily and noiselessly outward into utter darkness. Moving carefully and feeling forward for each step he passed out of the niche, closing the door behind him.

Feeling about, he discovered that he was in a narrow corridor which he followed cautiously for a few yards to be brought up suddenly by what appeared to be a ladder across the passageway. He felt of the obstruction carefully with his hands until he was assured that it was indeed a ladder and that a solid wall was just beyond it, ending the corridor. Therefore, as he could not go forward and as the ladder ended at the floor upon which he stood, and as he did not care to retrace his steps, there was no alternative but to climb upward, and this he did, his pistol ready in a side pocket of his blouse.

He had ascended but two or three rungs when his head came suddenly and painfully in contact with a hard surface above him. Groping about with one hand over his head he discovered that the obstacle seemed to be the covering to a trap door in the ceiling which, with a little effort, he succeeded in raising a couple of inches, revealing through the cracks the stars of a clear African night.

With a sigh of relief, but with unabated caution, he gently slid the trapdoor to one side far enough to permit him to raise his eyes above the level of the roof. A quick glance assured him that there was none near enough to observe his movements, nor, in fact, as far as he could see, was anyone in sight.

Drawing himself quickly through the aperture he replaced the cover and endeavored to regain his bearings. Directly to the south of him the low roof he stood upon adjoined a much loftier portion of the building, which rose several stories above his head. A few yards to the west he could see the flickering light of the flares of a winding street, and toward this he made his way.

From the edge of the roof he looked down upon the night life of the mad city. He saw men and women and children and lions, and of all that he saw it was quite evident to him that only the lions were sane. With the aid of the stars he easily picked out the points of the compass, and following carefully in his memory the steps that had led him into the city and to the roof upon which he now stood, he knew that the thoroughfare upon which he looked was the same along which he and Bertha Kircher had been led as prisoners earlier in the day.

If he could reach this he might be able to pass undetected in the shadows of the arcade to the city gate. He had already given up as futile the thought of seeking out the girl and attempting to succor her, for he knew that alone and with the few remaining rounds of ammunition he possessed, he could do nothing against this city-full of armed men. That he could live to cross the lion-infested forest beyond the city was doubtful, and having, by some miracle, won to the desert beyond, his fate would be certainly sealed; but yet he was consumed with but one desire—to leave behind him as far as possible this horrid city of maniacs.

He saw that the roofs rose to the same level as that upon which he stood unbroken to the north to the next street intersection. Directly below him was a flare. To reach the pavement in safety it was necessary that he find as dark a portion of the avenue as possible. And so he sought along the edge of the roofs for a place where he might descend in comparative concealment.

He had proceeded some little way beyond a point where the street curved abruptly to the east before he discovered a location sufficiently to his liking. But even here he was compelled to wait a considerable time for a satisfactory moment for his descent, which he had decided to make down one of the pillars of the arcade. Each time he prepared to lower himself over the edge of the roofs, footsteps approaching in one direction or another deterred him until at last he had almost come to the conclusion that he would have to wait for the entire city to sleep before continuing his flight.

But finally came a moment which he felt propitious and though with inward qualms, it was with outward calm that he commenced the descent to the street below.

When at last he stood beneath the arcade he was congratulating himself upon the success that had attended his efforts up to this point when, at a slight sound behind him, he turned to see a tall figure in the yellow tunic of a warrior confronting him.

CHAPTER XXII—OUT OF THE NICHE

Numa, the lion, growled futilely in baffled rage as he slipped back to the ground at the foot of the wall after his unsuccessful attempt to drag down the fleeing ape-man. He poised to make a second effort to follow his escaping quarry when his nose picked up a hitherto unnoticed quality in the scent spoor of his intended prey. Sniffing at the ground that Tarzan's feet had barely touched, Numa's growl changed to a low whine, for he had recognized the scent spoor of the man-thing that had rescued him from the pit of the Wamabos.

What thoughts passed through that massive head? Who may say? But now there was no indication of baffled rage as the great lion turned and moved majestically eastward along the wall. At the eastern end of the city he turned toward the south, continuing his way to the south side of the wall along which were the pens and corrals where the herbivorous flocks were fattened for the herds of domesticated lions within the city. The great black lions of the forest fed with almost equal impartiality upon the flesh of the grass-eaters and man. Like Numa of the pit they occasionally made excursions across the desert to the fertile valley of the Wamabos, but principally they took their toll of meat from the herds of the walled city of Herog, the mad king, or seized upon some of his luckless subjects.

Numa of the pit was in some respects an exception to the rule which guided his fellows of the forest in that as a cub he had been trapped and carried into the city, where he was kept for breeding purposes, only to escape in his second year. They had tried to teach him in the city of maniacs that he must not eat the flesh of man, and the result of their schooling was that only when aroused to anger or upon that one occasion that he had been impelled by the pangs of hunger, did he ever attack man.

The animal corrals of the maniacs are protected by an outer wall or palisade of upright logs, the lower ends of which are imbedded in the ground, the logs themselves being placed as close together as possible and further reinforced and bound together by withes. At intervals there are gates through which the flocks are turned on to the grazing land south of the city during the daytime. It is at such times that the black lions of the forest take their greatest toll from the herds, and it is infrequent that a lion attempts to enter the corrals at night. But Numa of the pit, having scented the spoor of his benefactor, was minded again to pass into the walled city, and with that idea in his cunning brain he crept stealthily along the outer side of the palisade, testing each gateway with a padded foot until at last he discovered one which seemed insecurely fastened. Lowering his great head he pressed against the gate, surging forward with all the weight of his huge body and the strength of his giant sinews—one mighty effort and Numa was within the corral.

The enclosure contained a herd of goats which immediately upon the advent of the carnivore started a mad stampede to the opposite end of the corral which was bounded by the south wall of the city. Numa had been within such a corral as this before, so that he knew that somewhere in the wall was a small door through which the goatherd might pass from the city to his flock; toward this door he made his way, whether by plan or accident it is difficult to say, though in the light of ensuing events it seems possible that the former was the case.

To reach the gate he must pass directly through the herd which had huddled affrightedly close to the opening so that once again there was a furious rush of hoofs as Numa strode quickly to the side of the portal. If Numa had planned, he had planned well, for scarcely had he reached his position when the door opened and a herder's head was projected into the enclosure, the fellow evidently seeking an explanation of the disturbance among his flock. Possibly he discovered the cause of the commotion, but it is doubtful, for it was dark and the great, taloned paw that reached up and struck downward a mighty blow that almost severed his head from his body, moved so quickly and silently that the man was dead within a fraction of a second from the moment that he opened the door, and then Numa, knowing now his way, passed through the wall into the dimly lighted streets of the city beyond.

Smith-Oldwick's first thought when he was accosted by the figure in the yellow tunic of a soldier was to shoot the man dead and trust to his legs and the dimly lighted, winding streets to permit his escape, for he knew that to be accosted was equivalent to recapture since no inhabitant of this weird city but would recognize him as an alien. It would be a simple thing to shoot the man from the pocket where the pistol lay without drawing the weapon, and with this purpose in mind the Englishman slipped his hands into the side pocket of his blouse, but simultaneously with this action his wrist was seized in a powerful grasp and a low voice whispered in English: "Lieutenant, it is I, Tarzan of the Apes."

The relief from the nervous strain under which he had been laboring for so long, left Smith-Oldwick suddenly as weak as a babe, so that he was forced to grasp the ape-man's arm for support—and when he found his voice all he could do was to repeat: "You? You? I thought you were dead!"

"No, not dead," replied Tarzan, "and I see that you are not either. But how about the girl?"

"I haven't seen her," replied the Englishman, "since we were brought here. We were taken into a building on the plaza close by and there we were separated. She was led away by guards and I was put into a den of lions. I haven't seen her since."

"How did you escape?" asked the ape-man.

"The lions didn't seem to pay much attention to me and I climbed out of the place by way of a tree and through a window into a room on the second floor. Had a little scrimmage there with a fellow and was hidden by one of their women in a hole in the wall. The loony thing then betrayed me to another bounder who happened in, but I found a way out and up onto the roof where I have been for quite some time now waiting for a chance to get down into the street without being seen. That's all I know, but I haven't the slightest idea in the world where to look for Miss Kircher."

"Where were you going now?" asked Tarzan.

Smith-Oldwick hesitated. "I—well, I couldn't do anything here alone and I was going to try to get out of the city and in some way reach the British forces east and bring help."

"You couldn't do it," said Tarzan. "Even if you got through the forest alive you could never cross the desert country without food or water."

"What shall we do, then?" asked the Englishman.

"We will see if we can find the girl," replied the ape-man, and then, as though he had forgotten the presence of the Englishman and was arguing to convince himself, "She may be a German and a spy, but she is a woman—a white woman—I can't leave her here."

"But how are we going to find her?" asked the Englishman.

"I have followed her this far," replied Tarzan, "and unless I am greatly mistaken I can follow her still farther."

"But I cannot accompany you in these clothes without exposing us both to detection and arrest," argued Smith-Oldwick.

"We will get you other clothes, then," said Tarzan.

"How?" asked the Englishman.

"Go back to the roof beside the city wall where I entered," replied the ape-man with a grim smile, "and ask the naked dead man there how I got my disguise."

Smith-Oldwick looked quickly up at his companion. "I have it," he exclaimed. "I know where there is a fellow who doesn't need his clothes anymore, and if we can get back on this roof I think we can find him and get his apparel without much resistance. Only a girl and a young fellow whom we could easily surprise and overcome."

"What do you mean?" asked Tarzan. "How do you know that the man doesn't need his clothes any more."

"I know he doesn't need them," replied the Englishman, "because I killed him."

"Oh!" exclaimed the ape-man, "I see. I guess it might be easier that way than to tackle one of these fellows in the street where there is more chance of our being interrupted."

"But how are we going to reach the roof again, after all?" queried Smith-Oldwick.

"The same way you came down," replied Tarzan. "This roof is low and there is a little ledge formed by the capital of each column; I noticed that when you descended. Some of the buildings wouldn't have been so easy to negotiate."

Smith-Oldwick looked up toward the eaves of the low roof. "It's not very high," he said, "but I am afraid I can't make it. I'll try—I've been pretty weak since a lion mauled me and the guards beat me up, and too, I haven't eaten since yesterday."

Tarzan thought a moment. "You've got to go with me," he said at last. "I can't leave you here. The only chance you have of escape is through me and I can't go with you now until we have found the girl."

"I want to go with you," replied Smith-Oldwick. "I'm not much good now but at that two of us may be better than one."

"All right," said Tarzan, "come on," and before the Englishman realized what the other contemplated Tarzan had picked him up and thrown him across his shoulder. "Now, hang on," whispered the ape-man, and with a short run he clambered apelike up the front of the low arcade. So quickly and easily was it done that the Englishman scarcely had time to realize what was happening before he was deposited safely upon the roof.

"There," remarked Tarzan. "Now, lead me to the place you speak of."

Smith-Oldwick had no difficulty in locating the trap in the roof through which he had escaped. Removing the cover the ape-man bent low, listening and sniffing. "Come," he said after a moment's investigation and lowered himself to the floor beneath. Smith-Oldwick followed him, and together the two crept through the darkness toward the door in the back wall of the niche in which the Englishman had been hidden by the girl. They found the door ajar and opening it Tarzan saw a streak of light showing through the hangings that separated it from the alcove.

Placing his eye close to the aperture he saw the girl and the young man of which the Englishman had spoken seated on opposite sides of a low table upon which food was spread. Serving them was a giant Negro and it was he whom the ape-man watched most closely. Familiar with the tribal idiosyncrasies of a great number of African tribes over a considerable proportion of the Dark Continent, the Tarmangani at last felt reasonably assured that he knew from what part of Africa this slave had come, and the dialect of his people. There was, however, the chance that the fellow had been captured in childhood and that through long years of non-use his native language had become lost to him, but then there always had been an element of chance connected with nearly every event of Tarzan's life, so he waited patiently until in the performance of his duties the black man approached a little table which stood near the niche in which Tarzan and the Englishman hid.

As the slave bent over some dish which stood upon the table his ear was not far from the aperture through which Tarzan looked. Apparently from a solid wall, for the Negro had no knowledge of the existence of the niche, came to him in the tongue of his own people, the whispered words: "If you would return to the land of the Wamabo say nothing, but do as I bid you."

The black rolled terrified eyes toward the hangings at his side. The ape-man could see him tremble and for a moment was fearful that in his terror he would betray them. "Fear not," he whispered, "we are your friends."

At last the Negro spoke in a low whisper, scarcely audible even to the keen ears of the ape-man. "What," he asked, "can poor Otobu do for the god who speaks to him out of the solid wall?"

"This," replied Tarzan. "Two of us are coming into this room. Help us prevent this man and woman from escaping or raising an outcry that will bring others to their aid."

"I will help you," replied the Negro, "to keep them within this room, but do not fear that their outcries will bring others. These walls are built so that no sound may pass through, and even if it did what difference would it make in this village which is constantly filled with the screams of its mad people. Do not fear their cries. No one will notice them. I go to do your bidding."

Tarzan saw the black cross the room to the table upon which he placed another dish of food before the feasters. Then he stepped to a place behind the man and as he did so raised his eyes to the point in the wall from which the ape-man's voice had come to him, as much as to say, "Master, I am ready."

Without more delay Tarzan threw aside the hangings and stepped into the room. As he did so the young man rose from the table to be instantly seized from behind by the black slave. The girl, whose back was toward the ape-man and his companion, was not at first aware of their presence but saw only the attack of the slave upon her lover, and with a loud scream she leaped forward to assist the latter. Tarzan sprang to her side and laid a heavy hand upon her arm before she could interfere with Otobu's attentions to the young man. At first, as she turned toward the ape-man, her face reflected only mad rage, but almost instantly this changed into the vapid smile with which Smith-Oldwick was already familiar and her slim fingers commenced their soft appraisement of the newcomer.

Almost immediately she discovered Smith-Oldwick but there was neither surprise nor anger upon her countenance. Evidently the poor mad creature knew but two principal moods, from one to the other of which she changed with lightning-like rapidity.

"Watch her a moment," said Tarzan to the Englishman, "while I disarm that fellow," and stepping to the side of the young man whom Otobu was having difficulty in subduing Tarzan relieved him of his saber. "Tell them," he said to the Negro, "if you speak their language, that we will not harm them if they leave us alone and let us depart in peace."

The black had been looking at Tarzan with wide eyes, evidently not comprehending how this god could appear in so material a form, and with the voice of a white bwana and the uniform of a warrior of this city to which he quite evidently did not belong. But nevertheless his first confidence in the voice that offered him freedom was not lessened and he did as Tarzan bid him.

"They want to know what you want," said Otobu, after he had spoken to the man and the girl.

"Tell them that we want food for one thing," said Tarzan, "and something else that we know where to find in this room. Take the man's spear, Otobu; I see it leaning against the wall in the corner of the room. And you, Lieutenant, take his saber," and then again to Otobu, "I will watch the man while you go and bring forth that which is beneath the couch over against this wall," and Tarzan indicated the location of the piece of furniture.

Otobu, trained to obey, did as he was bid. The eyes of the man and the girl followed him, and as he drew back the hangings and dragged forth the corpse of the man Smith-Oldwick had slain, the girl's lover voiced a loud scream and attempted to leap forward to the side of the corpse. Tarzan, however, seized him and then the fellow turned upon him with teeth and nails. It was with no little difficulty that Tarzan finally subdued the man, and while Otobu was removing the outer clothing from the corpse, Tarzan asked the black to question the young man as to his evident excitement at the sight of the body.

"I can tell you Bwana," replied Otobu. "This man was his father."

"What is he saying to the girl?" asked Tarzan.

"He is asking her if she knew that the body of his father was under the couch. And she is saying that she did not know it."

Tarzan repeated the conversation to Smith-Oldwick, who smiled. "If the chap could have seen her removing all evidence of the crime and arranging the hangings of the couch so that the body was concealed after she had helped me drag it across the room, he wouldn't have very much doubt as to her knowledge of the affair. The rug you see draped over the bench in the corner was arranged to hide the blood stain—in some ways they are not so loony after all."

The black man had now removed the outer garments from the dead man, and Smith-Oldwick was hastily drawing them on over his own clothing. "And now," said Tarzan, "we will sit down and eat. One accomplishes little on an empty stomach." As they ate the ape-man attempted to carry on a conversation with the two natives through Otobu. He learned that they were in the palace which had belonged to the dead man lying upon the floor beside them. He had held an official position of some nature, and he and his family were of the ruling class but were not members of the court.

When Tarzan questioned them about Bertha Kircher, the young man said that she had been taken to the king's palace; and when asked why replied: "For the king, of course."

During the conversation both the man and the girl appeared quite rational, even asking some questions as to the country from which their uninvited guests had come, and evidencing much surprise when informed that there was anything but waterless wastes beyond their own valley.

When Otobu asked the man, at Tarzan's suggestion, if he was familiar with the interior of the king's palace, he replied that he was; that he was a friend of Prince Metak, one of the king's sons, and that he often visited the palace and that Metak also came here to his father's palace frequently. As Tarzan ate he racked his brain for some plan whereby he might utilize the knowledge of the young man to gain entrance to the palace, but he had arrived at nothing which he considered feasible when there came a loud knocking upon the door of the outer room.

For a moment no one spoke and then the young man raised his voice and cried aloud to those without. Immediately Otobu sprang for the fellow and attempted to smother his words by clapping a palm over his mouth.

"What is he saying?" asked Tarzan.

"He is telling them to break down the door and rescue him and the girl from two strangers who entered and made them prisoners. If they enter they will kill us all."

"Tell him," said Tarzan, "to hold his peace or I will slay him."

Otobu did as he was instructed and the young maniac lapsed into scowling silence. Tarzan crossed the alcove and entered the outer room to note the effect of the assaults upon the door.

Smith-Oldwick followed him a few steps, leaving Otobu to guard the two prisoners. The ape-man saw that the door could not long withstand the heavy blows being dealt the panels from without. "I wanted to use that fellow in the other room," he said to Smith-Oldwick, "but I am afraid we will have to get out of here the way we came. We can't accomplish anything by waiting here and meeting these fellows. From the noise out there there must be a dozen of them. Come," he said, "you go first and I will follow."

As the two turned back from the alcove they witnessed an entirely different scene from that upon which they had turned their backs but a moment or two before. Stretched on the floor and apparently lifeless lay the body of the black slave, while the two prisoners had vanished completely.

CHAPTER XXIII—THE FLIGHT FROM XUJA

As Metak bore Bertha Kircher toward the edge of the pool, the girl at first had no conception of the deed he contemplated but when, as they approached the edge, he did not lessen his speed she guessed the frightful truth. As he leaped head foremost with her into the water, she closed her eyes and breathed a silent prayer, for she was confident that the maniac had no other purpose than to drown himself and her. And yet, so potent is the first law of nature that even in the face of certain death, as she surely believed herself, she clung tenaciously to life, and while she struggled to free herself from the powerful clutches of the madman, she held her breath against the final moment when the asphyxiating waters must inevitably flood her lungs.

Through the frightful ordeal she maintained absolute control of her senses so that, after the first plunge, she was aware that the man was swimming with her beneath the surface. He took perhaps not more than a dozen strokes directly toward the end wall of the pool and then he arose; and once again she knew that her head was above the surface. She opened her eyes to see that they were in a corridor dimly lighted by gratings set in its roof—a winding corridor, water filled from wall to wall.

Along this the man was swimming with easy powerful strokes, at the same time holding her chin above the water. For ten minutes he swam thus without stopping and the girl heard him speak to her, though she could not understand what he said, as he evidently immediately realized, for, half floating, he shifted his hold upon her so that he could touch her nose and mouth with the fingers of one hand. She grasped what he meant and immediately took a deep breath, whereat he dove quickly beneath the surface pulling her down with him and again for a dozen strokes or more he swam thus wholly submerged.

When they again came to the surface, Bertha Kircher saw that they were in a large lagoon and that the bright stars were shining high above them, while on either hand domed and minareted buildings were silhouetted sharply against the starlit sky. Metak swam swiftly to the north side of the lagoon where, by means of a ladder, the two climbed out upon the embankment. There were others in the plaza but they paid but little if any attention to the two bedraggled figures. As Metak walked quickly across the pavement with the girl at his side, Bertha Kircher could only guess at the man's intentions. She could see no way in which to escape and so she went docilely with him, hoping against hope that some fortuitous circumstance might eventually arise that would give her the coveted chance for freedom and life.

Metak led her toward a building which, as she entered, she recognized as the same to which she and Lieutenant Smith-Oldwick had been led when they were brought into the city. There was no man sitting behind the carved desk now, but about the room were a dozen or more warriors in the tunics of the house to which they were attached, in this case white with a small lion in the form of a crest or badge upon the breast and back of each.

As Metak entered and the men recognized him they arose, and in answer to a query he put, they pointed to an arched doorway at the rear of the room. Toward this Metak led the girl, and then, as though filled with a sudden suspicion, his eyes narrowed cunningly and turning toward the soldiery he issued an order which resulted in their all preceding him through the small doorway and up a flight of stairs a short distance beyond.

The stairway and the corridor above were lighted by small flares which revealed several doors in the walls of the upper passageway. To one of these the men led the prince. Bertha Kircher saw them knock upon the door and heard a voice reply faintly through the thick door to the summons. The effect upon those about her was electrical. Instantly excitement reigned, and in response to orders from the king's son the soldiers commenced to beat heavily upon the door, to throw their bodies against it and to attempt to hew away the panels with their sabers. The girl wondered at the cause of the evident excitement of her captors.

She saw the door giving to each renewed assault, but what she did not see just before it crashed inward was the figures of the two men who alone, in all the world, might have saved her, pass between the heavy hangings in an adjoining alcove and disappear into a dark corridor.

As the door gave and the warriors rushed into the apartment followed by the prince, the latter became immediately filled with baffled rage, for the rooms were deserted except for the dead body of the owner of the palace, and the still form of the black slave, Otobu, where they lay stretched upon the floor of the alcove.

The prince rushed to the windows and looked out, but as the suite overlooked the barred den of lions from which, the prince thought, there could be no escape, his puzzlement was only increased. Though he searched about the room for some clue to the whereabouts of its former occupants he did not discover the niche behind the hangings. With the fickleness of insanity he quickly tired of the search, and, turning to the soldiers who had accompanied him from the floor below, dismissed them.

After setting up the broken door as best they could, the men left the apartment and when they were again alone Metak turned toward the girl. As he approached her, his face distorted by a hideous leer, his features worked rapidly in spasmodic twitches. The girl, who was standing at the entrance of the alcove, shrank back, her horror reflected in her face. Step by step she backed across the room, while the crouching maniac crept stealthily after her with claw-like fingers poised in anticipation of the moment they should leap forth and seize her.

As she passed the body of the Negro, her foot touched some obstacle at her side, and glancing down she saw the spear with which Otobu had been supposed to hold the prisoners. Instantly she leaned forward and snatched it from the floor with its sharp point directed at the body of the madman. The effect upon Metak was electrical. From stealthy silence he broke into harsh peals of laughter, and drawing his saber danced to and fro before the girl, but whichever way he went the point of the spear still threatened him.

Gradually the girl noticed a change in the tone of the creature's screams that was also reflected in the changing expression upon his hideous countenance. His hysterical laughter was slowly changing into cries of rage while the silly leer upon his face was supplanted by a ferocious scowl and up-curled lips, which revealed the sharpened fangs beneath.

He now ran rapidly in almost to the spear's point, only to jump away, run a few steps to one side and again attempt to make an entrance, the while he slashed and hewed at the spear with such violence that it was with difficulty the girl maintained her guard, and all the time was forced to give ground step by step. She had reached the point where she was standing squarely against the couch at the side of the room when, with an incredibly swift movement, Metak stooped and grasping a low stool hurled it directly at her head.

She raised the spear to fend off the heavy missile, but she was not entirely successful, and the impact of the blow carried her backward upon the couch, and instantly Metak was upon her.

Tarzan and Smith-Oldwick gave little thought as to what had become of the other two occupants of the room. They were gone, and so far as these two were concerned they might never return. Tarzan's one desire was to reach the street again, where, now that both of them were in some sort of disguise, they should be able to proceed with comparative safety to the palace and continue their search for the girl.

Smith-Oldwick preceded Tarzan along the corridor and as they reached the ladder he climbed aloft to remove the trap. He worked for a moment and then, turning, addressed Tarzan.

"Did we replace the cover on this trap when we came down? I don't recall that we did."

"No," said Tarzan, "it was left open."

"So I thought," said Smith-Oldwick, "but it's closed now and locked. I cannot move it. Possibly you can," and he descended the ladder.

Even Tarzan's immense strength, however, had no effect other than to break one of the rungs of the ladder against which he was pushing, nearly precipitating him to the floor below. After the rung broke he rested for a moment before renewing his efforts, and as he stood with his head near the cover of the trap, he distinctly heard voices on the roof above him.

Dropping down to Oldwick's side he told him what he had heard. "We had better find some other way out," he said, and the two started to retrace their steps toward the alcove. Tarzan was again in the lead, and as he opened the door in the back of the niche, he was suddenly startled to hear, in tones of terror and in a woman's voice, the words: "O God, be merciful" from just beyond the hangings.

Here was no time for cautious investigation and, not even waiting to find the aperture and part the hangings, but with one sweep of a brawny hand dragging them from their support, the ape-man leaped from the niche into the alcove.

At the sound of his entry the maniac looked up, and as he saw at first only a man in the uniform of his father's soldiers, he shrieked forth an angry order, but at the second glance, which revealed the face of the newcomer, the madman leaped from the prostrate form of his victim and, apparently forgetful of the saber which he had dropped upon the floor beside the couch as he leaped to grapple with the girl, closed with bare hands upon his antagonist, his sharp-filed teeth searching for the other's throat.

Metak, the son of Herog, was no weakling. Powerful by nature and rendered still more so in the throes of one of his maniacal fits of fury he was no mean antagonist, even for the mighty ape-man, and to this a distinct advantage for him was added by the fact that almost at the outset of their battle Tarzan, in stepping backward, struck his heel against the corpse of the man whom Smith-Oldwick had killed, and fell heavily backward to the floor with Metak upon his breast.

With the quickness of a cat the maniac made an attempt to fasten his teeth in Tarzan's jugular, but a quick movement of the latter resulted in his finding a hold only upon the Tarmangani's shoulder. Here he clung while his fingers sought Tarzan's throat, and it was then that the ape-man, realizing the possibility of defeat, called to Smith-Oldwick to take the girl and seek to escape.

The Englishman looked questioningly at Bertha Kircher, who had now risen from the couch, shaking and trembling. She saw the question in his eyes and with an effort she drew herself to her full height. "No," she cried, "if he dies here I shall die with him. Go if you wish to. You can do nothing here, but I—I cannot go."

Tarzan had now regained his feet, but the maniac still clung to him tenaciously. The girl turned suddenly to Smith-Oldwick. "Your pistol!" she cried. "Why don't you shoot him?"

The man drew the weapon from his pocket and approached the two antagonists, but by this time they were moving so rapidly that there was no opportunity for shooting one without the danger of hitting the other. At the same time Bertha Kircher circled about them with the prince's saber, but neither could she find an opening. Again and again the two men fell to the floor, until presently Tarzan found a hold upon the other's throat, against which contingency Metak had been constantly battling, and slowly, as the giant fingers closed, the other's mad eyes protruded from his livid face, his jaws gaped and released their hold upon Tarzan's shoulder, and then in a sudden excess of disgust and rage the ape-man lifted the body of the prince high above his head and with all the strength of his great arms hurled it across the room and through the window where it fell with a sickening thud into the pit of lions beneath.

As Tarzan turned again toward his companions, the girl was standing with the saber still in her hand and an expression upon her face that he never had seen there before. Her eyes were wide and misty with unshed tears, while her sensitive lips trembled as though she were upon the point of giving way to some pent emotion which her rapidly rising and falling bosom plainly indicated she was fighting to control.

"If we are going to get out of here," said the ape-man, "we can't lose any time. We are together at last and nothing can be gained by delay. The question now is the safest way. The couple who escaped us evidently departed through the passageway to the roof and secured the trap against us so that we are cut off in that direction. What chance have we below? You came that way," and he turned toward the girl.

"At the foot of the stairs," she said, "is a room full of armed men. I doubt if we could pass that way."

It was then that Otobu raised himself to a sitting posture. "So you are not dead after all," exclaimed the ape-man. "Come, how badly are you hurt?"

The Negro rose gingerly to his feet, moved his arms and legs and felt of his head.

"Otobu does not seem to be hurt at all, Bwana," he replied, "only for a great ache in his head."

"Good," said the ape-man. "You want to return to the Wamabo country?"

"Yes, Bwana."

"Then lead us from the city by the safest way."

"There is no safe way," replied the black, "and even if we reach the gates we shall have to fight. I can lead you from this building to a side street with little danger of meeting anyone on the way. Beyond that we must take our chance of discovery. You are all dressed as are the people of this wicked city so perhaps we may pass unnoticed, but at the gate it will be a different matter, for none is permitted to leave the city at night."

"Very well," replied the ape-man, "let us be on our way."

Otobu led them through the broken door of the outer room, and part way down the corridor he turned into another apartment at the right. This they crossed to a passageway beyond, and, finally, traversing several rooms and corridors, he led them down a flight of steps to a door which opened directly upon a side street in rear of the palace.

Two men, a woman, and a black slave were not so extraordinary a sight upon the streets of the city as to arouse comment. When passing beneath the flares the three Europeans were careful to choose a moment when no chance pedestrian might happen to get a view of their features, but in the shadow of the arcades there seemed little danger of detection. They had covered a good portion of the distance to the gate without mishap when there came to their ears from the central portion of the city sounds of a great commotion.

"What does that mean?" Tarzan asked of Otobu, who was now trembling violently.

"Master," he replied, "they have discovered that which has happened in the palace of Veza, mayor of the city. His son and the girl escaped and summoned soldiers who have now doubtless discovered the body of Veza."

"I wonder," said Tarzan, "if they have discovered the party I threw through the window."

Bertha Kircher, who understood enough of the dialect to follow their conversation, asked Tarzan if he knew that the man he had thrown from the window was the king's son. The ape-man laughed. "No," he said, "I did not. That rather complicates matters—at least if they have found him."

Suddenly there broke above the turmoil behind them the clear strains of a bugle. Otobu increased his pace. "Hurry, Master," he cried, "it is worse than I had thought."

"What do you mean?" asked Tarzan.

"For some reason the king's guard and the king's lions are being called out. I fear, O Bwana, that we cannot escape them. But why they should be called out for us I do not know."

But if Otobu did not know, Tarzan at least guessed that they had found the body of the king's son. Once again the notes of the bugle rose high and clear upon the night air. "Calling more lions?" asked Tarzan.

"No, Master," replied Otobu. "It is the parrots they are calling."

They moved on rapidly in silence for a few minutes when their attention was attracted by the flapping of the wings of a bird above them. They looked up to discover a parrot circling about over their heads.

"Here are the parrots, Otobu," said Tarzan with a grin. "Do they expect to kill us with parrots?"

The Negro moaned as the bird darted suddenly ahead of them toward the city wall. "Now indeed are we lost, Master," cried the black. "The bird that found us has flown to the gate to warn the guard."

"Come, Otobu, what are you talking about?" exclaimed Tarzan irritably. "Have you lived among these lunatics so long that you are yourself mad?"

"No, Master," replied Otobu. "I am not mad. You do not know them. These terrible birds are like human beings without hearts or souls. They speak the language of the people of this city of Xuja. They are demons, Master, and when in sufficient numbers they might even attack and kill us."

"How far are we from the gate?" asked Tarzan.

"We are not very far," replied the Negro. "Beyond this next turn we will see it a few paces ahead of us. But the bird has reached it before us and by now they are summoning the guard," the truth of which statement was almost immediately indicated by sounds of many voices raised evidently in commands just ahead of them, while from behind came increased evidence of approaching pursuit—loud screams and the roars of lions.

A few steps ahead a narrow alley opened from the east into the thoroughfare they were following and as they approached it there emerged from its dark shadows the figure of a mighty lion. Otobu halted in his tracks and shrank back against Tarzan. "Look, Master," he whimpered, "a great black lion of the forest!"

Tarzan drew the saber which still hung at his side. "We cannot go back," he said. "Lions, parrots, or men, it must be all the same," and he moved steadily forward in the direction of the gate. What wind was stirring in the city street moved from Tarzan toward the lion and when the ape-man had approached to within a few yards of the beast, who had stood silently eyeing them up to this time, instead of the expected roar, a whine broke from the beast's throat. The ape-man was conscious of a very decided feeling of relief. "It's Numa of the pit," he called back to his companions, and to Otobu, "Do not fear, this lion will not harm us."

Numa moved forward to the ape-man's side and then turning, paced beside him along the narrow street. At the next turn they came in sight of the gate, where, beneath several flares, they saw a group of at least twenty warriors prepared to seize them, while from the opposite direction the roars of the pursuing lions sounded close upon them, mingling with the screams of numerous parrots which now circled about their heads. Tarzan halted and turned to the young aviator. "How many rounds of ammunition have you left?" he asked.

"I have seven in the pistol," replied Smith-Oldwick, "and perhaps a dozen more cartridges in my blouse pocket."

"I'm going to rush them," said Tarzan. "Otobu, you stay at the side of the woman. Oldwick, you and I will go ahead, you upon my left. I think we need not try to tell Numa what to do," for even then the great lion was baring his fangs and growling ferociously at the guardsmen, who appeared uneasy in the face of this creature which, above all others, they feared.

"As we advance, Oldwick," said the ape-man, "fire one shot. It may frighten them, and after that fire only when necessary. All ready? Let's go!" and he moved forward toward the gate. At the same time, Smith-Oldwick discharged his weapon and a yellow-coated warrior screamed and crumpled forward upon his face. For a minute the others showed symptoms of panic but one, who seemed to be an officer, rallied them. "Now," said Tarzan, "all together!" and he started at a run for the gate. Simultaneously the lion, evidently scenting the purpose of the Tarmangani, broke into a full charge toward the guard.

Shaken by the report of the unfamiliar weapon, the ranks of the guardsmen broke before the furious assault of the great beast. The officer screamed forth a volley of commands in a mad fury of uncontrolled rage but the guardsmen, obeying the first law of nature as well as actuated by their inherent fear of the black denizen of the forest scattered to right and left to elude the monster. With ferocious growls Numa wheeled to the right, and with raking talons struck right and left among a little handful of terrified guardsmen who were endeavoring to elude him, and then Tarzan and Smith-Oldwick closed with the others.

For a moment their most formidable antagonist was the officer in command. He wielded his curved saber as only an adept might as he faced Tarzan, to whom the similar weapon in his own hand was most unfamiliar. Smith-Oldwick could not fire for fear of hitting the ape-man when suddenly to his dismay he saw Tarzan's weapon fly from his grasp as the Xujan warrior neatly disarmed his opponent. With a scream the fellow raised his saber for the final cut that would terminate the earthly career of Tarzan of the Apes when, to the astonishment of both the ape-man and Smith-Oldwick, the fellow stiffened rigidly, his weapon dropped from the nerveless fingers of his upraised hand, his mad eyes rolled upward and foam flecked his bared lip. Gasping as though in the throes of strangulation the fellow pitched forward at Tarzan's feet.

Tarzan stooped and picked up the dead man's weapon, a smile upon his face as he turned and glanced toward the young Englishman.

"The fellow is an epileptic," said Smith-Oldwick. "I suppose many of them are. Their nervous condition is not without its good points—a normal man would have gotten you."

The other guardsmen seemed utterly demoralized at the loss of their leader. They were huddled upon the opposite side of the street at the left of the gate, screaming at the tops of their voices and looking in the direction from which sounds of reinforcements were coming, as though urging on the men and lions that were already too close for the comfort of the fugitives. Six guardsmen still stood with their backs against the gate, their weapons flashing in the light of the flares and their parchment-like faces distorted in horrid grimaces of rage and terror.

Numa had pursued two fleeing warriors down the street which paralleled the wall for a short distance at this point. The ape-man turned to Smith-Oldwick. "You will have to use your pistol now," he said, "and we must get by these fellows at once;" and as the young Englishman fired, Tarzan rushed in to close quarters as though he had not already discovered that with the saber he was no match for these trained swordsmen. Two men fell to Smith-Oldwick's first two shots and then he missed, while the four remaining divided, two leaping for the aviator and two for Tarzan.

The ape-man rushed in in an effort to close with one of his antagonists where the other's saber would be comparatively useless. Smith-Oldwick dropped one of his assailants with a bullet through the chest and pulled his trigger on the second, only to have the hammer fall futilely upon an empty chamber. The cartridges in his weapon were exhausted and the warrior with his razor-edged, gleaming saber was upon him.

Tarzan raised his own weapon but once and that to divert a vicious cut for his head. Then he was upon one of his assailants and before the fellow could regain his equilibrium and leap back after delivering his cut, the ape-man had seized him by the neck and crotch. Tarzan's other antagonist was edging around to one side where he might use his weapon, and as he raised the blade to strike at the back of the Tarmangani's neck, the latter swung the body of his comrade upward so that it received the full force of the blow. The blade sank deep into the body of the warrior, eliciting a single frightful scream, and then Tarzan hurled the dying man in the face of his final adversary.

Smith-Oldwick, hard pressed and now utterly defenseless, had given up all hope in the instant that he realized his weapon was empty, when, from his left, a living bolt of black-maned ferocity shot past him to the breast of his opponent. Down went the Xujan, his face bitten away by one snap of the powerful jaws of Numa of the pit.

In the few seconds that had been required for the consummation of these rapidly ensuing events, Otobu had dragged Bertha Kircher to the gate which he had unbarred and thrown open, and with the vanquishing of the last of the active guardsmen, the party passed out of the maniac city of Xuja into the outer darkness beyond. At the same moment a half dozen lions rounded the last turn in the road leading back toward the plaza, and at sight of them Numa of the pit wheeled and charged. For a moment the lions of the city stood their ground, but only for a moment, and then before the black beast was upon them, they turned and fled, while Tarzan and his party moved rapidly toward the blackness of the forest beyond the garden.

"Will they follow us out of the city?" Tarzan asked Otobu.

"Not at night," replied the black. "I have been a slave here for five years but never have I known these people to leave the city by night. If they go beyond the forest in the daytime they usually wait until the dawn of another day before they return, as they fear to pass through the country of the black lions after dark. No, I think, Master, that they will not follow us tonight, but tomorrow they will come, and, O Bwana, then will they surely get us, or those that are left of us, for at least one among us must be the toll of the black lions as we pass through their forest."

As they crossed the garden, Smith-Oldwick refilled the magazine of his pistol and inserted a cartridge in the chamber. The girl moved silently at Tarzan's left, between him and the aviator. Suddenly the ape-man stopped and turned toward the city, his mighty frame, clothed in the yellow tunic of Herog's soldiery, plainly visible to the others beneath the light of the stars. They saw him raise his head and they heard break from his lips the plaintive note of a lion calling to his fellows. Smith-Oldwick felt a distinct shudder pass through his frame, while Otobu, rolling the whites of his eyes in terrified surprise, sank tremblingly to his knees. But the girl thrilled and she felt her heart beat in a strange exultation, and then she drew nearer to the beast-man until her shoulder touched his arm. The act was involuntary and for a moment she scarce realized what she had done, and then she stepped silently back, thankful that the light of the stars was not sufficient to reveal to the eyes of her companions the flush which she felt mantling her cheek. Yet she was not ashamed of the impulse that had prompted her, but rather of the act itself which she knew, had Tarzan noticed it, would have been repulsive to him.

From the open gate of the city of maniacs came the answering cry of a lion. The little group waited where they stood until presently they saw the majestic proportions of the black lion as he approached them along the trail. When he had rejoined them Tarzan fastened the fingers of one hand in the black mane and started on once more toward the forest. Behind them, from the city, rose a bedlam of horrid sounds, the roaring of lions mingling with the raucous voices of the screaming parrots and the mad shrieks of the maniacs. As they entered the Stygian darkness of the forest the girl once again involuntarily shrank closer to the ape-man, and this time Tarzan was aware of the contact.

Himself without fear, he yet instinctively appreciated how terrified the girl must be. Actuated by a sudden kindly impulse he found her hand and took it in his own and thus they continued upon their way, groping through the blackness of the trail. Twice they were approached by forest lions, but upon both occasions the deep growls of Numa of the pit drove off their assailants. Several times they were compelled to rest, for Smith-Oldwick was constantly upon the verge of exhaustion, and toward morning Tarzan was forced to carry him on the steep ascent from the bed of the valley.

CHAPTER XXIV—THE TOMMIES

Daylight overtook them after they had entered the gorge, but, tired as they all were with the exception of Tarzan, they realized that they must keep on at all costs until they found a spot where they might ascend the precipitous side of the gorge to the floor of the plateau above. Tarzan and Otobu were both equally confident that the Xujans would not follow them beyond the gorge, but though they scanned every inch of the frowning cliffs upon either hand noon came and there was still no indication of any avenue of escape to right or left. There were places where the ape-man alone might have negotiated the ascent but none where the others could hope successfully to reach the plateau, nor where Tarzan, powerful and agile as he was, could have ventured safely to carry them aloft.

For half a day the ape-man had been either carrying or supporting Smith-Oldwick and now, to his chagrin, he saw that the girl was faltering. He had realized well how much she had undergone and how greatly the hardships and dangers and the fatigue of the past weeks must have told upon her vitality. He saw how bravely she attempted to keep up, yet how often she stumbled and staggered as she labored through the sand and gravel of the gorge. Nor could he help but admire her fortitude and the uncomplaining effort she was making to push on.

The Englishman must have noticed her condition too, for some time after noon, he stopped suddenly and sat down in the sand. "It's no use," he said to Tarzan. "I can go no farther. Miss Kircher is rapidly weakening. You will have to go on without me."

"No," said the girl, "we cannot do that. We have all been through so much together and the chances of our escape are still so remote that whatever comes, let us remain together, unless," and she looked up at Tarzan, "you, who have done so much for us to whom you are under no obligations, will go on without us. I for one wish that you would. It must be as evident to you as it is to me that you cannot save us, for though you succeeded in dragging us from the path of our pursuers, even your great strength and endurance could never take one of us across the desert waste which lies between here and the nearest fertile country."

The ape-man returned her serious look with a smile. "You are not dead," he said to her, "nor is the lieutenant, nor Otobu, nor myself. One is either dead or alive, and until we are dead we should plan only upon continuing to live. Because we remain here and rest is no indication that we shall die here. I cannot carry you both to the country of the Wamabos, which is the nearest spot at which we may expect to find game and water, but we shall not give up on that account. So far we have found a way. Let us take things as they come. Let us rest now because you and Lieutenant Smith-Oldwick need the rest, and when you are stronger we will go on again."

"But the Xujans—?" she asked, "may they not follow us here?"

"Yes," he said, "they probably will. But we need not be concerned with them until they come."

"I wish," said the girl, "that I possessed your philosophy but I am afraid it is beyond me."

"You were not born and reared in the jungle by wild beasts and among wild beasts, or you would possess, as I do, the fatalism of the jungle."

And so they moved to the side of the gorge beneath the shade of an overhanging rock and lay down in the hot sand to rest. Numa wandered restlessly to and fro and finally, after sprawling for a moment close beside the ape-man, rose and moved off up the gorge to be lost to view a moment later beyond the nearest turn.

For an hour the little party rested and then Tarzan suddenly rose and, motioning the others to silence, listened. For a minute he stood motionless, his keen ears acutely receptive to sounds so faint and distant that none of the other three could detect the slightest break in the utter and deathlike quiet of the gorge. Finally the ape-man relaxed and turned toward them. "What is it?" asked the girl.

"They are coming," he replied. "They are yet some distance away, though not far, for the sandaled feet of the men and the pads of the lions make little noise upon the soft sands."

"What shall we do—try to go on?" asked Smith-Oldwick. "I believe I could make a go of it now for a short way. I am much rested. How about you Miss Kircher?"

"Oh, yes," she said, "I am much stronger. Yes, surely I can go on."

Tarzan knew that neither of them quite spoke the truth, that people do not recover so quickly from utter exhaustion, but he saw no other way and there was always the hope that just beyond the next turn would be a way out of the gorge.

"You help the lieutenant, Otobu," he said, turning to the black, "and I will carry Miss Kircher," and though the girl objected, saying that he must not waste his strength, he lifted her lightly in his arms and moved off up the canyon, followed by Otobu and the Englishman. They had gone no great distance when the others of the party became aware of the sounds of pursuit, for now the lions were whining as though the fresh scent spoor of their quarry had reached their nostrils.

"I wish that your Numa would return," said the girl.

"Yes," said Tarzan, "but we shall have to do the best we can without him. I should like to find some place where we can barricade ourselves against attack from all sides. Possibly then we might hold them off. Smith-Oldwick is a good shot and if there are not too many men he might be able to dispose of them provided they can only come at him one at a time. The lions don't bother me so much. Sometimes they are stupid animals, and I am sure that these that pursue us, and who are so dependent upon the masters that have raised and trained them, will be easily handled after the warriors are disposed of."

"You think there is some hope, then?" she asked.

"We are still alive," was his only answer.

"There," he said presently, "I thought I recalled this very spot." He pointed toward a fragment that had evidently fallen from the summit of the cliff and which now lay imbedded in the sand a few feet from the base. It was a jagged fragment of rock which rose some ten feet above the surface of the sand, leaving a narrow aperture between it and the cliff behind. Toward this they directed their steps and when finally they reached their goal they found a space about two feet wide and ten feet long between the rock and the cliff. To be sure it was open at both ends but at least they could not be attacked upon all sides at once.

They had scarcely concealed themselves before Tarzan's quick ears caught a sound upon the face of the cliff above them, and looking up he saw a diminutive monkey perched upon a slight projection—an ugly-faced little monkey who looked down upon them for a moment and then scampered away toward the south in the direction from which their pursuers were coming. Otobu had seen the monkey too. "He will tell the parrots," said the black, "and the parrots will tell the madmen."

"It is all the same," replied Tarzan; "the lions would have found us here. We could not hope to hide from them."

He placed Smith-Oldwick, with his pistol, at the north opening of their haven and told Otobu to stand with his spear at the Englishman's shoulder, while he himself prepared to guard the southern approach. Between them he had the girl lie down in the sand. "You will be safe there in the event that they use their spears," he said.

The minutes that dragged by seemed veritable eternities to Bertha Kircher and then at last, and almost with relief, she knew that the pursuers were upon them. She heard the angry roaring of the lions and the cries of the madmen. For several minutes the men seemed to be investigating the stronghold which their quarry had discovered. She could hear them both to the north and south and then from where she lay she saw a lion charging for the ape-man before her. She saw the giant arm swing back with the curved saber and she saw it fall with terrific velocity and meet the lion as he rose to grapple with the man, cleaving his skull as cleanly as a butcher opens up a sheep.

Then she heard footsteps running rapidly toward Smith-Oldwick and, as his pistol spoke, there was a scream and the sound of a falling body. Evidently disheartened by the failure of their first attempt the assaulters drew off, but only for a short time. Again they came, this time a man opposing Tarzan and a lion seeking to overcome Smith-Oldwick. Tarzan had cautioned the young Englishman not to waste his cartridges upon the lions and it was Otobu with the Xujan spear who met the beast, which was not subdued until both he and Smith-Oldwick had been mauled, and the latter had succeeded in running the point of the saber the girl had carried, into the beast's heart. The man who opposed Tarzan inadvertently came too close in an attempt to cut at the ape-man's head, with the result that an instant later his corpse lay with the neck broken upon the body of the lion.

Once again the enemy withdrew, but again only for a short time, and now they came in full force, the lions and the men, possibly a half dozen of each, the men casting their spears and the lions waiting just behind, evidently for the signal to charge.

"Is this the end?" asked the girl.

"No," cried the ape-man, "for we still live!"

The words had scarcely passed his lips when the remaining warriors, rushing in, cast their spears simultaneously from both sides. In attempting to shield the girl, Tarzan received one of the shafts in the shoulder, and so heavily had the weapon been hurled that it bore him backward to the ground. Smith-Oldwick fired his pistol twice when he too was struck down, the weapon entering his right leg midway between hip and knee. Only Otobu remained to face the enemy, for the Englishman, already weak from his wounds and from the latest mauling he had received at the claws of the lion, had lost consciousness as he sank to the ground with this new hurt.

As he fell his pistol dropped from his fingers, and the girl, seeing, snatched it up. As Tarzan struggled to rise, one of the warriors leaped full upon his breast and bore him back as, with fiendish shrieks, he raised the point of his saber above the other's heart. Before he could drive it home the girl leveled Smith-Oldwick's pistol and fired point-blank at the fiend's face.

Simultaneously there broke upon the astonished ears of both attackers and attacked a volley of shots from the gorge. With the sweetness of the voice of an angel from heaven the Europeans heard the sharp-barked commands of an English noncom. Even above the roars of the lions and the screams of the maniacs, those beloved tones reached the ears of Tarzan and the girl at the very moment that even the ape-man had given up the last vestige of hope.

Rolling the body of the warrior to one side Tarzan struggled to his feet, the spear still protruding from his shoulder. The girl rose too, and as Tarzan wrenched the weapon from his flesh and stepped out from behind the concealment of their refuge, she followed at his side. The skirmish that had resulted in their rescue was soon over. Most of the lions escaped but all of the pursuing Xujans had been slain. As Tarzan and the girl came into full view of the group, a British Tommy leveled his rifle at the ape-man. Seeing the fellow's actions and realizing instantly the natural error that Tarzan's yellow tunic had occasioned the girl sprang between him and the soldier. "Don't shoot," she cried to the latter, "we are both friends."

"Hold up your hands, you, then," he commanded Tarzan. "I ain't taking no chances with any duffer with a yellow shirt."

At this juncture the British sergeant who had been in command of the advance guard approached and when Tarzan and the girl spoke to him in English, explaining their disguises, he accepted their word, since they were evidently not of the same race as the creatures which lay dead about them. Ten minutes later the main body of the expedition came into view. Smith-Oldwick's wounds were dressed, as well as were those of the ape-man, and in half an hour they were on their way to the camp of their rescuers.

That night it was arranged that the following day Smith-Oldwick and Bertha Kircher should be transported to British headquarters near the coast by aeroplane, the two planes attached to the expeditionary force being requisitioned for the purpose. Tarzan and Otobu declined the offers of the British captain to accompany his force overland on the return march as Tarzan explained that his country lay to the west, as did Otobu's, and that they would travel together as far as the country of the Wamabos.

"You are not going back with us, then?" asked the girl.

"No," replied the ape-man. "My home is upon the west coast. I will continue my journey in that direction."

She cast appealing eyes toward him. "You will go back into that terrible jungle?" she asked. "We shall never see you again?"

He looked at her a moment in silence. "Never," he said, and without another word turned and walked away.

In the morning Colonel Capell came from the base camp in one of the planes that was to carry Smith-Oldwick and the girl to the east. Tarzan was standing some distance away as the ship landed and the officer descended to the ground. He saw the colonel greet his junior in command of the advance detachment, and then he saw him turn toward Bertha Kircher who was standing a few paces behind the captain. Tarzan wondered how the German spy felt in this situation, especially when she must know that there was one there who knew her real status. He saw Colonel Capell walk toward her with outstretched hands and smiling face and, although he could not hear the words of his greeting, he saw that it was friendly and cordial to a degree.

Tarzan turned away scowling, and if any had been close by they might have heard a low growl rumble from his chest. He knew that his country was at war with Germany and that not only his duty to the land of his fathers, but also his personal grievance against the enemy people and his hatred of them, demanded that he expose the girl's perfidy, and yet he hesitated, and because he hesitated he growled—not at the German spy but at himself for his weakness.

He did not see her again before she entered a plane and was borne away toward the east. He bid farewell to Smith-Oldwick and received again the oft-repeated thanks of the young Englishman. And then he saw him too borne aloft in the high circling plane and watched until the ship became a speck far above the eastern horizon to disappear at last high in air.

The Tommies, their packs and accouterments slung, were waiting the summons to continue their return march. Colonel Capell had, through a desire to personally observe the stretch of country between the camp of the advance detachment and the base, decided to march back his troops. Now that all was in readiness for departure he turned to Tarzan. "I wish you would come back with us, Greystoke," he said, "and if my appeal carries no inducement possibly that of Smith-Oldwick and the young lady who just left us may. They asked me to urge you to return to civilization."

"No;" said Tarzan, "I shall go my own way. Miss Kircher and Lieutenant Smith-Oldwick were only prompted by a sense of gratitude in considering my welfare."

"Miss Kircher?" exclaimed Capell and then he laughed, "You know her then as Bertha Kircher, the German spy?"

Tarzan looked at the other a moment in silence. It was beyond him to conceive that a British officer should thus laconically speak of an enemy spy whom he had had within his power and permitted to escape. "Yes," he replied, "I knew that she was Bertha Kircher, the German spy?"

"Is that all you knew?" asked Capell.

"That is all," said the ape-man.

"She is the Honorable Patricia Canby," said Capell, "one of the most valuable members of the British Intelligence Service attached to the East African forces. Her father and I served in India together and I have known her ever since she was born.

"Why, here's a packet of papers she took from a German officer and has been carrying it through all her vicissitudes—single-minded in the performance of her duty. Look! I haven't yet had time to examine them but as you see here is a military sketch map, a bundle of reports, and the diary of one Hauptmann Fritz Schneider."

"The diary of Hauptmann Fritz Schneider!" repeated Tarzan in a constrained voice. "May I see it, Capell? He is the man who murdered Lady Greystoke."

The Englishman handed the little volume over to the other without a word. Tarzan ran through the pages quickly looking for a certain date—the date that the horror had been committed—and when he found it he read rapidly. Suddenly a gasp of incredulity burst from his lips. Capell looked at him questioningly.

"God!" exclaimed the ape-man. "Can this be true? Listen!" and he read an excerpt from the closely written page:

"'Played a little joke on the English pig. When he comes home he will find the burned body of his wife in her boudoir—but he will only think it is his wife. Had von Goss substitute the body of a dead Negress and char it after putting Lady Greystoke's rings on it—Lady G will be of more value to the High Command alive than dead.'"

"She lives!" cried Tarzan.

"Thank God!" exclaimed Capell. "And now?"

"I will return with you, of course. How terribly I have wronged Miss Canby, but how could I know? I even told Smith-Oldwick, who loves her, that she was a German spy.

"Not only must I return to find my wife but I must right this wrong."

"Don't worry about that," said Capell, "she must have convinced him that she is no enemy spy, for just before they left this morning he told me she had promised to marry him."

TARZAN THE TERRIBLE

CHAPTER I—THE PITHECANTHROPUS

Silent as the shadows through which he moved, the great beast slunk through the midnight jungle, his yellow-green eyes round and staring, his sinewy tail undulating behind him, his head lowered and flattened, and every muscle vibrant to the thrill of the hunt. The jungle moon dappled an occasional clearing which the great cat was always careful to avoid. Though he moved through thick verdure across a carpet of innumerable twigs, broken branches, and leaves, his passing gave forth no sound that might have been apprehended by dull human ears.

Apparently less cautious was the hunted thing moving even as silently as the lion a hundred paces ahead of the tawny carnivore, for instead of skirting the moon-splashed natural clearings it passed directly across them, and by the tortuous record of its spoor it might indeed be guessed that it sought these avenues of least resistance, as well it might, since, unlike its grim stalker, it walked erect upon two feet—it walked upon two feet and was hairless except for a black thatch upon its head; its arms were well shaped and muscular; its hands powerful and slender with long tapering fingers and thumbs reaching almost to the first joint of the index fingers. Its legs too were shapely but its feet departed from the standards of all races of men, except possibly a few of the lowest races, in that the great toes protruded at right angles from the foot.

Pausing momentarily in the full light of the gorgeous African moon the creature turned an attentive ear to the rear and then, his head lifted, his features might readily have been discerned in the moonlight. They were strong, clean cut, and regular—features that would have attracted attention for their masculine beauty in any of the great capitals of the world. But was this thing a man? It would have been hard for a watcher in the trees to have decided as the lion's prey resumed its way across the silver tapestry that Luna had laid upon the floor of the dismal jungle, for from beneath the loin cloth of black fur that girdled its thighs there depended a long hairless, white tail.

In one hand the creature carried a stout club, and suspended at its left side from a shoulder belt was a short, sheathed knife, while a cross belt supported a pouch at its right hip. Confining these straps to the body and also apparently supporting the loin cloth was a broad girdle which glittered in the moonlight as though encrusted with virgin gold, and was clasped in the center of the belly with a huge buckle of ornate design that scintillated as with precious stones.

Closer and closer crept Numa, the lion, to his intended victim, and that the latter was not entirely unaware of his danger was evidenced by the increasing frequency with which he turned his ear and his sharp black eyes in the direction of the cat upon his trail. He did not greatly increase his speed, a long swinging walk where the open places permitted, but he loosened the knife in its scabbard and at all times kept his club in readiness for instant action.

Forging at last through a narrow strip of dense jungle vegetation the man-thing broke through into an almost treeless area of considerable extent. For an instant he hesitated, glancing quickly behind him and then up at the security of the branches of the great trees waving overhead, but some greater urge than fear or caution influenced his decision apparently, for he moved off again across the little plain leaving the safety of the trees behind him. At greater or less intervals leafy sanctuaries dotted the grassy expanse ahead of him and the route he took, leading from one to another, indicated that he had not entirely cast discretion to the winds. But after the second tree had been left behind the distance to the next was considerable, and it was then that Numa walked from the concealing cover of the jungle and, seeing his quarry apparently helpless before him, raised his tail stiffly erect and charged.

Two months—two long, weary months filled with hunger, with thirst, with hardships, with disappointment, and, greater than all, with gnawing pain—had passed since Tarzan of the Apes learned from the diary of the dead German captain that his wife still lived. A brief investigation in which he was enthusiastically aided by the Intelligence Department of the British East African Expedition revealed the fact that an attempt had been made to keep Lady Jane in hiding in the interior, for reasons of which only the German High Command might be cognizant.

In charge of Lieutenant Obergatz and a detachment of native German troops she had been sent across the border into the Congo Free State.

Starting out alone in search of her, Tarzan had succeeded in finding the village in which she had been incarcerated only to learn that she had escaped months before, and that the German officer had disappeared at the same time. From there on the stories of the chiefs and the warriors whom he quizzed, were vague and often contradictory. Even the direction that the fugitives had taken Tarzan could only guess at by piecing together bits of fragmentary evidence gleaned from various sources.

Sinister conjectures were forced upon him by various observations which he made in the village. One was incontrovertible proof that these people were man-eaters; the other, the presence in the village of various articles of native German uniforms and equipment. At great risk and in the face of surly objection on the part of the chief, the ape-man made a careful inspection of every hut in the village from which at least a little ray of hope resulted from the fact that he found no article that might have belonged to his wife.

Leaving the village he had made his way toward the southwest, crossing, after the most appalling hardships, a vast waterless steppe covered for the most part with dense thorn, coming at last into a district that had probably never been previously entered by any white man and which was known only in the legends of the tribes whose country bordered it. Here were precipitous mountains, well-watered plateaus, wide plains, and vast swampy morasses, but neither the plains, nor the plateaus, nor the mountains were accessible to him until after weeks of arduous effort he succeeded in finding a spot where he might cross the morasses—a hideous stretch infested by venomous snakes and other larger dangerous reptiles. On several occasions he glimpsed at distances or by night what might have been titanic reptilian monsters, but as there were hippopotami, rhinoceri, and elephants in great numbers in and about the marsh he was never positive that the forms he saw were not of these.

When at last he stood upon firm ground after crossing the morasses he realized why it was that for perhaps countless ages this territory had defied the courage and hardihood of the heroic races of the outer world that had, after innumerable reverses and unbelievable suffering penetrated to practically every other region, from pole to pole.

From the abundance and diversity of the game it might have appeared that every known species of bird and beast and reptile had sought here a refuge wherein they might take their last stand against the encroaching multitudes of men that had steadily spread themselves over the surface of the earth, wresting the hunting grounds from the lower orders, from the moment that the first ape shed his hair and ceased to walk upon his knuckles. Even the species with which Tarzan was familiar showed here either the results of a divergent line of evolution or an unaltered form that had been transmitted without variation for countless ages.

Too, there were many hybrid strains, not the least interesting of which to Tarzan was a yellow and black striped lion. Smaller than the species with which Tarzan was familiar, but still a most formidable beast, since it possessed in addition to sharp saber-like canines the disposition of a devil. To Tarzan it presented evidence that tigers had once roamed the jungles of Africa, possibly giant saber-tooths of another epoch, and these apparently had crossed with lions with the resultant terrors that he occasionally encountered at the present day.

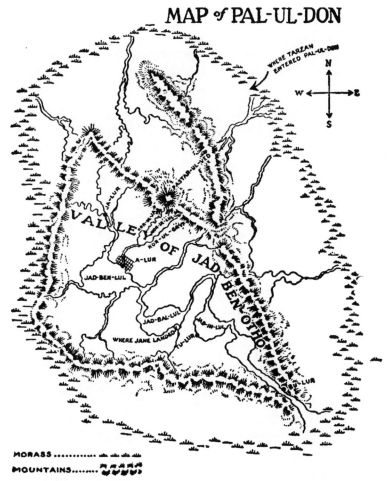

MAP of PAL-UL-DON

MORASS ....
MOUNTAINS........

The above map was copied and to some extent redrawn from a rough sketch found among the notes made by Lord Greystoke of his experiences in Pal-ul-don

The true lions of this new, Old World differed but little from those with which he was familiar; in size and conformation they were almost identical, but instead of shedding the leopard spots of cubhood, they retained them through life as definitely marked as those of the leopard.

Two months of effort had revealed no slightest evidence that she he sought had entered this beautiful yet forbidding land. His investigation, however, of the cannibal village and his questioning of other tribes in the neighborhood had convinced him that if Lady Jane still lived it must be in this direction that he seek her, since by a process of elimination he had reduced the direction of her flight to only this possibility. How she had crossed the morass he could not guess and yet something within seemed to urge upon him belief that she had crossed it, and that if she still lived it was here that she must be sought. But this unknown, untraversed wild was of vast extent; grim, forbidding mountains blocked his way, torrents tumbling from rocky fastnesses impeded his progress, and at every turn he was forced to match wits and muscles with the great carnivora that he might procure sustenance.

Time and again Tarzan and Numa stalked the same quarry and now one, now the other bore off the prize. Seldom however did the ape-man go hungry for the country was rich in game animals and birds and fish, in fruit and the countless other forms of vegetable life upon which the jungle-bred man may subsist.

Tarzan often wondered why in so rich a country he found no evidences of man and had at last come to the conclusion that the parched, thorn-covered steppe and the hideous morasses had formed a sufficient barrier to protect this country effectively from the inroads of mankind.

After days of searching he had succeeded finally in discovering a pass through the mountains and, coming down upon the opposite side, had found himself in a country practically identical with that which he had left. The hunting was good and at a water hole in the mouth of a canyon where it debouched upon a tree-covered plain Bara, the deer, fell an easy victim to the ape-man's cunning.

It was just at dusk. The voices of great four-footed hunters rose now and again from various directions, and as the canyon afforded among its trees no comfortable retreat the ape-man shouldered the carcass of the deer and started downward onto the plain. At its opposite side rose lofty trees—a great forest which suggested to his practiced eye a mighty jungle. Toward this the ape-man bent his step, but when midway of the plain he discovered standing alone such a tree as best suited him for a night's abode, swung lightly to its branches and, presently, a comfortable resting place.

Here he ate the flesh of Bara and when satisfied carried the balance of the carcass to the opposite side of the tree where he deposited it far above the ground in a secure place. Returning to his crotch he settled himself for sleep and in another moment the roars of the lions and the howlings of the lesser cats fell upon deaf ears.

The usual noises of the jungle composed rather than disturbed the ape-man but an unusual sound, however imperceptible to the awakened ear of civilized man, seldom failed to impinge upon the consciousness of Tarzan, however deep his slumber, and so it was that when the moon was high a sudden rush of feet across the grassy carpet in the vicinity of his tree brought him to alert and ready activity. Tarzan does not awaken as you and I with the weight of slumber still upon his eyes and brain, for did the creatures of the wild awaken thus, their awakenings would be few. As his eyes snapped open, clear and bright, so, clear and bright upon the nerve centers of his brain, were registered the various perceptions of all his senses.

Almost beneath him, racing toward his tree was what at first glance appeared to be an almost naked white man, yet even at the first instant of discovery the long, white tail projecting rearward did not escape the ape-man. Behind the fleeing figure, escaping, came Numa, the lion, in full charge. Voiceless the prey, voiceless the killer; as two spirits in a dead world the two moved in silent swiftness toward the culminating tragedy of this grim race.

Even as his eyes opened and took in the scene beneath him—even in that brief instant of perception, followed reason, judgment, and decision, so rapidly one upon the heels of the other that almost simultaneously the ape-man was in mid-air, for he had seen a white-skinned creature cast in a mold similar to his own, pursued by Tarzan's hereditary enemy. So close was the lion to the fleeing man-thing that Tarzan had no time carefully to choose the method of his attack. As a diver leaps from the springboard headforemost into the waters beneath, so Tarzan of the Apes dove straight for Numa, the lion; naked in his right hand the blade of his father that so many times before had tasted the blood of lions.

A raking talon caught Tarzan on the side, inflicting a long, deep wound and then the ape-man was on Numa's back and the blade was sinking again and again into the savage side. Nor was the man-thing either longer fleeing, or idle. He too, creature of the wild, had sensed on the instant the truth of the miracle of his saving, and turning in his tracks, had leaped forward with raised bludgeon to Tarzan's assistance and Numa's undoing. A single terrific blow upon the flattened skull of the beast laid him insensible and then as Tarzan's knife found the wild heart a few convulsive shudders and a sudden relaxation marked the passing of the carnivore.

Leaping to his feet the ape-man placed his foot upon the carcass of his kill and, raising his face to Goro, the moon, voiced the savage victory cry that had so often awakened the echoes of his native jungle.

As the hideous scream burst from the ape-man's lips the man-thing stepped quickly back as in sudden awe, but when Tarzan returned his hunting knife to its sheath and turned toward him the other saw in the quiet dignity of his demeanor no cause for apprehension.

For a moment the two stood appraising each other, and then the man-thing spoke. Tarzan realized that the creature before him was uttering articulate sounds which expressed in speech, though in a language with which Tarzan was unfamiliar, the thoughts of a man possessing to a greater or less extent the same powers of reason that he possessed. In other words, that though the creature before him had the tail and thumbs and great toes of a monkey, it was, in all other respects, quite evidently a man.

The blood, which was now flowing down Tarzan's side, caught the creature's attention. From the pocket-pouch at his side he took a small bag and approaching Tarzan indicated by signs that he wished the ape-man to lie down that he might treat the wound, whereupon, spreading the edges of the cut apart, he sprinkled the raw flesh with powder from the little bag. The pain of the wound was as nothing to the exquisite torture of the remedy but, accustomed to physical suffering, the ape-man withstood it stoically and in a few moments not only had the bleeding ceased but the pain as well.

In reply to the soft and far from unpleasant modulations of the other's voice, Tarzan spoke in various tribal dialects of the interior as well as in the language of the great apes, but it was evident that the man understood none of these. Seeing that they could not make each other understood, the pithecanthropus advanced toward Tarzan and placing his left hand over his own heart laid the palm of his right hand over the heart of the ape-man. To the latter the action appeared as a form of friendly greeting and, being versed in the ways of uncivilized races, he responded in kind as he realized it was doubtless intended that he should. His action seemed to satisfy and please his new-found acquaintance, who immediately fell to talking again and finally, with his head tipped back, sniffed the air in the direction of the tree above them and then suddenly pointing toward the carcass of Bara, the deer, he touched his stomach in a sign language which even the densest might interpret. With a wave of his hand Tarzan invited his guest to partake of the remains of his savage repast, and the other, leaping nimbly as a little monkey to the lower branches of the tree, made his way quickly to the flesh, assisted always by his long, strong sinuous tail.

The pithecanthropus ate in silence, cutting small strips from the deer's loin with his keen knife. From his crotch in the tree Tarzan watched his companion, noting the preponderance of human attributes which were doubtless accentuated by the paradoxical thumbs, great toes, and tail.

He wondered if this creature was representative of some strange race or if, what seemed more likely, but an atavism. Either supposition would have seemed preposterous enough did he not have before him the evidence of the creature's existence. There he was, however, a tailed man with distinctly arboreal hands and feet. His trappings, gold encrusted and jewel studded, could have been wrought only by skilled artisans; but whether they were the work of this individual or of others like him, or of an entirely different race, Tarzan could not, of course, determine.

His meal finished, the guest wiped his fingers and lips with leaves broken from a nearby branch, looked up at Tarzan with a pleasant smile that revealed a row of strong white teeth, the canines of which were no longer than Tarzan's own, spoke a few words which Tarzan judged were a polite expression of thanks and then sought a comfortable place in the tree for the night.

The earth was shadowed in the darkness which precedes the dawn when Tarzan was awakened by a violent shaking of the tree in which he had found shelter. As he opened his eyes he saw that his companion was also astir, and glancing around quickly to apprehend the cause of the disturbance, the ape-man was astounded at the sight which met his eyes.

The dim shadow of a colossal form reared close beside the tree and he saw that it was the scraping of the giant body against the branches that had awakened him. That such a tremendous creature could have approached so closely without disturbing him filled Tarzan with both wonderment and chagrin. In the gloom the ape-man at first conceived the intruder to be an elephant; yet, if so, one of greater proportions than any he had ever before seen, but as the dim outlines became less indistinct he saw on a line with his eyes and twenty feet above the ground the dim silhouette of a grotesquely serrated back that gave the impression of a creature whose each and every spinal vertebra grew a thick, heavy horn. Only a portion of the back was visible to the ape-man, the rest of the body being lost in the dense shadows beneath the tree, from whence there now arose the sound of giant jaws powerfully crunching flesh and bones. From the odors that rose to the ape-man's sensitive nostrils he presently realized that beneath him was some huge reptile feeding upon the carcass of the lion that had been slain there earlier in the night.

As Tarzan's eyes, straining with curiosity, bored futilely into the dark shadows he felt a light touch upon his shoulder, and, turning, saw that his companion was attempting to attract his attention. The creature, pressing a forefinger to his own lips as to enjoin silence, attempted by pulling on Tarzan's arm to indicate that they should leave at once.

Realizing that he was in a strange country, evidently infested by creatures of titanic size, with the habits and powers of which he was entirely unfamiliar, the ape-man permitted himself to be drawn away. With the utmost caution the pithecanthropus descended the tree upon the opposite side from the great nocturnal prowler, and, closely followed by Tarzan, moved silently away through the night across the plain.

The ape-man was rather loath thus to relinquish an opportunity to inspect a creature which he realized was probably entirely different from anything in his past experience; yet he was wise enough to know when discretion was the better part of valor and now, as in the past, he yielded to that law which dominates the kindred of the wild, preventing them from courting danger uselessly, whose lives are sufficiently filled with danger in their ordinary routine of feeding and mating.

As the rising sun dispelled the shadows of the night, Tarzan found himself again upon the verge of a great forest into which his guide plunged, taking nimbly to the branches of the trees through which he made his way with the celerity of long habitude and hereditary instinct, but though aided by a prehensile tail, fingers, and toes, the man-thing moved through the forest with no greater ease or surety than did the giant ape-man.

It was during this journey that Tarzan recalled the wound in his side inflicted upon him the previous night by the raking talons of Numa, the lion, and examining it was surprised to discover that not only was it painless but along its edges were no indications of inflammation, the results doubtless of the antiseptic powder his strange companion had sprinkled upon it.

They had proceeded for a mile or two when Tarzan's companion came to earth upon a grassy slope beneath a great tree whose branches overhung a clear brook. Here they drank and Tarzan discovered the water to be not only deliciously pure and fresh but of an icy temperature that indicated its rapid descent from the lofty mountains of its origin.

Casting aside his loin cloth and weapons Tarzan entered the little pool beneath the tree and after a moment emerged, greatly refreshed and filled with a keen desire to breakfast. As he came out of the pool he noticed his companion examining him with a puzzled expression upon his face. Taking the ape-man by the shoulder he turned him around so that Tarzan's back was toward him and then, touching the end of Tarzan's spine with his forefinger, he curled his own tail up over his shoulder and, wheeling the ape-man about again, pointed first at Tarzan and then at his own caudal appendage, a look of puzzlement upon his face, the while he jabbered excitedly in his strange tongue.

The ape-man realized that probably for the first time his companion had discovered that he was tailless by nature rather than by accident, and so he called attention to his own great toes and thumbs to further impress upon the creature that they were of different species.

The fellow shook his head dubiously as though entirely unable to comprehend why Tarzan should differ so from him but at last, apparently giving the problem up with a shrug, he laid aside his own harness, skin, and weapons and entered the pool.

His ablutions completed and his meager apparel redonned he seated himself at the foot of the tree and motioning Tarzan to a place beside him, opened the pouch that hung at his right side taking from it strips of dried flesh and a couple of handfuls of thin-shelled nuts with which Tarzan was unfamiliar. Seeing the other break them with his teeth and eat the kernel, Tarzan followed the example thus set him, discovering the meat to be rich and well flavored. The dried flesh also was far from unpalatable, though it had evidently been jerked without salt, a commodity which Tarzan imagined might be rather difficult to obtain in this locality.

As they ate Tarzan's companion pointed to the nuts, the dried meat, and various other nearby objects, in each instance repeating what Tarzan readily discovered must be the names of these things in the creature's native language. The ape-man could but smile at this evident desire upon the part of his new-found acquaintance to impart to him instructions that eventually might lead to an exchange of thoughts between them. Having already mastered several languages and a multitude of dialects the ape-man felt that he could readily assimilate another even though this appeared one entirely unrelated to any with which he was familiar.

So occupied were they with their breakfast and the lesson that neither was aware of the beady eyes glittering down upon them from above; nor was Tarzan cognizant of any impending danger until the instant that a huge, hairy body leaped full upon his companion from the branches above them.

CHAPTER II—"TO THE DEATH!"

In the moment of discovery Tarzan saw that the creature was almost a counterpart of his companion in size and conformation, with the exception that his body was entirely clothed with a coat of shaggy black hair which almost concealed his features, while his harness and weapons were similar to those of the creature he had attacked. Ere Tarzan could prevent the creature had struck the ape-man's companion a blow upon the head with his knotted club that felled him, unconscious, to the earth; but before he could inflict further injury upon his defenseless prey the ape-man had closed with him.

Instantly Tarzan realized that he was locked with a creature of almost superhuman strength. The sinewy fingers of a powerful hand sought his throat while the other lifted the bludgeon above his head. But if the strength of the hairy attacker was great, great too was that of his smooth-skinned antagonist. Swinging a single terrific blow with clenched fist to the point of the other's chin, Tarzan momentarily staggered his assailant and then his own fingers closed upon the shaggy throat, as with the other hand he seized the wrist of the arm that swung the club. With equal celerity he shot his right leg behind the shaggy brute and throwing his weight forward hurled the thing over his hip heavily to the ground, at the same time precipitating his own body upon the other's chest.

With the shock of the impact the club fell from the brute's hand and Tarzan's hold was wrenched from its throat. Instantly the two were locked in a deathlike embrace. Though the creature bit at Tarzan the latter was quickly aware that this was not a particularly formidable method of offense or defense, since its canines were scarcely more developed than his own. The thing that he had principally to guard against was the sinuous tail which sought steadily to wrap itself about his throat and against which experience had afforded him no defense.

Struggling and snarling the two rolled growling about the sward at the foot of the tree, first one on top and then the other but each more occupied at present in defending his throat from the other's choking grasp than in aggressive, offensive tactics. But presently the ape-man saw his opportunity and as they rolled about he forced the creature closer and closer to the pool, upon the banks of which the battle was progressing. At last they lay upon the very verge of the water and now it remained for Tarzan to precipitate them both beneath the surface but in such a way that he might remain on top.

At the same instant there came within range of Tarzan's vision, just behind the prostrate form of his companion, the crouching, devil-faced figure of the striped saber-tooth hybrid, eyeing him with snarling, malevolent face.

Almost simultaneously Tarzan's shaggy antagonist discovered the menacing figure of the great cat. Immediately he ceased his belligerent activities against Tarzan and, jabbering and chattering to the ape-man, he tried to disengage himself from Tarzan's hold but in such a way that indicated that as far as he was concerned their battle was over. Appreciating the danger to his unconscious companion and being anxious to protect him from the saber-tooth the ape-man relinquished his hold upon his adversary and together the two rose to their feet.

Drawing his knife Tarzan moved slowly toward the body of his companion, expecting that his recent antagonist would grasp the opportunity for escape. To his surprise, however, the beast, after regaining its club, advanced at his side.

The great cat, flattened upon its belly, remained motionless except for twitching tail and snarling lips where it lay perhaps fifty feet beyond the body of the pithecanthropus. As Tarzan stepped over the body of the latter he saw the eyelids quiver and open, and in his heart he felt a strange sense of relief that the creature was not dead and a realization that without his suspecting it there had arisen within his savage bosom a bond of attachment for this strange new friend.

Tarzan continued to approach the saber-tooth, nor did the shaggy beast at his right lag behind. Closer and closer they came until at a distance of about twenty feet the hybrid charged. Its rush was directed toward the shaggy manlike ape who halted in his tracks with upraised bludgeon to meet the assault. Tarzan, on the contrary, leaped forward and with a celerity second not even to that of the swift-moving cat, he threw himself headlong upon him as might a Rugby tackler on an American gridiron. His right arm circled the beast's neck in front of the right shoulder, his left behind the left foreleg, and so great was the force of the impact that the two rolled over and over several times upon the ground, the cat screaming and clawing to liberate itself that it might turn upon its attacker, the man clinging desperately to his hold.

Seemingly the attack was one of mad, senseless ferocity unguided by either reason or skill. Nothing, however, could have been farther from the truth than such an assumption since every muscle in the ape-man's giant frame obeyed the dictates of the cunning mind that long experience had trained to meet every exigency of such an encounter. The long, powerful legs, though seemingly inextricably entangled with the hind feet of the clawing cat, ever as by a miracle, escaped the raking talons and yet at just the proper instant in the midst of all the rolling and tossing they were where they should be to carry out the ape-man's plan of offense. So that on the instant that the cat believed it had won the mastery of its antagonist it was jerked suddenly upward as the ape-man rose to his feet, holding the striped back close against his body as he rose and forcing it backward until it could but claw the air helplessly.

Instantly the shaggy black rushed in with drawn knife which it buried in the beast's heart. For a few moments Tarzan retained his hold but when the body had relaxed in final dissolution he pushed it from him and the two who had formerly been locked in mortal combat stood facing each other across the body of the common foe.

Tarzan waited, ready either for peace or war. Presently two shaggy black hands were raised; the left was laid upon its own heart and the right extended until the palm touched Tarzan's breast. It was the same form of friendly salutation with which the pithecanthropus had sealed his alliance with the ape-man and Tarzan, glad of every ally he could win in this strange and savage world, quickly accepted the proffered friendship.

At the conclusion of the brief ceremony Tarzan, glancing in the direction of the hairless pithecanthropus, discovered that the latter had recovered consciousness and was sitting erect watching them intently. He now rose slowly and at the same time the shaggy black turned in his direction and addressed him in what evidently was their common language. The hairless one replied and the two approached each other slowly. Tarzan watched interestedly the outcome of their meeting. They halted a few paces apart, first one and then the other speaking rapidly but without apparent excitement, each occasionally glancing or nodding toward Tarzan, indicating that he was to some extent the subject of their conversation.

Presently they advanced again until they met, whereupon was repeated the brief ceremony of alliance which had previously marked the cessation of hostilities between Tarzan and the black. They then advanced toward the ape-man addressing him earnestly as though endeavoring to convey to him some important information. Presently, however, they gave it up as an unprofitable job and, resorting to sign language, conveyed to Tarzan that they were proceeding upon their way together and were urging him to accompany them.

As the direction they indicated was a route which Tarzan had not previously traversed he was extremely willing to accede to their request, as he had determined thoroughly to explore this unknown land before definitely abandoning search for Lady Jane therein.

For several days their way led through the foothills parallel to the lofty range towering above. Often were they menaced by the savage denizens of this remote fastness, and occasionally Tarzan glimpsed weird forms of gigantic proportions amidst the shadows of the nights.

On the third day they came upon a large natural cave in the face of a low cliff at the foot of which tumbled one of the numerous mountain brooks that watered the plain below and fed the morasses in the lowlands at the country's edge. Here the three took up their temporary abode where Tarzan's instruction in the language of his companions progressed more rapidly than while on the march.

The cave gave evidence of having harbored other manlike forms in the past. Remnants of a crude, rock fireplace remained and the walls and ceiling were blackened with the smoke of many fires. Scratched in the soot, and sometimes deeply into the rock beneath, were strange hieroglyphics and the outlines of beasts and birds and reptiles, some of the latter of weird form suggesting the extinct creatures of Jurassic times. Some of the more recently made hieroglyphics Tarzan's companions read with interest and commented upon, and then with the points of their knives they too added to the possibly age-old record of the blackened walls.

Tarzan's curiosity was aroused, but the only explanation at which he could arrive was that he was looking upon possibly the world's most primitive hotel register. At least it gave him a further insight into the development of the strange creatures with which Fate had thrown him. Here were men with the tails of monkeys, one of them as hair covered as any fur-bearing brute of the lower orders, and yet it was evident that they possessed not only a spoken, but a written language. The former he was slowly mastering and at this new evidence of unlooked-for civilization in creatures possessing so many of the physical attributes of beasts, Tarzan's curiosity was still further piqued and his desire quickly to master their tongue strengthened, with the result that he fell to with even greater assiduity to the task he had set himself. Already he knew the names of his companions and the common names of the fauna and flora with which they had most often come in contact.

Ta-den, he of the hairless, white skin, having assumed the role of tutor, prosecuted his task with a singleness of purpose that was reflected in his pupil's rapid mastery of Ta-den's mother tongue. Om-at, the hairy black, also seemed to feel that there rested upon his broad shoulders a portion of the burden of responsibility for Tarzan's education, with the result that either one or the other of them was almost constantly coaching the ape-man during his waking hours. The result was only what might have been expected—a rapid assimilation of the teachings to the end that before any of them realized it, communication by word of mouth became an accomplished fact.

Tarzan explained to his companions the purpose of his mission but neither could give him any slightest thread of hope to weave into the fabric of his longing. Never had there been in their country a woman such as he described, nor any tailless man other than himself that they ever had seen.

"I have been gone from A-lur while Bu, the moon, has eaten seven times," said Ta-den. "Many things may happen in seven times twenty-eight days; but I doubt that your woman could have entered our country across the terrible morasses which even you found an almost insurmountable obstacle, and if she had, could she have survived the perils that you already have encountered beside those of which you have yet to learn? Not even our own women venture into the savage lands beyond the cities."

"'A-lur,' Light-city, City of Light," mused Tarzan, translating the word into his own tongue. "And where is A-lur?" he asked. "Is it your city, Ta-den, and Om-at's?"

"It is mine," replied the hairless one; "but not Om-at's. The Waz-don have no cities—they live in the trees of the forests and the caves of the hills—is it not so, black man?" he concluded, turning toward the hairy giant beside him.

"Yes," replied Om-at, "We Waz-don are free—only the Hodon imprison themselves in cities. I would not be a white man!"

Tarzan smiled. Even here was the racial distinction between white man and black man—Hodon and Waz-don. Not even the fact that they appeared to be equals in the matter of intelligence made any difference—one was white and one was black, and it was easy to see that the white considered himself superior to the other—one could see it in his quiet smile.

"Where is A-lur?" Tarzan asked again. "You are returning to it?"

"It is beyond the mountains," replied Ta-den. "I do not return to it—not yet. Not until Ko-tan is no more."

"Ko-tan?" queried Tarzan.

"Ko-tan is king," explained the pithecanthropus. "He rules this land. I was one of his warriors. I lived in the palace of Ko-tan and there I met O-lo-a, his daughter. We loved, Likestar-light, and I; but Ko-tan would have none of me. He sent me away to fight with the men of the village of Dak-at, who had refused to pay his tribute to the king, thinking that I would be killed, for Dak-at is famous for his many fine warriors. And I was not killed. Instead I returned victorious with the tribute and with Dak-at himself my prisoner; but Ko-tan was not pleased because he saw that O-lo-a loved me even more than before, her love being strengthened and fortified by pride in my achievement.

"Powerful is my father, Ja-don, the Lion-man, chief of the largest village outside of A-lur. Him Ko-tan hesitated to affront and so he could not but praise me for my success, though he did it with half a smile. But you do not understand! It is what we call a smile that moves only the muscles of the face and affects not the light of the eyes—it means hypocrisy and duplicity. I must be praised and rewarded. What better than that he reward me with the hand of O-lo-a, his daughter? But no, he saves O-lo-a for Bu-lot, son of Mo-sar, the chief whose great-grandfather was king and who thinks that he should be king. Thus would Ko-tan appease the wrath of Mo-sar and win the friendship of those who think with Mo-sar that Mo-sar should be king.

"But what reward shall repay the faithful Ta-den? Greatly do we honor our priests. Within the temples even the chiefs and the king himself bow down to them. No greater honor could Ko-tan confer upon a subject—who wished to be a priest, but I did not so wish. Priests other than the high priest must become eunuchs for they may never marry.

"It was O-lo-a herself who brought word to me that her father had given the commands that would set in motion the machinery of the temple. A messenger was on his way in search of me to summon me to Ko-tan's presence. To have refused the priesthood once it was offered me by the king would have been to have affronted the temple and the gods—that would have meant death; but if I did not appear before Ko-tan I would not have to refuse anything. O-lo-a and I decided that I must not appear. It was better to fly, carrying in my bosom a shred of hope, than to remain and, with my priesthood, abandon hope forever.

"Beneath the shadows of the great trees that grow within the palace grounds I pressed her to me for, perhaps, the last time and then, lest by ill-fate I meet the messenger, I scaled the great wall that guards the palace and passed through the darkened city. My name and rank carried me beyond the city gate. Since then I have wandered far from the haunts of the Ho-don but strong within me is the urge to return if even but to look from without her walls upon the city that holds her most dear to me and again to visit the village of my birth, to see again my father and my mother."

"But the risk is too great?" asked Tarzan.

"It is great, but not too great," replied Ta-den. "I shall go."

"And I shall go with you, if I may," said the ape-man, "for I must see this City of Light, this A-lur of yours, and search there for my lost mate even though you believe that there is little chance that I find her. And you, Om-at, do you come with us?"

"Why not?" asked the hairy one. "The lairs of my tribe lie in the crags above A-lur and though Es-sat, our chief, drove me out I should like to return again, for there is a she there upon whom I should be glad to look once more and who would be glad to look upon me. Yes, I will go with you. Es-sat feared that I might become chief and who knows but that Es-sat was right. But Pan-at-lee! it is she I seek first even before a chieftainship."

"We three, then, shall travel together," said Tarzan.

"And fight together," added Ta-den; "the three as one," and as he spoke he drew his knife and held it above his head.

"The three as one," repeated Om-at, drawing his weapon and duplicating Ta-den's act. "It is spoken!"

"The three as one!" cried Tarzan of the Apes. "To the death!" and his blade flashed in the sunlight.

"Let us go, then," said Om-at; "my knife is dry and cries aloud for the blood of Es-sat."

The trail over which Ta-den and Om-at led and which scarcely could be dignified even by the name of trail was suited more to mountain sheep, monkeys, or birds than to man; but the three that followed it were trained to ways which no ordinary man might essay. Now, upon the lower slopes, it led through dense forests where the ground was so matted with fallen trees and over-rioting vines and brush that the way held always to the swaying branches high above the tangle; again it skirted yawning gorges whose slippery-faced rocks gave but momentary foothold even to the bare feet that lightly touched them as the three leaped chamois-like from one precarious foothold to the next. Dizzy and terrifying was the way that Om-at chose across the summit as he led them around the shoulder of a towering crag that rose a sheer two thousand feet of perpendicular rock above a tumbling river. And when at last they stood upon comparatively level ground again Om-at turned and looked at them both intently and especially at Tarzan of the Apes.

"You will both do," he said. "You are fit companions for Om-at, the Waz-don."

"What do you mean?" asked Tarzan.

"I brought you this way," replied the black, "to learn if either lacked the courage to follow where Om-at led. It is here that the young warriors of Es-sat come to prove their courage. And yet, though we are born and raised upon cliff sides, it is considered no disgrace to admit that Pastar-ul-ved, the Father of Mountains, has defeated us, for of those who try it only a few succeed—the bones of the others lie at the feet of Pastar-ul-ved."

Ta-den laughed. "I would not care to come this way often," he said.

"No," replied Om-at; "but it has shortened our journey by at least a full day. So much the sooner shall Tarzan look upon the Valley of Jad-ben-Otho. Come!" and he led the way upward along the shoulder of Pastar-ul-ved until there lay spread below them a scene of mystery and of beauty—a green valley girt by towering cliffs of marble whiteness—a green valley dotted by deep blue lakes and crossed by the blue trail of a winding river. In the center a city of the whiteness of the marble cliffs—a city which even at so great a distance evidenced a strange, yet artistic architecture. Outside the city there were visible about the valley isolated groups of buildings—sometimes one, again two and three and four in a cluster—but always of the same glaring whiteness, and always in some fantastic form.

About the valley the cliffs were occasionally cleft by deep gorges, verdure filled, giving the appearance of green rivers rioting downward toward a central sea of green.

"Jad Pele ul Jad-ben-Otho," murmured Tarzan in the tongue of the pithecanthropi; "The Valley of the Great God—it is beautiful!"

"Here, in A-lur, lives Ko-tan, the king, ruler over all Pal-ul-don," said Ta-den.

"And here in these gorges live the Waz-don," exclaimed Om-at, "who do not acknowledge that Ko-tan is the ruler over all the Land-of-man."

Ta-den smiled and shrugged. "We will not quarrel, you and I," he said to Om-at, "over that which all the ages have not proved sufficient time in which to reconcile the Ho-don and Waz-don; but let me whisper to you a secret, Om-at. The Ho-don live together in greater or less peace under one ruler so that when danger threatens them they face the enemy with many warriors, for every fighting Ho-don of Pal-ul-don is there. But you Waz-don, how is it with you? You have a dozen kings who fight not only with the Ho-don but with one another. When one of your tribes goes forth upon the fighting trail, even against the Ho-don, it must leave behind sufficient warriors to protect its women and its children from the neighbors upon either hand. When we want eunuchs for the temples or servants for the fields or the homes we march forth in great numbers upon one of your villages. You cannot even flee, for upon either side of you are enemies and though you fight bravely we come back with those who will presently be eunuchs in the temples and servants in our fields and homes. So long as the Waz-don are thus foolish the Ho-don will dominate and their king will be king of Pal-ul-don."

"Perhaps you are right," admitted Om-at. "It is because our neighbors are fools, each thinking that his tribe is the greatest and should rule among the Waz-don. They will not admit that the warriors of my tribe are the bravest and our shes the most beautiful."

Ta-den grinned. "Each of the others presents precisely the same arguments that you present, Om-at," he said, "which, my friend, is the strongest bulwark of defense possessed by the Ho-don."

"Come!" exclaimed Tarzan; "such discussions often lead to quarrels and we three must have no quarrels. I, of course, am interested in learning what I can of the political and economic conditions of your land; I should like to know something of your religion; but not at the expense of bitterness between my only friends in Pal-ul-don. Possibly, however, you hold to the same god?"

"There indeed we do differ," cried Om-at, somewhat bitterly and with a trace of excitement in his voice.

"Differ!" almost shouted Ta-den; "and why should we not differ? Who could agree with the preposterous——"

"Stop!" cried Tarzan. "Now, indeed, have I stirred up a hornets' nest. Let us speak no more of matters political or religious."

"That is wiser," agreed Om-at; "but I might mention, for your information, that the one and only god has a long tail."

"It is sacrilege," cried Ta-den, laying his hand upon his knife; "Jad-ben-Otho has no tail!"

"Stop!" shrieked Om-at, springing forward; but instantly Tarzan interposed himself between them.

"Enough!" he snapped. "Let us be true to our oaths of friendship that we may be honorable in the sight of God in whatever form we conceive Him."

"You are right, Tailless One," said Ta-den. "Come, Om-at, let us look after our friendship and ourselves, secure in the conviction that Jad-ben-Otho is sufficiently powerful to look after himself."

"Done!" agreed Om-at, "but——"

"No 'buts,' Om-at," admonished Tarzan.

The shaggy black shrugged his shoulders and smiled. "Shall we make our way down toward the valley?" he asked. "The gorge below us is uninhabited; that to the left contains the caves of my people. I would see Pan-at-lee once more. Ta-den would visit his father in the valley below and Tarzan seeks entrance to A-lur in search of the mate that would be better dead than in the clutches of the Ho-don priests of Jad-ben-Otho. How shall we proceed?"

"Let us remain together as long as possible," urged Ta-den. "You, Om-at, must seek Pan-at-lee by night and by stealth, for three, even we three, may not hope to overcome Es-sat and all his warriors. At any time may we go to the village where my father is chief, for Ja-don always will welcome the friends of his son. But for Tarzan to enter A-lur is another matter, though there is a way and he has the courage to put it to the test—listen, come close for Jad-ben-Otho has keen ears and this he must not hear," and with his lips close to the ears of his companions Ta-den, the Tall-tree, son of Ja-don, the Lion-man, unfolded his daring plan.

And at the same moment, a hundred miles away, a lithe figure, naked but for a loin cloth and weapons, moved silently across a thorn-covered, waterless steppe, searching always along the ground before him with keen eyes and sensitive nostrils.

CHAPTER III—PAN-AT-LEE

Night had fallen upon unchartered Pal-ul-don. A slender moon, low in the west, bathed the white faces of the chalk cliffs presented to her, in a mellow, unearthly glow. Black were the shadows in Kor-ul-Ja, Gorge-of-lions, where dwelt the tribe of the same name under Es-sat, their chief. From an aperture near the summit of the lofty escarpment a hairy figure emerged—the head and shoulders first—and fierce eyes scanned the cliff side in every direction.

It was Es-sat, the chief. To right and left and below he looked as though to assure himself that he was unobserved, but no other figure moved upon the cliff face, nor did another hairy body protrude from any of the numerous cave mouths from the high-flung abode of the chief to the habitations of the more lowly members of the tribe nearer the cliff's base. Then he moved outward upon the sheer face of the white chalk wall. In the half-light of the baby moon it appeared that the heavy, shaggy black figure moved across the face of the perpendicular wall in some miraculous manner, but closer examination would have revealed stout pegs, as large around as a man's wrist protruding from holes in the cliff into which they were driven. Es-sat's four handlike members and his long, sinuous tail permitted him to move with consummate ease whither he chose—a gigantic rat upon a mighty wall. As he progressed upon his way he avoided the cave mouths, passing either above or below those that lay in his path.

The outward appearance of these caves was similar. An opening from eight to as much as twenty feet long by eight high and four to six feet deep was cut into the chalklike rock of the cliff, in the back of this large opening, which formed what might be described as the front veranda of the home, was an opening about three feet wide and six feet high, evidently forming the doorway to the interior apartment or apartments. On either side of this doorway were smaller openings which it were easy to assume were windows through which light and air might find their way to the inhabitants. Similar windows were also dotted over the cliff face between the entrance porches, suggesting that the entire face of the cliff was honeycombed with apartments. From many of these smaller apertures small streams of water trickled down the escarpment, and the walls above others was blackened as by smoke. Where the water ran the wall was eroded to a depth of from a few inches to as much as a foot, suggesting that some of the tiny streams had been trickling downward to the green carpet of vegetation below for ages.

In this primeval setting the great pithecanthropus aroused no jarring discord for he was as much a part of it as the trees that grew upon the summit of the cliff or those that hid their feet among the dank ferns in the bottom of the gorge.

Now he paused before an entrance-way and listened and then, noiselessly as the moonlight upon the trickling waters, he merged with the shadows of the outer porch. At the doorway leading into the interior he paused again, listening, and then quietly pushing aside the heavy skin that covered the aperture he passed within a large chamber hewn from the living rock. From the far end, through another doorway, shone a light, dimly. Toward this he crept with utmost stealth, his naked feet giving forth no sound. The knotted club that had been hanging at his back from a thong about his neck he now removed and carried in his left hand.

Beyond the second doorway was a corridor running parallel with the cliff face. In this corridor were three more doorways, one at each end and a third almost opposite that in which Es-sat stood. The light was coming from an apartment at the end of the corridor at his left. A sputtering flame rose and fell in a small stone receptacle that stood upon a table or bench of the same material, a monolithic bench fashioned at the time the room was excavated, rising massively from the floor, of which it was a part.

In one corner of the room beyond the table had been left a dais of stone about four feet wide and eight feet long. Upon this were piled a foot or so of softly tanned pelts from which the fur had not been removed. Upon the edge of this dais sat a young female Waz-don. In one hand she held a thin piece of metal, apparently of hammered gold, with serrated edges, and in the other a short, stiff brush. With these she was occupied in going over her smooth, glossy coat which bore a remarkable resemblance to plucked sealskin. Her loin cloth of yellow and black striped *Jato*-skin lay on the couch beside her with the circular breastplates of beaten gold, revealing the symmetrical lines of her nude figure in all its beauty and harmony of contour, for even though the creature was jet black and entirely covered with hair yet she was undeniably beautiful.

That she was beautiful in the eyes of Es-sat, the chief, was evidenced by the gloating expression upon his fierce countenance and the increased rapidity of his breathing. Moving quickly forward he entered the room and as he did so the young she looked up. Instantly her eyes filled with terror and as quickly she seized the loin cloth and with a few deft movements adjusted it about her. As she gathered up her breastplates Es-sat rounded the table and moved quickly toward her.

"What do you want?" she whispered, though she knew full well.

"Pan-at-lee," he said, "your chief has come for you."

"It was for this that you sent away my father and my brothers to spy upon the Kor-ul-lul? I will not have you. Leave the cave of my ancestors!"

Es-sat smiled. It was the smile of a strong and wicked man who knows his power—not a pleasant smile at all. "I will leave, Pan-at-lee," he said; "but you shall go with me—to the cave of Es-sat, the chief, to be the envied of the shes of Kor-ul-Ja. Come!"

"Never!" cried Pan-at-lee. "I hate you. Sooner would I mate with a Ho-don than with you, beater of women, murderer of babes."

A frightful scowl distorted the features of the chief. "She-*Jato*!" he cried. "I will tame you! I will break you! Es-sat, the chief, takes what he will and who dares question his right, or combat his least purpose, will first serve that purpose and then be broken as I break this," and he picked a stone platter from the table and broke it in his powerful hands. "You might have been first and most favored in the cave of the ancestors of Es-sat; but now shall you be last and least and when I am done with you you shall belong to all of the men of Es-sat's cave. Thus for those who spurn the love of their chief!"

He advanced quickly to seize her and as he laid a rough hand upon her she struck him heavily upon the side of his head with her golden breastplates. Without a sound Es-sat, the chief, sank to the floor of the apartment. For a moment Pan-at-lee bent over him, her improvised weapon raised to strike again should he show signs of returning consciousness, her glossy breasts rising and falling with her quickened breathing. Suddenly she stooped and removed Es-sat's knife with its scabbard and shoulder belt. Slipping it over her own shoulder she quickly adjusted her breastplates and keeping a watchful glance upon the figure of the fallen chief, backed from the room.

In a niche in the outer room, just beside the doorway leading to the balcony, were neatly piled a number of rounded pegs from eighteen to twenty inches in length. Selecting five of these she made them into a little bundle about which she twined the lower extremity of her sinuous tail and thus carrying them made her way to the outer edge of the balcony. Assuring herself that there was none about to see, or hinder her, she took quickly to the pegs already set in the face of the cliff and with the celerity of a monkey clambered swiftly aloft to the highest row of pegs which she followed in the direction of the lower end of the gorge for a matter of some hundred yards. Here, above her head, were a series of small round holes placed one above another in three parallel rows. Clinging only with her toes she removed two of the pegs from the bundle carried in her tail and taking one in either hand she inserted them in two opposite holes of the outer rows as far above her as she could reach. Hanging by these new holds she now took one of the three remaining pegs in each of her feet, leaving the fifth grasped securely in her tail. Reaching above her with this member she inserted the fifth peg in one of the holes of the center row and then, alternately hanging by her tail, her feet, or her hands, she moved the pegs upward to new holes, thus carrying her stairway with her as she ascended.

At the summit of the cliff a gnarled tree exposed its time-worn roots above the topmost holes forming the last step from the sheer face of the precipice to level footing. This was the last avenue of escape for members of the tribe hard pressed by enemies from below. There were three such emergency exits from the village and it were death to use them in other than an emergency. This Pan-at-lee well knew; but she knew, too, that it were worse than death to remain where the angered Es-sat might lay hands upon her.

When she had gained the summit, the girl moved quickly through the darkness in the direction of the next gorge which cut the mountain-side a mile beyond Kor-ul-Ja. It was the Gorge-of-water, Kor-ul-lul, to which her father and two brothers had been sent by Es-sat ostensibly to spy upon the neighboring tribe. There was a chance, a slender chance, that she might find them; if not there was the deserted Kor-ul-*gryf* several miles beyond, where she might hide indefinitely from man if she could elude the frightful monster from which the gorge derived its name and whose presence there had rendered its caves uninhabitable for generations.

Pan-at-lee crept stealthily along the rim of the Kor-ul-lul. Just where her father and brothers would watch she did not know. Sometimes their spies remained upon the rim, sometimes they watched from the gorge's bottom. Pan-at-lee was at a loss to know what to do or where to go. She felt very small and helpless alone in the vast darkness of the night. Strange noises fell upon her ears. They came from the lonely reaches of the towering mountains above her, from far away in the invisible valley and from the nearer foothills and once, in the distance, she heard what she thought was the bellow of a bull *gryf*. It came from the direction of the Kor-ul-*gryf*. She shuddered.

Presently there came to her keen ears another sound. Something approached her along the rim of the gorge. It was coming from above. She halted, listening. Perhaps it was her father, or a brother. It was coming closer. She strained her eyes through the darkness. She did not move—she scarcely breathed. And then, of a sudden, quite close it seemed, there blazed through the black night two yellow-green spots of fire.

Pan-at-lee was brave, but as always with the primitive, the darkness held infinite terrors for her. Not alone the terrors of the known but more frightful ones as well—those of the unknown. She had passed through much this night and her nerves were keyed to the highest pitch—raw, taut nerves, they were, ready to react in an exaggerated form to the slightest shock.

But this was no slight shock. To hope for a father and a brother and to see death instead glaring out of the darkness! Yes, Pan-at-lee was brave, but she was not of iron. With a shriek that reverberated among the hills she turned and fled along the rim of Kor-ul-lul and behind her, swiftly, came the devil-eyed lion of the mountains of Pal-ul-don.

Pan-at-lee was lost. Death was inevitable. Of this there could be no doubt, but to die beneath the rending fangs of the carnivore, congenital terror of her kind—it was unthinkable. But there was an alternative. The lion was almost upon her—another instant and he would seize her. Pan-at-lee turned sharply to her left. Just a few steps she took in the new direction before she disappeared over the rim of Kor-ul-lul. The baffled lion, planting all four feet, barely stopped upon the verge of the abyss. Glaring down into the black shadows beneath he mounted an angry roar.

Through the darkness at the bottom of Kor-ul-Ja, Om-at led the way toward the caves of his people. Behind him came Tarzan and Ta-den. Presently they halted beneath a great tree that grew close to the cliff.

"First," whispered Om-at, "I will go to the cave of Pan-at-lee. Then will I seek the cave of my ancestors to have speech with my own blood. It will not take long. Wait here—I shall return soon. Afterward shall we go together to Ta-den's people."

He moved silently toward the foot of the cliff up which Tarzan could presently see him ascending like a great fly on a wall. In the dim light the ape-man could not see the pegs set in the face of the cliff. Om-at moved warily. In the lower tier of caves there should be a sentry. His knowledge of his people and their customs told him, however, that in all probability the sentry was asleep. In this he was not mistaken, yet he did not in any way abate his wariness. Smoothly and swiftly he ascended toward the cave of Pan-at-lee while from below Tarzan and Ta-den watched him.

"How does he do it?" asked Tarzan. "I can see no foothold upon that vertical surface and yet he appears to be climbing with the utmost ease."

Ta-den explained the stairway of pegs. "You could ascend easily," he said, "although a tail would be of great assistance."

They watched until Om-at was about to enter the cave of Pan-at-lee without seeing any indication that he had been observed and then, simultaneously, both saw a head appear in the mouth of one of the lower caves. It was quickly evident that its owner had discovered Om-at for immediately he started upward in pursuit. Without a word Tarzan and Ta-den sprang forward toward the foot of the cliff. The pithecanthropus was the first to reach it and the ape-man saw him spring upward for a handhold on the lowest peg above him. Now Tarzan saw other pegs roughly paralleling each other in zigzag rows up the cliff face. He sprang and caught one of these, pulled himself upward by one hand until he could reach a second with his other hand; and when he had ascended far enough to use his feet, discovered that he could make rapid progress. Ta-den was outstripping him, however, for these precarious ladders were no novelty to him and, further, he had an advantage in possessing a tail.

Nevertheless, the ape-man gave a good account of himself, being presently urged to redoubled efforts by the fact that the Waz-don above Ta-den glanced down and discovered his pursuers just before the Ho-don overtook him. Instantly a wild cry shattered the silence of the gorge—a cry that was immediately answered by hundreds of savage throats as warrior after warrior emerged from the entrance to his cave.

The creature who had raised the alarm had now reached the recess before Pan-at-lee's cave and here he halted and turned to give battle to Ta-den. Unslinging his club which had hung down his back from a thong about his neck he stood upon the level floor of the entrance-way effectually blocking Ta-den's ascent. From all directions the warriors of Kor-ul-Ja were swarming toward the interlopers. Tarzan, who had reached a point on the same level with Ta-den but a little to the latter's left, saw that nothing short of a miracle could save them. Just at the ape-man's left was the entrance to a cave that either was deserted or whose occupants had not as yet been aroused, for the level recess remained unoccupied. Resourceful was the alert mind of Tarzan of the Apes and quick to respond were the trained muscles. In the time that you or I might give to debating an action he would accomplish it and now, though only seconds separated his nearest antagonist from him, in the brief span of time at his disposal he had stepped into the recess, unslung his long rope and leaning far out shot the sinuous noose, with the precision of long habitude, toward the menacing figure wielding its heavy club above Ta-den. There was a momentary pause of the rope-hand as the noose sped toward its goal, a quick movement of the right wrist that closed it upon its victim as it settled over his head and then a surging tug as, seizing the rope in both hands, Tarzan threw back upon it all the weight of his great frame.

Voicing a terrified shriek, the Waz-don lunged headforemost from the recess above Ta-den. Tarzan braced himself for the coming shock when the creature's body should have fallen the full length of the rope and as it did there was a snap of the vertebrae that rose sickeningly in the momentary silence that had followed the doomed man's departing scream. Unshaken by the stress of the suddenly arrested weight at the end of the rope, Tarzan quickly pulled the body to his side that he might remove the noose from about its neck, for he could not afford to lose so priceless a weapon.

During the several seconds that had elapsed since he cast the rope the Waz-don warriors had remained inert as though paralyzed by wonder or by terror. Now, again, one of them found his voice and his head and straightway, shrieking invectives at the strange intruder, started upward for the ape-man, urging his fellows to attack. This man was the closest to Tarzan. But for him the ape-man could easily have reached Ta-den's side as the latter was urging him to do. Tarzan raised the body of the dead Waz-don above his head, held it poised there for a moment as with face raised to the heavens he screamed forth the horrid challenge of the bull apes of the tribe of Kerchak, and with all the strength of his giant sinews he hurled the corpse heavily upon the ascending warrior. So great was the force of the impact that not only was the Waz-don torn from his hold but two of the pegs to which he clung were broken short in their sockets.

As the two bodies, the living and the dead, hurtled downward toward the foot of the cliff a great cry arose from the Waz-don. "Jad-guru-don! Jad-guru-don!" they screamed, and then: "Kill him! Kill him!"

And now Tarzan stood in the recess beside Ta-den. "Jad-guru-don!" repeated the latter, smiling—"The terrible man! Tarzan the Terrible! They may kill you, but they will never forget you."

"They shall not ki—What have we here?" Tarzan's statement as to what "they" should not do was interrupted by a sudden ejaculation as two figures, locked in deathlike embrace, stumbled through the doorway of the cave to the outer porch. One was Om-at, the other a creature of his own kind but with a rough coat, the hairs of which seemed to grow straight outward from the skin, stiffly, unlike Om-at's sleek covering. The two were quite evidently well matched and equally evident was the fact that each was bent upon murder. They fought almost in silence except for an occasional low growl as one or the other acknowledged thus some new hurt.

Tarzan, following a natural impulse to aid his ally, leaped forward to enter the dispute only to be checked by a grunted admonition from Om-at. "Back!" he said. "This fight is mine, alone."

The ape-man understood and stepped aside.

"It is a gund-bar," explained Ta-den, "a chief-battle. This fellow must be Es-sat, the chief. If Om-at kills him without assistance Om-at may become chief."

Tarzan smiled. It was the law of his own jungle—the law of the tribe of Kerchak, the bull ape—the ancient law of primitive man that needed but the refining influences of civilization to introduce the hired dagger and the poison cup. Then his attention was drawn to the outer edge of the vestibule. Above it appeared the shaggy face of one of Es-sat's warriors. Tarzan sprang to intercept the man; but Ta-den was there ahead of him. "Back!" cried the Ho-don to the newcomer. "It is gund-bar." The fellow looked scrutinizingly at the two fighters, then turned his face downward toward his fellows. "Back!" he cried, "it is gund-bar between Es-sat and Om-at." Then he looked back at Ta-den and Tarzan. "Who are you?" he asked.

"We are Om-at's friends," replied Ta-den.

The fellow nodded. "We will attend to you later," he said and disappeared below the edge of the recess.

The battle upon the ledge continued with unabated ferocity, Tarzan and Ta-den having difficulty in keeping out of the way of the contestants who tore and beat at each other with hands and feet and lashing tails. Es-sat was unarmed—Pan-at-lee had seen to that—but at Om-at's side swung a sheathed knife which he made no effort to draw. That would have been contrary to their savage and primitive code for the chief-battle must be fought with nature's weapons.

Sometimes they separated for an instant only to rush upon each other again with all the ferocity and nearly the strength of mad bulls. Presently one of them tripped the other but in that viselike embrace one could not fall alone—Es-sat dragged Om-at with him, toppling upon the brink of the niche. Even Tarzan held his breath. There they surged to and fro perilously for a moment and then the inevitable happened—the two, locked in murderous embrace, rolled over the edge and disappeared from the ape-man's view.

Tarzan voiced a suppressed sigh for he had liked Om-at and then, with Ta-den, approached the edge and looked over. Far below, in the dim light of the coming dawn, two inert forms should be lying stark in death; but, to Tarzan's amazement, such was far from the sight that met his eyes.

Instead, there were the two figures still vibrant with life and still battling only a few feet below him. Clinging always to the pegs with two holds—a hand and a foot, or a foot and a tail, they seemed as much at home upon the perpendicular wall as upon the level surface of the vestibule; but now their tactics were slightly altered, for each seemed particularly bent upon dislodging his antagonist from his holds and precipitating him to certain death below. It was soon evident that Om-at, younger and with greater powers of endurance than Es-sat, was gaining an advantage. Now was the chief almost wholly on the defensive. Holding him by the cross belt with one mighty hand Om-at was forcing his foeman straight out from the cliff, and with the other hand and one foot was rapidly breaking first one of Es-sat's holds and then another, alternating his efforts, or rather punctuating them, with vicious blows to the pit of his adversary's stomach. Rapidly was Es-sat weakening and with the knowledge of impending death there came, as there comes to every coward and bully under similar circumstances, a crumbling of the veneer of bravado which had long masqueraded as courage and with it crumbled his code of ethics. Now was Es-sat no longer chief of Kor-ul-Ja—instead he was a whimpering craven battling for life. Clutching at Om-at, clutching at the nearest pegs he sought any support that would save him from that awful fall, and as he strove to push aside the hand of death, whose cold fingers he already felt upon his heart, his tail sought Om-at's side and the handle of the knife that hung there.

Tarzan saw and even as Es-sat drew the blade from its sheath he dropped catlike to the pegs beside the battling men. Es-sat's tail had drawn back for the cowardly fatal thrust. Now many others saw the perfidious act and a great cry of rage and disgust arose from savage throats; but as the blade sped toward its goal, the ape-man seized the hairy member that wielded it, and at the same instant Om-at thrust the body of Es-sat from him with such force that its weakened holds were broken and it hurtled downward, a brief meteor of screaming fear, to death.

CHAPTER IV—TARZAN-JAD-GURU

As Tarzan and Om-at clambered back to the vestibule of Pan-at-lee's cave and took their stand beside Ta-den in readiness for whatever eventuality might follow the death of Es-sat, the sun that topped the eastern hills touched also the figure of a sleeper upon a distant, thorn-covered steppe awakening him to another day of tireless tracking along a faint and rapidly disappearing spoor.

For a time silence reigned in the Kor-ul-Ja. The tribesmen waited, looking now down upon the dead thing that had been their chief, now at one another, and now at Om-at and the two who stood upon his either side. Presently Om-at spoke. "I am Om-at," he cried. "Who will say that Om-at is not gund of Kor-ul-Ja?"

He waited for a taker of his challenge. One or two of the larger young bucks fidgeted restlessly and eyed him; but there was no reply.

"Then Om-at is gund," he said with finality. "Now tell me, where are Pan-at-lee, her father, and her brothers?"

An old warrior spoke. "Pan-at-lee should be in her cave. Who should know that better than you who are there now? Her father and her brothers were sent to watch Kor-ul-lul; but neither of these questions arouse any tumult in our breasts. There is one that does: Can Om-at be chief of

Kor-ul-Ja and yet stand at bay against his own people with a Ho-don and that terrible man at his side—that terrible man who has no tail? Hand the strangers over to your people to be slain as is the way of the Waz-don and then may Om-at be gund."

Neither Tarzan nor Ta-den spoke then, they but stood watching Om-at and waiting for his decision, the ghost of a smile upon the lips of the ape-man. Ta-den, at least, knew that the old warrior had spoken the truth—the Waz-don entertain no strangers and take no prisoners of an alien race.

Then spoke Om-at. "Always there is change," he said. "Even the old hills of Pal-ul-don appear never twice alike—the brilliant sun, a passing cloud, the moon, a mist, the changing seasons, the sharp clearness following a storm; these things bring each a new change in our hills. From birth to death, day by day, there is constant change in each of us. Change, then, is one of Jad-ben-Otho's laws.

"And now I, Om-at, your gund, bring another change. Strangers who are brave men and good friends shall no longer be slain by the Waz-don of Kor-ul-Ja!"

There were growls and murmurings and a restless moving among the warriors as each eyed the others to see who would take the initiative against Om-at, the iconoclast.

"Cease your mutterings," admonished the new gund. "I am your chief. My word is your law. You had no part in making me chief. Some of you helped Es-sat to drive me from the cave of my ancestors; the rest of you permitted it. I owe you nothing. Only these two, whom you would have me kill, were loyal to me. I am gund and if there be any who doubts it let him speak—he cannot die younger."

Tarzan was pleased. Here was a man after his own heart. He admired the fearlessness of Om-at's challenge and he was a sufficiently good judge of men to know that he had listened to no idle bluff—Om-at would back up his words to the death, if necessary, and the chances were that he would not be the one to die. Evidently the majority of the Kor-ul-Jaians entertained the same conviction.

"I will make you a good gund," said Om-at, seeing that no one appeared inclined to dispute his rights. "Your wives and daughters will be safe—they were not safe while Es-sat ruled. Go now to your crops and your hunting. I leave to search for Pan-at-lee. Ab-on will be gund while I am away—look to him for guidance and to me for an accounting when I return—and may Jad-ben-Otho smile upon you."

He turned toward Tarzan and the Ho-don. "And you, my friends," he said, "are free to go among my people; the cave of my ancestors is yours, do what you will."

"I," said Tarzan, "will go with Om-at to search for Pan-at-lee."

"And I," said Ta-den.

Om-at smiled. "Good!" he exclaimed. "And when we have found her we shall go together upon Tarzan's business and Ta-den's. Where first shall we search?" He turned toward his warriors. "Who knows where she may be?"

None knew other than that Pan-at-lee had gone to her cave with the others the previous evening—there was no clew, no suggestion as to her whereabouts.

"Show me where she sleeps," said Tarzan; "let me see something that belongs to her—an article of her apparel—then, doubtless, I can help you."

Two young warriors climbed closer to the ledge upon which Om-at stood. They were In-sad and O-dan. It was the latter who spoke.

"Gund of Kor-ul-Ja," he said, "we would go with you to search for Pan-at-lee."

It was the first acknowledgment of Om-at's chieftainship and immediately following it the tenseness that had prevailed seemed to relax—the warriors spoke aloud instead of in whispers, and the women appeared from the mouths of caves as with the passing of a sudden storm. In-sad and O-dan had taken the lead and now all seemed glad to follow. Some came to talk with Om-at and to look more closely at Tarzan; others, heads of caves, gathered their hunters and discussed the business of the day. The women and children prepared to descend to the fields with the youths and the old men, whose duty it was to guard them.

"O-dan and In-sad shall go with us," announced Om-at, "we shall not need more. Tarzan, come with me and I shall show you where Pan-at-lee sleeps, though why you should wish to know I cannot guess—she is not there. I have looked for myself."

The two entered the cave where Om-at led the way to the apartment in which Es-sat had surprised Pan-at-lee the previous night.

"All here are hers," said Om-at, "except the war club lying on the floor—that was Es-sat's."

The ape-man moved silently about the apartment, the quivering of his sensitive nostrils scarcely apparent to his companion who only wondered what good purpose could be served here and chafed at the delay.

"Come!" said the ape-man, presently, and led the way toward the outer recess.

Here their three companions were awaiting them. Tarzan passed to the left side of the niche and examined the pegs that lay within reach. He looked at them but it was not his eyes that were examining them. Keener than his keen eyes was that marvelously trained sense of scent that had first been developed in him during infancy under the tutorage of his foster mother, Kala, the she-ape, and further sharpened in the grim jungles by that master teacher—the instinct of self-preservation.

From the left side of the niche he turned to the right. Om-at was becoming impatient.

"Let us be off," he said. "We must search for Pan-at-lee if we would ever find her."

"Where shall we search?" asked Tarzan.

Om-at scratched his head. "Where?" he repeated. "Why all Pal-ul-don, if necessary."

"A large job," said Tarzan. "Come," he added, "she went this way," and he took to the pegs that led aloft toward the summit of the cliff. Here he followed the scent easily since none had passed that way since Pan-at-lee had fled. At the point at which she had left the permanent pegs and resorted to those carried with her Tarzan came to an abrupt halt. "She went this way to the summit," he called back to Om-at who was directly behind him; "but there are no pegs here."

"I do not know how you know that she went this way," said Om-at; "but we will get pegs. In-sad, return and fetch climbing pegs for five."

The young warrior was soon back and the pegs distributed. Om-at handed five to Tarzan and explained their use. The ape-man returned one. "I need but four," he said.

Om-at smiled. "What a wonderful creature you would be if you were not deformed," he said, glancing with pride at his own strong tail.

"I admit that I am handicapped," replied Tarzan. "You others go ahead and leave the pegs in place for me. I am afraid that otherwise it will be slow work as I cannot hold the pegs in my toes as you do."

"All right," agreed Om-at; "Ta-den, In-sad, and I will go first, you follow and O-dan bring up the rear and collect the pegs—we cannot leave them here for our enemies."

"Can't your enemies bring their own pegs?" asked Tarzan.

"Yes; but it delays them and makes easier our defense and—they do not know which of all the holes you see are deep enough for pegs—the others are made to confuse our enemies and are too shallow to hold a peg."

At the top of the cliff beside the gnarled tree Tarzan again took up the trail. Here the scent was fully as strong as upon the pegs and the ape-man moved rapidly across the ridge in the direction of the Kor-ul-lul.

Presently he paused and turned toward Om-at. "Here she moved swiftly, running at top speed, and, Om-at, she was pursued by a lion."

"You can read that in the grass?" asked O-dan as the others gathered about the ape-man.

Tarzan nodded. "I do not think the lion got her," he added; "but that we shall determine quickly. No, he did not get her—look!" and he pointed toward the southwest, down the ridge.

Following the direction indicated by his finger, the others presently detected a movement in some bushes a couple of hundred yards away.

"What is it?" asked Om-at. "It is she?" and he started toward the spot.

"Wait," advised Tarzan. "It is the lion which pursued her."

"You can see him?" asked Ta-den.

"No, I can smell him."

The others looked their astonishment and incredulity; but of the fact that it was indeed a lion they were not left long in doubt. Presently the bushes parted and the creature stepped out in full view, facing them. It was a magnificent beast, large and beautifully maned, with the brilliant leopard spots of its kind well marked and symmetrical. For a moment it eyed them and then, still chafing at the loss of its prey earlier in the morning, it charged.

The Pal-ul-donians unslung their clubs and stood waiting the onrushing beast. Tarzan of the Apes drew his hunting knife and crouched in the path of the fanged fury. It was almost upon him when it swerved to the right and leaped for Om-at only to be sent to earth with a staggering blow upon the head. Almost instantly it was up and though the men rushed fearlessly in, it managed to sweep aside their weapons with its mighty paws. A single blow wrenched O-dan's club from his hand and sent it hurtling against Ta-den, knocking him from his feet. Taking advantage of its opportunity the lion rose to throw itself upon O-dan and at the same instant Tarzan flung himself upon its back. Strong, white teeth buried themselves in the spotted neck, mighty arms encircled the savage throat and the sinewy legs of the ape-man locked themselves about the gaunt belly.

The others, powerless to aid, stood breathlessly about as the great lion lunged hither and thither, clawing and biting fearfully and futilely at the savage creature that had fastened itself upon him. Over and over they rolled and now the onlookers saw a brown hand raised above the lion's side—a brown hand grasping a keen blade. They saw it fall and rise and fall again—each time with terrific force and in its wake they saw a crimson stream trickling down *Ja's* gorgeous coat.

Now from the lion's throat rose hideous screams of hate and rage and pain as he redoubled his efforts to dislodge and punish his tormentor; but always the tousled black head remained half buried in the dark brown mane and the mighty arm rose and fell to plunge the knife again and again into the dying beast.

The Pal-ul-donians stood in mute wonder and admiration. Brave men and mighty hunters they were and as such the first to accord honor to a mightier.

"And you would have had me slay him!" cried Om-at, glancing at In-sad and O-dan.

"Jad-ben-Otho reward you that you did not," breathed In-sad.

And now the lion lunged suddenly to earth and with a few spasmodic quiverings lay still. The ape-man rose and shook himself, even as might *Ja*, the leopard-coated lion of Pal-ul-don, had he been the one to survive.

O-dan advanced quickly toward Tarzan. Placing a palm upon his own breast and the other on Tarzan's, "Tarzan the Terrible," he said, "I ask no greater honor than your friendship."

"And I no more than the friendship of Om-at's friends," replied the ape-man simply, returning the other's salute.

"Do you think," asked Om-at, coming close to Tarzan and laying a hand upon the other's shoulder, "that he got her?"

"No, my friend; it was a hungry lion that charged us."

"You seem to know much of lions," said In-sad.

"Had I a brother I could not know him better," replied Tarzan.

"Then where can she be?" continued Om-at.

"We can but follow while the spoor is fresh," answered the ape-man and again taking up his interrupted tracking he led them down the ridge and at a sharp turning of the trail to the left brought them to the verge of the cliff that dropped into the Kor-ul-lul. For a moment Tarzan examined the ground to the right and to the left, then he stood erect and looking at Om-at pointed into the gorge.

For a moment the Waz-don gazed down into the green rift at the bottom of which a tumultuous river tumbled downward along its rocky bed, then he closed his eyes as to a sudden spasm of pain and turned away.

"You—mean—she jumped?" he asked.

"To escape the lion," replied Tarzan. "He was right behind her—look, you can see where his four paws left their impress in the turf as he checked his charge upon the very verge of the abyss."

"Is there any chance—" commenced Om-at, to be suddenly silenced by a warning gesture from Tarzan.

"Down!" whispered the ape-man, "many men are coming. They are running—from down the ridge." He flattened himself upon his belly in the grass, the others following his example.

For some minutes they waited thus and then the others, too, heard the sound of running feet and now a hoarse shout followed by many more.

"It is the war cry of the Kor-ul-lul," whispered Om-at—"the hunting cry of men who hunt men. Presently shall we see them and if Jad-ben-Otho is pleased with us they shall not too greatly outnumber us."

"They are many," said Tarzan, "forty or fifty, I should say; but how many are the pursued and how many the pursuers we cannot even guess, except that the latter must greatly outnumber the former, else these would not run so fast."

"Here they come," said Ta-den.

"It is An-un, father of Pan-at-lee, and his two sons," exclaimed O-dan. "They will pass without seeing us if we do not hurry," he added looking at Om-at, the chief, for a sign.

"Come!" cried the latter, springing to his feet and running rapidly to intercept the three fugitives. The others followed him.

"Five friends!" shouted Om-at as An-un and his sons discovered them.

"Adenen yo!" echoed O-dan and In-sad.

The fugitives scarcely paused as these unexpected reinforcements joined them but they eyed Ta-den and Tarzan with puzzled glances.

"The Kor-ul-lul are many," shouted An-un. "Would that we might pause and fight; but first we must warn Es-sat and our people."

"Yes," said Om-at, "we must warn our people."

"Es-sat is dead," said In-sad.

"Who is chief?" asked one of An-un's sons.

"Om-at," replied O-dan.

"It is well," cried An-un. "Pan-at-lee said that you would come back and slay Es-sat."

Now the enemy broke into sight behind them.

"Come!" cried Tarzan, "let us turn and charge them, raising a great cry. They pursued but three and when they see eight charging upon them they will think that many men have come to do battle. They will believe that there are more even than they see and then one who is swift will have time to reach the gorge and warn your people."

"It is well," said Om-at. "Id-an, you are swift—carry word to the warriors of Kor-ul-Ja that we fight the Kor-ul-lul upon the ridge and that Ab-on shall send a hundred men."

Id-an, the son of An-un, sped swiftly toward the cliff-dwellings of the Kor-ul-Ja while the others charged the oncoming Kor-ul-lul, the war cries of the two tribes rising and falling in a certain grim harmony. The leaders of the Kor-ul-lul paused at sight of the reinforcements, waiting apparently for those behind to catch up with them and, possibly, also to learn how great a force confronted them. The leaders, swifter runners than their fellows, perhaps, were far in advance while the balance of their number had not yet emerged from the brush; and now as Om-at and his companions fell upon them with a ferocity born of necessity they fell back, so that when their companions at last came in sight of them they appeared to be in full rout. The natural result was that the others turned and fled.

Encouraged by this first success Om-at followed them into the brush, his little company charging valiantly upon his either side, and loud and terrifying were the savage yells with which they pursued the fleeing enemy. The brush, while not growing so closely together as to impede progress, was of such height as to hide the members of the party from one another when they became separated by even a few yards. The result was that Tarzan, always swift and always keen for battle, was soon pursuing the enemy far in the lead of the others—a lack of prudence which was to prove his undoing.

The warriors of Kor-ul-lul, doubtless as valorous as their foemen, retreated only to a more strategic position in the brush, nor were they long in guessing that the number of their pursuers was fewer than their own. They made a stand then where the brush was densest—an ambush it was, and into this ran Tarzan of the Apes. They tricked him neatly. Yes, sad as is the narration of it, they tricked the wily jungle lord. But then they were fighting on their own ground, every foot of which they knew as you know your front parlor, and they were following their own tactics, of which Tarzan knew nothing.

A single black warrior appeared to Tarzan a laggard in the rear of the retreating enemy and thus retreating he lured Tarzan on. At last he turned at bay confronting the ape-man with bludgeon and drawn knife and as Tarzan charged him a score of burly Waz-don leaped from the surrounding brush. Instantly, but too late, the giant Tarmangani realized his peril. There flashed before him a vision of his lost mate and a great and sickening regret surged through him with the realization that if she still lived she might no longer hope, for though she might never know of the passing of her lord the fact of it must inevitably seal her doom.

And consequent to this thought there enveloped him a blind frenzy of hatred for these creatures who dared thwart his purpose and menace the welfare of his wife. With a savage growl he threw himself upon the warrior before him twisting the heavy club from the creature's hand as if he had been a little child, and with his left fist backed by the weight and sinew of his giant frame, he crashed a shattering blow to the center of the Waz-don's face—a blow that crushed the bones and dropped the fellow in his tracks. Then he swung upon the others with their fallen comrade's bludgeon striking to right and left mighty, unmerciful blows that drove down their own weapons until that wielded by the ape-man was splintered and shattered. On either hand they fell before his cudgel; so rapid the delivery of his blows, so catlike his recovery that in the first few moments of the battle he seemed invulnerable to their attack; but it could not last—he was outnumbered twenty to one and his undoing came from a thrown club. It struck him upon the back of the head. For a moment he stood swaying and then like a great pine beneath the woodsman's ax he crashed to earth.

Others of the Kor-ul-lul had rushed to engage the balance of Om-at's party. They could be heard fighting at a short distance and it was evident that the Kor-ul-Ja were falling slowly back and as they fell Om-at called to the missing one: "Tarzan the Terrible! Tarzan the Terrible!"

"Jad-guru, indeed," repeated one of the Kor-ul-lul rising from where Tarzan had dropped him. "Tarzan-jad-guru! He was worse than that."

CHAPTER V—IN THE KOR-UL-*GRYF*

As Tarzan fell among his enemies a man halted many miles away upon the outer verge of the morass that encircles Pal-ul-don. Naked he was except for a loin cloth and three belts of cartridges, two of which passed over his shoulders, crossing upon his chest and back, while the third encircled his waist. Slung to his back by its leathern sling-strap was an Enfield, and he carried too a long knife, a bow and a quiver of arrows. He had come far, through wild and savage lands, menaced by fierce beasts and fiercer men, yet intact to the last cartridge was the ammunition that had filled his belts the day that he set out.

The bow and the arrows and the long knife had brought him thus far safely, yet often in the face of great risks that could have been minimized by a single shot from the well-kept rifle at his back. What purpose might he have for conserving this precious ammunition? in risking his life to bring the last bright shining missile to his unknown goal? For what, for whom were these death-dealing bits of metal preserved? In all the world only he knew.

When Pan-at-lee stepped over the edge of the cliff above Kor-ul-lul she expected to be dashed to instant death upon the rocks below; but she had chosen this in preference to the rending fangs of *Ja*. Instead, chance had ordained that she make the frightful plunge at a point where the tumbling river swung close beneath the overhanging cliff to eddy for a slow moment in a deep pool before plunging madly downward again in a cataract of boiling foam, and water thundering against rocks.

Into this icy pool the girl shot, and down and down beneath the watery surface until, half choked, yet fighting bravely, she battled her way once more to air. Swimming strongly she made the opposite shore and there dragged herself out upon the bank to lie panting and spent until the approaching dawn warned her to seek concealment, for she was in the country of her people's enemies.

Rising, she moved into the concealment of the rank vegetation that grows so riotously in the well-watered kors[1] of Pal-ul-don.

Hidden amidst the plant life from the sight of any who might chance to pass along the well-beaten trail that skirted the river Pan-at-lee sought rest and food, the latter growing in abundance all about her in the form of fruits and berries and succulent tubers which she scooped from the earth with the knife of the dead Es-sat.

Ah! if she had but known that he was dead! What trials and risks and terrors she might have been saved; but she thought that he still lived and so she dared not return to Kor-ul-Ja. At least not yet while his rage was at white heat. Later, perhaps, her father and brothers returned to their cave, she might risk it; but not now—not now. Nor could she for long remain here in the neighborhood of the hostile Kor-ul-lul and somewhere she must find safety from beasts before the night set in.

As she sat upon the bole of a fallen tree seeking some solution of the problem of existence that confronted her, there broke upon her ears from up the gorge the voices of shouting men—a sound that she recognized all too well. It was the war cry of the Kor-ul-lul. Closer and closer it approached her hiding place. Then, through the veil of foliage she caught glimpses of three figures fleeing along the trail, and behind them the shouting of the pursuers rose louder and louder as

---

[1] I have used the Pal-ul-don word for gorge with the English plural, which is not the correct native plural form. The latter, it seems to me, is awkward for us and so I have generally ignored it throughout my manuscript, permitting, for example, Kor-ul-Ja to answer for both singular and plural. However, for the benefit of those who may be interested in such things I may say that the plurals are formed simply for all words in the Pal-ul-don language by doubling the initial letter of the word, as k'kor, gorges, pronounced as though written kakor, the a having the sound of a in sofa. Lions, d' don.

they neared her. Again she caught sight of the fugitives crossing the river below the cataract and again they were lost to sight. And now the pursuers came into view—shouting Kor-ul-lul warriors, fierce and implacable. Forty, perhaps fifty of them. She waited breathless; but they did not swerve from the trail and passed her, unguessing that an enemy she lay hid within a few yards of them.

Once again she caught sight of the pursued—three Waz-don warriors clambering the cliff face at a point where portions of the summit had fallen away presenting a steep slope that might be ascended by such as these. Suddenly her attention was riveted upon the three. Could it be? O Jad-ben-Otho! had she but known a moment before. When they passed she might have joined them, for they were her father and two brothers. Now it was too late. With bated breath and tense muscles she watched the race. Would they reach the summit? Would the Kor-ul-lul overhaul them? They climbed well, but, oh, so slowly. Now one lost his footing in the loose shale and slipped back! The Kor-ul-lul were ascending—one hurled his club at the nearest fugitive. The Great God was pleased with the brother of Pan-at-lee, for he caused the club to fall short of its target, and to fall, rolling and bounding, back upon its owner carrying him from his feet and precipitating him to the bottom of the gorge.

Standing now, her hands pressed tight above her golden breastplates, Pan-at-lee watched the race for life. Now one, her older brother, reached the summit and clinging there to something that she could not see he lowered his body and his long tail to the father beneath him. The latter, seizing this support, extended his own tail to the son below—the one who had slipped back—and thus, upon a living ladder of their own making, the three reached the summit and disappeared from view before the Kor-ul-lul overtook them. But the latter did not abandon the chase. On they went until they too had disappeared from sight and only a faint shouting came down to Pan-at-lee to tell her that the pursuit continued.

The girl knew that she must move on. At any moment now might come a hunting party, combing the gorge for the smaller animals that fed or bedded there.

Behind her were Es-sat and the returning party of Kor-ul-lul that had pursued her kin; before her, across the next ridge, was the Kor-ul-*gryf*, the lair of the terrifying monsters that brought the chill of fear to every inhabitant of Pal-ul-don; below her, in the valley, was the country of the Ho-don, where she could look for only slavery, or death; here were the Kor-ul-lul, the ancient enemies of her people and everywhere were the wild beasts that eat the flesh of man.

For but a moment she debated and then turning her face toward the southeast she set out across the gorge of water toward the Kor-ul-*gryf*—at least there were no men there. As it is now, so it was in the beginning, back to the primitive progenitor of man which is typified by Pan-at-lee and her kind today, of all the hunters that woman fears, man is the most relentless, the most terrible. To the dangers of man she preferred the dangers of the *gryf*.

Moving cautiously she reached the foot of the cliff at the far side of Kor-ul-lul and here, toward noon, she found a comparatively easy ascent. Crossing the ridge she stood at last upon the brink of Kor-ul-*gryf*—the horror place of the folklore of her race. Dank and mysterious grew the vegetation below; giant trees waved their plumed tops almost level with the summit of the cliff; and over all brooded an ominous silence.

Pan-at-lee lay upon her belly and stretching over the edge scanned the cliff face below her. She could see caves there and the stone pegs which the ancients had fashioned so laboriously by hand. She had heard of these in the firelight tales of her childhood and of how the gryfs had come from the morasses across the mountains and of how at last the people had fled after many had been seized and devoured by the hideous creatures, leaving their caves untenanted for no man living knew how long. Some said that Jad-ben-Otho, who has lived forever, was still a little boy. Pan-at-lee shuddered; but there were caves and in them she would be safe even from the gryfs.

She found a place where the stone pegs reached to the very summit of the cliff, left there no doubt in the final exodus of the tribe when there was no longer need of safeguarding the deserted caves against invasion. Pan-at-lee clambered slowly down toward the uppermost cave. She found the recess in front of the doorway almost identical with those of her own tribe. The floor of it, though, was littered with twigs and old nests and the droppings of birds, until it was half choked. She moved along to another recess and still another, but all were alike in the accumulated filth. Evidently there was no need in looking further. This one seemed large and commodious. With her knife she fell to work cleaning away the debris by the simple expedient of pushing it over the edge, and always her eyes turned constantly toward the silent gorge where lurked the fearsome creatures of Pal-ul-don. And other eyes there were, eyes she did not see, but that saw her and watched her every move—fierce eyes, greedy eyes, cunning and cruel. They watched her, and a red tongue licked flabby, pendulous lips. They watched her, and a half-human brain laboriously evolved a brutish design.

As in her own Kor-ul-Ja, the natural springs in the cliff had been developed by the long-dead builders of the caves so that fresh, pure water trickled now, as it had for ages, within easy access to the cave entrances. Her only difficulty would be in procuring food and for that she must take the risk at least once in two days, for she was sure that she could find fruits and tubers and perhaps small animals, birds, and eggs near the foot of the cliff, the last two, possibly, in the caves themselves. Thus might she live on here indefinitely. She felt now a certain sense of security imparted doubtless by the impregnability of her high-flung sanctuary that she knew to be safe from all the more dangerous beasts, and this one from men, too, since it lay in the abjured Kor-ul-*gryf*.

Now she determined to inspect the interior of her new home. The sun still in the south, lighted the interior of the first apartment. It was similar to those of her experience—the same beasts and men were depicted in the same crude fashion in the carvings on the walls—evidently there had been little progress in the race of Waz-don during the generations that had come and departed since Kor-ul-*gryf* had been abandoned by men. Of course Pan-at-lee thought no such thoughts, for evolution and progress existed not for her, or her kind. Things were as they had always been and would always be as they were.

That these strange creatures have existed thus for incalculable ages it can scarce be doubted, so marked are the indications of antiquity about their dwellings—deep furrows worn by naked feet in living rock; the hollow in the jamb of a stone doorway where many arms have touched in passing; the endless carvings that cover, ofttimes, the entire face of a great cliff and all the walls and ceilings of every cave and each carving wrought by a different hand, for each is the coat of arms, one might say, of the adult male who traced it.

And so Pan-at-lee found this ancient cave homelike and familiar. There was less litter within than she had found without and what there was was mostly an accumulation of dust. Beside the doorway was the niche in which wood and tinder were kept, but there remained nothing now other than mere dust. She had however saved a little pile of twigs from the debris on the porch. In a short time she had made a light by firing a bundle of twigs and lighting others from this fire she explored some of the inner rooms. Nor here did she find aught that was new or strange nor any relic of the departed owners other than a few broken stone dishes. She had been looking for something soft to sleep upon, but was doomed to disappointment as the former owners had evidently made a leisurely departure, carrying all their belongings with them. Below, in the gorge were leaves and grasses and fragrant branches, but Pan-at-lee felt no stomach for descending into that horrid abyss for the gratification of mere creature comfort—only the necessity for food would drive her there.

And so, as the shadows lengthened and night approached she prepared to make as comfortable a bed as she could by gathering the dust of ages into a little pile and spreading it between her soft body and the hard floor—at best it was only better than nothing. But Pan-at-lee was very tired. She had not slept since two nights before and in the interval she had experienced many dangers and hardships. What wonder then that despite the hard bed, she was asleep almost immediately she had composed herself for rest.

She slept and the moon rose, casting its silver light upon the cliff's white face and lessening the gloom of the dark forest and the dismal gorge. In the distance a lion roared. There was a long silence. From the upper reaches of the gorge came a deep bellow. There was a movement in the trees at the cliff's foot. Again the bellow, low and ominous. It was answered from below the deserted village. Something dropped from the foliage of a tree directly below the cave in which Pan-at-lee slept—it dropped to the ground among the dense shadows. Now it moved, cautiously. It moved toward the foot of the cliff, taking form and shape in the moonlight. It moved like the creature of a bad dream—slowly, sluggishly. It might have been a huge sloth—it might have been a man, with so grotesque a brush does the moon paint—master cubist.

Slowly it moved up the face of the cliff—like a great grubworm it moved, but now the moon-brush touched it again and it had hands and feet and with them it clung to the stone pegs and raised itself laboriously aloft toward the cave where Pan-at-lee slept. From the lower reaches of the gorge came again the sound of bellowing, and it was answered from above the village.

Tarzan of the Apes opened his eyes. He was conscious of a pain in his head, and at first that was about all. A moment later grotesque shadows, rising and falling, focused his arousing perceptions. Presently he saw that he was in a cave. A dozen Waz-don warriors squatted about, talking. A rude stone cresset containing burning oil lighted the interior and as the flame rose and fell the exaggerated shadows of the warriors danced upon the walls behind them.

"We brought him to you alive, Gund," he heard one of them saying, "because never before was Ho-don like him seen. He has no tail—he was born without one, for there is no scar to mark where a tail had been cut off. The thumbs upon his hands and feet are unlike those of the races of Pal-ul-don. He is more powerful than many men put together and he attacks with the fearlessness of *Ja*. We brought him alive, that you might see him before he is slain."

The chief rose and approached the ape-man, who closed his eyes and feigned unconsciousness. He felt hairy hands upon him as he was turned over, none too gently. The gund examined him from head to foot, making comments, especially upon the shape and size of his thumbs and great toes.

"With these and with no tail," he said, "it cannot climb."

"No," agreed one of the warriors, "it would surely fall even from the cliff pegs."

"I have never seen a thing like it," said the chief. "It is neither Waz-don nor Ho-don. I wonder from whence it came and what it is called."

"The Kor-ul-Ja shouted aloud, 'Tarzan-jad-guru!' and we thought that they might be calling this one," said a warrior. "Shall we kill it now?"

"No," replied the chief, "we will wait until its life returns into its head that I may question it. Remain here, In-tan, and watch it. When it can again hear and speak call me."

He turned and departed from the cave, the others, except In-tan, following him. As they moved past him and out of the chamber Tarzan caught snatches of their conversation which indicated that the Kor-ul-Ja reinforcements had fallen upon their little party in great numbers and driven them away. Evidently the swift feet of Id-an had saved the day for the warriors of Om-at. The ape-man smiled, then he partially opened an eye and cast it upon In-tan. The warrior stood at the entrance to the cave looking out—his back was toward his prisoner. Tarzan tested the bonds that secured his wrists. They seemed none too stout and they had tied his hands in front of him! Evidence indeed that the Waz-don took few prisoners—if any.

Cautiously he raised his wrists until he could examine the thongs that confined them. A grim smile lighted his features. Instantly he was at work upon the bonds with his strong teeth, but ever a wary eye was upon In-tan, the warrior of Kor-ul-lul. The last knot had been loosened and Tarzan's hands were free when In-tan turned to cast an appraising eye upon his ward. He saw that the prisoner's position was changed—he no longer lay upon his back as they had left him, but upon his side and his hands were drawn up against his face. In-tan came closer and bent down. The bonds seemed very loose upon the prisoner's wrists. He extended his hand to examine them with his fingers and instantly the two hands leaped from their bonds—one to seize his own wrist, the other his throat. So unexpected the catlike attack that In-tan had not even time to cry out before steel fingers silenced him. The creature pulled him suddenly forward so that he lost his balance and rolled over upon the prisoner and to the floor beyond to stop with Tarzan upon his breast. In-tan struggled to release himself—struggled to draw his knife; but Tarzan found it before him. The Waz-don's tail leaped to the other's throat, encircling it—he too could choke; but his own knife, in the hands of his antagonist, severed the beloved member close to its root.

The Waz-don's struggles became weaker—a film was obscuring his vision. He knew that he was dying and he was right. A moment later he was dead. Tarzan rose to his feet and placed one foot upon the breast of his dead foe. How the urge seized him to roar forth the victory cry of his kind! But he dared not. He discovered that they had not removed his rope from his shoulders and that they had replaced his knife in its sheath. It had been in his hand when he was felled. Strange creatures! He did not know that they held a superstitious fear of the weapons of a dead enemy, believing that if buried without them he would forever haunt his slayers in search of them and that when he found them he would kill the man who killed him. Against the wall leaned his bow and quiver of arrows.

Tarzan stepped toward the doorway of the cave and looked out. Night had just fallen. He could hear voices from the nearer caves and there floated to his nostrils the odor of cooking food. He looked down and experienced a sensation of relief. The cave in which he had been held was in the lowest tier—scarce thirty feet from the base of the cliff. He was about to chance an immediate descent when there occurred to him a thought that brought a grin to his savage lips—

a thought that was born of the name the Waz-don had given him—Tarzan-jad-guru—Tarzan the Terrible—and a recollection of the days when he had delighted in baiting the blacks of the distant jungle of his birth. He turned back into the cave where lay the dead body of In-tan. With his knife he severed the warrior's head and carrying it to the outer edge of the recess tossed it to the ground below, then he dropped swiftly and silently down the ladder of pegs in a way that would have surprised the Kor-ul-lul who had been so sure that he could not climb.

At the bottom he picked up the head of In-tan and disappeared among the shadows of the trees carrying the grisly trophy by its shock of shaggy hair. Horrible? But you are judging a wild beast by the standards of civilization. You may teach a lion tricks, but he is still a lion. Tarzan looked well in a Tuxedo, but he was still a Tarmangani and beneath his pleated shirt beat a wild and savage heart.

Nor was his madness lacking in method. He knew that the hearts of the Kor-ul-lul would be filled with rage when they discovered the thing that he had done and he knew too, that mixed with the rage would be a leaven of fear and it was fear of him that had made Tarzan master of many jungles—one does not win the respect of the killers with bonbons.

Below the village Tarzan returned to the foot of the cliff searching for a point where he could make the ascent to the ridge and thus back to the village of Om-at, the Kor-ul-Ja. He came at last to a place where the river ran so close to the rocky wall that he was forced to swim it in search of a trail upon the opposite side and here it was that his keen nostrils detected a familiar spoor. It was the scent of Pan-at-lee at the spot where she had emerged from the pool and taken to the safety of the jungle.

Immediately the ape-man's plans were changed. Pan-at-lee lived, or at least she had lived after the leap from the cliff's summit. He had started in search of her for Om-at, his friend, and for Om-at he would continue upon the trail he had picked up thus fortuitously by accident. It led him into the jungle and across the gorge and then to the point at which Pan-at-lee had commenced the ascent of the opposite cliffs. Here Tarzan abandoned the head of In-tan, tying it to the lower branch of a tree, for he knew that it would handicap him in his ascent of the steep escarpment. Apelike he ascended, following easily the scent spoor of Pan-at-lee. Over the summit and across the ridge the trail lay, plain as a printed page to the delicate senses of the jungle-bred tracker.

Tarzan knew naught of the Kor-ul-*gryf*. He had seen, dimly in the shadows of the night, strange, monstrous forms and Ta-den and Om-at had spoken of great creatures that all men feared; but always, everywhere, by night and by day, there were dangers. From infancy death had stalked, grim and terrible, at his heels. He knew little of any other existence. To cope with danger was his life and he lived his life as simply and as naturally as you live yours amidst the dangers of the crowded city streets. The black man who goes abroad in the jungle by night is afraid, for he has spent his life since infancy surrounded by numbers of his own kind and safeguarded, especially at night, by such crude means as lie within his powers. But Tarzan had lived as the lion lives and the panther and the elephant and the ape—a true jungle creature dependent solely upon his prowess and his wits, playing a lone hand against creation. Therefore he was surprised at nothing and feared nothing and so he walked through the strange night as undisturbed and unapprehensive as the farmer to the cow lot in the darkness before the dawn.

Once more Pan-at-lee's trail ended at the verge of a cliff; but this time there was no indication that she had leaped over the edge and a moment's search revealed to Tarzan the stone pegs upon which she had made her descent. As he lay upon his belly leaning over the top of the cliff examining the pegs his attention was suddenly attracted by something at the foot of the cliff. He could not distinguish its identity, but he saw that it moved and presently that it was ascending slowly, apparently by means of pegs similar to those directly below him. He watched it intently as it rose higher and higher until he was able to distinguish its form more clearly, with the result that he became convinced that it more nearly resembled some form of great ape than a lower order. It had a tail, though, and in other respects it did not seem a true ape.

Slowly it ascended to the upper tier of caves, into one of which it disappeared. Then Tarzan took up again the trail of Pan-at-lee. He followed it down the stone pegs to the nearest cave and then further along the upper tier. The ape-man raised his eyebrows when he saw the direction in which it led, and quickened his pace. He had almost reached the third cave when the echoes of Kor-ul-*gryf* were awakened by a shrill scream of terror.

CHAPTER VI—THE TOR-O-DON

Pan-at-lee slept—the troubled sleep, of physical and nervous exhaustion, filled with weird dreamings. She dreamed that she slept beneath a great tree in the bottom of the Kor-ul-*gryf* and that one of the fearsome beasts was creeping upon her but she could not open her eyes nor move. She tried to scream but no sound issued from her lips. She felt the thing touch her throat, her breast, her arm, and there it closed and seemed to be dragging her toward it. With a super-human effort of will she opened her eyes. In the instant she knew that she was dreaming and that quickly the hallucination of the dream would fade—it had happened to her many times before. But it persisted. In the dim light that filtered into the dark chamber she saw a form beside her, she felt hairy fingers upon her and a hairy breast against which she was being drawn. Jad-ben-Otho! this was no dream. And then she screamed and tried to fight the thing from her; but her scream was answered by a low growl and another hairy hand seized her by the hair of the head. The beast rose now upon its hind legs and dragged her from the cave to the moonlit recess without and at the same instant she saw the figure of what she took to be a Ho-don rise above the outer edge of the niche.

The beast that held her saw it too and growled ominously but it did not relinquish its hold upon her hair. It crouched as though waiting an attack, and it increased the volume and frequency of its growls until the horrid sounds reverberated through the gorge, drowning even the deep bellowings of the beasts below, whose mighty thunderings had broken out anew with the sudden commotion from the high-flung cave. The beast that held her crouched and the creature that faced it crouched also, and growled—as hideously as the other. Pan-at-lee trembled. This was no Ho-don and though she feared the Ho-don she feared this thing more, with its catlike crouch and its beastly growls. She was lost—that Pan-at-lee knew. The two things might fight for her, but whichever won she was lost. Perhaps, during the battle, if it came to that, she might find the opportunity to throw herself over into the Kor-ul-*gryf*.

The thing that held her she had recognized now as a Tor-o-don, but the other thing she could not place, though in the moonlight she could see it very distinctly. It had no tail. She could see its hands and its feet, and they were not the hands and feet of the races of Pal-ul-don. It was slowly closing upon the Tor-o-don and in one hand it held a gleaming knife. Now it spoke and to Pan-at-lee's terror was added an equal weight of consternation.

"When it leaves go of you," it said, "as it will presently to defend itself, run quickly behind me, Pan-at-lee, and go to the cave nearest the pegs you descended from the cliff top. Watch from there. If I am defeated you will have time to escape this slow thing; if I am not I will come to you there. I am Om-at's friend and yours."

The last words took the keen edge from Pan-at-lee's terror; but she did not understand. How did this strange creature know her name? How did it know that she had descended the pegs by a certain cave? It must, then, have been here when she came. Pan-at-lee was puzzled.

"Who are you?" she asked, "and from whence do you come?"

"I am Tarzan," he replied, "and just now I came from Om-at, of Kor-ul-Ja, in search of you."

Om-at, gund of Kor-ul-Ja! What wild talk was this? She would have questioned him further, but now he was approaching the Tor-o-don and the latter was screaming and growling so loudly as to drown the sound of her voice. And then it did what the strange creature had said that it would do—it released its hold upon her hair as it prepared to charge. Charge it did and in those close quarters there was no room to fence for openings. Instantly the two beasts locked in deadly embrace, each seeking the other's throat. Pan-at-lee watched, taking no advantage of the opportunity to escape which their preoccupation gave her. She watched and waited, for into her savage little brain had come the resolve to pin her faith to this strange creature who had unlocked her heart with those four words—"I am Om-at's friend!" And so she waited, with drawn knife, the opportunity to do her bit in the vanquishing of the Tor-o-don. That the newcomer could do it unaided she well knew to be beyond the realms of possibility, for she knew well the prowess of the beastlike man with whom it fought. There were not many of them in Pal-ul-don, but what few there were were a terror to the women of the Waz-don and the Ho-don, for the old Tor-o-don bulls roamed the mountains and the valleys of Pal-ul-don between rutting seasons and woe betide the women who fell in their paths.

With his tail the Tor-o-don sought one of Tarzan's ankles, and finding it, tripped him. The two fell heavily, but so agile was the ape-man and so quick his powerful muscles that even in falling he twisted the beast beneath him, so that Tarzan fell on top and now the tail that had tripped him sought his throat as had the tail of In-tan, the Kor-ul-lul. In the effort of turning his antagonist's body during the fall Tarzan had had to relinquish his knife that he might seize the shaggy body with both hands and now the weapon lay out of reach at the very edge of the recess. Both hands were occupied for the moment in fending off the clutching fingers that sought to seize him and drag his throat within reach of his foe's formidable fangs and now the tail was seeking its deadly hold with a formidable persistence that would not be denied.

Pan-at-lee hovered about, breathless, her dagger ready, but there was no opening that did not also endanger Tarzan, so constantly were the two duelists changing their positions. Tarzan felt the tail slowly but surely insinuating itself about his neck though he had drawn his head down between the muscles of his shoulders in an effort to protect this vulnerable part. The battle seemed to be going against him for the giant beast against which he strove would have been a fair match in weight and strength for Bolgani, the gorilla. And knowing this he suddenly exerted a single super-human effort, thrust far apart the giant hands and with the swiftness of a striking snake buried his fangs in the jugular of the Tor-o-don. At the same instant the creature's tail coiled about his own throat and then commenced a battle royal of turning and twisting bodies as each sought to dislodge the fatal hold of the other, but the acts of the ape-man were guided by a human brain and thus it was that the rolling bodies rolled in the direction that Tarzan wished— toward the edge of the recess.

The choking tail had shut the air from his lungs, he knew that his gasping lips were parted and his tongue protruding; and now his brain reeled and his sight grew dim; but not before he reached his goal and a quick hand shot out to seize the knife that now lay within reach as the two bodies tottered perilously upon the brink of the chasm.

With all his remaining strength the ape-man drove home the blade—once, twice, thrice, and then all went black before him as he felt himself, still in the clutches of the Tor-o-don, topple from the recess.

Fortunate it was for Tarzan that Pan-at-lee had not obeyed his injunction to make good her escape while he engaged the Tor-o-don, for it was to this fact that he owed his life. Close beside the struggling forms during the brief moments of the terrific climax she had realized every detail of the danger to Tarzan with which the emergency was fraught and as she saw the two rolling over the outer edge of the niche she seized the ape-man by an ankle at the same time throwing herself prone upon the rocky floor. The muscles of the Tor-o-don relaxed in death with the last thrust of Tarzan's knife and with its hold upon the ape-man released it shot from sight into the gorge below.

It was with infinite difficulty that Pan-at-lee retained her hold upon the ankle of her protector, but she did so and then, slowly, she sought to drag the dead weight back to the safety of the niche. This, however, was beyond her strength and she could but hold on tightly, hoping that some plan would suggest itself before her powers of endurance failed. She wondered if, after all, the creature was already dead, but that she could not bring herself to believe—and if not dead how long it would be before he regained consciousness. If he did not regain it soon he never would regain it, that she knew, for she felt her fingers numbing to the strain upon them and slipping, slowly, slowly, from their hold. It was then that Tarzan regained consciousness. He could not know what power upheld him, but he felt that whatever it was it was slowly releasing its hold upon his ankle. Within easy reach of his hands were two pegs and these he seized upon just as Pan-at-lee's fingers slipped from their hold.

As it was he came near to being precipitated into the gorge—only his great strength saved him. He was upright now and his feet found other pegs. His first thought was of his foe. Where was he? Waiting above there to finish him? Tarzan looked up just as the frightened face of Pan-at-lee appeared over the threshold of the recess.

"You live?" she cried.

"Yes," replied Tarzan. "Where is the shaggy one?"

Pan-at-lee pointed downward. "There," she said, "dead."

"Good!" exclaimed the ape-man, clambering to her side. "You are unharmed?" he asked.

"You came just in time," replied Pan-at-lee; "but who are you and how did you know that I was here and what do you know of Om-at and where did you come from and what did you mean by calling Om-at, gund?"

"Wait, wait," cried Tarzan; "one at a time. My, but you are all alike—the shes of the tribe of Kerchak, the ladies of England, and their sisters of Pal-ul-don. Have patience and I will try to tell you all that you wish to know. Four of us set out with Om-at from Kor-ul-Ja to search for you. We were attacked by the Kor-ul-lul and separated. I was taken prisoner, but escaped. Again I stumbled upon your trail and followed it, reaching the summit of this cliff just as the hairy one was climbing up after you. I was coming to investigate when I heard your scream—the rest you know."

"But you called Om-at, gund of Kor-ul-Ja," she insisted. "Es-sat is gund."

"Es-sat is dead," explained the ape-man. "Om-at slew him and now Om-at is gund. Om-at came back seeking you. He found Es-sat in your cave and killed him."

"Yes," said the girl, "Es-sat came to my cave and I struck him down with my golden breastplates and escaped."

"And a lion pursued you," continued Tarzan, "and you leaped from the cliff into Kor-ul-lul, but why you were not killed is beyond me."

"Is there anything beyond you?" exclaimed Pan-at-lee. "How could you know that a lion pursued me and that I leaped from the cliff and not know that it was the pool of deep water below that saved me?"

"I would have known that, too, had not the Kor-ul-lul come then and prevented me continuing upon your trail. But now I would ask you a question—by what name do you call the thing with which I just fought?"

"It was a Tor-o-don," she replied. "I have seen but one before. They are terrible creatures with the cunning of man and the ferocity of a beast. Great indeed must be the warrior who slays one single-handed." She gazed at him in open admiration.

"And now," said Tarzan, "you must sleep, for tomorrow we shall return to Kor-ul-Ja and Om-at, and I doubt that you have had much rest these two nights."

Pan-at-lee, lulled by a feeling of security, slept peacefully into the morning while Tarzan stretched himself upon the hard floor of the recess just outside her cave.

The sun was high in the heavens when he awoke; for two hours it had looked down upon another heroic figure miles away—the figure of a godlike man fighting his way through the hideous morass that lies like a filthy moat defending Pal-ul-don from the creatures of the outer world. Now waist deep in the sucking ooze, now menaced by loathsome reptiles, the man advanced only by virtue of Herculean efforts gaining laboriously by inches along the devious way that he was forced to choose in selecting the least precarious footing. Near the center of the morass was open water—slimy, green-hued water. He reached it at last after more than two hours of such effort as would have left an ordinary man spent and dying in the sticky mud, yet he was less than halfway across the marsh. Greasy with slime and mud was his smooth, brown hide, and greasy with slime and mud was his beloved Enfield that had shone so brightly in the first rays of the rising sun.

He paused a moment upon the edge of the open water and then throwing himself forward struck out to swim across. He swam with long, easy, powerful strokes calculated less for speed than for endurance, for his was, primarily, a test of the latter, since beyond the open water was another two hours or more of gruelling effort between it and solid ground. He was, perhaps, halfway across and congratulating himself upon the ease of the achievement of this portion of his task when there arose from the depths directly in his path a hideous reptile, which, with wide-distended jaws, bore down upon him, hissing shrilly.

Tarzan arose and stretched, expanded his great chest and drank in deep draughts of the fresh morning air. His clear eyes scanned the wondrous beauties of the landscape spread out before them. Directly below lay Kor-ul-*gryf*, a dense, somber green of gently moving tree tops. To Tarzan it was neither grim, nor forbidding—it was jungle, beloved jungle. To his right there spread a panorama of the lower reaches of the Valley of Jad-ben-Otho, with its winding streams and its blue lakes. Gleaming whitely in the sunlight were scattered groups of dwellings—the feudal strongholds of the lesser chiefs of the Ho-don. A-lur, the City of Light, he could not see as it was hidden by the shoulder of the cliff in which the deserted village lay.

For a moment Tarzan gave himself over to that spiritual enjoyment of beauty that only the man-mind may attain and then Nature asserted herself and the belly of the beast called aloud that it was hungry. Again Tarzan looked down at Kor-ul-*gryf*. There was the jungle! Grew there a jungle that would not feed Tarzan? The ape-man smiled and commenced the descent to the gorge. Was there danger there? Of course. Who knew it better than Tarzan? In all jungles lies death, for life and death go hand in hand and where life teems death reaps his fullest harvest. Never had Tarzan met a creature of the jungle with which he could not cope—sometimes by virtue of brute strength alone, again by a combination of brute strength and the cunning of the man-mind; but Tarzan had never met a *gryf*.

He had heard the bellowings in the gorge the night before after he had lain down to sleep and he had meant to ask Pan-at-lee this morning what manner of beast so disturbed the slumbers of its betters. He reached the foot of the cliff and strode into the jungle and here he halted, his keen eyes and ears watchful and alert, his sensitive nostrils searching each shifting air current for the scent spoor of game. Again he advanced deeper into the .wood, his light step giving forth no sound, his bow and arrows in readiness. A light morning breeze was blowing from up the gorge and in this direction he bent his steps. Many odors impinged upon his organs of scent. Some of these he classified without effort, but others were strange—the odors of beasts and of birds, of trees and shrubs and flowers with which he was unfamiliar. He sensed faintly the reptilian odor that he had learned to connect with the strange, nocturnal forms that had loomed dim and bulky on several occasions since his introduction to Pal-ul-don.

And then, suddenly he caught plainly the strong, sweet odor of Bara, the deer. Were the belly vocal, Tarzan's would have given a little cry of joy, for it loved the flesh of Bara. The ape-man moved rapidly, but cautiously forward. The prey was not far distant and as the hunter approached it, he took silently to the trees and still in his nostrils was the faint reptilian odor that spoke of a great creature which he had never yet seen except as a denser shadow among the dense shadows of the night; but the odor was of such a faintness as suggests to the jungle bred the distance of absolute safety.

And now, moving noiselessly, Tarzan came within sight of Bara drinking at a pool where the stream that waters Kor-ul-*gryf* crosses an open place in the jungle. The deer was too far from the nearest tree to risk a charge, so the ape-man must depend upon the accuracy and force of his first arrow, which must drop the deer in its tracks or forfeit both deer and shaft. Far back came the right hand and the bow, that you or I might not move, bent easily beneath the muscles of the forest god. There was a singing twang and Bara, leaping high in air, collapsed upon the ground, an arrow through his heart. Tarzan dropped to earth and ran to his kill, lest the animal might even yet rise and escape; but Bara was safely dead. As Tarzan stooped to lift it to his shoulder there fell upon his ears a thunderous bellow that seemed almost at his right elbow, and as his eyes shot in the direction of the sound, there broke upon his vision such a creature as paleontologists have dreamed as having possibly existed in the dimmest vistas of Earth's infancy—a gigantic creature, vibrant with mad rage, that charged, bellowing, upon him.

When Pan-at-lee awoke she looked out upon the niche in search of Tarzan. He was not there. She sprang to her feet and rushed out, looking down into Kor-ul-*gryf* guessing that he had gone down in search of food and there she caught a glimpse of him disappearing into the forest. For an instant she was panic-stricken. She knew that he was a stranger in Pal-ul-don and that, so, he might not realize the dangers that lay in that gorge of terror. Why did she not call to him to return? You or I might have done so, but no Pal-ul-don, for they know the ways of the *gryf*—they know the weak eyes and the keen ears, and that at the sound of a human voice they come. To have called to Tarzan, then, would but have been to invite disaster and so she did not call. Instead, afraid though she was, she descended into the gorge for the purpose of overhauling Tarzan and warning him in whispers of his danger. It was a brave act, since it was performed in the face of countless ages of inherited fear of the creatures that she might be called upon to face. Men have been decorated for less.

Pan-at-lee, descended from a long line of hunters, assumed that Tarzan would move up wind and in this direction she sought his tracks, which she soon found well marked, since he had made no effort to conceal them. She moved rapidly until she reached the point at which Tarzan had taken to the trees. Of course she knew what had happened; since her own people were semi-arboreal; but she could not track him through the trees, having no such well-developed sense of scent as he.

She could but hope that he had continued on up wind and in this direction she moved, her heart pounding in terror against her ribs, her eyes glancing first in one direction and then another. She had reached the edge of a clearing when two things happened—she caught sight of Tarzan bending over a dead deer and at the same instant a deafening roar sounded almost beside her. It terrified her beyond description, but it brought no paralysis of fear. Instead it galvanized her into instant action with the result that Pan-at-lee swarmed up the nearest tree to the very loftiest branch that would sustain her weight. Then she looked down.

The thing that Tarzan saw charging him when the warning bellow attracted his surprised eyes loomed terrifically monstrous before him—monstrous and awe-inspiring; but it did not terrify Tarzan, it only angered him, for he saw that it was beyond even his powers to combat and that meant that it might cause him to lose his kill, and Tarzan was hungry. There was but a single alternative to remaining for annihilation and that was flight—swift and immediate. And Tarzan fled, but he carried the carcass of Bara, the deer, with him. He had not more than a dozen paces start, but on the other hand the nearest tree was almost as close. His greatest danger lay, he imagined, in the great, towering height of the creature pursuing him, for even though he reached the tree he would have to climb high in an incredibly short time as, unless appearances were deceiving, the thing could reach up and pluck him down from any branch under thirty feet above the ground, and possibly from those up to fifty feet, if it reared up on its hind legs.

But Tarzan was no sluggard and though the *gryf* was incredibly fast despite its great bulk, it was no match for Tarzan, and when it comes to climbing, the little monkeys gaze with envy upon the feats of the ape-man. And so it was that the bellowing *gryf* came to a baffled stop at the foot of the tree and even though he reared up and sought to seize his prey among the branches, as Tarzan had guessed he might, he failed in this also. And then, well out of reach, Tarzan came to a stop and there, just above him, he saw Pan-at-lee sitting, wide-eyed and trembling.

"How came you here?" he asked.

She told him. "You came to warn me!" he said. "It was very brave and unselfish of you. I am chagrined that I should have been thus surprised. The creature was up wind from me and yet I did not sense its near presence until it charged. I cannot understand it."

"It is not strange," said Pan-at-lee. "That is one of the peculiarities of the *gryf*—it is said that man never knows of its presence until it is upon him—so silently does it move despite its great size."

"But I should have smelled it," cried Tarzan, disgustedly.

"Smelled it!" ejaculated Pan-at-lee. "Smelled it?"

"Certainly. How do you suppose I found this deer so quickly? And I sensed the *gryf*, too, but faintly as at a great distance." Tarzan suddenly ceased speaking and looked down at the bellowing creature below them—his nostrils quivered as though searching for a scent. "Ah!" he exclaimed. "I have it!"

"What?" asked Pan-at-lee.

"I was deceived because the creature gives off practically no odor," explained the ape-man. "What I smelled was the faint aroma that doubtless permeates the entire jungle because of the long presence of many of the creatures—it is the sort of odor that would remain for a long time, faint as it is.

"Pan-at-lee, did you ever hear of a triceratops? No? Well this thing that you call a *gryf* is a triceratops and it has been extinct for hundreds of thousands of years. I have seen its skeleton in the museum in London and a figure of one restored. I always thought that the scientists who did such work depended principally upon an overwrought imagination, but I see that I was wrong. This living thing is not an exact counterpart of the restoration that I saw; but it is so similar as to be easily recognizable, and then, too, we must remember that during the ages that have elapsed since the paleontologist's specimen lived many changes might have been wrought by evolution in the living line that has quite evidently persisted in Pal-ul-don."

"Triceratops, London, paleo—I don't know what you are talking about," cried Pan-at-lee.

Tarzan smiled and threw a piece of dead wood at the face of the angry creature below them. Instantly the great bony hood over the neck was erected and a mad bellow rolled upward from the gigantic body. Full twenty feet at the shoulder the thing stood, a dirty slate-blue in color except for its yellow face with the blue bands encircling the eyes, the red hood with the yellow lining and the yellow belly. The three parallel lines of bony protuberances down the back gave a further touch of color to the body, those following the line of the spine being red, while those on either side are yellow. The five- and three-toed hoofs of the ancient horned dinosaurs had become talons in the *gryf*, but the three horns, two large ones above the eyes and a median horn on the nose, had persisted through all the ages. Weird and terrible as was its appearance Tarzan could not but admire the mighty creature looming big below him, its seventy-five feet of length majestically typifying those things which all his life the ape-man had admired—courage and strength. In that massive tail alone was the strength of an elephant.

The wicked little eyes looked up at him and the horny beak opened to disclose a full set of powerful teeth.

"Herbivorous!" murmured the ape-man. "Your ancestors may have been, but not you," and then to Pan-at-lee: "Let us go now. At the cave we will have deer meat and then—back to Kor-ul-Ja and Om-at."

The girl shuddered. "Go?" she repeated. "We will never go from here."

"Why not?" asked Tarzan.

For answer she but pointed to the *gryf*.

"Nonsense!" exclaimed the man. "It cannot climb. We can reach the cliff through the trees and be back in the cave before it knows what has become of us."

"You do not know the *gryf*," replied Pan-at-lee gloomily.

"Wherever we go it will follow and always it will be ready at the foot of each tree when we would descend. It will never give us up."

"We can live in the trees for a long time if necessary," replied Tarzan, "and sometime the thing will leave."

The girl shook her head. "Never," she said, "and then there are the Tor-o-don. They will come and kill us and after eating a little will throw the balance to the *gryf*—the *gryf* and Tor-o-don are friends, because the Tor-o-don shares his food with the *gryf*."

"You may be right," said Tarzan; "but even so I don't intend waiting here for someone to come along and eat part of me and then feed the balance to that beast below. If I don't get out of this place whole it won't be my fault. Come along now and we'll make a try at it," and so saying he moved off through the tree tops with Pan-at-lee close behind. Below them, on the ground, moved the horned dinosaur and when they reached the edge of the forest where there lay fifty yards of open ground to cross to the foot of the cliff he was there with them, at the bottom of the tree, waiting.

Tarzan looked ruefully down and scratched his head.

CHAPTER VII—JUNGLE CRAFT

Presently he looked up and at Pan-at-lee. "Can you cross the gorge through the trees very rapidly?" he questioned.

"Alone?" she asked.

"No," replied Tarzan.

"I can follow wherever you can lead," she said then.

"Across and back again?"

"Yes."

"Then come, and do exactly as I bid." He started back again through the trees, swiftly, swinging monkey-like from limb to limb, following a zigzag course that he tried to select with an eye for the difficulties of the trail beneath. Where the underbrush was heaviest, where fallen trees blocked the way, he led the footsteps of the creature below them; but all to no avail. When they reached the opposite side of the gorge the *gryf* was with them.

"Back again," said Tarzan, and, turning, the two retraced their high-flung way through the upper terraces of the ancient forest of Kor-ul-*gryf*. But the result was the same—no, not quite; it was worse, for another *gryf* had joined the first and now two waited beneath the tree in which they stopped.

The cliff looming high above them with its innumerable cave mouths seemed to beckon and to taunt them. It was so near, yet eternity yawned between. The body of the Tor-o-don lay at the cliff's foot where it had fallen. It was in plain view of the two in the tree. One of the gryfs walked over and sniffed about it, but did not offer to devour it. Tarzan had examined it casually as he had passed earlier in the morning. He guessed that it represented either a very high order of ape or a very low order of man—something akin to the Java man, perhaps; a truer example of the pithecanthropi than either the Ho-don or the Waz-don; possibly the precursor of them both. As his eyes wandered idly over the scene below his active brain was working out the details of the plan that he had made to permit Pan-at-lee's escape from the gorge. His thoughts were interrupted by a strange cry from above them in the gorge.

"Whee-oo! Whee-oo!" it sounded, coming closer.

The gryfs below raised their heads and looked in the direction of the interruption. One of them made a low, rumbling sound in its throat. It was not a bellow and it did not indicate anger. Immediately the "Whee-oo!" responded. The gryfs repeated the rumbling and at intervals the "Whee-oo!" was repeated, coming ever closer.

Tarzan looked at Pan-at-lee. "What is it?" he asked.

"I do not know," she replied. "Perhaps a strange bird, or another horrid beast that dwells in this frightful place."

"Ah," exclaimed Tarzan; "there it is. Look!"

Pan-at-lee voiced a cry of despair. "A Tor-o-don!"

The creature, walking erect and carrying a stick in one hand, advanced at a slow, lumbering gait. It walked directly toward the gryfs who moved aside, as though afraid. Tarzan watched intently. The Tor-o-don was now quite close to one of the triceratops. It swung its head and snapped at him viciously. Instantly the Tor-o-don sprang in and commenced to belabor the huge beast across the face with his stick. To the ape-man's amazement the *gryf*, that might have annihilated the comparatively puny Tor-o-don instantly in any of a dozen ways, cringed like a whipped cur.

"Whee-oo! Whee-oo!" shouted the Tor-o-don and the *gryf* came slowly toward him. A whack on the median horn brought it to a stop. Then the Tor-o-don walked around behind it, clambered up its tail and seated himself astraddle of the huge back. "Whee-oo!" he shouted and prodded the beast with a sharp point of his stick. The *gryf* commenced to move off.

So rapt had Tarzan been in the scene below him that he had given no thought to escape, for he realized that for him and Pan-at-lee time had in these brief moments turned back countless ages to spread before their eyes a page of the dim and distant past. They two had looked upon the first man and his primitive beasts of burden.

And now the ridden *gryf* halted and looked up at them, bellowing. It was sufficient. The creature had warned its master of their presence. Instantly the Tor-o-don urged the beast close beneath the tree which held them, at the same time leaping to his feet upon the horny back. Tarzan saw the bestial face, the great fangs, the mighty muscles. From the loins of such had sprung the human race—and only from such could it have sprung, for only such as this might have survived the horrid dangers of the age that was theirs.

The Tor-o-don beat upon his breast and growled horribly—hideous, uncouth, beastly. Tarzan rose to his full height upon a swaying branch—straight and beautiful as a demigod—unspoiled by the taint of civilization—a perfect specimen of what the human race might have been had the laws of man not interfered with the laws of nature.

The Present fitted an arrow to his bow and drew the shaft far back. The Past basing its claims upon brute strength sought to reach the other and drag him down; but the loosed arrow sank deep into the savage heart and the Past sank back into the oblivion that had claimed his kind.

"Tarzan-jad-guru!" murmured Pan-at-lee, unknowingly giving him out of the fullness of her admiration the same title that the warriors of her tribe had bestowed upon him.

The ape-man turned to her. "Pan-at-lee," he said, "these beasts may keep us treed here indefinitely. I doubt if we can escape together, but I have a plan. You remain here, hiding yourself in the foliage, while I start back across the gorge in sight of them and yelling to attract their attention. Unless they have more brains than I suspect they will follow me. When they are gone you make for the cliff. Wait for me in the cave not longer than today. If I do not come by tomorrow's sun you will have to start back for Kor-ul-Ja alone. Here is a joint of deer meat for you." He had severed one of the deer's hind legs and this he passed up to her.

"I cannot desert you," she said simply; "it is not the way of my people to desert a friend and ally. Om-at would never forgive me."

"Tell Om-at that I commanded you to go," replied Tarzan.

"It is a command?" she asked.

"It is! Good-bye, Pan-at-lee. Hasten back to Om-at—you are a fitting mate for the chief of Kor-ul-Ja." He moved off slowly through the trees.

"Good-bye, Tarzan-jad-guru!" she called after him. "Fortunate are my Om-at and his Pan-at-lee in owning such a friend."

Tarzan, shouting aloud, continued upon his way and the great gryfs, lured by his voice, followed beneath. His ruse was evidently proving successful and he was filled with elation as he led the bellowing beasts farther and farther from Pan-at-lee. He hoped that she would take advantage of the opportunity afforded her for escape, yet at the same time he was filled with concern as to her ability to survive the dangers which lay between Kor-ul-*gryf* and Kor-ul-Ja. There were lions and Tor-o-dons and the unfriendly tribe of Kor-ul-lul to hinder her progress, though the distance in itself to the cliffs of her people was not great.

He realized her bravery and understood the resourcefulness that she must share in common with all primitive people who, day by day, must contend face to face with nature's law of the survival of the fittest, unaided by any of the numerous artificial protections that civilization has thrown around its brood of weaklings.

Several times during this crossing of the gorge Tarzan endeavored to outwit his keen pursuers, but all to no avail. Double as he would he could not throw them off his track and ever as he changed his course they changed theirs to conform. Along the verge of the forest upon the southeastern side of the gorge he sought some point at which the trees touched some negotiable portion of the cliff, but though he traveled far both up and down the gorge he discovered no such easy avenue of escape. The ape-man finally commenced to entertain an idea of the hopelessness of his case and to realize to the full why the Kor-ul-*gryf* had been religiously abjured by the races of Pal-ul-don for all these many ages.

Night was falling and though since early morning he had sought diligently a way out of this cul-de-sac he was no nearer to liberty than at the moment the first bellowing *gryf* had charged him as he stooped over the carcass of his kill: but with the falling of night came renewed hope for, in common with the great cats, Tarzan was, to a greater or lesser extent, a nocturnal beast. It is true he could not see by night as well as they, but that lack was largely recompensed for by the keenness of his scent and the highly developed sensitiveness of his other organs of perception. As the blind follow and interpret their Braille characters with deft fingers, so Tarzan reads the book of the jungle with feet and hands and eyes and ears and nose; each contributing its share to the quick and accurate translation of the text.

But again he was doomed to be thwarted by one vital weakness—he did not know the *gryf*, and before the night was over he wondered if the things never slept, for wheresoever he moved they moved also, and always they barred his road to liberty. Finally, just before dawn, he relinquished his immediate effort and sought rest in a friendly tree crotch in the safety of the middle terrace.

Once again was the sun high when Tarzan awoke, rested and refreshed. Keen to the necessities of the moment he made no effort to locate his jailers lest in the act he might apprise them of his movements. Instead he sought cautiously and silently to melt away among the foliage of the trees. His first move, however, was heralded by a deep bellow from below.

Among the numerous refinements of civilization that Tarzan had failed to acquire was that of profanity, and possibly it is to be regretted since there are circumstances under which it is at least a relief to pent emotion. And it may be that in effect Tarzan resorted to profanity if there can be physical as well as vocal swearing, since immediately the bellow announced that his hopes had been again frustrated, he turned quickly and seeing the hideous face of the *gryf* below him seized a large fruit from a nearby branch and hurled it viciously at the horned snout. The missile struck full between the creature's eyes, resulting in a reaction that surprised the ape-man; it did not arouse the beast to a show of revengeful rage as Tarzan had expected and hoped; instead the creature gave a single vicious side snap at the fruit as it bounded from his skull and then turned sulkily away, walking off a few steps.

There was that in the act that recalled immediately to Tarzan's mind similar action on the preceding day when the Tor-o-don had struck one of the creatures across the face with his staff, and instantly there sprung to the cunning and courageous brain a plan of escape from his predicament that might have blanched the cheek of the most heroic.

The gambling instinct is not strong among creatures of the wild; the chances of their daily life are sufficient stimuli for the beneficial excitement of their nerve centers. It has remained for civilized man, protected in a measure from the natural dangers of existence, to invent artificial stimulants in the form of cards and dice and roulette wheels. Yet when necessity bids there are no greater gamblers than the savage denizens of the jungle, the forest, and the hills, for as lightly as you roll the ivory cubes upon the green cloth they will gamble with death—their own lives the stake.

And so Tarzan would gamble now, pitting the seemingly wild deductions of his shrewd brain against all the proofs of the bestial ferocity of his antagonists that his experience of them had adduced—against all the age-old folklore and legend that had been handed down for countless generations and passed on to him through the lips of Pan-at-lee.

Yet as he worked in preparation for the greatest play that man can make in the game of life, he smiled; nor was there any indication of haste or excitement or nervousness in his demeanor.

First he selected a long, straight branch about two inches in diameter at its base. This he cut from the tree with his knife, removed the smaller branches and twigs until he had fashioned a pole about ten feet in length. This he sharpened at the smaller end. The staff finished to his satisfaction he looked down upon the triceratops.

"Whee-oo!" he cried.

Instantly the beasts raised their heads and looked at him. From the throat of one of them came faintly a low rumbling sound.

"Whee-oo!" repeated Tarzan and hurled the balance of the carcass of the deer to them.

Instantly the gryfs fell upon it with much bellowing, one of them attempting to seize it and keep it from the other: but finally the second obtained a hold and an instant later it had been torn asunder and greedily devoured. Once again they looked up at the ape-man and this time they saw him descending to the ground.

One of them started toward him. Again Tarzan repeated the weird cry of the Tor-o-don. The *gryf* halted in his track, apparently puzzled, while Tarzan slipped lightly to the earth and advanced toward the nearer beast, his staff raised menacingly and the call of the first-man upon his lips.

Would the cry be answered by the low rumbling of the beast of burden or the horrid bellow of the man-eater? Upon the answer to this question hung the fate of the ape-man.

Pan-at-lee was listening intently to the sounds of the departing gryfs as Tarzan led them cunningly from her, and when she was sure that they were far enough away to insure her safe retreat she dropped swiftly from the branches to the ground and sped like a frightened deer across the open space to the foot of the cliff, stepped over the body of the Tor-o-don who had attacked her the night before and was soon climbing rapidly up the ancient stone pegs of the deserted cliff village. In the mouth of the cave near that which she had occupied she kindled a fire and cooked the haunch of venison that Tarzan had left her, and from one of the trickling streams that ran down the face of the escarpment she obtained water to satisfy her thirst.

All day she waited, hearing in the distance, and sometimes close at hand, the bellowing of the gryfs which pursued the strange creature that had dropped so miraculously into her life. For him she felt the same keen, almost fanatical loyalty that many another had experienced for Tarzan of the Apes. Beast and human, he had held them to him with bonds that were stronger than steel—those of them that were clean and courageous, and the weak and the helpless; but never could Tarzan claim among his admirers the coward, the ingrate or the scoundrel; from such, both man and beast, he had won fear and hatred.

To Pan-at-lee he was all that was brave and noble and heroic and, too, he was Om-at's friend—the friend of the man she loved. For any one of these reasons Pan-at-lee would have died for Tarzan, for such is the loyalty of the simple-minded children of nature. It has remained for civilization to teach us to weigh the relative rewards of loyalty and its antithesis. The loyalty of the primitive is spontaneous, unreasoning, unselfish and such was the loyalty of Pan-at-lee for the Tarmangani.

And so it was that she waited that day and night, hoping that he would return that she might accompany him back to Om-at, for her experience had taught her that in the face of danger two have a better chance than one. But Tarzan-jad-guru had not come, and so upon the following morning Pan-at-lee set out upon her return to Kor-ul-Ja.

She knew the dangers and yet she faced them with the stolid indifference of her race. When they directly confronted and menaced her would be time enough to experience fear or excitement or confidence. In the meantime it was unnecessary to waste nerve energy by anticipating them. She moved therefore through her savage land with no greater show of concern than might mark your sauntering to a corner drug-store for a sundae. But this is your life and that is Pan-at-lee's and even now as you read this Pan-at-lee may be sitting upon the edge of the recess of Om-at's cave while the *Ja* and *Jato* roar from the gorge below and from the ridge above, and the Kor-ul-lul threaten upon the south and the Ho-don from the Valley of Jad-ben-Otho far below, for Pan-at-lee still lives and preens her silky coat of jet beneath the tropical moonlight of Pal-ul-don.

But she was not to reach Kor-ul-Ja this day, nor the next, nor for many days after though the danger that threatened her was neither Waz-don enemy nor savage beast.

She came without misadventure to the Kor-ul-lul and after descending its rocky southern wall without catching the slightest glimpse of the hereditary enemies of her people, she experienced a renewal of confidence that was little short of practical assurance that she would successfully terminate her venture and be restored once more to her own people and the lover she had not seen for so many long and weary moons.

She was almost across the gorge now and moving with an extreme caution abated no wit by her confidence, for wariness is an instinctive trait of the primitive, something which cannot be laid aside even momentarily if one would survive. And so she came to the trail that follows the windings of Kor-ul-lul from its uppermost reaches down into the broad and fertile Valley of Jad-ben-Otho.

And as she stepped into the trail there arose on either side of her from out of the bushes that border the path, as though materialized from thin air, a score of tall, white warriors of the Ho-don. Like a frightened deer Pan-at-lee cast a single startled look at these menacers of her freedom and leaped quickly toward the bushes in an effort to escape; but the warriors were too close at hand. They closed upon her from every side and then, drawing her knife she turned at bay, metamorphosed by the fires of fear and hate from a startled deer to a raging tiger-cat. They did not try to kill her, but only to subdue and capture her; and so it was that more than a single Ho-don warrior felt the keen edge of her blade in his flesh before they had succeeded in overpowering her by numbers. And still she fought and scratched and bit after they had taken the knife from her until it was necessary to tie her hands and fasten a piece of wood between her teeth by means of thongs passed behind her head.

At first she refused to walk when they started off in the direction of the valley but after two of them had seized her by the hair and dragged her for a number of yards she thought better of her original decision and came along with them, though still as defiant as her bound wrists and gagged mouth would permit.

Near the entrance to Kor-ul-lul they came upon another body of their warriors with which were several Waz-don prisoners from the tribe of Kor-ul-lul. It was a raiding party come up from a Ho-don city of the valley after slaves. This Pan-at-lee knew for the occurrence was by no means unusual. During her lifetime the tribe to which she belonged had been sufficiently fortunate, or powerful, to withstand successfully the majority of such raids made upon them, but yet Pan-at-lee had known of friends and relatives who had been carried into slavery by the Ho-don and she knew, too, another thing which gave her hope, as doubtless it did to each of the other captives— that occasionally the prisoners escaped from the cities of the hairless whites.

After they had joined the other party the entire band set forth into the valley and presently, from the conversation of her captors, Pan-at-lee knew that she was headed for A-lur, the City of Light; while in the cave of his ancestors, Om-at, chief of the Kor-ul-Ja, bemoaned the loss of both his friend and she that was to have been his mate.

CHAPTER VIII—A-LUR

As the hissing reptile bore down upon the stranger swimming in the open water near the center of the morass on the frontier of Pal-ul-don it seemed to the man that this indeed must be the futile termination of an arduous and danger-filled journey. It seemed, too, equally futile to pit his puny knife against this frightful creature. Had he been attacked on land it is possible that he might as a last resort have used his Enfield, though he had come thus far through all these weary, danger-ridden miles without recourse to it, though again and again had his life hung in the balance in the face of the savage denizens of forest, jungle, and steppe. For whatever it may have been for which he was preserving his precious ammunition he evidently held it more sacred even than his life, for as yet he had not used a single round and now the decision was not required of him, since it would have been impossible for him to have unslung his Enfield, loaded and fired with the necessary celerity while swimming.

Though his chance for survival seemed slender, and hope at its lowest ebb, he was not minded therefore to give up without a struggle. Instead he drew his blade and awaited the oncoming reptile. The creature was like no living thing he ever before had seen although possibly it resembled a crocodile in some respects more than it did anything with which he was familiar.

As this frightful survivor of some extinct progenitor charged upon him with distended jaws there came to the man quickly a full consciousness of the futility of endeavoring to stay the mad rush or pierce the armor-coated hide with his little knife. The thing was almost upon him now and whatever form of defense he chose must be made quickly. There seemed but a single alternative to instant death, and this he took at almost the instant the great reptile towered directly above him.

With the celerity of a seal he dove headforemost beneath the oncoming body and at the same instant, turning upon his back, he plunged his blade into the soft, cold surface of the slimy belly as the momentum of the hurtling reptile carried it swiftly over him; and then with powerful strokes he swam on beneath the surface for a dozen yards before he rose. A glance showed him the stricken monster plunging madly in pain and rage upon the surface of the water behind him. That it was writhing in its death agonies was evidenced by the fact that it made no effort to pursue him, and so, to the accompaniment of the shrill screaming of the dying monster, the man won at last to the farther edge of the open water to take up once more the almost superhuman effort of crossing the last stretch of clinging mud which separated him from the solid ground of Pal-ul-don.

A good two hours it took him to drag his now weary body through the clinging, stinking muck, but at last, mud covered and spent, he dragged himself out upon the soft grasses of the bank. A hundred yards away a stream, winding its way down from the distant mountains, emptied into the morass, and, after a short rest, he made his way to this and seeking a quiet pool, bathed himself and washed the mud and slime from his weapons, accouterments, and loin cloth. Another hour was spent beneath the rays of the hot sun in wiping, polishing, and oiling his Enfield though the means at hand for drying it consisted principally of dry grasses. It was afternoon before he had satisfied himself that his precious weapon was safe from any harm by dirt, or dampness, and then he arose and took up the search for the spoor he had followed to the opposite side of the swamp.

Would he find again the trail that had led into the opposite side of the morass, to be lost there, even to his trained senses? If he found it not again upon this side of the almost impassable barrier he might assume that his long journey had ended in failure. And so he sought up and down the verge of the stagnant water for traces of an old spoor that would have been invisible to your eyes or mine, even had we followed directly in the tracks of its maker.

As Tarzan advanced upon the gryfs he imitated as closely as he could recall them the methods and mannerisms of the Tor-o-don, but up to the instant that he stood close beside one of the huge creatures he realized that his fate still hung in the balance, for the thing gave forth no sign, either menacing or otherwise. It only stood there, watching him out of its cold, reptilian eyes and then Tarzan raised his staff and with a menacing "Whee-oo!" struck the *gryf* a vicious blow across the face.

The creature made a sudden side snap in his direction, a snap that did not reach him, and then turned sullenly away, precisely as it had when the Tor-o-don commanded it. Walking around to its rear as he had seen the shaggy first-man do, Tarzan ran up the broad tail and seated himself upon the creature's back, and then again imitating the acts of the Tor-o-don he prodded it with the sharpened point of his staff, and thus goading it forward and guiding it with blows, first upon one side and then upon the other, he started it down the gorge in the direction of the valley.

At first it had been in his mind only to determine if he could successfully assert any authority over the great monsters, realizing that in this possibility lay his only hope of immediate escape from his jailers. But once seated upon the back of his titanic mount the ape-man experienced the sensation of a new thrill that recalled to him the day in his boyhood that he had first clambered to the broad head of Tantor, the elephant, and this, together with the sense of mastery that was always meat and drink to the lord of the jungle, decided him to put his newly acquired power to some utilitarian purpose.

Pan-at-lee he judged must either have already reached safety or met with death. At least, no longer could he be of service to her, while below Kor-ul-*gryf*, in the soft green valley, lay A-lur, the City of Light, which, since he had gazed upon it from the shoulder of Pastar-ul-ved, had been his ambition and his goal.

Whether or not its gleaming walls held the secret of his lost mate he could not even guess but if she lived at all within the precincts of Pal-ul-don it must be among the Ho-don, since the hairy black men of this forgotten world took no prisoners. And so to A-lur he would go, and how more effectively than upon the back of this grim and terrible creature that the races of Pal-ul-don held in such awe?

A little mountain stream tumbles down from Kor-ul-*gryf* to be joined in the foothills with that which empties the waters of Kor-ul-lul into the valley, forming a small river which runs southwest, eventually entering the valley's largest lake at the City of A-lur, through the center of which the stream passes. An ancient trail, well marked by countless generations of naked feet of man and beast, leads down toward A-lur beside the river, and along this Tarzan guided the *gryf*. Once clear of the forest which ran below the mouth of the gorge, Tarzan caught occasional glimpses of the city gleaming in the distance far below him.

The country through which he passed was resplendent with the riotous beauties of tropical verdure. Thick, lush grasses grew waist high upon either side of the trail and the way was broken now and again by patches of open park-like forest, or perhaps a little patch of dense jungle where the trees overarched the way and trailing creepers depended in graceful loops from branch to branch.

At times the ape-man had difficulty in commanding obedience upon the part of his unruly beast, but always in the end its fear of the relatively puny goad urged it on to obedience. Late in the afternoon as they approached the confluence of the stream they were skirting and another which appeared to come from the direction of Kor-ul-Ja the ape-man, emerging from one of the jungle patches, discovered a considerable party of Ho-don upon the opposite bank. Simultaneously they saw him and the mighty creature he bestrode. For a moment they stood in wide-eyed amazement and then, in answer to the command of their leader, they turned and bolted for the shelter of the nearby wood.

The ape-man had but a brief glimpse of them but it was sufficient indication that there were Waz-don with them, doubtless prisoners taken in one of the raids upon the Waz-don villages of which Ta-den and Om-at had told him.

At the sound of their voices the *gryf* had bellowed terrifically and started in pursuit even though a river intervened, but by dint of much prodding and beating, Tarzan had succeeded in heading the animal back into the path though thereafter for a long time it was sullen and more intractable than ever.

As the sun dropped nearer the summit of the western hills Tarzan became aware that his plan to enter A-lur upon the back of a *gryf* was likely doomed to failure, since the stubbornness of the great beast was increasing momentarily, doubtless due to the fact that its huge belly was crying out for food. The ape-man wondered if the Tor-o-dons had any means of picketing their beasts for the night, but as he did not know and as no plan suggested itself, he determined that he should have to trust to the chance of finding it again in the morning.

There now arose in his mind a question as to what would be their relationship when Tarzan had dismounted. Would it again revert to that of hunter and quarry or would fear of the goad continue to hold its supremacy over the natural instinct of the hunting flesh-eater? Tarzan wondered but as he could not remain upon the *gryf* forever, and as he preferred dismounting and putting the matter to a final test while it was still light, he decided to act at once.

How to stop the creature he did not know, as up to this time his sole desire had been to urge it forward. By experimenting with his staff, however, he found that he could bring it to a halt by reaching forward and striking the thing upon its beaklike snout. Close by grew a number of leafy trees, in any one of which the ape-man could have found sanctuary, but it had occurred to him that should he immediately take to the trees it might suggest to the mind of the *gryf* that the creature that had been commanding him all day feared him, with the result that Tarzan would once again be held a prisoner by the triceratops.

And so, when the *gryf* halted, Tarzan slid to the ground, struck the creature a careless blow across the flank as though in dismissal and walked indifferently away. From the throat of the beast came a low rumbling sound and without even a glance at Tarzan it turned and entered the river where it stood drinking for a long time.

Convinced that the *gryf* no longer constituted a menace to him the ape-man, spurred on himself by the gnawing of hunger, unslung his bow and selecting a handful of arrows set forth cautiously in search of food, evidence of the near presence of which was being borne up to him by a breeze from down river.

Ten minutes later he had made his kill, again one of the Pal-ul-don specimens of antelope, all species of which Tarzan had known since childhood as Bara, the deer, since in the little primer that had been the basis of his education the picture of a deer had been the nearest approach to the likeness of the antelope, from the giant eland to the smaller bushbuck of the hunting grounds of his youth.

Cutting off a haunch he cached it in a nearby tree, and throwing the balance of the carcass across his shoulder trotted back toward the spot at which he had left the *gryf*. The great beast was just emerging from the river when Tarzan, seeing it, issued the weird cry of the Tor-o-don. The creature looked in the direction of the sound voicing at the same time the low rumble with which it answered the call of its master. Twice Tarzan repeated his cry before the beast moved slowly toward him, and when it had come within a few paces he tossed the carcass of the deer to it, upon which it fell with greedy jaws.

"If anything will keep it within call," mused the ape-man as he returned to the tree in which he had cached his own portion of his kill, "it is the knowledge that I will feed it." But as he finished his repast and settled himself comfortably for the night high among the swaying branches of his eyrie he had little confidence that he would ride into A-lur the following day upon his prehistoric steed.

When Tarzan awoke early the following morning he dropped lightly to the ground and made his way to the stream. Removing his weapons and loin cloth he entered the cold waters of the little pool, and after his refreshing bath returned to the tree to breakfast upon another portion of Bara, the deer, adding to his repast some fruits and berries which grew in abundance nearby.

His meal over he sought the ground again and raising his voice in the weird cry that he had learned, he called aloud on the chance of attracting the *gryf*, but though he waited for some time and continued calling there was no response, and he was finally forced to the conclusion that he had seen the last of his great mount of the preceding day.

And so he set his face toward A-lur, pinning his faith upon his knowledge of the Ho-don tongue, his great strength and his native wit.

Refreshed by food and rest, the journey toward A-lur, made in the cool of the morning along the bank of the joyous river, he found delightful in the extreme. Differentiating him from his fellows of the savage jungle were many characteristics other than those physical and mental. Not the least of these were in a measure spiritual, and one that had doubtless been as strong as another in influencing Tarzan's love of the jungle had been his appreciation of the beauties of nature. The apes cared more for a grubworm in a rotten log than for all the majestic grandeur of the forest giants waving above them. The only beauties that Numa acknowledged were those of his own person as he paraded them before the admiring eyes of his mate, but in all the manifestations of the creative power of nature of which Tarzan was cognizant he appreciated the beauties.

As Tarzan neared the city his interest became centered upon the architecture of the outlying buildings which were hewn from the chalklike limestone of what had once been a group of low hills, similar to the many grass-covered hillocks that dotted the valley in every direction. Ta-den's explanation of the Ho-don methods of house construction accounted for the ofttimes remarkable shapes and proportions of the buildings which, during the ages that must have been required for their construction, had been hewn from the limestone hills, the exteriors chiseled to such architectural forms as appealed to the eyes of the builders while at the same time following roughly the original outlines of the hills in an evident desire to economize both labor and space. The excavation of the apartments within had been similarly governed by necessity.

As he came nearer Tarzan saw that the waste material from these building operations had been utilized in the construction of outer walls about each building or group of buildings resulting from a single hillock, and later he was to learn that it had also been used for the filling of inequalities between the hills and the forming of paved streets throughout the city, the result, possibly, more of the adoption of an easy method of disposing of the quantities of broken limestone than by any real necessity for pavements.

There were people moving about within the city and upon the narrow ledges and terraces that broke the lines of the buildings and which seemed to be a peculiarity of Ho-don architecture, a concession, no doubt, to some inherent instinct that might be traced back to their early cliff-dwelling progenitors.

Tarzan was not surprised that at a short distance he aroused no suspicion or curiosity in the minds of those who saw him, since, until closer scrutiny was possible, there was little to distinguish him from a native either in his general conformation or his color. He had, of course, formulated a plan of action and, having decided, he did not hesitate in the carrying out his plan.

With the same assurance that you might venture upon the main street of a neighboring city Tarzan strode into the Ho-don city of A-lur. The first person to detect his spuriousness was a little child playing in the arched gateway of one of the walled buildings. "No tail! no tail!" it shouted, throwing a stone at him, and then it suddenly grew dumb and its eyes wide as it sensed that this creature was something other than a mere Ho-don warrior who had lost his tail. With a gasp the child turned and fled screaming into the courtyard of its home.

Tarzan continued on his way, fully realizing that the moment was imminent when the fate of his plan would be decided. Nor had he long to wait since at the next turning of the winding street he came face to face with a Ho-don warrior. He saw the sudden surprise in the latter's eyes, followed instantly by one of suspicion, but before the fellow could speak Tarzan addressed him.

"I am a stranger from another land," he said; "I would speak with Ko-tan, your king."

The fellow stepped back, laying his hand upon his knife. "There are no strangers that come to the gates of A-lur," he said, "other than as enemies or slaves."

"I come neither as a slave nor an enemy," replied Tarzan. "I come directly from Jad-ben-Otho. Look!" and he held out his hands that the Ho-don might see how greatly they differed from his own, and then wheeled about that the other might see that he was tailless, for it was upon this fact that his plan had been based, due to his recollection of the quarrel between Ta-den and Om-at, in which the Waz-don had claimed that Jad-ben-Otho had a long tail while the Ho-don had been equally willing to fight for his faith in the taillessness of his god.

The warrior's eyes widened and an expression of awe crept into them, though it was still tinged with suspicion. "Jad-ben-Otho!" he murmured, and then, "It is true that you are neither Ho-don nor Waz-don, and it is also true that Jad-ben-Otho has no tail. Come," he said, "I will take you to Ko-tan, for this is a matter in which no common warrior may interfere. Follow me," and still clutching the handle of his knife and keeping a wary side glance upon the ape-man he led the way through A-lur.

The city covered a large area. Sometimes there was a considerable distance between groups of buildings, and again were quite close together. There were numerous imposing groups, evidently hewn from the larger hills, often rising to a height of a hundred feet or more. As they advanced they met numerous warriors and women, all of whom showed great curiosity in the stranger, but there was no attempt to menace him when it was found that he was being conducted to the palace of the king.

They came at last to a great pile that sprawled over a considerable area, its western front facing upon a large blue lake and evidently hewn from what had once been a natural cliff. This group of buildings was surrounded by a wall of considerably greater height than any that Tarzan had before seen. His guide led him to a gateway before which waited a dozen or more warriors who had risen to their feet and formed a barrier across the entrance-way as Tarzan and his party appeared around the corner of the palace wall, for by this time he had accumulated such a following of the curious as presented to the guards the appearance of a formidable mob.

The guide's story told, Tarzan was conducted into the courtyard where he was held while one of the warriors entered the palace, evidently with the intention of notifying Ko-tan. Fifteen minutes later a large warrior appeared, followed by several others, all of whom examined Tarzan with every sign of curiosity as they approached.

The leader of the party halted before the ape-man. "Who are you?" he asked, "and what do you want of Ko-tan, the king?"

"I am a friend," replied the ape-man, "and I have come from the country of Jad-ben-Otho to visit Ko-tan of Pal-ul-don."

The warrior and his followers seemed impressed. Tarzan could see the latter whispering among themselves.

"How come you here," asked the spokesman, "and what do you want of Ko-tan?"

Tarzan drew himself to his full height. "Enough!" he cried. "Must the messenger of Jad-ben-Otho be subjected to the treatment that might be accorded to a wandering Waz-don? Take me to the king at once lest the wrath of Jad-ben-Otho fall upon you."

There was some question in the mind of the ape-man as to how far he might carry his unwarranted show of assurance, and he waited therefore with amused interest the result of his demand. He did not, however, have long to wait for almost immediately the attitude of his questioner changed. He whitened, cast an apprehensive glance toward the eastern sky and then extended his right palm toward Tarzan, placing his left over his own heart in the sign of amity that was common among the peoples of Pal-ul-don.

Tarzan stepped quickly back as though from a profaning hand, a feigned expression of horror and disgust upon his face.

"Stop!" he cried, "who would dare touch the sacred person of the messenger of Jad-ben-Otho? Only as a special mark of favor from Jad-ben-Otho may even Ko-tan himself receive this honor from me. Hasten! Already now have I waited too long! What manner of reception the Ho-don of A-lur would extend to the son of my father!"

At first Tarzan had been inclined to adopt the role of Jad-ben-Otho himself but it occurred to him that it might prove embarrassing and considerable of a bore to be compelled constantly to portray the character of a god, but with the growing success of his scheme it had suddenly occurred to him that the authority of the son of Jad-ben-Otho would be far greater than that of an ordinary messenger of a god, while at the same time giving him some leeway in the matter of his acts and demeanor, the ape-man reasoning that a young god would not be held so strictly accountable in the matter of his dignity and bearing as an older and greater god.

This time the effect of his words was immediately and painfully noticeable upon all those near him. With one accord they shrank back, the spokesman almost collapsing in evident terror. His apologies, when finally the paralysis of his fear would permit him to voice them, were so abject that the ape-man could scarce repress a smile of amused contempt.

"Have mercy, O Dor-ul-Otho," he pleaded, "on poor old Dak-lot. Precede me and I will show you to where Ko-tan, the king, awaits you, trembling. Aside, snakes and vermin," he cried pushing his warriors to right and left for the purpose of forming an avenue for Tarzan.

"Come!" cried the ape-man peremptorily, "lead the way, and let these others follow."

The now thoroughly frightened Dak-lot did as he was bid, and Tarzan of the Apes was ushered into the palace of Kotan, King of Pal-ul-don.

CHAPTER IX—BLOOD-STAINED ALTARS

The entrance through which he caught his first glimpse of the interior was rather beautifully carved in geometric designs, and within the walls were similarly treated, though as he proceeded from one apartment to another he found also the figures of animals, birds, and men taking their places among the more formal figures of the mural decorator's art. Stone vessels were much in evidence as well as ornaments of gold and the skins of many animals, but nowhere did he see an indication of any woven fabric, indicating that in that respect at least the Ho-don were still low in the scale of evolution, and yet the proportions and symmetry of the corridors and apartments bespoke a degree of civilization.

The way led through several apartments and long corridors, up at least three flights of stone stairs and finally out upon a ledge upon the western side of the building overlooking the blue lake. Along this ledge, or arcade, his guide led him for a hundred yards, to stop at last before a wide entrance-way leading into another apartment of the palace.

Here Tarzan beheld a considerable concourse of warriors in an enormous apartment, the domed ceiling of which was fully fifty feet above the floor. Almost filling the chamber was a great pyramid ascending in broad steps well up under the dome in which were a number of round apertures which let in the light. The steps of the pyramid were occupied by warriors to the very pinnacle, upon which sat a large, imposing figure of a man whose golden trappings shone brightly in the light of the afternoon sun, a shaft of which poured through one of the tiny apertures of the dome.

"Ko-tan!" cried Dak-lot, addressing the resplendent figure at the pinnacle of the pyramid. "Ko-tan and warriors of Pal-ul-don! Behold the honor that Jad-ben-Otho has done you in sending as his messenger his own son," and Dak-lot, stepping aside, indicated Tarzan with a dramatic sweep of his hand.

Ko-tan rose to his feet and every warrior within sight craned his neck to have a better view of the newcomer. Those upon the opposite side of the pyramid crowded to the front as the words of the old warrior reached them. Skeptical were the expressions on most of the faces; but theirs was a skepticism marked with caution. No matter which way fortune jumped they wished to be upon the right side of the fence. For a moment all eyes were centered upon Tarzan and then gradually they drifted to Ko-tan, for from his attitude would they receive the cue that would determine theirs. But Ko-tan was evidently in the same quandary as they—the very attitude of his body indicated it—it was one of indecision and of doubt.

The ape-man stood erect, his arms folded upon his broad breast, an expression of haughty disdain upon his handsome face; but to Dak-lot there seemed to be indications also of growing anger. The situation was becoming strained. Dak-lot fidgeted, casting apprehensive glances at Tarzan and appealing ones at Ko-tan. The silence of the tomb wrapped the great chamber of the throneroom of Pal-ul-don.

At last Ko-tan spoke. "Who says that he is Dor-ul-Otho?" he asked, casting a terrible look at Dak-lot.

"He does!" almost shouted that terrified noble.

"And so it must be true?" queried Ko-tan.

Could it be that there was a trace of irony in the chief's tone? Otho forbid! Dak-lot cast a side glance at Tarzan—a glance that he intended should carry the assurance of his own faith; but that succeeded only in impressing the ape-man with the other's pitiable terror.

"O Ko-tan!" pleaded Dak-lot, "your own eyes must convince you that indeed he is the son of Otho. Behold his godlike figure, his hands, and his feet, that are not as ours, and that he is entirely tailless as is his mighty father."

Ko-tan appeared to be perceiving these facts for the first time and there was an indication that his skepticism was faltering. At that moment a young warrior who had pushed his way forward from the opposite side of the pyramid to where he could obtain a good look at Tarzan raised his voice.

"Ko-tan," he cried, "it must be even as Dak-lot says, for I am sure now that I have seen Dor-ul-Otho before. Yesterday as we were returning with the Kor-ul-lul prisoners we beheld him seated upon the back of a great *gryf*. We hid in the woods before he came too near, but I saw enough to make sure that he who rode upon the great beast was none other than the messenger who stands here now."

This evidence seemed to be quite enough to convince the majority of the warriors that they indeed stood in the presence of deity—their faces showed it only too plainly, and a sudden modesty that caused them to shrink behind their neighbors. As their neighbors were attempting to do the same thing, the result was a sudden melting away of those who stood nearest the ape-man, until the steps of the pyramid directly before him lay vacant to the very apex and to Ko-tan. The latter, possibly influenced as much by the fearful attitude of his followers as by the evidence adduced, now altered his tone and his manner in such a degree as might comport with the requirements if the stranger was indeed the Dor-ul-Otho while leaving his dignity a loophole of escape should it appear that he had entertained an impostor.

"If indeed you are the Dor-ul-Otho," he said, addressing Tarzan, "you will know that our doubts were but natural since we have received no sign from Jad-ben-Otho that he intended honoring us so greatly, nor how could we know, even, that the Great God had a son? If you are he, all Pal-ul-don rejoices to honor you; if you are not he, swift and terrible shall be the punishment of your temerity. I, Ko-tan, King of Pal-ul-don, have spoken."

"And spoken well, as a king should speak," said Tarzan, breaking his long silence, "who fears and honors the god of his people. It is well that you insist that I indeed be the Dor-ul-Otho before you accord me the homage that is my due. Jad-ben-Otho charged me specially to ascertain if you were fit to rule his people. My first experience of you indicates that Jad-ben-Otho chose well when he breathed the spirit of a king into the babe at your mother's breast."

The effect of this statement, made so casually, was marked in the expressions and excited whispers of the now awe-struck assemblage. At last they knew how kings were made! It was decided by Jad-ben-Otho while the candidate was still a suckling babe! Wonderful! A miracle! and this divine creature in whose presence they stood knew all about it. Doubtless he even discussed such matters with their god daily. If there had been an atheist among them before, or an agnostic, there was none now, for had they not looked with their own eyes upon the son of god?

"It is well then," continued the ape-man, "that you should assure yourself that I am no impostor. Come closer that you may see that I am not as are men. Furthermore it is not meet that you stand upon a higher level than the son of your god." There was a sudden scramble to reach the floor of the throne-room, nor was Ko-tan far behind his warriors, though he managed to maintain a certain majestic dignity as he descended the broad stairs that countless naked feet had polished to a gleaming smoothness through the ages. "And now," said Tarzan as the king stood before him, "you can have no doubt that I am not of the same race as you. Your priests have told you that Jad-ben-Otho is tailless. Tailless, therefore, must be the race of gods that spring from his loins. But enough of such proofs as these! You know the power of Jad-ben-Otho; how his lightnings gleaming out of the sky carry death as he wills it; how the rains come at his bidding, and the fruits and the berries and the grains, the grasses, the trees and the flowers spring to life at his divine direction; you have witnessed birth and death, and those who honor their god honor him because he controls these things. How would it fare then with an impostor who claimed to be the son of this all-powerful god? This then is all the proof that you require, for as he would strike you down should you deny me, so would he strike down one who wrongfully claimed kinship with him."

This line of argument being unanswerable must needs be convincing. There could be no questioning of this creature's statements without the tacit admission of lack of faith in the omnipotence of Jad-ben-Otho. Ko-tan was satisfied that he was entertaining deity, but as to just what form his entertainment should take he was rather at a loss to know. His conception of god had been rather a vague and hazy affair, though in common with all primitive people his god was a personal one as were his devils and demons. The pleasures of Jad-ben-Otho he had assumed to be the excesses which he himself enjoyed, but devoid of any unpleasant reaction. It therefore occurred to him that the Dor-ul-Otho would be greatly entertained by eating—eating large quantities of everything that Ko-tan liked best and that he had found most injurious; and there was also a drink that the women of the Ho-don made by allowing corn to soak in the juices of succulent fruits, to which they had added certain other ingredients best known to themselves. Ko-tan knew by experience that a single draught of this potent liquor would bring happiness and surcease from worry, while several would cause even a king to do things and enjoy things that he would never even think of doing or enjoying while not under the magical influence of the potion, but unfortunately the next morning brought suffering in direct ratio to the joy of the preceding day. A god, Ko-tan reasoned, could experience all the pleasure without the headache, but for the immediate present he must think of the necessary dignities and honors to be accorded his immortal guest.

No foot other than a king's had touched the surface of the apex of the pyramid in the throneroom at A-lur during all the forgotten ages through which the kings of Pal-ul-don had ruled from its high eminence. So what higher honor could Ko-tan offer than to give place beside him to the Dor-ul-Otho? And so he invited Tarzan to ascend the pyramid and take his place upon the stone bench that topped it. As they reached the step below the sacred pinnacle Ko-tan continued as though to mount to his throne, but Tarzan laid a detaining hand upon his arm.

"None may sit upon a level with the gods," he admonished, stepping confidently up and seating himself upon the throne. The abashed Ko-tan showed his embarrassment, an embarrassment he feared to voice lest he incur the wrath of the king of kings.

"But," added Tarzan, "a god may honor his faithful servant by inviting him to a place at his side. Come, Ko-tan; thus would I honor you in the name of Jad-ben-Otho."

The ape-man's policy had for its basis an attempt not only to arouse the fearful respect of Ko-tan but to do it without making of him an enemy at heart, for he did not know how strong a hold the religion of the Ho-don had upon them, for since the time that he had prevented Ta-den and Om-at from quarreling over a religious difference the subject had been utterly taboo among them. He was therefore quick to note the evident though wordless resentment of Ko-tan at the suggestion that he entirely relinquish his throne to his guest. On the whole, however, the effect had been satisfactory as he could see from the renewed evidence of awe upon the faces of the warriors.

At Tarzan's direction the business of the court continued where it had been interrupted by his advent. It consisted principally in the settling of disputes between warriors. There was present one who stood upon the step just below the throne and which Tarzan was to learn was the place reserved for the higher chiefs of the allied tribes which made up Ko-tan's kingdom. The one who attracted Tarzan's attention was a stalwart warrior of powerful physique and massive, lion-like features. He was addressing Ko-tan on a question that is as old as government and that will continue in unabated importance until man ceases to exist. It had to do with a boundary dispute with one of his neighbors.

The matter itself held little or no interest for Tarzan, but he was impressed by the appearance of the speaker and when Ko-tan addressed him as Ja-don the ape-man's interest was permanently crystallized, for Ja-don was the father of Ta-den. That the knowledge would benefit him in any way seemed rather a remote possibility since he could not reveal to Ja-don his friendly relations with his son without admitting the falsity of his claims to godship.

When the affairs of the audience were concluded Ko-tan suggested that the son of Jad-ben-Otho might wish to visit the temple in which were performed the religious rites coincident to the worship of the Great God. And so the ape-man was conducted by the king himself, followed by the warriors of his court, through the corridors of the palace toward the northern end of the group of buildings within the royal enclosure.

The temple itself was really a part of the palace and similar in architecture. There were several ceremonial places of varying sizes, the purposes of which Tarzan could only conjecture. Each had an altar in the west end and another in the east and were oval in shape, their longest diameter lying due east and west. Each was excavated from the summit of a small hillock and all were without roofs. The western altars invariably were a single block of stone the top of which was hollowed into an oblong basin. Those at the eastern ends were similar blocks of stone with flat tops and these latter, unlike those at the opposite ends of the ovals were invariably stained or painted a reddish brown, nor did Tarzan need to examine them closely to be assured of what his keen nostrils already had told him—that the brown stains were dried and drying human blood.

Below these temple courts were corridors and apartments reaching far into the bowels of the hills, dim, gloomy passages that Tarzan glimpsed as he was led from place to place on his tour of inspection of the temple. A messenger had been dispatched by Ko-tan to announce the coming visit of the son of Jad-ben-Otho with the result that they were accompanied through the temple by a considerable procession of priests whose distinguishing mark of profession seemed to consist in grotesque headdresses; sometimes hideous faces carved from wood and entirely concealing the countenances of their wearers, or again, the head of a wild beast cunningly fitted over the head of a man. The high priest alone wore no such head-dress. He was an old man with close-set, cunning eyes and a cruel, thin-lipped mouth.

At first sight of him Tarzan realized that here lay the greatest danger to his ruse, for he saw at a glance that the man was antagonistic toward him and his pretensions, and he knew too that doubtless of all the people of Pal-ul-don the high priest was most likely to harbor the truest estimate of Jad-ben-Otho, and, therefore, would look with suspicion on one who claimed to be the son of a fabulous god.

No matter what suspicion lurked within his crafty mind, Lu-don, the high priest of A-lur, did not openly question Tarzan's right to the title of Dor-ul-Otho, and it may be that he was restrained by the same doubts which had originally restrained Ko-tan and his warriors—the doubt that is at the bottom of the minds of all blasphemers even and which is based upon the fear that after all there may be a god. So, for the time being at least Lu-don played safe. Yet Tarzan knew as well as though the man had spoken aloud his inmost thoughts that it was in the heart of the high priest to tear the veil from his imposture.

At the entrance to the temple Ko-tan had relinquished the guidance of the guest to Lu-don and now the latter led Tarzan through those portions of the temple that he wished him to see. He showed him the great room where the votive offerings were kept, gifts from the barbaric chiefs of Pal-ul-don and from their followers. These things ranged in value from presents of dried fruits to massive vessels of beaten gold, so that in the great main storeroom and its connecting chambers and corridors was an accumulation of wealth that amazed even the eyes of the owner of the secret of the treasure vaults of Opar.

Moving to and fro throughout the temple were sleek black Waz-don slaves, fruits of the Ho-don raids upon the villages of their less civilized neighbors. As they passed the barred entrance to a dim corridor, Tarzan saw within a great company of pithecanthropi of all ages and of both sexes, Ho-don as well as Waz-don, the majority of them squatted upon the stone floor in attitudes of utter dejection while some paced back and forth, their features stamped with the despair of utter hopelessness.

"And who are these who lie here thus unhappily?" he asked of Lu-don. It was the first question that he had put to the high priest since entering the temple, and instantly he regretted that he had asked it, for Lu-don turned upon him a face upon which the expression of suspicion was but thinly veiled.

"Who should know better than the son of Jad-ben-Otho?" he retorted.

"The questions of Dor-ul-Otho are not with impunity answered with other questions," said the ape-man quietly, "and it may interest Lu-don, the high priest, to know that the blood of a false priest upon the altar of his temple is not displeasing in the eyes of Jad-ben-Otho."

Lu-don paled as he answered Tarzan's question. "They are the offerings whose blood must refresh the eastern altars as the sun returns to your father at the day's end."

"And who told you," asked Tarzan, "that Jad-ben-Otho was pleased that his people were slain upon his altars? What if you were mistaken?"

"Then countless thousands have died in vain," replied Lu-don.

Ko-tan and the surrounding warriors and priests were listening attentively to the dialogue. Some of the poor victims behind the barred gateway had heard and rising, pressed close to the barrier through which one was conducted just before sunset each day, never to return.

"Liberate them!" cried Tarzan with a wave of his hand toward the imprisoned victims of a cruel superstition, "for I can tell you in the name of Jad-ben-Otho that you are mistaken."

CHAPTER X—THE FORBIDDEN GARDEN

Lu-don paled. "It is sacrilege," he cried; "for countless ages have the priests of the Great God offered each night a life to the spirit of Jad-ben-Otho as it returned below the western horizon to its master, and never has the Great God given sign that he was displeased."

"Stop!" commanded Tarzan. "It is the blindness of the priesthood that has failed to read the messages of their god. Your warriors die beneath the knives and clubs of the Wazdon; your hunters are taken by *Ja* and *Jato*; no day goes by but witnesses the deaths of few or many in the villages of the Ho-don, and one death each day of those that die are the toll which Jad-ben-Otho has exacted for the lives you take upon the eastern altar. What greater sign of his displeasure could you require, O stupid priest?"

Lu-don was silent. There was raging within him a great conflict between his fear that this indeed might be the son of god and his hope that it was not, but at last his fear won and he bowed his head. "The son of Jad-ben-Otho has spoken," he said, and turning to one of the lesser priests: "Remove the bars and return these people from whence they came."

He thus addressed did as he was bid and as the bars came down the prisoners, now all fully aware of the miracle that had saved them, crowded forward and throwing themselves upon their knees before Tarzan raised their voices in thanksgiving.

Ko-tan was almost as staggered as the high priest by this ruthless overturning of an age-old religious rite. "But what," he cried, "may we do that will be pleasing in the eyes of Jad-ben-Otho?" turning a look of puzzled apprehension toward the ape-man.

"If you seek to please your god," he replied, "place upon your altars such gifts of food and apparel as are most welcome in the city of your people. These things will Jad-ben-Otho bless, when you may distribute them among those of the city who need them most. With such things are your storerooms filled as I have seen with mine own eyes, and other gifts will be brought when the priests tell the people that in this way they find favor before their god," and Tarzan turned and signified that he would leave the temple.

As they were leaving the precincts devoted to the worship of their deity, the ape-man noticed a small but rather ornate building that stood entirely detached from the others as though it had been cut from a little pinnacle of limestone which had stood out from its fellows. As his interested glance passed over it he noticed that its door and windows were barred.

"To what purpose is that building dedicated?" he asked of Lu-don. "Who do you keep imprisoned there?"

"It is nothing," replied the high priest nervously, "there is no one there. The place is vacant. Once it was used but not now for many years," and he moved on toward the gateway which led back into the palace. Here he and the priests halted while Tarzan with Ko-tan and his warriors passed out from the sacred precincts of the temple grounds.

The one question which Tarzan would have asked he had feared to ask for he knew that in the hearts of many lay a suspicion as to his genuineness, but he determined that before he slept he would put the question to Ko-tan, either directly or indirectly—as to whether there was, or had been recently within the city of A-lur a female of the same race as his.

As their evening meal was being served to them in the banquet hall of Ko-tan's palace by a part of the army of black slaves upon whose shoulders fell the burden of all the heavy and menial tasks of the city, Tarzan noticed that there came to the eyes of one of the slaves what was apparently an expression of startled recognition, as he looked upon the ape-man for the first time in the banquet hall of Ko-tan. And again later he saw the fellow whisper to another slave and nod his head in his direction. The ape-man did not recall ever having seen this Waz-don before and he was at a loss to account for an explanation of the fellow's interest in him, and presently the incident was all but forgotten.

Ko-tan was surprised and inwardly disgusted to discover that his godly guest had no desire to gorge himself upon rich foods and that he would not even so much as taste the villainous brew of the Ho-don. To Tarzan the banquet was a dismal and tiresome affair, since so great was the interest of the guests in gorging themselves with food and drink that they had no time for conversation, the only vocal sounds being confined to a continuous grunting which, together with their table manners reminded Tarzan of a visit he had once made to the famous Berkshire herd of His Grace, the Duke of Westminster at Woodhouse, Chester.

One by one the diners succumbed to the stupefying effects of the liquor with the result that the grunting gave place to snores, so presently Tarzan and the slaves were the only conscious creatures in the banquet hall.

Rising, the ape-man turned to a tall black who stood behind him. "I would sleep," he said, "show me to my apartment."

As the fellow conducted him from the chamber the slave who had shown surprise earlier in the evening at sight of him, spoke again at length to one of his fellows. The latter cast a half-frightened look in the direction of the departing ape-man. "If you are right," he said, "they should reward us with our liberty, but if you are wrong, O Jad-ben-Otho, what will be our fate?"

"But I am not wrong!" cried the other.

"Then there is but one to tell this to, for I have heard that he looked sour when this Dor-ul-Otho was brought to the temple and that while the so-called son of Jad-ben-Otho was there he gave this one every cause to fear and hate him. I mean Lu-don, the high priest."

"You know him?" asked the other slave.

"I have worked in the temple," replied his companion.

"Then go to him at once and tell him, but be sure to exact the promise of our freedom for the proof."

And so a black Waz-don came to the temple gate and asked to see Lu-don, the high priest, on a matter of great importance, and though the hour was late Lu-don saw him, and when he had heard his story he promised him and his friend not only their freedom but many gifts if they could prove the correctness of their claims.

And as the slave talked with the high priest in the temple at A-lur the figure of a man groped its way around the shoulder of Pastar-ul-ved and the moonlight glistened from the shiny barrel of an Enfield that was strapped to the naked back, and brass cartridges shed tiny rays of reflected light from their polished cases where they hung in the bandoliers across the broad brown shoulders and the lean waist.

Tarzan's guide conducted him to a chamber overlooking the blue lake where he found a bed similar to that which he had seen in the villages of the Waz-don, merely a raised dais of stone upon which was piled great quantities of furry pelts. And so he lay down to sleep, the question that he most wished to put still unasked and unanswered.

With the coming of a new day he was awake and wandering about the palace and the palace grounds before there was sign of any of the inmates of the palace other than slaves, or at least he saw no others at first, though presently he stumbled upon an enclosure which lay almost within the center of the palace grounds surrounded by a wall that piqued the ape-man's curiosity, since he had determined to investigate as fully as possible every part of the palace and its environs.

This place, whatever it might be, was apparently without doors or windows but that it was at least partially roofless was evidenced by the sight of the waving branches of a tree which spread above the top of the wall near him. Finding no other method of access, the ape-man uncoiled his rope and throwing it over the branch of the tree where it projected beyond the wall, was soon climbing with the ease of a monkey to the summit.

There he found that the wall surrounded an enclosed garden in which grew trees and shrubs and flowers in riotous profusion. Without waiting to ascertain whether the garden was empty or contained Ho-don, Waz-don, or wild beasts, Tarzan dropped lightly to the sward on the inside and without further loss of time commenced a systematic investigation of the enclosure.

His curiosity was aroused by the very evident fact that the place was not for general use, even by those who had free access to other parts of the palace grounds and so there was added to its natural beauties an absence of mortals which rendered its exploration all the more alluring to Tarzan since it suggested that in such a place might he hope to come upon the object of his long and difficult search.

In the garden were tiny artificial streams and little pools of water, flanked by flowering bushes, as though it all had been designed by the cunning hand of some master gardener, so faithfully did it carry out the beauties and contours of nature upon a miniature scale.

The interior surface of the wall was fashioned to represent the white cliffs of Pal-ul-don, broken occasionally by small replicas of the verdure-filled gorges of the original.

Filled with admiration and thoroughly enjoying each new surprise which the scene offered, Tarzan moved slowly around the garden, and as always he moved silently. Passing through a miniature forest he came presently upon a tiny area of flowerstudded sward and at the same time beheld before him the first Ho-don female he had seen since entering the palace. A young and beautiful woman stood in the center of the little open space, stroking the head of a bird which she held against her golden breastplate with one hand. Her profile was presented to the ape-man and he saw that by the standards of any land she would have been accounted more than lovely.

Seated in the grass at her feet, with her back toward him, was a female Waz-don slave. Seeing that she he sought was not there and apprehensive that an alarm be raised were he discovered by the two women, Tarzan moved back to hide himself in the foliage, but before he had succeeded the Ho-don girl turned quickly toward him as though apprised of his presence by that unnamed sense, the manifestations of which are more or less familiar to us all.

At sight of him her eyes registered only her surprise though there was no expression of terror reflected in them, nor did she scream or even raise her well-modulated voice as she addressed him.

"Who are you," she asked, "who enters thus boldly the Forbidden Garden?"

At sound of her mistress' voice the slave maiden turned quickly, rising to her feet. "Tarzan-jad-guru!" she exclaimed in tones of mingled astonishment and relief.

"You know him?" cried her mistress turning toward the slave and affording Tarzan an opportunity to raise a cautioning finger to his lips lest Pan-at-lee further betray him, for it was Pan-at-lee indeed who stood before him, no less a source of surprise to him than had his presence been to her.

Thus questioned by her mistress and simultaneously admonished to silence by Tarzan, Pan-at-lee was momentarily silenced and then haltingly she groped for a way to extricate herself from her dilemma. "I thought—" she faltered, "but no, I am mistaken—I thought that he was one whom I had seen before near the Kor-ul-*gryf*."

The Ho-don looked first at one and then at the other an expression of doubt and questioning in her eyes. "But you have not answered me," she continued presently; "who are you?"

"You have not heard then," asked Tarzan, "of the visitor who arrived at your king's court yesterday?"

"You mean," she exclaimed, "that you are the Dor-ul-Otho?" And now the erstwhile doubting eyes reflected naught but awe.

"I am he," replied Tarzan; "and you?"

"I am O-lo-a, daughter of Ko-tan, the king," she replied.

So this was O-lo-a, for love of whom Ta-den had chosen exile rather than priesthood. Tarzan had approached more closely the dainty barbarian princess. "Daughter of Ko-tan," he said, "Jad-ben-Otho is pleased with you and as a mark of his favor he has preserved for you through many dangers him whom you love."

"I do not understand," replied the girl but the flush that mounted to her cheek belied her words. "Bu-lat is a guest in the palace of Ko-tan, my father. I do not know that he has faced any danger. It is to Bu-lat that I am betrothed."

"But it is not Bu-lat whom you love," said Tarzan.

Again the flush and the girl half turned her face away. "Have I then displeased the Great God?" she asked.

"No," replied Tarzan; "as I told you he is well satisfied and for your sake he has saved Ta-den for you."

"Jad-ben-Otho knows all," whispered the girl, "and his son shares his great knowledge."

"No," Tarzan hastened to correct her lest a reputation for omniscience might prove embarrassing. "I know only what Jad-ben-Otho wishes me to know."

"But tell me," she said, "I shall be reunited with Ta-den? Surely the son of god can read the future."

The ape-man was glad that he had left himself an avenue of escape. "I know nothing of the future," he replied, "other than what Jad-ben-Otho tells me. But I think you need have no fear for the future if you remain faithful to Ta-den and Ta-den's friends."

"You have seen him?" asked O-lo-a. "Tell me, where is he?"

"Yes," replied Tarzan, "I have seen him. He was with Om-at, the gund of Kor-ul-Ja."

"A prisoner of the Waz-don?" interrupted the girl.

"Not a prisoner but an honored guest," replied the ape-man.

"Wait," he exclaimed, raising his face toward the heavens; "do not speak. I am receiving a message from Jad-ben-Otho, my father."

The two women dropped to their knees, covering their faces with their hands, stricken with awe at the thought of the awful nearness of the Great God. Presently Tarzan touched O-lo-a on the shoulder.

"Rise," he said. "Jad-ben-Otho has spoken. He has told me that this slave girl is from the tribe of Kor-ul-Ja, where Ta-den is, and that she is betrothed to Om-at, their chief. Her name is Pan-at-lee."

O-lo-a turned questioningly toward Pan-at-lee. The latter nodded, her simple mind unable to determine whether or not she and her mistress were the victims of a colossal hoax. "It is even as he says," she whispered.

O-lo-a fell upon her knees and touched her forehead to Tarzan's feet. "Great is the honor that Jad-ben-Otho has done his poor servant," she cried. "Carry to him my poor thanks for the happiness that he has brought to O-lo-a."

"It would please my father," said Tarzan, "if you were to cause Pan-at-lee to be returned in safety to the village of her people."

"What cares Jad-ben-Otho for such as she?" asked O-lo-a, a slight trace of hauteur in her tone.

"There is but one god," replied Tarzan, "and he is the god of the Waz-don as well as of the Ho-don; of the birds and the beasts and the flowers and of everything that grows upon the earth or beneath the waters. If Pan-at-lee does right she is greater in the eyes of Jad-ben-Otho than would be the daughter of Ko-tan should she do wrong."

It was evident that O-lo-a did not quite understand this interpretation of divine favor, so contrary was it to the teachings of the priesthood of her people. In one respect only did Tarzan's teachings coincide with her belief—that there was but one god. For the rest she had always been taught that he was solely the god of the Ho-don in every sense, other than that other creatures were created by Jad-ben-Otho to serve some useful purpose for the benefit of the Ho-don race. And now to be told by the son of god that she stood no higher in divine esteem than the black handmaiden at her side was indeed a shock to her pride, her vanity, and her faith. But who could question the word of Dor-ul-Otho, especially when she had with her own eyes seen him in actual communion with god in heaven?

"The will of Jad-ben-Otho be done," said O-lo-a meekly, "if it lies within my power. But it would be best, O Dor-ul-Otho, to communicate your father's wish directly to the king."

"Then keep her with you," said Tarzan, "and see that no harm befalls her."

O-lo-a looked ruefully at Pan-at-lee. "She was brought to me but yesterday," she said, "and never have I had slave woman who pleased me better. I shall hate to part with her."

"But there are others," said Tarzan.

"Yes," replied O-lo-a, "there are others, but there is only one Pan-at-lee."

"Many slaves are brought to the city?" asked Tarzan.

"Yes," she replied.

"And many strangers come from other lands?" he asked.

She shook her head negatively. "Only the Ho-don from the other side of the Valley of Jad-ben-Otho," she replied, "and they are not strangers."

"Am I then the first stranger to enter the gates of A-lur?" he asked.

"Can it be," she parried, "that the son of Jad-ben-Otho need question a poor ignorant mortal like O-lo-a?"

"As I told you before," replied Tarzan, "Jad-ben-Otho alone is all-knowing."

"Then if he wished you to know this thing," retorted O-lo-a quickly, "you would know it."

Inwardly the ape-man smiled that this little heathen's astuteness should beat him at his own game, yet in a measure her evasion of the question might be an answer to it. "There have been other strangers here then recently?" he persisted.

"I cannot tell you what I do not know," she replied. "Always is the palace of Ko-tan filled with rumors, but how much fact and how much fancy how may a woman of the palace know?"

"There has been such a rumor then?" he asked.

"It was only rumor that reached the Forbidden Garden," she replied.

"It described, perhaps, a woman of another race?" As he put the question and awaited her answer he thought that his heart ceased to beat, so grave to him was the issue at stake.

The girl hesitated before replying, and then. "No," she said, "I cannot speak of this thing, for if it be of sufficient importance to elicit the interest of the gods then indeed would I be subject to the wrath of my father should I discuss it."

"In the name of Jad-ben-Otho I command you to speak," said Tarzan. "In the name of Jad-ben-Otho in whose hands lies the fate of Ta-den!"

The girl paled. "Have mercy!" she cried, "and for the sake of Ta-den I will tell you all that I know."

"Tell what?" demanded a stern voice from the shrubbery behind them. The three turned to see the figure of Ko-tan emerging from the foliage. An angry scowl distorted his kingly features but at sight of Tarzan it gave place to an expression of surprise not unmixed with fear. "Dor-ul-Otho!" he exclaimed, "I did not know that it was you," and then, raising his head and squaring his shoulders he said, "but there are places where even the son of the Great God may not walk and this, the Forbidden Garden of Ko-tan, is one."

It was a challenge but despite the king's bold front there was a note of apology in it, indicating that in his superstitious mind there flourished the inherent fear of man for his Maker. "Come, Dor-ul-Otho," he continued, "I do not know all this foolish child has said to you but whatever you would know Ko-tan, the king, will tell you. O-lo-a, go to your quarters immediately," and he pointed with stern finger toward the opposite end of the garden.

The princess, followed by Pan-at-lee, turned at once and left them.

"We will go this way," said Ko-tan and preceding, led Tarzan in another direction. Close to that part of the wall which they approached Tarzan perceived a grotto in the miniature cliff into the interior of which Ko-tan led him, and down a rocky stairway to a gloomy corridor the opposite end of which opened into the palace proper. Two armed warriors stood at this entrance to the Forbidden Garden, evidencing how jealously were the sacred precincts of the place guarded.

In silence Ko-tan led the way back to his own quarters in the palace. A large chamber just outside the room toward which Ko-tan was leading his guest was filled with chiefs and warriors awaiting the pleasure of their ruler. As the two entered, an aisle was formed for them the length of the chamber, down which they passed in silence.

Close to the farther door and half hidden by the warriors who stood before him was Lu-don, the high priest. Tarzan glimpsed him but briefly but in that short period he was aware of a cunning and malevolent expression upon the cruel countenance that he was subconsciously aware boded him no good, and then with Ko-tan he passed into the adjoining room and the hangings dropped.

At the same moment the hideous headdress of an under priest appeared in the entrance of the outer chamber. Its owner, pausing for a moment, glanced quickly around the interior and then having located him whom he sought moved rapidly in the direction of Lu-don. There was a whispered conversation which was terminated by the high priest.

"Return immediately to the quarters of the princess," he said, "and see that the slave is sent to me at the temple at once." The under priest turned and departed upon his mission while Lu-don also left the apartment and directed his footsteps toward the sacred enclosure over which he ruled.

A half-hour later a warrior was ushered into the presence of Ko-tan. "Lu-don, the high priest, desires the presence of Ko-tan, the king, in the temple," he announced, "and it is his wish that he come alone."

Ko-tan nodded to indicate that he accepted the command which even the king must obey. "I will return presently, Dor-ul-Otho," he said to Tarzan, "and in the meantime my warriors and my slaves are yours to command."

CHAPTER XI—THE SENTENCE OF DEATH

But it was an hour before the king re-entered the apartment and in the meantime the ape-man had occupied himself in examining the carvings upon the walls and the numerous specimens of the handicraft of Pal-ul-donian artisans which combined to impart an atmosphere of richness and luxury to the apartment.

The limestone of the country, close-grained and of marble whiteness yet worked with comparative ease with crude implements, had been wrought by cunning craftsmen into bowls and urns and vases of considerable grace and beauty. Into the carved designs of many of these virgin gold had been hammered, presenting the effect of a rich and magnificent cloisonne. A barbarian himself the art of barbarians had always appealed to the ape-man to whom they represented a natural expression of man's love of the beautiful to even a greater extent than the studied and artificial efforts of civilization. Here was the real art of old masters, the other the cheap imitation of the chromo.

It was while he was thus pleasurably engaged that Ko-tan returned. As Tarzan, attracted by the movement of the hangings through which the king entered, turned and faced him he was almost shocked by the remarkable alteration of the king's appearance. His face was livid; his hands trembled as with palsy, and his eyes were wide as with fright. His appearance was one apparently of a combination of consuming anger and withering fear. Tarzan looked at him questioningly.

"You have had bad news, Ko-tan?" he asked.

The king mumbled an unintelligible reply. Behind there thronged into the apartment so great a number of warriors that they choked the entrance-way. The king looked apprehensively to right and left. He cast terrified glances at the ape-man and then raising his face and turning his eyes upward he cried: "Jad-ben-Otho be my witness that I do not this thing of my own accord." There was a moment's silence which was again broken by Ko-tan. "Seize him," he cried to the warriors about him, "for Lu-don, the high priest, swears that he is an impostor."

To have offered armed resistance to this great concourse of warriors in the very heart of the palace of their king would have been worse than fatal. Already Tarzan had come far by his wits and now that within a few hours he had had his hopes and his suspicions partially verified by the vague admissions of O-lo-a he was impressed with the necessity of inviting no mortal risk that he could avoid.

"Stop!" he cried, raising his palm against them. "What is the meaning of this?"

"Lu-don claims he has proof that you are not the son of Jad-ben-Otho," replied Ko-tan. "He demands that you be brought to the throneroom to face your accusers. If you are what you claim to be none knows better than you that you need have no fear in acquiescing to his demands, but remember always that in such matters the high priest commands the king and that I am only the bearer of these commands, not their author."

Tarzan saw that Ko-tan was not entirely convinced of his duplicity as was evidenced by his palpable design to play safe.

"Let not your warriors seize me," he said to Ko-tan, "lest Jad-ben-Otho, mistaking their intention, strike them dead." The effect of his words was immediate upon the men in the front rank of those who faced him, each seeming suddenly to acquire a new modesty that compelled him to self-effacement behind those directly in his rear—a modesty that became rapidly contagious.

The ape-man smiled. "Fear not," he said, "I will go willingly to the audience chamber to face the blasphemers who accuse me."

Arrived at the great throneroom a new complication arose. Ko-tan would not acknowledge the right of Lu-don to occupy the apex of the pyramid and Lu-don would not consent to occupying an inferior position while Tarzan, to remain consistent with his high claims, insisted that no one should stand above him, but only to the ape-man was the humor of the situation apparent.

To relieve the situation Ja-don suggested that all three of them occupy the throne, but this suggestion was repudiated by Ko-tan who argued that no mortal other than a king of Pal-ul-don had ever sat upon the high eminence, and that furthermore there was not room for three there.

"But who," said Tarzan, "is my accuser and who is my judge?"

"Lu-don is your accuser," explained Ko-tan.

"And Lu-don is your judge," cried the high priest.

"I am to be judged by him who accuses me then," said Tarzan. "It were better to dispense then with any formalities and ask Lu-don to sentence me." His tone was ironical and his sneering face, looking straight into that of the high priest, but caused the latter's hatred to rise to still greater proportions.

It was evident that Ko-tan and his warriors saw the justice of Tarzan's implied objection to this unfair method of dispensing justice. "Only Ko-tan can judge in the throneroom of his palace," said Ja-don, "let him hear Lu-don's charges and the testimony of his witnesses, and then let Ko-tan's judgment be final."

Ko-tan, however, was not particularly enthusiastic over the prospect of sitting in trial upon one who might after all very possibly be the son of his god, and so he temporized, seeking for an avenue of escape. "It is purely a religious matter," he said, "and it is traditional that the kings of Pal-ul-don interfere not in questions of the church."

"Then let the trial be held in the temple," cried one of the chiefs, for the warriors were as anxious as their king to be relieved of all responsibility in the matter. This suggestion was more than satisfactory to the high priest who inwardly condemned himself for not having thought of it before.

"It is true," he said, "this man's sin is against the temple. Let him be dragged thither then for trial."

"The son of Jad-ben-Otho will be dragged nowhere," cried Tarzan. "But when this trial is over it is possible that the corpse of Lu-don, the high priest, will be dragged from the temple of the god he would desecrate. Think well, then, Lu-don before you commit this folly."

His words, intended to frighten the high priest from his position failed utterly in consummating their purpose. Lu-don showed no terror at the suggestion the ape-man's words implied.

"Here is one," thought Tarzan, "who, knowing more of his religion than any of his fellows, realizes fully the falsity of my claims as he does the falsity of the faith he preaches."

He realized, however, that his only hope lay in seeming indifference to the charges. Ko-tan and the warriors were still under the spell of their belief in him and upon this fact must he depend in the final act of the drama that Lu-don was staging for his rescue from the jealous priest whom he knew had already passed sentence upon him in his own heart.

With a shrug he descended the steps of the pyramid. "It matters not to Dor-ul-Otho," he said, "where Lu-don enrages his god, for Jad-ben-Otho can reach as easily into the chambers of the temple as into the throneroom of Ko-tan."

Immeasurably relieved by this easy solution of their problem the king and the warriors thronged from the throneroom toward the temple grounds, their faith in Tarzan increased by his apparent indifference to the charges against him. Lu-don led them to the largest of the altar courts.

Taking his place behind the western altar he motioned Ko-tan to a place upon the platform at the left hand of the altar and directed Tarzan to a similar place at the right.

As Tarzan ascended the platform his eyes narrowed angrily at the sight which met them. The basin hollowed in the top of the altar was filled with water in which floated the naked corpse of a new-born babe. "What means this?" he cried angrily, turning upon Lu-don.

The latter smiled malevolently. "That you do not know," he replied, "is but added evidence of the falsity of your claim. He who poses as the son of god did not know that as the last rays of the setting sun flood the eastern altar of the temple the lifeblood of an adult reddens the white stone for the edification of Jad-ben-Otho, and that when the sun rises again from the body of its maker it looks first upon this western altar and rejoices in the death of a new-born babe each day, the ghost of which accompanies it across the heavens by day as the ghost of the adult returns with it to Jad-ben-Otho at night.

"Even the little children of the Ho-don know these things, while he who claims to be the son of Jad-ben-Otho knows them not; and if this proof be not enough, there is more. Come, Waz-don," he cried, pointing to a tall slave who stood with a group of other blacks and priests on the temple floor at the left of the altar.

The fellow came forward fearfully. "Tell us what you know of this creature," cried Lu-don, pointing to Tarzan.

"I have seen him before," said the Waz-don. "I am of the tribe of Kor-ul-lul, and one day recently a party of which I was one encountered a few of the warriors of the Kor-ul-Ja upon the ridge which separates our villages. Among the enemy was this strange creature whom they called Tarzan-jad-guru; and terrible indeed was he for he fought with the strength of many men so that it required twenty of us to subdue him. But he did not fight as a god fights, and when a club struck him upon the head he sank unconscious as might an ordinary mortal.

"We carried him with us to our village as a prisoner but he escaped after cutting off the head of the warrior we left to guard him and carrying it down into the gorge and tying it to the branch of a tree upon the opposite side."

"The word of a slave against that of a god!" cried Ja-don, who had shown previously a friendly interest in the pseudo godling.

"It is only a step in the progress toward truth," interjected Lu-don. "Possibly the evidence of the only princess of the house of Ko-tan will have greater weight with the great chief from the north, though the father of a son who fled the holy offer of the priesthood may not receive with willing ears any testimony against another blasphemer."

Ja-don's hand leaped to his knife, but the warriors next him laid detaining fingers upon his arms. "You are in the temple of Jad-ben-Otho, Ja-don," they cautioned and the great chief was forced to swallow Lu-don's affront though it left in his heart bitter hatred of the high priest.

And now Ko-tan turned toward Lu-don. "What knoweth my daughter of this matter?" he asked. "You would not bring a princess of my house to testify thus publicly?"

"No," replied Lu-don, "not in person, but I have here one who will testify for her." He beckoned to an under priest. "Fetch the slave of the princess," he said.

His grotesque headdress adding a touch of the hideous to the scene, the priest stepped forward dragging the reluctant Pan-at-lee by the wrist.

"The Princess O-lo-a was alone in the Forbidden Garden with but this one slave," explained the priest, "when there suddenly appeared from the foliage nearby this creature who claims to be the Dor-ul-Otho. When the slave saw him the princess says that she cried aloud in startled recognition and called the creature by name—Tarzan-jad-guru—the same name that the slave from Kor-ul-lul gave him. This woman is not from Kor-ul-lul but from Kor-ul-Ja, the very tribe with which the Kor-ul-lul says the creature was associating when he first saw him. And further the princess said that when this woman, whose name is Pan-at-lee, was brought to her yesterday she told a strange story of having been rescued from a Tor-o-don in the Kor-ul-*gryf* by a creature such as this, whom she spoke of then as Tarzan-jad-guru; and of how the two were pursued in the bottom of the gorge by two monster gryfs, and of how the man led them away while Pan-at-lee escaped, only to be taken prisoner in the Kor-ul-lul as she was seeking to return to her own tribe.

"Is it not plain now," cried Lu-don, "that this creature is no god. Did he tell you that he was the son of god?" he almost shouted, turning suddenly upon Pan-at-lee.

The girl shrank back terrified. "Answer me, slave!" cried the high priest.

"He seemed more than mortal," parried Pan-at-lee.

"Did he tell you that he was the son of god? Answer my question," insisted Lu-don.

"No," she admitted in a low voice, casting an appealing look of forgiveness at Tarzan who returned a smile of encouragement and friendship.

"That is no proof that he is not the son of god," cried Ja-don. "Dost think Jad-ben-Otho goes about crying 'I am god! I am god!' Hast ever heard him Lu-don? No, you have not. Why should his son do that which the father does not do?"

"Enough," cried Lu-don. "The evidence is clear. The creature is an impostor and I, the head priest of Jad-ben-Otho in the city of A-lur, do condemn him to die." There was a moment's silence during which Lu-don evidently paused for the dramatic effect of his climax. "And if I am wrong may Jad-ben-Otho pierce my heart with his lightnings as I stand here before you all."

The lapping of the wavelets of the lake against the foot of the palace wall was distinctly audible in the utter and almost breathless silence which ensued. Lu-don stood with his face turned toward the heavens and his arms outstretched in the attitude of one who bares his breast to the dagger of an executioner. The warriors and the priests and the slaves gathered in the sacred court awaited the consuming vengeance of their god.

It was Tarzan who broke the silence. "Your god ignores you Lu-don," he taunted, with a sneer that he meant to still further anger the high priest, "he ignores you and I can prove it before the eyes of your priests and your people."

"Prove it, blasphemer! How can you prove it?"

"You have called me a blasphemer," replied Tarzan, "you have proved to your own satisfaction that I am an impostor, that I, an ordinary mortal, have posed as the son of god. Demand then that Jad-ben-Otho uphold his godship and the dignity of his priesthood by directing his consuming fires through my own bosom."

Again there ensued a brief silence while the onlookers waited for Lu-don to thus consummate the destruction of this presumptuous impostor.

"You dare not," taunted Tarzan, "for you know that I would be struck dead no quicker than were you."

"You lie," cried Lu-don, "and I would do it had I not but just received a message from Jad-ben-Otho directing that your fate be different."

A chorus of admiring and reverential "Ahs" arose from the priesthood. Ko-tan and his warriors were in a state of mental confusion. Secretly they hated and feared Lu-don, but so ingrained was their sense of reverence for the office of the high priest that none dared raise a voice against him.

None? Well, there was Ja-don, fearless old Lion-man of the north. "The proposition was a fair one," he cried. "Invoke the lightnings of Jad-ben-Otho upon this man if you would ever convince us of his guilt."

"Enough of this," snapped Lu-don. "Since when was Ja-don created high priest? Seize the prisoner," he cried to the priests and warriors, "and on the morrow he shall die in the manner that Jad-ben-Otho has willed."

There was no immediate movement on the part of any of the warriors to obey the high priest's command, but the lesser priests on the other hand, imbued with the courage of fanaticism leaped eagerly forward like a flock of hideous harpies to seize upon their prey.

The game was up. That Tarzan knew. No longer could cunning and diplomacy usurp the functions of the weapons of defense he best loved. And so the first hideous priest who leaped to the platform was confronted by no suave ambassador from heaven, but rather a grim and ferocious beast whose temper savored more of hell.

The altar stood close to the western wall of the enclosure. There was just room between the two for the high priest to stand during the performance of the sacrificial ceremonies and only Lu-don stood there now behind Tarzan, while before him were perhaps two hundred warriors and priests.

The presumptuous one who would have had the glory of first laying arresting hands upon the blasphemous impersonator rushed forward with outstretched hand to seize the ape-man. Instead it was he who was seized; seized by steel fingers that snapped him up as though he had been a dummy of straw, grasped him by one leg and the harness at his back and raised him with giant arms high above the altar. Close at his heels were others ready to seize the ape-man and drag him down, and beyond the altar was Lu-don with drawn knife advancing toward him.

There was no instant to waste, nor was it the way of the ape-man to fritter away precious moments in the uncertainty of belated decision. Before Lu-don or any other could guess what was in the mind of the condemned, Tarzan with all the force of his great muscles dashed the screaming hierophant in the face of the high priest, and, as though the two actions were one, so quickly did he move, he had leaped to the top of the altar and from there to a handhold upon the summit of the temple wall. As he gained a footing there he turned and looked down upon those beneath. For a moment he stood in silence and then he spoke.

"Who dare believe," he cried, "that Jad-ben-Otho would forsake his son?" and then he dropped from their sight upon the other side.

There were two at least left within the enclosure whose hearts leaped with involuntary elation at the success of the ape-man's maneuver, and one of them smiled openly. This was Ja-don, and the other, Pan-at-lee.

The brains of the priest that Tarzan had thrown at the head of Lu-don had been dashed out against the temple wall while the high priest himself had escaped with only a few bruises, sustained in his fall to the hard pavement. Quickly scrambling to his feet he looked around in fear, in terror and finally in bewilderment, for he had not been a witness to the ape-man's escape. "Seize him," he cried; "seize the blasphemer," and he continued to look around in search of his victim with such a ridiculous expression of bewilderment that more than a single warrior was compelled to hide his smiles beneath his palm.

The priests were rushing around wildly, exhorting the warriors to pursue the fugitive but these awaited now stolidly the command of their king or high priest. Ko-tan, more or less secretly pleased by the discomfiture of Lu-don, waited for that worthy to give the necessary directions which he presently did when one of his acolytes excitedly explained to him the manner of Tarzan's escape.

Instantly the necessary orders were issued and priests and warriors sought the temple exit in pursuit of the ape-man. His departing words, hurled at them from the summit of the temple wall, had had little effect in impressing the majority that his claims had not been disproven by Lu-don, but in the hearts of the warriors was admiration for a brave man and in many the same unholy gratification that had risen in that of their ruler at the discomfiture of Lu-don.

A careful search of the temple grounds revealed no trace of the quarry. The secret recesses of the subterranean chambers, familiar only to the priesthood, were examined by these while the warriors scattered through the palace and the palace grounds without the temple. Swift runners were dispatched to the city to arouse the people there that all might be upon the lookout for Tarzan the Terrible. The story of his imposture and of his escape, and the tales that the Waz-don slaves had brought into the city concerning him were soon spread throughout A-lur, nor did they lose aught in the spreading, so that before an hour had passed the women and children were hiding behind barred doorways while the warriors crept apprehensively through the streets expecting momentarily to be pounced upon by a ferocious demon who, bare-handed, did victorious battle with huge gryfs and whose lightest pastime consisted in tearing strong men limb from limb.

CHAPTER XII—THE GIANT STRANGER

And while the warriors and the priests of A-lur searched the temple and the palace and the city for the vanished ape-man there entered the head of Kor-ul-Ja down the precipitous trail from the mountains, a naked stranger bearing an Enfield upon his back. Silently he moved downward toward the bottom of the gorge and there where the ancient trail unfolded more levelly before him he swung along with easy strides, though always with the utmost alertness against possible dangers. A gentle breeze came down from the mountains behind him so that only his ears and his eyes were of value in detecting the presence of danger ahead. Generally the trail followed along the banks of the winding brooklet at the bottom of the gorge, but in some places where the waters tumbled over a precipitous ledge the trail made a detour along the side of the gorge, and again it wound in and out among rocky outcroppings, and presently where it rounded sharply the projecting shoulder of a cliff the stranger came suddenly face to face with one who was ascending the gorge.

Separated by a hundred paces the two halted simultaneously. Before him the stranger saw a tall white warrior, naked but for a loin cloth, cross belts, and a girdle. The man was armed with a heavy, knotted club and a short knife, the latter hanging in its sheath at his left hip from the end of one of his cross belts, the opposite belt supporting a leathern pouch at his right side. It was Ta-den hunting alone in the gorge of his friend, the chief of Kor-ul-Ja. He contemplated the stranger with surprise but no wonder, since he recognized in him a member of the race with which his experience of Tarzan the Terrible had made him familiar and also, thanks to his friendship for the ape-man, he looked upon the newcomer without hostility.

The latter was the first to make outward sign of his intentions, raising his palm toward Ta-den in that gesture which has been a symbol of peace from pole to pole since man ceased to walk upon his knuckles. Simultaneously he advanced a few paces and halted.

Ta-den, assuming that one so like Tarzan the Terrible must be a fellow-tribesman of his lost friend, was more than glad to accept this overture of peace, the sign of which he returned in kind as he ascended the trail to where the other stood. "Who are you?" he asked, but the newcomer only shook his head to indicate that he did not understand.

By signs he tried to carry to the Ho-don the fact that he was following a trail that had led him over a period of many days from some place beyond the mountains and Ta-den was convinced that the newcomer sought Tarzan-jad-guru. He wished, however, that he might discover whether as friend or foe.

The stranger perceived the Ho-don's prehensile thumbs and great toes and his long tail with an astonishment which he sought to conceal, but greater than all was the sense of relief that the first inhabitant of this strange country whom he had met had proven friendly, so greatly would he have been handicapped by the necessity for forcing his way through a hostile land.

Ta-den, who had been hunting for some of the smaller mammals, the meat of which is especially relished by the Ho-don, forgot his intended sport in the greater interest of his new discovery. He would take the stranger to Om-at and possibly together the two would find some way of discovering the true intentions of the newcomer. And so again through signs he apprised the other that he would accompany him and together they descended toward the cliffs of Om-at's people.

As they approached these they came upon the women and children working under guard of the old men and the youths—gathering the wild fruits and herbs which constitute a part of their diet, as well as tending the small acres of growing crops which they cultivate. The fields lay in small level patches that had been cleared of trees and brush. Their farm implements consisted of metal-shod poles which bore a closer resemblance to spears than to tools of peaceful agriculture. Supplementing these were others with flattened blades that were neither hoes nor spades, but instead possessed the appearance of an unhappy attempt to combine the two implements in one.

At first sight of these people the stranger halted and unslung his bow for these creatures were black as night, their bodies entirely covered with hair. But Ta-den, interpreting the doubt in the other's mind, reassured him with a gesture and a smile. The Waz-don, however, gathered around excitedly jabbering questions in a language which the stranger discovered his guide understood though it was entirely unintelligible to the former. They made no attempt to molest him and he was now sure that he had fallen among a peaceful and friendly people.

It was but a short distance now to the caves and when they reached these Ta-den led the way aloft upon the wooden pegs, assured that this creature whom he had discovered would have no more difficulty in following him than had Tarzan the Terrible. Nor was he mistaken for the other mounted with ease until presently the two stood within the recess before the cave of Om-at, the chief.

The latter was not there and it was mid-afternoon before he returned, but in the meantime many warriors came to look upon the visitor and in each instance the latter was more thoroughly impressed with the friendly and peaceable spirit of his hosts, little guessing that he was being entertained by a ferocious and warlike tribe who never before the coming of Ta-den and Tarzan had suffered a stranger among them.

At last Om-at returned and the guest sensed intuitively that he was in the presence of a great man among these people, possibly a chief or king, for not only did the attitude of the other black warriors indicate this but it was written also in the mien and bearing of the splendid creature who stood looking at him while Ta-den explained the circumstances of their meeting. "And I believe, Om-at," concluded the Ho-don, "that he seeks Tarzan the Terrible."

At the sound of that name, the first intelligible word that had fallen upon the ears of the stranger since he had come among them, his face lightened. "Tarzan!" he cried, "Tarzan of the Apes!" and by signs he tried to tell them that it was he whom he sought.

They understood, and also they guessed from the expression of his face that he sought Tarzan from motives of affection rather than the reverse, but of this Om-at wished to make sure. He pointed to the stranger's knife, and repeating Tarzan's name, seized Ta-den and pretended to stab him, immediately turning questioningly toward the stranger.

The latter shook his head vehemently and then first placing a hand above his heart he raised his palm in the symbol of peace.

"He is a friend of Tarzan-jad-guru," exclaimed Ta-den.

"Either a friend or a great liar," replied Om-at.

"Tarzan," continued the stranger, "you know him? He lives? O God, if I could only speak your language." And again reverting to sign language he sought to ascertain where Tarzan was. He would pronounce the name and point in different directions, in the cave, down into the gorge, back toward the mountains, or out upon the valley below, and each time he would raise his brows questioningly and voice the universal "eh?" of interrogation which they could not fail to understand. But always Om-at shook his head and spread his palms in a gesture which indicated that while he understood the question he was ignorant as to the whereabouts of the ape-man, and then the black chief attempted as best he might to explain to the stranger what he knew of the whereabouts of Tarzan.

He called the newcomer Jar-don, which in the language of Pal-ul-don means "stranger," and he pointed to the sun and said as. This he repeated several times and then he held up one hand with the fingers outspread and touching them one by one, including the thumb, repeated the word adenen until the stranger understood that he meant five. Again he pointed to the sun and describing an arc with his forefinger starting at the eastern horizon and terminating at the western, he repeated again the words as adenen. It was plain to the stranger that the words meant that the sun had crossed the heavens five times. In other words, five days had passed. Om-at then pointed to the cave where they stood, pronouncing Tarzan's name and imitating a walking man with the first and second fingers of his right hand upon the floor of the recess, sought to show that Tarzan had walked out of the cave and climbed upward on the pegs five days before, but this was as far as the sign language would permit him to go.

This far the stranger followed him and, indicating that he understood he pointed to himself and then indicating the pegs leading above announced that he would follow Tarzan.

"Let us go with him," said Om-at, "for as yet we have not punished the Kor-ul-lul for killing our friend and ally."

"Persuade him to wait until morning," said Ta-den, "that you may take with you many warriors and make a great raid upon the Kor-ul-lul, and this time, Om-at, do not kill your prisoners. Take as many as you can alive and from some of them we may learn the fate of Tarzan-jad-guru."

"Great is the wisdom of the Ho-don," replied Om-at. "It shall be as you say, and having made prisoners of all the Kor-ul-lul we shall make them tell us what we wish to know. And then we shall march them to the rim of Kor-ul-*gryf* and push them over the edge of the cliff."

Ta-den smiled. He knew that they would not take prisoner all the Kor-ul-lul warriors—that they would be fortunate if they took one and it was also possible that they might even be driven back in defeat, but he knew too that Om-at would not hesitate to carry out his threat if he had the opportunity, so implacable was the hatred of these neighbors for each other.

It was not difficult to explain Om-at's plan to the stranger or to win his consent since he was aware, when the great black had made it plain that they would be accompanied by many warriors, that their venture would probably lead them into a hostile country and every safeguard that he could employ he was glad to avail himself of, since the furtherance of his quest was the paramount issue.

He slept that night upon a pile of furs in one of the compartments of Om-at's ancestral cave, and early the next day following the morning meal they sallied forth, a hundred savage warriors swarming up the face of the sheer cliff and out upon the summit of the ridge, the main body preceded by two warriors whose duties coincided with those of the point of modern military maneuvers, safeguarding the column against the danger of too sudden contact with the enemy.

Across the ridge they went and down into the Kor-ul-lul and there almost immediately they came upon a lone and unarmed Waz-don who was making his way fearfully up the gorge toward the village of his tribe. Him they took prisoner which, strangely, only added to his terror since from the moment that he had seen them and realized that escape was impossible, he had expected to be slain immediately.

"Take him back to Kor-ul-Ja," said Om-at, to one of his warriors, "and hold him there unharmed until I return."

And so the puzzled Kor-ul-lul was led away while the savage company moved stealthily from tree to tree in its closer advance upon the village. Fortune smiled upon Om-at in that it gave him quickly what he sought—a battle royal, for they had not yet come in sight of the caves of the Kor-ul-lul when they encountered a considerable band of warriors headed down the gorge upon some expedition.

Like shadows the Kor-ul-Ja melted into the concealment of the foliage upon either side of the trail. Ignorant of impending danger, safe in the knowledge that they trod their own domain where each rock and stone was as familiar as the features of their mates, the Kor-ul-lul walked innocently into the ambush. Suddenly the quiet of that seeming peace was shattered by a savage cry and a hurled club felled a Kor-ul-lul.

The cry was a signal for a savage chorus from a hundred Kor-ul-Ja throats with which were soon mingled the war cries of their enemies. The air was filled with flying clubs and then as the two forces mingled, the battle resolved itself into a number of individual encounters as each warrior singled out a foe and closed upon him. Knives gleamed and flashed in the mottling sunlight that filtered through the foliage of the trees above. Sleek black coats were streaked with crimson stains.

In the thick of the fight the smooth brown skin of the stranger mingled with the black bodies of friend and foe. Only his keen eyes and his quick wit had shown him how to differentiate between Kor-ul-lul and Kor-ul-Ja since with the single exception of apparel they were identical, but at the first rush of the enemy he had noticed that their loin cloths were not of the leopard-matted hides such as were worn by his allies.

Om-at, after dispatching his first antagonist, glanced at Jar-don. "He fights with the ferocity of *Jato*," mused the chief. "Powerful indeed must be the tribe from which he and Tarzan-jad-guru come," and then his whole attention was occupied by a new assailant.

The fighters surged to and fro through the forest until those who survived were spent with exhaustion. All but the stranger who seemed not to know the sense of fatigue. He fought on when each new antagonist would have gladly quit, and when there were no more Kor-ul-lul who were not engaged, he leaped upon those who stood pantingly facing the exhausted Kor-ul-Ja.

And always he carried upon his back the peculiar thing which Om-at had thought was some manner of strange weapon but the purpose of which he could not now account for in view of the fact that Jar-don never used it, and that for the most part it seemed but a nuisance and needless encumbrance since it banged and smashed against its owner as he leaped, catlike, hither and thither in the course of his victorious duels. The bow and arrows he had tossed aside at the beginning of the fight but the Enfield he would not discard, for where he went he meant that it should go until its mission had been fulfilled.

Presently the Kor-ul-Ja, seemingly shamed by the example of Jar-don closed once more with the enemy, but the latter, moved no doubt to terror by the presence of the stranger, a tireless demon who appeared invulnerable to their attacks, lost heart and sought to flee. And then it was that at Om-at's command his warriors surrounded a half-dozen of the most exhausted and made them prisoners.

It was a tired, bloody, and elated company that returned victorious to the Kor-ul-Ja. Twenty of their number were carried back and six of these were dead men. It was the most glorious and successful raid that the Kor-ul-Ja had made upon the Kor-ul-lul in the memory of man, and it marked Om-at as the greatest of chiefs, but that fierce warrior knew that advantage had lain upon his side largely because of the presence of his strange ally. Nor did he hesitate to give credit where credit belonged, with the result that Jar-don and his exploits were upon the tongue of every member of the tribe of Kor-ul-Ja and great was the fame of the race that could produce two such as he and Tarzan-jad-guru.

And in the gorge of Kor-ul-lul beyond the ridge the survivors spoke in bated breath of this second demon that had joined forces with their ancient enemy.

Returned to his cave Om-at caused the Kor-ul-lul prisoners to be brought into his presence singly, and each he questioned as to the fate of Tarzan. Without exception they told him the same story—that Tarzan had been taken prisoner by them five days before but that he had slain the warrior left to guard him and escaped, carrying the head of the unfortunate sentry to the opposite side of Kor-ul-lul where he had left it suspended by its hair from the branch of a tree. But what had become of him after, they did not know; not one of them, until the last prisoner was examined, he whom they had taken first—the unarmed Kor-ul-lul making his way from the direction of the Valley of Jad-ben-Otho toward the caves of his people.

This one, when he discovered the purpose of their questioning, bartered with them for the lives and liberty of himself and his fellows. "I can tell you much of this terrible man of whom you ask, Kor-ul-Ja," he said. "I saw him yesterday and I know where he is, and if you will promise to let me and my fellows return in safety to the caves of our ancestors I will tell you all, and truthfully, that which I know."

"You will tell us anyway," replied Om-at, "or we shall kill you."

"You will kill me anyway," retorted the prisoner, "unless you make me this promise; so if I am to be killed the thing I know shall go with me."

"He is right, Om-at," said Ta-den, "promise him that they shall have their liberty."

"Very well," said Om-at. "Speak Kor-ul-lul, and when you have told me all, you and your fellows may return unharmed to your tribe."

"It was thus," commenced the prisoner. "Three days since I was hunting with a party of my fellows near the mouth of Kor-ul-lul not far from where you captured me this morning, when we were surprised and set upon by a large number of Ho-don who took us prisoners and carried us to A-lur where a few were chosen to be slaves and the rest were cast into a chamber beneath the temple where are held for sacrifice the victims that are offered by the Ho-don to Jad-ben-Otho upon the sacrificial altars of the temple at A-lur.

"It seemed then that indeed was my fate sealed and that lucky were those who had been selected for slaves among the Ho-don, for they at least might hope to escape—those in the chamber with me must be without hope.

"But yesterday a strange thing happened. There came to the temple, accompanied by all the priests and by the king and many of his warriors, one whom all did great reverence, and when he came to the barred gateway leading to the chamber in which we wretched ones awaited our fate,

I saw to my surprise that it was none other than that terrible man who had so recently been a prisoner in the village of Kor-ul-lul—he whom you call Tarzan-jad-guru but whom they addressed as Dor-ul-Otho. And he looked upon us and questioned the high priest and when he was told of the purpose for which we were imprisoned there he grew angry and cried that it was not the will of Jad-ben-Otho that his people be thus sacrificed, and he commanded the high priest to liberate us, and this was done.

"The Ho-don prisoners were permitted to return to their homes and we were led beyond the City of A-lur and set upon our way toward Kor-ul-lul. There were three of us, but many are the dangers that lie between A-lur and Kor-ul-lul and we were only three and unarmed. Therefore none of us reached the village of our people and only one of us lives. I have spoken."

"That is all you know concerning Tarzan-jad-guru?" asked Om-at.

"That is all I know," replied the prisoner, "other than that he whom they call Lu-don, the high priest at A-lur, was very angry, and that one of the two priests who guided us out of the city said to the other that the stranger was not Dor-ul-Otho at all; that Lu-don had said so and that he had also said that he would expose him and that he should be punished with death for his presumption. That is all they said within my hearing.

"And now, chief of Kor-ul-Ja, let us depart."

Om-at nodded. "Go your way," he said, "and Ab-on, send warriors to guard them until they are safely within the Kor-ul-lul.

"Jar-don," he said beckoning to the stranger, "come with me," and rising he led the way toward the summit of the cliff, and when they stood upon the ridge Om-at pointed down into the valley toward the City of A-lur gleaming in the light of the western sun.

"There is Tarzan-jad-guru," he said, and Jar-don understood.

CHAPTER XIII—THE MASQUERADER

As Tarzan dropped to the ground beyond the temple wall there was in his mind no intention to escape from the City of A-lur until he had satisfied himself that his mate was not a prisoner there, but how, in this strange city in which every man's hand must be now against him, he was to live and prosecute his search was far from clear to him.

There was only one place of which he knew that he might find even temporary sanctuary and that was the Forbidden Garden of the king. There was thick shrubbery in which a man might hide, and water and fruits. A cunning jungle creature, if he could reach the spot unsuspected, might remain concealed there for a considerable time, but how he was to traverse the distance between the temple grounds and the garden unseen was a question the seriousness of which he fully appreciated.

"Mighty is Tarzan," he soliloquized, "in his native jungle, but in the cities of man he is little better than they."

Depending upon his keen observation and sense of location he felt safe in assuming that he could reach the palace grounds by means of the subterranean corridors and chambers of the temple through which he had been conducted the day before, nor any slightest detail of which had escaped his keen eyes. That would be better, he reasoned, than crossing the open grounds above where his pursuers would naturally immediately follow him from the temple and quickly discover him.

And so a dozen paces from the temple wall he disappeared from sight of any chance observer above, down one of the stone stairways that led to the apartments beneath. The way that he had been conducted the previous day had followed the windings and turnings of numerous corridors and apartments, but Tarzan, sure of himself in such matters, retraced the route accurately without hesitation.

He had little fear of immediate apprehension here since he believed that all the priests of the temple had assembled in the court above to witness his trial and his humiliation and his death, and with this idea firmly implanted in his mind he rounded the turn of the corridor and came face to face with an under priest, his grotesque headdress concealing whatever emotion the sight of Tarzan may have aroused.

However, Tarzan had one advantage over the masked votary of Jad-ben-Otho in that the moment he saw the priest he knew his intention concerning him, and therefore was not compelled to delay action. And so it was that before the priest could determine on any suitable line of conduct in the premises a long, keen knife had been slipped into his heart.

As the body lunged toward the floor Tarzan caught it and snatched the headdress from its shoulders, for the first sight of the creature had suggested to his ever-alert mind a bold scheme for deceiving his enemies.

The headdress saved from such possible damage as it must have sustained had it fallen to the floor with the body of its owner, Tarzan relinquished his hold upon the corpse, set the headdress carefully upon the floor and stooping down severed the tail of the Ho-don close to its root. Near by at his right was a small chamber from which the priest had evidently just emerged and into this Tarzan dragged the corpse, the headdress, and the tail.

Quickly cutting a thin strip of hide from the loin cloth of the priest, Tarzan tied it securely about the upper end of the severed member and then tucking the tail under his loin cloth behind him, secured it in place as best he could. Then he fitted the headdress over his shoulders and stepped from the apartment, to all appearances a priest of the temple of Jad-ben-Otho unless one examined too closely his thumbs and his great toes.

He had noticed that among both the Ho-don and the Waz-don it was not at all unusual that the end of the tail be carried in one hand, and so he caught his own tail up thus lest the lifeless appearance of it dragging along behind him should arouse suspicion.

Passing along the corridor and through the various chambers he emerged at last into the palace grounds beyond the temple. The pursuit had not yet reached this point though he was conscious of a commotion not far behind him. He met now both warriors and slaves but none gave him more than a passing glance, a priest being too common a sight about the palace.

And so, passing the guards unchallenged, he came at last to the inner entrance to the Forbidden Garden and there he paused and scanned quickly that portion of the beautiful spot that lay before his eyes. To his relief it seemed unoccupied and congratulating himself upon the ease with which he had so far outwitted the high powers of A-lur he moved rapidly to the opposite end of the enclosure. Here he found a patch of flowering shrubbery that might safely have concealed a dozen men.

Crawling well within he removed the uncomfortable headdress and sat down to await whatever eventualities fate might have in store for him the while he formulated plans for the future. The one night that he had spent in A-lur had kept him up to a late hour, apprising him of the fact that while there were few abroad in the temple grounds at night, there were yet enough to make it possible for him to fare forth under cover of his disguise without attracting the unpleasant attention of the guards, and, too, he had noticed that the priesthood constituted a privileged class that seemed to come and go at will and unchallenged throughout the palace as well as the temple. Altogether then, he decided, night furnished the most propitious hours for his investigation—by day he could lie up in the shrubbery of the Forbidden Garden, reasonably free from detection. From beyond the garden he heard the voices of men calling to one another both far and near, and he guessed that diligent was the search that was being prosecuted for him.

The idle moments afforded him an opportunity to evolve a more satisfactory scheme for attaching his stolen caudal appendage. He arranged it in such a way that it might be quickly assumed or discarded, and this done he fell to examining the weird mask that had so effectively hidden his features.

The thing had been very cunningly wrought from a single block of wood, very probably a section of a tree, upon which the features had been carved and afterward the interior hollowed out until only a comparatively thin shell remained. Two-semicircular notches had been rounded out from opposite sides of the lower edge. These fitted snugly over his shoulders, aprons of wood extending downward a few inches upon his chest and back. From these aprons hung long tassels or switches of hair tapering from the outer edges toward the center which reached below the bottom of his torso. It required but the most cursory examination to indicate to the ape-man that these ornaments consisted of human scalps, taken, doubtless, from the heads of the sacrifices upon the eastern altars. The headdress itself had been carved to depict in formal design a hideous face that suggested both man and *gryf*. There were the three white horns, the yellow face with the blue bands encircling the eyes and the red hood which took the form of the posterior and anterior aprons.

As Tarzan sat within the concealing foliage of the shrubbery meditating upon the hideous priest-mask which he held in his hands he became aware that he was not alone in the garden. He sensed another presence and presently his trained ears detected the slow approach of naked feet across the sward. At first he suspected that it might be one stealthily searching the Forbidden Garden for him but a little later the figure came within the limited area of his vision which was circumscribed by stems and foliage and flowers. He saw then that it was the princess O-lo-a and that she was alone and walking with bowed head as though in meditation—sorrowful meditation for there were traces of tears upon her lids.

Shortly after his ears warned him that others had entered the garden—men they were and their footsteps proclaimed that they walked neither slowly nor meditatively. They came directly toward the princess and when Tarzan could see them he discovered that both were priests.

"O-lo-a, Princess of Pal-ul-don," said one, addressing her, "the stranger who told us that he was the son of Jad-ben-Otho has but just fled from the wrath of Lu-don, the high priest, who exposed him and all his wicked blasphemy. The temple, and the palace, and the city are being searched and we have been sent to search the Forbidden Garden, since Ko-tan, the king, said that only this morning he found him here, though how he passed the guards he could not guess."

"He is not here," said O-lo-a. "I have been in the garden for some time and have seen nor heard no other than myself. However, search it if you will."

"No," said the priest who had before spoken, "it is not necessary since he could not have entered without your knowledge and the connivance of the guards, and even had he, the priest who preceded us must have seen him."

"What priest?" asked O-lo-a.

"One passed the guards shortly before us," explained the man.

"I did not see him," said O-lo-a.

"Doubtless he left by another exit," remarked the second priest.

"Yes, doubtless," acquiesced O-lo-a, "but it is strange that I did not see him." The two priests made their obeisance and turned to depart.

"Stupid as Buto, the rhinoceros," soliloquized Tarzan, who considered Buto a very stupid creature indeed. "It should be easy to outwit such as these."

The priests had scarce departed when there came the sound of feet running rapidly across the garden in the direction of the princess to an accompaniment of rapid breathing as of one almost spent, either from fatigue or excitement.

"Pan-at-lee," exclaimed O-lo-a, "what has happened? You look as terrified as the doe for which you were named!"

"O Princess of Pal-ul-don," cried Pan-at-lee, "they would have killed him in the temple. They would have killed the wondrous stranger who claimed to be the Dor-ul-Otho."

"But he escaped," said O-lo-a. "You were there. Tell me about it."

"The head priest would have had him seized and slain, but when they rushed upon him he hurled one in the face of Lu-don with the same ease that you might cast your breastplates at me, and then he leaped upon the altar and from there to the top of the temple wall and disappeared below. They are searching for him, but, O Princess, I pray that they do not find him."

"And why do you pray that?" asked O-lo-a. "Has not one who has so blasphemed earned death?"

"Ah, but you do not know him," replied Pan-at-lee.

"And you do, then?" retorted O-lo-a quickly. "This morning you betrayed yourself and then attempted to deceive me. The slaves of O-lo-a do not such things with impunity. He is then the same Tarzan-jad-guru of whom you told me? Speak woman and speak only the truth."

Pan-at-lee drew herself up very erect, her little chin held high, for was not she too among her own people already as good as a princess? "Pan-at-lee, the Kor-ul-Ja does not lie," she said, "to protect herself."

"Then tell me what you know of this Tarzan-jad-guru," insisted O-lo-a.

"I know that he is a wondrous man and very brave," said Pan-at-lee, "and that he saved me from the Tor-o-don and the *gryf* as I told you, and that he is indeed the same who came into the garden this morning; and even now I do not know that he is not the son of Jad-ben-Otho for his courage and his strength are more than those of mortal man, as are also his kindness and his honor: for when he might have harmed me he protected me, and when he might have saved himself he thought only of me. And all this he did because of his friendship for Om-at, who is gund of Kor-ul-Ja and with whom I should have mated had the Ho-don not captured me."

"He was indeed a wonderful man to look upon," mused O-lo-a, "and he was not as are other men, not alone in the conformation of his hands and feet or the fact that he was tailless, but there was that about him which made him seem different in ways more important than these."

"And," supplemented Pan-at-lee, her savage little heart loyal to the man who had befriended her and hoping to win for him the consideration of the princess even though it might not avail him; "and," she said, "did he not know all about Ta-den and even his whereabouts. Tell me, O Princess, could mortal know such things as these?"

"Perhaps he saw Ta-den," suggested O-lo-a.

"But how would he know that you loved Ta-den," parried Pan-at-lee. "I tell you, my Princess, that if he is not a god he is at least more than Ho-don or Waz-don. He followed me from the cave of Es-sat in Kor-ul-Ja across Kor-ul-lul and two wide ridges to the very cave in Kor-ul-*gryf* where I hid, though many hours had passed since I had come that way and my bare feet left no impress upon the ground. What mortal man could do such things as these? And where in all Pal-ul-don would virgin maid find friend and protector in a strange male other than he?"

"Perhaps Lu-don may be mistaken—perhaps he is a god," said O-lo-a, influenced by her slave's enthusiastic championing of the stranger.

"But whether god or man he is too wonderful to die," cried Pan-at-lee. "Would that I might save him. If he lived he might even find a way to give you your Ta-den, Princess."

"Ah, if he only could," sighed O-lo-a, "but alas it is too late for tomorrow I am to be given to Bu-lot."

"He who came to your quarters yesterday with your father?" asked Pan-at-lee.

"Yes; the one with the awful round face and the big belly," exclaimed the Princess disgustedly. "He is so lazy he will neither hunt nor fight. To eat and to drink is all that Bu-lot is fit for, and he thinks of naught else except these things and his slave women. But come, Pan-at-lee, gather for me some of these beautiful blossoms. I would have them spread around my couch tonight that I may carry away with me in the morning the memory of the fragrance that I love best and which I know that I shall not find in the village of Mo-sar, the father of Bu-lot. I will help you, Pan-at-lee, and we will gather armfuls of them, for I love to gather them as I love nothing else—they were Ta-den's favorite flowers."

The two approached the flowering shrubbery where Tarzan hid, but as the blooms grew plentifully upon every bush the ape-man guessed there would be no necessity for them to enter the patch far enough to discover him. With little exclamations of pleasure as they found particularly large or perfect blooms the two moved from place to place upon the outskirts of Tarzan's retreat.

"Oh, look, Pan-at-lee," cried O-lo-a presently; "there is the king of them all. Never did I see so wonderful a flower—No! I will get it myself—it is so large and wonderful no other hand shall touch it," and the princess wound in among the bushes toward the point where the great flower bloomed upon a bush above the ape-man's head.

So sudden and unexpected her approach that there was no opportunity to escape and Tarzan sat silently trusting that fate might be kind to him and lead Ko-tan's daughter away before her eyes dropped from the high-growing bloom to him. But as the girl cut the long stem with her knife she looked down straight into the smiling face of Tarzan-jad-guru.

With a stifled scream she drew back and the ape-man rose and faced her.

"Have no fear, Princess," he assured her. "It is the friend of Ta-den who salutes you," raising her fingers to his lips.

Pan-at-lee came now excitedly forward. "O Jad-ben-Otho, it is he!"

"And now that you have found me," queried Tarzan, "will you give me up to Lu-don, the high priest?"

Pan-at-lee threw herself upon her knees at O-lo-a's feet. "Princess! Princess!" she beseeched, "do not discover him to his enemies."

"But Ko-tan, my father," whispered O-lo-a fearfully, "if he knew of my perfidy his rage would be beyond naming. Even though I am a princess Lu-don might demand that I be sacrificed to appease the wrath of Jad-ben-Otho, and between the two of them I should be lost."

"But they need never know," cried Pan-at-lee, "that you have seen him unless you tell them yourself for as Jad-ben-Otho is my witness I will never betray you."

"Oh, tell me, stranger," implored O-lo-a, "are you indeed a god?"

"Jad-ben-Otho is not more so," replied Tarzan truthfully.

"But why do you seek to escape then from the hands of mortals if you are a god?" she asked.

"When gods mingle with mortals," replied Tarzan, "they are no less vulnerable than mortals. Even Jad-ben-Otho, should he appear before you in the flesh, might be slain."

"You have seen Ta-den and spoken with him?" she asked with apparent irrelevancy.

"Yes, I have seen him and spoken with him," replied the ape-man. "For the duration of a moon I was with him constantly."

"And—" she hesitated—"he—" she cast her eyes toward the ground and a flush mantled her cheek—"he still loves me?" and Tarzan knew that she had been won over.

"Yes," he said, "Ta-den speaks only of O-lo-a and he waits and hopes for the day when he can claim her."

"But tomorrow they give me to Bu-lot," she said sadly.

"May it be always tomorrow," replied Tarzan, "for tomorrow never comes."

"Ah, but this unhappiness will come, and for all the tomorrows of my life I must pine in misery for the Ta-den who will never be mine."

"But for Lu-don I might have helped you," said the ape-man. "And who knows that I may not help you yet?"

"Ah, if you only could, Dor-ul-Otho," cried the girl, "and I know that you would if it were possible for Pan-at-lee has told me how brave you are, and at the same time how kind."

"Only Jad-ben-Otho knows what the future may bring," said Tarzan. "And now you two go your way lest someone should discover you and become suspicious."

"We will go," said O-lo-a, "but Pan-at-lee will return with food. I hope that you escape and that Jad-ben-Otho is pleased with what I have done." She turned and walked away and Pan-at-lee followed while the ape-man again resumed his hiding.

At dusk Pan-at-lee came with food and having her alone Tarzan put the question that he had been anxious to put since his conversation earlier in the day with O-lo-a.

"Tell me," he said, "what you know of the rumors of which O-lo-a spoke of the mysterious stranger which is supposed to be hidden in A-lur. Have you too heard of this during the short time that you have been here?"

"Yes," said Pan-at-lee, "I have heard it spoken of among the other slaves. It is something of which all whisper among themselves but of which none dares to speak aloud. They say that there is a strange she hidden in the temple and that Lu-don wants her for a priestess and that Ko-tan wants her for a wife and that neither as yet dares take her for fear of the other."

"Do you know where she is hidden in the temple?" asked Tarzan.

"No," said Pan-at-lee. "How should I know? I do not even know that it is more than a story and I but tell you that which I have heard others say."

"There was only one," asked Tarzan, "whom they spoke of?"

"No, they speak of another who came with her but none seems to know what became of this one."

Tarzan nodded. "Thank you Pan-at-lee," he said. "You may have helped me more than either of us guess."

"I hope that I have helped you," said the girl as she turned back toward the palace.

"And I hope so too," exclaimed Tarzan emphatically.

CHAPTER XIV—THE TEMPLE OF THE GRYF

When night had fallen Tarzan donned the mask and the dead tail of the priest he had slain in the vaults beneath the temple. He judged that it would not do to attempt again to pass the guard, especially so late at night as it would be likely to arouse comment and suspicion, and so he swung into the tree that overhung the garden wall and from its branches dropped to the ground beyond.

Avoiding too grave risk of apprehension the ape-man passed through the grounds to the court of the palace, approaching the temple from the side opposite to that at which he had left it at the time of his escape. He came thus it is true through a portion of the grounds with which he was unfamiliar but he preferred this to the danger of following the beaten track between the palace apartments and those of the temple. Having a definite goal in mind and endowed as he was with an almost miraculous sense of location he moved with great assurance through the shadows of the temple yard.

Taking advantage of the denser shadows close to the walls and of what shrubs and trees there were he came without mishap at last to the ornate building concerning the purpose of which he had asked Lu-don only to be put off with the assertion that it was forgotten—nothing strange in itself but given possible importance by the apparent hesitancy of the priest to discuss its use and the impression the ape-man had gained at the time that Lu-don lied.

And now he stood at last alone before the structure which was three stories in height and detached from all the other temple buildings. It had a single barred entrance which was carved from the living rock in representation of the head of a *gryf*, whose wide-open mouth constituted the doorway. The head, hood, and front paws of the creature were depicted as though it lay crouching with its lower jaw on the ground between its outspread paws. Small oval windows, which were likewise barred, flanked the doorway.

Seeing that the coast was clear, Tarzan stepped into the darkened entrance where he tried the bars only to discover that they were ingeniously locked in place by some device with which he was unfamiliar and that they also were probably too strong to be broken even if he could have risked the noise which would have resulted. Nothing was visible within the darkened interior and so, momentarily baffled, he sought the windows. Here also the bars refused to yield up their secret, but again Tarzan was not dismayed since he had counted upon nothing different.

If the bars would not yield to his cunning they would yield to his giant strength if there proved no other means of ingress, but first he would assure himself that this latter was the case. Moving entirely around the building he examined it carefully. There were other windows but they were similarly barred. He stopped often to look and listen but he saw no one and the sounds that he heard were too far away to cause him any apprehension.

He glanced above him at the wall of the building. Like so many of the other walls of the city, palace, and temple, it was ornately carved and there were too the peculiar ledges that ran sometimes in a horizontal plane and again were tilted at an angle, giving ofttimes an impression of irregularity and even crookedness to the buildings. It was not a difficult wall to climb, at least not difficult for the ape-man.

But he found the bulky and awkward headdress a considerable handicap and so he laid it aside upon the ground at the foot of the wall. Nimbly he ascended to find the windows of the second floor not only barred but curtained within. He did not delay long at the second floor since he had in mind an idea that he would find the easiest entrance through the roof which he had noticed was roughly dome shaped like the throneroom of Ko-tan. Here there were apertures. He had seen them from the ground, and if the construction of the interior resembled even slightly that of the throneroom, bars would not be necessary upon these apertures, since no one could reach them from the floor of the room.

There was but a single question: would they be large enough to admit the broad shoulders of the ape-man.

He paused again at the third floor, and here, in spite of the hangings, he saw that the interior was lighted and simultaneously there came to his nostrils from within a scent that stripped from him temporarily any remnant of civilization that might have remained and left him a fierce and terrible bull of the jungles of Kerchak. So sudden and complete was the metamorphosis that there almost broke from the savage lips the hideous challenge of his kind, but the cunning brute-mind saved him this blunder.

And now he heard voices within—the voice of Lu-don he could have sworn, demanding. And haughty and disdainful came the answering words though utter hopelessness spoke in the tones of this other voice which brought Tarzan to the pinnacle of frenzy.

The dome with its possible apertures was forgotten. Every consideration of stealth and quiet was cast aside as the ape-man drew back his mighty fist and struck a single terrific blow upon the bars of the small window before him, a blow that sent the bars and the casing that held them clattering to the floor of the apartment within.

Instantly Tarzan dove headforemost through the aperture carrying the hangings of antelope hide with him to the floor below. Leaping to his feet he tore the entangling pelt from about his head only to find himself in utter darkness and in silence. He called aloud a name that had not passed his lips for many weary months. "Jane, Jane," he cried, "where are you?" But there was only silence in reply.

Again and again he called, groping with outstretched hands through the Stygian blackness of the room, his nostrils assailed and his brain tantalized by the delicate effluvia that had first assured him that his mate had been within this very room. And he had heard her dear voice combatting the base demands of the vile priest. Ah, if he had but acted with greater caution! If he had but continued to move with quiet and stealth he might even at this moment be holding her in his arms while the body of Lu-don, beneath his foot, spoke eloquently of vengeance achieved. But there was no time now for idle self-reproaches.

He stumbled blindly forward, groping for he knew not what till suddenly the floor beneath him tilted and he shot downward into a darkness even more utter than that above. He felt his body strike a smooth surface and he realized that he was hurtling downward as through a polished chute while from above there came the mocking tones of a taunting laugh and the voice of Lu-don screamed after him: "Return to thy father, O Dor-ul-Otho!"

The ape-man came to a sudden and painful stop upon a rocky floor. Directly before him was an oval window crossed by many bars, and beyond he saw the moonlight playing on the waters of the blue lake below. Simultaneously he was conscious of a familiar odor in the air of the chamber, which a quick glance revealed in the semidarkness as of considerable proportion.

It was the faint, but unmistakable odor of the *gryf*, and now Tarzan stood silently listening. At first he detected no sounds other than those of the city that came to him through the window overlooking the lake; but presently, faintly, as though from a distance he heard the shuffling of padded feet along a stone pavement, and as he listened he was aware that the sound approached.

Nearer and nearer it came, and now even the breathing of the beast was audible. Evidently attracted by the noise of his descent into its cavernous retreat it was approaching to investigate. He could not see it but he knew that it was not far distant, and then, deafeningly there reverberated through those gloomy corridors the mad bellow of the *gryf*.

Aware of the poor eyesight of the beast, and his own eyes now grown accustomed to the darkness of the cavern, the ape-man sought to elude the infuriated charge which he well knew no living creature could withstand. Neither did he dare risk the chance of experimenting upon this strange *gryf* with the tactics of the Tor-o-don that he had found so efficacious upon that other occasion when his life and liberty had been the stakes for which he cast. In many respects the conditions were dissimilar. Before, in broad daylight, he had been able to approach the *gryf* under normal conditions in its natural state, and the *gryf* itself was one that he had seen subjected to the authority of man, or at least of a manlike creature; but here he was confronted by an imprisoned beast in the full swing of a furious charge and he had every reason to suspect that this *gryf* might never have felt the restraining influence of authority, confined as it was in this gloomy pit to serve likely but the single purpose that Tarzan had already seen so graphically portrayed in his own experience of the past few moments.

To elude the creature, then, upon the possibility of discovering some loophole of escape from his predicament seemed to the ape-man the wisest course to pursue. Too much was at stake to risk an encounter that might be avoided—an encounter the outcome of which there was every reason to apprehend would seal the fate of the mate that he had just found, only to lose again so harrowingly. Yet high as his disappointment and chagrin ran, hopeless as his present estate now appeared, there tingled in the veins of the savage lord a warm glow of thanksgiving and elation. She lived! After all these weary months of hopelessness and fear he had found her. She lived!

To the opposite side of the chamber, silently as the wraith of a disembodied soul, the swift jungle creature moved from the path of the charging Titan that, guided solely in the semi-darkness by its keen ears, bore down upon the spot toward which Tarzan's noisy entrance into its lair had attracted it. Along the further wall the ape-man hurried. Before him now appeared the black opening of the corridor from which the beast had emerged into the larger chamber. Without hesitation Tarzan plunged into it. Even here his eyes, long accustomed to darkness that would have seemed total to you or to me, saw dimly the floor and the walls within a radius of a few feet—enough at least to prevent him plunging into any unguessed abyss, or dashing himself upon solid rock at a sudden turning.

The corridor was both wide and lofty, which indeed it must be to accommodate the colossal proportions of the creature whose habitat it was, and so Tarzan encountered no difficulty in moving with reasonable speed along its winding trail. He was aware as he proceeded that the trend of the passage was downward, though not steeply, but it seemed interminable and he wondered to what distant subterranean lair it might lead. There was a feeling that perhaps after all he might better have remained in the larger chamber and risked all on the chance of subduing the *gryf* where there was at least sufficient room and light to lend to the experiment some slight chance of success. To be overtaken here in the narrow confines of the black corridor where he was assured the *gryf* could not see him at all would spell almost certain death and now he heard the thing approaching from behind. Its thunderous bellows fairly shook the cliff from which the cavernous chambers were excavated. To halt and meet this monstrous incarnation of fury with a futile whee-oo! seemed to Tarzan the height of insanity and so he continued along the corridor, increasing his pace as he realized that the *gryf* was overhauling him.

Presently the darkness lessened and at the final turning of the passage he saw before him an area of moonlight. With renewed hope he sprang rapidly forward and emerged from the mouth of the corridor to find himself in a large circular enclosure the towering white walls of which rose high upon every side—smooth perpendicular walls upon the sheer face of which was no slightest foothold. To his left lay a pool of water, one side of which lapped the foot of the wall at this point. It was, doubtless, the wallow and the drinking pool of the *gryf*.

And now the creature emerged from the corridor and Tarzan retreated to the edge of the pool to make his last stand. There was no staff with which to enforce the authority of his voice, but yet he made his stand for there seemed naught else to do. Just beyond the entrance to the corridor the *gryf* paused, turning its weak eyes in all directions as though searching for its prey. This then seemed the psychological moment for his attempt and raising his voice in peremptory command the ape-man voiced the weird whee-oo! of the Tor-o-don. Its effect upon the *gryf* was instantaneous and complete—with a terrific bellow it lowered its three horns and dashed madly in the direction of the sound.

To right nor to left was any avenue of escape, for behind him lay the placid waters of the pool, while down upon him from before thundered annihilation. The mighty body seemed already to tower above him as the ape-man turned and dove into the dark waters.

Dead in her breast lay hope. Battling for life during harrowing months of imprisonment and danger and hardship it had fitfully flickered and flamed only to sink after each renewal to smaller proportions than before and now it had died out entirely leaving only cold, charred embers that Jane Clayton knew would never again be rekindled. Hope was dead as she faced Lu-don, the high priest, in her prison quarters in the Temple of the Gryf at A-lur. Both time and hardship had failed to leave their impress upon her physical beauty—the contours of her perfect form, the glory of her radiant loveliness had defied them, yet to these very attributes she owed the danger which now confronted her, for Lu-don desired her. From the lesser priests she had been safe, but from Lu-don, she was not safe, for Lu-don was not as they, since the high priestship of Pal-ul-don may descend from father to son.

Ko-tan, the king, had wanted her and all that had so far saved her from either was the fear of each for the other, but at last Lu-don had cast aside discretion and had come in the silent watches of the night to claim her. Haughtily had she repulsed him, seeking ever to gain time, though what time might bring her of relief or renewed hope she could not even remotely conjecture. A leer of lust and greed shone hungrily upon his cruel countenance as he advanced across the room to seize her. She did not shrink nor cower, but stood there very erect, her chin up, her level gaze freighted with the loathing and contempt she felt for him. He read her expression and while it angered him, it but increased his desire for possession. Here indeed was a queen, perhaps a goddess; fit mate for the high priest.

"You shall not!" she said as he would have touched her. "One of us shall die before ever your purpose is accomplished."

He was close beside her now. His laugh grated upon her ears. "Love does not kill," he replied mockingly.

He reached for her arm and at the same instant something clashed against the bars of one of the windows, crashing them inward to the floor, to be followed almost simultaneously by a human figure which dove headforemost into the room, its head enveloped in the skin window hangings which it carried with it in its impetuous entry.

Jane Clayton saw surprise and something of terror too leap to the countenance of the high priest and then she saw him spring forward and jerk upon a leather thong that depended from the ceiling of the apartment. Instantly there dropped from above a cunningly contrived partition that fell between them and the intruder, effectively barring him from them and at the same time leaving him to grope upon its opposite side in darkness, since the only cresset the room contained was upon their side of the partition.

Faintly from beyond the wall Jane heard a voice calling, but whose it was and what the words she could not distinguish. Then she saw Lu-don jerk upon another thong and wait in evident expectancy of some consequent happening. He did not have long to wait. She saw the thong move suddenly as though jerked from above and then Lu-don smiled and with another signal put in motion whatever machinery it was that raised the partition again to its place in the ceiling.

Advancing into that portion of the room that the partition had shut off from them, the high priest knelt upon the floor, and down tilting a section of it, revealed the dark mouth of a shaft leading below. Laughing loudly he shouted into the hole: "Return to thy father, O Dor-ul-Otho!"

Making fast the catch that prevented the trapdoor from opening beneath the feet of the unwary until such time as Lu-don chose the high priest rose again to his feet.

"Now, Beautiful One!" he cried, and then, "Ja-don! what do you here?"

Jane Clayton turned to follow the direction of Lu-don's eyes and there she saw framed in the entrance-way to the apartment the mighty figure of a warrior, upon whose massive features sat an expression of stern and uncompromising authority.

"I come from Ko-tan, the king," replied Ja-don, "to remove the beautiful stranger to the Forbidden Garden."

"The king defies me, the high priest of Jad-ben-Otho?" cried Lu-don.

"It is the king's command—I have spoken," snapped Ja-don, in whose manner was no sign of either fear or respect for the priest.

Lu-don well knew why the king had chosen this messenger whose heresy was notorious, but whose power had as yet protected him from the machinations of the priest. Lu-don cast a surreptitious glance at the thongs hanging from the ceiling. Why not? If he could but maneuver to entice Ja-don to the opposite side of the chamber!

"Come," he said in a conciliatory tone, "let us discuss the matter," and moved toward the spot where he would have Ja-don follow him.

"There is nothing to discuss," replied Ja-don, yet he followed the priest, fearing treachery.

Jane watched them. In the face and figure of the warrior she found reflected those admirable traits of courage and honor that the profession of arms best develops. In the hypocritical priest there was no redeeming quality. Of the two then she might best choose the warrior. With him there was a chance—with Lu-don, none. Even the very process of exchange from one prison to another might offer some possibility of escape. She weighed all these things and decided, for Lu-don's quick glance at the thongs had not gone unnoticed nor uninterpreted by her.

"Warrior," she said, addressing Ja-don, "if you would live enter not that portion of the room."

Lu-don cast an angry glance upon her. "Silence, slave!" he cried.

"And where lies the danger?" Ja-don asked of Jane, ignoring Lu-don.

The woman pointed to the thongs. "Look," she said, and before the high priest could prevent she had seized that which controlled the partition which shot downward separating Lu-don from the warrior and herself.

Ja-don looked inquiringly at her. "He would have tricked me neatly but for you," he said; "kept me imprisoned there while he secreted you elsewhere in the mazes of his temple."

"He would have done more than that," replied Jane, as she pulled upon the other thong. "This releases the fastenings of a trapdoor in the floor beyond the partition. When you stepped on that you would have been precipitated into a pit beneath the temple. Lu-don has threatened me with this fate often. I do not know that he speaks the truth, but he says that a demon of the temple is imprisoned there—a huge *gryf*."

"There is a *gryf* within the temple," said Ja-don. "What with it and the sacrifices, the priests keep us busy supplying them with prisoners, though the victims are sometimes those for whom Lu-don has conceived hatred among our own people. He has had his eyes upon me for a long time. This would have been his chance but for you. Tell me, woman, why you warned me. Are we not all equally your jailers and your enemies?"

"None could be more horrible than Lu-don," she replied; "and you have the appearance of a brave and honorable warrior. I could not hope, for hope has died and yet there is the possibility that among so many fighting men, even though they be of another race than mine, there is one who would accord honorable treatment to a stranger within his gates—even though she be a woman."

Ja-don looked at her for a long minute. "Ko-tan would make you his queen," he said. "That he told me himself and surely that were honorable treatment from one who might make you a slave."

"Why, then, would he make me queen?" she asked.

Ja-don came closer as though in fear his words might be overheard. "He believes, although he did not tell me so in fact, that you are of the race of gods. And why not? Jad-ben-Otho is tailless, therefore it is not strange that Ko-tan should suspect that only the gods are thus. His queen is dead leaving only a single daughter. He craves a son and what more desirable than that he should found a line of rulers for Pal-ul-don descended from the gods?"

"But I am already wed," cried Jane. "I cannot wed another. I do not want him or his throne."

"Ko-tan is king," replied Ja-don simply as though that explained and simplified everything.

"You will not save me then?" she asked.

"If you were in Ja-lur," he replied, "I might protect you, even against the king."

"What and where is Ja-lur?" she asked, grasping at any straw.

"It is the city where I rule," he answered. "I am chief there and of all the valley beyond."

"Where is it?" she insisted, and "is it far?"

"No," he replied, smiling, "it is not far, but do not think of that—you could never reach it. There are too many to pursue and capture you. If you wish to know, however, it lies up the river that empties into Jad-ben-lul whose waters kiss the walls of A-lur—up the western fork it lies with water upon three sides. Impregnable city of Pal-ul-don—alone of all the cities it has never been entered by a foeman since it was built there while Jad-ben-Otho was a boy."

"And there I would be safe?" she asked.

"Perhaps," he replied.

Ah, dead Hope; upon what slender provocation would you seek to glow again! She sighed and shook her head, realizing the inutility of Hope—yet the tempting bait dangled before her mind's eye—Ja-lur!

"You are wise," commented Ja-don interpreting her sigh. "Come now, we will go to the quarters of the princess beside the Forbidden Garden. There you will remain with O-lo-a, the king's daughter. It will be better than this prison you have occupied."

"And Ko-tan?" she asked, a shudder passing through her slender frame.

"There are ceremonies," explained Ja-don, "that may occupy several days before you become queen, and one of them may be difficult of arrangement." He laughed, then.

"What?" she asked.

"Only the high priest may perform the marriage ceremony for a king," he explained.

"Delay!" she murmured; "blessed delay!" Tenacious indeed of life is Hope even though it be reduced to cold and lifeless char—a veritable phoenix.

CHAPTER XV—"THE KING IS DEAD!"

As they conversed Ja-don had led her down the stone stairway that leads from the upper floors of the Temple of the Gryf to the chambers and the corridors that honeycomb the rocky hills from which the temple and the palace are hewn and now they passed from one to the other through a doorway upon one side of which two priests stood guard and upon the other two warriors. The former would have halted Ja-don when they saw who it was that accompanied him for well known throughout the temple was the quarrel between king and high priest for possession of this beautiful stranger.

"Only by order of Lu-don may she pass," said one, placing himself directly in front of Jane Clayton, barring her progress. Through the hollow eyes of the hideous mask the woman could see those of the priest beneath gleaming with the fires of fanaticism. Ja-don placed an arm about her shoulders and laid his hand upon his knife.

"She passes by order of Ko-tan, the king," he said, "and by virtue of the fact that Ja-don, the chief, is her guide. Stand aside!"

The two warriors upon the palace side pressed forward. "We are here, gund of Ja-lur," said one, addressing Ja-don, "to receive and obey your commands."

The second priest now interposed. "Let them pass," he admonished his companion. "We have received no direct commands from Lu-don to the contrary and it is a law of the temple and the palace that chiefs and priests may come and go without interference."

"But I know Lu-don's wishes," insisted the other.

"He told you then that Ja-don must not pass with the stranger?"

"No—but—"

"Then let them pass, for they are three to two and will pass anyway—we have done our best."

Grumbling, the priest stepped aside. "Lu-don will exact an accounting," he cried angrily.

Ja-don turned upon him. "And get it when and where he will," he snapped.

They came at last to the quarters of the Princess O-lo-a where, in the main entrance-way, loitered a small guard of palace warriors and several stalwart black eunuchs belonging to the princess, or her women. To one of the latter Ja-don relinquished his charge.

"Take her to the princess," he commanded, "and see that she does not escape."

Through a number of corridors and apartments lighted by stone cressets the eunuch led Lady Greystoke halting at last before a doorway concealed by hangings of *Jato* skin, where the guide beat with his staff upon the wall beside the door.

"O-lo-a, Princess of Pal-ul-don," he called, "here is the stranger woman, the prisoner from the temple."

"Bid her enter," Jane heard a sweet voice from within command.

The eunuch drew aside the hangings and Lady Greystoke stepped within. Before her was a low-ceiled room of moderate size. In each of the four corners a kneeling figure of stone seemed to be bearing its portion of the weight of the ceiling upon its shoulders. These figures were evidently intended to represent Waz-don slaves and were not without bold artistic beauty. The ceiling itself was slightly arched to a central dome which was pierced to admit light by day, and air. Upon one side of the room were many windows, the other three walls being blank except for a doorway in each. The princess lay upon a pile of furs which were arranged over a low stone dais in one corner of the apartment and was alone except for a single Waz-don slave girl who sat upon the edge of the dais near her feet.

As Jane entered O-lo-a beckoned her to approach and when she stood beside the couch the girl half rose upon an elbow and surveyed her critically.

"How beautiful you are," she said simply.

Jane smiled, sadly; for she had found that beauty may be a curse.

"That is indeed a compliment," she replied quickly, "from one so radiant as the Princess O-lo-a."

"Ah!" exclaimed the princess delightedly; "you speak my language! I was told that you were of another race and from some far land of which we of Pal-ul-don have never heard."

"Lu-don saw to it that the priests instructed me," explained Jane; "but I am from a far country, Princess; one to which I long to return—and I am very unhappy."

"But Ko-tan, my father, would make you his queen," cried the girl; "that should make you very happy."

"But it does not," replied the prisoner; "I love another to whom I am already wed. Ah, Princess, if you had known what it was to love and to be forced into marriage with another you would sympathize with me."

The Princess O-lo-a was silent for a long moment. "I know," she said at last, "and I am very sorry for you; but if the king's daughter cannot save herself from such a fate who may save a slave woman? for such in fact you are."

The drinking in the great banquet hall of the palace of Ko-tan, king of Pal-ul-don had commenced earlier this night than was usual, for the king was celebrating the morrow's betrothal of his only daughter to Bu-lot, son of Mo-sar, the chief, whose great-grandfather had been king of Pal-ul-don and who thought that he should be king, and Mo-sar was drunk and so was Bu-lot, his son. For that matter nearly all of the warriors, including the king himself, were drunk. In the heart of Ko-tan was no love either for Mo-sar, or Bu-lot, nor did either of these love the king. Ko-tan was giving his daughter to Bu-lot in the hope that the alliance would prevent Mo-sar from insisting upon his claims to the throne, for, next to Ja-don, Mo-sar was the most powerful of the chiefs and while Ko-tan looked with fear upon Ja-don, too, he had no fear that the old Lion-man would attempt to seize the throne, though which way he would throw his influence and his warriors in the event that Mo-sar declare war upon Ko-tan, the king could not guess.

Primitive people who are also warlike are seldom inclined toward either tact or diplomacy even when sober; but drunk they know not the words, if aroused. It was really Bu-lot who started it.

"This," he said, "I drink to O-lo-a," and he emptied his tankard at a single gulp. "And this," seizing a full one from a neighbor, "to her son and mine who will bring back the throne of Pal-ul-don to its rightful owners!"

"The king is not yet dead!" cried Ko-tan, rising to his feet; "nor is Bu-lot yet married to his daughter—and there is yet time to save Pal-ul-don from the spawn of the rabbit breed."

The king's angry tone and his insulting reference to Bu-lot's well-known cowardice brought a sudden, sobering silence upon the roistering company. Every eye turned upon Bu-lot and Mo-sar, who sat together directly opposite the king. The first was very drunk though suddenly he seemed quite sober. He was so drunk that for an instant he forgot to be a coward, since his reasoning powers were so effectually paralyzed by the fumes of liquor that he could not intelligently weigh the consequences of his acts. It is reasonably conceivable that a drunk and angry rabbit might commit a rash deed. Upon no other hypothesis is the thing that Bu-lot now did explicable. He rose suddenly from the seat to which he had sunk after delivering his toast and seizing the knife from the sheath of the warrior upon his right hurled it with terrific force at Ko-tan. Skilled in the art of throwing both their knives and their clubs are the warriors of Pal-ul-don and at this short distance and coming as it did without warning there was no defense and but one possible result—Ko-tan, the king, lunged forward across the table, the blade buried in his heart.

A brief silence followed the assassin's cowardly act. White with terror, now, Bu-lot fell slowly back toward the doorway at his rear, when suddenly angry warriors leaped with drawn knives to prevent his escape and to avenge their king. But Mo-sar now took his stand beside his son.

"Ko-tan is dead!" he cried. "Mo-sar is king! Let the loyal warriors of Pal-ul-don protect their ruler!"

Mo-sar commanded a goodly following and these quickly surrounded him and Bu-lot, but there were many knives against them and now Ja-don pressed forward through those who confronted the pretender.

"Take them both!" he shouted. "The warriors of Pal-ul-don will choose their own king after the assassin of Ko-tan has paid the penalty of his treachery."

Directed now by a leader whom they both respected and admired those who had been loyal to Ko-tan rushed forward upon the faction that had surrounded Mo-sar. Fierce and terrible was the fighting, devoid, apparently, of all else than the ferocious lust to kill and while it was at its height Mo-sar and Bu-lot slipped unnoticed from the banquet hall.

To that part of the palace assigned to them during their visit to A-lur they hastened. Here were their servants and the lesser warriors of their party who had not been bidden to the feast of Ko-tan. These were directed quickly to gather together their belongings for immediate departure. When all was ready, and it did not take long, since the warriors of Pal-ul-don require but little impedimenta on the march, they moved toward the palace gate.

Suddenly Mo-sar approached his son. "The princess," he whispered. "We must not leave the city without her—she is half the battle for the throne."

Bu-lot, now entirely sober, demurred. He had had enough of fighting and of risk. "Let us get out of A-lur quickly," he urged, "or we shall have the whole city upon us. She would not come without a struggle and that would delay us too long."

"There is plenty of time," insisted Mo-sar. "They are still fighting in the pal-e-don-so. It will be long before they miss us and, with Ko-tan dead, long before any will think to look to the safety of the princess. Our time is now—it was made for us by Jad-ben-Otho. Come!"

Reluctantly Bu-lot followed his father, who first instructed the warriors to await them just inside the gateway of the palace. Rapidly the two approached the quarters of the princess. Within the entrance-way only a handful of warriors were on guard. The eunuchs had retired.

"There is fighting in the pal-e-don-so," Mo-sar announced in feigned excitement as they entered the presence of the guards. "The king desires you to come at once and has sent us to guard the apartments of the princess. Make haste!" he commanded as the men hesitated.

The warriors knew him and that on the morrow the princess was to be betrothed to Bu-lot, his son. If there was trouble what more natural than that Mo-sar and Bu-lot should be intrusted with the safety of the princess. And then, too, was not Mo-sar a powerful chief to whose orders disobedience might prove a dangerous thing? They were but common fighting men disciplined in the rough school of tribal warfare, but they had learned to obey a superior and so they departed for the banquet hall—the place-where-men-eat.

Barely waiting until they had disappeared Mo-sar crossed to the hangings at the opposite end of the entrance-hall and followed by Bu-lot made his way toward the sleeping apartment of O-lo-a and a moment later, without warning, the two men burst in upon the three occupants of the room. At sight of them O-lo-a sprang to her feet.

"What is the meaning of this?" she demanded angrily.

Mo-sar advanced and halted before her. Into his cunning mind had entered a plan to trick her. If it succeeded it would prove easier than taking her by force, and then his eyes fell upon Jane Clayton and he almost gasped in astonishment and admiration, but he caught himself and returned to the business of the moment.

"O-lo-a," he cried, "when you know the urgency of our mission you will forgive us. We have sad news for you. There has been an uprising in the palace and Ko-tan, the king, has been slain. The rebels are drunk with liquor and now on their way here. We must get you out of A-lur at once—there is not a moment to lose. Come, and quickly!"

"My father dead?" cried O-lo-a, and suddenly her eyes went wide. "Then my place is here with my people," she cried. "If Ko-tan is dead I am queen until the warriors choose a new ruler—that is the law of Pal-ul-don. And if I am queen none can make me wed whom I do not wish to wed—and Jad-ben-Otho knows I never wished to wed thy cowardly son. Go!" She pointed a slim forefinger imperiously toward the doorway.

Mo-sar saw that neither trickery nor persuasion would avail now and every precious minute counted. He looked again at the beautiful woman who stood beside O-lo-a. He had never before seen her but he well knew from palace gossip that she could be no other than the godlike stranger whom Ko-tan had planned to make his queen.

"Bu-lot," he cried to his son, "take you your own woman and I will take—mine!" and with that he sprang suddenly forward and seizing Jane about the waist lifted her in his arms, so that before O-lo-a or Pan-at-lee might even guess his purpose he had disappeared through the hangings near the foot of the dais and was gone with the stranger woman struggling and fighting in his grasp.

And then Bu-lot sought to seize O-lo-a, but O-lo-a had her Pan-at-lee—fierce little tiger-girl of the savage Kor-ul-Ja—Pan-at-lee whose name belied her—and Bu-lot found that with the two of them his hands were full. When he would have lifted O-lo-a and borne her away Pan-at-lee seized him around the legs and strove to drag him down. Viciously he kicked her, but she would not desist, and finally, realizing that he might not only lose his princess but be so delayed as to invite capture if he did not rid himself of this clawing, scratching she-*Jato*, he hurled O-lo-a to the floor and seizing Pan-at-lee by the hair drew his knife and—

The curtains behind him suddenly parted. In two swift bounds a lithe figure crossed the room and before ever the knife of Bu-lot reached its goal his wrist was seized from behind and a terrific blow crashing to the base of his brain dropped him, lifeless, to the floor. Bu-lot, coward, traitor, and assassin, died without knowing who struck him down.

As Tarzan of the Apes leaped into the pool in the *gryf* pit of the temple at A-lur one might have accounted for his act on the hypothesis that it was the last blind urge of self-preservation to delay, even for a moment, the inevitable tragedy in which each some day must play the leading role upon his little stage; but no—those cool, gray eyes had caught the sole possibility for escape that the surroundings and the circumstances offered—a tiny, moonlit patch of water glimmering through a small aperture in the cliff at the surface of the pool upon its farther side. With swift, bold strokes he swam for speed alone knowing that the water would in no way deter his pursuer. Nor did it. Tarzan heard the great splash as the huge creature plunged into the pool behind him; he heard the churning waters as it forged rapidly onward in his wake. He was nearing the opening—would it be large enough to permit the passage of his body? That portion of it which showed above the surface of the water most certainly would not. His life, then, depended upon how much of the aperture was submerged. And now it was directly before him and the *gryf* directly behind. There was no alternative—there was no other hope. The ape-man threw all the resources of his great strength into the last few strokes, extended his hands before him as a cutwater, submerged to the water's level and shot forward toward the hole.

Frothing with rage was the baffled Lu-don as he realized how neatly the stranger she had turned his own tables upon him. He could of course escape the Temple of the Gryf in which her quick wit had temporarily imprisoned him; but during the delay, however brief, Ja-don would find time to steal her from the temple and deliver her to Ko-tan. But he would have her yet— that the high priest swore in the names of Jad-ben-Otho and all the demons of his faith. He hated Ko-tan. Secretly he had espoused the cause of Mo-sar, in whom he would have a willing tool. Perhaps, then, this would give him the opportunity he had long awaited—a pretext for inciting the revolt that would dethrone Ko-tan and place Mo-sar in power—with Lu-don the real ruler of Pal-ul-don. He licked his thin lips as he sought the window through which Tarzan had entered and now Lu-don's only avenue of escape. Cautiously he made his way across the floor, feeling before him with his hands, and when they discovered that the trap was set for him an ugly snarl broke from the priest's lips. "The she-devil!" he muttered; "but she shall pay, she shall pay—ah, Jad-ben-Otho; how she shall pay for the trick she has played upon Lu-don!"

He crawled through the window and climbed easily downward to the ground. Should he pursue Ja-don and the woman, chancing an encounter with the fierce chief, or bide his time until treachery and intrigue should accomplish his design? He chose the latter solution, as might have been expected of such as he.

Going to his quarters he summoned several of his priests—those who were most in his confidence and who shared his ambitions for absolute power of the temple over the palace—all men who hated Ko-tan.

"The time has come," he told them, "when the authority of the temple must be placed definitely above that of the palace. Ko-tan must make way for Mo-sar, for Ko-tan has defied your high priest. Go then, Pan-sat, and summon Mo-sar secretly to the temple, and you others go to the city and prepare the faithful warriors that they may be in readiness when the time comes."

For another hour they discussed the details of the coup d'état that was to overthrow the government of Pal-ul-don. One knew a slave who, as the signal sounded from the temple gong, would thrust a knife into the heart of Ko-tan, for the price of liberty. Another held personal knowledge of an officer of the palace that he could use to compel the latter to admit a number of Lu-don's warriors to various parts of the palace. With Mo-sar as the cat's paw, the plan seemed scarce possible of failure and so they separated, going upon their immediate errands to palace and to city.

As Pan-sat entered the palace grounds he was aware of a sudden commotion in the direction of the pal-e-don-so and a few minutes later Lu-don was surprised to see him return to the apartments of the high priest, breathless and excited.

"What now, Pan-sat?" cried Lu-don. "Are you pursued by demons?"

"O master, our time has come and gone while we sat here planning. Ko-tan is already dead and Mo-sar fled. His friends are fighting with the warriors of the palace but they have no head, while Ja-don leads the others. I could learn but little from frightened slaves who had fled at the outburst of the quarrel. One told me that Bu-lot had slain the king and that he had seen Mo-sar and the assassin hurrying from the palace."

"Ja-don," muttered the high priest. "The fools will make him king if we do not act and act quickly. Get into the city, Pan-sat—let your feet fly and raise the cry that Ja-don has killed the king and is seeking to wrest the throne from O-lo-a. Spread the word as you know best how to spread it that Ja-don has threatened to destroy the priests and hurl the altars of the temple into Jad-ben-lul. Rouse the warriors of the city and urge them to attack at once. Lead them into the temple by the secret way that only the priests know and from here we may spew them out upon the palace before they learn the truth. Go, Pan-sat, immediately—delay not an instant."

"But stay," he called as the under priest turned to leave the apartment; "saw or heard you anything of the strange white woman that Ja-don stole from the Temple of the Gryf where we have had her imprisoned?"

"Only that Ja-don took her into the palace where he threatened the priests with violence if they did not permit him to pass," replied Pan-sat. "This they told me, but where within the palace she is hidden I know not."

"Ko-tan ordered her to the Forbidden Garden," said Lu-don, "doubtless we shall find her there. And now, Pan-sat, be upon your errand."

In a corridor by Lu-don's chamber a hideously masked priest leaned close to the curtained aperture that led within. Were he listening he must have heard all that passed between Pan-sat and the high priest, and that he had listened was evidenced by his hasty withdrawal to the shadows of a nearby passage as the lesser priest moved across the chamber toward the doorway. Pan-sat went his way in ignorance of the near presence that he almost brushed against as he hurried toward the secret passage that leads from the temple of Jad-ben-Otho, far beneath the palace, to the city beyond, nor did he sense the silent creature following in his footsteps.

CHAPTER XVI—THE SECRET WAY

It was a baffled *gryf* that bellowed in angry rage as Tarzan's sleek brown body cutting the moonlit waters shot through the aperture in the wall of the *gryf* pool and out into the lake beyond. The ape-man smiled as he thought of the comparative ease with which he had defeated the purpose of the high priest but his face clouded again at the ensuing remembrance of the grave danger that threatened his mate. His sole object now must be to return as quickly as he might to the chamber where he had last seen her on the third floor of the Temple of the Gryf, but how he was to find his way again into the temple grounds was a question not easy of solution.

In the moonlight he could see the sheer cliff rising from the water for a great distance along the shore—far beyond the precincts of the temple and the palace—towering high above him, a seemingly impregnable barrier against his return. Swimming close in, he skirted the wall searching diligently for some foothold, however slight, upon its smooth, forbidding surface. Above him and quite out of reach were numerous apertures, but there were no means at hand by which he could reach them. Presently, however, his hopes were raised by the sight of an opening level with the surface of the water. It lay just ahead and a few strokes brought him to it—cautious strokes that brought forth no sound from the yielding waters. At the nearer side of the opening he stopped and reconnoitered. There was no one in sight. Carefully he raised his body to the threshold of the entrance-way, his smooth brown hide glistening in the moonlight as it shed the water in tiny sparkling rivulets.

Before him stretched a gloomy corridor, unlighted save for the faint illumination of the diffused moonlight that penetrated it for but a short distance from the opening. Moving as rapidly as reasonable caution warranted, Tarzan followed the corridor into the bowels of the cave. There was an abrupt turn and then a flight of steps at the top of which lay another corridor running parallel with the face of the cliff. This passage was dimly lighted by flickering cressets set in niches in the walls at considerable distances apart. A quick survey showed the ape-man numerous openings upon each side of the corridor and his quick ears caught sounds that indicated that there were other beings not far distant—priests, he concluded, in some of the apartments letting upon the passageway.

To pass undetected through this hive of enemies appeared quite beyond the range of possibility. He must again seek disguise and knowing from experience how best to secure such he crept stealthily along the corridor toward the nearest doorway. Like Numa, the lion, stalking a wary prey he crept with quivering nostrils to the hangings that shut off his view from the interior of the apartment beyond. A moment later his head disappeared within; then his shoulders, and his lithe body, and the hangings dropped quietly into place again. A moment later there filtered to the vacant corridor without a brief, gasping gurgle and again silence. A minute passed; a second, and a third, and then the hangings were thrust aside and a grimly masked priest of the temple of Jad-ben-Otho strode into the passageway.

With bold steps he moved along and was about to turn into a diverging gallery when his attention was aroused by voices coming from a room upon his left. Instantly the figure halted and crossing the corridor stood with an ear close to the skins that concealed the occupants of the room from him, and him from them. Presently he leaped back into the concealing shadows of the diverging gallery and immediately thereafter the hangings by which he had been listening parted and a priest emerged to turn quickly down the main corridor. The eavesdropper waited until the other had gained a little distance and then stepping from his place of concealment followed silently behind.

The way led along the corridor which ran parallel with the face of the cliff for some little distance and then Pan-sat, taking a cresset from one of the wall niches, turned abruptly into a small apartment at his left. The tracker followed cautiously in time to see the rays of the flickering light dimly visible from an aperture in the floor before him. Here he found a series of steps, similar to those used by the Waz-don in scaling the cliff to their caves, leading to a lower level.

First satisfying himself that his guide was continuing upon his way unsuspecting, the other descended after him and continued his stealthy stalking. The passageway was now both narrow and low, giving but bare headroom to a tall man, and it was broken often by flights of steps leading always downward. The steps in each unit seldom numbered more than six and sometimes there was only one or two but in the aggregate the tracker imagined that they had descended between fifty and seventy-five feet from the level of the upper corridor when the passageway terminated in a small apartment at one side of which was a little pile of rubble.

Setting his cresset upon the ground, Pan-sat commenced hurriedly to toss the bits of broken stone aside, presently revealing a small aperture at the base of the wall upon the opposite side of which there appeared to be a further accumulation of rubble. This he also removed until he had a hole of sufficient size to permit the passage of his body, and leaving the cresset still burning upon the floor the priest crawled through the opening he had made and disappeared from the sight of the watcher hiding in the shadows of the narrow passageway behind him.

No sooner, however, was he safely gone than the other followed, finding himself, after passing through the hole, on a little ledge about halfway between the surface of the lake and the top of the cliff above. The ledge inclined steeply upward, ending at the rear of a building which stood upon the edge of the cliff and which the second priest entered just in time to see Pan-sat pass out into the city beyond.

As the latter turned a nearby corner the other emerged from the doorway and quickly surveyed his surroundings. He was satisfied the priest who had led him hither had served his purpose in so far as the tracker was concerned. Above him, and perhaps a hundred yards away, the white walls of the palace gleamed against the northern sky. The time that it had taken him to acquire definite knowledge concerning the secret passageway between the temple and the city he did not count as lost, though he begrudged every instant that kept him from the prosecution of his main objective. It had seemed to him, however, necessary to the success of a bold plan that he had formulated upon overhearing the conversation between Lu-don and Pan-sat as he stood without the hangings of the apartment of the high priest.

Alone against a nation of suspicious and half-savage enemies he could scarce hope for a successful outcome to the one great issue upon which hung the life and happiness of the creature he loved best. For her sake he must win allies and it was for this purpose that he had sacrificed these precious moments, but now he lost no further time in seeking to regain entrance to the palace grounds that he might search out whatever new prison they had found in which to incarcerate his lost love.

He found no difficulty in passing the guards at the entrance to the palace for, as he had guessed, his priestly disguise disarmed all suspicion. As he approached the warriors he kept his hands behind him and trusted to fate that the sickly light of the single torch which stood beside the doorway would not reveal his un-Pal-ul-donian feet. As a matter of fact so accustomed were they to the comings and goings of the priesthood that they paid scant attention to him and he passed on into the palace grounds without even a moment's delay.

His goal now was the Forbidden Garden and this he had little difficulty in reaching though he elected to enter it over the wall rather than to chance arousing any suspicion on the part of the guards at the inner entrance, since he could imagine no reason why a priest should seek entrance there thus late at night.

He found the garden deserted, nor any sign of her he sought. That she had been brought hither he had learned from the conversation he had overheard between Lu-don and Pan-sat, and he was sure that there had been no time or opportunity for the high priest to remove her from the palace grounds. The garden he knew to be devoted exclusively to the uses of the princess and her women and it was only reasonable to assume therefore that if Jane had been brought to the garden it could only have been upon an order from Ko-tan. This being the case the natural assumption would follow that he would find her in some other portion of O-lo-a's quarters.

Just where these lay he could only conjecture, but it seemed reasonable to believe that they must be adjacent to the garden, so once more he scaled the wall and passing around its end directed his steps toward an entrance-way which he judged must lead to that portion of the palace nearest the Forbidden Garden.

To his surprise he found the place unguarded and then there fell upon his ear from an interior apartment the sound of voices raised in anger and excitement. Guided by the sound he quickly traversed several corridors and chambers until he stood before the hangings which separated him from the chamber from which issued the sounds of altercation. Raising the skins slightly he looked within. There were two women battling with a Ho-don warrior. One was the daughter of Ko-tan and the other Pan-at-lee, the Kor-ul-Ja.

At the moment that Tarzan lifted the hangings, the warrior threw O-lo-a viciously to the ground and seizing Pan-at-lee by the hair drew his knife and raised it above her head. Casting the encumbering headdress of the dead priest from his shoulders the ape-man leaped across the intervening space and seizing the brute from behind struck him a single terrible blow.

As the man fell forward dead, the two women recognized Tarzan simultaneously. Pan-at-lee fell upon her knees and would have bowed her head upon his feet had he not, with an impatient gesture, commanded her to rise. He had no time to listen to their protestations of gratitude or answer the numerous questions which he knew would soon be flowing from those two feminine tongues.

"Tell me," he cried, "where is the woman of my own race whom Ja-don brought here from the temple?"

"She is but this moment gone," cried O-lo-a. "Mo-sar, the father of this thing here," and she indicated the body of Bu-lot with a scornful finger, "seized her and carried her away."

"Which way?" he cried. "Tell me quickly, in what direction he took her."

"That way," cried Pan-at-lee, pointing to the doorway through which Mo-sar had passed. "They would have taken the princess and the stranger woman to Tu-lur, Mo-sar's city by the Dark Lake."

"I go to find her," he said to Pan-at-lee, "she is my mate. And if I survive I shall find means to liberate you too and return you to Om-at."

Before the girl could reply he had disappeared behind the hangings of the door near the foot of the dais. The corridor through which he ran was illy lighted and like nearly all its kind in the Ho-don city wound in and out and up and down, but at last it terminated at a sudden turn which brought him into a courtyard filled with warriors, a portion of the palace guard that had just been summoned by one of the lesser palace chiefs to join the warriors of Ko-tan in the battle that was raging in the banquet hall.

At sight of Tarzan, who in his haste had forgotten to recover his disguising headdress, a great shout arose. "Blasphemer!" "Defiler of the temple!" burst hoarsely from savage throats, and mingling with these were a few who cried, "Dor-ul-Otho!" evidencing the fact that there were among them still some who clung to their belief in his divinity.

To cross the courtyard armed only with a knife, in the face of this great throng of savage fighting men seemed even to the giant ape-man a thing impossible of achievement. He must use his wits now and quickly too, for they were closing upon him. He might have turned and fled back through the corridor but flight now even in the face of dire necessity would but delay him in his pursuit of Mo-sar and his mate.

"Stop!" he cried, raising his palm against them. "I am the Dor-ul-Otho and I come to you with a word from Ja-don, who it is my father's will shall be your king now that Ko-tan is slain. Lu-don, the high priest, has planned to seize the palace and destroy the loyal warriors that Mo-sar may be made king—Mo-sar who will be the tool and creature of Lu-don. Follow me. There is no time to lose if you would prevent the traitors whom Lu-don has organized in the city from entering the palace by a secret way and overpowering Ja-don and the faithful band within."

For a moment they hesitated. At last one spoke. "What guarantee have we," he demanded, "that it is not you who would betray us and by leading us now away from the fighting in the banquet hall cause those who fight at Ja-don's side to be defeated?"

"My life will be your guarantee," replied Tarzan. "If you find that I have not spoken the truth you are sufficient in numbers to execute whatever penalty you choose. But come, there is not time to lose. Already are the lesser priests gathering their warriors in the city below," and without waiting for any further parley he strode directly toward them in the direction of the gate upon the opposite side of the courtyard which led toward the principal entrance to the palace ground.

Slower in wit than he, they were swept away by his greater initiative and that compelling power which is inherent to all natural leaders. And so they followed him, the giant ape-man with a dead tail dragging the ground behind him—a demi-god where another would have been ridiculous. Out into the city he led them and down toward the unpretentious building that hid Lu-don's secret passageway from the city to the temple, and as they rounded the last turn they saw before them a gathering of warriors which was being rapidly augmented from all directions as the traitors of A-lur mobilized at the call of the priesthood.

"You spoke the truth, stranger," said the chief who marched at Tarzan's side, "for there are the warriors with the priests among them, even as you told us."

"And now," replied the ape-man, "that I have fulfilled my promise I will go my way after Mo-sar, who has done me a great wrong. Tell Ja-don that Jad-ben-Otho is upon his side, nor do you forget to tell him also that it was the Dor-ul-Otho who thwarted Lu-don's plan to seize the palace."

"I will not forget," replied the chief. "Go your way. We are enough to overpower the traitors."

"Tell me," asked Tarzan, "how I may know this city of Tu-lur?"

"It lies upon the south shore of the second lake below A-lur," replied the chief, "the lake that is called Jad-in-lul."

They were now approaching the band of traitors, who evidently thought that this was another contingent of their own party since they made no effort either toward defense or retreat. Suddenly the chief raised his voice in a savage war cry that was immediately taken up by his followers, and simultaneously, as though the cry were a command, the entire party broke into a mad charge upon the surprised rebels.

Satisfied with the outcome of his suddenly conceived plan and sure that it would work to the disadvantage of Lu-don, Tarzan turned into a side street and pointed his steps toward the outskirts of the city in search of the trail that led southward toward Tu-lur.

CHAPTER XVII—BY JAD-BAL-LUL

As Mo-sar carried Jane Clayton from the palace of Ko-tan, the king, the woman struggled incessantly to regain her freedom. He tried to compel her to walk, but despite his threats and his abuse she would not voluntarily take a single step in the direction in which he wished her to go. Instead she threw herself to the ground each time he sought to place her upon her feet, and so of necessity he was compelled to carry her though at last he tied her hands and gagged her to save himself from further lacerations, for the beauty and slenderness of the woman belied her strength and courage. When he came at last to where his men had gathered he was glad indeed to turn her over to a couple of stalwart warriors, but these too were forced to carry her since Mo-sar's fear of the vengeance of Ko-tan's retainers would brook no delays.

And thus they came down out of the hills from which A-lur is carved, to the meadows that skirt the lower end of Jad-ben-lul, with Jane Clayton carried between two of Mo-sar's men. At the edge of the lake lay a fleet of strong canoes, hollowed from the trunks of trees, their bows and sterns carved in the semblance of grotesque beasts or birds and vividly colored by some master in that primitive school of art, which fortunately is not without its devotees today.

Into the stern of one of these canoes the warriors tossed their captive at a sign from Mo-sar, who came and stood beside her as the warriors were finding their places in the canoes and selecting their paddles.

"Come, Beautiful One," he said, "let us be friends and you shall not be harmed. You will find Mo-sar a kind master if you do his bidding," and thinking to make a good impression on her he removed the gag from her mouth and the thongs from her wrists, knowing well that she could not escape surrounded as she was by his warriors, and presently, when they were out on the lake, she would be as safely imprisoned as though he held her behind bars.

And so the fleet moved off to the accompaniment of the gentle splashing of a hundred paddles, to follow the windings of the rivers and lakes through which the waters of the Valley of Jad-ben-Otho empty into the great morass to the south. The warriors, resting upon one knee, faced the bow and in the last canoe Mo-sar tiring of his fruitless attempts to win responses from his sullen captive, squatted in the bottom of the canoe with his back toward her and resting his head upon the gunwale sought sleep.

Thus they moved in silence between the verdure-clad banks of the little river through which the waters of Jad-ben-lul emptied—now in the moonlight, now in dense shadow where great trees overhung the stream, and at last out upon the waters of another lake, the black shores of which seemed far away under the weird influence of a moonlight night.

Jane Clayton sat alert in the stern of the last canoe. For months she had been under constant surveillance, the prisoner first of one ruthless race and now the prisoner of another. Since the long-gone day that Hauptmann Fritz Schneider and his band of native German troops had treacherously wrought the Kaiser's work of rapine and destruction on the Greystoke bungalow and carried her away to captivity she had not drawn a free breath. That she had survived unharmed the countless dangers through which she had passed she attributed solely to the beneficence of a kind and watchful Providence.

At first she had been held on the orders of the German High Command with a view of her ultimate value as a hostage and during these months she had been subjected to neither hardship nor oppression, but when the Germans had become hard pressed toward the close of their unsuccessful campaign in East Africa it had been determined to take her further into the interior and now there was an element of revenge in their motives, since it must have been apparent that she could no longer be of any possible military value.

Bitter indeed were the Germans against that half-savage mate of hers who had cunningly annoyed and harassed them with a fiendishness of persistence and ingenuity that had resulted in a noticeable loss in morale in the sector he had chosen for his operations. They had to charge against him the lives of certain officers that he had deliberately taken with his own hands, and one entire section of trench that had made possible a disastrous turning movement by the British. Tarzan had out-generaled them at every point. He had met cunning with cunning and cruelty with cruelties until they feared and loathed his very name. The cunning trick that they had played upon him in destroying his home, murdering his retainers, and covering the abduction of his wife in such a way as to lead him to believe that she had been killed, they had regretted a thousand times, for a thousandfold had they paid the price for their senseless ruthlessness, and now, unable to wreak their vengeance directly upon him, they had conceived the idea of inflicting further suffering upon his mate.

In sending her into the interior to avoid the path of the victorious British, they had chosen as her escort Lieutenant Erich Obergatz who had been second in command of Schneider's company, and who alone of its officers had escaped the consuming vengeance of the ape-man. For a long time Obergatz had held her in a native village, the chief of which was still under the domination of his fear of the ruthless German oppressors. While here only hardships and discomforts assailed her, Obergatz himself being held in leash by the orders of his distant superior but as time went on the life in the village grew to be a veritable hell of cruelties and oppressions practiced by the arrogant Prussian upon the villagers and the members of his native command—for time hung heavily upon the hands of the lieutenant and with idleness combining with the personal discomforts he was compelled to endure, his none too agreeable temper found an outlet first in petty interference with the chiefs and later in the practice of absolute cruelties upon them.

What the self-sufficient German could not see was plain to Jane Clayton—that the sympathies of Obergatz' native soldiers lay with the villagers and that all were so heartily sickened by his abuse that it needed now but the slightest spark to detonate the mine of revenge and hatred that the pig-headed Hun had been assiduously fabricating beneath his own person.

And at last it came, but from an unexpected source in the form of a German native deserter from the theater of war. Footsore, weary, and spent, he dragged himself into the village late one afternoon, and before Obergatz was even aware of his presence the whole village knew that the power of Germany in Africa was at an end. It did not take long for the lieutenant's native soldiers to realize that the authority that held them in service no longer existed and that with it had gone the power to pay them their miserable wage. Or at least, so they reasoned. To them Obergatz no longer represented aught else than a powerless and hated foreigner, and short indeed would have been his shrift had not a native woman who had conceived a doglike affection for Jane Clayton hurried to her with word of the murderous plan, for the fate of the innocent white woman lay in the balance beside that of the guilty Teuton.

"Already they are quarreling as to which one shall possess you," she told Jane.

"When will they come for us?" asked Jane. "Did you hear them say?"

"Tonight," replied the woman, "for even now that he has none to fight for him they still fear the white man. And so they will come at night and kill him while he sleeps."

Jane thanked the woman and sent her away lest the suspicion of her fellows be aroused against her when they discovered that the two whites had learned of their intentions. The woman went at once to the hut occupied by Obergatz. She had never gone there before and the German looked up in surprise as he saw who his visitor was.

Briefly she told him what she had heard. At first he was inclined to bluster arrogantly, with a great display of bravado but she silenced him peremptorily.

"Such talk is useless," she said shortly. "You have brought upon yourself the just hatred of these people. Regardless of the truth or falsity of the report which has been brought to them, they believe in it and there is nothing now between you and your Maker other than flight. We shall both be dead before morning if we are unable to escape from the village unseen. If you go to them now with your silly protestations of authority you will be dead a little sooner, that is all."

"You think it is as bad as that?" he said, a noticeable alteration in his tone and manner.

"It is precisely as I have told you," she replied. "They will come tonight and kill you while you sleep. Find me pistols and a rifle and ammunition and we will pretend that we go into the jungle to hunt. That you have done often. Perhaps it will arouse suspicion that I accompany you but that we must chance. And be sure my dear Herr Lieutenant to bluster and curse and abuse your servants unless they note a change in your manner and realizing your fear know that you suspect their intention. If all goes well then we can go out into the jungle to hunt and we need not return.

"But first and now you must swear never to harm me, or otherwise it would be better that I called the chief and turned you over to him and then put a bullet into my own head, for unless you swear as I have asked I were no better alone in the jungle with you than here at the mercies of these degraded blacks."

"I swear," he replied solemnly, "in the names of my God and my Kaiser that no harm shall befall you at my hands, Lady Greystoke."

"Very well," she said, "we will make this pact to assist each other to return to civilization, but let it be understood that there is and never can be any semblance even of respect for you upon my part. I am drowning and you are the straw. Carry that always in your mind, German."

If Obergatz had held any doubt as to the sincerity of her word it would have been wholly dissipated by the scathing contempt of her tone. And so Obergatz, without further parley, got pistols and an extra rifle for Jane, as well as bandoleers of cartridges. In his usual arrogant and disagreeable manner he called his servants, telling them that he and the white kali were going out into the brush to hunt. The beaters would go north as far as the little hill and then circle back to the east and in toward the village. The gun carriers he directed to take the extra pieces and precede himself and Jane slowly toward the east, waiting for them at the ford about half a mile distant. The blacks responded with greater alacrity than usual and it was noticeable to both Jane and Obergatz that they left the village whispering and laughing.

"The swine think it is a great joke," growled Obergatz, "that the afternoon before I die I go out and hunt meat for them."

As soon as the gun bearers disappeared in the jungle beyond the village the two Europeans followed along the same trail, nor was there any attempt upon the part of Obergatz' native soldiers, or the warriors of the chief to detain them, for they too doubtless were more than willing that the whites should bring them in one more mess of meat before they killed them.

A quarter of a mile from the village, Obergatz turned toward the south from the trail that led to the ford and hurrying onward the two put as great a distance as possible between them and the village before night fell. They knew from the habits of their erstwhile hosts that there was little danger of pursuit by night since the villagers held Numa, the lion, in too great respect to venture needlessly beyond their stockade during the hours that the king of beasts was prone to choose for hunting.

And thus began a seemingly endless sequence of frightful days and horror-laden nights as the two fought their way toward the south in the face of almost inconceivable hardships, privations, and dangers. The east coast was nearer but Obergatz positively refused to chance throwing himself into the hands of the British by returning to the territory which they now controlled, insisting instead upon attempting to make his way through an unknown wilderness to South Africa where, among the Boers, he was convinced he would find willing sympathizers who would find some way to return him in safety to Germany, and the woman was perforce compelled to accompany him.

And so they had crossed the great thorny, waterless steppe and come at last to the edge of the morass before Pal-ul-don. They had reached this point just before the rainy season when the waters of the morass were at their lowest ebb. At this time a hard crust is baked upon the dried surface of the marsh and there is only the open water at the center to materially impede progress. It is a condition that exists perhaps not more than a few weeks, or even days at the termination of long periods of drought, and so the two crossed the otherwise almost impassable barrier without realizing its latent terrors. Even the open water in the center chanced to be deserted at the time by its frightful denizens which the drought and the receding waters had driven southward toward the mouth of Pal-ul-don's largest river which carries the waters out of the Valley of Jad-ben-Otho.

Their wanderings carried them across the mountains and into the Valley of Jad-ben-Otho at the source of one of the larger streams which bears the mountain waters down into the valley to empty them into the main river just below The Great Lake on whose northern shore lies A-lur. As they had come down out of the mountains they had been surprised by a party of Ho-don hunters. Obergatz had escaped while Jane had been taken prisoner and brought to A-lur. She had neither seen nor heard aught of the German since that time and she did not know whether he had perished in this strange land, or succeeded in successfully eluding its savage denizens and making his way at last into South Africa.

For her part, she had been incarcerated alternately in the palace and the temple as either Ko-tan or Lu-don succeeded in wresting her temporarily from the other by various strokes of cunning and intrigue. And now at last she was in the power of a new captor, one whom she knew from the gossip of the temple and the palace to be cruel and degraded. And she was in the stern of the last canoe, and every enemy back was toward her, while almost at her feet Mo-sar's loud snores gave ample evidence of his unconsciousness to his immediate surroundings.

The dark shore loomed closer to the south as Jane Clayton, Lady Greystoke, slid quietly over the stern of the canoe into the chill waters of the lake. She scarcely moved other than to keep her nostrils above the surface while the canoe was yet discernible in the last rays of the declining moon. Then she struck out toward the southern shore.

Alone, unarmed, all but naked, in a country overrun by savage beasts and hostile men, she yet felt for the first time in many months a sensation of elation and relief. She was free! What if the next moment brought death, she knew again, at least a brief instant of absolute freedom. Her blood tingled to the almost forgotten sensation and it was with difficulty that she restrained a glad triumphant cry as she clambered from the quiet waters and stood upon the silent beach.

Before her loomed a forest, darkly, and from its depths came those nameless sounds that are a part of the night life of the jungle—the rustling of leaves in the wind, the rubbing together of contiguous branches, the scurrying of a rodent, all magnified by the darkness to sinister and awe-inspiring proportions; the hoot of an owl, the distant scream of a great cat, the barking of wild dogs, attested the presence of the myriad life she could not see—the savage life, the free life of which she was now a part. And then there came to her, possibly for the first time since the giant ape-man had come into her life, a fuller realization of what the jungle meant to him, for though alone and unprotected from its hideous dangers she yet felt its lure upon her and an exaltation that she had not dared hope to feel again.

Ah, if that mighty mate of hers were but by her side! What utter joy and bliss would be hers! She longed for no more than this. The parade of cities, the comforts and luxuries of civilization held forth no allure half as insistent as the glorious freedom of the jungle.

A lion moaned in the blackness to her right, eliciting delicious thrills that crept along her spine. The hair at the back of her head seemed to stand erect—yet she was unafraid. The muscles bequeathed her by some primordial ancestor reacted instinctively to the presence of an ancient enemy—that was all. The woman moved slowly and deliberately toward the wood. Again the lion moaned; this time nearer. She sought a low-hanging branch and finding it swung easily into the friendly shelter of the tree. The long and perilous journey with Obergatz had trained her muscles and her nerves to such unaccustomed habits. She found a safe resting place such as Tarzan had taught her was best and there she curled herself, thirty feet above the ground, for a night's rest. She was cold and uncomfortable and yet she slept, for her heart was warm with renewed hope and her tired brain had found temporary surcease from worry.

She slept until the heat of the sun, high in the heavens, awakened her. She was rested and now her body was well as her heart was warm. A sensation of ease and comfort and happiness pervaded her being. She rose upon her gently swaying couch and stretched luxuriously, her naked limbs and lithe body mottled by the sunlight filtering through the foliage above combined with the lazy gesture to impart to her appearance something of the leopard. With careful eye she scrutinized the ground below and with attentive ear she listened for any warning sound that might suggest the near presence of enemies, either man or beast. Satisfied at last that there was nothing close of which she need have fear she clambered to the ground. She wished to bathe but the lake was too exposed and just a bit too far from the safety of the trees for her to risk it until she became more familiar with her surroundings. She wandered aimlessly through the forest searching for food which she found in abundance. She ate and rested, for she had no objective as yet. Her freedom was too new to be spoiled by plannings for the future. The haunts of civilized man seemed to her now as vague and unattainable as the half-forgotten substance of a dream. If she could but live on here in peace, waiting, waiting for—*him*. It was the old hope revived. She knew that he would come some day, if he lived. She had always known that, though recently she had believed that he would come too late. If he lived! Yes, he would come if he lived, and if he did not live she were as well off here as elsewhere, for then nothing mattered, only to wait for the end as patiently as might be.

Her wanderings brought her to a crystal brook and there she drank and bathed beneath an overhanging tree that offered her quick asylum in the event of danger. It was a quiet and beautiful spot and she loved it from the first. The bottom of the brook was paved with pretty stones and bits of glassy obsidian. As she gathered a handful of the pebbles and held them up to look at them she noticed that one of her fingers was bleeding from a clean, straight cut. She fell to searching for the cause and presently discovered it in one of the fragments of volcanic glass which revealed an edge that was almost razor-like. Jane Clayton was elated. Here, God-given to her hands, was the first beginning with which she might eventually arrive at both weapons and tools—a cutting edge. Everything was possible to him who possessed it—nothing without.

She sought until she had collected many of the precious bits of stone—until the pouch that hung at her right side was almost filled. Then she climbed into the great tree to examine them at leisure. There were some that looked like knife blades, and some that could easily be fashioned into spear heads, and many smaller ones that nature seemed to have intended for the tips of savage arrows.

The spear she would essay first—that would be easiest. There was a hollow in the bole of the tree in a great crotch high above the ground. Here she cached all of her treasure except a single knifelike sliver. With this she descended to the ground and searching out a slender sapling that grew arrow-straight she hacked and sawed until she could break it off without splitting the wood. It was just the right diameter for the shaft of a spear—a hunting spear such as her beloved Waziri had liked best. How often had she watched them fashioning them, and they had taught her how to use them, too—them and the heavy war spears—laughing and clapping their hands as her proficiency increased.

She knew the arborescent grasses that yielded the longest and toughest fibers and these she sought and carried to her tree with the spear shaft that was to be. Clambering to her crotch she bent to her work, humming softly a little tune. She caught herself and smiled—it was the first time in all these bitter months that song had passed her lips or such a smile.

"I feel," she sighed, "I almost feel that John is near—my John—my Tarzan!"

She cut the spear shaft to the proper length and removed the twigs and branches and the bark, whittling and scraping at the nubs until the surface was all smooth and straight. Then she split one end and inserted a spear point, shaping the wood until it fitted perfectly. This done she laid the shaft aside and fell to splitting the thick grass stems and pounding and twisting them until she had separated and partially cleaned the fibers. These she took down to the brook and washed and brought back again and wound tightly around the cleft end of the shaft, which she had notched to receive them, and the upper part of the spear head which she had also notched slightly with a bit of stone. It was a crude spear but the best that she could attain in so short a time. Later, she promised herself, she should have others—many of them—and they would be spears of which even the greatest of the Waziri spear-men might be proud.

CHAPTER XVIII—THE LION PIT OF TU-LUR

Though Tarzan searched the outskirts of the city until nearly dawn he discovered nowhere the spoor of his mate. The breeze coming down from the mountains brought to his nostrils a diversity of scents but there was not among them the slightest suggestion of her whom he sought. The natural deduction was therefore that she had been taken in some other direction. In his search he had many times crossed the fresh tracks of many men leading toward the lake and these he concluded had probably been made by Jane Clayton's abductors. It had only been to minimize the chance of error by the process of elimination that he had carefully reconnoitered every other avenue leading from A-lur toward the southeast where lay Mo-sar's city of Tu-lur, and now he followed the trail to the shores of Jad-ben-lul where the party had embarked upon the quiet waters in their sturdy canoes.

He found many other craft of the same description moored along the shore and one of these he commandeered for the purpose of pursuit. It was daylight when he passed through the lake which lies next below Jad-ben-lul and paddling strongly passed within sight of the very tree in which his lost mate lay sleeping.

Had the gentle wind that caressed the bosom of the lake been blowing from a southerly direction the giant ape-man and Jane Clayton would have been reunited then, but an unkind fate had willed otherwise and the opportunity passed with the passing of his canoe which presently his powerful strokes carried out of sight into the stream at the lower end of the lake.

Following the winding river which bore a considerable distance to the north before doubling back to empty into the Jad-in-lul, the ape-man missed a portage that would have saved him hours of paddling.

It was at the upper end of this portage where Mo-sar and his warriors had debarked that the chief discovered the absence of his captive. As Mo-sar had been asleep since shortly after their departure from A-lur, and as none of the warriors recalled when she had last been seen, it was impossible to conjecture with any degree of accuracy the place where she had escaped. The consensus of opinion was, however, that it had been in the narrow river connecting Jad-ben-lul with the lake next below it, which is called Jad-bal-lul, which freely translated means the lake of gold. Mo-sar had been very wroth and having himself been the only one at fault he naturally sought with great diligence to fix the blame upon another.

He would have returned in search of her had he not feared to meet a pursuing company dispatched either by Ja-don or the high priest, both of whom, he knew, had just grievances against him. He would not even spare a boatload of his warriors from his own protection to return in quest of the fugitive but hastened onward with as little delay as possible across the portage and out upon the waters of Jad-in-lul.

The morning sun was just touching the white domes of Tu-lur when Mo-sar's paddlers brought their canoes against the shore at the city's edge. Safe once more behind his own walls and protected by many warriors, the courage of the chief returned sufficiently at least to permit him to dispatch three canoes in search of Jane Clayton, and also to go as far as A-lur if possible to learn what had delayed Bu-lot, whose failure to reach the canoes with the balance of the party at the time of the flight from the northern city had in no way delayed Mo-sar's departure, his own safety being of far greater moment than that of his son.

As the three canoes reached the portage on their return journey the warriors who were dragging them from the water were suddenly startled by the appearance of two priests, carrying a light canoe in the direction of Jad-in-lul. At first they thought them the advance guard of a larger force of Lu-don's followers, although the correctness of such a theory was belied by their knowledge that priests never accepted the risks or perils of a warrior's vocation, nor even fought until driven into a corner and forced to do so. Secretly the warriors of Pal-ul-don held the emasculated priesthood in contempt and so instead of immediately taking up the offensive as they would have had the two men been warriors from A-lur instead of priests, they waited to question them.

At sight of the warriors the priests made the sign of peace and upon being asked if they were alone they answered in the affirmative.

The leader of Mo-sar's warriors permitted them to approach. "What do you here," he asked, "in the country of Mo-sar, so far from your own city?"

"We carry a message from Lu-don, the high priest, to Mo-sar," explained one.

"Is it a message of peace or of war?" asked the warrior.

"It is an offer of peace," replied the priest.

"And Lu-don is sending no warriors behind you?" queried the fighting man.

"We are alone," the priest assured him. "None in A-lur save Lu-don knows that we have come upon this errand."

"Then go your way," said the warrior.

"Who is that?" asked one of the priests suddenly, pointing toward the upper end of the lake at the point where the river from Jad-bal-lul entered it.

All eyes turned in the direction that he had indicated to see a lone warrior paddling rapidly into Jad-in-lul, the prow of his canoe pointing toward Tu-lur. The warriors and the priests drew into the concealment of the bushes on either side of the portage.

"It is the terrible man who called himself the Dor-ul-Otho," whispered one of the priests. "I would know that figure among a great multitude as far as I could see it."

"You are right, priest," cried one of the warriors who had seen Tarzan the day that he had first entered Ko-tan's palace. "It is indeed he who has been rightly called Tarzan-jad-guru."

"Hasten priests," cried the leader of the party. "You are two paddles in a light canoe. Easily can you reach Tu-lur ahead of him and warn Mo-sar of his coming, for he has but only entered the lake."

For a moment the priests demurred for they had no stomach for an encounter with this terrible man, but the warrior insisted and even went so far as to threaten them. Their canoe was taken from them and pushed into the lake and they were all but lifted bodily from their feet and put aboard it. Still protesting they were shoved out upon the water where they were immediately in full view of the lone paddler above them. Now there was no alternative. The city of Tu-lur offered the only safety and bending to their paddles the two priests sent their craft swiftly in the direction of the city.

The warriors withdrew again to the concealment of the foliage. If Tarzan had seen them and should come hither to investigate there were thirty of them against one and naturally they had no fear of the outcome, but they did not consider it necessary to go out upon the lake to meet him since they had been sent to look for the escaped prisoner and not to intercept the strange warrior, the stories of whose ferocity and prowess doubtless helped them to arrive at their decision to provoke no uncalled-for quarrel with him.

If he had seen them he gave no sign, but continued paddling steadily and strongly toward the city, nor did he increase his speed as the two priests shot out in full view. The moment the priests' canoe touched the shore by the city its occupants leaped out and hurried swiftly toward the palace gate, casting affrighted glances behind them. They sought immediate audience with Mo-sar, after warning the warriors on guard that Tarzan was approaching.

They were conducted at once to the chief, whose court was a smaller replica of that of the king of A-lur. "We come from Lu-don, the high priest," explained the spokesman. "He wishes the friendship of Mo-sar, who has always been his friend. Ja-don is gathering warriors to make himself king. Throughout the villages of the Ho-don are thousands who will obey the commands of Lu-don, the high priest. Only with Lu-don's assistance can Mo-sar become king, and the message from Lu-don is that if Mo-sar would retain the friendship of Lu-don he must return immediately the woman he took from the quarters of the Princess O-lo-a."

At this juncture a warrior entered. His excitement was evident. "The Dor-ul-Otho has come to Tu-lur and demands to see Mo-sar at once," he said.

"The Dor-ul-Otho!" exclaimed Mo-sar.

"That is the message he sent," replied the warrior, "and indeed he is not as are the people of Pal-ul-don. He is, we think, the same of whom the warriors that returned from A-lur today told us and whom some call Tarzan-jad-guru and some Dor-ul-Otho. But indeed only the son of god would dare come thus alone to a strange city, so it must be that he speaks the truth."

Mo-sar, his heart filled with terror and indecision, turned questioningly toward the priests.

"Receive him graciously, Mo-sar," counseled he who had spoken before, his advice prompted by the petty shrewdness of his defective brain which, under the added influence of Lu-don's tutorage leaned always toward duplicity. "Receive him graciously and when he is quite convinced of your friendship he will be off his guard, and then you may do with him as you will. But if possible, Mo-sar, and you would win the undying gratitude of Lu-don, the high-priest, save him alive for my master."

Mo-sar nodded understandingly and turning to the warrior commanded that he conduct the visitor to him.

"We must not be seen by the creature," said one of the priests. "Give us your answer to Lu-don, Mo-sar, and we will go our way."

"Tell Lu-don," replied the chief, "that the woman would have been lost to him entirely had it not been for me. I sought to bring her to Tu-lur that I might save her for him from the clutches of Ja-don, but during the night she escaped. Tell Lu-don that I have sent thirty warriors to search for her. It is strange you did not see them as you came."

"We did," replied the priests, "but they told us nothing of the purpose of their journey."

"It is as I have told you," said Mo-sar, "and if they find her, assure your master that she will be kept unharmed in Tu-lur for him. Also tell him that I will send my warriors to join with his against Ja-don whenever he sends word that he wants them. Now go, for Tarzan-jad-guru will soon be here."

He signaled to a slave. "Lead the priests to the temple," he commanded, "and ask the high priest of Tu-lur to see that they are fed and permitted to return to A-lur when they will."

The two priests were conducted from the apartment by the slave through a doorway other than that at which they had entered, and a moment later Tarzan-jad-guru strode into the presence of Mo-sar, ahead of the warrior whose duty it had been to conduct and announce him. The ape-man made no sign of greeting or of peace but strode directly toward the chief who, only by the exertion of his utmost powers of will, hid the terror that was in his heart at sight of the giant figure and the scowling face.

"I am the Dor-ul-Otho," said the ape-man in level tones that carried to the mind of Mo-sar a suggestion of cold steel; "I am Dor-ul-Otho, and I come to Tu-lur for the woman you stole from the apartments of O-lo-a, the princess."

The very boldness of Tarzan's entry into this hostile city had had the effect of giving him a great moral advantage over Mo-sar and the savage warriors who stood upon either side of the chief. Truly it seemed to them that no other than the son of Jad-ben-Otho would dare so heroic an act. Would any mortal warrior act thus boldly, and alone enter the presence of a powerful chief and, in the midst of a score of warriors, arrogantly demand an accounting? No, it was beyond reason. Mo-sar was faltering in his decision to betray the stranger by seeming friendliness. He even paled to a sudden thought—Jad-ben-Otho knew everything, even our inmost thoughts. Was it not therefore possible that this creature, if after all it should prove true that he was the Dor-ul-Otho, might even now be reading the wicked design that the priests had implanted in the brain of Mo-sar and which he had entertained so favorably? The chief squirmed and fidgeted upon the bench of hewn rock that was his throne.

"Quick," snapped the ape-man, "Where is she?"

"She is not here," cried Mo-sar.

"You lie," replied Tarzan.

"As Jad-ben-Otho is my witness, she is not in Tu-lur," insisted the chief. "You may search the palace and the temple and the entire city but you will not find her, for she is not here."

"Where is she, then?" demanded the ape-man. "You took her from the palace at A-lur. If she is not here, where is she? Tell me not that harm has befallen her," and he took a sudden threatening step toward Mo-sar, that sent the chief shrinking back in terror.

"Wait," he cried, "if you are indeed the Dor-ul-Otho you will know that I speak the truth. I took her from the palace of Ko-tan to save her for Lu-don, the high priest, lest with Ko-tan dead Ja-don seize her. But during the night she escaped from me between here and A-lur, and I have but just sent three canoes full-manned in search of her."

Something in the chief's tone and manner assured the ape-man that he spoke in part the truth, and that once again he had braved incalculable dangers and suffered loss of time futilely.

"What wanted the priests of Lu-don that preceded me here?" demanded Tarzan chancing a shrewd guess that the two he had seen paddling so frantically to avoid a meeting with him had indeed come from the high priest at A-lur.

"They came upon an errand similar to yours," replied Mo-sar; "to demand the return of the woman whom Lu-don thought I had stolen from him, thus wronging me as deeply, O Dor-ul-Otho, as have you."

"I would question the priests," said Tarzan. "Bring them hither." His peremptory and arrogant manner left Mo-sar in doubt as to whether to be more incensed, or terrified, but ever as is the way with such as he, he concluded that the first consideration was his own safety. If he could transfer the attention and the wrath of this terrible man from himself to Lu-don's priests it would more than satisfy him and if they should conspire to harm him, then Mo-sar would be safe in the eyes of Jad-ben-Otho if it finally developed that the stranger was in reality the son of god. He felt uncomfortable in Tarzan's presence and this fact rather accentuated his doubt, for thus indeed would mortal feel in the presence of a god. Now he saw a way to escape, at least temporarily.

"I will fetch them myself, Dor-ul-Otho," he said, and turning, left the apartment. His hurried steps brought him quickly to the temple, for the palace grounds of Tu-lur, which also included the temple as in all of the Ho-don cities, covered a much smaller area than those of the larger city of A-lur. He found Lu-don's messengers with the high priest of his own temple and quickly transmitted to them the commands of the ape-man.

"What do you intend to do with him?" asked one of the priests.

"I have no quarrel with him," replied Mo-sar. "He came in peace and he may depart in peace, for who knows but that he is indeed the Dor-ul-Otho?"

"We know that he is not," replied Lu-don's emissary. "We have every proof that he is only mortal, a strange creature from another country. Already has Lu-don offered his life to Jad-ben-Otho if he is wrong in his belief that this creature is not the son of god. If the high priest of A-lur, who is the highest priest of all the high priests of Pal-ul-don is thus so sure that the creature is an impostor as to stake his life upon his judgment then who are we to give credence to the claims of this stranger? No, Mo-sar, you need not fear him. He is only a warrior who may be overcome with the same weapons that subdue your own fighting men. Were it not for Lu-don's command that he be taken alive I would urge you to set your warriors upon him and slay him, but the commands of Lu-don are the commands of Jad-ben-Otho himself, and those we may not disobey."

But still the remnant of a doubt stirred within the cowardly breast of Mo-sar, urging him to let another take the initiative against the stranger.

"He is yours then," he replied, "to do with as you will. I have no quarrel with him. What you may command shall be the command of Lu-don, the high priest, and further than that I shall have nothing to do in the matter."

The priests turned to him who guided the destinies of the temple at Tu-lur. "Have you no plan?" they asked. "High indeed will he stand in the counsels of Lu-don and in the eyes of Jad-ben-Otho who finds the means to capture this impostor alive."

"There is the lion pit," whispered the high priest. "It is now vacant and what will hold *Ja* and *Jato* will hold this stranger if he is not the Dor-ul-Otho."

"It will hold him," said Mo-sar; "doubtless too it would hold a *gryf*, but first you would have to get the *gryf* into it."

The priests pondered this bit of wisdom thoughtfully and then one of those from A-lur spoke. "It should not be difficult," he said, "if we use the wits that Jad-ben-Otho gave us instead of the worldly muscles which were handed down to us from our fathers and our mothers and which have not even the power possessed by those of the beasts that run about on four feet."

"Lu-don matched his wits with the stranger and lost," suggested Mo-sar. "But this is your own affair. Carry it out as you see best."

"At A-lur, Ko-tan made much of this Dor-ul-Otho and the priests conducted him through the temple. It would arouse in his mind no suspicion were you to do the same, and let the high priest of Tu-lur invite him to the temple and gathering all the priests make a great show of belief in his kinship to Jad-ben-Otho. And what more natural then than that the high priest should wish to show him through the temple as did Lu-don at A-lur when Ko-tan commanded it, and if by chance he should be led through the lion pit it would be a simple matter for those who bear the torches to extinguish them suddenly and before the stranger was aware of what had happened, the stone gates could be dropped, thus safely securing him."

"But there are windows in the pit that let in light," interposed the high priest, "and even though the torches were extinguished he could still see and might escape before the stone door could be lowered."

"Send one who will cover the windows tightly with hides," said the priest from A-lur.

"The plan is a good one," said Mo-sar, seeing an opportunity for entirely eliminating himself from any suspicion of complicity, "for it will require the presence of no warriors, and thus with only priests about him his mind will entertain no suspicion of harm."

They were interrupted at this point by a messenger from the palace who brought word that the Dor-ul-Otho was becoming impatient and if the priests from A-lur were not brought to him at once he would come himself to the temple and get them. Mo-sar shook his head. He could not conceive of such brazen courage in mortal breast and glad he was that the plan evolved for Tarzan's undoing did not necessitate his active participation.

And so, while Mo-sar left for a secret corner of the palace by a roundabout way, three priests were dispatched to Tarzan and with whining words that did not entirely deceive him, they acknowledged his kinship to Jad-ben-Otho and begged him in the name of the high priest to honor the temple with a visit, when the priests from A-lur would be brought to him and would answer any questions that he put to them.

Confident that a continuation of his bravado would best serve his purpose, and also that if suspicion against him should crystallize into conviction on the part of Mo-sar and his followers that he would be no worse off in the temple than in the palace, the ape-man haughtily accepted the invitation of the high priest.

And so he came into the temple and was received in a manner befitting his high claims. He questioned the two priests of A-lur from whom he obtained only a repetition of the story that Mo-sar had told him, and then the high priest invited him to inspect the temple.

They took him first to the altar court, of which there was only one in Tu-lur. It was almost identical in every respect with those at A-lur. There was a bloody altar at the east end and the drowning basin at the west, and the grizzly fringes upon the headdresses of the priests attested the fact that the eastern altar was an active force in the rites of the temple. Through the chambers and corridors beneath they led him, and finally, with torch bearers to light their steps, into a damp and gloomy labyrinth at a low level and here in a large chamber, the air of which was still heavy with the odor of lions, the crafty priests of Tu-lur encompassed their shrewd design.

The torches were suddenly extinguished. There was a hurried confusion of bare feet moving rapidly across the stone floor. There was a loud crash as of a heavy weight of stone falling upon stone, and then surrounding the ape-man naught but the darkness and the silence of the tomb.

CHAPTER XIX—DIANA OF THE JUNGLE

Jane had made her first kill and she was very proud of it. It was not a very formidable animal—only a hare; but it marked an epoch in her existence. Just as in the dim past the first hunter had shaped the destinies of mankind so it seemed that this event might shape hers in some new mold. No longer was she dependent upon the wild fruits and vegetables for sustenance. Now she might command meat, the giver of the strength and endurance she would require successfully to cope with the necessities of her primitive existence.

The next step was fire. She might learn to eat raw flesh as had her lord and master; but she shrank from that. The thought even was repulsive. She had, however, a plan for fire. She had given the matter thought, but had been too busy to put it into execution so long as fire could be of no immediate use to her. Now it was different—she had something to cook and her mouth watered for the flesh of her kill. She would grill it above glowing embers. Jane hastened to her tree. Among the treasures she had gathered in the bed of the stream were several pieces of volcanic glass, clear as crystal. She sought until she had found the one in mind, which was convex. Then she hurried to the ground and gathered a little pile of powdered bark that was very dry, and some dead leaves and grasses that had lain long in the hot sun. Near at hand she arranged a supply of dead twigs and branches—small and large.

Vibrant with suppressed excitement she held the bit of glass above the tinder, moving it slowly until she had focused the sun's rays upon a tiny spot. She waited breathlessly. How slow it was! Were her high hopes to be dashed in spite of all her clever planning? No! A thin thread of smoke rose gracefully into the quiet air. Presently the tinder glowed and broke suddenly into flame. Jane clasped her hands beneath her chin with a little gurgling exclamation of delight. She had achieved fire!

She piled on twigs and then larger branches and at last dragged a small log to the flames and pushed an end of it into the fire which was crackling merrily. It was the sweetest sound that she had heard for many a month. But she could not wait for the mass of embers that would be required to cook her hare. As quickly as might be she skinned and cleaned her kill, burying the hide and entrails. That she had learned from Tarzan. It served two purposes. One was the necessity for keeping a sanitary camp and the other the obliteration of the scent that most quickly attracts the man-eaters.

Then she ran a stick through the carcass and held it above the flames. By turning it often she prevented burning and at the same time permitted the meat to cook thoroughly all the way through. When it was done she scampered high into the safety of her tree to enjoy her meal in quiet and peace. Never, thought Lady Greystoke, had aught more delicious passed her lips. She patted her spear affectionately. It had brought her this toothsome dainty and with it a feeling of greater confidence and safety than she had enjoyed since that frightful day that she and Obergatz had spent their last cartridge. She would never forget that day—it had seemed one hideous succession of frightful beast after frightful beast. They had not been long in this strange country, yet they thought that they were hardened to dangers, for daily they had had encounters with ferocious creatures; but this day—she shuddered when she thought of it. And with her last cartridge she had killed a black and yellow striped lion-thing with great saber teeth just as it was about to spring upon Obergatz who had futilely emptied his rifle into it—the last shot—his final cartridge. For another day they had carried the now useless rifles; but at last they had discarded them and thrown away the cumbersome bandoleers, as well. How they had managed to survive during the ensuing week she could never quite understand, and then the Ho-don had come upon them and captured her. Obergatz had escaped—she was living it all over again. Doubtless he was dead unless he had been able to reach this side of the valley which was quite evidently less overrun with savage beasts.

Jane's days were very full ones now, and the daylight hours seemed all too short in which to accomplish the many things she had determined upon, since she had concluded that this spot presented as ideal a place as she could find to live until she could fashion the weapons she considered necessary for the obtaining of meat and for self-defense.

She felt that she must have, in addition to a good spear, a knife, and bow and arrows. Possibly when these had been achieved she might seriously consider an attempt to fight her way to one of civilization's nearest outposts. In the meantime it was necessary to construct some sort of protective shelter in which she might feel a greater sense of security by night, for she knew that there was a possibility that any night she might receive a visit from a prowling panther, although she had as yet seen none upon this side of the valley. Aside from this danger she felt comparatively safe in her aerial retreat.

The cutting of the long poles for her home occupied all of the daylight hours that were not engaged in the search for food. These poles she carried high into her tree and with them constructed a flooring across two stout branches binding the poles together and also to the branches with fibers from the tough arboraceous grasses that grew in profusion near the stream. Similarly she built walls and a roof, the latter thatched with many layers of great leaves. The fashioning of the barred windows and the door were matters of great importance and consuming interest. The windows, there were two of them, were large and the bars permanently fixed; but the door was small, the opening just large enough to permit her to pass through easily on hands and knees, which made it easier to barricade. She lost count of the days that the house cost her; but time was a cheap commodity—she had more of it than of anything else. It meant so little to her that she had not even any desire to keep account of it. How long since she and Obergatz had fled from the wrath of the Negro villagers she did not know and she could only roughly guess at the seasons. She worked hard for two reasons; one was to hasten the completion of her little place of refuge, and the other a desire for such physical exhaustion at night that she would sleep through those dreaded hours to a new day. As a matter of fact the house was finished in less than a week—that is, it was made as safe as it ever would be, though regardless of how long she might occupy it she would keep on adding touches and refinements here and there.

Her daily life was filled with her house building and her hunting, to which was added an occasional spice of excitement contributed by roving lions. To the woodcraft that she had learned from Tarzan, that master of the art, was added a considerable store of practical experience derived from her own past adventures in the jungle and the long months with Obergatz, nor was any day now lacking in some added store of useful knowledge. To these facts was attributable her apparent immunity from harm, since they told her when *Ja* was approaching before he crept close enough for a successful charge and, too, they kept her close to those never-failing havens of retreat—the trees.

The nights, filled with their weird noises, were lonely and depressing. Only her ability to sleep quickly and soundly made them endurable. The first night that she spent in her completed house behind barred windows and barricaded door was one of almost undiluted peace and happiness. The night noises seemed far removed and impersonal and the soughing of the wind in the trees was gently soothing. Before, it had carried a mournful note and was sinister in that it might hide the approach of some real danger. That night she slept indeed.

She went further afield now in search of food. So far nothing but rodents had fallen to her spear—her ambition was an antelope, since beside the flesh it would give her, and the gut for her bow, the hide would prove invaluable during the colder weather that she knew would accompany the rainy season. She had caught glimpses of these wary animals and was sure that they always crossed the stream at a certain spot above her camp. It was to this place that she went to hunt them. With the stealth and cunning of a panther she crept through the forest, circling about to get up wind from the ford, pausing often to look and listen for aught that might menace her—herself the personification of a hunted deer. Now she moved silently down upon the chosen spot. What luck! A beautiful buck stood drinking in the stream. The woman wormed her way closer. Now she lay upon her belly behind a small bush within throwing distance of the quarry. She must rise to her full height and throw her spear almost in the same instant and she must throw it with great force and perfect accuracy. She thrilled with the excitement of the minute, yet cool and steady were her swift muscles as she rose and cast her missile. Scarce by the width of a finger did the point strike from the spot at which it had been directed. The buck leaped high, landed upon the bank of the stream, and fell dead. Jane Clayton sprang quickly forward toward her kill.

"Bravo!" A man's voice spoke in English from the shrubbery upon the opposite side of the stream. Jane Clayton halted in her tracks—stunned, almost, by surprise. And then a strange, unkempt figure of a man stepped into view. At first she did not recognize him, but when she did, instinctively she stepped back.

"Lieutenant Obergatz!" she cried. "Can it be you?"

"It can. It is," replied the German. "I am a strange sight, no doubt; but still it is I, Erich Obergatz. And you? You have changed too, is it not?"

He was looking at her naked limbs and her golden breastplates, the loin cloth of *Jato*-hide, the harness and ornaments that constitute the apparel of a Ho-don woman—the things that Lu-don had dressed her in as his passion for her grew. Not Ko-tan's daughter, even, had finer trappings.

"But why are you here?" Jane insisted. "I had thought you safely among civilized men by this time, if you still lived."

"Gott!" he exclaimed. "I do not know why I continue to live. I have prayed to die and yet I cling to life. There is no hope. We are doomed to remain in this horrible land until we die. The bog! The frightful bog! I have searched its shores for a place to cross until I have entirely circled the hideous country. Easily enough we entered; but the rains have come since and now no living man could pass that slough of slimy mud and hungry reptiles. Have I not tried it! And the beasts that roam this accursed land. They hunt me by day and by night."

"But how have you escaped them?" she asked.

"I do not know," he replied gloomily. "I have fled and fled and fled. I have remained hungry and thirsty in tree tops for days at a time. I have fashioned weapons—clubs and spears—and I have learned to use them. I have slain a lion with my club. So even will a cornered rat fight. And we are no better than rats in this land of stupendous dangers, you and I. But tell me about yourself. If it is surprising that I live, how much more so that you still survive."

Briefly she told him and all the while she was wondering what she might do to rid herself of him. She could not conceive of a prolonged existence with him as her sole companion. Better, a thousand times better, to be alone. Never had her hatred and contempt for him lessened through the long weeks and months of their constant companionship, and now that he could be of no service in returning her to civilization, she shrank from the thought of seeing him daily. And, too, she feared him. Never had she trusted him; but now there was a strange light in his eye that had not been there when last she saw him. She could not interpret it—all she knew was that it gave her a feeling of apprehension—a nameless dread.

"You lived long then in the city of A-lur?" he said, speaking in the language of Pal-ul-don.

"You have learned this tongue?" she asked. "How?"

"I fell in with a band of half-breeds," he replied, "members of a proscribed race that dwells in the rock-bound gut through which the principal river of the valley empties into the morass. They are called Waz-ho-don and their village is partly made up of cave dwellings and partly of houses carved from the soft rock at the foot of the cliff. They are very ignorant and superstitious and when they first saw me and realized that I had no tail and that my hands and feet were not like theirs they were afraid of me. They thought that I was either god or demon. Being in a position where I could neither escape them nor defend myself, I made a bold front and succeeded in impressing them to such an extent that they conducted me to their city, which they call Bu-lur, and there they fed me and treated me with kindness. As I learned their language I sought to impress them more and more with the idea that I was a god, and I succeeded, too, until an old fellow who was something of a priest among them, or medicine-man, became jealous of my growing power. That was the beginning of the end and came near to being the end in fact. He told them that if I was a god I would not bleed if a knife was stuck into me—if I did bleed it would prove conclusively that I was not a god. Without my knowledge he arranged to stage the ordeal before the whole village upon a certain night—it was upon one of those numerous occasions when they eat and drink to Jad-ben-Otho, their pagan deity. Under the influence of their vile liquor they would be ripe for any bloodthirsty scheme the medicine-man might evolve. One of the women told me about the plan—not with any intent to warn me of danger, but prompted merely by feminine curiosity as to whether or not I would bleed if stuck with a dagger. She could not wait, it seemed, for the orderly procedure of the ordeal—she wanted to know at once, and when I caught her trying to slip a knife into my side and questioned her she explained the whole thing with the utmost naivete. The warriors already had commenced drinking—it would have been futile to make any sort of appeal either to their intellects or their superstitions. There was but one alternative to death and that was flight. I told the woman that I was very much outraged and offended at this reflection upon my godhood and that as a mark of my disfavor I should abandon them to their fate.

"'I shall return to heaven at once!' I exclaimed.

"She wanted to hang around and see me go, but I told her that her eyes would be blasted by the fire surrounding my departure and that she must leave at once and not return to the spot for at least an hour. I also impressed upon her the fact that should any other approach this part of the village within that time not only they, but she as well, would burst into flames and be consumed.

"She was very much impressed and lost no time in leaving, calling back as she departed that if I were indeed gone in an hour she and all the village would know that I was no less than Jad-ben-Otho himself, and so they must think me, for I can assure you that I was gone in much less than an hour, nor have I ventured close to the neighborhood of the city of Bu-lur since," and he fell to laughing in harsh, cackling notes that sent a shiver through the woman's frame.

As Obergatz talked Jane had recovered her spear from the carcass of the antelope and commenced busying herself with the removal of the hide. The man made no attempt to assist her, but stood by talking and watching her, the while he continually ran his filthy fingers through his matted hair and beard. His face and body were caked with dirt and he was naked except for a torn greasy hide about his loins. His weapons consisted of a club and knife of Waz-don pattern, that he had stolen from the city of Bu-lur; but what more greatly concerned the woman than his filth or his armament were his cackling laughter and the strange expression in his eyes.

She went on with her work, however, removing those parts of the buck she wanted, taking only as much meat as she might consume before it spoiled, as she was not sufficiently a true jungle creature to relish it beyond that stage, and then she straightened up and faced the man.

"Lieutenant Obergatz," she said, "by a chance of accident we have met again. Certainly you would not have sought the meeting any more than I. We have nothing in common other than those sentiments which may have been engendered by my natural dislike and suspicion of you, one of the authors of all the misery and sorrow that I have endured for endless months. This little corner of the world is mine by right of discovery and occupation. Go away and leave me to enjoy here what peace I may. It is the least that you can do to amend the wrong that you have done me and mine."

The man stared at her through his fishy eyes for a moment in silence, then there broke from his lips a peal of mirthless, uncanny laughter.

"Go away! Leave you alone!" he cried. "I have found you. We are going to be good friends. There is no one else in the world but us. No one will ever know what we do or what becomes of us and now you ask me to go away and live alone in this hellish solitude." Again he laughed, though neither the muscles of his eyes or his mouth reflected any mirth—it was just a hollow sound that imitated laughter.

"Remember your promise," she said.

"Promise! Promise! What are promises? They are made to be broken—we taught the world that at Liege and Louvain. No, no! I will not go away. I shall stay and protect you."

"I do not need your protection," she insisted. "You have already seen that I can use a spear."

"Yes," he said; "but it would not be right to leave you here alone—you are but a woman. No, no; I am an officer of the Kaiser and I cannot abandon you."

Once more he laughed. "We could be very happy here together," he added.

The woman could not repress a shudder, nor, in fact, did she attempt to hide her aversion.

"You do not like me?" he asked. "Ah, well; it is too sad. But some day you will love me," and again the hideous laughter.

The woman had wrapped the pieces of the buck in the hide and this she now raised and threw across her shoulder. In her other hand she held her spear and faced the German.

"Go!" she commanded. "We have wasted enough words. This is my country and I shall defend it. If I see you about again I shall kill you. Do you understand?"

An expression of rage contorted Obergatz' features. He raised his club and started toward her.

"Stop!" she commanded, throwing her spear-hand backward for a cast. "You saw me kill this buck and you have said truthfully that no one will ever know what we do here. Put these two facts together, German, and draw your own conclusions before you take another step in my direction."

The man halted and his club-hand dropped to his side. "Come," he begged in what he intended as a conciliatory tone. "Let us be friends, Lady Greystoke. We can be of great assistance to each other and I promise not to harm you."

"Remember Liege and Louvain," she reminded him with a sneer. "I am going now—be sure that you do not follow me. As far as you can walk in a day from this spot in any direction you may consider the limits of my domain. If ever again I see you within these limits I shall kill you."

There could be no question that she meant what she said and the man seemed convinced for he but stood sullenly eyeing her as she backed from sight beyond a turn in the game trail that crossed the ford where they had met, and disappeared in the forest.

CHAPTER XX—SILENTLY IN THE NIGHT

In A-lur the fortunes of the city had been tossed from hand to hand. The party of Ko-tan's loyal warriors that Tarzan had led to the rendezvous at the entrance to the secret passage below the palace gates had met with disaster. Their first rush had been met with soft words from the priests. They had been exhorted to defend the faith of their fathers from blasphemers. Ja-don was painted to them as a defiler of temples, and the wrath of Jad-ben-Otho was prophesied for those who embraced his cause. The priests insisted that Lu-don's only wish was to prevent the seizure of the throne by Ja-don until a new king could be chosen according to the laws of the Ho-don.

The result was that many of the palace warriors joined their fellows of the city, and when the priests saw that those whom they could influence outnumbered those who remained loyal to the palace, they caused the former to fall upon the latter with the result that many were killed and only a handful succeeded in reaching the safety of the palace gates, which they quickly barred.

The priests led their own forces through the secret passageway into the temple, while some of the loyal ones sought out Ja-don and told him all that had happened. The fight in the banquet hall had spread over a considerable portion of the palace grounds and had at last resulted in the temporary defeat of those who had opposed Ja-don. This force, counseled by under priests sent for the purpose by Lu-don, had withdrawn within the temple grounds so that now the issue was plainly marked as between Ja-don on the one side and Lu-don on the other.

The former had been told of all that had occurred in the apartments of O-lo-a to whose safety he had attended at the first opportunity and he had also learned of Tarzan's part in leading his men to the gathering of Lu-don's warriors.

These things had naturally increased the old warrior's former inclinations of friendliness toward the ape-man, and now he regretted that the other had departed from the city.

The testimony of O-lo-a and Pan-at-lee was such as to strengthen whatever belief in the godliness of the stranger Ja-don and others of the warriors had previously entertained, until presently there appeared a strong tendency upon the part of this palace faction to make the Dor-ul-otho an issue of their original quarrel with Lu-don. Whether this occurred as the natural sequence to repeated narrations of the ape-man's exploits, which lost nothing by repetition, in conjunction with Lu-don's enmity toward him, or whether it was the shrewd design of some wily old warrior such as Ja-don, who realized the value of adding a religious cause to their temporal one, it were difficult to determine; but the fact remained that Ja-don's followers developed bitter hatred for the followers of Lu-don because of the high priest's antagonism to Tarzan.

Unfortunately however Tarzan was not there to inspire the followers of Ja-don with the holy zeal that might have quickly settled the dispute in the old chieftain's favor. Instead, he was miles away and because their repeated prayers for his presence were unanswered, the weaker spirits among them commenced to suspect that their cause did not have divine favor. There was also another and a potent cause for defection from the ranks of Ja-don. It emanated from the city where the friends and relatives of the palace warriors, who were largely also the friends and relatives of Lu-don's forces, found the means, urged on by the priesthood, to circulate throughout the palace pernicious propaganda aimed at Ja-don's cause.

The result was that Lu-don's power increased while that of Ja-don waned. Then followed a sortie from the temple which resulted in the defeat of the palace forces, and though they were able to withdraw in decent order withdraw they did, leaving the palace to Lu-don, who was now virtually ruler of Pal-ul-don.

Ja-don, taking with him the princess, her women, and their slaves, including Pan-at-lee, as well as the women and children of his faithful followers, retreated not only from the palace but from the city of A-lur as well and fell back upon his own city of Ja-lur. Here he remained, recruiting his forces from the surrounding villages of the north which, being far removed from the influence of the priesthood of A-lur, were enthusiastic partisans in any cause that the old chieftain espoused, since for years he had been revered as their friend and protector.

And while these events were transpiring in the north, Tarzan-jad-guru lay in the lion pit at Tu-lur while messengers passed back and forth between Mo-sar and Lu-don as the two dickered for the throne of Pal-ul-don. Mo-sar was cunning enough to guess that should an open breach occur between himself and the high priest he might use his prisoner to his own advantage, for he had heard whisperings among even his own people that suggested that there were those who were more than a trifle inclined to belief in the divinity of the stranger and that he might indeed be the Dor-ul-Otho. Lu-don wanted Tarzan himself. He wanted to sacrifice him upon the eastern altar with his own hands before a multitude of people, since he was not without evidence that his own standing and authority had been lessened by the claims of the bold and heroic figure of the stranger.

The method that the high priest of Tu-lur had employed to trap Tarzan had left the ape-man in possession of his weapons though there seemed little likelihood of their being of any service to him. He also had his pouch, in which were the various odds and ends which are the natural accumulation of all receptacles from a gold meshbag to an attic. There were bits of obsidian and choice feathers for arrows, some pieces of flint and a couple of steel, an old knife, a heavy bone needle, and strips of dried gut. Nothing very useful to you or me, perhaps; but nothing useless to the savage life of the ape-man.

When Tarzan realized the trick that had been so neatly played upon him he had awaited expectantly the coming of the lion, for though the scent of *Ja* was old he was sure that sooner or later they would let one of the beasts in upon him. His first consideration was a thorough exploration of his prison. He had noticed the hide-covered windows and these he immediately uncovered, letting in the light, and revealing the fact that though the chamber was far below the level of the temple courts it was yet many feet above the base of the hill from which the temple was hewn. The windows were so closely barred that he could not see over the edge of the thick wall in which they were cut to determine what lay close in below him. At a little distance were the blue waters of Jad-in-lul and beyond, the verdure-clad farther shore, and beyond that the mountains. It was a beautiful picture upon which he looked—a picture of peace and harmony and quiet. Nor anywhere a slightest suggestion of the savage men and beasts that claimed this lovely landscape as their own. What a paradise! And some day civilized man would come and—spoil it! Ruthless axes would raze that age-old wood; black, sticky smoke would rise from ugly chimneys against that azure sky; grimy little boats with wheels behind or upon either side would churn the mud from the bottom of Jad-in-lul, turning its blue waters to a dirty brown; hideous piers would project into the lake from squalid buildings of corrugated iron, doubtless, for of such are the pioneer cities of the world.

But would civilized man come? Tarzan hoped not. For countless generations civilization had ramped about the globe; it had dispatched its emissaries to the North Pole and the South; it had circled Pal-ul-don once, perhaps many times, but it had never touched her. God grant that it never would. Perhaps He was saving this little spot to be always just as He had made it, for the scratching of the Ho-don and the Waz-don upon His rocks had not altered the fair face of Nature.

Through the windows came sufficient light to reveal the whole interior to Tarzan. The room was fairly large and there was a door at each end—a large door for men and a smaller one for lions. Both were closed with heavy masses of stone that had been lowered in grooves running to the floor. The two windows were small and closely barred with the first iron that Tarzan had seen in Pal-ul-don. The bars were let into holes in the casing, and the whole so strongly and neatly contrived that escape seemed impossible. Yet within a few minutes of his incarceration Tarzan had commenced to undertake his escape. The old knife in his pouch was brought into requisition and slowly the ape-man began to scrape and chip away the stone from about the bars of one of the windows. It was slow work but Tarzan had the patience of absolute health.

Each day food and water were brought him and slipped quickly beneath the smaller door which was raised just sufficiently to allow the stone receptacles to pass in. The prisoner began to believe that he was being preserved for something beside lions. However that was immaterial. If they would but hold off for a few more days they might select what fate they would—he would not be there when they arrived to announce it.

And then one day came Pan-sat, Lu-don's chief tool, to the city of Tu-lur. He came ostensibly with a fair message for Mo-sar from the high priest at A-lur. Lu-don had decided that Mo-sar should be king and he invited Mo-sar to come at once to A-lur and then Pan-sat, having delivered the message, asked that he might go to the temple of Tu-lur and pray, and there he sought the high priest of Tu-lur to whom was the true message that Lu-don had sent. The two were closeted alone in a little chamber and Pan-sat whispered into the ear of the high priest.

"Mo-sar wishes to be king," he said, "and Lu-don wishes to be king. Mo-sar wishes to retain the stranger who claims to be the Dor-ul-Otho and Lu-don wishes to kill him, and now," he leaned even closer to the ear of the high priest of Tu-lur, "if you would be high priest at A-lur it is within your power."

Pan-sat ceased speaking and waited for the other's reply. The high priest was visibly affected. To be high priest at A-lur! That was almost as good as being king of all Pal-ul-don, for great were the powers of him who conducted the sacrifices upon the altars of A-lur.

"How?" whispered the high priest. "How may I become high priest at A-lur?"

Again Pan-sat leaned close: "By killing the one and bringing the other to A-lur," replied he. Then he rose and departed knowing that the other had swallowed the bait and could be depended upon to do whatever was required to win him the great prize.

Nor was Pan-sat mistaken other than in one trivial consideration. This high priest would indeed commit murder and treason to attain the high office at A-lur; but he had misunderstood which of his victims was to be killed and which to be delivered to Lu-don. Pan-sat, knowing himself all the details of the plannings of Lu-don, had made the quite natural error of assuming that the other was perfectly aware that only by publicly sacrificing the false Dor-ul-Otho could the high priest at A-lur bolster his waning power and that the assassination of Mo-sar, the pretender, would remove from Lu-don's camp the only obstacle to his combining the offices of high priest and king. The high priest at Tu-lur thought that he had been commissioned to kill Tarzan and bring Mo-sar to A-lur. He also thought that when he had done these things he would be made high priest at A-lur; but he did not know that already the priest had been selected who was to murder him within the hour that he arrived at A-lur, nor did he know that a secret grave had been prepared for him in the floor of a subterranean chamber in the very temple he dreamed of controlling.

And so when he should have been arranging the assassination of his chief he was leading a dozen heavily bribed warriors through the dark corridors beneath the temple to slay Tarzan in the lion pit. Night had fallen. A single torch guided the footsteps of the murderers as they crept stealthily upon their evil way, for they knew that they were doing the thing that their chief did not want done and their guilty consciences warned them to stealth.

In the dark of his cell the ape-man worked at his seemingly endless chipping and scraping. His keen ears detected the coming of footsteps along the corridor without—footsteps that approached the larger door. Always before had they come to the smaller door—the footsteps of a single slave who brought his food. This time there were many more than one and their coming at this time of night carried a sinister suggestion. Tarzan continued to work at his scraping and chipping. He heard them stop beyond the door. All was silence broken only by the scrape, scrape, scrape of the ape-man's tireless blade.

Those without heard it and listening sought to explain it. They whispered in low tones making their plans. Two would raise the door quickly and the others would rush in and hurl their clubs at the prisoner. They would take no chances, for the stories that had circulated in A-lur had been brought to Tu-lur—stories of the great strength and wonderful prowess of Tarzan-jad-guru that caused the sweat to stand upon the brows of the warriors, though it was cool in the damp corridor and they were twelve to one.

And then the high priest gave the signal—the door shot upward and ten warriors leaped into the chamber with poised clubs. Three of the heavy weapons flew across the room toward a darker shadow that lay in the shadow of the opposite wall, then the flare of the torch in the priest's hand lighted the interior and they saw that the thing at which they had flung their clubs was a pile of skins torn from the windows and that except for themselves the chamber was vacant.

One of them hastened to a window. All but a single bar was gone and to this was tied one end of a braided rope fashioned from strips cut from the leather window hangings.

To the ordinary dangers of Jane Clayton's existence was now added the menace of Obergatz' knowledge of her whereabouts. The lion and the panther had given her less cause for anxiety than did the return of the unscrupulous Hun, whom she had always distrusted and feared, and whose repulsiveness was now immeasurably augmented by his unkempt and filthy appearance, his strange and mirthless laughter, and his unnatural demeanor. She feared him now with a new fear as though he had suddenly become the personification of some nameless horror. The wholesome, outdoor life that she had been leading had strengthened and rebuilt her nervous system yet it seemed to her as she thought of him that if this man should ever touch her she should scream, and, possibly, even faint. Again and again during the day following their unexpected meeting the woman reproached herself for not having killed him as she would *Ja* or *Jato* or any other predatory beast that menaced her existence or her safety. There was no attempt at self-justification for these sinister reflections—they needed no justification. The standards by which the acts of such as you or I may be judged could not apply to hers. We have recourse to the protection of friends and relatives and the civil soldiery that upholds the majesty of the law and which may be invoked to protect the righteous weak against the unrighteous strong; but Jane Clayton comprised within herself not only the righteous weak but all the various agencies for the protection of the weak. To her, then, Lieutenant Erich Obergatz presented no different problem than did *Ja*, the lion, other than that she considered the former the more dangerous animal. And so she determined that should he ignore her warning there would be no temporizing upon the occasion of their next meeting—the same swift spear that would meet *Ja*'s advances would meet his.

That night her snug little nest perched high in the great tree seemed less the sanctuary that it had before. What might resist the sanguinary intentions of a prowling panther would prove no great barrier to man, and influenced by this thought she slept less well than before. The slightest noise that broke the monotonous hum of the nocturnal jungle startled her into alert wakefulness to lie with straining ears in an attempt to classify the origin of the disturbance, and once she was awakened thus by a sound that seemed to come from something moving in her own tree. She listened intently—scarce breathing. Yes, there it was again. A scuffing of something soft against the hard bark of the tree. The woman reached out in the darkness and grasped her spear. Now she felt a slight sagging of one of the limbs that supported her shelter as though the thing, whatever it was, was slowly raising its weight to the branch. It came nearer. Now she thought that she could detect its breathing. It was at the door. She could hear it fumbling with the frail barrier. What could it be? It made no sound by which she might identify it. She raised herself upon her hands and knees and crept stealthily the little distance to the doorway, her spear clutched tightly in her hand. Whatever the thing was, it was evidently attempting to gain entrance without awakening her. It was just beyond the pitiful little contraption of slender boughs that she had bound together with grasses and called a door—only a few inches lay between the thing and her. Rising to her knees she reached out with her left hand and felt until she found a place where a crooked branch had left an opening a couple of inches wide near the center of the barrier. Into this she inserted the point of her spear. The thing must have heard her move within for suddenly it abandoned its efforts for stealth and tore angrily at the obstacle. At the same moment Jane thrust her spear forward with all her strength. She felt it enter flesh. There was a scream and a curse from without, followed by the crashing of a body through limbs and foliage. Her spear was almost dragged from her grasp, but she held to it until it broke free from the thing it had pierced.

It was Obergatz; the curse had told her that. From below came no further sound. Had she, then, killed him? She prayed so—with all her heart she prayed it. To be freed from the menace of this loathsome creature were relief indeed. During all the balance of the night she lay there awake, listening. Below her, she imagined, she could see the dead man with his hideous face bathed in the cold light of the moon—lying there upon his back staring up at her.

She prayed that *Ja* might come and drag it away, but all during the remainder of the night she heard never another sound above the drowsy hum of the jungle. She was glad that he was dead, but she dreaded the gruesome ordeal that awaited her on the morrow, for she must bury the thing that had been Erich Obergatz and live on there above the shallow grave of the man she had slain.

She reproached herself for her weakness, repeating over and over that she had killed in self-defense, that her act was justified; but she was still a woman of today, and strong upon her were the iron mandates of the social order from which she had sprung, its interdictions and its superstitions.

At last came the tardy dawn. Slowly the sun topped the distant mountains beyond Jad-in-lul. And yet she hesitated to loosen the fastenings of her door and look out upon the thing below. But it must be done. She steeled herself and untied the rawhide thong that secured the barrier. She looked down and only the grass and the flowers looked up at her. She came from her shelter and examined the ground upon the opposite side of the tree—there was no dead man there, nor anywhere as far as she could see. Slowly she descended, keeping a wary eye and an alert ear ready for the first intimation of danger.

At the foot of the tree was a pool of blood and a little trail of crimson drops upon the grass, leading away parallel with the shore of Jad-ben-lul. Then she had not slain him! She was vaguely aware of a peculiar, double sensation of relief and regret. Now she would be always in doubt. He might return; but at least she would not have to live above his grave.

She thought some of following the bloody spoor on the chance that he might have crawled away to die later, but she gave up the idea for fear that she might find him dead nearby, or, worse yet badly wounded. What then could she do? She could not finish him with her spear—no, she knew that she could not do that, nor could she bring him back and nurse him, nor could she leave him there to die of hunger or of thirst, or to become the prey of some prowling beast. It were better then not to search for him for fear that she might find him.

That day was one of nervous starting to every sudden sound. The day before she would have said that her nerves were of iron; but not today. She knew now the shock that she had suffered and that this was the reaction. Tomorrow it might be different, but something told her that never again would her little shelter and the patch of forest and jungle that she called her own be the same. There would hang over them always the menace of this man. No longer would she pass restful nights of deep slumber. The peace of her little world was shattered forever.

That night she made her door doubly secure with additional thongs of rawhide cut from the pelt of the buck she had slain the day that she met Obergatz. She was very tired for she had lost much sleep the night before; but for a long time she lay with wide-open eyes staring into the darkness. What saw she there? Visions that brought tears to those brave and beautiful eyes— visions of a rambling bungalow that had been home to her and that was no more, destroyed by the same cruel force that haunted her even now in this remote, uncharted corner of the earth; visions of a strong man whose protecting arm would never press her close again; visions of a tall, straight son who looked at her adoringly out of brave, smiling eyes that were like his father's. Always the vision of the crude simple bungalow rather than of the stately halls that had been as much a part of her life as the other. But he had loved the bungalow and the broad, free acres best and so she had come to love them best, too.

At last she slept, the sleep of utter exhaustion. How long it lasted she did not know; but suddenly she was wide awake and once again she heard the scuffing of a body against the bark of her tree and again the limb bent to a heavy weight. He had returned! She went cold, trembling as with ague. Was it he, or, O God! had she killed him then and was this—? She tried to drive the horrid thought from her mind, for this way, she knew, lay madness.

And once again she crept to the door, for the thing was outside just as it had been last night. Her hands trembled as she placed the point of her weapon to the opening. She wondered if it would scream as it fell.

CHAPTER XXI—THE MANIAC

The last bar that would make the opening large enough to permit his body to pass had been removed as Tarzan heard the warriors whispering beyond the stone door of his prison. Long since had the rope of hide been braided. To secure one end to the remaining bar that he had left for this purpose was the work of but a moment, and while the warriors whispered without, the brown body of the ape-man slipped through the small aperture and disappeared below the sill.

Tarzan's escape from the cell left him still within the walled area that comprised the palace and temple grounds and buildings. He had reconnoitered as best he might from the window after he had removed enough bars to permit him to pass his head through the opening, so that he knew what lay immediately before him—a winding and usually deserted alleyway leading in the direction of the outer gate that opened from the palace grounds into the city.

The darkness would facilitate his escape. He might even pass out of the palace and the city without detection. If he could elude the guard at the palace gate the rest would be easy. He strode along confidently, exhibiting no fear of detection, for he reasoned that thus would he disarm suspicion. In the darkness he easily could pass for a Ho-don and in truth, though he passed several after leaving the deserted alley, no one accosted or detained him, and thus he came at last to the guard of a half-dozen warriors before the palace gate. These he attempted to pass in the same unconcerned fashion and he might have succeeded had it not been for one who came running rapidly from the direction of the temple shouting: "Let no one pass the gates! The prisoner has escaped from the pal-ul-Ja!"

Instantly a warrior barred his way and simultaneously the fellow recognized him. "Xot tor!" he exclaimed: "Here he is now. Fall upon him! Fall upon him! Back! Back before I kill you."

The others came forward. It cannot be said that they rushed forward. If it was their wish to fall upon him there was a noticeable lack of enthusiasm other than that which directed their efforts to persuade someone else to fall upon him. His fame as a fighter had been too long a topic of conversation for the good of the morale of Mo-sar's warriors. It were safer to stand at a distance and hurl their clubs and this they did, but the ape-man had learned something of the use of this weapon since he had arrived in Pal-ul-don. And as he learned great had grown his respect for this most primitive of arms. He had come to realize that the black savages he had known had never appreciated the possibilities of their knob sticks, nor had he, and he had discovered, too, why the Pal-ul-donians had turned their ancient spears into plowshares and pinned their faith to the heavy-ended club alone. In deadly execution it was far more effective than a spear and it answered, too, every purpose of a shield, combining the two in one and thus reducing the burden of the warrior. Thrown as they throw it, after the manner of the hammer-throwers of the Olympian games, an ordinary shield would prove more a weakness than a strength while one that would be strong enough to prove a protection would be too heavy to carry. Only another club, deftly wielded to deflect the course of an enemy missile, is in any way effective against these formidable weapons and, too, the war club of Pal-ul-don can be thrown with accuracy a far greater distance than any spear.

And now was put to the test that which Tarzan had learned from Om-at and Ta-den. His eyes and his muscles trained by a lifetime of necessity moved with the rapidity of light and his brain functioned with an uncanny celerity that suggested nothing less than prescience, and these things more than compensated for his lack of experience with the war club he handled so dexterously. Weapon after weapon he warded off and always he moved with a single idea in mind—to place himself within reach of one of his antagonists. But they were wary for they feared this strange creature to whom the superstitious fears of many of them attributed the miraculous powers of deity. They managed to keep between Tarzan and the gateway and all the time they bawled lustily for reinforcements. Should these come before he had made his escape the ape-man realized that the odds against him would be unsurmountable, and so he redoubled his efforts to carry out his design.

Following their usual tactics two or three of the warriors were always circling behind him collecting the thrown clubs when Tarzan's attention was directed elsewhere. He himself retrieved several of them which he hurled with such deadly effect as to dispose of two of his antagonists, but now he heard the approach of hurrying warriors, the patter of their bare feet upon the stone pavement and then the savage cries which were to bolster the courage of their fellows and fill the enemy with fear.

There was no time to lose. Tarzan held a club in either hand and, swinging one he hurled it at a warrior before him and as the man dodged he rushed in and seized him, at the same time casting his second club at another of his opponents. The Ho-don with whom he grappled reached instantly for his knife but the ape-man grasped his wrist. There was a sudden twist, the snapping of a bone and an agonized scream, then the warrior was lifted bodily from his feet and held as a shield between his fellows and the fugitive as the latter backed through the gateway. Beside Tarzan stood the single torch that lighted the entrance to the palace grounds. The warriors were advancing to the succor of their fellow when the ape-man raised his captive high above his head and flung him full in the face of the foremost attacker. The fellow went down and two directly behind him sprawled headlong over their companion as the ape-man seized the torch and cast it back into the palace grounds to be extinguished as it struck the bodies of those who led the charging reinforcements.

In the ensuing darkness Tarzan disappeared in the streets of Tu-lur beyond the palace gate. For a time he was aware of sounds of pursuit but the fact that they trailed away and died in the direction of Jad-in-lul informed him that they were searching in the wrong direction, for he had turned south out of Tu-lur purposely to throw them off his track. Beyond the outskirts of the city he turned directly toward the northwest, in which direction lay A-lur.

In his path he knew lay Jad-bal-lul, the shore of which he was compelled to skirt, and there would be a river to cross at the lower end of the great lake upon the shores of which lay A-lur. What other obstacles lay in his way he did not know but he believed that he could make better time on foot than by attempting to steal a canoe and force his way up stream with a single paddle. It was his intention to put as much distance as possible between himself and Tu-lur before he slept for he was sure that Mo-sar would not lightly accept his loss, but that with the coming of day, or possibly even before, he would dispatch warriors in search of him.

A mile or two from the city he entered a forest and here at last he felt such a measure of safety as he never knew in open spaces or in cities. The forest and the jungle were his birthright. No creature that went upon the ground upon four feet, or climbed among the trees, or crawled upon its belly had any advantage over the ape-man in his native heath. As myrrh and frankincense were the dank odors of rotting vegetation in the nostrils of the great Tarmangani. He squared his broad shoulders and lifting his head filled his lungs with the air that he loved best. The heavy fragrance of tropical blooms, the commingled odors of the myriad-scented life of the jungle went to his head with a pleasurable intoxication far more potent than aught contained in the oldest vintages of civilization.

He took to the trees now, not from necessity but from pure love of the wild freedom that had been denied him so long. Though it was dark and the forest strange yet he moved with a surety and ease that bespoke more a strange uncanny sense than wondrous skill. He heard *Ja* moaning somewhere ahead and an owl hooted mournfully to the right of him—long familiar sounds that imparted to him no sense of loneliness as they might to you or to me, but on the contrary one of companionship for they betokened the presence of his fellows of the jungle, and whether friend or foe it was all the same to the ape-man.

He came at last to a little stream at a spot where the trees did not meet above it so he was forced to descend to the ground and wade through the water and upon the opposite shore he stopped as though suddenly his godlike figure had been transmuted from flesh to marble. Only his dilating nostrils bespoke his pulsing vitality. For a long moment he stood there thus and then swiftly, but with a caution and silence that were inherent in him he moved forward again, but now his whole attitude bespoke a new urge. There was a definite and masterful purpose in every movement of those steel muscles rolling softly beneath the smooth brown hide. He moved now toward a certain goal that quite evidently filled him with far greater enthusiasm than had the possible event of his return to A-lur.

And so he came at last to the foot of a great tree and there he stopped and looked up above him among the foliage where the dim outlines of a roughly rectangular bulk loomed darkly. There was a choking sensation in Tarzan's throat as he raised himself gently into the branches. It was as though his heart were swelling either to a great happiness or a great fear.

Before the rude shelter built among the branches he paused listening. From within there came to his sensitive nostrils the same delicate aroma that had arrested his eager attention at the little stream a mile away. He crouched upon the branch close to the little door.

"Jane," he called, "heart of my heart, it is I."

The only answer from within was as the sudden indrawing of a breath that was half gasp and half sigh, and the sound of a body falling to the floor. Hurriedly Tarzan sought to release the thongs which held the door but they were fastened from the inside, and at last, impatient with further delay, he seized the frail barrier in one giant hand and with a single effort tore it completely away. And then he entered to find the seemingly lifeless body of his mate stretched upon the floor.

He gathered her in his arms; her heart beat; she still breathed, and presently he realized that she had but swooned.

When Jane Clayton regained consciousness it was to find herself held tightly in two strong arms, her head pillowed upon the broad shoulder where so often before her fears had been soothed and her sorrows comforted. At first she was not sure but that it was all a dream. Timidly her hand stole to his cheek.

"John," she murmured, "tell me, is it really you?"

In reply he drew her more closely to him. "It is I," he replied. "But there is something in my throat," he said haltingly, "that makes it hard for me to speak."

She smiled and snuggled closer to him. "God has been good to us, Tarzan of the Apes," she said.

For some time neither spoke. It was enough that they were reunited and that each knew that the other was alive and safe. But at last they found their voices and when the sun rose they were still talking, so much had each to tell the other; so many questions there were to be asked and answered.

"And Jack," she asked, "where is he?"

"I do not know," replied Tarzan. "The last I heard of him he was on the Argonne Front."

"Ah, then our happiness is not quite complete," she said, a little note of sadness creeping into her voice.

"No," he replied, "but the same is true in countless other English homes today, and pride is learning to take the place of happiness in these."

She shook her head, "I want my boy," she said.

"And I too," replied Tarzan, "and we may have him yet. He was safe and unwounded the last word I had. And now," he said, "we must plan upon our return. Would you like to rebuild the bungalow and gather together the remnants of our Waziri or would you rather return to London?"

"Only to find Jack," she said. "I dream always of the bungalow and never of the city, but John, we can only dream, for Obergatz told me that he had circled this whole country and found no place where he might cross the morass."

"I am not Obergatz," Tarzan reminded her, smiling. "We will rest today and tomorrow we will set out toward the north. It is a savage country, but we have crossed it once and we can cross it again."

And so, upon the following morning, the Tarmangani and his mate went forth upon their journey across the Valley of Jad-ben-Otho, and ahead of them were fierce men and savage beasts, and the lofty mountains of Pal-ul-don; and beyond the mountains the reptiles and the morass, and beyond that the arid, thorn-covered steppe, and other savage beasts and men and weary, hostile miles of untracked wilderness between them and the charred ruins of their home.

Lieutenant Erich Obergatz crawled through the grass upon all fours, leaving a trail of blood behind him after Jane's spear had sent him crashing to the ground beneath her tree. He made no sound after the one piercing scream that had acknowledged the severity of his wound. He was quiet because of a great fear that had crept into his warped brain that the devil woman would pursue and slay him. And so he crawled away like some filthy beast of prey, seeking a thicket where he might lie down and hide.

He thought that he was going to die, but he did not, and with the coming of the new day he discovered that his wound was superficial. The rough obsidian-shod spear had entered the muscles of his side beneath his right arm inflicting a painful, but not a fatal wound. With the realization of this fact came a renewed desire to put as much distance as possible between himself and Jane Clayton. And so he moved on, still going upon all fours because of a persistent hallucination that in this way he might escape observation. Yet though he fled his mind still revolved muddily about a central desire—while he fled from her he still planned to pursue her, and to his lust of possession was added a desire for revenge. She should pay for the suffering she had inflicted upon him. She should pay for rebuffing him, but for some reason which he did not try to explain to himself he would crawl away and hide. He would come back though. He would come back and when he had finished with her, he would take that smooth throat in his two hands and crush the life from her.

He kept repeating this over and over to himself and then he fell to laughing out loud, the cackling, hideous laughter that had terrified Jane. Presently he realized his knees were bleeding and that they hurt him. He looked cautiously behind. No one was in sight. He listened. He could hear no indications of pursuit and so he rose to his feet and continued upon his way a sorry sight—covered with filth and blood, his beard and hair tangled and matted and filled with burrs and dried mud and unspeakable filth. He kept no track of time. He ate fruits and berries and tubers that he dug from the earth with his fingers. He followed the shore of the lake and the river that he might be near water, and when *Ja* roared or moaned he climbed a tree and hid there, shivering.

And so after a time he came up the southern shore of Jad-ben-lul until a wide river stopped his progress. Across the blue water a white city glimmered in the sun. He looked at it for a long time, blinking his eyes like an owl. Slowly a recollection forced itself through his tangled brain. This was A-lur, the City of Light. The association of ideas recalled Bu-lur and the Waz-ho-don. They had called him Jad-ben-Otho. He commenced to laugh aloud and stood up very straight and strode back and forth along the shore. "I am Jad-ben-Otho," he cried, "I am the Great God. In A-lur is my temple and my high priests. What is Jad-ben-Otho doing here alone in the jungle?"

He stepped out into the water and raising his voice shrieked loudly across toward A-lur. "I am Jad-ben-Otho!" he screamed. "Come hither slaves and take your god to his temple." But the distance was great and they did not hear him and no one came, and the feeble mind was distracted by other things—a bird flying in the air, a school of minnows swimming around his feet. He lunged at them trying to catch them, and falling upon his hands and knees he crawled through the water grasping futilely at the elusive fish.

Presently it occurred to him that he was a sea lion and he forgot the fish and lay down and tried to swim by wriggling his feet in the water as though they were a tail. The hardships, the privations, the terrors, and for the past few weeks the lack of proper nourishment had reduced Erich Obergatz to little more than a gibbering idiot.

A water snake swam out upon the surface of the lake and the man pursued it, crawling upon his hands and knees. The snake swam toward the shore just within the mouth of the river where tall reeds grew thickly and Obergatz followed, making grunting noises like a pig. He lost the snake within the reeds but he came upon something else—a canoe hidden there close to the bank. He examined it with cackling laughter. There were two paddles within it which he took and threw out into the current of the river. He watched them for a while and then he sat down beside the canoe and commenced to splash his hands up and down upon the water. He liked to hear the noise and see the little splashes of spray. He rubbed his left forearm with his right palm and the dirt came off and left a white spot that drew his attention. He rubbed again upon the now thoroughly soaked blood and grime that covered his body. He was not attempting to wash himself; he was merely amused by the strange results. "I am turning white," he cried. His glance wandered from his body now that the grime and blood were all removed and caught again the white city shimmering beneath the hot sun.

"A-lur—City of Light!" he shrieked and that reminded him again of Tu-lur and by the same process of associated ideas that had before suggested it, he recalled that the Waz-ho-don had thought him Jad-ben-Otho.

"I am Jad-ben-Otho!" he screamed and then his eyes fell again upon the canoe. A new idea came and persisted. He looked down at himself, examining his body, and seeing the filthy loin cloth, now water soaked and more bedraggled than before, he tore it from him and flung it into the lake. "Gods do not wear dirty rags," he said aloud. "They do not wear anything but wreaths and garlands of flowers and I am a god—I am Jad-ben-Otho—and I go in state to my sacred city of A-lur."

He ran his fingers through his matted hair and beard. The water had softened the burrs but had not removed them. The man shook his head. His hair and beard failed to harmonize with his other godly attributes. He was commencing to think more clearly now, for the great idea had taken hold of his scattered wits and concentrated them upon a single purpose, but he was still a maniac. The only difference being that he was now a maniac with a fixed intent. He went out on the shore and gathered flowers and ferns and wove them in his beard and hair—blazing blooms of different colors—green ferns that trailed about his ears or rose bravely upward like the plumes in a lady's hat.

When he was satisfied that his appearance would impress the most casual observer with his evident deity he returned to the canoe, pushed it from shore and jumped in. The impetus carried it into the river's current and the current bore it out upon the lake. The naked man stood erect in the center of the little craft, his arms folded upon his chest. He screamed aloud his message to the city: "I am Jad-ben-Otho! Let the high priest and the under priests attend upon me!"

As the current of the river was dissipated by the waters of the lake the wind caught him and his craft and carried them bravely forward. Sometimes he drifted with his back toward A-lur and sometimes with his face toward it, and at intervals he shrieked his message and his commands. He was still in the middle of the lake when someone discovered him from the palace wall, and as he drew nearer, a crowd of warriors and women and children were congregated there watching him and along the temple walls were many priests and among them Lu-don, the high priest. When the boat had drifted close enough for them to distinguish the bizarre figure standing in it and for them to catch the meaning of his words Lu-don's cunning eyes narrowed. The high priest had learned of the escape of Tarzan and he feared that should he join Ja-don's forces, as seemed likely, he would attract many recruits who might still believe in him, and the Dor-ul-Otho, even if a false one, upon the side of the enemy might easily work havoc with Lu-don's plans.

The man was drifting close in. His canoe would soon be caught in the current that ran close to shore here and carried toward the river that emptied the waters of Jad-ben-lul into Jad-bal-lul. The under priests were looking toward Lu-don for instructions.

"Fetch him hither!" he commanded. "If he is Jad-ben-Otho I shall know him."

The priests hurried to the palace grounds and summoned warriors. "Go, bring the stranger to Lu-don. If he is Jad-ben-Otho we shall know him."

And so Lieutenant Erich Obergatz was brought before the high priest at A-lur. Lu-don looked closely at the naked man with the fantastic headdress.

"Where did you come from?" he asked.

"I am Jad-ben-Otho," cried the German. "I came from heaven. Where is my high priest?"

"I am the high priest," replied Lu-don.

Obergatz clapped his hands. "Have my feet bathed and food brought to me," he commanded.

Lu-don's eyes narrowed to mere slits of crafty cunning. He bowed low until his forehead touched the feet of the stranger. Before the eyes of many priests, and warriors from the palace he did it.

"Ho, slaves," he cried, rising; "fetch water and food for the Great God," and thus the high priest acknowledged before his people the godhood of Lieutenant Erich Obergatz, nor was it long before the story ran like wildfire through the palace and out into the city and beyond that to the lesser villages all the way from A-lur to Tu-lur.

The real god had come—Jad-ben-Otho himself, and he had espoused the cause of Lu-don, the high priest. Mo-sar lost no time in placing himself at the disposal of Lu-don, nor did he mention aught about his claims to the throne. It was Mo-sar's opinion that he might consider himself fortunate were he allowed to remain in peaceful occupation of his chieftainship at Tu-lur, nor was Mo-sar wrong in his deductions.

But Lu-don could still use him and so he let him live and sent word to him to come to A-lur with all his warriors, for it was rumored that Ja-don was raising a great army in the north and might soon march upon the City of Light.

Obergatz thoroughly enjoyed being a god. Plenty of food and peace of mind and rest partially brought back to him the reason that had been so rapidly slipping from him; but in one respect he was madder than ever, since now no power on earth would ever be able to convince him that he was not a god. Slaves were put at his disposal and these he ordered about in godly fashion. The same portion of his naturally cruel mind met upon common ground the mind of Lu-don, so that the two seemed always in accord. The high priest saw in the stranger a mighty force wherewith to hold forever his power over all Pal-ul-don and thus the future of Obergatz was assured so long as he cared to play god to Lu-don's high priest.

A throne was erected in the main temple court before the eastern altar where Jad-ben-Otho might sit in person and behold the sacrifices that were offered up to him there each day at sunset. So much did the cruel, half-crazed mind enjoy these spectacles that at times he even insisted upon wielding the sacrificial knife himself and upon such occasions the priests and the people fell upon their faces in awe of the dread deity.

If Obergatz taught them not to love their god more he taught them to fear him as they never had before, so that the name of Jad-ben-Otho was whispered in the city and little children were frightened into obedience by the mere mention of it. Lu-don, through his priests and slaves, circulated the information that Jad-ben-Otho had commanded all his faithful followers to flock to the standard of the high priest at A-lur and that all others were cursed, especially Ja-don and the base impostor who had posed as the Dor-ul-Otho. The curse was to take the form of early death following terrible suffering, and Lu-don caused it to be published abroad that the name of any warrior who complained of a pain should be brought to him, for such might be deemed to be under suspicion, since the first effects of the curse would result in slight pains attacking the unholy. He counseled those who felt pains to look carefully to their loyalty. The result was remarkable and immediate—half a nation without a pain, and recruits pouring into A-lur to offer their services to Lu-don while secretly hoping that the little pains they had felt in arm or leg or belly would not recur in aggravated form.

CHAPTER XXII—A JOURNEY ON A *GRYF*

Tarzan and Jane skirted the shore of Jad-bal-lul and crossed the river at the head of the lake. They moved in leisurely fashion with an eye to comfort and safety, for the ape-man, now that he had found his mate, was determined to court no chance that might again separate them, or delay or prevent their escape from Pal-ul-don. How they were to recross the morass was a matter of little concern to him as yet—it would be time enough to consider that matter when it became of more immediate moment. Their hours were filled with the happiness and content of reunion after long separation; they had much to talk of, for each had passed through many trials and vicissitudes and strange adventures, and no important hour might go unaccounted for since last they met.

It was Tarzan's intention to choose a way above A-lur and the scattered Ho-don villages below it, passing about midway between them and the mountains, thus avoiding, in so far as possible, both the Ho-don and Waz-don, for in this area lay the neutral territory that was uninhabited by either. Thus he would travel northwest until opposite the Kor-ul-Ja where he planned to stop to pay his respects to Om-at and give the gund word of Pan-at-lee, and a plan Tarzan had for insuring her safe return to her people. It was upon the third day of their journey and they had almost reached the river that passes through A-lur when Jane suddenly clutched Tarzan's arm and pointed ahead toward the edge of a forest that they were approaching. Beneath the shadows of the trees loomed a great bulk that the ape-man instantly recognized.

"What is it?" whispered Jane.

"A *gryf*," replied the ape-man, "and we have met him in the worst place that we could possibly have found. There is not a large tree within a quarter of a mile, other than those among which he stands. Come, we shall have to go back, Jane; I cannot risk it with you along. The best we can do is to pray that he does not discover us."

"And if he does?"

"Then I shall have to risk it."

"Risk what?"

"The chance that I can subdue him as I subdued one of his fellows," replied Tarzan. "I told you—you recall?"

"Yes, but I did not picture so huge a creature. Why, John, he is as big as a battleship."

The ape-man laughed. "Not quite, though I'll admit he looks quite as formidable as one when he charges."

They were moving away slowly so as not to attract the attention of the beast.

"I believe we're going to make it," whispered the woman, her voice tense with suppressed excitement. A low rumble rolled like distant thunder from the wood. Tarzan shook his head.

"'The big show is about to commence in the main tent,'" he quoted, grinning. He caught the woman suddenly to his breast and kissed her. "One can never tell, Jane," he said. "We'll do our best—that is all we can do. Give me your spear, and—don't run. The only hope we have lies in that little brain more than in us. If I can control it—well, let us see."

The beast had emerged from the forest and was looking about through his weak eyes, evidently in search of them. Tarzan raised his voice in the weird notes of the Tor-o-don's cry, "Whee-oo! Whee-oo! Whee-oo!" For a moment the great beast stood motionless, his attention riveted by the call. The ape-man advanced straight toward him, Jane Clayton at his elbow. "Whee-oo!" he cried again peremptorily. A low rumble rolled from the *gryf*'s cavernous chest in answer to the call, and the beast moved slowly toward them.

"Fine!" exclaimed Tarzan. "The odds are in our favor now. You can keep your nerve?—but I do not need to ask."

"I know no fear when I am with Tarzan of the Apes," she replied softly, and he felt the pressure of her soft fingers on his arm.

And thus the two approached the giant monster of a forgotten epoch until they stood close in the shadow of a mighty shoulder. "Whee-oo!" shouted Tarzan and struck the hideous snout with the shaft of the spear. The vicious side snap that did not reach its mark—that evidently was not intended to reach its mark—was the hoped-for answer.

"Come," said Tarzan, and taking Jane by the hand he led her around behind the monster and up the broad tail to the great, horned back. "Now will we ride in the state that our forebears knew, before which the pomp of modern kings pales into cheap and tawdry insignificance. How would you like to canter through Hyde Park on a mount like this?"

"I am afraid the Bobbies would be shocked by our riding habits, John," she cried, laughingly.

Tarzan guided the *gryf* in the direction that they wished to go. Steep embankments and rivers proved no slightest obstacle to the ponderous creature.

"A prehistoric tank, this," Jane assured him, and laughing and talking they continued on their way. Once they came unexpectedly upon a dozen Ho-don warriors as the *gryf* emerged suddenly into a small clearing. The fellows were lying about in the shade of a single tree that grew alone. When they saw the beast they leaped to their feet in consternation and at their shouts the *gryf* issued his hideous, challenging bellow and charged them. The warriors fled in all directions while Tarzan belabored the beast across the snout with his spear in an effort to control him, and at last he succeeded, just as the *gryf* was almost upon one poor devil that it seemed to have singled out for its special prey. With an angry grunt the *gryf* stopped and the man, with a single backward glance that showed a face white with terror, disappeared in the jungle he had been seeking to reach.

The ape-man was elated. He had doubted that he could control the beast should it take it into its head to charge a victim and had intended abandoning it before they reached the Kor-ul-Ja. Now he altered his plans—they would ride to the very village of Om-at upon the *gryf*, and the Kor-ul-Ja would have food for conversation for many generations to come. Nor was it the theatric instinct of the ape-man alone that gave favor to this plan. The element of Jane's safety entered into the matter for he knew that she would be safe from man and beast alike so long as she rode upon the back of Pal-ul-don's most formidable creature.

As they proceeded slowly in the direction of the Kor-ul-Ja, for the natural gait of the *gryf* is far from rapid, a handful of terrified warriors came panting into A-lur, spreading a weird story of the Dor-ul-Otho, only none dared call him the Dor-ul-Otho aloud. Instead they spoke of him as Tarzan-jad-guru and they told of meeting him mounted upon a mighty *gryf* beside the beautiful stranger woman whom Ko-tan would have made queen of Pal-ul-don. This story was brought to Lu-don who caused the warriors to be hailed to his presence, when he questioned them closely until finally he was convinced that they spoke the truth and when they had told him the direction in which the two were traveling, Lu-don guessed that they were on their way to Ja-lur to join Ja-don, a contingency that he felt must be prevented at any cost. As was his wont in the stress of emergency, he called Pan-sat into consultation and for long the two sat in close conference. When they arose a plan had been developed. Pan-sat went immediately to his own quarters where he removed the headdress and trappings of a priest to don in their stead the harness and weapons of a warrior. Then he returned to Lu-don.

"Good!" cried the latter, when he saw him. "Not even your fellow-priests or the slaves that wait upon you daily would know you now. Lose no time, Pan-sat, for all depends upon the speed with which you strike and—remember! Kill the man if you can; but in any event bring the woman to me here, alive. You understand?"

"Yes, master," replied the priest, and so it was that a lone warrior set out from A-lur and made his way northwest in the direction of Ja-lur.

The gorge next above Kor-ul-Ja is uninhabited and here the wily Ja-don had chosen to mobilize his army for its descent upon A-lur. Two considerations influenced him—one being the fact that could he keep his plans a secret from the enemy he would have the advantage of delivering a surprise attack upon the forces of Lu-don from a direction that they would not expect attack, and in the meantime he would be able to keep his men from the gossip of the cities where strange tales were already circulating relative to the coming of Jad-ben-Otho in person to aid the high priest in his war against Ja-don. It took stout hearts and loyal ones to ignore the implied threats of divine vengeance that these tales suggested. Already there had been desertions and the cause of Ja-don seemed tottering to destruction.

Such was the state of affairs when a sentry posted on the knoll in the mouth of the gorge sent word that he had observed in the valley below what appeared at a distance to be nothing less than two people mounted upon the back of a *gryf*. He said that he had caught glimpses of them, as they passed open spaces, and they seemed to be traveling up the river in the direction of the Kor-ul-Ja.

At first Ja-don was inclined to doubt the veracity of his informant; but, like all good generals, he could not permit even palpably false information to go uninvestigated and so he determined to visit the knoll himself and learn precisely what it was that the sentry had observed through the distorting spectacles of fear. He had scarce taken his place beside the man ere the fellow touched his arm and pointed. "They are closer now," he whispered, "you can see them plainly." And sure enough, not a quarter of a mile away Ja-don saw that which in his long experience in Pal-ul-don he had never before seen—two humans riding upon the broad back of a *gryf*.

At first he could scarce credit even this testimony of his own eyes, but soon he realized that the creatures below could be naught else than they appeared, and then he recognized the man and rose to his feet with a loud cry.

"It is he!" he shouted to those about him. "It is the Dor-ul-Otho himself."

The *gryf* and his riders heard the shout though not the words. The former bellowed terrifically and started in the direction of the knoll, and Ja-don, followed by a few of his more intrepid warriors, ran to meet him. Tarzan, loath to enter an unnecessary quarrel, tried to turn the animal, but as the beast was far from tractable it always took a few minutes to force the will of its master upon it; and so the two parties were quite close before the ape-man succeeded in stopping the mad charge of his furious mount.

Ja-don and his warriors, however, had come to the realization that this bellowing creature was bearing down upon them with evil intent and they had assumed the better part of valor and taken to trees, accordingly. It was beneath these trees that Tarzan finally stopped the *gryf*. Ja-don called down to him.

"We are friends," he cried. "I am Ja-don, Chief of Ja-lur. I and my warriors lay our foreheads upon the feet of Dor-ul-Otho and pray that he will aid us in our righteous fight with Lu-don, the high priest."

"You have not defeated him yet?" asked Tarzan. "Why I thought you would be king of Pal-ul-don long before this."

"No," replied Ja-don. "The people fear the high priest and now that he has in the temple one whom he claims to be Jad-ben-Otho many of my warriors are afraid. If they but knew that the Dor-ul-Otho had returned and that he had blessed the cause of Ja-don I am sure that victory would be ours."

Tarzan thought for a long minute and then he spoke. "Ja-don," he said, "was one of the few who believed in me and who wished to accord me fair treatment. I have a debt to pay to Ja-don and an account to settle with Lu-don, not alone on my own behalf, but principally upon that of my mate. I will go with you Ja-don to mete to Lu-don the punishment he deserves. Tell me, chief, how may the Dor-ul-Otho best serve his father's people?"

"By coming with me to Ja-lur and the villages between," replied Ja-don quickly, "that the people may see that it is indeed the Dor-ul-Otho and that he smiles upon the cause of Ja-don."

"You think that they will believe in me more now than before?" asked the ape-man.

"Who will dare doubt that he who rides upon the great *gryf* is less than a god?" returned the old chief.

"And if I go with you to the battle at A-lur," asked Tarzan, "can you assure the safety of my mate while I am gone from her?"

"She shall remain in Ja-lur with the Princess O-lo-a and my own women," replied Ja-don. "There she will be safe for there I shall leave trusted warriors to protect them. Say that you will come, O Dor-ul-Otho, and my cup of happiness will be full, for even now Ta-den, my son, marches toward A-lur with a force from the northwest and if we can attack, with the Dor-ul-Otho at our head, from the northeast our arms should be victorious."

"It shall be as you wish, Ja-don," replied the ape-man; "but first you must have meat fetched for my *gryf*."

"There are many carcasses in the camp above," replied Ja-don, "for my men have little else to do than hunt."

"Good," exclaimed Tarzan. "Have them brought at once."

And when the meat was brought and laid at a distance the ape-man slipped from the back of his fierce charger and fed him with his own hand. "See that there is always plenty of flesh for him," he said to Ja-don, for he guessed that his mastery might be short-lived should the vicious beast become over-hungry.

It was morning before they could leave for Ja-lur, but Tarzan found the *gryf* lying where he had left him the night before beside the carcasses of two antelope and a lion; but now there was nothing but the *gryf*.

"The paleontologists say that he was herbivorous," said Tarzan as he and Jane approached the beast.

The journey to Ja-lur was made through the scattered villages where Ja-don hoped to arouse a keener enthusiasm for his cause. A party of warriors preceded Tarzan that the people might properly be prepared, not only for the sight of the *gryf* but to receive the Dor-ul-Otho as became his high station. The results were all that Ja-don could have hoped and in no village through which they passed was there one who doubted the deity of the ape-man.

As they approached Ja-lur a strange warrior joined them, one whom none of Ja-don's following knew. He said he came from one of the villages to the south and that he had been treated unfairly by one of Lu-don's chiefs. For this reason he had deserted the cause of the high priest and come north in the hope of finding a home in Ja-lur. As every addition to his forces was welcome to the old chief he permitted the stranger to accompany them, and so he came into Ja-lur with them.

There arose now the question as to what was to be done with the *gryf* while they remained in the city. It was with difficulty that Tarzan had prevented the savage beast from attacking all who came near it when they had first entered the camp of Ja-don in the uninhabited gorge next to the Kor-ul-Ja, but during the march to Ja-lur the creature had seemed to become accustomed to the presence of the Ho-don. The latter, however, gave him no cause for annoyance since they kept as far from him as possible and when he passed through the streets of the city he was viewed from the safety of lofty windows and roofs. However tractable he appeared to have become there would have been no enthusiastic seconding of a suggestion to turn him loose within the city. It was finally suggested that he be turned into a walled enclosure within the palace grounds and this was done, Tarzan driving him in after Jane had dismounted. More meat was thrown to him and he was left to his own devices, the awe-struck inhabitants of the palace not even venturing to climb upon the walls to look at him.

Ja-don led Tarzan and Jane to the quarters of the Princess O-lo-a who, the moment that she beheld the ape-man, threw herself to the ground and touched her forehead to his feet. Pan-at-lee was there with her and she too seemed happy to see Tarzan-jad-guru again. When they found that Jane was his mate they looked with almost equal awe upon her, since even the most skeptical of the warriors of Ja-don were now convinced that they were entertaining a god and a goddess within the city of Ja-lur, and that with the assistance of the power of these two, the cause of Ja-don would soon be victorious and the old Lion-man set upon the throne of Pal-ul-don.

From O-lo-a Tarzan learned that Ta-den had returned and that they were to be united in marriage with the weird rites of their religion and in accordance with the custom of their people as soon as Ta-den came home from the battle that was to be fought at A-lur.

The recruits were now gathering at the city and it was decided that the next day Ja-don and Tarzan would return to the main body in the hidden camp and immediately under cover of night the attack should be made in force upon Lu-don's forces at A-lur. Word of this was sent to Ta-den where he awaited with his warriors upon the north side of Jad-ben-lul, only a few miles from A-lur.

In the carrying out of these plans it was necessary to leave Jane behind in Ja-don's palace at Ja-lur, but O-lo-a and her women were with her and there were many warriors to guard them, so Tarzan bid his mate good-bye with no feelings of apprehension as to her safety, and again seated upon the *gryf* made his way out of the city with Ja-don and his warriors.

At the mouth of the gorge the ape-man abandoned his huge mount since it had served its purpose and could be of no further value to him in their attack upon A-lur, which was to be made just before dawn the following day when, as he could not have been seen by the enemy, the effect of his entry to the city upon the *gryf* would have been totally lost. A couple of sharp blows with the spear sent the big animal rumbling and growling in the direction of the Kor-ul-*gryf* nor was the ape-man sorry to see it depart since he had never known at what instant its short temper and insatiable appetite for flesh might turn it upon some of his companions.

Immediately upon their arrival at the gorge the march on A-lur was commenced.

CHAPTER XXIII—TAKEN ALIVE

As night fell a warrior from the palace of Ja-lur slipped into the temple grounds. He made his way to where the lesser priests were quartered. His presence aroused no suspicion as it was not unusual for warriors to have business within the temple. He came at last to a chamber where several priests were congregated after the evening meal. The rites and ceremonies of the sacrifice had been concluded and there was nothing more of a religious nature to make call upon their time until the rites at sunrise.

Now the warrior knew, as in fact nearly all Pal-ul-don knew, that there was no strong bond between the temple and the palace at Ja-lur and that Ja-don only suffered the presence of the priests and permitted their cruel and abhorrent acts because of the fact that these things had been the custom of the Ho-don of Pal-ul-don for countless ages, and rash indeed must have been the man who would have attempted to interfere with the priests or their ceremonies. That Ja-don never entered the temple was well known, and that his high priest never entered the palace, but the people came to the temple with their votive offerings and the sacrifices were made night and morning as in every other temple in Pal-ul-don.

The warriors knew these things, knew them better perhaps than a simple warrior should have known them. And so it was here in the temple that he looked for the aid that he sought in the carrying out of whatever design he had.

As he entered the apartment where the priests were he greeted them after the manner which was customary in Pal-ul-don, but at the same time he made a sign with his finger that might have attracted little attention or scarcely been noticed at all by one who knew not its meaning. That there were those within the room who noticed it and interpreted it was quickly apparent, through the fact that two of the priests rose and came close to him as he stood just within the doorway and each of them, as he came, returned the signal that the warrior had made.

The three talked for but a moment and then the warrior turned and left the apartment. A little later one of the priests who had talked with him left also and shortly after that the other.

In the corridor they found the warrior waiting, and led him to a little chamber which opened upon a smaller corridor just beyond where it joined the larger. Here the three remained in whispered conversation for some little time and then the warrior returned to the palace and the two priests to their quarters.

The apartments of the women of the palace at Ja-lur are all upon the same side of a long, straight corridor. Each has a single door leading into the corridor and at the opposite end several windows overlooking a garden. It was in one of these rooms that Jane slept alone. At each end of the corridor was a sentinel, the main body of the guard being stationed in a room near the outer entrance to the women's quarters.

The palace slept for they kept early hours there where Ja-don ruled. The pal-e-don-so of the great chieftain of the north knew no such wild orgies as had resounded through the palace of the king at A-lur. Ja-lur was a quiet city by comparison with the capital, yet there was always a guard kept at every entrance to the chambers of Ja-don and his immediate family as well as at the gate leading into the temple and that which opened upon the city.

These guards, however, were small, consisting usually of not more than five or six warriors, one of whom remained awake while the others slept. Such were the conditions then when two warriors presented themselves, one at either end of the corridor, to the sentries who watched over the safety of Jane Clayton and the Princess O-lo-a, and each of the newcomers repeated to the sentinels the stereotyped words which announced that they were relieved and these others sent to watch in their stead. Never is a warrior loath to be relieved of sentry duty. Where, under different circumstances he might ask numerous questions he is now too well satisfied to escape the monotonies of that universally hated duty. And so these two men accepted their relief without question and hastened away to their pallets.

And then a third warrior entered the corridor and all of the newcomers came together before the door of the ape-man's slumbering mate. And one was the strange warrior who had met Ja-don and Tarzan outside the city of Ja-lur as they had approached it the previous day; and he was the same warrior who had entered the temple a short hour before, but the faces of his fellows were unfamiliar, even to one another, since it is seldom that a priest removes his hideous headdress in the presence even of his associates.

Silently they lifted the hangings that hid the interior of the room from the view of those who passed through the corridor, and stealthily slunk within. Upon a pile of furs in a far corner lay the sleeping form of Lady Greystoke. The bare feet of the intruders gave forth no sound as they crossed the stone floor toward her. A ray of moonlight entering through a window near her couch shone full upon her, revealing the beautiful contours of an arm and shoulder in cameo-distinctness against the dark furry pelt beneath which she slept, and the perfect profile that was turned toward the skulking three.

But neither the beauty nor the helplessness of the sleeper aroused such sentiments of passion or pity as might stir in the breasts of normal men. To the three priests she was but a lump of clay, nor could they conceive aught of that passion which had aroused men to intrigue and to murder for possession of this beautiful American girl, and which even now was influencing the destiny of undiscovered Pal-ul-don.

Upon the floor of the chamber were numerous pelts and as the leader of the trio came close to the sleeping woman he stooped and gathered up one of the smaller of these. Standing close to her head he held the rug outspread above her face. "Now," he whispered and simultaneously he threw the rug over the woman's head and his two fellows leaped upon her, seizing her arms and pinioning her body while their leader stifled her cries with the furry pelt. Quickly and silently they bound her wrists and gagged her and during the brief time that their work required there was no sound that might have been heard by occupants of the adjoining apartments.

Jerking her roughly to her feet they forced her toward a window but she refused to walk, throwing herself instead upon the floor. They were very angry and would have resorted to cruelties to compel her obedience but dared not, since the wrath of Lu-don might fall heavily upon whoever mutilated his fair prize.

And so they were forced to lift and carry her bodily. Nor was the task any sinecure since the captive kicked and struggled as best she might, making their labor as arduous as possible. But finally they succeeded in getting her through the window and into the garden beyond where one of the two priests from the Ja-lur temple directed their steps toward a small barred gateway in the south wall of the enclosure.

Immediately beyond this a flight of stone stairs led downward toward the river and at the foot of the stairs were moored several canoes. Pan-sat had indeed been fortunate in enlisting aid from those who knew the temple and the palace so well, or otherwise he might never have escaped from Ja-lur with his captive. Placing the woman in the bottom of a light canoe Pan-sat entered it and took up the paddle. His companions unfastened the moorings and shoved the little craft out into the current of the stream. Their traitorous work completed they turned and retraced their steps toward the temple, while Pan-sat, paddling strongly with the current, moved rapidly down the river that would carry him to the Jad-ben-lul and A-lur.

The moon had set and the eastern horizon still gave no hint of approaching day as a long file of warriors wound stealthily through the darkness into the city of A-lur. Their plans were all laid and there seemed no likelihood of their miscarriage. A messenger had been dispatched to Ta-den whose forces lay northwest of the city. Tarzan, with a small contingent, was to enter the temple through the secret passageway, the location of which he alone knew, while Ja-don, with the greater proportion of the warriors, was to attack the palace gates.

The ape-man, leading his little band, moved stealthily through the winding alleys of A-lur, arriving undetected at the building which hid the entrance to the secret passageway. This spot being best protected by the fact that its existence was unknown to others than the priests, was unguarded. To facilitate the passage of his little company through the narrow winding, uneven tunnel, Tarzan lighted a torch which had been brought for the purpose and preceding his warriors led the way toward the temple.

That he could accomplish much once he reached the inner chambers of the temple with his little band of picked warriors the ape-man was confident since an attack at this point would bring confusion and consternation to the easily overpowered priests, and permit Tarzan to attack the palace forces in the rear at the same time that Ja-don engaged them at the palace gates, while Ta-den and his forces swarmed the northern walls. Great value had been placed by Ja-don on the moral effect of the Dor-ul-Otho's mysterious appearance in the heart of the temple and he had urged Tarzan to take every advantage of the old chieftain's belief that many of Lu-don's warriors still wavered in their allegiance between the high priest and the Dor-ul-Otho, being held to the former more by the fear which he engendered in the breasts of all his followers than by any love or loyalty they might feel toward him.

There is a Pal-ul-donian proverb setting forth a truth similar to that contained in the old Scotch adage that "The best laid schemes o' mice and men gang aft a-gley." Freely translated it might read, "He who follows the right trail sometimes reaches the wrong destination," and such apparently was the fate that lay in the footsteps of the great chieftain of the north and his godlike ally.

Tarzan, more familiar with the windings of the corridors than his fellows and having the advantage of the full light of the torch, which at best was but a dim and flickering affair, was some distance ahead of the others, and in his keen anxiety to close with the enemy he gave too little thought to those who were to support him. Nor is this strange, since from childhood the ape-man had been accustomed to fight the battles of life single-handed so that it had become habitual for him to depend solely upon his own cunning and prowess.

And so it was that he came into the upper corridor from which opened the chambers of Lu-don and the lesser priests far in advance of his warriors, and as he turned into this corridor with its dim cressets flickering somberly, he saw another enter it from a corridor before him—a warrior half carrying, half dragging the figure of a woman. Instantly Tarzan recognized the gagged and fettered captive whom he had thought safe in the palace of Ja-don at Ja-lur.

The warrior with the woman had seen Tarzan at the same instant that the latter had discovered him. He heard the low beastlike growl that broke from the ape-man's lips as he sprang forward to wrest his mate from her captor and wreak upon him the vengeance that was in the Tarmangani's savage heart. Across the corridor from Pan-sat was the entrance to a smaller chamber. Into this he leaped carrying the woman with him.

Close behind came Tarzan of the Apes. He had cast aside his torch and drawn the long knife that had been his father's. With the impetuosity of a charging bull he rushed into the chamber in pursuit of Pan-sat to find himself, when the hangings dropped behind him, in utter darkness. Almost immediately there was a crash of stone on stone before him followed a moment later by a similar crash behind. No other evidence was necessary to announce to the ape-man that he was again a prisoner in Lu-don's temple.

He stood perfectly still where he had halted at the first sound of the descending stone door. Not again would he easily be precipitated to the *gryf* pit, or some similar danger, as had occurred when Lu-don had trapped him in the Temple of the Gryf. As he stood there his eyes slowly grew accustomed to the darkness and he became aware that a dim light was entering the chamber through some opening, though it was several minutes before he discovered its source. In the roof of the chamber he finally discerned a small aperture, possibly three feet in diameter and it was through this that what was really only a lesser darkness rather than a light was penetrating its Stygian blackness of the chamber in which he was imprisoned.

Since the doors had fallen he had heard no sound though his keen ears were constantly strained in an effort to discover a clue to the direction taken by the abductor of his mate. Presently he could discern the outlines of his prison cell. It was a small room, not over fifteen feet across. On hands and knees, with the utmost caution, he examined the entire area of the floor. In the exact center, directly beneath the opening in the roof, was a trap, but otherwise the floor was solid. With this knowledge it was only necessary to avoid this spot in so far as the floor was concerned. The walls next received his attention. There were only two openings. One the doorway through which he had entered, and upon the opposite side that through which the warrior had borne Jane Clayton. These were both closed by the slabs of stone which the fleeing warrior had released as he departed.

Lu-don, the high priest, licked his thin lips and rubbed his bony white hands together in gratification as Pan-sat bore Jane Clayton into his presence and laid her on the floor of the chamber before him.

"Good, Pan-sat!" he exclaimed. "You shall be well rewarded for this service. Now, if we but had the false Dor-ul-Otho in our power all Pal-ul-don would be at our feet."

"Master, I have him!" cried Pan-sat.

"What!" exclaimed Lu-don, "you have Tarzan-jad-guru? You have slain him perhaps. Tell me, my wonderful Pan-sat, tell me quickly. My breast is bursting with a desire to know."

"I have taken him alive, Lu-don, my master," replied Pan-sat. "He is in the little chamber that the ancients built to trap those who were too powerful to take alive in personal encounter."

"You have done well, Pan-sat, I——"

A frightened priest burst into the apartment. "Quick, master, quick," he cried, "the corridors are filled with the warriors of Ja-don."

"You are mad," cried the high priest. "My warriors hold the palace and the temple."

"I speak the truth, master," replied the priest, "there are warriors in the corridor approaching this very chamber, and they come from the direction of the secret passage which leads hither from the city."

"It may be even as he says," exclaimed Pan-sat. "It was from that direction that Tarzan-jad-guru was coming when I discovered and trapped him. He was leading his warriors to the very holy of holies."

Lu-don ran quickly to the doorway and looked out into the corridor. At a glance he saw that the fears of the frightened priest were well founded. A dozen warriors were moving along the corridor toward him but they seemed confused and far from sure of themselves. The high priest guessed that deprived of the leadership of Tarzan they were little better than lost in the unknown mazes of the subterranean precincts of the temple.

Stepping back into the apartment he seized a leathern thong that depended from the ceiling. He pulled upon it sharply and through the temple boomed the deep tones of a metal gong. Five times the clanging notes rang through the corridors, then he turned toward the two priests. "Bring the woman and follow me," he directed.

Crossing the chamber he passed through a small doorway, the others lifting Jane Clayton from the floor and following him. Through a narrow corridor and up a flight of steps they went, turning to right and left and doubling back through a maze of winding passageways which terminated in a spiral staircase that gave forth at the surface of the ground within the largest of the inner altar courts close beside the eastern altar.

From all directions now, in the corridors below and the grounds above, came the sound of hurrying footsteps. The five strokes of the great gong had summoned the faithful to the defense of Lu-don in his private chambers. The priests who knew the way led the less familiar warriors to the spot and presently those who had accompanied Tarzan found themselves not only leaderless but facing a vastly superior force. They were brave men but under the circumstances they were helpless and so they fell back the way they had come, and when they reached the narrow confines of the smaller passageway their safety was assured since only one foeman could attack them at a time. But their plans were frustrated and possibly also their entire cause lost, so heavily had Ja-don banked upon the success of their venture.

With the clanging of the temple gong Ja-don assumed that Tarzan and his party had struck their initial blow and so he launched his attack upon the palace gate. To the ears of Lu-don in the inner temple court came the savage war cries that announced the beginning of the battle. Leaving Pan-sat and the other priest to guard the woman he hastened toward the palace personally to direct his force and as he passed through the temple grounds he dispatched a messenger to learn the outcome of the fight in the corridors below, and other messengers to spread the news among his followers that the false Dor-ul-Otho was a prisoner in the temple.

As the din of battle rose above A-lur, Lieutenant Erich Obergatz turned upon his bed of soft hides and sat up. He rubbed his eyes and looked about him. It was still dark without.

"I am Jad-ben-Otho," he cried, "who dares disturb my slumber?"

A slave squatting upon the floor at the foot of his couch shuddered and touched her forehead to the floor. "It must be that the enemy have come, O Jad-ben-Otho." She spoke soothingly for she had reason to know the terrors of the mad frenzy into which trivial things sometimes threw the Great God.

A priest burst suddenly through the hangings of the doorway and falling upon his hands and knees rubbed his forehead against the stone flagging. "O Jad-ben-Otho," he cried, "the warriors of Ja-don have attacked the palace and the temple. Even now they are fighting in the corridors near the quarters of Lu-don, and the high priest begs that you come to the palace and encourage your faithful warriors by your presence."

Obergatz sprang to his feet. "I am Jad-ben-Otho," he screamed. "With lightning I will blast the blasphemers who dare attack the holy city of A-lur."

For a moment he rushed aimlessly and madly about the room, while the priest and the slave remained upon hands and knees with their foreheads against the floor.

"Come," cried Obergatz, planting a vicious kick in the side of the slave girl. "Come! Would you wait here all day while the forces of darkness overwhelm the City of Light?"

Thoroughly frightened as were all those who were forced to serve the Great God, the two arose and followed Obergatz towards the palace.

Above the shouting of the warriors rose constantly the cries of the temple priests: "Jad-ben-Otho is here and the false Dor-ul-Otho is a prisoner in the temple." The persistent cries reached even to the ears of the enemy as it was intended that they should.

CHAPTER XXIV—THE MESSENGER OF DEATH

The sun rose to see the forces of Ja-don still held at the palace gate. The old warrior had seized the tall structure that stood just beyond the palace and at the summit of this he kept a warrior stationed to look toward the northern wall of the palace where Ta-den was to make his attack; but as the minutes wore into hours no sign of the other force appeared, and now in the full light of the new sun upon the roof of one of the palace buildings appeared Lu-don, the high priest, Mo-sar, the pretender, and the strange, naked figure of a man, into whose long hair and beard were woven fresh ferns and flowers. Behind them were banked a score of lesser priests who chanted in unison: "This is Jad-ben-Otho. Lay down your arms and surrender." This they repeated again and again, alternating it with the cry: "The false Dor-ul-Otho is a prisoner."

In one of those lulls which are common in battles between forces armed with weapons that require great physical effort in their use, a voice suddenly arose from among the followers of Ja-don: "Show us the Dor-ul-Otho. We do not believe you!"

"Wait," cried Lu-don. "If I do not produce him before the sun has moved his own width, the gates of the palace shall be opened to you and my warriors will lay down their arms."

He turned to one of his priests and issued brief instructions.

The ape-man paced the confines of his narrow cell. Bitterly he reproached himself for the stupidity which had led him into this trap, and yet was it stupidity? What else might he have done other than rush to the succor of his mate? He wondered how they had stolen her from Ja-lur, and then suddenly there flashed to his mind the features of the warrior whom he had just seen with her. They were strangely familiar. He racked his brain to recall where he had seen the man before and then it came to him. He was the strange warrior who had joined Ja-don's forces outside of Ja-lur the day that Tarzan had ridden upon the great *gryf* from the uninhabited gorge next to the Kor-ul-Ja down to the capital city of the chieftain of the north. But who could the man be? Tarzan knew that never before that other day had he seen him.

Presently he heard the clanging of a gong from the corridor without and very faintly the rush of feet, and shouts. He guessed that his warriors had been discovered and a fight was in progress. He fretted and chafed at the chance that had denied him participation in it.

Again and again he tried the doors of his prison and the trap in the center of the floor, but none would give to his utmost endeavors. He strained his eyes toward the aperture above but he could see nothing, and then he continued his futile pacing to and fro like a caged lion behind its bars.

The minutes dragged slowly into hours. Faintly sounds came to him as of shouting men at a great distance. The battle was in progress. He wondered if Ja-don would be victorious and should he be, would his friends ever discover him in this hidden chamber in the bowels of the hill? He doubted it.

And now as he looked again toward the aperture in the roof there appeared to be something depending through its center. He came closer and strained his eyes to see. Yes, there was something there. It appeared to be a rope. Tarzan wondered if it had been there all the time. It must have, he reasoned, since he had heard no sound from above and it was so dark within the chamber that he might easily have overlooked it.

He raised his hand toward it. The end of it was just within his reach. He bore his weight upon it to see if it would hold him. Then he released it and backed away, still watching it, as you have seen an animal do after investigating some unfamiliar object, one of the little traits that differentiated Tarzan from other men, accentuating his similarity to the savage beasts of his native jungle. Again and again he touched and tested the braided leather rope, and always he listened for any warning sound from above.

He was very careful not to step upon the trap at any time and when finally he bore all his weight upon the rope and took his feet from the floor he spread them wide apart so that if he fell he would fall astride the trap. The rope held him. There was no sound from above, nor any from the trap below.

Slowly and cautiously he drew himself upward, hand over hand. Nearer and nearer the roof he came. In a moment his eyes would be above the level of the floor above. Already his extended arms projected into the upper chamber and then something closed suddenly upon both his forearms, pinioning them tightly and leaving him hanging in mid-air unable to advance or retreat.

Immediately a light appeared in the room above him and presently he saw the hideous mask of a priest peering down upon him. In the priest's hands were leathern thongs and these he tied about Tarzan's wrists and forearms until they were completely bound together from his elbows almost to his fingers. Behind this priest Tarzan presently saw others and soon several lay hold of him and pulled him up through the hole.

Almost instantly his eyes were above the level of the floor he understood how they had trapped him. Two nooses had lain encircling the aperture into the cell below. A priest had waited at the end of each of these ropes and at opposite sides of the chamber. When he had climbed to a sufficient height upon the rope that had dangled into his prison below and his arms were well within the encircling snares the two priests had pulled quickly upon their ropes and he had been made an easy captive without any opportunity of defending himself or inflicting injury upon his captors.

And now they bound his legs from his ankles to his knees and picking him up carried him from the chamber. No word did they speak to him as they bore him upward to the temple yard.

The din of battle had risen again as Ja-don had urged his forces to renewed efforts. Ta-den had not arrived and the forces of the old chieftain were revealing in their lessened efforts their increasing demoralization, and then it was that the priests carried Tarzan-jad-guru to the roof of the palace and exhibited him in the sight of the warriors of both factions.

"Here is the false Dor-ul-Otho," screamed Lu-don.

Obergatz, his shattered mentality having never grasped fully the meaning of much that was going on about him, cast a casual glance at the bound and helpless prisoner, and as his eyes fell upon the noble features of the ape-man, they went wide in astonishment and fright, and his pasty countenance turned a sickly blue. Once before had he seen Tarzan of the Apes, but many times had he dreamed that he had seen him and always was the giant ape-man avenging the wrongs that had been committed upon him and his by the ruthless hands of the three German officers who had led their native troops in the ravishing of Tarzan's peaceful home. Hauptmann Fritz Schneider had paid the penalty of his needless cruelties; Unter-lieutenant von Goss, too, had paid; and now Obergatz, the last of the three, stood face to face with the Nemesis that had trailed him through his dreams for long, weary months. That he was bound and helpless lessened not the German's terror—he seemed not to realize that the man could not harm him. He but stood cringing and jibbering and Lu-don saw and was filled with apprehension that others might see and seeing realize that this bewhiskered idiot was no god—that of the two Tarzan-jad-guru was the more godly figure. Already the high priest noted that some of the palace warriors standing near were whispering together and pointing. He stepped closer to Obergatz. "You are Jad-ben-Otho," he whispered, "denounce him!"

The German shook himself. His mind cleared of all but his great terror and the words of the high priest gave him the clue to safety.

"I am Jad-ben-Otho!" he screamed.

Tarzan looked him straight in the eye. "You are Lieutenant Obergatz of the German Army," he said in excellent German. "You are the last of the three I have sought so long and in your putrid heart you know that God has not brought us together at last for nothing."

The mind of Lieutenant Obergatz was functioning clearly and rapidly at last. He too saw the questioning looks upon the faces of some of those around them. He saw the opposing warriors of both cities standing by the gate inactive, every eye turned upon him, and the trussed figure of the ape-man. He realized that indecision now meant ruin, and ruin, death. He raised his voice in the sharp barking tones of a Prussian officer, so unlike his former maniacal screaming as to quickly arouse the attention of every ear and to cause an expression of puzzlement to cross the crafty face of Lu-don.

"I am Jad-ben-Otho," snapped Obergatz. "This creature is no son of mine. As a lesson to all blasphemers he shall die upon the altar at the hand of the god he has profaned. Take him from my sight, and when the sun stands at zenith let the faithful congregate in the temple court and witness the wrath of this divine hand," and he held aloft his right palm.

Those who had brought Tarzan took him away then as Obergatz had directed, and the German turned once more to the warriors by the gate. "Throw down your arms, warriors of Ja-don," he cried, "lest I call down my lightnings to blast you where you stand. Those who do as I bid shall be forgiven. Come! Throw down your arms."

The warriors of Ja-don moved uneasily, casting looks of appeal at their leader and of apprehension toward the figures upon the palace roof. Ja-don sprang forward among his men. "Let the cowards and knaves throw down their arms and enter the palace," he cried, "but never will Ja-don and the warriors of Ja-lur touch their foreheads to the feet of Lu-don and his false god. Make your decision now," he cried to his followers.

A few threw down their arms and with sheepish looks passed through the gateway into the palace, and with the example of these to bolster their courage others joined in the desertion from the old chieftain of the north, but staunch and true around him stood the majority of his warriors and when the last weakling had left their ranks Ja-don voiced the savage cry with which he led his followers to the attack, and once again the battle raged about the palace gate.

At times Ja-don's forces pushed the defenders far into the palace ground and then the wave of combat would recede and pass out into the city again. And still Ta-den and the reinforcements did not come. It was drawing close to noon. Lu-don had mustered every available man that was not actually needed for the defense of the gate within the temple, and these he sent, under the leadership of Pan-sat, out into the city through the secret passageway and there they fell upon Ja-don's forces from the rear while those at the gate hammered them in front.

Attacked on two sides by a vastly superior force the result was inevitable and finally the last remnant of Ja-don's little army capitulated and the old chief was taken a prisoner before Lu-don. "Take him to the temple court," cried the high priest. "He shall witness the death of his accomplice and perhaps Jad-ben-Otho shall pass a similar sentence upon him as well."

The inner temple court was packed with humanity. At either end of the western altar stood Tarzan and his mate, bound and helpless. The sounds of battle had ceased and presently the ape-man saw Ja-don being led into the inner court, his wrists bound tightly together before him. Tarzan turned his eyes toward Jane and nodded in the direction of Ja-don. "This looks like the end," he said quietly. "He was our last and only hope."

"We have at least found each other, John," she replied, "and our last days have been spent together. My only prayer now is that if they take you they do not leave me."

Tarzan made no reply for in his heart was the same bitter thought that her own contained— not the fear that they would kill him but the fear that they would not kill her. The ape-man strained at his bonds but they were too many and too strong. A priest near him saw and with a jeering laugh struck the defenseless ape-man in the face.

"The brute!" cried Jane Clayton.

Tarzan smiled. "I have been struck thus before, Jane," he said, "and always has the striker died."

"You still have hope?" she asked.

"I am still alive," he said as though that were sufficient answer. She was a woman and she did not have the courage of this man who knew no fear. In her heart of hearts she knew that he would die upon the altar at high noon for he had told her, after he had been brought to the inner court, of the sentence of death that Obergatz had pronounced upon him, and she knew too that Tarzan knew that he would die, but that he was too courageous to admit it even to himself.

As she looked upon him standing there so straight and wonderful and brave among his savage captors her heart cried out against the cruelty of the fate that had overtaken him. It seemed a gross and hideous wrong that that wonderful creature, now so quick with exuberant life and strength and purpose should be presently naught but a bleeding lump of clay—and all so uselessly and wantonly. Gladly would she have offered her life for his but she knew that it was a waste of words since their captors would work upon them whatever it was their will to do—for him, death; for her—she shuddered at the thought.

And now came Lu-don and the naked Obergatz, and the high priest led the German to his place behind the altar, himself standing upon the other's left. Lu-don whispered a word to Obergatz, at the same time nodding in the direction of Ja-don. The Hun cast a scowling look upon the old warrior.

"And after the false god," he cried, "the false prophet," and he pointed an accusing finger at Ja-don. Then his eyes wandered to the form of Jane Clayton.

"And the woman, too?" asked Lu-don.

"The case of the woman I will attend to later," replied Obergatz. "I will talk with her tonight after she has had a chance to meditate upon the consequences of arousing the wrath of Jad-ben-Otho."

He cast his eyes upward at the sun. "The time approaches," he said to Lu-don. "Prepare the sacrifice."

Lu-don nodded to the priests who were gathered about Tarzan. They seized the ape-man and lifted him bodily to the altar where they laid him upon his back with his head at the south end of the monolith, but a few feet from where Jane Clayton stood. Impulsively and before they could restrain her the woman rushed forward and bending quickly kissed her mate upon the forehead. "Good-bye, John," she whispered.

"Good-bye," he answered, smiling.

The priests seized her and dragged her away. Lu-don handed the sacrificial knife to Obergatz. "I am the Great God," cried the German, "thus falleth the divine wrath upon all my enemies!" He looked up at the sun and then raised the knife high above his head.

"Thus die the blasphemers of God!" he screamed, and at the same instant a sharp staccato note rang out above the silent, spell-bound multitude. There was a screaming whistle in the air and Jad-ben-Otho crumpled forward across the body of his intended victim. Again the same alarming noise and Lu-don fell, a third and Mo-sar crumpled to the ground. And now the warriors and the people, locating the direction of this new and unknown sound turned toward the western end of the court.

Upon the summit of the temple wall they saw two figures—a Ho-don warrior and beside him an almost naked creature of the race of Tarzan-jad-guru, across his shoulders and about his hips were strange broad belts studded with beautiful cylinders that glinted in the mid-day sun, and in his hands a shining thing of wood and metal from the end of which rose a thin wreath of blue-gray smoke.

And then the voice of the Ho-don warrior rang clear upon the ears of the silent throng. "Thus speaks the true Jad-ben-Otho," he cried, "through this his Messenger of Death. Cut the bonds of the prisoners. Cut the bonds of the Dor-ul-Otho and of Ja-don, King of Pal-ul-don, and of the woman who is the mate of the son of god."

Pan-sat, filled with the frenzy of fanaticism saw the power and the glory of the regime he had served crumpled and gone. To one and only one did he attribute the blame for the disaster that had but just overwhelmed him. It was the creature who lay upon the sacrificial altar who had brought Lu-don to his death and toppled the dreams of power that day by day had been growing in the brain of the under priest.

The sacrificial knife lay upon the altar where it had fallen from the dead fingers of Obergatz. Pan-sat crept closer and then with a sudden lunge he reached forth to seize the handle of the blade, and even as his clutching fingers were poised above it, the strange thing in the hands of the strange creature upon the temple wall cried out its crashing word of doom and Pan-sat the under priest, screaming, fell back upon the dead body of his master.

"Seize all the priests," cried Ta-den to the warriors, "and let none hesitate lest Jad-ben-Otho's messenger send forth still other bolts of lightning."

The warriors and the people had now witnessed such an exhibition of divine power as might have convinced an even less superstitious and more enlightened people, and since many of them had but lately wavered between the Jad-ben-Otho of Lu-don and the Dor-ul-Otho of Ja-don it was not difficult for them to swing quickly back to the latter, especially in view of the unanswerable argument in the hands of him whom Ta-den had described as the Messenger of the Great God.

And so the warriors sprang forward now with alacrity and surrounded the priests, and when they looked again at the western wall of the temple court they saw pouring over it a great force of warriors. And the thing that startled and appalled them was the fact that many of these were black and hairy Waz-don.

At their head came the stranger with the shiny weapon and on his right was Ta-den, the Ho-don, and on his left Om-at, the black gund of Kor-ul-Ja.

A warrior near the altar had seized the sacrificial knife and cut Tarzan's bonds and also those of Ja-don and Jane Clayton, and now the three stood together beside the altar and as the newcomers from the western end of the temple court pushed their way toward them the eyes of the woman went wide in mingled astonishment, incredulity, and hope. And the stranger, slinging his weapon across his back by a leather strap, rushed forward and took her in his arms.

"Jack!" she cried, sobbing on his shoulder. "Jack, my son!"

And Tarzan of the Apes came then and put his arms around them both, and the King of Pal-ul-don and the warriors and the people kneeled in the temple court and placed their foreheads to the ground before the altar where the three stood.

CHAPTER XXV—HOME

Within an hour of the fall of Lu-don and Mo-sar, the chiefs and principal warriors of Pal-ul-don gathered in the great throneroom of the palace at A-lur upon the steps of the lofty pyramid and placing Ja-don at the apex proclaimed him king. Upon one side of the old chieftain stood Tarzan of the Apes, and upon the other Korak, the Killer, worthy son of the mighty ape-man.

And when the brief ceremony was over and the warriors with upraised clubs had sworn fealty to their new ruler, Ja-don dispatched a trusted company to fetch O-lo-a and Pan-at-lee and the women of his own household from Ja-lur.

And then the warriors discussed the future of Pal-ul-don and the question arose as to the administration of the temples and the fate of the priests, who practically without exception had been disloyal to the government of the king, seeking always only their own power and comfort and aggrandizement. And then it was that Ja-don turned to Tarzan. "Let the Dor-ul-Otho transmit to his people the wishes of his father," he said.

"Your problem is a simple one," said the ape-man, "if you but wish to do that which shall be pleasing in the eyes of God. Your priests, to increase their power, have taught you that Jad-ben-Otho is a cruel god, that his eyes love to dwell upon blood and upon suffering. But the falsity of their teachings has been demonstrated to you today in the utter defeat of the priesthood.

"Take then the temples from the men and give them instead to the women that they may be administered in kindness and charity and love. Wash the blood from your eastern altar and drain forever the water from the western.

"Once I gave Lu-don the opportunity to do these things but he ignored my commands, and again is the corridor of sacrifice filled with its victims. Liberate these from every temple in Pal-ul-don. Bring offerings of such gifts as your people like and place them upon the altars of your god. And there he will bless them and the priestesses of Jad-ben-Otho can distribute them among those who need them most."

As he ceased speaking a murmur of evident approval ran through the throng. Long had they been weary of the avarice and cruelty of the priests and now that authority had come from a high source with a feasible plan for ridding themselves of the old religious order without necessitating any change in the faith of the people they welcomed it.

"And the priests," cried one. "We shall put them to death upon their own altars if it pleases the Dor-ul-Otho to give the word."

"No," cried Tarzan. "Let no more blood be spilled. Give them their freedom and the right to take up such occupations as they choose."

That night a great feast was spread in the pal-e-don-so and for the first time in the history of ancient Pal-ul-don black warriors sat in peace and friendship with white. And a pact was sealed between Ja-don and Om-at that would ever make his tribe and the Ho-don allies and friends.

It was here that Tarzan learned the cause of Ta-den's failure to attack at the stipulated time. A messenger had come from Ja-don carrying instructions to delay the attack until noon, nor had they discovered until almost too late that the messenger was a disguised priest of Lu-don. And they had put him to death and scaled the walls and come to the inner temple court with not a moment to spare.

The following day O-lo-a and Pan-at-lee and the women of Ja-don's family arrived at the palace at A-lur and in the great throneroom Ta-den and O-lo-a were wed, and Om-at and Pan-at-lee.

For a week Tarzan and Jane and Korak remained the guests of Ja-don, as did Om-at and his black warriors. And then the ape-man announced that he would depart from Pal-ul-don. Hazy in the minds of their hosts was the location of heaven and equally so the means by which the gods traveled between their celestial homes and the haunts of men and so no questionings arose when it was found that the Dor-ul-Otho with his mate and son would travel overland across the mountains and out of Pal-ul-don toward the north.

They went by way of the Kor-ul-Ja accompanied by the warriors of that tribe and a great contingent of Ho-don warriors under Ta-den. The king and many warriors and a multitude of people accompanied them beyond the limits of A-lur and after they had bid them good-bye and Tarzan had invoked the blessings of God upon them the three Europeans saw their simple, loyal friends prostrate in the dust behind them until the cavalcade had wound out of the city and disappeared among the trees of the nearby forest.

They rested for a day among the Kor-ul-Ja while Jane investigated the ancient caves of these strange people and then they moved on, avoiding the rugged shoulder of Pastar-ul-ved and winding down the opposite slope toward the great morass. They moved in comfort and in safety, surrounded by their escort of Ho-don and Waz-don.

In the minds of many there was doubtless a question as to how the three would cross the great morass but least of all was Tarzan worried by the problem. In the course of his life he had been confronted by many obstacles only to learn that he who will may always pass. In his mind lurked an easy solution of the passage but it was one which depended wholly upon chance.

It was the morning of the last day that, as they were breaking camp to take up the march, a deep bellow thundered from a nearby grove. The ape-man smiled. The chance had come. Fittingly then would the Dor-ul-Otho and his mate and their son depart from unmapped Pal-ul-don.

He still carried the spear that Jane had made, which he had prized so highly because it was her handiwork that he had caused a search to be made for it through the temple in A-lur after his release, and it had been found and brought to him. He had told her laughingly that it should have the place of honor above their hearth as the ancient flintlock of her Puritan grandsire had held a similar place of honor above the fireplace of Professor Porter, her father.

At the sound of the bellowing the Ho-don warriors, some of whom had accompanied Tarzan from Ja-don's camp to Ja-lur, looked questioningly at the ape-man while Om-at's Waz-don looked for trees, since the *gryf* was the one creature of Pal-ul-don which might not be safely encountered even by a great multitude of warriors. Its tough, armored hide was impregnable to their knife thrusts while their thrown clubs rattled from it as futilely as if hurled at the rocky shoulder of Pastar-ul-ved.

"Wait," said the ape-man, and with his spear in hand he advanced toward the *gryf*, voicing the weird cry of the Tor-o-don. The bellowing ceased and turned to low rumblings and presently the huge beast appeared. What followed was but a repetition of the ape-man's previous experience with these huge and ferocious creatures.

And so it was that Jane and Korak and Tarzan rode through the morass that hems Pal-ul-don, upon the back of a prehistoric triceratops while the lesser reptiles of the swamp fled hissing in terror. Upon the opposite shore they turned and called back their farewells to Ta-den and Om-at and the brave warriors they had learned to admire and respect. And then Tarzan urged their titanic mount onward toward the north, abandoning him only when he was assured that the Waz-don and the Ho-don had had time to reach a point of comparative safety among the craggy ravines of the foothills.

Turning the beast's head again toward Pal-ul-don the three dismounted and a sharp blow upon the thick hide sent the creature lumbering majestically back in the direction of its native haunts. For a time they stood looking back upon the land they had just quit—the land of Tor-o-don and *gryf*; of Ja and Jato; of Waz-don and Ho-don; a primitive land of terror and sudden death and peace and beauty; a land that they all had learned to love.

And then they turned once more toward the north and with light hearts and brave hearts took up their long journey toward the land that is best of all—home.

GLOSSARY

From conversations with Lord Greystoke and from his notes, there have been gleaned a number of interesting items relative to the language and customs of the inhabitants of Pal-ul-don that are not brought out in the story. For the benefit of those who may care to delve into the derivation of the proper names used in the text, and thus obtain some slight insight into the language of the race, there is appended an incomplete glossary taken from some of Lord Greystoke's notes.

A point of particular interest hinges upon the fact that the names of all male hairless pithecanthropi begin with a consonant, have an even number of syllables, and end with a consonant, while the names of the females of the same species begin with a vowel, have an odd number of syllables, and end with a vowel. On the contrary, the names of the male hairy black pithecanthropi while having an even number of syllables begin with a vowel and end with a consonant; while the females of this species have an odd number of syllables in their names which begin always with a consonant and end with a vowel.

A.	Light.
ab.	Boy.
Ab-on.	Acting *gund* of Kor-ul-Ja.
Ad.	Three.
Adad.	Six.
Adadad.	Nine.
Adaden.	Seven.
Aden.	Four.
Adenaden.	Eight.
Adenen.	Five.
A-lur.	City of light.
An.	Spear.
An-un.	Father of Pan-at-lee.
As.	The sun.
At.	Tail.
Bal.	Gold or golden.
Bar.	Battle.
Ben.	Great.
Bu.	Moon.
Bu-lot (moon face).	Son of chief Mo-sar.
Bu-lur (moon city).	The city of the Waz-ho-don.
Dak.	Fat.
Dak-at (fat tail).	Chief of a Ho-don village.
Dak-lot.	One of Ko-tan's palace warriors.
Dan.	Rock.
Den.	Tree.
Don.	Man.

Dor.	Son.
Dor-ul-Otho (son of god).	Tarzan.
E.	Where.
Ed.	Seventy.
El.	Grace or graceful.
En.	One.
Enen.	Two.
Es.	Rough.
Es-sat (rough skin).	Chief of Om-at's tribe of hairy blacks.
Et.	Eighty.
Fur.	Thirty.
Ged.	Forty.
Go.	Clear.
Gryf.	"Triceratops—A genus of huge herbivorous dinosaurs of the group Ceratopsia. The skull had two large horns above the eyes, a median horn on the nose, a horny beak, and a great bony hood or transverse crest over the neck. Their toes, five in front and three behind, were provided with hoofs, and thetail was large and strong." Webster's Dict. The *gryf* of Pal-ul-don similar except that it is omnivorous, has strong, powerfully armed jaws and talons instead of hoofs. Coloration: face yellow with blue bands encircling the eyes; hood red on top, yellow underneath; belly yellow; body a dirty slate blue; legs same. Bony protuberances yellow except along the spine—these are red. Tail conforms with body and belly. Horns, ivory.
Gund.	Chief.
Guru.	Terrible.
Het.	Fifty.
Ho.	White.
Ho-don.	The hairless white men of Pal-ul-don.
Id.	Silver.
Id-an.	One of Pan-at-lee's two brothers.
In.	Dark.
In-sad.	Kor-ul-Ja warrior accompanying Tarzan, Om-at, andTa-den in search of Pan-at-lee.
In-tan.	Kor-ul-lul left to guard Tarzan
Ja.	Lion.

Jad.	The
Jad-bal-lul.	The golden lake.
Jad-ben-lul.	The big lake.
Jad-ben-Otho.	The Great God.
Jad-guru-don.	The terrible man.
Jad-in-lul.	The dark lake.
Ja-don (thelion-man).	Chief of a Ho-don village and father of Ta-den.
Jad Pele ul Jad-ben-Otho	The valley of the Great God
Ja-lur (lion city).	Ja-don'scapital.
Jar.	Strange.
Jar-don.	Name given Korak by Om-at.
Jato.	Saber-tooth hybrid.
Ko.	Mighty.
Kor.	Gorge.
Kor-ul-gryf.	Gorge of the *gryf*.
Kor-ul-Ja.	Name of Es-sat's gorge and tribe.
Kor-ul-lul.	Name of another Waz-don gorge and tribe.
Ko-tan.	King of the Ho-don.
Lav.	Run or running.
Lee.	Doe.
Lo.	Star.
Lot.	Face.
Lu.	Fierce.
Lu-don(fierceman).	High priest of A-lur.
Lul.	Water.
Lur.	City.
Ma.	Child.
Mo.	Short.
Mo-sar (short nose).	Chief and pretender.
Mu.	Strong.
No.	Brook.
O.	Like or similar.
Od.	Ninety.
O-dan.	Kor-ul-Ja warrior accompanying Tarzan, Om-at, and Ta-den in search of Pan-at-lee.
Og.	Sixty.
O-lo-a (like-star-light).	Ko-tan's daughter.
Om.	Long.
Om-at(longtail).	Ablack.
On.	Ten.
Otho.	God.
Pal.	Place; land; country.

Pal-e-don-so (place where men eat).	Banquet hall.
Pal-ul-don (land of man).	Name of the country.
Pal-ul-Ja.	Place of lions.
Pan.	Soft.
Pan-at-lee.	Om-at's sweetheart.
Pan-sat (soft skin).	A priest.
Pastar.	Father.
Pastar-ul-ved.	Father of Mountains.
Pele.	Valley.
Ro.	Flower.
Sad.	Forest.
San.	One hundred.
Sar.	Nose.
Sat.	Skin.
So.	Eat.
Sod.	Eaten.
Sog.	Eating.
Son.	Ate.
Ta.	Tall.
Ta-den (tall tree).	A white.
Tan.	Warrior.
Tarzan-jad-guru.	Tarzan the Terrible.
To.	Purple.
Ton.	Twenty.
Tor.	Beast.
Tor-o-don.	Beastlike man.
Tu.	Bright.
Tu-lur (bright city).	Mo-sar's city.
Ul.	Of.
Un.	Eye.
Ut.	Corn.
Ved.	Mountain
Waz.	Black.
Waz-don.	The hairy black men of Pal-ul-don.
Waz-ho-don (black white men).	A mixed race.
Xot.	One thousand.
Yo.	Friend.
Za.	Girl.

TARZAN AND THE GOLDEN LION

CHAPTER I—THE GOLDEN LION

Sabor, the lioness, suckled her young—a single fuzzy ball, spotted like Sheeta, the leopard. She lay in the warm sunshine before the rocky cavern that was her lair, stretched out upon her side with half closed eyes, yet Sabor was alert. There had been three of these little, fuzzy balls at first—two daughters and a son—and Sabor and Numa, their sire, had been proud of them; proud and happy. But kills had not been plentiful, and Sabor, undernourished, had been unable to produce sufficient milk to nourish properly three lusty cubs, and then a cold rain had come, and the little ones had sickened. Only the strongest survived—the two daughters had died. Sabor had mourned, pacing to and fro beside the pitiful bits of bedraggled fur, whining moaning. Now and again she would nose them with her muzzle as though she would awaken them from the long sleep that knows no waking.

At last, however, she abandoned her efforts, and now her whole savage heart was filled with concern for the little male cub that remained to her. That was why Sabor was more alert than usual.

Numa, the lion, was away. Two nights before he had made a kill and dragged it to their lair and last night he had fared forth again, but he had not returned. Sabor was thinking, as she half dozed, of Wappi, the plump antelope, that her splendid mate might this very minute be dragging through the tangled jungle to her. Or perhaps it would be Pacco, the zebra, whose flesh was the best beloved of her kind—juicy, succulent Pacco. Sabor's mouth watered.

Ah, what was that? The shadow of a sound had come to those keen ears. She raised her head, cocking it first upon one side and then the other, as with up-pricked ears she sought to catch the faintest repetition of that which had disturbed her.

Her nose sniffed the air. There was but the suggestion of a breeze, but what there was moved toward her from the direction of the sound she had heard, and which she still heard in a slightly increasing volume that told her that whatever was making it was approaching her. As it drew closer the beast's nervousness increased and she rolled over on her belly, shutting off the milk supply from the cub, which vented its disapproval in miniature growls until a low, querulous whine from the lioness silenced him, then he stood at her side, looking first at her and then in the direction toward which she looked, cocking his little head first on one side and then on the other.

Evidently there was a disturbing quality in the sound that Sabor heard-[-]something that inspired a certain restlessness, if not actual apprehension—though she could not be sure as yet that it boded ill. It might be her great lord returning, but it did not sound like the movement of a lion, certainly not like a lion dragging a heavy kill. She glanced at her cub, breathing as she did so

439

a plaintive whine. There was always the fear that some danger menaced him—this last of her little family—but she, Sabor the lioness, was there to defend him.

Presently the breeze brought to her nostrils the scent-spoor of the thing that moved toward her through the jungle. Instantly the troubled mother-face was metamorphosed into a bare-fanged, glittering-eyed mask of savage rage, for the scent that had come up to her through the jungle was the hated man-scent. She rose to her feet, her head flattened, her sinuous tail twitching nervously. Through that strange medium by which animals communicate with one another she cautioned her cub to lie down and remain where he was until she returned, then she moved rapidly and[dele.] silently to meet the intruder.

The cub had heard what its mother heard and now he caught the smell of man—an unfamiliar smell that had never impinged upon his nostrils before, yet a smell that he knew at once for that of an enemy—a smell that brought a reaction as typical as that which marked the attitude of the grown lioness, bringing the hairs along his little spine erect and baring his tiny fangs. As the adult moved quickly and stealthily into the underbrush the small cub, ignoring her injunction, followed after her, his hind quarters wobbling from side to side, after the manner of the very young of his kind, the ridiculous gait comporting ill with the dignified bearing of his fore quarters; but the lioness, intent upon that which lay before her, did not know that he followed her.

There was dense jungle before the two for a hundred yards, but through it the lions had worn a tunnel-like path to their lair; and then there was a small clearing through which ran a well-worn jungle trail, out of the jungle at one end of the clearing and into the jungle again at the other. As Sabor reached the clearing she saw the object of her fear and hatred well within it. What if the man-thing were not hunting her or hers? What if he even dreamed not of their presence? These facts were as nothing to Sabor, the lioness, today.[dele.] Ordinarily she would have let him pass unmolested, so long as he did not come close enough to threaten the safety of her cub; or, cubless, she would have slunk away at the first intimation of his approach. But today the lioness was nervous and fearful—fearful because of the single cub that remained to her—her maternal instincts centered threefold, perhaps, upon this lone and triply loved survivor —and so she did not wait for the man to threaten the safety of her little one; but instead she moved to meet him and to stop him. From the soft mother she had become a terrifying creature of destruction, her brain obsessed by a single thought—to kill.

She did not hesitate an instant at the edge of the clearing, nor did she give the slightest warning. The first intimation that the black warrior had that there was a lion within twenty miles of him, was the terrifying apparition of this devil-faced cat charging across the clearing toward him with the speed of an arrow. The black was not searching for lions. Had he known that there was one near he would have given it a wide berth. He would have fled now had there been anywhere to flee. The nearest tree was farther from him than was the lioness. She could overhaul him before he would have covered a quarter of the distance. There was no hope and there was only one thing to do. The beast was almost upon him and behind her he saw a tiny cub. The man bore a heavy spear. He carried it far back with his right hand and hurled it at the very instant that Sabor rose to seize him. The spear passed through the savage heart and almost simultaneously the giant jaws closed upon the face and skull of the warrior. The momentum of the lioness carried the two heavily to the ground, dead except for a few spasmodic twitchings of their muscles.

The orphaned cub stopped twenty feet away and surveyed the first great catastrophe of his life with questioning eyes. He wanted to approach his dam but a natural fear of the man-scent held him away. Presently he commenced to whine in a tone that always brought his mother to him hurriedly; but this time she did not come—she did not even rise and look toward him. He was puzzled—he could not understand it. He continued to cry, feeling all the while more sad and more lonely. Gradually he crept closer to his mother. He saw that the strange creature she had killed did not move and after a while he felt less terror of it, so that at last he found the courage to come quite close to his mother and sniff at her. He still whined to her, but she did not answer. It dawned on him at last that there was something wrong—that his great, beautiful mother was not as she had been—a change had come over her; yet still he clung to her, crying much until at last he fell asleep, cuddled close to her dead body.

It was thus that Tarzan found him—Tarzan and Jane, his wife, and their son, Korak the Killer, returning from the mysterious land of Pal-ul-don from which the two men had rescued Jane Clayton. At the sound of their approach the cub opened his eyes and rising, flattened his ears and snarled at them, backing close against his dead mother. At sight of him the ape-man smiled.

"Plucky little devil," he commented, taking in the story of the tragedy at a single glance. He approached the spitting cub, expecting it to turn and run away; but it did nothing of the sort. Instead it snarled more ferociously and struck at his extended hand as he stooped and reached for it.

"What a brave little fellow," cried Jane. "Poor little orphan!"

"He's going to make a great lion, or he would have if his dam had lived," said Korak. "Look at that back—as straight and strong as a spear. Too bad the rascal has got to die."

"He doesn't have to die," returned Tarzan.

"There's not much chance for him—he'll need milk for a couple of months more, and who's going to get it for him?"

"I am," replied Tarzan.

"You're going to adopt him?"

Tarzan nodded.

Korak and Jane laughed. "That'll be fine," commented the former.

"Lord Greystoke, foster mother to the son of Numa," laughed Jane.

Tarzan smiled with them, but he did not cease his attentions toward the cub. Reaching out suddenly he caught the little lion by the scruff of its neck and then stroking it gently he talked to it in a low, crooning tone. I do not know what he said; but perhaps the cub did, for presently it ceased its struggles and no longer sought to scratch or bite the caressing hand. After that he picked it up and held it against his breast. It did not seem afraid now, nor did it even bare its fangs against this close proximity to the erstwhile hated man-scent.

"How do you do it?" [dele']exclaimed Jane Clayton.

Tarzan shrugged his broad shoulders. "Your kind are not afraid of you—these are really my kind, try to civilize me as you will, and perhaps that is why they are not afraid of me when I give them the signs of friendship. Even this little rascal seems to know it, doesn't he?"

"I can never understand it," commented Korak. "I think I am rather familiar with African animals, yet I haven't the power over them or the understanding that you have. Why is it?"

"There is but one Tarzan," said Lady Greystoke, smiling at her son teasingly, and yet her tone was not without a note of pride.

"Remember that I was born among beasts and raised by beasts," Tarzan reminded him. "Perhaps after all my father was an ape—you know Kala always insisted that he was."

"John! How can you?" exclaimed Jane. "You know perfectly well who your father and mother were."

Tarzan looked solemnly at his son and closed one eye. "Your mother never can learn to appreciate the fine qualities of the anthropoids. One might almost think that she objected to the suggestion that she had mated with one of them."

"John Clayton, I shall never speak to you again if you don't stop saying such hideous things. I am ashamed of you. It is bad enough that you are an unregenerate wild-man, without trying to suggest that you may be an ape into the bargain."

The long journey from Pal-ul-don was almost completed— inside the week they should be again at the site of their former home. Whether anything now remained of the ruins the Germans had left was problematical. The barns and outhouses had all been burned and the interior of the bungalow partially wrecked. Those of the Waziri, the faithful native retainers of the Greystokes, who had not been killed by Hauptman Fritz Schneider's soldiers, had rallied to the beat of the war-drum and gone to place themselves at the disposal of the English in whatever capacity they might be found useful to the great cause of humanity. This much Tarzan had known before he set out in search of Lady Jane; but how many of his war-like Waziri had survived the war and what further had befallen his vast estates he did not know. Wandering tribes of natives, or raiding bands of Arab slavers might have completed the demolition inaugurated by the Hun, and it was likely, too, that the jungle had swept up and reclaimed its own, covering his dearings and burying amidst its riot of lush verdure every sign of man's brief trespass upon its world-old preserves.

Following the adoption of the tiny Numa, Tarzan was compelled to an immediate consideration of the needs of his protege in planning his marches and his halts, for the cub must have sustenance and that sustenance could be naught but milk.

Lion's milk was out of the question, but fortunately they were now in a comparatively well peopled country where villages were not infrequent and where the great Lord of the Jungle was known, feared, and respected, and so it was that upon the afternoon of the day he had found the young lion Tarzan approached a village for the purpose of obtaining milk for the cub.

At first the natives appeared sullen and indifferent, looking with contempt upon whites who traveled without a large safari—with contempt and without fear. With no safari these strangers could carry no presents for them, nor anything wherewith to repay for the food they would doubtless desire, and with no askari they could not demand food, or rather they could not enforce an order, nor could they protect themselves should it seem worth while to molest them. Sullen and indifferent the natives seemed, yet they were scarce unconcerned, their curiosity being aroused by the unusual apparel and ornamentation of these whites. They saw them almost as naked as themselves and armed similarly except that one, the younger man, carried a rifle. All three wore the trappings of Pal-ul-don, primitive and barbaric, and entirely strange to the eyes of the simple blacks.

"Where is your chief?" asked Tarzan as he strode into the village amongst the women, the children, and the yapping dogs.

A few dozing warriors rose from the shadows of the huts where they had been lying and approached the newcomers.

"The chief sleeps," replied one. "Who are you to awaken him? What do you want?"

"I wish to speak to your chief. Go and fetch him!"

The warrior looked at him in wide-eyed amaze, and then broke into a loud laugh.

"The chief must be brought to him," he cried, addressing his fellows, and then, laughing loudly, he slapped his thigh and nudged those nearest him with his elbows.

"Tell him," continued the ape-man, "that Tarzan would speak with him."

Instantly the attitude of his auditors underwent a remarkable transformation—they fell back from him and they ceased laughing—their eyes very wide and round. He who had laughed loudest became suddenly solemn. "Bring mats," he cried, "for Tarzan and his people to sit upon, while I fetch Umanga the chief," and off he ran as fast as he could as though glad of the excuse to escape the presence of the mighty one he feared he had offended.

It made no difference now that they had no safari, no askari, nor any presents. The villagers were vying with one another to do them honor. Even before the chief came many had already brought presents of food and ornaments. Presently Umanga appeared. He was an old man who had been a chief even before Tarzan of the Apes was born. His manner was patriarchal and dignified and he greeted his guest as one great man might greet another, yet he was undeniably pleased that the Lord of the Jungle had honored his village with a visit.

When Tarzan explained his wishes and exhibited the lion cub Umanga assured him that there would be milk a-plenty so long as Tarzan honored them with his presence—warm milk, fresh from the chief's own goats. As they palavered the ape-man's keen eyes took in every detail of the village and its people, and presently they alighted upon a large bitch among the numerous curs that overran the huts and the street. Her udder was swollen with milk and the sight of it suggested a plan to Tarzan. He jerked a thumb in the direction of the animal. "I would buy her," he said to Umanga.

"She is yours, Bwana, without payment," replied the chief. "She whelped two days since and last night her pups were all stolen from her nest, doubtless by a great snake; but if you will accept them I will give you instead as many younger and fatter dogs as you wish, for I am sure that this one would prove poor eating."

"I do not wish to eat her," replied Tarzan. "I will take her along with me to furnish milk for the cub. Have her brought to me."

Some boys then caught the animal and tying a thong about its neck dragged it to the ape-man. Like the lion, the dog was at first afraid, for the scent of the Tarmangani was not as the scent of the blacks, and it snarled and snapped at its new master; but at length he won the animal's confidence so that it lay quietly beside him while he stroked its head. To get the lion close to it was, however, another matter, for here both were terrified by the enemy scent of the other— the lion snarling and spitting arid the dog bare-fanged and growling. It required patience—infinite patience—but at last the thing was an accomplished fact and the cur bitch suckled the son of Numa. Hunger had succeeded in overcoming the natural suspicion of the lion, while the firm yet kindly attitude of the ape-man had won the confidence of the canine, which had been accustomed through life to more of cuffs and kicks than kindness.

That night Tarzan had the dog tied ill[??] the hut he occupied, and twice before morning he made her lie while the cub fed. The next day they took leave of Umanga and his people and with the dog still upon a leash trotting beside them they set off once more toward home, the young lion cuddled in the hollow of one of Tarzan's arms or carried in a sack slung across his shoulder.

They named the lion Jad-bal-ja, which in the language of the pithecanthropi of Pal-ul-don, means the Golden Lion, because of his color. Every day he became more accustomed to them and to his foster mother, who finally came to accept him as flesh of her flesh. The bitch they called Za, meaning girl. The second day they removed her leash and she followed them willingly through the jungle, nor ever after did she seek to leave them, nor was happy unless she was near one of the three.

As the moment approached when the trail should break from the jungle onto the edge of the rolling plain where their home had been, the three were filled with suppressed excitement, though none uttered a syllable of the hope and fear that was in the heart of each. What would they find? What could they find other than the same tangled mass of vegetation that the ape-man had cleared away to build his home when first he had come there with his bride?

At last they stepped from the concealing verdure of the forest to look out across the plain where, in the distance, the outlines of the bungalow had once been clearly discernible nestled amidst the trees and shrubs that had been retained or imported to beautify the grounds.

"Look!" cried Lady Jane. "It is there—it is still there!"

"But what are those other things to the left, beyond it?" asked Korak.

"They are the huts of natives," replied Tarzan.

"The fields are being cultivated!" exclaimed the woman.

"And some of the outbuildings have been rebuilt," said Tarzan. "It can mean but one thing— the Waziri have come back from the war—my faithful Waziri. They have restored what the Hun destroyed and are watching over our home until we return."

CHAPTER II—THE TRAINING OF JAD-BAL-JA

And so Tarzan of the Apes, and Jane Clayton, and Korak came home after a long absence and with them came Jad-bal-ja, the golden lion, and Za, the bitch. Among the first to meet them and to welcome them home was old Muviro, father of Wasimbu, who had given his life in defense of the home and wife of the ape-man.

"Ah, Bwana," cried the faithful black, "my old eyes are made young again by the sight of you. It has been long that you have been gone, but though many doubted that you would return, old Muviro knew that the great world held nothing that might overcome his master. And so he knew, too, that his master would return to the home of his love and the land where his faithful Waziri awaited him; but that she, whom we have mourned as dead, should have returned is beyond belief, and great shall be the rejoicing in the huts of the Waziri tonight. And the earth shall tremble to the dancing feet of the warriors and the heavens ring with the glad cries of their women, since the three they love most on earth have come back to them."

And in truth, great indeed was the rejoicing in the huts of the Waziri. And not for one night alone, but for many nights did the dancing and the rejoicing continue until Tarzan was compelled to put a stop to the festivities that he and his family might gain a few hours of unbroken slumber.

The ape-man found that not only had his faithful Waziri, under the equally faithful guidance of his English foreman, Jervis, completely rehabilitated his stables, corrals, and outbuildings as well as the native huts, but had restored the interior of the bungalow, so that in all outward appearances the place was precisely as it had been before the raid of the Germans.

Jervis was at Nairobi on the business of the estate, and it was some days after their arrival that he returned to the ranch. His surprise and happiness were no less genuine than those of the Waziri. With the chief and warriors he sat for hours at the feet of the Big Bwana, listening to an account of the strange land of Pal-ul-don and the adventures that had befallen the three during Lady Greystoke's captivity there, and with the Waziri he marveled at the queer pets the ape-man had brought back with him. That Tarzan might have fancied a mongrel native cur was strange enough, but that he should have adopted a cub of his hereditary enemies, Numa and Sabor, seemed beyond all belief. And equally surprising to them all was the manner of Tarzan's education of the cub.

The golden lion and his foster mother occupied a corner of the ape-man's bedroom, and many was the hour each day that he spent in training and educating the little spotted, yellow ball—all playfulness and affection now, but one day to grow into a great, savage beast of prey.

As the days passed and the golden lion grew, Tarzan taught it many tricks—to fetch and carry, to lie motionless in hiding at his almost inaudible word of command, to move from point to point as he indicated, to hunt for hidden things by scent and to retrieve them, and when meat was added to its diet he fed it always in a way that brought grim smiles to the savage lips of the Waziri warriors, for Tarzan had built for him a dummy in the semblance of a man and the meat that the lion was to eat was fastened always at the throat of the dummy. Never did the manner of feeding vary. At a word from the ape-man the golden lion would crouch, belly to the ground, and then Tarzan would point at the dummy and whisper the single word "kill." However hungry he might be, the lion learned never to move toward his meat until that single word had been uttered by its master; and then with a rush and a savage growl it drove straight for the flesh. While it was little it had difficulty at first in clambering up the dummy to the savory morsel fastened at the figure's throat, but as it grew older and larger it gained the objective more easily, and finally a single leap would carry it to its goal and down would go the dummy upon its back with the young lion tearing at its throat.

There was one lesson that, of all the others, was most difficult to learn and it is doubtful that any other than Tarzan of the Apes, reared by beasts, among beasts, could have overcome the savage blood-lust of the carnivore and rendered his natural instinct subservient to the will of his master. It took weeks and months of patient endeavor to accomplish this single item of the lion's education, which consisted in teaching him that at the word "fetch" he must find any indicated object and return with it to his master, even the dummy with raw meat tied at its throat, and that he must not touch the meat nor harm the dummy nor any other article that he was fetching, but place it carefully at the ape-man's feet. Afterward he learned always to be sure of his reward, which usually consisted in a double portion of the meat that he loved best.

Lady Greystoke and Korak were often interested spectators of the education of the golden lion, though the former expressed mystification as to the purpose of such elaborate training of the young cub and some misgivings as to the wisdom of the ape-man's program.

"What in the world can you do with such a brute after he is grown?" she asked. "He bids fair to be a mighty Numa. Being accustomed to men he will be utterly fearless of them, and having fed always at the throat of a dummy he will look there at the throat of living men for his food hereafter."

"He will feed only upon what I tell him to feed," replied the ape-man.

"But you do not expect him to feed always upon men?" she interrogated, laughingly.

"He will never feed upon men."

"But how can you prevent it, having taught him from cubhood always to feed upon men?"

"I am afraid, Jane, that you under-estimate the intelligence of a lion, or else I very much over-estimate it. If your theory is correct the hardest part of my work is yet before me, but if I am right it is practically complete now. However, we will experiment a bit and see which is right. We shall take Jad-bal-ja out upon the plain with us this afternoon. Game is plentiful and we shall have no difficulty in ascertaining just how much control I have over young Numa after all."

"I'll wager a hundred pounds," said Korak, laughing, "that he does just what he jolly well pleases after he gets a taste of live blood."

"You're on, my son," said the ape-man. I think I am going to show you and your mother this afternoon what you or anyone else never dreamed could be accomplished."

"Lord Greystoke, the world's premier animal trainer!" cried Lady Greystoke, and Tarzan joined them in their laughter.

"It is not animal training," said the ape-man. "The plan upon which I work would be impossible to anyone but Tarzan of the Apes. Let us take a hypothetical case to illustrate what I mean. There comes to you some creature whom you hate, whom by instinct and heredity you consider a deadly enemy. You are afraid of him. You understand no word that he speaks. Finally, by means sometimes brutal he impresses upon your mind his wishes. You may do the thing he wants, but do you do it with a spirit of unselfish loyalty? You do not— you do it under compulsion, hating the creature that forces his will upon you. At any moment that you felt it was in your power to do so, you would disobey him. You would even go further—you would turn upon him and destroy him. On the other hand, there comes to you one with whom you are familiar; he is a friend, a protector. He understands and speaks the language that you understand and speak. He has fed you, he has gained your confidence by kindness and protection, he asks you to do something for him. Do you refuse? No, you obey willingly. It is thus that the golden lion will obey me."

"As long as it suits his purpose to do so," commented Korak.

"Let me go a step farther then," said the ape-man. "Suppose that this creature, whom you love and obey, has the power to punish, even to kill you, if it is necessary so to do to enforce his commands. How then about your obedience?"

"We'll see," said Korak, "how easily the golden lion will make one hundred pounds for me."

That afternoon they set out across the plain, Jad-bal-ja following Tarzan's horse's heels. They dismounted at a little clump of trees some distance from the bungalow and from there proceeded onward warily toward a swale in which antelopes were usually to be found, moving up which they came cautiously to the heavy brush that bordered the swale upon their side. There was Tarzan, Jane, and Korak, and close beside Tarzan the golden lion—four jungle hunters —and of the four Jad-bal-ja, the lion, was the least accomplished. Stealthily they crawled through the brush, scarce a leaf rustling to their passage, until at last they looked down into the swale upon a small herd of antelope grazing peacefully below. Closest to them was an old buck, and him Tarzan pointed out in some mysterious manner to Jad-bal-ja.

"Fetch him," he whispered, and the golden lion rumbled a scarce audible acknowledgment of the command.

Stealthily he worked his way through the brush. The antelopes fed on, unsuspecting. The distance separating the lion from his prey was over great for a successful charge, and so Jad-bal-ja waited, hiding in the brush, until the antelope should either graze closer to him or turn its back toward him. No sound came from the four watching the grazing herbivora, nor did the latter give any indication of a suspicion of the nearness of danger. The old buck moved slowly closer to Jad-bal-ja. Almost imperceptibly the lion was gathering for the charge. The only noticeable movement was the twitching of his tail's tip, and then, as lightning from the sky, as an arrow from a bow, he shot from immobility to tremendous speed in an instant. He was almost upon the buck before the latter realized the proximity of danger, and then it was too late, for scarcely had the antelope wheeled than the lion rose upon its hind legs and seized it, while the balance of the herd broke into precipitate flight.

"Now," said Korak, "we shall see."

"He will bring the antelope to me," said Tarzan confidently.

The golden lion hesitated a moment, growling over the carcass of his kill. Then he seized it by the back and with his head turned to one side dragged it along the ground beside him, as he made his way slowly back toward Tarzan. Through the brush he dragged the slain antelope until he had dropped it at the feet of his master, where he stood, looking up at the face of the ape-man with an expression that could not have been construed into aught but pride in his achievement and a plea for commendation.

Tarzan stroked his head and spoke to him in a low voice, praising him, and then, drawing his hunting knife, he cut the jugular of the antelope and let the blood from the carcass. Jane and Korak stood close, watching Jad-bal-ja— what would the lion do with the smell of fresh, hot blood in his nostrils? He sniffed at it and growled, and with bared fangs he eyed the three wickedly. The ape-man pushed him away with his open palm and the lion growled again angrily and snapped at him.

Quick is Numa, quick is Bara, the deer, but Tarzan of the Apes is lightning. So swiftly did he strike, and so heavily, that Jad-bal-ja was falling on his back almost in the very instant that he had growled at his master. Swiftly he came to his feet again and the two stood facing one another.

"Down!" commanded the ape-man. "Lie down, Jad-bal-ja!" His voice was low and firm. The lion hesitated but for an instant, and then lay down as Tarzan of the Apes had taught him to do at the word of command. Tarzan turned and lifted the carcass of the antelope to his shoulder.

"Come," he said to Jad-bal-ja. "Heel!" and without another glance at the carnivore he moved off toward the horses.

"I might have known it," said Korak, with a laugh, "and saved my hundred pounds."

"Of course you might have known it," said his mother.

CHAPTER III—A MEETING OF MYSTERY

A rather attractive-looking, though over-dressed, young woman was dining in a second-rate chop-house in London. She was noticeable, not so much for her fine figure and coarsely beautiful face as for the size and appearance of her companion, a large, well-proportioned man in the mid-twenties, with such a tremendous beard that it gave him the appearance of hiding in ambush. He stood fully three inches over six feet. His shoulders were broad, his chest deep, and his hips narrow. His physique, his carriage, everything about him, suggested indubitably the trained athlete.

The two were in close conversation, a conversation that occasionally gave every evidence of bordering upon heated argument.

"I tell you," said the man, "that I do not see what we need of the others. Why should they share with us—why divide into six portions that which you and I might have alone?"

"It takes money to carry the plan through," she replied, "and neither you nor I have any money. They have it and they will back us with it—me for my knowledge and you for your appearance and your strength. They searched for you, Esteban, for two years, and, now that they have found you, I should not care to be in your shoes if you betrayed them. They would just as soon slit your throat as not, Esteban, if they no more than thought they couldn't use you, now that you have all the details of their plan. But if you should try to take all the profit from them—"

She paused, shrugging her shoulders. "No, my dear, I love life too well to join you in any such conspiracy as that."

"But I tell you, Flora, we ought to get more out of it than they want to give. You furnish all the knowledge and I take all the risk—why shouldn't we have more than a sixth apiece?"

"Talk to them yourself, then, Esteban," said the girl, with a shrug, "but if you will take my advice you will be satisfied with what you are offered. Not only have I the information, without which they can do nothing, but I found you into the bargain, yet I do not ask it all—I shall be perfectly satisfied with one-sixth, and I can assure you that if you do not muddle the thing, one-sixth of what you bring out will be enough for any one of us for the rest of his natural life."

The man did not seem convinced, and the young woman had a feeling that he would bear watching. Really, she knew very little about him, and had seen him in person only a few times since her first discovery of him some two months before. upon the screen of a London cinema house in a spectacular feature in which he had played the role of a Roman soldier of the Pretorian Guard.

Here his heroic size and perfect physique had alone entitled him to consideration, for his part was a minor one, and doubtless of all the thousands who saw him upon the silver sheet Flora Hawkes was the only one who took more than a passing interest in him, and her interest was aroused, not by his histrionic ability, but rather because for some two years she and her confederates had been searching for such a type as Esteban Miranda so admirably represented. To find him in the flesh bade fair to prove difficult of accomplishment, but after a month of seemingly fruitless searching she finally discovered him among a score of extra men at the studio of one of London's lesser producing companies. She needed no other credentials than her good looks to form his acquaintance, and while that was ripening into intimacy she made no mention to him of the real purpose of her association with him.

That he was a Spaniard and apparently of good family was evident to her, and that he was unscrupulous was to be guessed by the celerity with which he agreed to take part in the shady transaction that had been conceived in the mind of Flora Hawkes, and the details of which had been perfected by her and her four confederates. So, therefore, knowing that he was unscrupulous, she was aware that every precaution must be taken to prevent him taking advantage of the knowledge of their plan that he must one day have in detail, the key to which she, up to the present moment, had kept entirely to herself, not even confiding it to any one of her four other confederates.

They sat for a moment in silence, toying with the empty glasses from which they had been drinking. Presently she looked up to find his gaze fixed upon her and an expression in his eyes that even a less sophisticated woman than Flora Hawkes might readily have interpreted.

"You can make me do anything you want, Flora," he said, "for when I am with you I forget the gold, and think only of that other reward which you continually deny me, but which one day I shall win."

"Love and business do not mix well," replied the girl. "Wait until you have succeeded in this work, Esteban, and then we may talk of love."

"You do not love me," he whispered, hoarsely. "I know—I have seen—that each of the others loves you. That is why I could hate them. And if I thought that you loved one of them, I could cut his heart out. Sometimes I have thought that you did—first one of them and then another. You are too familiar with them, Flora. I have seen John Peebles squeeze your hand when he thought no one was looking, and when you dance with Dick Throck he holds you too close and you dance cheek to cheek. I tell you I do not like it, Flora, and one of these days I shall forget all about the gold and think only of you, and then something will happen and there will not be so many to divide the ingots that I shall bring back from Africa. And Bluber and Kraski are almost as bad; perhaps Kraski is the worst of all, for he is a good-looking devil and I do not like the way in which you cast sheep's eyes at him."

The fire of growing anger was leaping to the girl's eyes. With an angry gesture she silenced him.

"What business is it of yours, Senor Miranda, who I choose for my friends, or how I treat them or how they treat me? I will have you understand that I have known these men for years, while I have known you for but a few weeks, and if any has a right to dictate my behavior, which, thank God, none has, it would be one of them rather than you."

His eyes blazed angrily.

"It is as I thought!" he cried. "You love one of them." He half rose from the table and leaned across it toward her, menacingly. "Just let me find out which one it is and I will cut him into pieces!"

He ran his fingers through his long, black hair until it stood up on end like the mane of an angry lion. His eyes were blazing with a light that sent a chill of dread through the girl's heart. He appeared a man temporarily bereft of reason—if he were not a maniac he most certainly looked one, and the girl was afraid and realized that she must placate him.

"Come, come, Esteban," she whispered softly, there is no need for working yourself into a towering rage over nothing. I have not said that I loved one of these, nor have I said that I do not love you, but I am not used to being wooed in such fashion. Perhaps your Spanish senoritas like it, but I am an English girl and if you love me treat me as an English lover would treat me.

"You have not said that you loved one of these others—no, but on the other hand you have not said that you do not love one of them—tell me, Flora, which one of them is it that you love?"

His eyes were still blazing, and his great frame trembling with suppressed passion.

"I do not love any of them, Esteban," she replied, "nor, as yet, do I love you. But I could, Esteban, that much I will tell you. I could love you, Esteban, as I could never love another, but I shall not permit myself to do so until after you have returned and we are free to live where and how we like. Then, maybe—but, even so, I do not promise."

"You had better promise," he said, sullenly, though evidently somewhat mollified. "You had better promise, Flora, for I care nothing for the gold if I may not have you also."

"Hush," she cautioned, "here they come now, and it is about time; they are fully a half-hour late."

The man turned his eyes in the direction of her gaze, and the two sat watching the approach of four men who had just entered the chop-house. Two of them were evidently Englishmen—big, meaty fellows of the middle class, who looked what they really were, former pugilists; the third, Adolph Bluber, was a short, fat German, with a round, red face and a bull neck; the other, the youngest of the four, was by far the best looking. His smooth face, clear complexion, and large dark eyes might of themselves have proven sufficient grounds for Miranda's jealousy, but supplementing these were a mop of wavy, brown hair, the figure of a Greek god and the grace of a Russian dancer, which, in truth, was what Carl Kraski was when he chose to be other than a rogue.

The girl greeted the four pleasantly, while the Spaniard vouchsafed them but a single, surly nod, as they found chairs and seated themselves at the table.

"Hale!" [cried] Peebles, pounding the table to attract the attention of a waiter, "let us 'ave hale."

The suggestion met with unanimous approval, and as they waited for their drink they spoke casually of unimportant things; the heat, the circumstance that had delayed them, the trivial occurrences since they had last met; throughout which Esteban sat in sullen silence, but after the waiter had returned and they drank to Flora, with which ceremony it had long been their custom to signalize each gathering, they got down to business.

"Now," cried Peebles, pounding the table with his meaty fist, "'ere we are, and that's that! We 'ave everything, Flora—the plans, the money, Senor Miranda—and are jolly well ready, old dear, for your part of it.

"How much money have you?" asked Flora. "It is going to take a lot of money, and there is no use starting unless you have plenty to carry on with."

Peebles turned to Bluber. "There," he said, pointing a pudgy finger at him, "is the bloomin' treasurer. 'E can tell you 'ow much we 'ave, the fat rascal of a Dutchman."

Bluber smiled an oily smile and rubbed his fat palms together. "Vell," he said, "how much you t'ink, Miss Flora, ve should have?"

"Not less than two thousand pounds to be on the safe side," she replied quickly.

"Oi! Oi!" exclaimed Bluber. "But dot is a lot of money— two t'ousand pounds. Oi! Oi!"

The girl made a gesture of disgust. "I told you in the first place that I wouldn't have anything to do with a bunch of cheap screws, and that until you had enough money to carry the thing out properly I would not give you the maps and directions, without which you cannot hope to reach the vaults, where there is stored enough gold to buy this whole, tight, little island if half that what I have heard them say about it is true. You can go along and spend your own money, but you've got to show me that you have at least two thousand pounds to spend before I give up the information that will make you the richest men in the world."

"The blighter's got the money," growled Throck. "Blime if I know what he's beefin' about."

"He can't help it," [growled] the Russian, "it's a racial characteristic; Bluber would try to jew down the marriage license clerk if he were going to get married."

"Oh, vell," sighed Bluber, "for vy should we spend more money than is necessary? If ve can do it for vone t'ousand pounds so much the better."

"Certainly," snapped the girl, "and if it don't take but one thousand, that is all that you will have to spend, but you've got to have the two thousand in case of emergencies, and from what I have seen of that country you are likely to run up against more emergencies than anything else."

"Oi! Oi!" cried Bluber.

"'E's got the money all right," said Peebles, "now let's get busy."

"He may have it, but I want to see it first," replied the girl.

"Vat you t'ink; I carry all dot money around in my pocket?" cried Bluber.

"Can't you take our word for it?" grumbled Throck.

"You're a nice bunch of crooks to ask me that," she replied, laughing in the face of the burly ruffians. "I'll take Carl's word for it, though; if he tells me that you have it, and that it is in such shape that it can, and will, be used to pay all the necessary expenses of our expedition, I will believe him."

Peebles and Throck scowled angrily, and Miranda's eyes closed to two narrow, nasty slits, as he directed his gaze upon the Russian. Bluber, on the contrary, was affected not at all; the more he was insulted, the better, apparently, he liked it. Toward one who treated him with consideration. or respect he would have become arrogant, while he fawned upon the hand that struck him. Kraski, alone, smiled a self-satisfied smile that set the blood of the Spaniard boiling.

"Bluber has the money, Flora," he said; "each of us has contributed his share. We'll make Bluber treasurer, because we know that he will squeeze the last farthing until it shrieks before he will let it escape him. It is our plan now to set out from London in pairs."

He drew a map from his pocket, and unfolding it, spread it out upon the table before them. With his finger he indicated a point marked X. "Here we will meet and here we will equip our expedition. Bluber and Miranda will go first; then Peebles and Throck. By the time that you and I arrive everything will be in shape for moving immediately into the interior, where we shall establish a permanent camp, off the beaten track and as near our objective as possible. Miranda will disport himself behind his whiskers until he is ready to set out upon the final stage of his long journey. I understand that he is well schooled in the part that he is to play and that he can depict the character to perfection. As he will have only ignorant natives and wild beasts to deceive it should not tax his histrionic ability too greatly." There was a veiled note of sarcasm in the soft, drawling tone that caused the black eyes of the Spaniard to gleam wickedly.

"Do I understand," asked Miranda, his soft tone belying his angry scowl, "that you and Miss Hawkes travel alone to X?"

"You do, unless your understanding is poor," replied the Russian.

The Spaniard half rose from the table and leaned across it menacingly toward Kraski. The girl, who was sitting next to him, seized his coat.

"None of that!" she said, dragging him back into his chair. "There has been too much of it among you already, and if there is any more I shall cut you all and seek more congenial companions for my expedition."

"Yes, cut it out; 'ere we are, and that's that!" exclaimed Peebles belligerently.

"John's right," rumbled Throck, in his deep bass, "and I'm here to back him up. Flora's right, and I'm here to back her up. And if there is any more of it, blime if I don't bash a couple of you pretty 'uns," and he looked first at Miranda and then at Kraski.

"Now," soothed Bluber, "let's all shake hands and be good friends."

"Right-o," cried Peebles, "that's the talk. Give 'im your 'and, Esteban. Come, Carl, bury the 'atchet. We can't start in on this thing with no hanimosities, and 'ere we are, and that's that."

The Russian, feeling secure in his position with Flora, and therefore in a magnanimous mood, extended his hand across the table toward the Spaniard. For a moment Esteban hesitated.

"Come, man, shake!" growled Throck, "or you can go back to your job as an extra man, blime, and we'll find someone else to do your work and divvy the swag with."

Suddenly the dark countenance of the Spaniard was lighted by a pleasant smile. He extended his hand quickly and clasped Kraski's. "Forgive me," he said, "I am hot-tempered, but I mean nothing. Miss Hawkes is right, we must all be friends, and here's my hand on it, Kraski, as far as I am concerned."

"Good," said Kraski, "and I am sorry if I offended you;" but he forgot that the other was an actor, and if he could have seen into the depths of that dark soul he would have shuddered.

"Und now, dot ve are all good friends," said Bluber, rubbing his hands together unctuously, vy not arrange for vhen ve shall commence starting to finish up everyt'ings? Miss Flora, she gives me the map und der directions und we start commencing immediately."

"Loan me a pencil, Carl," said the girl, and when the man had handed her one she searched out a spot upon the map some distance into the interior from X, where she drew a tiny circle. "This is O," she said. "When we all reach here you shall have the final directions and not before."

Bluber threw up his hands. "Oi! Miss Flora, vhat you t'ink, ve spend two t'ousand pounds to buy a pig in a poke? Oi! Oi! you vouldn't ask us to do dot? Ve must see everyt'ing, ve must know everyt'ing, before ve spend vun farthing."

"Yes, and 'ere we are, and that's that!" roared John Peebles, striking the table with his fist.

The girl rose leisurely from her seat. "Oh, very well," she said with a shrug. "If you feel that way about it we might as well call it all off."

"Oh, vait, vait, Miss Flora," cried Bluber, rising hurriedly. "Don't be ogcited. But can't you see vere ve are? Two t'ousand pounds is a lot of money, and ve are good business men. Ve shouldn't be spending it all vit'out getting not'ings for it."

"I am not asking you to spend it and get nothing for it," replied the girl, tartly; "but if anyone has got to trust anyone else in this outfit, it is you who are going to trust me. If I give you all the information I have, there is nothing in the world that could prevent you from going ahead and leaving me out in the cold, and I don't intend that that shall happen."

"But we are not gonoffs, Miss Flora," insisted the Jew. "Ve would not t'ink for vun minute of cheating you."

"You're not angels, either, Bluber, any of you," retorted the girl. "If you want to go ahead with this you've got to do it in my way, and I am going to be there at the finish to see that I get what is coming to me. You've taken my word for it, up to the present time, that I had the dope, and now you've got to take it the rest of the way or all bets are off. What good would it do me to go over into a bally jungle and suffer all the hardships that we are bound to suffer, dragging you along with me, if I were not going to be able to deliver the goods when I got there? And I am not such a softy as to think I could get away with it with a bunch of bandits like you if I tried to put anything of that kind over on you. And as long as I do play straight I feel perfectly safe, for I know that either Esteban or Carl will look after me, and I don't know but what the rest of you would, too. Is it a go or isn't it?"

"Vell, John, vot do you und Dick t'ink?" asked Bluber, addressing the two ex-prize-fighters. "Carl, I know he vill t'ink vhatever Flora t'inks. Hey? V'at?"

"Blime," said Throck, "I never was much of a hand at trusting nobody unless I had to, but it looks now as though we had to trust Flora."

"Same 'ere," said John Peebles. "If you try any funny work, Flora—" He made a significant movement with his finger across his throat.

"I understand, John," said the girl with a smile, "and I know that you would do it as quickly for two pounds as you would for two thousand. But you are all agreed, then, to carry on according to my plans? You too, Carl?"

The Russian nodded. "Whatever the rest say goes with me," he remarked.

And so the gentle little coterie discussed their plans in so far as they could—each minutest detail that would be necessary to place them all at the O which the girl had drawn upon the map.

CHAPTER IV—WHAT THE FOOTPRINTS TOLD

When Jad-bal-ja, the golden lion, was two years old, he was as magnificent a specimen of his kind as the Greystokes had ever looked upon. In size he was far above the average of that attained by mature males; in conformation he was superb, his noble head and his great black mane giving him the appearance of a full-grown male, while in intelligence he far outranked his savage brothers of the forest.

Jad-bal-ja was a never-ending source of pride and delight to the ape-man who had trained him so carefully, and nourished him cunningly for the purpose of developing to the full all the latent powers within him. The lion no longer slept at the foot of his master's bed, but occupied a strong cage that Tarzan had had constructed for him at the rear of the bungalow, for who knew better than the ape-man that a lion, wherever he may be or however he may have been raised, is yet a lion—a savage flesh-eater. For the first year he had roamed at will about the house and grounds; after that he went abroad only in the company of Tarzan. Often the two roamed the plain and the jungle hunting together. In a way the lion was almost equally as familiar with Jane and Korak, and neither of them feared or mistrusted him, but toward Tarzan of the Apes did he show the greatest affection. The blacks of Tarzan's household he tolerated, nor did he ever offer to molest any of the domestic animals or fowl, after Tarzan had impressed upon him in his early cubhood that appropriate punishment followed immediately upon any predatory excursion into the corrals or henhouses. The fact that he was never permitted to become ravenously hungry was doubtless the deciding factor in safeguarding the livestock of the farm.

The man and the beast seemed to understand one another perfectly. It is doubtful that the lion understood all that Tarzan said to him, but be that as it may the ease with which he communicated his wishes to the lion bordered upon the uncanny. The obedience that a combination of sternness and affection had elicited from the cub had become largely habit in the grown lion. At Tarzan's command he would go to great distances and bring back antelope or zebra, laying his kill at his master's feet without offering to taste the flesh himself, and he had even retrieved living animals without harming them. Such, then, was the golden lion that roamed the primeval forest with his godlike master.

It was at about this time that there commenced to drift in to the ape-man rumors of a predatory band to the west and south of his estate; ugly stories of ivory-raiding, slave-running and torture, such as had not disturbed the quiet of the ape-man's savage jungle since the days of Sheik Amor Ben Khatour, and there came other tales, too, that caused Tarzan of the Apes to pucker his brows in puzzlement and thought, and then a month elapsed during which Tarzan heard no more of the rumors from the west.

* * * * *

The war had reduced the resources of the Greystokes to but a meager income. They had given practically all to the cause of the Allies, and now what little had remained to them had been all but exhausted in the rehabilitation of Tarzan's African estate.

"It looks very much, Jane," he said to his wife one night, "as though another trip to Opar were on the books."

"I dread to think of it. I do not want you to go," she said. "You have come away from that awful city twice, but barely with your life. The third time you may not be so fortunate. We have enough, John, to permit us to live here in comfort and in happiness. Why jeopardize those two things which are greater than all wealth in another attempt to raid the treasure vaults?"

"There is no danger, Jane," he assured her. "The last time Werper dogged my footsteps, and between him and the earthquake I was nearly done for. But there is no chance of any such combination of circumstances thwarting me again.

"You will not go alone, John?" she asked. "You will take Korak with you?"

"No," he said, "I shall not take him. He must remain here with you, for really my long absences are more dangerous to you than to me. I shall take fifty of the Waziri, as porters, to carry the gold, and thus we should be able to bring out enough to last us for a long time.

"And Jad-bal-ja," she asked, "shall you take him?"

"No, he had better remain here; Korak can look after him and take him out for a hunt occasionally. I am going to travel light and fast and it would be too hard a trip for him— lions don't care to move around much in the hot sun, and as we shall travel mostly by day I doubt if Jad-bal-ja would last long."

And so it befell that Tarzan of the Apes set out once more upon the long trail that leads to Opar. Behind him marched fifty giant Waziri, the pick of the warlike tribe that had adopted Tarzan as its Chief. Upon the veranda of the bungalow stood Jane and Korak waving their adieux, while from the rear of the building there came to the ape-man's ears the rumbling roar of Jad-bal-ja, the golden lion. And as they marched away the voice of Numa accompanied them out upon the rolling plain, until at last it trailed off to nothingness in the distance.

His speed determined by that of the slowest of the blacks, Tarzan made but comparatively rapid progress. Opar lay a good twenty-five days' trek from the farm for men traveling light, as were these, but upon the return journey, laden as they would be with the ingots of gold, their progress would be slower. And because of this the ape-man had allotted two months for the venture. His safari, consisting of seasoned warriors only, permitted of really rapid progress. They carried no supplies, for they were all hunters and were moving through a country in which game was abundant—no need then for burdening themselves with the cumbersome impedimenta of white huntsmen.

A thorn boma and a few leaves furnished their shelter for the night, while spears and arrows and the powers of their great white chief ensured that their bellies would never go empty. With the picked men that he had brought with him, Tarzan expected to make the trip to Opar in twenty-one days, though had he been traveling alone he would have moved two or three times as fast, since, when Tarzan elected to travel with speed, he fairly flew through the jungle, equally at home in it by day or by night and practically tireless.

It was a mid-afternoon the third week of the march that Tarzan, ranging far ahead of his blacks in search of game, came suddenly upon the carcass of Bara, the deer, a feathered arrow protruding from its flank. It was evident that Bara had been wounded at some little distance from where it had lain down to die, for the location of the missile indicated that the wound could not have caused immediate death. But what particularly caught the attention of the ape-man, even before he had come close enough to make a minute examination, was the design of the arrow, and immediately he withdrew it from the body of the deer he knew it for what it was, and was filled with such wonderment as might come to you or to me were we to see a native Swazi headdress upon Broadway or the Strand, for the arrow was precisely such as one may purchase in most any sporting-goods house in any large city of the world—such an arrow as is sold and used for archery practice in the parks and suburbs. Nothing could have been more incongruous than this silly toy in the heart of savage Africa, and yet that it had done its work effectively was evident by the dead body of Bara, though the ape-man guessed that the shaft had been sped by no practiced savage hand.

Tarzan's curiosity was aroused and also his inherent jungle caution. One must know his jungle well to survive long the jungle, and if one would know it well he must let no unusual occurrence or circumstance go unexplained. And so it was that Tarzan set out upon the back track of Bara for the purpose of ascertaining, if possible, the nature of Bara's slayer. The bloody spoor was easily followed and the ape-man wondered why it was that the hunter had not tracked and overtaken his quarry, which had evidently been dead since the previous day. He found that Bara had traveled far, and the sun was already low in the west before Tarzan came upon the first indications of the slayer of the animal. These were in the nature of footprints that filled him with quite as much surprise as had the arrow. He examined them carefully, and, stooping low, even sniffed at them with his sensitive nostrils. Improbable, nay impossible though it seemed, the naked footprints were those of a white man—a large man, probably as large as Tarzan himself. As the foster-son of Kala stood gazing upon the spoor of the mysterious stranger he ran the fingers of one hand through his thick, black hair in a characteristic gesture indicative of deep puzzlement.

What naked white man could there be in Tarzan's jungle who slew Tarzan's game with the pretty arrow of an archery club? It was incredible that there should be such a one, and yet there recurred to the ape-man's mind the vague rumors that he had heard weeks before. Determined to solve the mystery he set out now upon the trail of the stranger—an erratic trail which wound about through the jungle, apparently aimlessly, prompted, Tarzan guessed, by the ignorance of an inexperienced hunter. But night fell before he had arrived at a solution of the riddle, and it was pitch dark as the ape-man turned his steps toward camp.

He knew that his Waziri would be expecting meat and it was not Tarzan's intention to disappoint them, though he then discovered that he was not the only carnivore hunting the district that night. The coughing grunt of a lion close by apprised him of it first, and then, from the distance, the deep roar of another. But of what moment was it to the ape-man that others hunted? It would not be the first time that he had pitted his cunning, his strength, and his agility against the other hunters of his savage world— both man and beast.

And so it was that Tarzan made his kill at last, snatching it almost from under the nose of a disappointed and infuriated lion—a fat antelope that the latter had marked as his own. Throwing his kill to his shoulder almost in the path of the charging Numa, the ape-man swung lightly to the lower terraces and with a taunting laugh for the infuriated cat, vanished noiselessly into the night.

He found the camp and his hungry Waziri without trouble, and so great was their faith in him that they not for a moment doubted but that he would return with meat for them.

Early the following morning Tarzan set out again toward Opar, and directing his Waziri to continue the march in the most direct way, he left them that he might pursue further his investigations of the mysterious presence in his jungle that the arrow and the footsteps had apprised him of.

Coming again to the spot at which darkness had forced him to abandon his investigations, he took up the spoor of the stranger. Nor had he followed it far before he came upon further evidence of the presence of this new and malign personality—stretched before him in the trail was the body of a giant ape, one of the tribe of great anthropoids among whom Tarzan had been raised. Protruding from the hairy abdomen of the Mangani was another of the machine-made arrows of civilization. The ape-man's eyes narrowed and a scowl darkened his brow. Who was this who dared invade his sacred preserves and slaughter thus ruthlessly Tarzan's people?

A low growl rumbled in the throat of the ape-man. Sloughed with the habiliments of civilization was the thin veneer of civilization that Tarzan wore among white men. No English lord was this who looked upon the corpse of his hairy cousin, but another jungle beast in whose breast raged the unquenchable fire of suspicion and hatred for the man-thing that is the heritage of the jungle-bred. A beast of prey viewed the bloody work of ruthless man. Nor was there in the consciousness of Tarzan any acknowledgment of his blood relationship to the killer.

Realizing that the trail had been made upon the second day before, Tarzan hastened on in pursuit of the slayer. There was no doubt in his mind but that plain murder had been committed, for he was sufficiently familiar with the traits of the Mangani to know that none of them would provoke assault unless driven to it.

Tarzan was traveling up wind, and some half-hour after he had discovered the body of the ape his keen nostrils caught the scent-spoor of others of its kind. Knowing the timidity of these fierce denizens of the jungle he moved forward now with great wariness, lest, warned of his approach, they take flight before they were aware of his identity. He did not see them often, yet he knew that there were always those among them who recalled him, and that through these he could always establish amicable relations with the balance of the tribe.

Owing to the denseness of the undergrowth Tarzan chose the middle terraces for his advance, and here, swinging freely and swiftly among the leafy boughs, he came presently upon the giant anthropoids. There were about twenty of them in the band, and they were engaged, in a little natural clearing, in their never-ending search for caterpillars and beetles, which formed important items in the diet of the Mangani.

A faint smile overspread the ape-man's face as he paused upon a great branch, himself hidden by the leafy foliage about him, and watched the little band below him. Every action, every movement of the great apes, recalled vividly to Tarzan's mind the long years of his childhood, when, protected by the fierce mother-love of Kala, the she-ape, he had ranged the jungle with the tribe of Kerchak. In the romping young, he saw again Neeta and his other childhood playmates and in the adults all the great, savage brutes he had feared in youth and conquered in manhood. The ways of man may change but the ways of the ape are the same, yesterday, today and forever.

He watched them in silence for some minutes. How glad they would be to see him when they discovered his identity! For Tarzan of the Apes was known the length and the breadth of the great jungle as the friend and protector of the Mangani. At first they would growl at him and threaten him, for they would not depend solely on either their eyes or their ears for confirmation of his identity. Not until he had entered the clearing, and bristling bulls with bared fighting fangs had circled him stiffly until they had come close enough for their nostrils to verify the evidence of their eyes and ears, would they finally accept him. Then doubtless there would be great excitement for a few minutes, until, following the instincts of the ape mind, their attention was weaned from him by a blowing leaf, a caterpillar, or a bird's egg, and then they would move about their business, taking no further notice of him more than of any other member of the tribe. But this would not come until after each individual had smelled of him, and perhaps, pawed his flesh with calloused hands.

Now it was that Tarzan made a friendly sound of greeting, and, as the apes looked up, stepped from his concealment into plain view of them. "I am Tarzan of the Apes," he said, "mighty fighter, friend of the Mangani. Tarzan comes in friendship to his people," and with these words he dropped lightly to the lush grass of the clearing.

Instantly pandemonium reigned. Screaming warnings, the shes raced with the young for the opposite side of the clearing, while the bulls, bristling and growling, faced the intruder.

"Come," cried Tarzan, "do you not know me? I am Tarzan of the Apes, friend of the Mangani, son of Kala, and king of the tribe of Kerchak."

"We know you," growled one of the old bulls; "yesterday we saw you when you killed Gobu. Go away or we shall kill you."

"I did not kill Gobu," replied the ape-man. "I found his dead body yesterday and I was following the spoor of his slayer, when I came upon you."

"We saw you," repeated the old bull; "go away or we shall kill you. You are no longer the friend of the Mangani."

The ape-man stood with brows contracted in thought. It was evident that these apes really believed that they had seen him kill their fellow. What was the explanation? How could it be accounted for? Did the naked footprints of the great white man whom he had been following mean more, then, than he had guessed? Tarzan wondered. He raised his eyes and again addressed the bulls.

"It was not I who killed Gobu," he insisted. "Many of you have known me all your lives. You know that only in fair fight, as one bull fights another, have I ever killed a Mangani. You know that, of all the jungle people, the Mangani are my best friends, and that Tarzan of the Apes is the best friend the Mangani have. How, then, could I slay one of my own people?"

"We only know," replied the old bull, "that we saw you kill Gobu. With our own eyes we saw you kill him. Go away quickly, therefore, or we shall kill you. Mighty fighter is Tarzan of the Apes, but mightier even than he are all the great bulls of Pagth. I am Pagth, king of the tribe of Pagth. Go away before we kill you."

Tarzan tried to reason with them but they would not listen, so confident were they that it was he who had slain their fellow, the bull Gobu. Finally, rather than chance a quarrel in which some of them must inevitably be killed, he turned sorrowfully away. But more than ever, now, was he determined to seek out the slayer of Gobu that he might demand an accounting of one who dared thus invade his lifelong domain.

Tarzan trailed the spoor until it mingled with the tracks of many men—barefooted blacks, mostly, but among them the footprints of booted white men, and once he saw the footprints of a woman or a child, which, he could not tell. The trail led apparently toward the rocky hills which protected the barren valley of Opar.

Forgetful now of his original mission and imbued only with a savage desire to wrest from the interlopers a full accounting for their presence in the jungle, and to mete out to the slayer of Gobu his just deserts, Tarzan forged ahead upon the now broad and well-marked trail of the considerable party which could not now be much more than a half-day's march ahead of him, which meant that they were doubtless now already upon the rim of the valley of Opar, if this was their ultimate destination. And what other they could have in view Tarzan could not imagine.

He had always kept closely to himself the location of Opar. In so far as he knew no white person other than Jane, and their son, Korak, knew of the location of the forgotten city of the ancient Atlantians. Yet what else could have drawn these white men, with so large a party, into the savage, unexplored wilderness which hemmed Opar upon all sides?

Such were the thoughts that occupied Tarzan's mind as he followed swiftly the trail that led toward Opar. Darkness fell, but so fresh was the spoor that the ape-man could follow it by scent even when he could not see the imprints upon the ground, and presently, in the distance, he saw the light of a camp ahead of him.

CHAPTER V—THE FATAL DROPS

At home, the life in the bungalow and at the farm followed its usual routine as it had before the departure of Tarzan. Korak, sometimes on foot and sometimes on horseback, followed the activities of the farm hands and the herders, sometimes alone, but more often in company with the white foreman, Jervis, and often, especially when they rode, Jane accompanied them.

The golden lion Korak exercised upon a leash, since he was not at all confident of his powers of control over the beast, and feared lest, in the absence of his master, Jad-bal-ja might take to the forest and revert to his natural savage state. Such a lion, abroad in the jungle, would be a distinct menace to human life, for Jad-bal-ja, reared among men, lacked that natural timidity of men that is so marked a trait of all wild beasts. Trained as he had been to make his kill at the throat of a human effigy, it required no considerable powers of imagination upon the part of Korak to visualize what might occur should the golden lion, loosed from all restraint, be thrown upon his own resources in the surrounding jungle.

It was during the first week of Tarzan's absence that a runner from Nairobi brought a cable message to Lady Greystoke, announcing the serious illness of her father in London. Mother and son discussed the situation. It would be five or six weeks before Tarzan could return, even if they sent a runner after him, and, were Jane to await him, there would be little likelihood of her reaching her father in time. Even should she depart at once, there seemed only a faint hope that she would arrive early enough to see him alive. It was decided, therefore, that she should set out immediately, Korak accompanying her as far as Nairobi, and then returning to the ranch and resuming its general supervision until his father's return.

It is a long trek from the Greystoke estate to Nairobi, and Korak had not yet returned when, about three weeks after Tarzan's departure, a black, whose duty it was to feed and care for Jad-bal-ja, carelessly left the door of the cage unfastened while he was cleaning it. The golden lion paced back and forth while the black wielded his broom within the cage. They were old friends, and the Waziri felt no fear of the great lion, with the result that his back was as often turned to him as not. The black was working in the far corner of the cage when Jad-bal-ja paused a moment at the door at the opposite end. The beast saw that the gate hung slightly ajar upon its hinges. Silently he raised a great padded paw and inserted it in the opening—a slight pull and the gate swung in.

Instantly the golden lion inserted his snout in the widened aperture, and as he swung the barrier aside the horrified black looked up to see his charge drop softly to the ground outside.

"Stop! Jad-bal-ja! Stop!" screamed the frightened black, leaping after him. But the golden lion only increased his pace, and leaping the fence, loped off in the direction of the forest.

The black pursued him with brandishing broom, emitting loud yells that brought the inmates of the Waziri huts into the open, where they joined their fellow in pursuit of the lion. Across the rolling plains they followed him, but as well have sought to snare the elusive will-o'-the-wisp as this swift and wary fugitive, who heeded neither their blandishments nor their threats. And so it was that they saw the golden lion disappear into the primeval forest and, though they searched diligently until almost dark, they were forced at length to give up their quest and return crestfallen to the farm.

Ah," cried the unhappy black, who had been responsible for the escape of Jad-bal-ja, "what will the Big Bwana say to me, what will he do to me when he finds that I have permitted the golden lion to get away!"

"You will be banished from the bungalow for a long time, Keewazi," old Muviro assured him. "And doubtless you will be sent to the grazing ground far to the east to guard the herd there, where. you will have plenty of lions for company, though they will not be as friendly as was Jad-bal-ja. It is not half what you deserve, and were the heart of the Big Bwana not filled with love for his black children—were he like other white Bwanas old Muviro has seen—you would be lashed until you could not stand, perhaps until you died."

"I am a man," replied Keewazi. "I am a warrior and a Waziri. Whatever punishment the Big Bwana inflicts I will accept as a man should."

It was that same night that Tarzan approached the camp-fires of the strange party he had been tracking. Unseen by them, he halted in the foliage of a tree directly in the center of their camp, which was surrounded by an enormous thorn boma, and brilliantly lighted by numerous fires which blacks were diligently feeding with branches from an enormous pile of firewood that they had evidently gathered earlier in the day for this purpose. Near the center of the camp were several tents, and before one, in the light of a fire, sat four white men. Two of them were great, bull-necked, red-faced fellows, apparently Englishmen of the lower class, the third appeared to be a short, fat, German Jew, while the fourth was a tall, slender, handsome fellow, with dark, wavy brown hair and regular features. He and the German were most meticulously garbed for Central African traveling, after the highly idealized standard of motion pictures, in fact either one of them might have stepped directly from a screening of the latest jungle thriller. The young man was evidently not of English descent and Tarzan mentally cataloged him, almost immediately, as a Slav. Shortly after Tarzan's arrival this one arose and entered one of the nearby tents, from which Tarzan immediately heard the sound of voices in low conversation. He could not distinguish the words, but the tones of one seemed quite distinctly feminine. The three remaining at the fire were carrying on a desultory conversation, when suddenly from near at hand beyond the boma wall, a lion's roar broke the silence of the jungle.

With a startled shriek the Jew leaped to his feet, so suddenly that he cleared the ground a good foot, and then, stepping backward, he lost his balance, tripped over his camp-stool, and sprawled upon his back.

"My Gord, Adolph!" roared one of his companions. "If you do that again, damn me if I don't break your neck. 'Ere we are, and that's that."

"Blime if 'e aint worse' n a bloomin' lion," growled the other.

The Jew crawled to his feet. "Mein Gott!" he cried, his voice quavering, "I t'ought sure he vas coming over the fence. S'elp me if I ever get out of diss, neffer again— not for all der gold in Africa vould I go t'rough vat I haf been t'rough dese past t'ree mont's. Oi! Oi! ven I t'ink of it, Oi! Oi! Lions, und leopards, und rhinoceroses und hippopotamuses, Oi! Oi!"

His companions laughed. "Dick and I tells you right along from the beginning that you 'adn't oughter come into the interior," said one of them.

"But for vy I buy all dese clo's?" wailed the German. "Mein Gott, dis suit, it stands me tventy guineas, vot I stand in. Ach, had I know somet'ing, vun guinea vould have bought me my whole wardrobe—tventy guineas for dis und no vun to see it but niggers und lions."

"And you look like 'ell in it, besides," commented one of his friends.

"Und look at it, it's all dirty and torn. How should I know it I spoil dis suit? Mit mine own eyes I see it at der Princess Teayter, how der hero spend t'ree mont's in Africa hunting lions und killing cannibals, und ven he comes ouid he hasn't even got a grease spot on his pants—how should I know it Africa was so dirty und full of thorns?"

It was at this point that Tarzan of the Apes elected to drop quietly into the circle of firelight before them. The two Englishmen leaped to their feet, quite evidently startled, and the Jew turned and took a half step as though in flight, but immediately his eyes rested upon the ape-man he halted, a look of relief supplanting that of terror which had overspread his countenance, as Tarzan had dropped upon them apparently from the heavens.

"Mein Gott, Esteban," shrilled the German, "vy you come back so soon, and for vy you come back like dot, sudden—don't you suppose ve got nerves?"

Tarzan was angry, angry at these raw intruders, who dared enter without his permission, the wide, domain in which he kept peace and order. When Tarzan was angry there flamed upon his forehead the scar that Bolgani, the gorilla, had placed there upon that long-gone day when the boy Tarzan had met the great beast in mortal combat, and first learned the true value of his father's hunting knife—the knife that had placed him, the comparatively weak little Tarmangani, upon an even footing with the great beasts of the jungle.

His gray eyes were narrowed, his voice came cold and level as he addressed them. "Who are you," he demanded, "who dare thus invade the country of the Waziri, the land of Tarzan, without permission from the Lord of the Jungle?"

"Where do you get that stuff, Esteban," demanded one of the Englishmen, "and wat in 'ell are you doin' back 'ere alone and so soon? Where are your porters, where is the bloomin' gold?"

The ape-man eyed the speaker in silence for a moment. "I am Tarzan of the Apes," he said. "I do not know what you are talking about. I only know that I come in search of him who slew Gobu, the great ape; him who slew Bara, the deer, without my permission."

"Oh, 'ell," exploded the other Englishman, "stow the guff, Esteban—if you're tryin' for to be funny we don't see the joke, 'ere we are, and that's that."

Inside the tent, which the fourth white man had entered while Tarzan was watching the camp from his hiding place in the tree above, a woman, evidently suddenly stirred by terror, touched the arm of her companion frantically, and pointed toward the tall, almost naked figure of the ape-man as he stood revealed in the full light of the beast fires. "God, Carl," she whispered, in trembling tones, "look!"

"What's wrong, Flora?" inquired her companion. "I see only Esteban."

"It is not Esteban," hissed the girl. "It is Lord Greystoke himself—it is Tarzan of the Apes!"

"You are mad, Flora," replied the man, "it cannot be he."

"It is he, though," she insisted. "Do you suppose that I do not know him? Did I not work in his town house for years? Did I not see him nearly every day? Do you suppose that I do not know Tarzan of the Apes? Look at that red scar flaming on his forehead—I have heard the story of that scar and I have seen it burn scarlet when he was aroused to anger. It is scarlet now, and Tarzan of the Apes is angry."

"Well, suppose it is Tarzan of the Apes, what can he do?"

"You do not know him," replied the girl. "You do not guess the tremendous power he wields here—the power of life and death over man and beast. If he knew our mission here, not one of us would ever reach the coast alive. The very fact that he is here now makes me believe that he may have discovered our purpose, and if he has, God help us—unless —unless—"

"Unless what?" demanded the man.

The girl was silent in thought for a moment. "There is only one way," she said finally. "We dare not kill him. His savage blacks would learn of it, and no power on earth could save us then. There is a way, though, if we act quickly." She turned and searched for a moment in one of her bags, and presently she handed the man a small bottle, containing liquid. "Go out and talk to him," she said, "make friends with him. Lie to him. Tell him anything. Promise anything. But get on friendly enough terms with him so that you can offer him coffee. He does not drink wine or anything with alcohol in it, but I know that he likes coffee. I have often served it to him in his room late at night upon his return from the theater or a ball. Get him to drink coffee and then you will know what to do with this." And she indicated the bottle which the man still held in his hand.

Kraski nodded. "I understand," he said, and, turning, left the tent.

He had taken but a step when the girl recalled him. "Do not let him see me. Do not let him guess that I am here or that you know me."

The man nodded and left her. Approaching the tense figures before the fire he greeted Tarzan with a pleasant smile and a cheery word.

"Welcome," he said, "we are always glad to see a stranger in our camp. Sit down. Hand the gentleman a stool, John," he said to Peebles.

The ape-man eyed Kraski as he had eyed the others. There was no answering friendly light in his eyes responding to the Russian's greeting.

"I have been trying to find out what your party is doing here," he said sharply to the Russian, "but they still insist that I am someone whom I am not. They are either fools or knaves, and I intend to find out which, and deal with them accordingly."

"Come, come," cried Kraski, soothingly. "There must be some mistake, I am sure. But tell me, who are you?"

"I am Tarzan of the Apes," replied the ape-man. "No hunters enter this part of Africa without my permission. That fact is so well known that there is no chance of your having passed the coast without having been so advised. I seek an explanation, and that quickly."

"Ah, you are Tarzan of the Apes," exclaimed Kraski. "Fortunate indeed are we, for now may we be set straight upon our way, and escape from our frightful dilemma is assured. We are lost, sir, inextricably lost, due to the ignorance or knavery of our guide, who deserted us several weeks ago. Surely we knew of you; who does not know of Tarzan of the Apes? But it was not our intention to cross the boundaries of your territory. We were searching farther south for specimens of the fauna of the district, which our good friend and employer, here, Mr. Adolph Bluber, is collecting at great expense for presentation to a museum in his home city in America. Now I am sure that you can tell us where we are and direct us upon our proper course."

Peebles, Throck, and Bluber stood fascinated by Kraski's glib lies, but it was the German Jew who first rose to the occasion. Too thick were the skulls of the English pugs to grasp quickly the clever ruse of the Russian.

"Vy yes," said the oily Bluber, rubbing his palms together, "dot iss it, yust vot I vas going to tell you."

Tarzan turned sharply upon him. "Then what was all this talk about Esteban?" he asked. "Was it not by that name that these others addressed me?"

"Ah," cried Bluber, "John will haf his leetle joke. He iss ignorant of Africa; he has neffer been here before. He t'ought perhaps dat you vere a native John he calls all der natives Esteban, und he has great jokes by himself mit dem, because he knows dey cannot onderstand vot he says. Hey John, iss it not so, vot it iss I say?" But the shrewd Bluber did not wait for John to reply. "You see," he went on, "ve are lost, und you take us ouid mit dis jungle, ve pay you anyt'ing—you name your own price."

The ape-man only half believed him, yet he was somewhat mollified by their evidently friendly intentions. Perhaps after all they were telling him a half-truth and had, really, wandered into his territory unwittingly. That, however, he would find out definitely from their native carriers, from whom his own Waziri would wean the truth. But the matter of his having been mistaken for Esteban still piqued his curiosity, also he was still desirous of learning the identity of the slayer of Gobu, the great ape.

"Please sit down," urged Kraski. "We were about to have coffee and we should be delighted to have you join us. We meant no wrong in coming here, and I can assure you that we will gladly and willingly make full amends to you, or to whomever else we may have unintentionally wronged."

To take coffee with these men would do no harm. Perhaps he had wronged them, but however that might be a cup of their coffee would place no great obligation upon him. Flora had been right in her assertion that if Tarzan of the Apes had any weakness whatsoever it was for an occasional cup of black coffee late at night. He did not accept the proffered camp stool, but squatted, ape-fashion, before them, the flickering light of the beast fires playing upon his bronzed hide and bringing into relief the gracefully contoured muscles of his godlike frame. Not as the muscles of the blacksmith or the professional strong man were the muscles of Tarzan of the Apes, but rather those of Mercury or Apollo, so symmetrically balanced were their proportions, suggesting only the great strength that lay in them. Trained to speed and agility were they as well as to strength, and thus, clothing as they did his giant frame, they imparted to him the appearance of a demi-god.

Throck, Peebles, and Bluber sat watching him in spellbound fascination, while Kraski walked over to the cook fire to arrange for the coffee. The two Englishmen were as yet only half awakened to the fact that they had mistaken this newcomer for another, and as it was, Peebles still scratched his head and grumbled to himself in inarticulate half-denial of Kraski's assumption of the new identity of Tarzan. Bluber was inwardly terror-stricken. His keener intelligence had quickly grasped the truth of Kraski's recognition of the man for what he was rather than for what Peebles and Throck thought him to be, and, as Bluber knew nothing of Flora's plan, he was in quite a state of funk as he tried to visualize the outcome of Tarzan's discovery of them at the very threshold of Opar. He did not realize, as did Flora, that their very lives were in danger—that it was Tarzan of the Apes, a beast of the jungle, with whom they had to deal, and not John Clayton, Lord Greystoke, an English peer. Rather was Bluber considering the two thousand pounds that they stood to lose through this deplorable termination of their expedition, for he was sufficiently familiar with the reputation of the ape-man to know that they would never be permitted to take with them the gold that Esteban was very likely, at this moment, pilfering from the vaults of Opar. Really Bluber was almost upon the verge of tears when Kraski returned with the coffee, which he brought himself.

From the dark shadows of the tent's interior Flora Hawkes looked nervously out upon the scene before her. She was terrified at the possibility of discovery by her former employer, for she had been a maid in the Greystokes' London town house as well as at the African bungalow and knew that Lord Greystoke would recognize her instantly should he chance to see her. She entertained for him, now, in his jungle haunts, a fear that was possibly greater than Tarzan's true character warranted, but none the less real was it to the girl whose guilty conscience conjured all sorts of possible punishments for her disloyalty to those who had always treated her with uniform kindliness and consideration.

Constant dreaming of the fabulous wealth of the treasure vaults of Opar, concerning which she had heard so much in detail from the conversations of the Greystokes, had aroused within her naturally crafty and unscrupulous mind a desire for possession, and in consequence thereof she had slowly visualized a scheme whereby she might loot the treasure vaults of a sufficient number of the golden ingots to make her independently wealthy for life. The entire plan had been hers. She had at first interested Kraski, who had in turn enlisted the cooperation of the two Englishmen and Bluber, and these four had raised the necessary money to defray the cost of the expedition. It had been Flora who had searched for a type of man who might successfully impersonate Tarzan in his own jungle, and she had found Esteban Miranda, a handsome, powerful, and unscrupulous Spaniard, whose histrionic ability aided by the art of make-up, of which he was a past master, permitted him to almost faultlessly impersonate the character they desired him to portray, in so far, as least, as outward appearances were concerned.

The Spaniard was not only powerful and active, but physically courageous as well, and since he had shaved his beard and donned the jungle habiliments of a Tarzan, he had lost no opportunity for emulating the ape-man in every way that lay within his ability. Of jungle craft he had none of course, and personal combats with the more savage jungle beasts caution prompted him to eschew, but he hunted the lesser game with spear and with arrow and practiced continually with the grass rope that was a part of his make-up.

And now Flora Hawkes saw all her well-laid plans upon the verge of destruction. She trembled as she watched the men before the fire, for her fear of Tarzan was very real, and then she became tense with nervous anticipation as she saw Kraski approaching the group with the coffee pot in one hand and cups in the other. Kraski set the pot and the cups upon the ground a little in the rear of Tarzan, and, as he filled the latter, she saw him pour a portion of the contents of the bottle she had given him into one of the cups. A cold sweat broke out upon her forehead as Kraski lifted this cup and offered it to the ape-man. Would he take it? Would he suspect? If he did suspect what horrible punishment would be meted to them all for their temerity? She saw Kraski hand another cup to Peebles, Throck, and Bluber, then return to the circle with the last one for himself. As the Russian raised it before his face and bowed politely to the ape-man, she saw the five men drink. The reaction which ensued left her weak and spent. Turning she collapsed upon her cot, and lay there trembling, her face buried in her arm. And, outside, Tarzan of the Apes drained his cup to the last drop.

CHAPTER VI—DEATH STEALS BEHIND

During the afternoon of the day that Tarzan discovered the camp of the conspirators, a watcher upon the crumbling outer wall of the ruined city of Opar descried a party of men moving downward into the valley from the summit of the encircling cliff. Tarzan, Jane Clayton, and their black Waziri were the only strangers that the denizens of Opar had ever seen within their valley during the lifetime of the oldest among them, and only in half-forgotten legends of a by-gone past was there any suggestion that strangers other than these had ever visited Opar. Yet from time immemorial a guard had always remained upon the summit of the outer wall. Now a single knurled and crippled man-like creature was all that recalled the numerous, lithe warriors of lost Atlantis. For down through the long ages the race had deteriorated and finally, through occasional mating with the great apes, the men had become the beast-like things of modern Opar. Strange and inexplicable had been the providence of nature that had confined this deterioration almost solely to the males, leaving the females straight, well-formed, often of comely and even beautiful features, a condition that might be largely attributable to the fact that female infants possessing ape-like characteristics were immediately destroyed, while, on the other hand, boy babies who possessed purely human attributes were also done away with.

Typical indeed of the male inhabitants of Opar was the lone watcher upon the outer city wall, a short, stocky man with matted hair and beard, his tangled locks growing low upon a low, receding forehead; small, close-set eyes and fang-like teeth bore evidence of his simian ancestry, as did his short, crooked legs and long, muscular ape-like arms, all scantily hair-covered as was his torso.

As his wicked, blood-rimmed eyes watched the progress of the party across the valley toward Opar, evidences of his growing excitement were manifested in the increased rapidity of his breathing, and low, almost inaudible growls that issued from his throat. The strangers were too far distant to be recognizable only as human beings, and their number to be roughly approximated as between two and three score. Having assured himself of these two facts the watcher descended from the outer wall, crossed the space between it and the inner wall, through which he passed, and at a rapid trot crossed the broad avenue beyond and disappeared within the crumbling but still magnificent temple beyond.

Cadj, the High Priest of Opar, squatted beneath the shade of the giant trees which now overgrew what had once been one of the gardens of the ancient temple. With him were a dozen members of the lesser priesthood, the intimate cronies of the High Priest, who were star tied by the sudden advent of one of the inferior members of the clan of Opar. The fellow hurried breathlessly to Cadj.

"Cadj," he cried, "strange men descend upon Opar! From the northwest they have come into the valley from beyond the barrier cliffs—fifty of them at least, perhaps half again that number. I saw them as I watched from the summit of the outer wall, but further than they are men I cannot say, for they are still a great distance away. Not since the great Tarmangani came among us last have there been strangers within Opar."

"It has been many moons since the great Tarmangani who called himself Tarzan of the Apes was among us," said Cadj. "He promised us to return before the rain to see that no harm had befallen La, but he did not come back and La has always insisted that he is dead. Have you told any other of what you have seen?" he demanded, turning suddenly upon the messenger.

"No," replied the latter.

"Good!" exclaimed Cadj. "Come, we will all go to the outer wall and see who it is who dares enter forbidden Opar, and let no one breathe a word of what Blagh has told us until I give permission."

"The word of Cadj is law until La speaks," murmured one of the priests.

Cadj turned a scowling face upon the speaker. "I am High Priest of Opar," he growled. "Who dares disobey me?"

"But La is High Priestess," said one, "and the High Priestess is the queen of Opar."

"But the High Priest can offer whom he will as sacrifice in the Chamber of the Dead or to the Flaming God," Cadj reminded the other meaningly.

"We shall keep silence, Cadj," replied the priest, cringing.

"Good!" growled the High Priest and led the way from the garden through the corridors of the temple back toward the outer wall of Opar. From here they watched the approaching party that was in plain view of them, far out across the valley. The watchers conversed in low gutturals in the language of the great apes, interspersed with which were occasional words and phrases of a strange tongue that were doubtless corrupted forms of the ancient language of Atlantis handed down through countless generations from their human progenitors—that now extinct race whose cities and civilization lie buried deep beneath the tossing waves of the Atlantic, and whose adventurous spirit had, in remote ages, caused them to penetrate into the heart of Africa in search of gold and to build there, in duplication of their far home cities, the magnificent city of Opar.

As Cadj and his followers watched from beneath shaggy brows the strangers plodding laboriously beneath the now declining equatorial sun across the rocky, barren valley, a gray little monkey eyed them from amidst the foliage of one of the giant trees that had forced its way through the pavement of the ancient avenue behind them. A solemn, sad-faced little monkey it was, but like all his kind overcome by curiosity, and finally to such an extent that his fear of the fierce males of Opar was so considerably overcome that he at last swung lightly from the tree to the pavement, made his way through the inner wall and up the inside of the outer wall to a position in their rear where he could hide behind one of the massive granite blocks of the crumbling wall in comparative safety from detection, the while he might overhear the conversation of the Oparians, all of which that was carried on in the language of the great apes he could understand perfectly.

The afternoon was drawing to a close before the slowly moving company approaching Opar was close enough for individuals to be recognizable in any way, and then presently one of the younger priests exclaimed excitedly. "It is he, Cadj. It is the great Tarmangani who calls himself Tarzan of the Apes. I can see him plainly; the others are all black men. He is urging them on prodding them with his spear. They act as though they were afraid and very tired, but he is forcing them forward."

"You are sure," demanded Cadj, "you are sure that it is Tarzan of the Apes?"

"I am positive," replied the speaker, and then another of the priests joined his assurances to that of his fellow. At last they were close enough so that Cadj himself, whose eyesight was not as good as that of the younger members of the company, realized that it was indeed Tarzan of the Apes who was returning to Opar. The High Priest scowled angrily in thought. Suddenly he turned upon the others.

"He must not come," he cried; "he must not enter Opar. Hasten and fetch a hundred fighting men. We will meet them as they come through the outer wall and slay them one by one."

But La," cried he who had aroused Cadj's anger in the garden, "I distinctly recall that La offered the friendship of Opar to Tarzan of the Apes upon that time, many moons ago, that he saved her from the tusks of infuriated Tantor."

"Silence," growled Cadj, "he shall not enter; we shall slay them all, though we need not know their identity until it is too late. Do you understand? And know, too, that whosoever attempts to thwart my purpose shall die—and he die not as a sacrifice, he shall die at my hands, but die he shall. You hear me?" And he pointed an unclean finger at the trembling priest.

Manu, the monkey, hearing this, was almost bursting with excitement. He knew Tarzan of the Apes—as all the migratory monkeys the length and breadth of Africa knew him —he knew him for friend and protector. To Manu the males of Opar were neither beast, nor man, nor friend. He knew them as cruel and surly creatures who ate the flesh of his kind, and he hated them accordingly. He was therefore greatly exercised at the plot that he had heard discussed which was aimed at the life of the great Tarmangani. He scratched his little gray head, and the root of his tail, and his belly, as he attempted to mentally digest what he had heard, and bring forth from the dim recesses of his little brain a plan to foil the priests and save Tarzan of the Apes. He made grotesque grimaces that were aimed at the unsuspecting Cadj and his followers, but which failed to perturb them, possibly because a huge granite block hid the little monkey from them. This was quite the most momentous thing that had occurred in the life of Manu. He wanted to jump up and down and dance and screech and jabber—to scold and threaten the hated Oparians, but something told him that nothing would be gained by this, other than, perhaps, to launch in his direction a shower of granite missiles, which the priests knew only too well how to throw with accuracy. Now Manu is not a deep thinker, but upon this occasion he quite outdid himself, and managed to concentrate his mind upon the thing at hand rather than permit its being distracted by each falling leaf or buzzing insect. He even permitted a succulent caterpillar to crawl within his reach and out again with impunity.

Just before darkness fell, Cadj saw a little gray monkey disappear over the summit of the outer wall fifty paces from where he crouched with his fellows, waiting for the coming of the fighting men. But so numerous were the monkeys about the ruins of Opar that the occurrence left Cadj's mind almost as quickly as the monkey disappeared from his view, and in the gathering gloom he did not see the little gray figure scampering off across the valley toward the band of intruders who now appeared to have stopped to rest at the foot of a large kopje that stood alone out in the valley, about a mile from the city.

Little Manu was very much afraid out there alone in the growing dusk, and he scampered very fast with his tail bowed up and out behind him. All the time he cast affrighted glances to the right and left. The moment he reached the kopje he scampered up its face as fast as he could. It was really a huge, precipitous granite rock with almost perpendicular sides, but sufficiently weather-worn to make its ascent easy to little Manu. He paused a moment at the summit to get his breath and still the beatings of his frightened little heart, and then he made his way around to a point where he could look down upon the party beneath.

There, indeed, was the great Tarmangani Tarzan, and with him were some fifty Gomangani. The latter were splicing together a number of long, straight poles, which they had laid upon the ground in two parallel lines. Across these two, at intervals of a foot or more, they were lashing smaller straight branches about eighteen inches in length, the whole forming a crude but substantial ladder. The purpose of all this Manu, of course, did not understand, nor did he know that it had been evolved from the fertile brain of Flora Hawkes as a means of scaling the precipitous kopje, at the summit of which lay the outer entrance to the treasure vaults of Opar. Nor did Manu know that the party had no intention of entering the city of Opar and were therefore in no danger of becoming victims of Cadj's hidden assassins. To him, the danger to Tarzan of the Apes was very real, and so, having regained his breath, he lost no time in delivering his warning to the friend of his people.

"Tarzan," he cried, in the language that was common to both.

The white man and the blacks looked up at the sound of his chattering voice.

"It is Manu, Tarzan," continued the little monkey, "who has come to tell you not to go to Opar. Cadj and his people await within the outer wall to slay you."

The blacks, having discovered that the author of the disturbance was nothing but a little gray monkey, returned immediately to their work, while the white man similarly ignored his words of warning. Manu was not surprised at the lack of interest displayed by the blacks, for he knew that they did not understand his language, but he could not comprehend why Tarzan failed to pay any attention whatsoever to him. Again and again he called Tarzan by name. Again and again he shrieked his warning to the ape-man, but without eliciting any reply or any information that the great Tarmangani had either heard or understood him. Manu was mystified. What had occurred to render Tarzan of the Apes so indifferent to the warnings of his old friend?

At last the little monkey gave it up and looked longingly back in the direction of the trees within the walled city of Opar. It was now very dark and he trembled at the thought of recrossing the valley, where he knew enemies might prowl by night. He scratched his head and he hugged his knees, then sat there whimpering, a very forlorn and unhappy little ball of a monkey. But however uncomfortable he was upon the high kopje, he was comparatively safe, and so he decided to remain there during the night rather than venture the terrifying return trip through the darkness. Thus it was that he saw the ladder completed and erected against the side of the kopje; and when the moon rose at last and lighted the scene, he saw Tarzan of the Apes urging his men to mount the ladder. He had never seen Tarzan thus rough and cruel with the blacks who accompanied him. Manu knew how ferocious the great Tarmangani could be with an enemy, whether man or beast, but he had never seen him accord such treatment to the blacks who were his friends.

One by one and with evident reluctance the blacks ascended the ladder, continually urged forward to greater speed by the sharp spear of the white man; when they had all ascended Tarzan followed, and Manu saw them disappear apparently into the heart of the great rock.

It was only a short time later that they commenced to reappear, and now each was burdened by two heavy objects which appeared to Manu to be very similar to some of the smaller stone blocks that had been used in the construction of the buildings in Opar. He saw them take the blocks to the edge of the kopje and cast them over to the ground beneath, and when the last of the blacks had emerged with his load and cast it to the valley below, one by one the party descended the ladder to the foot of the kopje. But this time Tarzan of the Apes went first. Then they lowered the ladder and took it apart and laid its pieces close to the foot of the cliff, after which they took up the blocks which they had brought from the heart of the kopje, and following Tarzan, who set out in the lead, they commenced to retrace their steps toward the rim of the valley.

Manu would have been very much mystified had he been a man, but being only a monkey he saw only what he saw without attempting to reason very much about it. He knew that the ways of men were peculiar, and oftentimes unaccountable. For example, the Gomangani who could not travel through the jungle and the forest with the ease of any other of the animals which frequented them, added to their difficulties by loading themselves down with additional weights in the form of metal anklets and armlets, with necklaces and girdles, and with skins of animals, which did nothing more than impede their progress and render life much more complicated than that which the untrammeled beasts enjoyed. Manu, whenever he gave the matter a thought, congratulated himself that he was not a man—he pitied the foolish, unreasonable creatures.

Manu must have slept. He thought that he had only closed his eyes a moment, but when he opened them the rosy light of dawn had overspread the desolate valley. Just disappearing over the cliffs to the northeast he could see the last of Tarzan's party commencing the descent of the barrier, then Manu turned his face toward Opar and prepared to descend from the kopje, and scamper back to the safety of his trees within the walls of Opar.

But first he would reconnoiter—Sheeta, the panther, might be still abroad, and so he scampered around the edge of the kopje to a point where he could see the entire valley floor between himself and Opar. And there it was that he saw again that which filled him with greatest excitement. For, debouching from the ruined outer wall of Opar was a large company of Opar's frightful men—fully a hundred of them Manu could have counted had Manu been able to count.

They seemed to be coming toward the kopje, and he sat and watched them as they approached, to defer his return to the city until after the path was cleared of hated Oparians. It occurred to him that they were coming after him, for the egotism of the lower animals is inordinate. Because he was a monkey, the idea did not seem at all ridiculous and so he hid behind a jutting rock, with only one little, bright eye exposed to the enemy. He saw them come closer and he grew very much excited, though he was not at all afraid, for he knew that if they ascended one side of the kopje he could descend the other and be half-way to Opar before they could possibly locate him again.

On and on they came, but they did not stop at the kopje— as a matter of fact they did not come very close to it, but continued on beyond it. Then it was that the truth of the matter flashed into the little brain of the monkey—Cadj and his people were pursuing Tarzan of the Apes to slay him. If Manu had been offended by Tarzan's indifference to him upon the night before, he had evidently forgotten it, for now he was quite as excited about the danger which he saw menace the ape-man as he had been upon the afternoon previous. At first he thought of running ahead, and again warning Tarzan, but he feared to venture so far from the trees of Opar, even if the thought of having to pass the hated Oparians had not been sufficient to deter him from carrying out this plan. For a few minutes he sat watching them, until they had all passed the kopje, and then it became quite clear to him that they were heading directly for the spot at which the last of Tarzan's party had disappeared from the valley—there could be no doubt that they were in pursuit of the ape-man.

Manu scanned the valley once more toward Opar. There was nothing in sight to deter him from an attempted return, and so, with the agility of his kind, he scampered down the vertical face of the kopje and was off at great speed toward the city's wall. Just when he formulated the plan that he eventually followed it is difficult to say. Perhaps he thought it all out as he sat upon the kopje, watching Cadj and his people upon the trail of the ape-man, or perhaps it occurred to him while he was scampering across the barren waste toward Opar. It may just have popped into his mind from a clear sky after he had regained the leafy sanctuary of his own trees. Be that, however as it may, the fact remains, that as La, High Priestess and princess of Opar, in company with several of her priestesses, was bathing in a pool in one of the temple gardens, she was startled by the screaming of a monkey, swinging frantically by his tail from the branch of a great tree which overspread the pool—it was a little gray monkey with a face so wise and serious that one might easily have imagined that the fate of nations lay constantly upon the shoulders of its owner.

"La, La," it screamed, "they have gone to kill Tarzan. They have gone to kill Tarzan."

At the sound of that name La was instantly all attention. Standing waist deep in the pool she looked up at the little monkey questioningly. What do you mean, Manu?" she asked. "It has been many moons since Tarzan was at Opar. He is not here now. What are you talking about?"

"I saw him," screamed Manu, "I saw him last night with many Gomangani. He came to the great rock that lies in the valley before Opar; with all his men he climbed to the top of it, went into the heart of it, and came out with stones which they threw down into the valley. Afterward they descended from the rock, and picked up the stones again and left the valley there," and Manu pointed toward the northeast with one of his hairy little fingers.

"How do you know it was Tarzan of the Apes?" asked La.

"Does Manu not know his cousin and his friend?" demanded the monkey. "With my eyes I saw him—it was Tarzan of the Apes."

La of Opar puckered her brows in thought. Deep in her heart smoldered the tires of her great love for Tarzan. Fires that had been quenched by the necessity that had compelled her marriage with Cadj since last she had seen the ape-man. For it is written among the laws of Opar that the High Priestess of the Flaming God must take a mate within a certain number of years after her consecration. For many moons had La longed to make Tarzan that mate. The ape-man had not loved her, and finally she had come to a realization that he could never love her. Afterward she had bowed to the frightful fate that had placed her in the arms of Cadj.

As month after month had passed and Tarzan bad not returned to Opar, as he had promised he would do, to see that no harm befell La, she had come to accept the opinion of Cadj that the ape-man was dead, and though she hated the repulsive Cadj none the less, her love for Tarzan had gradually become little more than a sorrowful memory. Now to learn that he was alive and had been so near was like re-opening an old wound. At first she comprehended little else than that Tarzan had been close to Opar, but presently the cries of Manu aroused her to a realization that the ape-man was in danger—just what the danger was, she did not know.

"Who has gone to kill Tarzan of the Apes? she demanded suddenly.

"Cadj, Cadj!" shrieked Manu. "He has gone with many, many men, and is following upon the spoor of Tarzan."

La sprang quickly from the pool, seized her girdle and ornaments from her attendant and adjusting them hurriedly, sped through the garden and into the temple.

CHAPTER VII—"YOU MUST SACRIFICE HIM"

Warily Cadj and his hundred frightful followers, armed with their bludgeons and knives, crept stealthily down the face of the barrier into the valley below, upon the trail of the white man and his black companions. They made no haste, for they had noted from the summit of Opar's outer wall, that the party they were pursuing moved very slowly, though why, they did not know, for they had been at too great a distance to see the burden that each of the blacks carried. Nor was it Cadj's desire to overtake his quarry by daylight, his plans contemplating a stealthy night attack, the suddenness of which, together with the great number of his followers, might easily confuse and overwhelm a sleeping camp.

The spoor they followed was well marked. There could be no mistaking it, and they moved slowly down the now gentle declivity, toward the bottom of the valley. It was close to noon that they were brought to a sudden halt by the discovery of a thorn boma recently constructed in a small clearing just ahead of them. From the center of the boma arose the thin smoke of a dying fire. Here, then, was the camp of the ape-man.

Cadj drew his followers into the concealment of the thick bushes that ordered the trail, and from there he sent ahead a single man to reconnoiter. It was but a few moments later that the latter returned to say that the camp was deserted, and once again Cadj moved forward with his men. Entering the boma they examined it in an effort to estimate the size of the party that accompanied Tarzan. As they were thus occupied Cadj saw something lying half concealed by bushes at the far end of the boma. Very warily he approached it, for there was that about it which not only aroused his curiosity but prompted him to caution, for it resembled indistinctly the figure of a man, lying huddled upon the ground.

With ready bludgeons a dozen of them approached the thing that had aroused Cadj's curiosity, and when they had come close to it they saw lying before them the lifeless figure of Tarzan of the Apes.

"The Flaming God has reached forth to avenge his desecrated altar," cried the High Priest, his eyes glowing with the maniacal fires of fanaticism.

But another priest, more practical, perhaps, or at least more cautious, kneeled beside the figure of the ape-man and placed his ear against the latter's heart.

"He is not dead," he whispered; "perhaps he only sleeps."

"Seize him, then, quickly," cried Cadj, and an instant later Tarzan's body was covered by the hairy forms of as many of the frightful men as could pile upon him. He offered no resistance—he did not even open his eyes, and presently his arms were securely bound behind him.

"Drag him forth where the eye of the Flaming God may rest upon him," cried Cadj. They dragged Tarzan out into the center of the boma into the full light of the sun, and Cadj, the High Priest, drawing his knife from his loin cloth, raised it above his head and stood over the prostrate form of his intended victim. Cadj's followers formed a rough circle about the ape-man and some of them pressed close behind their leader. They appeared uneasy, looking alternately at Tarzan and their High Priest, and then casting furtive glances at the sun, riding high in a cloud- mottled sky. But whatever the thoughts that troubled their half-savage brains, there was only one who dared voice his, and he was the same priest who, upon the preceding day, had questioned Cadj's proposal to slay the ape-man.

"Cadj," he said now, "who are you to offer up a sacrifice to the Flaming God? It is the privilege alone of La, our High Priestess and our queen, and indeed will she be angry when she learns what you have done."

"Silence, Dooth!" cried Cadj; "I, Cadj, am the High Priest of Opar. I, Cadj, am the mate of La, the queen. My word, too, is law in Opar. And you would remain a priest, and you would remain alive, keep silence."

"Your word is not law," replied Dooth, angrily, "and if you anger La, the High Priestess, or if you anger the Flaming God, you may be punished as another. If you make this sacrifice both will be angry."

"Enough," cried Cadj; "the Flaming God has spoken to me and has demanded that I offer up as sacrifice this defiler of his temple."

He knelt beside the ape-man and touched his breast above the heart with the point of his sharp blade, and then he raised the weapon high above him, preparatory to the fatal plunge into the living heart. At that instant a cloud passed before the face of the sun and a shadow rested upon them. A murmur rose from the surrounding priests.

"Look," cried Dooth, "the Flaming God is angry. He has hidden his face from the people of Opar."

Cadj paused. He cast a half-defiant, half-frightened look at the cloud obscuring the face of the sun. Then he rose slowly to his feet, and extending his arms upward toward the hidden god of day, he remained for a moment silent in apparently attentive and listening attitude. Then, suddenly, he turned upon his followers.

"Priests of Opar," he cried, "the Flaming God has spoken to his High Priest, Cadj. He is not angered. He but wishes to speak to me alone, and he directs that you go away into the jungle and wait until he has come and spoken to Cadj, after which I shall call you to return. Go!"

For the most part they seemed to accept the word of Cadj as law, but Dooth and a few others, doubtless prompted by a certain skepticism, hesitated.

"Be gone!" commanded Cadj. And so powerful is the habit of obedience that the doubters finally turned away and melted into the jungle with the others. A crafty smile lighted the cruel face of the High Priest as the last of them disappeared from sight, and then he once again turned his attention to the ape-man. That, deep within his breast however, lurked an inherent fear of his deity, was evidenced by the fact that he turned questioning glances toward the sky. He had determined to slay the ape-man while Dooth and the others were absent, yet the fear of his god restrained his hand until the light of his deity should shine forth upon him once more and assure him that the thing he contemplated might meet with favor.

It was a large cloud that overcast the sun, and while Cadj waited his nervousness increased. Six times he raised his knife for the fatal blow, yet in each instance his superstition prevented the consummation of the act. Five, ten, fifteen minutes passed, and still the sun remained obscured. But now at last Cadj could see that it was nearing the edge of the cloud, and once again he took his position kneeling beside the ape-man with his blade ready for the moment that the sunlight should flood again, for the last time, the living Tarzan. He saw it sweeping slowly across the boma toward him, and as it came a look of demoniacal hatred shone in his close-set, wicked eyes. Another instant and the Flaming God would have set the seal of his approval upon the sacrifice. Cadj trembled in anticipation. He raised the knife a trifle higher, his muscles tensed for the downward plunge, and then the silence of the jungle was broken by a woman's voice, raised almost to a scream.

"Cadj" came the single word, but with all the suddenness and all the surprising effect of lightning from a clear sky.

His knife still poised on high, the High Priest turned in the direction of the interruption to see at the clearing's edge the figure of La, the High Priestess, and behind her Dooth and a score of the lesser priests.

"What means this, Cadj?" demanded La, angrily, approaching rapidly toward him across the clearing. Sullenly the High Priest rose.

"The Flaming God demanded the life of this unbeliever," he cried.

"Speaker of lies," retorted La, "the Flaming God communicates with men through the lips of his High Priestess only. Too often already have you attempted to thwart the will of your queen. Know, then, Cadj, that the power of life and death which your queen holds is as potent over you as another. During the long ages that Opar has endured, our legends tell us that more than one High Priest has been offered upon the altar to the Flaming God. And it is not unlikely that yet another may go the way of the presumptuous. Curb, therefore, your vanity and your lust for power, lest they prove your undoing."

Cadj sheathed his knife and turned sullenly away, casting a venomous look at Dooth, to whom he evidently attributed his undoing. That he was temporarily abashed by the presence of his queen was evident, but to those who knew Cadj there was little doubt that he still harbored his intention to despatch the ape-man, and if the opportunity ever presented itself that he would do so, for Cadj had a strong following among the people and priests of Opar. There were many who doubted that La would ever dare to incur the displeasure and anger of so important a portion of her followers as to cause the death or degradation of their high priest, who occupied his office by virtue of laws and customs so old that their origin had been long lost in antiquity.

For years she had found first one excuse and then another to delay the ceremonies that would unite her in marriage to the High Priest. She had further aroused the antagonism of her people by palpable proofs of her infatuation for the ape-man, and even though at last she had been compelled to mate with Cadj, she had made no effort whatsoever to conceal her hatred and loathing for the man. How much further she could go with impunity was a question that often troubled those whose position in Opar depended upon her favor, and, knowing all these conditions as he did, it was not strange that Cadj should entertain treasonable thoughts toward his queen. Leagued with him in his treachery was Oah, a priestess who aspired to the power and offices of La. If La could be done away with, then Cadj had the influence to see that Oah became High Priestess. He also had Oah's promise to mate with him and permit him to rule as king, but as yet both were bound by the superstitious fear of their flaming deity, and because of this fact was the life of La temporarily made safe. It required, however, but the slightest spark to ignite the flames of treason that were smoldering about her.

So far, she was well within her rights in' forbidding the sacrifice of Tarzan by the High Priest. But her fate, her very life, perhaps, depended upon her future treatment of the prisoner. Should she spare him, should she evidence in any way a return of the great love she had once almost publicly avowed for him, it was likely that her doom would be sealed. It was even questionable whether or not she might with impunity spare his life and set him at liberty.

Cadj and the others watched her closely now as she crossed to the side of Tarzan. Standing there silently for several moments she looked down upon him.

"He is already dead?" she asked.

"He was not dead when Cadj sent us away," volunteered Dooth. "If he is dead now it is because Cadj killed him while we were away."

"I did not kill him," said Cadj. "That remains, as La, our queen, has told you, for her to do. The eye of the Flaming God looks down upon you, High Priestess of Opar. The knife is at your hip, the sacrifice lies before you."

La ignored the man's words and turned toward Dooth. "If he still lives," she said, "construct a litter and bear him back to Opar."

Thus, once more, came Tarzan of the Apes into the ancient colonial city of the Atlantians. The effects of the narcotic that Kraski had administered to him did not wear off for many hours. It was night when he opened his eyes, and for a moment he was bewildered by the darkness and the silence that surrounded him. All that he could scent at first was that he lay upon a pile of furs and that he was uninjured; for he felt no pain. Slowly there broke through the fog of his drugged brain recollection of the last moment before unconsciousness had overcome him, and presently he realized the trick that had been played upon him. For how long he had been unconscious and where he then was he could not imagine. Slowly he arose to his feet, finding that except for a slight dizziness he was quite himself. Cautiously he felt around in the darkness, moving with care, a hand out-stretched, and always feeling carefully with his feet for a secure footing. Almost immediately a stone wall stopped his progress, and this he followed around four sides of what he soon realized was a small room in which there were but two openings, a door upon each of the opposite sides. Only his senses of touch and smell were of value to him here. These told him only at first that he was imprisoned in a subterranean chamber, but as the effects of the narcotic diminished, the keenness of the latter returned, and with its return there was borne in upon Tarzan's brain an insistent impression of familiarity in certain fragrant odors that impinged upon his olfactory organs—a haunting suggestion that he had known them before under similar circumstances. Presently from above, through earth and masonry, came the shadow of an uncanny scream—just the faintest suggestion of it reached the keen ears of the ape-man, but it was sufficient to flood his mind with vivid recollections, and, by association of ideas, to fix the identity of the familiar odors about him. He knew at last that he was in the dark pit beneath Opar.

Above him, in her chamber in the temple, La, the High Priestess, tossed upon a sleepless couch. She knew all too well the temper of her people and the treachery of the High Priest, Cadj. She knew the religious fanaticism which prompted the ofttime maniacal actions of her bestial and ignorant followers, and she guessed truly that Cadj would inflame them against her should she fail this time in sacrificing the ape-man to the Flaming God. And it was the effort to find an escape from her dilemma that left her sleepless, for it was not in the heart of La to sacrifice Tarzan of the

Apes. High Priestess of a horrid cult, though she was, and queen of a race of half-beasts, yet she was a woman, too, a woman who had loved but once and given that love to the godlike ape-man who was again within her power. Twice before had he escaped her sacrificial knife; in the final instance love had at last triumphed over jealousy and fanaticism, and La, the woman, had realized that never again could she place in jeopardy the life of the man she loved, however hopeless she knew that love to be.

Tonight she was faced with a problem that she felt almost beyond her powers of solution. The fact that she was mated with Cadj removed the last vestige of hope that she had ever had of becoming the wife of the ape-man. Yet she was no less determined to save Tarzan if it were possible. Twice had he saved her life, once from a mad priest, and once from Tantor in must. Then, too, she had given her word that when Tarzan came again to Opar he came in friendship and would be received in friendship. But the influence of Cadj was great, and she knew that that influence had been directed unremittingly against the ape-man—she had seen it in the attitude of her followers from the very moment that they had placed Tarzan upon a litter to bear him back to Opar—she had seen it in the evil glances that had been cast at her. Sooner or later they would dare denounce her—all that they needed was some slight, new excuse, that, she knew, they eagerly awaited in her forthcoming attitude toward Tarzan. It was well after midnight when there came to her one of the priestesses who remained always upon guard outside her chamber door.

"Dooth would speak with you," whispered the hand-maiden.

"It is late," replied La, "and men are not permitted in this part of the temple. How came he here, and why?"

"He says that he comes in the service of La, who is in great danger," replied the girl.

"Fetch him here then," said La, "and as you value your life see that you tell no one."

"I shall be as voiceless as the stones of the altar," replied the girl, as she turned and left the chamber.

A moment later she returned, bringing Dooth, who halted a few feet from the High Priestess and saluted her. La signaled to the girl who had brought him, to depart, and then she turned questioningly to the man.

"Speak, Dooth!" she commanded.

"We all know," he said, "of La's love for the strange ape-man, and it is not for me, a lesser priest, to question the thoughts or acts of my High Priestess. It is only for me to serve, as those would do better to serve who now plot against you."

"What do you mean, Dooth? Who plots against me?"

"Even at this minute are Cadj and Oah and several of the priests and priestesses carrying out a plan for your undoing. They are setting spies to watch you, knowing that you would liberate the ape-man, because there will come to you one who will tell you that to permit him to escape will be the easiest solution of your problem. This one will be sent by Cadj, and then those who watch you will report to the people and to the priests that they have seen you lead the sacrifice to liberty. But even that will avail you nothing, for Cadj and Oah and the others have placed upon the trail from Opar many men in hiding, who will fall upon the ape-man and slay him before the Flaming God has descended twice into the western forest. In but one way only may you save yourself, La of Opar."

"And what is that way?" she asked.

"You must, with your own hands, upon the altar of our temple, sacrifice the ape-man to the Flaming God."

CHAPTER VIII—MYSTERY OF THE PAST

La had breakfasted the following morning, and had sent Dooth with food for Tarzan, when there came to her a young priestess, who was the sister of Oah. Even before the girl had spoken La knew that she was an emissary from Cadj, and that the treachery of which Dooth had warned her was already under way. The girl was ill at ease and quite evidently frightened, for she was young and held in high revere the queen whom she had good reason to know was all-powerful, and who might even inflict death upon her if she so wished. La, who had already determined upon a plan of action that she knew would be most embarrassing to Cadj and his conspirators, waited in silence for the girl to speak. But it was some time before the girl could muster up her courage or find a proper opening. Instead, she spoke of many things that had no bearing whatsoever upon her subject, and La, the High Priestess, was amused at her discomfiture.

"It is not often," said La, "that the sister of Oah comes to the apartments of her queen unless she is bidden. I am glad to see that she at last realizes the service that she owes to the High Priestess of the Flaming God."

"I come," said the girl, at last, speaking almost as one who has learned a part, "to tell you that I have overheard that which may be of interest to you, and which I am sure that you will be glad to hear."

"Yes?" interrogated La, raising her arched eyebrows.

"I overheard Cadj speaking with the lesser priests," the girl continued, "and I distinctly heard him say that he would be glad if the ape-man escaped, as that would relieve you, and Cadj as well, of much embarrassment. I thought that La, the queen, would be glad to know this, for it is known by all of us that La has promised friendship to the ape-man, and therefore does not wish to sacrifice him upon the altar of the Flaming God."

"My duty is plain to me," replied La, in a haughty voice, "and I do not need Cadj nor any hand-maiden to interpret it to me. I also know the prerogatives of a High Priestess, and that the right of sacrifice is one of them. For this reason I prevented Cadj from sacrificing the stranger. No other hand than mine may offer his heart's blood to the Flaming God, and upon the third day he shall die beneath my knife upon the altar of our temple."

The effect of these words upon the girl were precisely what La had anticipated. She saw disappointment and chagrin written upon the face of Cadj's messenger, who now had no answer, for her instructions had not foreseen this attitude upon the part of La. Presently the girl found some lame pretext upon which to withdraw, and when she had left the presence of the High Priestess, La could scarcely restrain a smile. She had no intention of sacrificing Tarzan, but this, of course, the sister of Oah did not know. So she returned to Cadj and repeated as nearly as she could recall it, all that La had said to her. The High Priest was much chagrined, for his plan had been now, not so much to encompass the destruction of Tarzan as to lead La into the commission of an act that would bring upon her the wrath of the priests and people of Opar, who, properly instigated, would demand her life in expiation. Oah, who was present when her sister returned, bit her lips, for great was her disappointment. Never before had she seen so close at hand the longed-for possibility of becoming High Priestess. For several minutes she paced to and fro in deep thought, and then, suddenly, she halted before Cadj.

"La loves this ape-man," she said, "and even though she may sacrifice him, it is only because of fear of her people. She loves him still—loves him better, Cadj, than she has ever loved you. The ape-man knows it, and trusts her, and because he knows it there is a way. Listen, Cadj, to Oah. We will send one to the ape-man who shall tell him that she comes from La, and that La has instructed her to lead him out of Opar and set him free. This one shall lead him into our ambush and when he is killed we shall go, many of us, before La, and accuse her of treachery. The one who led the ape-man from Opar shall say that La ordered her to do it, and the priests and the people will be very angry, and then you shall demand the life of La. It will be very easy and we shall be rid of both of them."

"Good!" exclaimed Cadj. "We shall do this thing at dawn upon the morrow, and before the Flaming God goes to his rest at night he shall look upon a new High Priestess in Opar."

That night Tarzan was aroused from his sleep by a sound at one of the doors of his prison cell. He heard the bolt slipped back and the door creak slowly open upon its ancient hinges. In the inky darkness he could discern no presence, but he heard the stealthy movement of sandaled feet upon the concrete floor, and then, out of the darkness, his name was whispered, in a woman's voice.

"I am here," he replied. "Who are you and what do you want of Tarzan of the Apes?"

"Your life is in danger," replied the voice. "Come, follow me."

"Who sent you?" demanded the ape-man, his sensitive nostrils searching for a clue to the identity of the nocturnal visitor, but so heavily was the air laden with the pungent odor of some heavy perfume with which the body of the woman seemed to have been anointed, that there was no distinguishing clue by which he might judge as to whether she was one of the priestesses he had known upon the occasion of his former visits to Opar, or an entire stranger to him.

"La sent me," she said, "to lead you from the pits of Opar to the freedom of the outside world beyond the city's walls." Groping in the darkness she finally found him. "Here are your weapons," she said, handing them to him, and then she took his hand, turned and led him from the dungeon, through a long, winding, and equally black corridor, down flights of age-old concrete steps, through passages and corridors, opening and closing door after door that creaked and groaned upon rusty hinges. How far they traveled thus, and in what direction, Tarzan could not guess. He had gleaned enough from Dooth, when the latter brought him his food, to believe that in La he had a friend who would aid him, for Dooth had told him that she had saved him from Cadj when the latter had discovered him unconscious in the deserted boma of the Europeans who had drugged and left him. And so, the woman having said that she came from La, Tarzan followed her willingly. He could not but recall Jane's prophecy of the evils that he might expect to befall him should he persist in undertaking this third trip to Opar, and he wondered if, after all, his wife was right, that he should never again escape from the toils of the fanatical priests of the Flaming God. He had not, of course, expected to enter Opar, but there seemed to hang over the accursed city a guardian demon that threatened the life of whosoever dared approach the forbidden spot or wrest from the forgotten treasure vaults a portion of their great hoard.

For more than an hour his guide led him through the Stygian darkness of underground passages, until, ascending a flight of steps they emerged into the center of a clump of bushes, through which the pale light of the moon was barely discernible. The fresh air, however, told him that they had reached the surface of the ground, and now the woman, who had not spoken a word since she had led him from his cell, continued on in silence, following a devious trail that wound hither and thither in an erratic fashion through a heavy forest choked with undergrowth, and always upward.

From the location of the stars and moon, and from the upward trend of the trail, Tarzan knew that he was being led into the mountains that lie behind Opar—a place he had never thought of visiting, since the country appeared rough and uninviting, and not likely to harbor game such as Tarzan cared most to hunt. He was already surprised by the nature of the vegetation, for he had thought the hills barren except for stunted trees and scraggy bush. As they continued upon their way, climbing ever upward, the moon rose higher in the heavens, until its soft light revealed more clearly to the keen eyes of the ape-man the topography of the country they were traversing, and then it was that he saw they were ascending a narrow, thickly wooded gorge, and he understood why the heavy vegetation had been invisible from the plain before Opar. Himself naturally uncommunicative, the woman's silence made no particular impression upon Tarzan. Had he had anything to say he should have said it, and likewise he assumed that there was no necessity for her speaking unless there was some good reason for speaking, for those who travel far and fast have no breath to waste upon conversation.

The eastern stars were fading at the first hint of coming dawn when the two scrambled up a precipitous bank that formed the upper end of the ravine, and came out upon comparatively level ground. As they advanced the sky lightened, and presently the woman halted at the edge of a declivity, and as the day broke Tarzan saw below him a wooded basin in the heart of the mountain, and, showing through the trees at what appeared to be some two or three miles distant, the outlines of a building that glistened and sparkled and scintillated in the light of the new sun. Then he turned and looked at his companion, and surprise and consternation were writ upon his face, for standing before him was La, the High Priestess of Opar.

"You?" he exclaimed. "Now indeed will Cadj have the excuse that Dooth said he sought to put you out of the way."

"He will never have the opportunity to put me out of the way," replied La, "for I shall never return to Opar."

"Never return to Opar!" he exclaimed, "then where are you going? Where can you go?"

"I am going with you," she replied. "I do not ask that you love me. I only ask that you take me away from Opar and from the enemies who would slay me. There was no other way. Manu, the monkey, overheard them plotting, and he came to me and told me all that they would do. Whether I saved you or sacrificed you, it had all been the same with me. They were determined to do away with me, that Oah might be High Priestess and Cadj king of Opar. But I should not have sacrificed you, Tarzan, under any circumstances, and this, then, seemed the only way in which we might both be saved. We could not go to the north or the west across the plain of Opar for there Cadj has placed warriors in ambush to waylay you, and though you be Tarzan and a mighty fighter, they would overwhelm you by their very numbers and slay you."

"But where are you leading me?" asked Tarzan.

"I have chosen the lesser of two evils; in this direction lies an unknown country, filled for us Oparians with legends of grim monsters and strange people. Never has an Oparian ventured here and returned again to Opar. But if there lives in all the world a creature who could win through this unknown valley, it be you, Tarzan of the Apes."

"But if you know nothing of this country, or its inhabitants," demanded Tarzan, "how is it that you so well know the trail that leads to it?"

"We well know the trail to the summit, but that is as far as I have ever been before. The great apes and the lions use this trail when they come down into Opar. The lions, of course, cannot tell us where it leads, and the great apes will not, for usually we are at war with them. Along this trail they come down into Opar to steal our people, and upon this trail we await to capture them, for often we offer a great ape in sacrifice to the Flaming God, or rather that was our former custom, but for many years they have been too wary for us, the toll being upon the other side, though we do not know for what purpose they steal our people, unless it be that they eat them. They are a very powerful race, standing higher than Bolgani, the gorilla, and infinitely more cunning, for, as there is ape blood in our veins, so is there human blood in the veins of these great apes that dwell in the valley above Opar."

"Why is it, La, that we must pass through this valley in order to escape from Opar? There must be some other way.

"There is no other way, Tarzan of the Apes," she replied. "The avenues across the valley are guarded by Cadj's people. Our only chance of escape lies in this direction, and I have brought you along the only trail that pierces the precipitous cliffs that guard Opar upon the south. Across or around this valley we must go in an attempt to find an avenue across the mountain and down upon the other side."

The ape-man stood gazing down into the wooded basin below them, his mind occupied with the problems of the moment. Had he been alone he would not have come this way, for he was sufficiently confident of his own prowess to believe that he might easily have crossed the valley of Opar in comparative safety, regardless of Cadj's plans to the contrary. But he was not alone. He had now to think of La, and he realized that in her efforts to save him she had placed him under a moral obligation which he might not disregard.

To skirt the basin, keeping as far as possible from the building, which he could see in the distance, seemed the wisest course to pursue, since, of course, his sole purpose was to find a way across the mountain and out of this inhospitable country. But the glimpses he caught of the edifice, half concealed as it was amid the foliage of great trees, piqued his curiosity to such an extent that he felt an almost irresistible urge to investigate. He did not believe that the basin was inhabited by other than wild beasts, and he attributed the building which he saw to the handiwork of an extinct or departed people, either contemporaneous with the ancient Atlantians who had built Opar or, perhaps, built by the original Oparians themselves, but now forgotten by their descendants. The glimpses which he caught of the building suggested such size and magnificence as might belong to a palace.

The ape-man knew no fear, though he possessed to a reasonable extent that caution which is inherent in all wild beasts. He would not have hesitated to pit his cunning and his prowess against the lower orders, however ferocious they might be, for, unlike man, they could not band together to his undoing. But should men elect to hunt him in numbers he knew that a real danger would confront him, and that, in the face of their combined strength and intelligence, his own might not avail him. There was little likelihood, however, he reasoned, that the basin was inhabited by human beings. Doubtless closer investigation of the building he saw would reveal that it was but a deserted ruin, and that the most formidable foes he would encounter would be the great apes and the lions. Of neither of these had he any fear; with the former it was even reasonable to imagine that he might establish amicable relations. Believing as he did that he must look for egress from the basin upon its opposite side, it was only natural that he should wish to choose the most direct route across the basin. Therefore his inclinations to explore the valley were seconded by considerations of speed and expediency.

"Come," he said to La, and started down the declivity which led into the basin in the direction of the building ahead of them.

"You are not going that way?" she cried in astonishment.

"Why not?" he said. "It is the shortest way across the valley, and in so far as I can judge our trail over the mountains is more likely to lie in that direction than elsewhere."

"But I am afraid," she said. "The Flaming God alone knows what hideous dangers lurk in the depths of that forest below us.

"Only Numa and the Mangani," he said. "Of these we need have no fear."

"You fear nothing," she said, "but I am only a woman."

"We can die but once," replied Tarzan, "and that once we must die. To be always fearing, then, would not avert it, and would make life miserable. We shall go the short way, then, and perhaps we shall see enough to make the risk well worth while."

They followed a well-worn trail downward among the brush, the trees increasing in both size and number as they approached the floor of the basin, until at last they were walking beneath the foliage of a great forest. What wind there was was at their back, and the ape-man, though he moved at a swinging walk, was constantly on the alert. Upon the hard-packed earth of the trail there were few signs to indicate the nature of the animals that had passed to and fro, but here and there the spoor of a lion was in evidence. Several times Tarzan stopped and listened, often he raised his head and his sensitive nostrils dilated as he sought for whatever the surrounding air might hold for him.

"I think there are men in this valley," he said presently. "For some time I have been almost positive that we are being watched. But whoever is stalking us is clever beyond words, for it is only the barest suggestion of another presence that I can scent."

La looked about apprehensively and drew close to his side. "I see no one," she said, in a low voice.

"Nor I," he replied. "Nor can I catch any well-defined scent spoor, yet I am positive that someone is following us. Someone or something that trails by scent, and is clever enough to keep its scent from us. It is more than likely that, whatever it is, it is passing through the trees, at a sufficient height to keep its scent spoor always above us. The air is right for that, and even if he were up wind from us we might not catch his scentat all. Wait here, I will make sure," and he swung lightly into the branches of a nearby tree and swarmed upward with the agility of Manu, the monkey. A moment later he descended to the girl's side.

"I was right," he said, "there is someone, or something, not far off. But whether it is man or Mangani I cannot say, for the odor is a strange one to me, suggesting neither, yet both. But two can play at that game. Come!" And he swung the girl to his shoulder and a moment later had carried her high into the trees. "Unless he is close enough to watch us, which I doubt," he said, "our spoor will be carried over his head and it will be some time before he can pick it up again, unless he is wise enough to rise to a higher level."

La marveled at the strength of the ape-man as he carried her easily from tree to tree, and at the speed with which he traversed the swaying, leafy trail. For half an hour he continued onward, and then quite suddenly he stopped, poised high upon a swaying bough.

"Look!" he said, pointing ahead and below them. Looking in the direction that he indicated the girl saw through the leafy foliage a small, heavily stockaded compound, in which were some dozen huts that immediately riveted her surprised attention, nor no less was the ape-man's curiosity piqued by what he glimpsed vaguely through the foliage. Huts they evidently were, but they seemed to be moving to and fro in the air, some moving gently backward and forward, while others jumped up and down in more or less violent agitation. Tarzan swung to a nearer tree and descended to a sturdy branch, to which he lowered La from his shoulder. Then he crept forward stealthily, the girl following, for she was, in common with the other Oparians, slightly arboreal. Presently they reached a point where they could see plainly the village below them, and immediately the seeming mystery of the dancing huts was explained.

They were of the bee-hive type, common to many African tribes, and were about seven feet in diameter by six or seven in height, but instead of resting on the ground, each hut was suspended by a heavy hawser-like grass rope to a branch of one of the several giant trees that grew within the stockade. From the center of the bottom of each hut trailed another lighter rope. From his position above them Tarzan saw no openings in any of the huts large enough to admit the body of a man, though there were several openings four or five inches in diameter in the sides of each hut about three feet above the floor. Upon the ground, inside the compound, were several of the inhabitants of the village, if the little collection of swinging houses could be dignified by such a name. Nor were the people any less strange to Tarzan than their peculiar domiciles. That they were negroes wasevident, but of a type entirely unfamiliar to the ape-man. All were naked, and without any ornamentation whatsoever other than a few daubs of color, placed apparently at random upon their bodies. They were tall, and very muscular appearing, though their legs seemed much too short and their arms too long for perfect symmetry, while their faces were almost bestial in contour, their jaws being exaggeratedly prognathous while above their beetling brows there was no forehead, the skull running back in an almost horizontal plane to a point.

As Tarzan stood looking at them he saw another descend one of the ropes that dangled from the bottom of a hut, and immediately he understood the purpose of the ropes and the location of the entrances to the dwellings. The creatures squatting about upon their haunches were engaged in feeding. Several had bones from which they were tearing the uncooked flesh with their great teeth, while others ate fruit and tubers. There were individuals of both sexes and of various ages, from childhood to maturity, but there was none that seemed very old. They were practically hairless, except for scraggy, reddish brown locks upon their heads. They spoke but seldom and then in tones which resembled the growling of beasts, nor once, while Tarzan watched them, did he see one laugh or even smile, which, of all their traits, rendered them most unlike the average native of Africa. Though Tarzan's eyes searched the compound carefully he saw no indication of cooking utensils or of any fire. Upon the ground about them lay their weapons, short javelin-like spears and a sort of battle-ax with a sharpened, metal blade. Tarzan of the Apes was glad that he had come this way, for it had permitted him to see such a type of native as he had not dreamed existed—a type so low that it bordered closely upon the brute. Even the Waz-dons and Ho- dons of Pal-ul-don were far advanced in the scale of evolution compared to these.

As he looked at them he could not but wonder that they were sufficiently intelligent to manufacture the weapons they possessed, which he could see, even at a distance, were of fine workmanship and design. Their huts, too, seemed well and ingeniously made, while the stockade which surrounded the little compound was tall, strong, and well-built, evidently for the purpose of safeguarding them against the lions which infested the basin.

As Tarzan and La watched these people they became presently aware of the approach of some creature from their left, and a moment later they saw a man similar to those of the compound swing from a tree that overhung the stockade and drop within. The others acknowledged his coming with scarce more than indifferent glances. He came forward and, squatting among them, appeared to be telling them of something, and though Tarzan could not hear his words he judged from his gestures and the sign language which he used to supplement his meager speech, that he was telling his fellows of the strange creatures he had seen in the forest a short time before, and the ape-man immediately judged that this was the same who he had been aware was following them and whom he had successfully put off the scent. The narration evidently excited them, for some of them arose, and leaping up and down with bent knees, slapped their arms against their sides grotesquely. The expressions upon their faces scarcely changed, however, and after a moment each squatted down again as he had been before. It was while they were thus engaged that there echoed through the forest a loud scream that awakened in the mind of the ape-man many savage memories.

"Bolgani," he whispered to La.

"It is one of the great apes," she said, and shuddered.

Presently they saw him, swinging down the jungle trail toward the compound. A huge gorilla, but such a gorilla as Tarzan of the Apes had never looked on before. Of almost gigantic stature, the creature was walking erect with the stride of a man, not ever once touching his knuckles to the ground. His head and face were almost those of a gorilla, and yet there was a difference, as Tarzan could note as the creature came nearer—it was Bolgani, with the soul and brain of a man—nor was this all that rendered the creature startling and unique. Stranger perhaps than aught else was the fact that it wore ornaments—and such ornaments! Gold and diamonds sparkled against its shaggy coat, above its elbows were numerous armlets and there were anklets upon its legs, while from a girdle about its middle there depended before and behind a long narrow strip that almost touched the ground and which seemed to be entirely constructed of golden spangles set with small diamonds. Never before had John Clayton, Lord Greystoke, seen such a display of barbaric finery, nor even amidst the jewels of Opar such a wealth of priceless stones.

Immediately after the hideous scream had first broken the comparative silence of the forest, Tarzan had noticed its effects upon the inmates of the compound. Instantly they had arisen to their feet. The women and children scurried behind the boles of the trees or clambered up the ropes into their swinging cages, while some of the men advanced to what Tarzan now saw was the gate of the compound. Outside this gate the gorilla halted and again raised his voice, but this time in speech rather than his hideous scream.

CHAPTER IX—THE SHAFT OF DEATH

As the huge, man-like gorilla entered the compound the warriors closed the gate, and fell back respectfully as he advanced to the center of the village where he stood for a moment, looking about.

"Where are the shes and the balus?" he asked, tersely. "Call them."

The women and the children must have heard the command, but they did not emerge from their hiding places. The warriors moved about uneasily, evidently torn by the conflicting emotions of fear of the creature who had issued the order, and reluctance to fulfil his commands.

"Call them," he repeated, "or go and fetch them." But at last one of the warriors mustered the courage to address him.

"This village has already furnished one woman within the moon," he said. "It is the turn of another village."

"Silence!" roared the gorilla-man, advancing threateningly toward him. "You are a rash Gomangani to threaten the will of a Bolgani I speak with the voice of Numa, the Emperor; obey or die."

Trembling, the black turned and called the women and children, but none responded to his summons. The Bolgani gestured impatiently.

"Go and fetch them," he demanded. And the blacks, cringing, moved sullenly across the compound toward the hiding places of their women and children. Presently they returned, dragging them with them, by the arms sometimes, but usually by the hair. Although they had seemed loath to give them up, they showed no gentleness toward them, nor any indication of affection. Their attitude toward them, however, was presently explained to Tarzan by the next words of the warrior who had spoken previously.

"Great Bolgani," he said, addressing the gorilla man, "if Numa takes always from this village, there will soon be not enough women for the warriors here, and there will be too few children, and in a little time there will be none of us left."

"What of that?" growled the gorilla-man. "There are already too many Gomangani in the world. For what other purpose were you created than to serve Numa, the Emperor, and his chosen people, the Bolgani?" As he spoke he was examining the women and children, pinching their flesh and pounding upon their chests and backs. Presently he returned to a comparatively young woman, straddling whose hip was a small child.

"This one will do," he said, snatching the child from its mother and hurling it roughly across the compound, where it lay against the face of the palisade, moaning pitifully, and perchance broken and dying. The poor, stupid mother, apparently more beast than human, stood for a moment trembling in dumb anguish, and then she started to rush forward to her child. But the gorilla-man seized her with one of his great hands and hurled her to the ground. Simultaneously there arose from the silent foliage above them the fierce and terrible scream of the challenging bull ape. In terror the simple blacks cast affrighted glances upward, while the gorilla-man raised his hideous face in snarling anger toward the author of the bestial cry.

Swaying upon a leafy bough they beheld such a creature as none of them had ever looked upon before—a white man, a Tarmangani, with hide as hairless as the body of Histah, the snake. In the instant that they looked they saw the spear hand of the stranger drive forward, and the shaft, speeding with the swiftness of thought, bury itself in the breast of the Bolgani. With a single scream of rage and pain, the gorilla-man crumbled to the earth, where he struggled spasmodically for a moment and then lay still, in death.

The ape-man held no great love for the Gomangani as a race, but inherent in his English brain and heart was the spirit of fair play, which prompted him to spontaneous espousal of the cause of the weak. On the other hand Bolgani was his hereditary enemy. His first battle had been with Bolganil and his first kill.

The poor blacks were still standing in stupefied wonderment when he dropped from the tree to the ground among them. They stepped back in terror, and simultaneously they raised their spears menacingly against him.

"I am a friend," he said. "I am Tarzan of the Apes. Lower your spears." And then he turned and withdrew his own weapon from the carcass of Bolgani. "Who is this creature, that may come into your village and slay your balus and steal your shes? Who is he, that you dare not drive your spears through him?"

"He is one of the great Bolgani," said the warrior, who seemed to be spokesman, and the leader in the village. "He is one of the chosen people of Numa, the Emperor, and when Numa learns that he has been killed in our village we shall all die for what you have done."

"Who is Numa?" demanded the ape-man, to whom Numa, in the language of the great apes, meant only lion.

"Numa is the Emperor," replied the black, "who lives with the Bolgani in the Palace of Diamonds."

He did not express himself in just these words, for the meager language of the great apes, even though amplified by the higher intelligence and greater development of the Oparians, is still primitive in the extreme. What he had really said was more nearly "Numa, the king of kings, who lives in the king's hut of glittering stones," which carried to the ape-man's mind the faithful impression of the fact. Numa, evidently, was the name adopted by the king of the Bolgani, and the title emperor, indicated merely his preeminence among the chiefs.

The instant that Bolgani had fallen the bereaved mother rushed forward and gathered her injured infant into her arms. She squatted now against the palisade, cuddling it to her breast, and crooning softly to pacify its cries, which Tarzan suddenly discovered were more the result of fright than injury. At first the mother had been frightened when he had attempted to examine the child, drawing away and baring her fighting fangs, much after the manner of a wild beast. But presently there had seemed to come to her dull brain a realization that this creature had saved her from Bolgani, that he had permitted her to recover her infant and that he was making no effort to harm either of them. Convinced at last that the child was only bruised, Tarzan turned again toward the warriors, who were talking together in an excited little group a few paces away. As they saw him advancing, they spread into a semi-circle and stood facing him.

"The Bolgani will send and slay us all," they said, "when they learn what has happened in our village, unless we can take to them the creature that cast the spear. Therefore, Tarmangani, you shall go with us to the Palace of Diamonds, and there we shall give you over to the Bolgani and perhaps Numa will forgive us."

The ape-man smiled. What kind of creature did the simple blacks think him, to believe that he would permit himself to be easily led into the avenging hands of Numa, the Emperor of the

Bolgani. Although he was fully aware of the risk that he had taken in entering the village, he knew too that because he was Tarzan of the Apes there was a greater chance that he would be able to escape than that they could hold him. He had faced savage spearmen before and knew precisely what to expect in the event of hostilities. He preferred, however, to make peace with these people, for it had been in his mind to find some means of questioning them the moment that he had discovered their village hidden away in this wild forest.

"Wait," he said, therefore. "Would you betray a friend who enters your village to protect you from an enemy?"

"We will not slay you, Tarmangani. We will take you to the Bolgani for Numa, the Emperor."

"But that would amount to the same thing," returned Tarzan, "for you well know that Numa, the Emperor, will have me slain."

"That we cannot help," replied the spokesman. "If we could save you we would, but when the Bolgani discover what has happened in our village, it is we who must suffer, unless, perhaps, they are satisfied to punish you instead."

"But why need they know that the Bolgani has been slain in your village?" asked Tarzan.

"Will they not see his body next time they come?" asked the spokesman.

"Not if you remove his body," replied Tarzan.

The blacks scratched their heads. Into their dull, ignorant minds had crept no such suggestion of a solution of their problem. What the stranger said was true. None but they and he knew that Bolgani had been slain within their palisade. To remove the body, then, would be to remove all suspicion from their village. But where were they to take it? They put the question to Tarzan.

"I will dispose of him for you," replied the Tarmangani. "Answer my questions truthfully and I will promise to take him away and dispose of him in such a manner that no one will know how he died, or where."

"What are your questions?" asked the spokesman.

"I am a stranger in your country. I am lost here," replied the ape-man. "And I would find a way out of the valley in that direction." And he pointed toward the southeast.

The black shook his head. "There may be a way out of the valley in that direction," he said, "but what lies beyond no man knows; nor do I know whether there be a way out or whether there be anything beyond. It is said that all is fire beyond the mountain, and no one dares to go and see. As for myself, I have never been far from my village—at most only a day's march to hunt for game for the Bolgani, and to gather fruit and nuts and plantains for them. If there is a way out I do not know, nor would any man dare take it if there were."

"Does no one ever leave the valley?" asked Tarzan.

"I know not what others do," replied the spokesman, "but those of this village never leave the valley."

"What lies in that direction?" asked Tarzan, pointing toward Opar.

"I do not know," replied the black, "only that sometimes the Bolgani come from that way, bringing with them strange creatures; little men with white skins and much hair, with short, crooked legs and long arms, and sometimes white shes, who do not look at all like the strange little Tarmangani. But where they get them I do not know, nor do they ever tell us. Are these all the questions that you wish to ask?"

"Yes, that is all," replied Tarzan, seeing that he could gain no information whatsoever from these ignorant villagers. Realizing that he must find his own way out of the valley, and knowing that he could do so much more quickly and safely if he was alone, he decided to sound the blacks in relation to a plan that had entered his mind.

"If I take the Bolgani away, so that the others will not know that he was slain in your village, will you treat me as a friend?" he asked.

"Yes," replied the spokesman.

"Then," said Tarzan, "will you keep here for me my white she until I return again to your village? You can hide her in one of your huts if a Bolgani comes, and no one need ever know that she is among you. What do you say?"

The blacks looked around. "We do not see her," said the spokesman. "Where is she?"

"If you will promise to protect her and hide her, I will bring her here," replied the ape-man.

"I will not harm her," said the head man, "but I do not know about the others."

Tarzan turned toward the others who were clustered about, listening. "I am going to bring my mate into your village," he said, "and you are going to hide her, and feed her, and protect her until I return. I shall take away the body of Bolgani, so that no suspicion shall fall upon you, and when I come back I shall expect to find my mate safe and unharmed."

He had thought it best to describe La as his mate, since thus they might understand that she was under his protection, and if they felt either gratitude or fear toward him, La would be safer. Raising his face toward the tree where she was hidden, he called to La to descend, and a moment later she clambered down to the lower branches of one of the trees in the compound and dropped into Tarzan's arms.

"This is she," he said to the assembled blacks, "guard her well and hide her from the Bolgani. If, upon my return, I find that any harm has befallen her, I shall take word to the Bolgani that it was you who did this," and he pointed to the corpse of the gorilla-man.

La turned appealingly toward him, fear showing in her eyes. "You are not going to leave me here?" she asked.

"Temporarily only," replied Tarzan. "These poor people are afraid that if the death of this creature is traced to their village they shall all suffer the wrath of his fellows, and so I have promised that I will remove the evidence in such a way as to direct suspicion elsewhere. If they are sufficiently high in the scale of evolution to harbor sentiments of gratitude, which I doubt, they will feel obligated to me for having slain this beast, as well as for preventing suspicion falling upon them. For these reasons they should protect you, but to make assurance doubly sure I have appealed also to their fear of the Bolgani—a characteristic which I know they possess. I am sure that you will be as safe here as with me until I return, otherwise I would not leave you. But alone I can travel much faster, and while I am gone I intend to find a way out of this valley, then I shall return for you and together we may make our escape easily, or at least with greater assurance of success than were we to blunder slowly about together."

"You will come back?" she asked, a note of fear, longing, and appeal in her voice.

"I will come back," he replied, and then turning to the blacks: "Clear out one of these huts for my mate, and see that she is not molested, and that she is furnished with food and water. And remember what I said, upon her safety your lives depend."

Stooping, Tarzan lifted the dead gorilla-man to his shoulder, and the simple blacks marveled at his prowess. Of great physical strength themselves, there was not one of them but would have staggered under the weight of Bolgani, yet this strange Tarmangani walked easily beneath his burden, and when they had opened the gate in the palisade he trotted down the jungle trail as though he carried nothing but his own frame. A moment later he disappeared at a turn and was swallowed by the forest.

La turned to the blacks: "Prepare my hut," she said, for she was very tired and longed to rest. They eyed her askance and whispered among themselves. It was evident to her that there was a difference of opinion among them, and presently from snatches of conversation which she overheard she realized that while some of the blacks were in favor of obeying Tarzan's injunctions implicitly, there were others who objected strenuously and who wished to rid their village of her, lest she be discovered there by the Bolgani, and the villagers be punished accordingly.

"It would be better," she heard one of the blacks say, "to turn her over to the Bolgani at once and tell them that we saw her mate slay the messenger of Numa. We will say that we tried to capture the Tarmangani but that he escaped, and that we were only able to seize his mate. Thus will we win the favor of Numa, and perhaps then he will not take so many of our women and children."

"But the Tarmangani is great," replied one of the others. "He is more powerful even than Bolgani. He would make a terrible enemy, and, as the chances are that the Bolgani would not believe us we should then have not only them but the Tarmangani to fear."

"You are right," cried La, "the Tarmangani is great. Far better will it be for you to have him for friend than enemy. Single-handed he grapples with Numa, the lion, and slays him. You saw with what ease he lifted the body of the mighty Bolgani to his shoulder. You saw him trot lightly down the jungle trail beneath his burden. With equal ease will he carry the corpse through the trees of the forest, far above the ground. In all the world there is no other like him, no other like Tarzan of the Apes. If you are wise, Gomangani, you will have Tarzan for a friend."

The blacks listened to her, their dull faces revealing nothing of what was passing in their stupid brains. For a few moments they stood thus in silence, the hulking, ignorant blacks upon one side, the slender, beautiful white woman upon the other. Then La spoke.

"Go," she cried imperiously, "and prepare my hut." It was the High Priestess of the Flaming God; La, the queen of Opar, addressing slaves. Her regal mien, her commanding tones, wrought an instant change in the villagers, and La knew then that Tarzan was right in his assumption that they could be moved only through fear, for now they turned quickly, cowering like whipped dogs, and hastened to a nearby hut, which they quickly prepared for her, fetching fresh leaves and grasses for its floor, and fruit and nuts and plantains for her meal.

When all was ready, La clambered up the rope and through the circular opening in the floor of the hanging hut, which she found large and airy, and now reasonably clean. She drew the rope up after her and threw herself upon the soft bed they had prepared for her, and soon the gentle swaying of the swinging hut, the soft murmur of the leaves above her, the voices of the birds and insects combined with her own physical exhaustion to lull her into deep slumber.

CHAPTER X—MAD TREACHERY

To the northwest of the valley of Opar the smoke rose from the cook fires of a camp in which some hundred blacks and six whites were eating their evening meal. The negroes squatted sullen and morose, mumbling together in low tones over their meager fare, the whites, scowling and apprehensive, kept their firearms close at hand. One of them, a girl, and the only member of her sex in the party, was addressing her fellows:

"We have Adolph's stinginess and Esteban's braggadocio to thank for the condition in which we are," she said.

The fat Bluber shrugged his shoulder, the big Spaniard scowled.

"For vy," asked Adolph, "am I to blame?"

"You were too stingy to employ enough carriers. I told you at the time that we ought to have had two hundred blacks in our party, but you wanted to save a little money, and now what is the result? Fifty men carrying eighty pounds of gold apiece and the other carriers are overburdened with camp equipment, while there are scarce enough left for askari to guard us properly. We have to drive them like beasts to make any progress and to keep them from throwing away their loads, and they are fagged out and angry. They don't require much of an excuse to kill us all on the spot. On top of all this they are underfed. If we could keep their bellies filled we could probably keep them happy and reasonably contented, but I have learned enough about natives to know that if they are hungry they are neither happy nor contented, even in idleness. If Esteban had not bragged so much about his prowess as a hunter we should have brought enough provisions to last us through, but now, though we are barely started upon our return journey, we are upon less than half rations."

"I can't kill game when there isn't any game," growled the Spaniard.

"There is plenty of game," said Kraski, the Russian. "We see the tracks of it every day."

The Spaniard eyed him venomously. "If there is so much game," he said, "go out and get it yourself."

"I never claimed to be a hunter," replied Kraski, "though I could go out with a sling shot and a pea shooter and do as well as you have."

The Spaniard leaped to his feet menacingly, and instantly the Russian covered him with a heavy service revolver.

"Cut that business," cried the girl, sharply, leaping between them.

"Let the blighters fight," growled John Peebles. "If one of 'em kills the hother there'll be fewer to split the swag, and 'ere we are 'n that's that."

"For vy should ve quarrel?" demanded Bluber. "Dere is enough for all—over forty-tree t'ousand pounds apiece. Ven you get mad at me you call me a dirty Jew und say dat I am stingy, but Mein Gott! you Christians are vorser. You vould kill vun of your friends to get more money. Oi! Oi! tank Gott dat I am not a Christian."

"Shut up," growled Throck, "or we'll have forty-three thousand pounds more to divide."

Bluber eyed the big Englishman fearfully. "Come, come, Dick," he oozed, in his oiliest tones, "you vouldn't get mad at a leedle choke vould you, und me your best friend?"

"I'm sick of all this grousin'," said Throck. "I h'ain't no high-brow, I h'ain't nothin' but a pug. But I got sense enough to know that Flora's the only one in the bloomin' bunch whose brains wouldn't rattle around in a peanut shell. John, Bluber, Kraski and me, we're here because we could raise the money to carry out Flora's plan. The dago there" —and he indicated Esteban— "because his face and his figure filled the bill. There don't any of us need no brains for this work, and there ain't any of us got any more brains than we need. Flora's the brains of this outfit, and the sooner everyone understands that and takes orders from her, the better off we'll all be. She's been to Africa with this Lord Greystoke feller before—you wuz his wife's maid, wasn't you, Flora? And she knows somethin' about the country and the natives and the animals, and there don't none of us know nuttin'."

"Throck is right," said Kraski, quickly, "we've been muddling long enough. We haven't had a boss, and the thing to do is to make Flora boss from now on. If anyone can get us out of this, she can, and from the way those fellows over there are acting," and he nodded toward the blacks, "we'll be lucky if we ever get out with our skins, let alone taking any of the gold with us."

"Oi! Oi! You don't mean to leave the gold?" almost shrieked Bluber.

"I mean that we do whatever Flora thinks best," replied Kraski. "If she says to leave the gold, we'll leave it.

"That we do," seconded Throck.

"I'm for it," said Peebles. "Whatever Flora says goes."

The Spaniard nodded his assent sullenly.

"The rest of us are all for it, Bluber. How about you?" asked Kraski.

"O vell—sure—if you say so," said Bluber, "und as John says 'und here ve ain't und vat's dat.'"

"And now, Flora," said Peebles, "you're the big 'un. What you say goes. What'll we do next?"

"Very well," said the girl; "we shall camp here until these men are rested, and early tomorrow we'll start out intelligently and systematically, and get meat for them. With their help we can do it. When they are rested and well fed we will start on again for the coast, moving very slowly, so as not to tire them too much. This is my first plan, but it all hinges upon our ability to get meat. If we do not find it I shall bury the gold here, and we will do our best to reach the coast as quickly as possible. There we shall recruit new porters—twice as many as we have now —and purchase enough provisions to carry us in and out again. As we come back in, we will cache provisions at every camping place for our return trip, thus saving the necessity of carrying heavy loads all the way in and out again. In this way we can come out light, with twice as many porters as we actually need. And by working them in shifts we will travel much faster and there will be no grumbling. These are my two plans. I am not asking you what you think of them, because I do not care. You have made me chief, and I am going to run this from now on as I think best."

"Bully for you," roared Peebles; "that's the kind of talk I likes to hear."

"Tell the head man I want to see him, Carl," said the girl, turning to Kraski, and a moment later the Russian returned with a burly negro.

"Owaza," said the girl, as the black halted before her, "we are short of food and the men are burdened with loads twice as heavy as they should carry. Tell them that we shall wait here until they are rested and that tomorrow we shall all go out and hunt for meat. You will send your boys out under three good men, and they will act as beaters and drive the game in to us. In this way we should get plenty of meat, and when the men are rested and well fed we will move on slowly. Where game is plentiful we will hunt and rest. Tell them that if they do this and we reach the coast in safety and with all our loads, I shall pay them twice what they agreed to come for."

"Oi! Oi!" spluttered Bluber, "twice vat dey agreed to come for! Oh, Flora, vy not offer dem ten per cent? Dot vould be fine interest on their money.

"Shut up, you fool," snapped Kraski, and Bluber subsided, though he rocked back and forth, shaking his head in disapproval.

The black, who had presented himself for the interview with sullen and scowling demeanor, brightened visibly now. "I will tell them," he said, "and I think that you will have no more trouble."

"Good," said Flora, "go and tell them now," and the black turned and left.

"There," said the girl, with a sigh of relief, "I believe that we can see light ahead at last."

"Tvice vat ve promised to pay them!" bawled Bluber, "Oi! Oi!"

Early the following morning they prepared to set out upon the hunt. The blacks were now smiling and happy in anticipation of plenty of meat, and as they tramped off into the jungle they were singing gayly. Flora had divided them into three parties, each under a head man with explicit directions for the position each party was to take in the line of beaters. Others had been detailed to the whites as gun-bearers, while a small party of the askari were left behind to guard the camp. The whites, with the exception of Esteban, were armed with rifles. He alone seemed inclined to question Flora's authority, insisting that he preferred to hunt with spear and arrows in keeping with the part he was playing. The fact that, though he had hunted assiduously for weeks, yet had never brought in a single kill, was not sufficient to dampen his egotism. So genuinely had he entered his part that he really thought he was Tarzan of the Apes, and with such fidelity had he equipped himself in every detail, and such a master of the art of make-up was he, that, in conjunction with his splendid figure and his handsome face that were almost a counterpart of Tarzan's, it was scarcely to be wondered at that he almost fooled himself as successfully as he had fooled others, for there were men among the carriers who had known the great ape-man, and even these were deceived, though they wondered at the change in him, since in little things he did not deport himself as Tarzan, and in the matter of kills he was disappointing.

Flora Hawkes, who was endowed with more than a fair share of intelligence, realized that it would not be well to cross any of her companions unnecessarily, and so she permitted Esteban to hunt that morning in his own way, though some of the others grumbled a little at her decision.

"What is the difference?" she asked them, after the Spaniard had set out alone. "The chances are that he could use a rifle no better than he uses his spear and arrows. Carl and Dick are really the only shots among us, and it is upon them we depend principally for the success of our hunt today. Esteban's egotism has been so badly bumped that it is possible that he will go to the last extremity to make a kill today—let us hope that he is successful."

"I hope he breaks his fool neck," said Kraski. "He has served our purpose and we would be better off if we were rid of him."

The girl shook her head negatively. "No," she said, "we must not think or speak of anything of that kind. We went into this thing together, let us stick together until the end. If you are wishing that one of us is dead, how do you know that others are not wishing that you were dead?"

"I haven't any doubt but that Miranda wishes I were dead," replied Kraski. "I never go to bed at night without thinking that the damned greaser may try to stick a knife into me before morning. And it don't make me feel any kinder toward him to hear you defending him, Flora. You've been a bit soft on him from the start."

"If I have, it's none of your business," retorted the girl.

And so they started out upon their hunt, the Russian scowling and angry, harboring thoughts of vengeance or worse against Esteban, and Esteban, hunting through the jungle, was occupied with his hatred and his jealousy. His dark mind was open to every chance suggestion of a means for putting the other men of the party out of the way, and taking the woman and the gold for himself. He hated them all; in each he saw a possible rival for the affections of Flora, and in the death of each he saw not only one less suitor for the girl's affections, but forty-three thousand additional pounds to be divided among fewer people. His mind was thus occupied to the exclusion of the business of hunting, which should have occupied him solely, when he came through a patch of heavy underbrush, and stepped into the glaring sunlight of a large clearing, face to face with a party of some fifty magnificent ebon warriors. For just an instant Esteban stood frozen in a paralysis of terror, forgetting momentarily the part he was playing—thinking of himself only as a lone white man in the heart of savage Africa facing a large band of war-like natives—cannibals, perhaps. It was that moment of utter silence and inaction that saved him, for, as he stood thus before them, the Waziri saw in the silent, majestic figure their beloved lord in a characteristic pose.

"O Bwana, Bwana," cried one of the warriors, rushing forward, "it is indeed you, Tarzan of the Apes, Lord of the Jungle, whom we had given up as lost. We, your faithful Waziri, have been searching for you, and even now we were about to dare the dangers of Opar, fearing that you might have ventured there without us and had been captured."

The black, who had at one time accompanied Tarzan to London as a body servant, spoke broken English, an accomplishment of which he was inordinately proud, losing no opportunity to air his attainment before his less fortunate fellows. The fact that it had been he whom fate had chosen to act as spokesman was indeed a fortunate circumstance to Miranda. Although the latter had applied himself assiduously to mastering the dialect of the west coast carriers, he would have been hard put to it to carry on a conversation with one of them, while he understood nothing of the Waziri tongue. Flora had schooled him carefully and well in the lore of Tarzan, so that he realized now that he was in the presence of a band of the ape-man's faithful Waziri. Never before had he seen such magnificent blacks—clean-cut, powerful men, with intelligent faces and well molded features, appearing as much higher in the scale of evolution as were the west coast blacks above the apes.

Lucky indeed was Esteban Miranda that he was quick witted and a consummate actor. Otherwise must he have betrayed his terror and his chagrin upon learning that this band of Tarzan's fierce and faithful followers was in this part of the country. For a moment longer he stood in silence before them, gathering his wits, and then he spoke, realizing that his very life depended upon his plausibility. And as he thought a great light broke upon the shrewd brain of the unscrupulous Spaniard.

"Since I last saw you," he said, "I discovered that a party of white men had entered the country for the purpose of robbing the treasure vaults of Opar. I followed them until I found their camp, and then I came in search of you, for there are many of them and they have many ingots of gold, for they have already been to Opar. Follow me, and we will raid their camp and take the gold from them. Come!" and he turned back toward the camp that he had just quitted.

As they made their way along the jungle trail, Usula, the Waziri who had spoken English to him, walked at Esteban's side. Behind them the Spaniard could hear the other warriors speaking in their native tongue, no word of which he understood, and it occurred to him that his position would be most embarrassing should he be addressed in the Waziri language, which, of course, Tarzan must have understood perfectly. As he listened to the chatter of Usula his mind was working rapidly, and presently, as though it were an inspiration, there recurred to him the memory of an accident that had befallen Tarzan, which had been narrated to him by Flora—the story of the injury he had received in the treasure vaults of Opar upon the occasion that he had lost his memory because of a blow upon the head. Esteban wondered if he had committed himself too deeply at first to attribute to amnesia any shortcomings in the portrayal of the role he was acting. At its worst, however, it seemed to him the best that he could do. He turned suddenly upon Usula.

"Do you remember," he asked, "the accident that befell me in the treasure vaults of Opar, depriving me of my memory?"

"Yes, Bwana, I remember it well," replied the black.

"A similar accident has befallen me," said Esteban. "A great tree fell in my path, and in falling a branch struck me upon the head. It has not caused me to lose my memory entirely, but since then it is with difficulty that I recall many things, and there are others which I must have forgotten entirely, for I do not know your name, nor do I understand the words that my other Waziri are speaking about me."

Usula looked at him compassionately. "Ah, Bwana, sad indeed is the heart of Usula to hear that this accident has befallen you. Doubtless it will soon pass away as did the other, and in the meantime I, Usula, will be your memory for you."

"Good," said Esteban, "tell the others that they may understand, and tell them also that I have lost the memory of other things besides. I could not now find my way home without you, and my other senses are dull as well. But as you say, Usula, it will soon pass off, and I shall be myself again."

"Your faithful Waziri will rejoice indeed with the coming of that moment," said Usula.

As they approached the camp, Miranda cautioned Usula to warn his followers to silence, and presently he halted them at the outskirts of the clearing where they could attain a view of the boma and the tents, guarding which was a little band of a half-dozen askari.

"When they see our greater numbers they will make no resistance," said Esteban. "Let us surround the camp, therefore, and at a signal from me we will advance together, when you shall address them, saying that Tarzan of the Apes comes with his Waziri for the gold they have stolen, but that he will spare them if they will leave the country at once and never return."

Had it fulfilled his purpose as well, the Spaniard would have willingly ordered his Waziri to fall upon the men guarding the camp and destroy them all, but to his cunning brain had been born a cleverer scheme. He wanted these men to see him with the Waziri and to live to tell the others that they had seen him, and to repeat to Flora and her followers the thing that Esteban had in his mind to tell one of the askari, while the Waziri were gathering up the gold ingots from the camp.

In directing Usula to station his men about the camp, Esteban had him warn them that they were not to show themselves until he had crept out into the clearing and attracted the attention of the askari on guard. Fifteen minutes, perhaps, were consumed in stationing his men, and then Usula returned to Esteban to report that all was ready.

"When I raise my hand then you will know that they have recognized me and that you are to advance," Esteban cautioned him, and stepped forward slowly into the clearing. One of the askari saw him and recognized him as Esteban. The Spaniard took a few steps closer to the boma and then halted.

"I am Tarzan of the Apes," he said; "your camp is entirely surrounded by my warriors. Make no move against us and we shall not hurt you."

He waved his hand. Fifty stalwart Waziri stepped into view from the concealing verdure of the surrounding jungle. The askari eyed them in ill-concealed terror, fingering their rifles nervously.

"Do not shoot," cautioned Esteban, "or we shall slay you all." He approached more closely and his Waziri closed in about him, entirely surrounding the boma.

"Speak to them, Usula," said Esteban. The black stepped forward.

"We are the Waziri," he cried, "and this is Tarzan of the Apes, Lord of the Jungle, our master. We have come to recover the gold of Tarzan that you have stolen from the treasure vaults of Opar. This time we shall spare you on condition that you leave the country and never return. Tell this word to your masters; tell them that Tarzan watches, and that his Waziri watch with him. Lay down your rifles."

The askari, glad to escape so easily, complied with the demands of Usula, and a moment later the Waziri had entered the boma, and at Esteban's direction were gathering up the golden ingots. As they worked, Esteban approached one of the askari, whom he knew spoke broken English.

"Tell your master," he said, "to give thanks for the mercy of Tarzan who has exacted a toll of but one life for this invasion of his country and theft of his treasure. The creature who presumes to pose as Tarzan I have slain, and his body I shall take away with me and feed to the lions. Tell them that Tarzan forgives even their attempt to poison him upon the occasion that he visited their camp, but only upon the condition that they never return to Africa, and that they divulge the secret of Opar to no others. Tarzan watches and his Waziri watch, and no man may enter Africa without Tarzan's knowledge. Even before they left London I knew that they were coming. Tell them that."

It took but a few minutes for the Waziri to gather up the golden ingots, and before the askari had recovered from the surprise of their appearance, they had gone again into the jungle, with Tarzan, their master.

It was late in the afternoon before Flora and the four white men returned from their hunt, surrounded by happy, laughing blacks, bearing the fruits of a successful chase.

"Now that you are in charge, Flora," Kraski was saying, "fortune is smiling upon us indeed. We have enough meat here for several days, and with plenty of meat in their bellies they ought to make good progress."

"I vill say it myself dot t'ings look brighter," said Bluber.

"Blime, they do that," said Throck. "I'm tellin' yu Flora's a bright one."

"What the devil is this?" demanded Peebles. "What's wrong with them beggars?" And he pointed toward the boma which was now in sight, and from which the askari were issuing at a run, jabbering excitedly as they raced toward them.

"Tarzan of the Apes has been here," they cried excitedly. "He has been here with all his Waziri—a thousand great warriors—and though we fought, they overcame us, and taking the gold they went away. Tarzan of the Apes spoke strange words to me before they left. He said that he had killed one of your number who had dared to call himself Tarzan of the Apes. We do not understand it. He went away alone to hunt when you went in the morning, and he came back shortly with a thousand warriors, and he took all the gold and he threatened to kill us and you if you ever return to this country again.

"Vot, vot?" cried Bluber, "der gold iss gone? Oi! Oi!" And then they all commenced to ask questions at once until Flora silenced them.

"Come," she said to the leader of the askari, "we will return to the boma and then you shall tell me slowly and carefully all that has happened since we left."

She listened intently to his narrative, and then questioned him carefully upon various points several times. At last she dismissed him. Then she turned to her confederates.

"It is all clear to me," she said. "Tarzan recovered from the effects of the drug we administered. Then he followed us with his Waziri, caught Esteban and killed him and, finding the camp, has taken the gold away. We shall be fortunate indeed if we escape from Africa with our lives."

"Oi! Oi!" almost shrieked Bluber, "der dirty crook. He steals all our gold, und ve lose our two t'ousand pounds into the bargain. Oi! Oi!"

"Shut up, you dirty Jew," growled Throck. "If it hadn't a' been for you and the dago this 'ere thing would never a 'appened. With 'im abraggin' about 'is 'unting and not bein' able to kill anything, and you a-squeezin' every bloomin' hapenny, we're in a rotten mess—that we are. This 'ere Tarzan bounder he bumped off Esteban, which is the best work what 'e ever done. Too bloody bad you weren't 'ere to get it too, and what I got a good mind to do is to slit your throat meself."

"Stow the guff, Dick," roared Peebles; "it wasn't nobody's fault, as far as I can see. Instead of talkin' what we oughter do is to go after this 'ere Tarzan feller and take the bloomin' gold away from 'im."

Flora Hawkes laughed. "We haven't a chance in the world," she said. "I know this Tarzan bloke. If he was all alone we wouldn't be a match for him, but he's got a bunch of his Waziri with him, and there are no finer warriors in Africa than they. And they'd fight for him to the last man. You just tell Owaza that you're thinking of going after Tarzan of the Apes and his Waziri to take the gold away from them, and see how long it'd be before we wouldn't have a single nigger with us. The very name of Tarzan scares these west coast blacks out of a year's growth. They would sooner face the devil. No, sir, we've lost, and all we can do is to get out of the country, and thank our lucky stars if we manage to get out alive. The ape-man will watch us. I should not be surprised if he were watching us this minute." Her companions looked around apprehensively at this, casting nervous glances toward the jungle. "And he'd never let us get back to Opar for another load, even if we could prevail upon our blacks to return there."

"Two t'ousand pounds, two t'ousand pounds!" wailed Bluber. "Und all dis suit, vot it cost me twenty guineas vot I can't vear it again in England unless I go to a fancy dress ball, vich I never do."

Kraski had not spoken, but had sat with eyes upon the ground, listening to the others. Now he raised his head. "We have lost our gold," he said, and before we get back to England we stand to spend the balance of our two thousand pounds—in other words our expedition is a total loss. The rest of you may be satisfied to go back broke, but I am not. There are other things in Africa besides the gold of Opar, and when we leave the country there is no reason why we shouldn't take something with us that will repay us for our time and investment."

"What do you mean?" asked Peebles.

"I have spent a lot of time talking with Owaza," replied Kraski, "trying to learn their crazy language, and I have come to find out a lot about the old villain. He's as crooked as they make 'em, and if he were to be hanged for all his murders, he'd have to have more lives than a cat, but notwithstanding all that, he's a shrewd old fellow, and I've learned a lot more from him than just his monkey talk —I have learned enough, in fact, so that I feel safe in saying that if we stick together we can go out of Africa with a pretty good-sized stake. Personally, I haven't given up the gold of Opar yet. What we've lost, we've lost, but there's plenty left where that came from, and some day, after this blows over, I'm coming back to get my share."

"But how about this other thing?" asked Flora. "How can Owaza help us?"

"There's a little bunch of Arabs down here," explained Kraski, "stealing slaves and ivory. Owaza knows where they are working and where their main camp is. There are only a few of them, and their blacks are nearly all slaves who would turn on them in a minute. Now the idea is this: we have a big enough party to overpower them and take their ivory away from them if we can get their slaves to take our side. We don't want the slaves; we couldn't do anything with them if we had them, so we can promise them their freedom for their help, and give Owaza and his gang a share in the ivory."

"How do you know Owaza will help us?" asked Flora.

"The idea is his; that's the reason I know," replied Kraski.

"It sounds good to me," said Peebles; "I ain't fer goin' 'ome empty 'anded." And in turn the others signified their approval of the scheme.

CHAPTER XI—STRANGE INCENSE BURNS

As Tarzan carried the dead Bolgani from the village of the Gomangani, he set his steps in the direction of the building he had seen from the rim of the valley, the curiosity of the man overcoming the natural caution of the beast. He was traveling up wind and the odors wafted down to his nostrils told him that he was approaching the habitat of the Bolgani. Intermingled with the scent spoor of the gorilla-men was that of Gomangani and the odor of cooked food, and the suggestion of a heavily sweet scent, which the ape-man could connect only with burning incense, though it seemed impossible that such a fragrance could emanate from the dwellings of the Bolgani. Perhaps it came from the great edifice he had seen—a building which must have been constructed by human beings, and in which human beings might still dwell, though never among the multitudinous odors that assailed his nostrils did he once catch the faintest suggestion of the man scent of whites.

When he perceived from the increasing strength of their odor, that he was approaching close to the Bolgani, Tarzan took to the trees with his burden, that he might thus stand a better chance of avoiding discovery, and presently, through the foliage ahead, he saw a lofty wall, and, beyond, the outlines of the weird architecture of a strange and mysterious pile—outlines that suggested a building of another world, so unearthly were they, and from beyond the wall came the odor of the Bolgani and the fragrance of the incense, intermingled with the scent spoor of Numa, the lion. The jungle was cleared away for fifty feet outside the wall surrounding the building, so that there was no tree overhanging the wall, but Tarzan approached as closely as he could, while still remaining reasonably well concealed by the foliage. He had chosen a point at a sufficient height above the ground to permit him to see over the top of the wall.

The building within the enclosure was of great size, its different parts appearing to have been constructed at various periods, and each with utter disregard to uniformity, resulting in a conglomeration of connecting buildings and towers, no two of which were alike, though the whole presented a rather pleasing, if somewhat bizarre appearance. The building stood upon an artificial elevation about ten feet high, surrounded by a retaining wall of granite, a wide staircase leading to the ground level below. About the building were shrubbery and trees, some of the latter appearing to be of great antiquity, while one enormous tower was almost entirely covered by ivy. By far the most remarkable feature of the building, however, lay in its rich and barbaric ornamentation. Set into the polished granite of which it was composed was an intricate mosaic of gold and diamonds; glittering stones in countless thousands scintillated from facades, minarets, domes, and towers.

The enclosure, which comprised some fifteen or twenty acres, was occupied for the most part by the building. The terrace upon which it stood was devoted to walks, flowers, shrubs, and ornamental trees, while that part of the area below, which was within the range of Tarzan's vision, seemed to be given over to the raising of garden truck. In the garden and upon the terrace were naked blacks, such as he had seen in the village where he had left La. There were both men and women, and these were occupied with the care of growing things within the enclosure. Among them were several of the gorilla-like creatures such as Tarzan had slain in the village, but these performed no labor, devoting themselves, rather, it seemed, to directing the work of the blacks, toward whom their manner was haughty and domineering, sometimes even brutal. These gorilla-men were trapped in rich ornaments, similar to those upon the body which now rested in a crotch of the tree behind the ape-man.

As Tarzan watched with interest the scene below him, two Bolgani emerged from the main entrance, a huge portal, some thirty feet in width, and perhaps fifteen feet high. The two wore head-bands, supporting tall, white feathers. As they emerged they took post on either side of the entrance, and cupping their hands before their mouths gave voice to a series of shrill cries that bore a marked resemblance to trumpet calls. Immediately the blacks ceased work and hastened to the foot of the stairs descending from the terrace to the garden. Here they formed lines on either side of the stairway, and similarly the Bolgani formed two lines upon the terrace from the main portal to the stairway, forming a living aisle from one to the other. Presently from the interior of the building came other trumpet-like calls, and a moment later Tarzan saw the head of a procession emerging. First came four Bolgani abreast, each bedecked with an ornate feather headdress, and each carrying a huge bludgeon erect before him. Behind these came two trumpeters, and twenty feet behind the trumpeters paced a huge, black-maned lion, held in leash by four sturdy blacks, two upon either side, holding what appeared to be golden chains that ran to a scintillant diamond collar about the beast's neck. Behind the lion marched twenty more Bolgani, four abreast. These carried spears, but whether they were for the purpose of protecting the lion from the people or the people from the lion Tarzan was at a loss to know.

The attitude of the Bolgani lining either side of the way between the portal and the stairway indicated extreme deference, for they bent their bodies from their waists in a profound bow while Numa was passing between their lines. When the beast reached the top of the stairway the procession halted, and immediately the Gomangani ranged below prostrated themselves and placed their foreheads on the ground. Numa, who was evidently an old lion, stood with lordly mien surveying the prostrate humans before him. His evil eyes glared glassily, the while he bared his tusks in a savage grimace, and from his deep lungs rumbled forth an ominous roar, at the sound of which the Gomangani trembled in unfeigned terror. The ape-man knit his brows in thought. Never before had he been called upon to witness so remarkable a scene of the abasement of man before a beast. Presently the procession continued upon its way descending the staircase and turning to the right along a path through the garden, and when it had passed them the Gomangani and the Bolgani arose and resumed their interrupted duties.

Tarzan remained in his concealment watching them, trying to discover some explanation for the strange, paradoxical conditions that he had witnessed. The lion, with his retinue, had turned the far corner of the palace and disappeared from sight. What was he to these people, to these strange creatures? What did he represent? Why this topsy-turvy arrangement of species? Here man ranked lower than the half-beast, and above all, from the deference that had been accorded him, stood a true beast—a savage carnivore.

He had been occupied with his thoughts and his observations for some fifteen minutes following the disappearance of Numa around the eastern end of the palace, when his attention was attracted to the opposite end of the structure by the sound of other shrill trumpet calls. Turning his eyes in that direction, he saw the procession emerging again into view, and proceeding toward the staircase down which they had entered the garden. Immediately the notes of the shrill call sounded upon their ears the Gomangani and the Bolgani resumed their original positions from below the foot of the staircase to the entrance to the palace, and once again was homage paid to Numa as he made his triumphal entry into the building.

Tarzan of the Apes ran his fingers through his mass of tousled hair, but finally he was forced to shake his head in defeat. He could find no explanation whatsoever for all that he had witnessed. His curiosity, however, was so keenly piqued that he determined to investigate the palace and surrounding grounds further before continuing on his way in search of a trail out of the valley.

Leaving the body of Bolgani where he had cached it, he started slowly to circle the building that he might examine it from all sides from the concealing foliage of the surrounding forest. He found the architecture equally unique upon all sides, and that the garden extended entirely around the building, though a portion upon the south side of the palace was given over to corrals and pens in which were kept numerous goats and a considerable flock of chickens. Upon this side, also, were several hundred swinging, beehive huts, such as he had seen in the native village of the Gomangani. These he took to be the quarters of the black slaves, who performed all the arduous and menial labor connected with the palace.

The lofty granite wall which surrounded the entire enclosure was pierced by but a single gate which opened opposite the east end of the palace. This gate was large and of massive construction, appearing to have been built to withstand the assault of numerous and well-armed forces. So strong did it appear that the ape-man could not but harbor the opinion that it had been constructed to protect the interior against forces equipped with heavy battering rams. That such a force had ever existed within the vicinity in historic times seemed most unlikely, and Tarzan conjectured, therefore, that the wall and the gate were of almost unthinkable antiquity, dating, doubtless, from the forgotten age of the Atlantians, and constructed, perhaps, to protect the builders of the Palace of Diamonds from the well-armed forces that had come from Atlantis to work the gold mines of Opar and to colonize central Africa.

While the wall, the gate, and the palace itself, suggested in many ways almost unbelievable age, yet they were in such an excellent state of repair that it was evident that they were still inhabited by rational and intelligent creatures; while upon the south side Tarzan had seen a new tower in process of construction, where a number of blacks working under the direction of Bolgani were cutting and shaping granite blocks and putting them in place.

Tarzan had halted in a tree near the east gate to watch the life passing in and out of the palace grounds beneath the ancient portal, and as he watched, a long cavalcade of powerful Gomangani emerged from the forest and entered the enclosure. Swung in hides between two poles, this party was carrying rough-hewn blocks of granite, four men to a block. Two or three Bolgani accompanied the long line of carriers, which was preceded and followed by a detachment of black warriors, armed with battle-axes and spears. The demeanor and attitude of the black porters, as well as of the Bolgani, suggested to the ape-man nothing more nor less than a caravan of donkeys, plodding their stupid way at the behest of theirdrivers. If one lagged he was prodded with the point of a spear or struck with its haft. There was no greater brutality shown than in the ordinary handling of beasts of burden the world around, nor in the demeanor of the blacks was there any more indication of objection or revolt than you see depicted upon the faces of a long line of burden-bearing mules; to all intents and purposes they were dumb, driven cattle. Slowly they filed through the gate way and disappeared from sight.

A few moments later another party came out of the forest and passed into the palace grounds. This consisted of fully fifty armed Bolgani and twice as many black warriors with spears and axes. Entirely surrounded by these armed creatures were four brawny porters, carrying a small litter, upon which was fastened an ornate chest about two feet wide by four feet long, with a depth of approximately two feet. The chest itself was of some dark, weather-worn wood, and was reinforced by bands and corners of what appeared to be virgin gold in which were set many diamonds. What the chest contained Tarzan could not, of course, conceive, but that it was considered of great value was evidenced by the precautions for safety with which it had been surrounded. The chest was borne directly into the huge, ivy-covered tower at the northeast corner of the palace, the entrance to which, Tarzan now first observed, was secured by doors as large and heavy as the east gate itself.

At the first opportunity that he could seize to accomplish it undiscovered, Tarzan swung across the jungle trail and continued through the trees to that one in which he had left the body of the Bolgani. Throwing this across his shoulder he returned to a point close above the trail near the east gate, and seizing upon a moment when there was a lull in the traffic he hurled the body as close to the portal as possible.

"Now," thought the ape-man, "let them guess who slew their fellow if they can."

Making his way toward the southeast, Tarzan approached the mountains which lie back of the Valley of the Palace of Diamonds. He had often to make detours to avoid native villages and to keep out of sight of the numerous parties of Bolgani that seemed to be moving in all directions through the forest. Late in the afternoon he came out of the hills into full view of the mountains beyond—rough, granite hills they were, whose precipitous peaks arose far above the timber line. Directly before him a well-marked trail led into a canyon, which he could see wound far upward toward the summit. This, then, would be as good a place to commence his investigations as another. And so, seeing that the coast was clear, the ape-man descended from the trees, and taking advantage of the underbrush bordering the trail, made his way silently, yet swiftly, into the hills. For the most part he was compelled to worm his way through thickets, for the trail was in constant use by Gomangani and Bolgani, parties passing up it empty-handed and, returning, bearing blocks of granite. As he advanced more deeply into the hills the heavy underbrush gave way to a lighter growth of scrub, through which he could pass with far greater ease though with considerable more risk of discovery. However, the instinct of the beast that dominated Tarzan's jungle craft permitted him to find cover where another would have been in full view of every enemy. Half way up the mountain the trail passed through a narrow gorge, not more than twenty feet wide and eroded from solid granite cliffs. Here there was no concealment whatsoever, and the ape-man realized that to enter it would mean almost immediate discovery. Glancing about, he saw that by making a slight detour he could reach the summit of the gorge, where, amid tumbled, granite boulders and stunted trees and shrubs, he knew that he could find sufficient concealment, and perhaps a plainer view of the trail beyond.

Nor was he mistaken, for, when he had reached a vantage point far above the trail, he saw ahead an open pocket in the mountain, the cliffs surrounding which were honeycombed with numerous openings, which, it seemed to Tarzan, could be naught else than the mouths of tunnels. Rough wooden ladders reached to some of them, closer to the base of the cliffs, while from others knotted ropes dangled to the ground below. Out of these tunnels emerged men carrying little sacks of earth, which they dumped in a common pile beside a rivulet which ran through the gorge. Here other blacks, supervised by Bolgani, were engaged in washing the dirt, but what they hoped to find or what they did find, Tarzan could not guess.

Along one side of the rocky basin many other blacks were engaged in quarrying the granite from the cliffs, which had been cut away through similar operations into a series of terraces running from the floor of the basin to the summit of the cliff. Here naked blacks toiled with primitive tools under the supervision of savage Bolgani. The activities of the quarrymen were obvious enough, but what the others were bringing from the mouths of the tunnels Tarzan could not be positive, though the natural assumption was that it was gold. Where, then, did they obtain their diamonds? Certainly not from these solid granite cliffs.

A few minutes' observation convinced Tarzan that the trail he had followed from the forest ended in this little cul-de-sac, and so he sought a way upward and around it, in search of a pass across the range.

The balance of that day and nearly all the next he devoted to his efforts in this direction, only in the end to be forced to admit that there was no egress from the valley upon this side. To points far above the timber line he made his way, but there, always, he came face to face with sheer, perpendicular cliffs of granite towering high above him, upon the face of which not even the ape-man could find foothold. Along the southern and eastern sides of the basin he carried his investigation, but with similar disappointing results, and then at last he turned his steps back toward the forest with the intention of seeking a way out through the valley of Opar with La, after darkness had fallen.

The sun had just risen when Tarzan arrived at the native village in which he had left La, and no sooner did his eyes rest upon it than he became apprehensive that something was amiss, for, not only was the gate wide open but there was no sign of life within the palisade, nor was there any movement of the swinging huts that would indicate that they were occupied. Always wary of ambush, Tarzan reconnoitered carefully before descending into the village. To his trained observation it became evident that the village had been deserted for at least twenty-four hours. Running to the hut in which La had been hidden he hastily ascended the rope and examined the interior—it was vacant, nor was there any sign of the High Priestess. Descending to the ground, the ape-man started to make a thorough investigation of the village in search of clews to the fate of its inhabitants and of La. He had examined the interiors of several huts when his keen eyes noted a slight movement of one of the swinging, cage-like habitations some distance from him. Quickly he crossed the intervening space, and as he approached the hut he saw that no rope trailed from its doorway. Halting beneath, Tarzan raised his face to the aperture, through which nothing but the roof of the hut was visible.

"Gomangani," he cried, "it is I, Tarzan of the Apes. Come to the opening and tell me what has become of your fellows and of my mate, whom I left here under the protection of your warriors."

There was no answer, and again Tarzan called, for he was positive that someone was hiding in the hut.

"Come down," he called again, "or I will come up after you."

Still there was no reply. A grim smile touched the ape-man's lips as he drew his hunting knife from its sheath and placed it between his teeth, and then, with a cat-like spring, leaped for the opening, and catching its sides, drew his body up into the interior of the hut.

If he had expected opposition, he met with none, nor in the dimly lighted interior could he at first distinguish any presence, though, when his eyes became accustomed to the semi-darkness, he descried a bundle of leaves and grasses lying against the opposite wall of the structure. Crossing to these he tore them aside revealing the huddled form of a terrified woman. Seizing her by a shoulder he drew her to a sitting position.

"What has happened?" he demanded. "Where are the villagers? Where is my mate?"

"Do not kill me! Do not kill me!" she cried. "It was not I. It was not my fault."

"I do not intend to kill you," replied Tarzan. "Tell me the truth and you shall be safe."

"The Bolgani have taken them away," cried the woman. "They came when the sun was low upon the day that you arrived, and they were very angry, for they had found the body of their fellow outside the gate of the Palace of Diamonds. They knew that he had come here to our village, and no one had seen him alive since he had departed from the palace. They came, then, and threatened and tortured our people, until at last the warriors told them all. I hid. I do not know why they did not find me. But at last they went away, taking all the others with them; taking your mate, too. They will never come back."

"You think that the Bolgani will kill them?" asked Tarzan.

"Yes," she replied, "they kill all who displease them."

Alone, now, and relieved of the responsibility of La, Tarzan might easily make his way by night through the valley of Opar and to safety beyond the barrier. But perhaps such a thought never entered his head. Gratitude and loyalty were marked characteristics of the ape-man. La had saved him from the fanaticism and intrigue of her people. She had saved him at a cost of all that was most dear to her, power and position, peace and safety. She had jeopardized her life for him, and become an exile from her own country. The mere fact then that the Bolgani had taken her with the possible intention of slaying her, was not sufficient for the ape-man. He must know whether or not she lived, and if she lived he must devote his every energy to winning her release and her eventual escape from the dangers of this valley.

Tarzan spent the day reconnoitering outside the palace grounds, seeking an opportunity of gaining entrance without detection, but this he found impossible inasmuch as there was never a moment that there were not Gomangani or Bolgani in the outer garden. But with the approach of darkness the great east gate was closed, and the inmates of the huts and palace withdrew within their walls, leaving not even a single sentinel without—a fact that indicated clearly that the Bolgani had no reason to apprehend an attack. The subjugation of the Gomangani, then, was apparently complete, and so the towering wall surrounding their palace, which was more than sufficient to protect them from the inroads of lions, was but the reminder of an ancient day when a once powerful, but now vanished, enemy threatened their peace and safety.

When darkness had finally settled Tarzan approached the gate, and throwing the noose of his grass rope over one of the carved lions that capped the gate posts, ascended quickly to the summit of the wall, from where he dropped lightly into the garden below. To ensure an avenue for quick escape in the event that he found La, he unlatched the heavy gates and swung them open. Then he crept stealthily toward the ivy-covered east tower, which he had chosen after a day of investigation as offering easiest ingress to the palace. The success of his plan hinged largely upon the age and strength of the ivy which grew almost to the summit of the tower, and, to his immense relief, he found that it would easily support his weight.

Far above the ground, near the summit of the tower, he had seen from the trees surrounding the palace an open window, which, unlike the balance of those in this part of the palace, was without bars. Dim lights shone from several of the tower windows, as from those of other parts of the palace. Avoiding these lighted apertures, Tarzan ascended quickly, though carefully, toward the unbarred window above, and as he reached it and cautiously raised his eyes above the level of the sill, he was delighted to find that it opened into an unlighted chamber, the interior of which, however, was so shrouded in darkness that he could discern nothing within. Drawing himself carefully to the level of the sill he crept quietly into the apartment beyond. Groping through the blackness, he cautiously made the rounds of the room, which he found to contain a carved bedstead of peculiar design, a table, and a couple of benches. Upon the bedstead were stuffs of woven material, thrown over the softly tanned pelts of antelopes and leopards.

Opposite the window through which he had entered was a closed door. This he opened slowly and silently, until, through a tiny aperture he could look out upon a dimly lighted corridor or circular hallway, in the center of which was an opening about four feet in diameter, passing through which and disappearing beyond a similar opening in the ceiling directly above was a straight pole with short crosspieces fastened to it at intervals of about a foot— quite evidently the primitive staircase which gave communication between the various floors of the tower. Three upright columns, set at equal intervals about the circumference of the circular opening in the center of the floor helped to support the ceiling above. Around the outside of this circular hallway there were other doors, similar to that opening into the apartment in which he was.

Hearing no noise and seeing no evidence of another than himself, Tarzan opened the door and stepped into the hallway. His nostrils were now assailed strongly by the same heavy fragrance of incense that had first greeted him upon his approach to the palace several days before. In the interior of the tower, however, it was much more powerful, practically obliterating all other odors, and placing upon the ape-man an almost prohibitive handicap in his search for La. In fact as he viewed the doors upon this single stage of the tower, he was filled with consternation at the prospect of the well-nigh impossible task that confronted him. To search this great tower alone, without any assistance whatever from his keen sense of scent, seemed impossible of accomplishment, if he were to take even the most ordinary precautions against detection.

The ape-man's self-confidence was in no measure blundering egotism. Knowing his limitations, he knew that he would have little or no chance against even a few Bolgani were he to be discovered within their palace, where all was familiar to them and strange to him. Behind him was the open window, and the silent jungle night, and freedom. Ahead danger, predestined failure; and, quite likely, death. Which should he choose? For a moment he stood in silent thought, and then, raising his head and squaring his great shoulders, he shook his black locks defiantly and stepped boldly toward the nearest door. Room after room he had investigated until he had made the entire circle of the landing, but in so far as La or any clew to her were concerned his search was fruitless. He found quaint furniture and rugs and tapestries, and ornaments of gold and diamonds, and in one dimly lighted chamber he came upon a sleeping Bolgani, but so silent were the movements of the ape-man that the sleeper slept on undisturbed, even though Tarzan passed entirely around his bed, which was set in the center of the chamber, and investigated a curtained alcove beyond.

Having completed the rounds of this floor, Tarzan determined to work upward first and then, returning, investigate the lower stages later. Pursuant to this plan, therefore, he ascended the strange stairway. Three landings he passed before he reached the upper floor of the tower. Circling each floor was a ring of doors, all of which were closed, while dimly lighting each landing were feebly burning cressets—shallow, golden bowls—containing what appeared to be tallow, in which floated a tow-like wick.

Upon the upper landing there were but three doors, all of which were closed. The ceiling of this hallway was the dome-like roof of the tower, in the center of which was another circular opening, through which the stairway protruded into the darkness of the night above.

As Tarzan opened the door nearest him it creaked upon its hinges, giving forth the first audible sound that had resulted from his investigations up to this point. The interior of the apartment before him was unlighted, and as Tarzan stood there in the entrance in statuesque silence for a few seconds following the creaking of the hinge, he was suddenly aware of movement—of the faintest shadow of a sound—behind him. Wheeling quickly he saw the figure of a man standing in an open doorway upon the opposite side of the landing.

CHAPTER XII—THE GOLDEN INGOTS

Esteban Miranda had played the role of Tarzan of the Apes with the Waziri as his audience for less than twenty-four hours when he began to realize that, even with the lee-way that his supposedly injured brain gave him, it was going to be a very difficult thing to carry on the deception indefinitely. In the first place Usula did not seem at all pleased at the idea of merely taking the gold away from the intruders and then running from them. Nor did his fellow warriors seem any more enthusiastic over the plan than he. As a matter of fact they could not conceive that any number of bumps upon the head could render their Tarzan of the Apes a coward, and to run away from these west coast blacks and a handful of inexperienced whites seemed nothing less than cowardly.

Following all this, there had occurred in the afternoon that which finally decided the Spaniard that he was building for himself anything other than a bed of roses, and that the sooner he found an excuse for quitting the company of the Waziri the greater would be his life expectancy.

They were passing through rather open jungle at the time. The brush was not particularly heavy and the trees were at considerable distances apart, when suddenly, without warning, a rhinoceros charged them. To the consternation of the Waziri, Tarzan of the Apes turned and fled for the nearest tree the instant his eyes alighted upon charging Buto. In his haste Esteban tripped and fell, and when at last he reached the tree instead of leaping agilely into the lower branches, he attempted to shin up the huge bole as a schoolboy shins up a telegraph pole, only to slip and fall back again to the ground.

In the meantime Buto, who charges either by scent or hearing, rather than by eyesight, his powers of which are extremely poor, had been distracted from his original direction by one of the Waziri, and after missing the fellow had gone blundering on to disappear in the underbrush beyond.

When Esteban finally arose and discovered that the rhinoceros was gone, he saw surrounding him a semi-circle of huge blacks, upon whose faces were written expressions of pity and sorrow, not unmingled, in some instances, with a tinge of contempt. The Spaniard saw that he had been terrified into a practically irreparable blunder, yet he seized despairingly upon the only excuse he could conjure up.

"My poor head," he cried, pressing both palms to his temples.

"The blow was upon your head, Bwana," said Usula, "and your faithful Waziri thought that it was the heart of their master that knew no fear."

Esteban made no reply, and in silence they resumed their march. In silence they continued until they made camp before dark upon the bank of the river just above a waterfall. During the afternoon Esteban had evolved a plan of escape from his dilemma, and no sooner had he made camp than he ordered the Waziri to bury the treasure.

"We shall leave it here," he said, "and tomorrow we shall set forth in search of the thieves, for I have decided to punish them. They must be taught that they may not come into the jungle of Tarzan with impunity. It was only the injury to my head that prevented me from slaying them immediately I discovered their perfidy."

This attitude pleased the Waziri better. They commenced to see a ray of hope. Once again was Tarzan of the Apes becoming Tarzan. And so it was that with lighter hearts and a new cheerfulness they set forth the next morning in search of the camp of the Englishmen, and by shrewd guessing on Usula's part they cut across the jungle to intercept the probable line of march of the Europeans to such advantage that they came upon them just as they were making camp that night. Long before they reached them they smelled the smoke of their fires and heard the songs and chatter of the west coast carriers.

Then it was that Esteban gathered the Waziri about him. "My children," he said, addressing Usula in English, "these strangers have come here to wrong Tarzan. To Tarzan, then, belongs the vengeance. Go, therefore, and leave me to punish my enemies alone and in my own way. Return home, leave the gold where it is, for it will be a long time before I shall need it."

The Waziri were disappointed, for this new plan did not at all accord with their desires, which contemplated a cheerful massacre of the west coast blacks. But as yet the man before them was Tarzan, their Big Bwana, to whom they had never failed in implicit obedience. For a few moments following Esteban's declaration of his intention, they stood in silence shifting uneasily, and then at last they commenced to speak to one another in Waziri. What they said the Spaniard did not know, but evidently they were urging something upon Usula, who presently turned toward him.

"Oh, Bwana," cried the black. "How can we return home to the Lady Jane and tell her that we left you injured and alone to face the rifles of the white men and their askari? Do not ask us to do it, Bwana. If you were yourself we should not fear for your safety, but since the injury to your head you have not been the same, and we fear to leave you alone in the jungle. Let us, then, your faithful Waziri, punish these people, after which we will take you home in safety, where you may be cured of the evils that have fallen upon you."

The Spaniard laughed. "I am entirely recovered," he said, "and I am in no more danger alone than I would be with you," which he knew, even better than they, was but a mild statement of the facts. "You will obey my wishes," he continued sternly. "Go back at once the way that we have come. After you have gone at least two miles you may make camp for the night, and in the morning start out again for home. Make no noise, I do not want them to know that I am here. Do not worry about me. I am all right, and I shall probably overtake you before you reach home. Go!"

Sorrowfully the Waziri turned back upon the trail they had just covered and a moment later the last of them disappeared from the sight of the Spaniard.

With a sigh of relief Esteban Miranda turned toward the camp of his own people. Fearing that to surprise them suddenly might invite a volley of shots from the askari he whistled, and then called aloud as he approached.

"It is Tarzan!" cried the first of the blacks who saw him. "Now indeed shall we all be killed."

Esteban saw the growing excitement among the carriers and askari—he saw the latter seize their rifles and that they were fingering the triggers nervously.

"It is I, Esteban Miranda," he called aloud. "Flora! Flora, tell those fools to lay aside their rifles."

The whites, too, were standing watching him, and at the sound of his voice Flora turned toward the blacks. "It is all right," she said, "that is not Tarzan. Lay aside your rifles."

Esteban entered the camp, smiling. "Here I am," he said.

"We thought that you were dead," said Kraski. "Some of these fellows said that Tarzan said that he had killed you."

"He captured me," said Esteban, "but as you see he did not kill me. I thought that he was going to, but he did not, and finally he turned me loose in the jungle. He may have thought that I could not survive and that he would accomplish his end just as surely without having my blood upon his hands."

"'E must have knowed you," said Peebles. "You'd die, all right, if you were left alone very long in the jungle— you'd starve to death."

Esteban made no reply to the sally but turned toward Flora. "Are you not glad to see me, Flora?" he asked.

The girl shrugged her shoulders. "What is the difference?" she asked. "Our expedition is a failure. Some of them think you were largely to blame." She nodded her head in the general direction of the other whites.

The Spaniard scowled. None of them cared very much to see him. He did not care about the others, but he had hoped that Flora would show some enthusiasm about his return. Well, if she had known what he had in his mind, she might have been happier to see him, and only too glad to show some kind of affection. But she did not know. She did not know that Esteban Miranda had hidden the golden ingots where he might go another day and get them. It had been his intention to persuade her to desert the others, and then, later, the two would return and recover the treasure, but now he was piqued and offended—none of them should have a shilling of it— he would wait until they left Africa and then he would return and take it all for himself. The only fly in the ointment was the thought that the Waziri knew the location of the treasure, and that, sooner or later, they would return with Tarzan and get it. This weak spot in his calculations must be strengthened, and to strengthen it he must have assistance which would mean sharing his secret with another, but whom?

Outwardly oblivious of the sullen glances of his companions he took his place among them. It was evident to him that they were far from being glad to see him, but just why he did not know, for he had not heard of the plan that Kraski and Owaza had hatched to steal the loot of the ivory raiders, and that their main objection to his presence was the fear that they would be compelled to share the loot with him. It was Kraski who first voiced the thought that was in the minds of all but Esteban.

"Miranda," he said, "it is the consensus of opinion that you and Bluber are largely responsible for the failure of our venture. We are not finding fault. I just mention it as a fact. But since you have been away we have struck upon a plan to take something out of Africa that will partially recompense us for the loss of the gold. We have worked the thing all out carefully and made our plans. We don't need you to carry them out. We have no objection to your coming along with us, if you want to, for company, but we want to have it understood from the beginning that you are not to share in anything that we get out of this."

The Spaniard smiled and waved a gesture of unconcern. "It is perfectly all right," he said. "I shall ask for nothing. I would not wish to take anything from any of you." And he grinned inwardly as he thought of the more than quarter of a million pounds in gold which he would one day take out of Africa for himself, alone. At this unexpected attitude of acquiescence upon

Esteban's part the others were greatly relieved, and immediately the entire atmosphere of constraint was removed.

"You're a good fellow, Esteban," said Peebles. "I've been sayin' right along that you'd want to do the right thing, and I want to say that I'm mighty glad to see you back here safe an' sound. I felt terrible when I 'eard you was croaked, that I did."

"Yes," said Bluber, "John he feel so bad he cry himself to sleep every night, ain't it, John?"

"Don't try to start nothin', Bluber," growled Peebles, glaring at the Jew.

"I vasn't commencing to start nodding," replied Adolph, seeing that the big Englishman was angry; "of course ve vere all sorry dat ve t'ought Esteban was killed und ve is all glad dot he is back."

"And that he don't want any of the swag," added Throck.

"Don't worry," said Esteban, "If I get back to London I'll be happy enough—I've had enough of Africa to last me all the rest of my life."

Before he could get to sleep that night, the Spaniard spent a wakeful hour or two trying to evolve a plan whereby he might secure the gold absolutely to himself, without fear of its being removed by the Waziri later. He knew that he could easily find the spot where he had buried it and remove it to another close by, provided that he could return immediately over the trail along which Usula had led them that day, and he could do this alone, ensuring that no one but himself would know the new location of the hiding place of the gold, but he was equally positive that he could never again return later from the coast and find where he had hidden it. This meant that he must share his secret with another—one familiar with the country who could find the spot again at any time and from any direction. But who was there whom he might trust! In his mind he went carefully over the entire personnel of their safari, and continually his mind reverted to a single individual—Owaza. He had no confidence in the wily old scoundrel's integrity, but there was no other who suited his purpose as well, and finally he was forced to the conclusion that he must share his secret with this black, and depend upon avarice rather than honor for his protection. He could repay the fellow well—make him rich beyond his wildest dreams, and this the Spaniard could well afford to do in view of the tremendous fortune at stake. And so he fell asleep dreaming of what gold, to the value of over a quarter of a million pounds sterling, would accomplish in the gay capitals of the world.

The following morning while they were breakfasting, Esteban mentioned casually that he had passed a large herd of antelope not far from their camp the previous day, and suggested that he take four or five men and do a little hunting, joining the balance of the party at camp that night. No one raised any objection, possibly for the reason that they assumed that the more he hunted and the further from the safari he went the greater the chances of his being killed, a contingency that none of them would have regretted, since at heart they had neither liking nor trust for him.

"I will take Owaza," he said. "He is the cleverest hunter of them all, and five or six men of his choosing." But later, when he approached Owaza, the black interposed objections to the hunt.

"We have plenty of meat for two days," he said. "Let us go on as fast as we can, away from the land of the Waziri and Tarzan. I can find plenty of game anywhere between here and the coast. March for two days, and then I will hunt with you."

"Listen," said Esteban, in a whisper. "It is more than antelope that I would hunt. I cannot tell you here in camp, but when we have left the others I will explain. It will pay you better to come with me today than all the ivory you can hope to get from the raiders." Owaza cocked an attentive ear and scratched his woolly head.

"It is a good day to hunt, Bwana," he said. "I will come with you and bring five boys."

After Owaza had planned the march for the main party and arranged for the camping place for the night, so that he and the Spaniard could find them again, the hunting party set out upon the trail that Usula had followed from the buried treasure the preceding day. They had not gone far before Owaza discovered the fresh spoor of the Waziri.

"Many men passed here late yesterday," he said to Esteban, eyeing the Spaniard quizzically.

"I saw nothing of them," replied the latter. "They must have come this way after I passed."

"They came almost to our camp, and then they turned about and went away again," said Owaza. "Listen, Bwana, I carry a rifle and you shall march ahead of me. If these tracks were made by your people, and you are leading me into ambush, you shall be the first to die."

"Listen, Owaza," said Esteban, "we are far enough from camp now so that I may tell you all. These tracks were made by the Waziri of Tarzan of the Apes, who buried the gold for me a day's march from here. I have sent them home, and I wish you to go back with me and move the gold to another hiding place. After these others have gotten their ivory and returned to England, you and I will come back and get the gold, and then, indeed, shall you be well rewarded."

"Who are you, then?" asked Owaza. "Often have I doubted that you are Tarzan of the Apes. The day that we left the camp outside of Opar one of my men told me that you had been poisoned by your own people and left in the camp. He said that he saw it with his own eyes—your body lying hidden behind some bushes—and yet you were with us upon the march that day. I thought that he lied to me, but I saw the consternation in his face when he saw you, and so I have often wondered if there were two Tarzans of the Apes."

"I am not Tarzan of the Apes," said Esteban. "It was Tarzan of the Apes who was poisoned in our camp by the others. But they only gave him something that would put him to sleep for a long time, possibly with the hope that he would be killed by wild animals before he awoke. Whether or not he still lives we do not know. Therefore you have nothing to fear from the Waziri or Tarzan on my account, Owaza, for I want to keep out of their way even more than you."

The black nodded. "Perhaps you speak the truth," he said, but still he walked behind, with his rifle always ready in his hand.

They went warily, for fear of overtaking the Waziri, but shortly after passing the spot where the latter had camped they saw that they had taken another route and that there was now no danger of coming in contact with them.

When they had reached a point within about a mile of the spot where the gold had been buried, Esteban told Owaza to have his boys remain there while they went ahead alone to effect the transfer of the ingots.

"The fewer who know of this," he said to the black, "the safer we shall be."

"The Bwana speaks words of wisdom," replied the wily black.

Esteban found the spot near the waterfall without difficulty, and upon questioning Owaza he discovered that the latter knew the location perfectly, and would have no difficulty in coming directly to it again from the coast. They transferred the gold but a short distance, concealing it in a heavy thicket near the edge of the river, knowing that it would be as safe from discovery there as though they had transported it a hundred miles, for the chances were extremely slight that the

Waziri or anyone else who should learn of its original hiding place would imagine that anyone would go to the trouble of removing it but a matter of a hundred yards.

When they had finished Owaza looked at the sun.

"We will never reach camp tonight," he said, "and we will have to travel fast to overtake them even tomorrow."

"I did not expect to," replied Esteban, "but I could not tell them that. If we never find them again I shall be satisfied." Owaza grinned. In his crafty mind an idea was formed.

"Why," he thought, "risk death in a battle with the Arab ivory raiders on the chance of securing a few tusks, when all this gold awaits only transportation to the coast to be ours?"

CHAPTER XIII—A STRANGE, FLAT TOWER

Tarzan, turning, discovered the man standing behind him on the top level of the ivy covered east tower of the Palace of Diamonds. His knife leaped from its sheath at the touch of his quick fingers. But almost simultaneously his hand dropped to his side, and he stood contemplating the other, with an expression of incredulity upon his face that but reflected a similar emotion registered upon the countenance of the stranger. For what Tarzan saw was no Bolgani, nor a Gomangani, but a white man, bald and old and shriveled, with a long, white beard—a white man, naked but for barbaric ornaments of gold spangles and diamonds.

"God!" exclaimed the strange apparition.

Tarzan eyed the other quizzically. That single English word opened up such tremendous possibilities for conjecture as baffled the mind of the ape-man.

"What are you? Who are you?" continued the old man, but this time in the dialect of the great apes.

"You used an English word a moment ago," said Tarzan. "Do you speak that language?" Tarzan himself spoke in English.

"Ah, dear God!" cried the old man, "that I should have lived to hear that sweet tongue again." And he, too, now spoke in English, halting English, as might one who was long unaccustomed to voicing the language.

"Who are you?" asked Tarzan, "and what are you doing here?"

"It is the same question that I asked you," replied the old man. "Do not be afraid to answer me. You are evidently an Englishman, and you have nothing to fear from me."

"I am here after a woman, captured by the Bolgani," replied Tarzan.

The other nodded. "Yes," he said, "I know. She is here."

"Is she safe?" asked Tarzan.

"She has not been harmed. She will be safe until tomorrow or the next day," replied the old man. "But who are you, and how did you find your way here from the outer world?"

"I am Tarzan of the Apes," replied the ape-man. "I came into this valley looking for a way out of the valley of Opar where the life of my companion was in danger. And you?"

"I am an old man," replied the other, "and I have been here ever since I was a boy. I was a stowaway on the ship that brought Stanley to Africa after the establishment of the station on Stanley Pool, and I came into the interior with him. I went out from camp to hunt, alone, one day. I lost my way and later was captured by unfriendly natives. They took me farther into the interior to their village from which I finally escaped, but so utterly confused and lost that I had no idea what direction to take to find a trail to the coast. I wandered thus for months, until finally, upon an accursed day I found an entrance to this valley. I do not know why they did not put me to death at once, but they did not, and later they discovered that my knowledge could be turned to advantage to them. Since then I have helped them in their quarrying and mining and in their diamond cutting. I have given them iron drills with hardened points and drills tipped with diamonds. Now I am practically one of them, but always in my heart has been the hope that some day I might escape from the valley—a hopeless hope, though, I may assure you."

"There is no way out?" asked Tarzan.

"There is a way, but it is always guarded."

"Where is it?" queried Tarzan.

"It is a continuation of one of the mine tunnels, passing entirely through the mountain to the valley beyond. The mines have been worked by the ancestors of this race for an almost incalculable length of time. The mountains are honeycombed with their shafts and tunnels. Back of the gold-bearing quartz lies an enormous deposit of altered peridotite, which contains diamonds, in the search for which it evidently became necessary to extend one of the shafts to the opposite side of the mountain, possibly for purposes of ventilation. This tunnel and the trail leading down into Opar are the only means of ingress to the valley. From time immemorial they have kept the tunnel guarded, more particularly, I imagine, to prevent the escape of slaves than to thwart the inroads of an enemy, since they believe that there is no fear of the latter emergency. The trail to Opar they do not guard, because they no longer fear the Oparians, and know quite well that none of their Gomangani slaves would dare enter the valley of the sunworshipers. For the same reason, then, that the slaves cannot escape, we, too, must remain prisoners here forever."

"How is the tunnel guarded?" asked Tarzan.

"Two Bolgani and a dozen or more Gomangani warriors are always upon duty there," replied the old man.

"The Gomangani would like to escape?"

"They have tried it many times in the past, I am told," replied the old man, "though never since I have lived here, and always they were caught and tortured. And all their race was punished and worked the harder because of these attempts upon the part of a few."

"They are numerous—the Gomangani?"

"There are probably five thousand of them in the valley," replied the old man.

"And how many Bolgani?" the ape-man asked.

"Between ten and eleven hundred."

"Five to one," murmured Tarzan, "and yet they are afraid to attempt to escape."

"But you must remember," said the old man, "that the Bolgani are the dominant and intelligent race—the others are intellectually little above the beasts of the forest."

"Yet they are men," Tarzan reminded him.

"In figure only," replied the old man. "They cannot band together as men do. They have not as yet reached the community plane of evolution. It is true that families reside in a single village, but that idea, together with their weapons, was given to them by the Bolgani that they might not be entirely exterminated by the lions and panthers.

"Formerly, I am told, each individual Gomangani, when he became old enough to hunt for himself, constructed a hut apart from others and took up his solitary life, there being at that time no slightest semblance of family life. Then the Bolgani taught them how to build palisaded villages and compelled the men and women to remain in them and rear their children to maturity, after which the children were required to remain in the village, so that now some of the communities can claim as many as forty or fifty people. But the death rate is high among them, and they cannot multiply as rapidly as people living under normal conditions of peace and security. The brutalities of the Bolgani kill many; the carnivora take a considerable toll."

"Five to one, and still they remain in slavery—what cowards they must be," said the ape-man.

"On the contrary, they are far from cowardly," replied the old man. "They will face a lion with the utmost bravery. But for so many ages have they been subservient to the will of the Bolgani, that it has become a fixed habit in them—as the fear of God is inherent in us, so is the fear of the Bolgani inherent in the minds of the Gomangani from birth."

"It is interesting," said Tarzan. "But tell me now where the woman is of whom I have come in search."

"She is your mate?" asked the old man.

"No," replied Tarzan. "I told the Gomangani that she was, so that they would protect her. She is La, queen of Opar, High Priestess of the Flaming God."

The old man looked his incredulity. "Impossible!" he cried. "It cannot be that the queen of Opar has risked her life by coming to the home of her hereditary enemies."

"She was forced to it," replied Tarzan, "her life being threatened by a part of her people because she had refused to sacrifice me to their god."

"If the Bolgani knew this there would be great rejoicing," replied the old man.

"Tell me where she is," demanded Tarzan. "She preserved me from her people, and I must save her from whatever fate the Bolgani contemplate for her."

"It is hopeless," said the old man. "I can tell you where she is, but you cannot rescue her."

"I can try," replied the ape-man.

"But you will fail and die."

"If what you tell me is true, that there is absolutely no chance of my escaping from the valley, I might as well die," replied the ape-man. "However, I do not agree with you."

The old man shrugged. "You do not know the Bolgani," he said.

"Tell me where the woman is," said Tarzan.

"Look," replied the old man, motioning Tarzan to follow him into his apartment, and approaching a window which faced toward the west, he pointed towards a strange flat tower which rose above the roof of the main building near the west end of the palace. "She is probably somewhere in the interior of that tower," said the old man to Tarzan, "but as far as you are concerned, she might as well be at the north pole."

Tarzan stood in silence for a moment, his keen eyes taking in every salient detail of the prospect before him. He saw the strange, flat-topped tower, which it seemed to him might be reached from the roof of the main building. He saw, too, branches of the ancient trees that sometimes topped the roof itself, and except for the dim light shining through some of the palace windows he saw no signs of life. He turned suddenly upon the old man.

"I do not know you," he said, "but I believe that I may trust you, since after all blood ties are strong, and we are the only men of our race in this valley. You might gain something in favor by betraying me, but I cannot believe that you will do it."

"Do not fear," said the old man, "I hate them. If I could help you I would, but I know that there is no hope of success for whatever plan you may have in mind—the woman will never be rescued; you will never leave the Valley of the Palace of Diamonds—you will never leave the palace itself unless the Bolgani wish it."

The ape-man grinned. "You have been here so long," he said, "that you are beginning to assume the attitude of mind that keeps the Gomangani in perpetual slavery. If you want to escape, come with me. We may not succeed, but at least you will have a better chance if you try than as if you remained forever in this tower."

The old man shook his head. "No," he said, "it is hopeless. If escape had been possible I should have been away from here long ago."

"Good-bye then," said Tarzan, and swinging out of the window he clambered toward the roof below, along the stout stem of the old ivy.

The old man watched him for a moment until he saw him make his way carefully across the roof toward the flat-topped tower where he hoped to find and liberate La. Then the old fellow turned and hurried rapidly down the crude stairway that rose ladder-like to the center of the tower.

Tarzan made his way across the uneven roof of the main building, clambering up the sides of its higher elevations and dropping again to its lower levels as he covered a considerable distance between the east tower and that flat-topped structure of peculiar design in which La was supposed to be incarcerated. His progress was slow, for he moved with the caution of a beast of prey, stopping often in dense shadows to listen.

When at last he reached the tower, he found that it had many openings letting upon the roof-openings which were closed only with hangings of the heavy tapestried stuff which he had seen in the tower. Drawing one of these slightly aside he looked within upon a large chamber, bare of furnishings, from the center of which there protruded through a circular aperture the top of a stairway similar to that he had ascended in the east tower. There was no one in sight within the chamber, and Tarzan crossed immediately to the stairway. Peering cautiously into the opening Tarzan saw that the stairway descended for a great distance, passing many floors. How far it went he could not judge, except it seemed likely that it pierced subterranean chambers beneath the palace. Sounds of life came up to him through the shaft, and odors, too, but the latter largely nullified, in so far as the scent impressions which they offered Tarzan were concerned, by the heavy incense which pervaded the entire palace.

It was this perfume that was to prove the ape-man's undoing, for otherwise his keen nostrils would have detected the scent of a near-by Gomangani. The fellow lay behind one of the hangings at an aperture in the tower wall. He had been lying in such a position that he had seen Tarzan enter the chamber, and he was watching him now as the ape-man stood looking down the shaft of the stairway. The eyes of the black had at first gone wide in terror at sight of this strange apparition, the like of which he had never seen before. Had the creature been of sufficient intelligence to harbor superstition, he would have thought Tarzan a god descended from above. But being of too low an order to possess any imagination whatsoever, he merely knew that he saw a strange creature, and that all strange creatures must be enemies, he was convinced. His duty was to apprise his masters of this presence in the palace, but he did not dare to move until the apparition had reached a sufficient distance from him to ensure that the movements of the Gomangani would not be noticed by the intruder—he did not care to call attention to himself, for he had found that the more one effaced oneself in the presence of the Bolgani, the less one was likely to suffer.

For a long time the stranger peered down the shaft of the stairway, and for a long time the Gomangani lay quietly watching him. But at last the former descended the stairs and passed out of sight of the watcher, who immediately leaped to his feet and scurried away across the roof of the palace toward a large tower arising at its western end.

As Tarzan descended the ladder the fumes of the incense became more and more annoying. Where otherwise he might have investigated quickly by scent he was now compelled to listen for every sound, and in many cases to investigate the chambers opening upon the central corridor by entering them. Where the doors were locked, he lay flat and listened close to the aperture at their base. On several occasions he risked calling La by name, but in no case did he receive any reply.

He had investigated four landings and was descending to the fifth when he saw standing in one of the doorways upon this level an evidently much excited and possibly terrified black. The fellow was of giant proportions and entirely unarmed. He stood looking at the ape-man with wide eyes as the latter jumped lightly from the stairway and stood facing him upon the same level.

"What do you want?" finally stammered the black. "Are you looking for the white she, your mate, whom the Bolgani took?"

"Yes," replied Tarzan. "What do you know of her?"

"I know where she is hidden," replied the black, "and if you will follow me I will lead you to her."

"Why do you offer to do this for me?" asked Tarzan, immediately suspicious. "Why is it that you do not go at once to your masters and tell them that I am here that they may send men to capture me?"

"I do not know the reason that I was sent to tell you this," replied the black. "The Bolgani sent me. I did not wish to come for I was afraid."

"Where did they tell you to lead me?" asked Tarzan.

"I am to lead you into a chamber, the door of, which will be immediately bolted upon us. You will then be a prisoner."

"And you?" inquired Tarzan.

"I, too, shall be a prisoner with you. The Bolgani do not care what becomes of me. Perhaps you will kill me, but they do not care."

"If you lead me into a trap I shall kill you," replied Tarzan. "But if you lead me to the woman perhaps we shall all escape. You would like to escape, would you not?"

"I should like to escape, but I cannot."

"Have you ever tried?"

"No, I have not. Why should I try to do something that cannot be done?"

"If you lead me into the trap I shall surely kill you. If you lead me to the woman, you at least have the chance that I do to live. Which will you do?"

The black scratched his head in thought, the idea slowly filtering through his stupid mind. At last he spoke.

"You are very wise," he said. "I will lead you to the woman."

"Go ahead, then," said Tarzan, "and I will follow you."

The black descended to the next level and opening the door, entered a long, straight corridor. As the ape-man followed his guide he had leisure to reflect upon the means through which the Bolgani had learned of his presence in the tower, and the only conclusion he could arrive at was that the old man had betrayed him, since in so far as Tarzan was aware he alone knew that the ape-man was in the palace. The corridor along which the black was leading him was very dark, receiving a dim and inadequate illumination from the dimly lighted corridor they had just left, the door into which remained open behind them. Presently the black stopped before a closed door.

"The woman is in there," said the black, pointing to the door.

"She is alone?" asked Tarzan.

"No," replied the black. "Look," and he opened the door, revealing a heavy hanging, which he gently separated, revealing to Tarzan the interior of the chamber beyond.

Seizing the black by the wrist, that he might not escape, Tarzan stepped forward and put his eyes to the aperture. Before him lay a large chamber, at one end of which was a raised dais, the base of which was of a dark, ornately carved wood. The central figure upon this dais was a huge, black-maned lion—the same that Tarzan had seen escorted through the gardens of the palace. His golden chains were now fastened to rings in the floor, while the four blacks stood in statuesque rigidity, two upon either side of the beast. Upon golden thrones behind the lion sat three magnificently ornamented Bolgani. At the foot of the steps leading to the stair stood La, between two Gomangani guards. Upon either side of a central aisle were carved benches facing the dais, and occupying the front section of these were some fifty Bolgani, among whom Tarzan almost immediately espied the little old man that he had met in the tower, the sight of whom instantly crystallized the ape-man's conviction of the source of his betrayal.

The chamber was lighted by hundreds of cressets, burning a substance which gave forth both light and the heavy incense that had assailed Tarzan's nostrils since first he entered the domain of the Bolgani. The long, cathedralesque windows upon one side of the apartment were thrown wide, admitting the soft air of the jungle summer night. Through them Tarzan could see the palace grounds and that this chamber was upon the same level as the terrace upon which the palace stood. Beyond those windows was an open gateway to the jungle and freedom, but interposed between him and the windows were fifty armed gorilla-men. Perhaps, then, strategy would be a better weapon than force with which to carve his way to freedom with La. Yet to the forefront of his mind was evidently a belief in the probability that in the end it would be force rather than strategy upon which he must depend. He turned to the black at his side.

"Would the Gomangani guarding the lion like to escape from the Bolgani?" he asked.

"The Gomangani would all escape if they could," replied the black.

"If it is necessary for me to enter the room, then," said Tarzan to the black, "will you accompany me and tell the other Gomangani that if they will fight for me I will take them out of the valley?"

"I will tell them, but they will not believe," replied the black.

"Tell them that they will die if they do not help me, then," said Tarzan.

"I will tell them."

As Tarzan turned his attention again to the chamber before him he saw that the Bolgani occupying the central golden throne was speaking.

"Nobles of Numa, King of Beasts, Emperor of All Created Things," he said in deep, growling tones, "Numa has heard the words that this she has spoken, and it is the will of Numa that she die. The Great Emperor is hungry. He, himself, will devour her here in the presence of his Nobles and the Imperial Council of Three. It is the will of Numa."

A growl of approval arose from the beast-like audience, while the great lion bared his hideous fangs and roared until the palace trembled, his wicked, yellow-green eyes fixed terribly upon the woman before him, evidencing the fact that these ceremonies were of sufficient frequency to have accustomed the lion to what he might expect as the logical termination of them.

"Day after tomorrow," continued the speaker, "the mate of this creature, who is by this time safely imprisoned in the Tower of the Emperors, will be brought before Numa for judgment. Slaves," he cried suddenly in a loud voice, rising to his feet and glaring at the guards holding La, "drag the woman to your Emperor."

Instantly the lion became frantic, lashing its tail and straining at its stout chains, roaring and snarling as it reared upon its hind feet and sought to leap upon La, who was now being forcibly conducted up the steps of the dais toward the bejeweled man-eater so impatiently awaiting her.

She did not cry out in terror, but she sought to twist herself free from the detaining hands of the powerful Gomangani—all futilely, however.

They had reached the last step, and were about to push La into the claws of the lion, when they were arrested by a loud cry from one side of the chamber—a cry that halted the Gomangani and brought the assembled Bolgani to their feet in astonishment and anger, for the sight that met their eyes was well qualified to arouse the latter within them. Leaping into the room with raised spear was the almost naked white man of whom they had heard, but whom none of them had as yet seen. And so quick was he that in the very instant of entry—even before they could rise to their feet—he had launched his spear.

CHAPTER XIV—THE CHAMBER OF HORRORS

A black-maned lion moved through the jungle night. With majestic unconcern for all other created things he took his lordly way through the primeval forest. He was not hunting, for he made no efforts toward stealth, nor, on the other hand, did he utter any vocal sound. He moved swiftly, though sometimes stopping with uplifted nose to scent the air and to listen. And thus at last he came to a high wall, along the face of which he sniffed, until the wall was broken by a half-opened gateway, through which he passed into the enclosure.

Before him loomed a great building, and presently as he stood watching it and listening, there broke from the interior the thunderous roar of an angry lion.

He of the black mane cocked his head upon one side and moved stealthily forward.

At the very instant that La was about to be thrust into the clutches of Numa, Tarzan of the Apes leaped into the apartment with a loud cry that brought to momentary pause the Gomangani that were dragging her to her doom, and in that brief instant of respite which the ape-man knew would follow his interruption the swift spear was launched. To the rage and consternation of the Bolgani they saw it bury itself in the heart of their Emperor—the great, black- maned lion.

At Tarzan's side stood the Gomangani whom he had terrified into service, and as Tarzan rushed forward toward La the black accompanied him, crying to his fellows that if they would help this stranger they might be free and escape from the Bolgani forever.

"You have permitted the great Emperor to be slain," he cried to the poor Gomangani who guarded Numa. "For this the Bolgani will kill you. Help to save the strange Tarmangani and his mate and you have at least a chance for life and freedom. And you," he added, addressing the two who had been guarding La, "they will hold you responsible also—your only hope lies with us."

Tarzan had reached La's side and was dragging her up the steps of the dais where he hoped that he might make a momentary stand against the fifty Bolgani who were now rushing forward from their seats toward him.

"Slay the three who sit upon the dais," cried Tarzan to the Gomangani, who were now evidently hesitating as to which side they would cast their lot with. "Slay them if you wish your freedom! Slay them if you wish to live!"

The authoritative tones of his voice, the magnetic appeal of his personality, his natural leadership won them to him for the brief instant that was necessary to turn them upon the hated authority that the three Bolgani upon the dais represented, and as they drove their spears into the shaggy black bodies of their masters they became then and forever the creatures of Tarzan of the Apes, for there could be no future hope for them in the land of the Bolgani.

With one arm around La's waist the ape-man carried her to the summit of the dais, where he seized his spear and drew it from the body of the dead lion. Then, turning about, and facing the advancing Bolgani, he placed one foot upon the carcass of his kill and raised his voice in the terrifying victory cry of the apes of Kerchak.

Before him the Bolgani paused, behind him the Gomangani quailed in terror.

"Stop!" cried Tarzan, raising a palm toward the Bolgani. "Listen! I am Tarzan of the Apes. I sought no quarrel with your people. I but look for a passage through your country to my own. Let me go my way in peace with this woman, taking these Gomangani with me."

For answer a chorus of savage growls arose from the Bolgani as they started forward again toward the dais. From their ranks there suddenly leaped the old man of the east tower, who ran swiftly toward Tarzan.

"Ah, traitor," cried the ape-man, "you would be the first, then, to taste the wrath of Tarzan?"

He spoke in English and the old man replied in the same tongue.

"Traitor?" he exclaimed in surprise.

"Yes, traitor," thundered Tarzan. "Did you not hurry here to tell the Bolgani that I was in the palace, that they might send the Gomangani to lure me to a trap?"

"I did nothing of the kind," replied the other. "I came here to place myself near the white woman, with the thought that I might be of service to her or you if I were needed. I come now, Englishman, to stand at your side and die at your side, for die you shall, as sure as there is a God in heaven. Nothing can save you now from the wrath of the Bolgani whose Emperor you have killed."

"Come, then," cried Tarzan, "and prove your loyalty. It were better to die now than to live in slavery forever."

The six Gomangani had ranged themselves, three upon either side of Tarzan and La, while the seventh, who had entered the chamber with Tarzan unarmed, was taking weapons from the body of one of the three Bolgani who had been slain upon the dais.

Before this array of force so new to them, the Bolgani paused at the foot of the steps leading to the dais. But only for a moment they paused, for there were but nine against fifty, and as they surged up the steps, Tarzan and his Gomangani met them with battle ax, and spear, and bludgeon. For a moment they pressed them back, but the numbers against them were too great, and once again a wave swept up that seemed likely to overwhelm them, when there broke upon the ears of the contestants a frightful roar, which, coming from almost at their side, brought a sudden, momentary cessation of the battle.

Turning their eyes in the direction of the sound they saw a huge, black-maned lion standing upon the floor of the apartment, just within one of the windows. For an instant he stood like a statue of golden bronze, and then again the building trembled to the reverberations of his mighty roar.

Towering above them all Tarzan of the Apes looked down from the dais upon the great beast below him, and then in quick elation he raised his voice above the growlings of the Bolgani.

"Jad-bal-ja," he cried, and pointing toward the Bolgani, "Kill! Kill!"

Scarcely had the words been uttered ere the huge monster, a veritable devil incarnate, was upon the hairy gorilla-men. And simultaneously there occurred to the mind of the ape-man a daring plan of salvation for himself and the others who were dependent upon him.

"Quick," he cried to the Gomangani, "fall upon the Bolgani. Here at last is the true Numa, King of Beasts, and ruler of all creation. He slays his enemies but he will protect Tarzan of the Apes and the Gomangani, who are his friends."

Seeing their hated masters falling back before the terrific onslaughts of the lion, the Gomangani rushed in with battle axes and clubs, while Tarzan, casting aside his spear, took his place among them with drawn knife, and, keeping close to Jad-bal-ja, directed the lion from one victim to another, lest he fall by mistake upon the Gomangani or the little old white man, or even La, herself. Twenty of the Bolgani lay dead upon the floor before the balance managed to escape from the chamber, and then Tarzan, turning to Jad-bal-ja, called him to heel.

"Go!" he said, turning toward the Gomangani, "and drag the body of the false Numa from the dais. Remove it from the room, for the true Emperor has come to claim his throne."

The old man and La were eyeing Tarzan and the lion in amazement.

"Who are you," asked the former, "that you can work such miracles with a savage beast of the jungle? Who are you, and what do you intend to do?"

"Wait and see," said Tarzan with a grim smile. "I think that we shall all be safe now, and that the Gomangani may live in comfort for a long time hereafter."

When the blacks had removed the carcass of the lion from the dais and thrown it from one of the windows of the chamber, Tarzan sent Jad-bal-ja to sit in the place upon the dais that had formerly been occupied by the lion, Numa.

"There," he said, turning to the Gomangani, "you see the true Emperor, who does not have to be chained to his throne. Three of you will go to the huts of your people behind the palace and summon them to the throne room, that they, too, may see what has transpired. Hurry, that we may have many warriors here before the Bolgani return in force."

Filled with an excitement which almost shook their dull minds into a semblance of intelligence three of the Gomangani hastened to do Tarzan's bidding, while the others stood gazing at Tarzan with expressions of such awe that might only be engendered by the sight of deity. La came then and stood beside Tarzan, looking up into his face with eyes that reflected a reverence fully as deep as that held by the blacks.

"I have not thanked you, Tarzan of the Apes," she said, "for what you have risked and done for me. I know that you must have come here in search of me, to save me from these creatures, and I know that it was not love that impelled you to this heroic and well-nigh hopeless act. That you have succeeded thus far is little short of miraculous, but I, in the legends of whose people are recounted the exploits of the Bolgani, know that there can be no hope of eventual escape for us all, and so I beseech that you go at once and make good your escape alone, if possible, for you alone of us have any possible chance of escape."

"I do not agree with you that we have no chance to escape, La," replied the ape-man. "It seems to me that now we not only have every reason to believe that we are practically assured of escape, but that we may ensure also to these poor Gomangani freedom from slavery and from the tyranny of the Bolgani. But this is not all. With this I shall not be satisfied. Not only must these people who show no hospitality to strangers be punished, but your own disloyal priests as well. To this latter end I intend to march out of the Valley of the Palace of Diamonds, down upon the city of Opar with a force of Gomangani sufficient to compel Cadj to relinquish the power he has usurped and replace you upon the throne of Opar. Nothing less than this shall satisfy me, and nothing less than this shall I accomplish before I leave."

"You are a brave man," said the old man, "and you have succeeded beyond what I thought could be possible, but La is right, you do not know the ferocity or the resources of the Bolgani, or the power which they wield over the Gomangani. Could you raise from the stupid minds of the blacks the incubus of fear that rests so heavily upon them you might win over a sufficient number to make good your escape from the valley, but that, I fear, is beyond even you. Our only hope, therefore, is to escape from the palace while they are momentarily disorganized, and trust to fleetness and to luck to carry us beyond the limits of the valley before we are apprehended."

"See," cried La, pointing; "even now it is too late—they return."

Tarzan looked in the direction that she indicated and saw through the open doorway at the far end of the chamber a large number of gorilla-men approaching. His eyes moved swiftly to the windows in the other wall. "But wait," he said, "behold another factor in the equation!"

The others looked toward the windows which opened upon the terrace, and they saw beyond them what appeared to be a crowd of several hundred blacks running rapidly toward the windows. The other blacks upon the dais cried out excitedly: "They come! They come! We shall be free, and no longer shall the Bolgani be able to make us work until we drop from exhaustion, or beat us, or torture us, or feed us to Numa."

As the first of the Bolgani reached the doorway leading into the chamber, the Gomangani commenced to pour through the several windows in the opposite wall. They were led by the three who had been sent to fetch them, and to such good effect had these carried their message that the blacks already seemed like a new people, so transfigured were they by the thought of immediate freedom. At sight of them the leader of the Bolgani cried aloud for them to seize the intruders upon the dais, but his answer was a spear hurled by the nearest black, and as he lunged forward, dead, the battle was on.

The Bolgani in the palace greatly outnumbered the blacks, but the latter had the advantage of holding the interior of the throne room in sufficient numbers to prevent the entry of many Bolgani simultaneously. Tarzan, immediately he recognized the temper of the blacks, called Jad-bal-ja to follow him, and, descending from the dais, he took command of the Gomangani. At each opening he placed sufficient men to guard it, and at the center of the room he held the balance in reserve. Then he called the old man into consultation.

"The gate in the east wall is open," he said. "I left it so when I entered. Would it be possible for twenty or thirty blacks to reach it in safety and, entering the forest, carry word to the villagers of what is transpiring here in the palace, and prevail upon them to send all of their warriors immediately to complete the work of emancipation that we have begun?"

"It is an excellent plan," replied the old man. "The Bolgani are not upon that side of the palace between us and the gate, and if it may ever be accomplished, now is the time. I will pick your men for you. They must be head-men, whose words will carry some weight with the villagers outside the palace walls."

"Good!" exclaimed Tarzan. "Select them immediately; tell them what we want and urge upon them the necessity for haste."

One by one the old man chose thirty warriors, whose duty he carefully explained to each. They were delighted with the plan and assured Tarzan that in less than an hour the first of the reinforcements would come.

"As you leave the enclosure," said the ape-man, "destroy the lock if you can, so that the Bolgani may not lock it again and bar out our reinforcements. Carry also the word that the first who come are to remain outside the wall until a sufficient number have arrived to make entry into the palace grounds reasonably safe—at least as many as are within this room now.

The blacks signified their understanding, and a moment later passed out of the room through one of the windows and disappeared into the darkness of the night beyond.

Shortly after the blacks had left the Bolgani made a determined rush upon the Gomangani guarding the main entrance to the throne room, with the result that a score or more of the gorilla-men succeeded in cutting their way into the room. At this first indication of reversal the blacks showed signs of faltering, the fear of the Bolgani that was inherent in them showing in their wavering attitude and seeming reluctance to force a counter attack. As Tarzan leaped forward to assist in checking the rush of the Bolgani into the throne room he called to Jad-bal-ja, and as the great lion leaped from the dais the ape-man, pointing to the nearest Bolgani, cried: "Kill! Kill!"

Straight for the throat of the nearest leaped Jad-bal-ja. The great jaws closed upon the snarling face of the frightened gorilla-man but once, and then, at the command of his master the golden lion dropped the carcass after a single shake and leaped upon another. Three had died thus in quick succession when the balance of the Bolgani turned to flee this chamber of horrors; but the Gomangani, their confidence restored by the ease with which this fierce ally brought death and terror to the tyrants, interposed themselves between the Bolgani and the doorway, shutting off their retreat.

"Hold them! Hold them!" cried Tarzan. "Do not kill them!" And then to the Bolgani: "Surrender and you will not be harmed!"

Jad-bal-ja clung close to the side of his master, glaring and growling at the Bolgani, and casting an occasional beseeching look at the ape-man which said plainer than words, "Send me among them."

Fifteen of the Bolgani who had entered the room survived. For a moment they hesitated, and then one of them threw his weapons upon the floor. Immediately the others followed suit.

Tarzan turned toward Jad-bal-ja. "Back!" he said, pointing toward the dais, and as the lion wheeled and slunk away toward the platform, Tarzan turned again toward the Bolgani.

"Let one of your number go," he said, "and announce to your fellows that I demand their immediate surrender."

The Bolgani whispered among themselves for a few moments and finally one of them announced that he would go and see the others. After he had left the room the old man approached Tarzan.

"They will never surrender," he said. "Look out for treachery."

"It is all right," said Tarzan. "I am expecting that, but I am gaining time, and that is what we need most. If there were a place near where I might confine these others I should feel better, for it would cut down our antagonists by at least that many."

"There is a room there," said the old man, pointing toward one of the doorways in the throne room, "where you can confine them—there are many such rooms in the Tower of the Emperors."

"Good," said Tarzan, and a moment later, following his instructions the Bolgani were safely locked in a room adjoining the throne room. In the corridors without they could hear the main body of the gorilla-men in argument. It was evident that they were discussing the message sent to them by Tarzan. Fifteen minutes passed, and finally thirty, with no word from the Bolgani and no resumption of hostilities, and then there came to the main entrance of the throne room the fellow whom Tarzan had despatched with his demand for surrender.

"Well," asked the ape-man, "what is their answer?"

"They will not surrender," replied the Bolgani, "but they will permit you to leave the valley provided that you will release those whom you have taken prisoner and harm no others."

The ape-man shook his head. "That will not do," he replied. "I hold the power to crush the Bolgani of the Valley of Diamonds. Look," and he pointed toward Jad-bal-ja, "here is the true Numa. The creature you had upon your throne was but a wild beast, but this is Numa, King of Beasts, Emperor of All Created Things. Look at him. Must he be held in leash by golden chains like some prisoner or slave? No! He is indeed an Emperor. But there is one yet greater than he, one from whom he takes commands. And that one is I, Tarzan of the Apes. Anger me and you shall feel not only the wrath of Numa, but the wrath of Tarzan, as well. The Gomangani are my people, the Bolgani shall be my slaves. Go and tell your fellows that, and that if they would live at all they had best come soon and sue for mercy. Go!"

When the messenger had again departed, Tarzan looked at the old man, who was eyeing him with an expression which might have denoted either awe or reverence, were it not for the vaguest hint of a twinkle in the corners of the eyes. The ape-man breathed a deep sigh of relief. "That will give us at least another half hour," he said.

"We shall need it, and more, too," replied the old man, "though, at that, you have accomplished more than I had thought possible, for at least you have put a doubt in the minds of the Bolgani, who never before have had cause to question their own power."

Presently from the outer corridors the sounds of argument and discussion gave place to that of movement among the Bolgani. A company, comprising some fifty of the gorilla-men, took post directly outside the main entrance of the throne room where they stood in silence, their weapons ready, as though for the purpose of disputing any effort upon the part of the inmates of the room to escape. Beyond them the balance of the gorilla-men could be seen moving away and disappearing through doorways and corridors leading from the main hallway of the palace. The Gomangani, together with La and the old man, watched impatiently for the coming of the black reinforcements, while Tarzan sat upon the edge of the dais half-reclining, with an arm about the neck of Jad-bal-ja.

"They are up to something," said the old man. "We must watch carefully against a surprise. If the blacks would but come now, while the doorway is held by only fifty, we should overcome them easily, and have, I do verily believe, some slight chance of escaping from the palace grounds."

"Your long residence here," said Tarzan, "has filled you with the same senseless fear of the Bolgani that the Gomangani hold. From the attitude of mind which you hold toward them one would think them some manner of supermen— they are only beasts, my friend, and if we remain loyal to our cause we shall overcome them."

"Beasts they may be," replied the old man, "but they are beasts with the brains of men—their cunning and their cruelty are diabolical."

A long silence ensued, broken only by the nervous whisperings of the Gomangani, whose morale, it was evident, was slowly disintegrating under the nervous strain of the enforced wait, and the failure of their fellows of the forest to come quickly to their aid. To this was added the demoralizing effect of speculation upon what the Bolgani were planning or what plan they already were putting into effect. The very silence of the gorilla-men was more terrible than the din of actual assault. La was the first of the whites to break the silence.

"If thirty of the Gomangani could leave the palace so easily, why might not we leave also?" she asked.

"There were two reasons," replied Tarzan. "One was that should we have left simultaneously the Bolgani, greatly outnumbering us as they did, could have harassed us and detained us for a sufficient length of time to have permitted their messengers to reach the villagers ahead of us, with the result that in a short time we should have been surrounded by thousands of hostile warriors. The second reason is that I desire to punish the creatures, so that in future a stranger may be safe in the Valley of the Palace of Diamonds." He paused. "And now I shall give you a third reason why we may not seek to escape at this moment." He pointed toward the windows overlooking the terrace. "Look," he said, "the terrace and the gardens are filled with Bolgani. Whatever their plan I think its success depends upon our attempt to escape from this room through the windows, for, unless I am mistaken, the Bolgani upon the terrace and in the gardens are making an attempt to hide themselves from us."

The old man walked to a part of the room from which he could see the greater part of the terrace and gardens upon which the windows of the throne room looked.

"You are right," he said when he returned to the ape-man's side; "the Bolgani are all massed outside these windows with the exception of those who guard the entrance, and possibly some others at the doorways at other portions of the throne room. That, however, we must determine." He walked quickly to the opposite side of the chamber and drew back the hangings before one of the apertures, disclosing beyond a small band of Bolgani. They stood there motionless, not making any effort to seize or harm him. To another exit, and another, he went, and beyond each discovered to the occupants of the chamber the same silent gorilla guardians. He made the circle of the room, passing over the dais behind the three thrones, and then he came back to Tarzan and La.

"It is as I suspected," he said, "we are entirely surrounded. Unless help comes soon we are lost."

"But their force is divided," Tarzan reminded him.

"Even so, it is sufficient to account for us," replied the old man.

"Perhaps you are right," said Tarzan, "but at least we shall have a bully fight."

"What is that!" exclaimed La, and simultaneously, attracted by the same noise, the inmates of the throne room raised their eyes to the ceiling above them, where they saw that traps had been lifted from a dozen openings, revealing the scowling faces of several score of gorilla-men.

"What are they up to now!" exclaimed Tarzan, and as though in answer to the query the Bolgani above began hurling bundles of burning, oil-soaked rags, tied in goat skins, into the throne room, which immediately commenced to fill it with a thick, suffocating smoke, accompanied by the stench of burning hide and hair.

CHAPTER XV—THE MAP OF BLOOD

After Esteban and Owaza had buried the gold, they returned to the spot where they had left their five boys, and proceeding with them to the river made camp for the night. Here they discussed their plans, deciding to abandon the balance of the party to reach the coast as best they might, while they returned to another section of the coast where they could recruit sufficient porters to carry out the gold.

"Instead of going way back to the coast for porters," asked Esteban, "why could we not just as well recruit them from the nearest village?"

"Such men would not go with us way to the coast," replied Owaza. "They are not porters. At best they would but carry our gold to the next village."

"Why not that, then?" inquired the Spaniard. "And at the next village we could employ porters to carry us on still farther, until we could employ other men to continue on with us."

Owaza shook his head. "It is a good plan, Bwana, but we cannot do it, because we have nothing with which to pay our porters."

Esteban scratched his head. "You are right," he said, "but it would save us that damnable trip to the coast and return." They sat for some moments in silence, thinking. "I have it!" at last exclaimed the Spaniard. "Even if we had the porters now we could not go directly to the coast for fear of meeting Flora Hawkes's party—we must let them get out of Africa before we take the gold to the coast. Two months will be none too long to wait, for they are going to have a devil of a time getting to the coast at all with that bunch of mutinous porters. While we are waiting, therefore, let us take one of the ingots of gold to the nearest point at which we can dispose of it for trade goods. Then we can return and hire porters to carry it from village to village."

"The Bwana speaks words of wisdom," replied Owaza. "It is not as far to the nearest trading post as it is back to the coast, and thus we shall not only save time, but also many long, hard marches."

"In the morning, then, we shall return and unearth one of the ingots, but we must be sure that none of your men accompanies us, for no one must know until it is absolutely necessary where the gold is buried. When we return for it, of course, then others must know, too, but inasmuch as we shall be with it constantly thereafter there will be little danger of its being taken from us."

And so upon the following morning the Spaniard and Owaza returned to the buried treasure, where they unearthed a single ingot.

Before he left the spot the Spaniard drew upon the inner surface of the leopard skin that he wore across his shoulder an accurate map of the location of the treasure, making the drawing with a sharpened stick, dipped in the blood of a small rodent he had killed for the purpose. From Owaza he obtained the native names of the river and of such landmarks as were visible from the spot at which the treasure was buried, together with as explicit directions as possible for reaching the place from the coast. This information, too, he wrote below the map, and when he had finished he felt much relieved from the fear that should aught befall Owaza he might never be able to locate the gold.

When Jane Clayton reached the coast to take passage for London she found awaiting her a wire stating that her father was entirely out of danger, and that there was no necessity for her coming to him. She, therefore, after a few days of rest, turned her face again toward home, and commenced to retrace the steps of the long, hot, weary journey that she had just completed. When, finally, she arrived at the bungalow she learned, to her consternation, that Tarzan of the Apes had not yet returned from his expedition to the city of Opar after the gold from the treasure vaults. She found Korak, evidently much exercised, but unwilling to voice a doubt as to the ability of his father to care for himself. She learned of the escape of the golden lion with regret, for she knew that Tarzan had become much attached to the noble beast.

It was the second day after her return that the Waziri who had accompanied Tarzan returned without him. Then, indeed, was her heart filled with fear for her lord and master. She questioned the men carefully, and when she learned from them that Tarzan had suffered another accident that had again affected his memory, she immediately announced that she would set out on the following day in search of him, commanding the Waziri who had just returned to accompany her.

Korak attempted to dissuade her, but failing in that insisted upon accompanying her.

"We must not all be away at once," she said. "You remain here, my son. If I fail I shall return and let you go.

"I cannot let you go alone, Mother," replied Korak.

"I am not alone when the Waziri are with me," she laughed. "And you know perfectly well, boy, that I am as safe anywhere in the heart of Africa with them as I am here at the ranch."

"Yes, yes, I suppose so," he replied, "but I wish I might go, or that Meriem were here."

"Yes, I, too, wish that Meriem were here;" replied Lady Greystoke. "However, do not worry. You know that my jungle- craft, while not equal to that of Tarzan or Korak, is by no means a poor asset, and that, surrounded by the loyalty and bravery of the Waziri, I shall be safe."

"I suppose you are right," replied Korak, "but I do not like to see you go without me."

And so, notwithstanding his objections, Jane Clayton set out the next morning with fifty Waziri warriors in search of her savage mate.

When Esteban and Owaza had not returned to camp as they had promised, the other members of the party were at first inclined to anger, which was later replaced by concern, not so much for the safety of the Spaniard but for fear that Owaza might have met with an accident and would not return to take them in safety to the coast, for of all the blacks he alone seemed competent to handle the surly and mutinous carriers. The negroes scouted the idea that Owaza had become lost and were more inclined to the opinion that he and Esteban had deliberately deserted them. Luvini, who acted as head-man in Owaza's absence, had a theory of his own.

"Owaza and the Bwana have gone after the ivory raiders alone. By trickery they may accomplish as much as we could have accomplished by force, and there will only be two among whom to divide the ivory."

"But how may two men overcome a band of raiders?" inquired Flora, skeptically.

"You do not know Owaza," answered Luvini. "If he can gain the ears of their slaves he will win them over, and when the Arabs see that he who accompanies Owaza and who fights at the head of the mutinous slaves is Tarzan of the Apes, they will flee in terror."

"I believe he is right," muttered Kraski, "it sounds just like the Spaniard," and then suddenly he turned upon Luvini. "Can you lead us to the raiders' camp?" he demanded.

"Yes," replied the negro.

"Good," exclaimed Kraski; "and now, Flora, what do you think of this plan? Let us send a swift runner to the raiders, warning them against Owaza and the Spaniard, and telling them that the latter is not Tarzan of the Apes, but an impostor. We can ask them to capture and hold the two until we come, and after we arrive we can make such further plans as the circumstances permit. Very possibly we can carry out our original design after we have once entered their camp as friends."

"Yes, that sounds good," replied Flora, "and it is certainly crooked enough—just like you, yourself."

The Russian blushed. "'Birds of a feather'"—he quoted.

The girl shrugged her shoulders indifferently, but Bluber, who, with Peebles and Throck, had been silent listeners to the conversation, blustered.

"Vot do you mean birds vit fedders?" he demanded. "Who vas a crook? I tell you, Mister Carl Kraski, I am an honest man, dot is von t'ing dot no man don't say about Adolph Bluber, he is a crook."

"O shut up," snapped Kraski, "if there's anything in it you'll be for it—if there's no risk. These fellows stole the ivory themselves, and killed a lot of people, probably, to do it. In addition they have taken slaves, which we will free."

"O vell," said Bluber, "if it is fair und eqvitable, vy, all right, but just remember, Mister Kraski, dot I am an honest man."

"Blime!" exclaimed Throck, "we're all honest; I've never seen such a downy bunch of parsons in all me life."

"Sure we're honest," roared John Peebles, "and anyone 'at says we ain't gets 'is bally 'ead knocked off, and 'ere we are, 'n that's that."

The girl smiled wearily. "You can always tell honest men," she said. "They go around telling the world how honest they are. But never mind that; the thing now is to decide whether we want to follow Kraski's suggestion or not. It's something we've got all pretty well to agree upon before we undertake it. There are five of us. Let's leave it to a vote. Do we, or don't we?"

"Will the men accompany us?" asked Kraski, turning to Luvini.

"If they are promised a share of the ivory they will," replied the black.

"How many are in favor of Carl's plan?" asked Flora.

They were unanimously for it, and so it was decided that they would undertake the venture, and a half hour later a runner was despatched on the trail to the raiders' camp with a message for the raider chief. Shortly after, the party broke camp and took up its march in the same direction.

A week later, when they reached the camp of the raiders they found that their messenger had arrived safely and that they were expected. Esteban and Owaza had not put in an appearance nor had anything been seen or heard of them in the vicinity. The result was that the Arabs were inclined to be suspicious and surly, fearing that the message brought to them had been but a ruse to permit this considerable body of whites and armed blacks to enter their stockade in safety.

Jane Clayton and her Waziri moving rapidly, picked up the spoor of Flora Hawkes's safari at the camp where the Waziri had last seen Esteban, whom they still thought to have been Tarzan of the Apes. Following the plainly marked trail, and moving much more rapidly than the Hawkes safari, Jane and the Waziri made camp within a mile of the ivory raiders only about a week after the Hawkes party had arrived and where they still remained, waiting either for the coming of Owaza and Esteban, or for a propitious moment in which they could launch their traitorous assault upon the Arabs. In the meantime, Luvini and some of the other blacks had succeeded in secretly spreading the propaganda of revolt among the slaves of the Arabs. Though he reported his progress daily to Flora Hawkes, he did not report the steady growth and development of a little private plan of his own, which contemplated, in addition to the revolt of the slaves, and the slaying of the Arabs, the murder of all the whites in the camp, with the exception of Flora Hawkes, whom Luvini wished to preserve either for himself or for sale to some black sultan of the north. It was Luvini's shrewd plan to first slay the Arabs, with the assistance of the whites, and then to fall upon the whites and slay them, after their body servants had stolen their weapons from them.

That Luvini would have been able to carry out his plan with ease there is little doubt, had it not been for the loyalty and affection of a young black boy attached to Flora Hawkes for her personal service.

The young white woman, notwithstanding the length to which she would go in the satisfaction of her greed and avarice, was a kind and indulgent mistress. The kindnesses she had shown this ignorant little black boy were presently to return her dividends far beyond her investment.

Luvini had been to her upon a certain afternoon to advise her that all was ready, and that the revolt of the slaves and the murder of the Arabs should take place that evening, immediately after dark. The cupidity of the whites had long been aroused by the store of ivory possessed by the raiders, with the result that all were more than eager for the final step in the conspiracy that would put them in possession of considerable wealth.

It was just before the evening meal that the little negro boy crept into Flora Hawkes's tent. He was very wide-eyed, and terribly frightened.

"What is the matter?" she demanded.

"S-sh!" he cautioned. "Do not let them hear you speak to me, but put your ear close to me while I tell you in a low voice what Luvini is planning."

The girl bent her head close to the lips of the little black. "You have been kind to me," he whispered, "and now that Luvini would harm you I have come to tell you."

"What do you mean?" exclaimed Flora, in a low voice.

"I mean that Luvini, after the Arabs are killed, has given orders that the black boys kill all the white men and take you prisoner. He intends to either keep you for himself or to sell you in the north for a great sum of money."

"But how do you know all this?" demanded the girl.

"All the blacks in camp know it," replied the boy. "I was to have stolen your rifle and your pistol, as each of the boys will steal the weapons of his white master."

The girl sprang to her feet. "I'll teach that nigger a lesson," she cried, seizing her pistol and striding toward the flap of the tent.

The boy seized her about the knees and held her. "No! no!" he cried. "Do not do it. Do not say anything. It will only mean that they will kill the white men sooner and take you prisoner just the same. Every black boy in the camp is against you. Luvini has promised that the ivory shall be divided equally among them all. They are ready now, and if you should threaten Luvini, or if in any other way they should learn that you were aware of the plot, they would fall upon you immediately."

"What do you expect me to do then?" she asked.

"There is but one hope, and that is in flight. You and the white men must escape into the jungle. Not even I may accompany you."

The girl stood looking at the little boy in silence for a moment, and then finally she said, "Very well, I will do as you say. You have saved my life. Perhaps I may never be able to repay you, and perhaps, again, I may. Go, now, before suspicion alights upon you."

The black withdrew from the tent, crawling beneath the back wall to avoid being seen by any of his fellows who were in the center of the camp from which the front of the tent was in plain view. Immediately he was gone Flora walked casually into the open and went to Kraski's tent, which the Russian occupied in common with Bluber. She found the two men and in low whispers apprised them of what the black had told her. Kraski then called Peebles and Throck, it being decided that they should give no outward sign of holding any suspicion that aught was wrong. The Englishmen were for jumping in upon the blacks and annihilating them, but Flora Hawkes dissuaded them from any such rash act by pointing out how greatly they were outnumbered by the natives, and how hopeless it would be to attempt to overpower them.

Bluber, with his usual cunning and shrewdness which inclined always to double dealing where there was the slightest possibility for it, suggested that they secretly advise the Arabs of what they had learned, and joining forces with them take up as strong a position in the camp as possible and commence to fire into the blacks without waiting for their attack.

Again Flora Hawkes vetoed the suggestion. "It will not do," she said, "for the Arabs are at heart as much our enemies as the blacks. If we were successful in subduing the niggers it would be but a question of minutes before the Arabs knew every detail of the plot that we had laid against them, after which our lives would not be worth that," and she snapped her fingers.

"I guess Flora is right, as usual," growled Peebles, "but what in 'ell are we goin' to do wanderin' around in this 'ere jungle without no niggers to hunt for us, or cook for us, or carry things for us, or find our way for us, that's wot I'd like to know, and 'ere we are, 'n that's that."

"No, I guess there ain't nothin' else to do," said Throck; "but blime if I likes to run away, says I, leastwise not for no dirty niggers."

There came then to the ears of the whites, rumbling from the far distance in the jungle, the roar of a lion.

"Oi! Oi!" cried Bluber. "Ve go out all alone in dot jungle? Mein Gott! I just as soon stay here und get killed like a vite man."

"They won't kill you like a white man," said Kraski. "They'll torture you if you stay."

Bluber wrung his hands, and the sweat of fear rolled down his oily face. "Oi! vy did I done it? Vy did I done it?" he wailed. "Vy didn't I stay home in London vere I belong?"

"Shut up!" snapped Flora. "Don't you know that if you do anything to arouse the suspicion of these fellows they will be on us at once? There is only one thing for us to do and that is to wait until they precipitate the attack upon the Arabs. We will still have our weapons, for they do not plan to steal them from us until after the Arabs are killed. In the confusion of the fight, we must make our escape into the jungle, and after that—God knows—and God help us."

"Yes," blubbered Bluber, who was in a blue funk, "Gott help us!"

A moment later Luvini came to them. "All is ready, Bwanas," he said. "As soon as the evening meal has been eaten, be in readiness. You will hear a shot, that will be the signal. Then open fire upon the Arabs."

"Good," said Kraski; "we have just been talking about it and we have decided that we will take our stand near the gate to prevent their escape."

"It is well," said Luvini, "but you must remain here." He was addressing Flora. "It would not be safe for you to be where there is to be fighting. Remain here in your tent, and we will confine the fighting to the other side of the village and possibly to the gate, if any of them makes a break for escape."

"All right," said Flora, "I will remain here where it is safe."

Satisfied that things could not have worked into his hands to better advantage, the black left them, and presently the entire camp was occupied with the evening meal. There was an atmosphere of restraint, and high, nervous tension throughout the entire camp that must have been noticeable, even to the Arabs, though they, alone of the entire company, were ignorant as to its cause. Bluber was so terrified that he could not eat, but sat white and trembling with his eyes roving wildly about the camp—first to the blacks, then to the Arabs, and then to the gate, the distance to which he must have measured a hundred times as he sat there waiting for the shot that was to be the signal for the massacre that was to send him out into the jungle to be, he surely thought, the immediate prey of the first hunting lion that passed.

Peebles and Throck ate their meal stolidly, much to Bluber's disgust. Kraski, being of a highly nervous temperament, ate but little, but he showed no signs of fear. Nor did Flora Hawkes, though at heart she realized the hopelessness of their situation.

Darkness had fallen. Some of the blacks and Arabs were still eating, when suddenly the silence was shattered by the sharp staccato report of a rifle. An Arab sank silently to the earth. Kraski rose and grasped Flora by the arm. "Come!" he cried.

Followed by Peebles and Throck, and preceded by Bluber, to whose feet fright had lent wings, they hurried toward the gate of the palisade.

By now the air was filled with the hoarse cries of fighting men and the report of rifles. The Arabs, who had numbered but about a dozen, were putting up a game fight, and being far better marksmen than the blacks, the issue of the battle was still in doubt when Kraski opened the gate and the five whites fled into the darkness of the jungle.

The outcome of the fight within the camp could not have been other than it was, for so greatly did the blacks outnumber the Arabs, that eventually, notwithstanding their poor marksmanship, they succeeded in shooting down the last of the nomads of the north. Then it was that Luvini turned his attention to the other whites only to discover that they had fled the village. The black realized two things instantly. One was that someone had betrayed him, and the other, that the whites couldn't have gone far in the short time since they had left the camp.

Calling his warriors about him he explained to them what had happened, and impressing upon them that the whites, if permitted to escape, would eventually return with reinforcements to punish the blacks, he aroused his followers, who now numbered over two hundred warriors, to the necessity of setting out immediately upon the trail of the fugitives and overtaking them before they could carry word even to a neighboring village, the nearest of which was not more than a day's march distant.

CHAPTER XVI—THE DIAMOND HOARD

The primitive smoke bombs filled the throne room of the Tower of the Emperors with their suffocating fumes, the Gomangani clustered about Tarzan begging him to save them, for they, too, had seen the massed Bolgani before every entrance and the great body of them that awaited in the gardens and upon the terrace without.

Wait a minute," said Tarzan, "until the smoke is thick enough to hide our movements from the Bolgani, and then we will rush the windows overlooking the terrace, for they are nearer the east gate than any other exit, and thus some of us will have a better chance for escape."

"I have a better plan," said the old man. "When the smoke conceals us, follow me. There is one exit that is unguarded, probably because they do not dream that we would use it. When I passed over the dais behind the throne I took occasion to note that there were no Bolgani guarding it."

"Where does it lead?" asked Tarzan.

"Into the basement of the Tower of Diamonds—the tower in which I discovered you. That portion of the palace is nearest to the east gate, and if we can reach it before they suspect our purpose there will be little doubt that we can reach the forest at least."

"Splendid!" ejaculated the ape-man. "It will not be long now before the smoke hides us from the Bolgani."

In fact it was so thick by this time that the occupants of the throne room were finding difficulty in breathing. Many of them were coughing and choking and the eyes of all were watering from the effects of the acrid smoke. And yet they were not entirely hidden from the observation of the watchers all about them.

"I don't know how much more of this we can stand," said Tarzan. "I have about all I care for, now."

"It is thickening up a bit," said the old man. "Just a moment more and I think we can make it unseen."

"I can stand it no longer," cried La. "I am suffocating and I am half-blinded."

"Very well," said the old man; "I doubt if they can see us now. It is pretty thick. Come, follow me;" and he led the way up the steps of the dais and through an aperture behind the thrones—a small opening hidden by hangings. The old man went first, and then La, followed by Tarzan and Jad-bal-ja, who had about reached the limit of his endurance and patience, so that it had been with difficulty that Tarzan had restrained him, and who now was voicing his anger in deep growls which might have apprised the Bolgani of their avenue of escape. Behind Tarzan and the lion crowded the coughing Gomangani; but because Jad-bal-ja was just in front of them they did not crowd as closely upon the party ahead of them as they probably would have done otherwise.

The aperture opened into a dark corridor which led down a flight of rough steps to a lower level, and then straight through utter darkness for the rather considerable distance which separated the Tower of Diamonds from the Tower of the Emperors. So great was their relief at escaping the dense smoke of the throne room that none of the party minded the darkness of the corridor, but followed patiently the lead of the old man who had explained that the first stairs down which they had passed were the only obstacles to be encountered in the tunnel.

At the corridor's end the old man halted before a heavy door, which after considerable difficulty he managed to open.

"Wait a moment," he said, "until I find a cresset and make a light."

They heard him moving about beyond the doorway for a moment and then a dim light flared, and presently the wick in a cresset flickered. In the dim rays Tarzan saw before them a large rectangular chamber, the great size of which was only partially suggested in the wavering light of the cresset.

"Get them all in," said the old man, "and close the door;" and when that had been done he called to Tarzan. "Come!" he said. "Before we leave this chamber I want to show you such a sight as no other human eyes have ever rested upon."

He led him to the far side of the chamber where, in the light of the cresset, Tarzan saw tier after tier of shelves, upon which were stacked small sacks made of skins. The old man set the cresset upon one of the shelves and taking a sack opened it and spilled a portion of the contents into the palm of his hand. "Diamonds," he said. "Each of these packages weighs five pounds and each contains diamonds. They have been accumulating them for countless ages, for they mine far more than they can use themselves. In their legends is the belief that some day the Atlantians will return and they can sell the diamonds to them. And so they continue to mine them and store them as though there was a constant and ready market for them. Here, take one of the bags with you," he said. He handed one to Tarzan and another to La.

"I do not believe that we shall ever leave the valley alive, but we might;" and he took a third bag for himself.

From the diamond vault the old man led them up a primitive ladder to the floor above, and quickly to the main entrance of the Tower. Only two heavy doors, bolted upon the inside, now lay between them and the terrace, a short distance beyond which the east gate swung open. The old man was about to open the doors when Tarzan stopped him.

"Wait a moment," he said, "until the rest of the Gomangani come. It takes them some time to ascend the ladder. When they are all here behind us, swing the doors open, and you and La, with this ten or a dozen Gomangani that are immediately around us, make a break for the gate. The rest of us will bring up the rear and hold the Bolgani off in case they attack us. Get ready," he added a moment later, "I think they are all up."

Carefully Tarzan explained to the Gomangani the plan he had in mind, and then, turning to the old man, he commanded "Now!" The bolt slipped, the doors swung open, and simultaneously the entire party started at a run toward the east gate.

The Bolgani, who were still massed about the throne room, were not aware that their victims had eluded them until Tarzan, bringing up the rear with Jad-bal-ja was passing through the east gate. Then the Bolgani discovered him, and immediately set up a hue and cry that brought several hundred of them on a mad run in pursuit.

"Here they come," cried Tarzan to the other, "make a run of it—straight down the valley toward Opar, La."

"And you?" demanded the young woman.

"I shall remain a moment with the Gomangani, and attempt to punish these fellows."

La stopped in her tracks. "I shall not go a step without you, Tarzan of the Apes," she said. "Too great already are the risks you have taken for me. No; I shall not go without you."

The ape-man shrugged. "As you will," he said. "Here they come."

With great difficulty he rallied a portion of the Gomangani who, once through the gate, seemed imbued but with a single purpose, and that to put as much distance between the Palace of Diamonds and themselves as possible. Perhaps fifty warriors rallied to his call, and with these he stood in the gateway toward which several hundred Bolgani were now charging.

The old man came and touched Tarzan on the arm. "You had better fly," he said. "The Gomangani will break and run at the first assault."

"We will gain nothing by flying," said Tarzan, "for we should only lose what we have gained with the Gomangani, and then we should have the whole valley about us like hornets."

He had scarcely finished speaking when one of the Gomangani cried: "Look! Look! They come;" and pointed along the trail into the forest.

"And just in time, too," remarked Tarzan, as he saw the first of a swarm of Gomangani pouring out of the forest toward the east gate. "Come!" he cried to the advancing blacks, "the Bolgani are upon us. Come, and avenge your wrongs!" Then he turned, and calling to the blacks around him, leaped forward to meet the onrushing gorilla-men. Behind them wave after wave of Gomangani rolled through the east gate of the Palace of Diamonds, carrying everything before them to break at last like surf upon the wavering wall of Bolgani that was being relentlessly hurled back against the palace walls.

The shouting and the fighting and the blood worked Jad-bal-ja into such a frenzy of excitement that Tarzan with difficulty restrained him from springing upon friend and foe alike, with the result that it required so much of the ape-man's time to hold in leash his ferocious ally that he was able to take but little part in the battle, yet he saw that it was going his way, and that, but for the occurrence of some untoward event, the complete defeat of the Bolgani was assured.

Nor were his deductions erroneous. So frantic were the Gomangani with the blood-lust of revenge and so enthused by the first fruits of victory, that they went fully as mad as Jad-bal-ja himself. They neither gave nor asked quarter, and the fighting ended only when they could find no more Bolgani to slay.

The fighting over, Tarzan, with La and the old man, returned to the throne room, from which the fumes of the smoke bombs had now disappeared. To them they summoned the head-man of each village, and when they had assembled before the dais, above which stood the three whites, with the great, black-maned lion Jad-bal-ja, Tarzan addressed them.

"Gomangani of the Valley of the Palace of Diamonds," he said, 'you have this night won your freedom from the tyrannical masters that have oppressed you since far beyond the time the oldest of you may remember. For so many countless ages have you been oppressed that there has never developed among you a leader capable of ruling you wisely and justly. Therefore you must select a ruler from another race than your own."

"You! You!" cried voice after voice as the head-men clamored to make Tarzan of the Apes their king.

"No," cried the ape-man, holding up his hand for silence, "but there is one here who has lived long among you, and who knows your habits and your customs, your hopes and your needs better than any other. If he will stay with you and rule you he will, I am sure, make you a good king," and Tarzan pointed to the old man.

The old man looked at Tarzan in bewilderment. "But I want to go away from here," he said; "I want to get back into the world of civilization, from which I have been buried all these years."

"You do not know what you are talking about," replied the ape-man. "You have been gone very long. You will find no friends left back there from whence you came. You will find deceit, and hypocrisy, and greed, and avarice, and cruelty. You will find that no one will be interested in you and that you will be interested in no one there. I, Tarzan of the Apes, have left my jungle and gone to the cities built by men, but always I have been disgusted and been glad to return to my jungle—to the noble beasts that are honest in their loves and in their hates—to the freedom and genuineness of nature.

"If you return you will be disappointed, and you will realize that you have thrown away an opportunity of accomplishing a work well worth your while. These poor creatures need you. I cannot remain to guide them out of darkness, but you may, and you may so mold them that they will be an industrious, virtuous, and kindly people, not untrained, however, in the arts of warfare, for when we have that which is good, there will always be those who are envious and who, if they are more powerful than we, Will attempt to come and take what we have by force. Therefore, you must train your people to protect their country and their rights, and to protect them they must have the ability and the knowledge to fightsuccessfully, and the weapons wherewith to wage their wars."

"You speak the truth, Tarzan of the Apes," replied the Old man. "There is nothing for me in that other world, so, if the Gomangani wish me to be their chief I will remain here."

The head-men, when he questioned them, assured Tarzan that if they could not have him for chief they would be very glad to have the old man, whom they all knew, either by sight or reputation, as one who had never perpetrated any cruelties upon the Gomangani.

The few surviving Bolgani who had taken refuge in various parts of the palace were sought out and brought to the throne room. Here they were given the option of remaining in the valley as slaves, or leaving the country entirely. The Gomangani would have fallen upon them and slain them, but that their new king would not permit.

"But where shall we go if we leave the Valley of the Palace of Diamonds?" asked one of the Bolgani. "Beyond the city of Opar we know not what exists, and in Opar may we find only enemies."

Tarzan sat eyeing them quizzically, and in silence. For a long time he did not speak, while several of the Gomangani head-men, and others of the Bolgani, made suggestions for the future of the gorilla-men. Finally the ape-man arose and nodded toward the Bolgani.

"There are about a hundred of you," he said. "You are powerful creatures and should be ferocious fighters. Beside me sits La, the High Priestess and queen of Opar. A wicked priest, usurping her power, has driven her from her throne, but tomorrow we march upon Opar with the bravest Gomangani of the Valley of the Palace of Diamonds, and there we punish Cadj, the High Priest, who has proven a traitor to his queen; and La, once more, ascends the throne of Opar. But where the seeds of treason have once been broadcast the plant may spring up at any time and where least expected. It will be long, therefore, before La of Opar may have full confidence in the loyalty of her people—a fact which offers you an opportunity and a country. Accompany us, therefore, to Opar, and fight with us to re-place La upon her throne, and then, when the fighting is over, remain there as La's bodyguard to protect her, not only from enemies without, but from enemies within."

The Bolgani discussed the matter for several minutes, and then one of them came to Tarzan. "We will do as you suggest," he said.

"And you will be loyal to La?" asked the ape-man.

"A Bolgani is never a traitor," replied the gorilla-man.

"Good!" exclaimed Tarzan, "and you, La, are you satisfied with this arrangement?"

"I accept them in my service," replied she.

Early the next morning Tarzan and La set out with three thousand Gomangani and a hundred Bolgani to punish the traitorous Cadj. There was little or no attempt at strategy or deception. They simply marched down through the Valley of the Palace of Diamonds, descended the rocky ravine into the valley of Opar, and made straight for the rear of the palace of La.

A little gray monkey, sitting among the vines and creepers upon the top of the temple walls, saw them coming. He cocked his head, first upon one side and then upon the other, and became so interested and excited that for a moment he forgot to scratch his belly—an occupation he had been assiduously pursuing for some time. The closer the column approached the more excited became Manu, the monkey, and when he realized vaguely the great numbers of the Gomangani he was fairly beside himself, but the last straw that sent him scampering madly back to the palace of Opar was the sight of the Bolgani—the ogres of his little world.

Cadj was in the courtyard of the inner temple, where at sunrise he had performed a sacrifice to the Flaming God. With Cadj were a number of the lesser priests, and Oah and her priestesses. That there was dissension among them was evident by the scowling faces fully as much as by the words which Oah directed at Cadj.

"Once again have you gone too far, Cadj," she cried bitterly. "Only may the High Priestess of the Flaming God perform the act of sacrifice. Yet again and again do you persist in defiling the sacred knife with your unworthy hand."

"Silence, woman," growled the High Priest. "I am Cadj, king of Opar, High Priest of the Flaming God. You are what you are only because of the favor of Cadj. Try not my patience too far or you shall indeed know the feel of the sacred knife." There could be no mistaking the sinister menace in his words. Several of those about him could ill conceal the shocked surprise they felt at his sacrilegious attitude toward their High Priestess. However little they thought of Oah, the fact remained that she had been elevated to the highest place among them, and those that believed that La was dead, as Cadj had taken great pains to lead them all to believe, gave in full to Oah the reverence which her high office entitled her.

"Have a care, Cadj," warned one of the older priests. "There is a limit beyond which not even you may pass."

"You dare threaten me?" cried Cadj, the maniacal fury of fanaticism gleaming in his eyes. "You dare threaten me, Cadj, the High Priest of the Flaming God?" And as he spoke he leaped toward the offending man, the sacrificial knife raised menacingly above his head, and just at that moment a little gray monkey came chattering and screaming through an embrasure in the wall overlooking the court of the temple.

"The Bolgani! The Bolgani!" he shrieked. "They come! They come!"

Cadj stopped and wheeled toward Manu, the hand that held the knife dropping at his side. "You saw them, Manu?" he asked. "You are speaking the truth? If this is another of your tricks you will not live to play another joke upon Cadj."

"I speak the truth," chattered the little monkey. "I saw them with my own eyes."

"How many of them are there?" asked Cadj. "And how near to Opar have they come?"

"They are as many as the leaves upon the trees," replied Manu, "and they are already close to the temple wall—the Bolgani and the Gomangani, they come as the grasses that grow in the ravines where it is cool and damp."

Cadj turned and raised his face toward the sun, and throwing back his head gave voice to a long-drawn scream that ended in a piercing shriek. Three times he voiced the hideous cry, and then with a command to the others in the court to follow him he started at a brisk trot toward the palace proper. As Cadj directed his steps toward the ancient avenue, upon which the palace of Opar faced, there issued from every corridor and doorway groups of the knurled and hairy men of Opar, armed with their heavy bludgeons and their knives. Screaming and chattering in the trees above them were a score or more of little gray monkeys.

"Not here," they cried, "not here," and pointed toward the south side of the city.

Like an undisciplined mob the horde of priests and warriors reentered the palace at Cadj's heels, and retraced their steps toward the opposite side of the edifice. Here they scrambled to the summit of the lofty wall which guards the palace, just as Tarzan's forces came to a halt outside.

"Rocks! Rocks!" screamed Cadj, and in answer to his commands the women in the courtyard below commenced to gather the loose fragments of stone that had crumbled from the wall and from the palace, and to toss them up to the warriors above.

"Go away!" screamed Cadj to the army outside his gates. "Go away! I am Cadj, High Priest of the Flaming God, and this is his temple. Defile not the temple of the Flaming God or you shall know his wrath."

Tarzan stepped forward a little ahead of the others, and raised his hand for silence.

"La, your High Priestess and your queen, is here," he cried to the Oparians upon the wall. "Cadj is a traitor and an impostor. Open your gates and receive your queen. Give up the traitors to justice, and no harm will befall you; but refuse La entry to her city and we shall take by force and with bloodshed that which belongs to La rightfully."

As he ceased speaking La stepped to his side that all her people might see her, and immediately there were scattering cries for La and a voice or two raised against Cadj. Evidently realizing that it would not take much to turn the scale against him, Cadj shrieked to his men to attack, and simultaneously launched a stone at Tarzan. Only the wondrous agility that he possessed saved the ape-man, and the missile passed by, and striking a Gomangani over the heart, felled him. Instantly a shower of missiles fell upon them, and then Tarzan called to his followers to charge. Roaring and growling, the Bolgani and the Gomangani leaped forward to the attack. Cat-like they ran up the rough wall in the face of the menacing bludgeons above. Tarzan, who had chosen Cadj as his objective, was among the first to reach the summit. A hairy, crooked warrior struck at him with a bludgeon, and hanging to the summit of the wall with one hand, Tarzan caught the weapon in the other and wrested it from his assailant. At the same time he saw Cadj turn and disappear into the courtyard beyond. Then Tarzan drew himself to the top where he was immediately engaged by two other warriors of Opar. With the weapon he had wrested from their fellow he knocked them to right and left, so great an advantage his great height and strength gave him over them, and then, remembering only that Cadj, who was the ring-leader of the revolt against La, must not be permitted to escape, Tarzan leaped to the pavement below just as the High Priest disappeared through an archway at the opposite end of the courtyard.

Some priests and priestesses sought to impede his progress. Seizing one of the former by the ankles he swung the body in circles about him, clearing his own pathway as he ran for the opposite end of the courtyard, and there he halted and wheeled and putting all the strength of his great muscles into the effort, he swung the body of the priest once more and hurled it back into the faces of his pursuers.

Without waiting to note the effect of his act he turned again and continued in pursuit of Cadj. The fellow kept always just ahead of him, because Cadj knew his way through the labyrinthian mazes of the palace and temple and courtyards better than Tarzan. That the trail was leading toward the inner courts of the temple Tarzan was convinced. There Cadj would find easy ingress to the pits beneath the palace and a hiding place from which it would be difficult to dislodge him, so numerous and winding were the dark subterranean tunnels. And so Tarzan put forth every effort to reach the sacrificial court in time to prevent Cadj from gaining the comparative safety of the underground passages; but as he finally leaped through the doorway into the court, a noose, cunningly laid, closed about one of his ankles and he was hurled heavily to the ground. Almost instantly a number of the crooked little men of Opar leaped upon him, where he lay, half-stunned by the fall, and before he had fully regained his faculties they had trussed him securely.

Only about half conscious, he felt them raise him from the ground and carry him, and presently he was deposited upon a cold stone surface. Then it was that full consciousness returned to him, and he realized that he lay outstretched once more upon the sacrificial altar of the inner court of the Temple of the Flaming God and above him stood Cadj, the High Priest, his cruel face contorted in a grimace of hate and the anticipation of revenge long deferred.

"At last!" gloated the creature of hate. "This time, Tarzan of the Apes, you shall know the fury not of the Flaming God, but of Cadj, the man; nor shall there be any wait nor any interference."

He swung the sacrificial knife high above his head. Beyond the point of the knife Tarzan of the Apes saw the summit of the courtyard wall, and just surmounting it the head and shoulders of a mighty, black-maned lion.

"Jad-bal-ja!" he cried. "Kill! Kill!"

Cadj hesitated, his knife poised on high. He saw the direction of the ape-man's eyes and followed them, and in that instant the golden lion leaped to the pavement, and with two mighty bounds was upon the High Priest of Opar. The knife clattered to the floor and the great jaws closed upon the horrid face.

The lesser priests who had seized Tarzan, and who had remained to witness his death at the hands of Cadj, had fled screaming from the court the instant that the golden lion had leaped upon their master, and now Tarzan and Jad-bal-ja and the corpse of Cadj were the sole occupants of the sacrificial courtyard of the temple.

"Come, Jad-bal-ja," commanded Tarzan; "let no one harm Tarzan of the Apes."

An hour later the victorious forces of La were overrunning the ancient palace and temples of Opar. The priests and warriors who had not been killed had quickly surrendered and acknowledged La as their queen and High Priestess, and now at La's command the city was being searched for Tarzan and Cadj. It was thus that La, herself, leading a searching party, entered the sacrificial courtyard.

The sight that met her eyes brought her to a sudden halt, for there, bound upon the altar, lay Tarzan of the Apes, and standing above him, his snarling face and gleaming eyes glaring directly at her was Jad-bal-ja, the golden lion.

"Tarzan!" shrieked La, taking a step toward the altar. "Cadj has had his way at last. God of my fathers have pity on me —Tarzan is dead."

"No," cried the ape-man; "far from dead. Come and release me. I am only bound, but had it not been for Jad-bal-ja I had been dead beneath your sacrificial knife."

"Thank God," cried La, and started to approach the altar, but paused before the menacing attitude of the growling lion.

"Down!" cried Tarzan, "let her approach;" and Jad-bal-ja lay down beside his master and stretched his whiskered chin across the ape-man's breast.

La came then, and picking up the sacrificial knife, cut the bonds that held the lord of the jungle captive, and then she saw beyond the altar the corpse of Cadj.

"Your worst enemy is dead," said Tarzan, "and for his death you may thank Jad-bal-ja, as I thank him for my life. You should rule now in peace and happiness and in friendship with the people of the Valley of the Palace of Diamonds."

That night Tarzan and the Bolgani and the head-men of the Gomangani, and the priests and priestesses of Opar, sat in the great banquet hall of the Palace of Opar, as the guests of La, the queen, and ate from the golden platters of the ancient Atlantians—platters that had been fashioned on a Continent that exists today only in the legends of antiquity. And the following morning Tarzan and Jad-bal-ja set forth upon their return journey to the land of the Waziri and home.

CHAPTER XVII—THE TORTURE OF FIRE

Flora Hawkes and her four confederates, pursued by Luvini and his two hundred warriors, stumbled through the darkness of the jungle night. They had no objective, for, guided entirely as they had been by the blacks, they knew not where they were and were completely lost. The sole idea dominating the mind of each was to put as much distance between themselves and the camp of the ivory raiders as possible, for no matter what the outcome of the battle there might have been, their fate would be the same should the victorious party capture them. They had stumbled on for perhaps half an hour when, during a momentary rest, they heard plainly behind them the sound of pursuit, and again they plunged on in their aimless flight of terror.

Presently, to their surprise, they discerned the glow of a light ahead. What could it be? Had they made a complete circle, and was this again the camp they had been fleeing? They pushed on to reconnoiter, until at last they saw before them the outlines of a camp surrounded by a thorn boma, in the center of which was burning a small camp-fire. About the fire were congregated half-a-hundred black warriors, and as the fugitives crept closer they saw among the blacks a figure standing out clearly in the light of the camp-fire— a white woman—and behind them rose louder and louder the sound of pursuit.

From the gestures and gesticulations of the blacks around the camp-fire it was evident that they were discussing the sounds of the battle they had recently heard in the direction of the raiders' camp, for they often pointed in that direction, and now the woman raised her hand for silence and they all listened, and it was evident that they, too, heard the coming of the warriors who were pursuing Flora Hawkes and her confederates.

"There is a white woman there," said Flora to the others. "We do not know who she is, but she is our only hope, for those who are pursuing us will overtake us quickly. Perhaps this woman will protect us. Come, I am going to find out;" and without waiting for an answer she walked boldly toward the boma.

They had come but a short distance when the keen eyes of the Waziri discovered them, and instantly the boma wall was ringed with bristling spears.

"Stop!" cried one of the warriors. "We are the Waziri of Tarzan. Who are you?"

"I am an Englishwoman," called Flora in reply. "I and my companions are lost in the jungle. We have been betrayed by our safari—our head-man is pursuing us now with warriors. There are but five of us and we ask your protection."

"Let them come," said Jane to the Waziri.

As Flora Hawkes and the four men entered the boma beneath the scrutiny of Jane Clayton and the Waziri, another pair of eyes watched from the foliage of the great tree that overhung the camp upon the opposite side—gray eyes to which a strange light came as they recognized the girl and her companions.

As the newcomers approached Lady Greystoke the latter gave an exclamation of surprise. "Flora!" she exclaimed, in astonishment. "Flora Hawkes, what in the world are you doing here?"

The girl, startled too, came to a full stop. "Lady Greystoke!" she ejaculated.

"I do not understand," continued Lady Greystoke. "I did not know that you were in Africa."

For a moment the glib Flora was overcome by consternation, but presently her native wit came to her assistance. "I am here with Mr. Bluber and his friends," she said, "who came to make scientific researches, and brought me along because I had been to Africa with you and Lord Greystoke, and knew something of the manners and customs of the country, and now our boys have turned against us and unless you can help us we are lost."

"Are they west coast boys?" asked Jane.

"Yes," replied Flora.

"I think my Waziri can handle them. How many of them are there?"

"About two hundred," said Kraski.

Lady Greystoke shook her head. "The odds are pretty heavy," she commented, and then she called to Usula, who was in charge. "There are two hundred west coast boys coming after these people," she said; "we shall have to fight to defend them."

"We are Waziri," replied Usula, simply, and a moment later the van of Luvini's forces broke into view at the outer rim of the camp-fire's reach.

At sight of the glistening warriors ready to receive them the west coast boys halted. Luvini, taking in the inferior numbers of the enemy at a glance, stepped forward a few paces ahead of his men and commenced to shout taunts and insults, demanding the return of the whites to him. He accompanied his words with fantastic and grotesque steps, at the same time waving his rifle and shaking his fist. Presently his followers took up the refrain until the whole band of two hundred was shrieking and yelling and threatening, the while they leaped up and down as they worked themselves into a frenzy of excitement that would impart to them the courage necessary for the initiating of a charge.

The Waziri, behind the boma wall, schooled and disciplined by Tarzan of the Apes, had long since discarded the fantastic overture to battle so dear to the hearts of other warlike tribes and, instead, stood stolid and grim awaiting the coming of the foe.

"They have a number of rifles," commented Lady Greystoke; "that looks rather bad for us."

"There are not over half-a-dozen who can hit anything with their rifles," said Kraski.

"You men are all armed. Take your places among my Waziri. Warn your men to go away and leave us alone. Do not fire until they attack, but at the first overt act, commence firing, and keep it up—there is nothing that so discourages a west coast black as the rifle fire of white men. Flora and I will remain at the back of the camp, near that large tree." She spoke authoritatively, as one who is accustomed to command and knows whereof she speaks. The men obeyed her; even Bluber, though he trembled pitiably as he moved forward to take his place in the front ranks among the Waziri.

Their movements, in the light of the camp-fire, were all plainly discernible to Luvini, and also to that other who watched from the foliage of the tree beneath which Jane Clayton and Flora Hawkes took refuge. Luvini had not come to fight. He had come to capture Flora Hawkes. He turned to his men. "There are only fifty of them," he said. "We can kill them easily, but we did not come to make war. We came to get the white girl back again. Stay here and make a great show against those sons of jackals. Keep them always looking at you. Advance a little and then fall back again, and while you are thus keeping their attention attracted in this direction I will take fifty men and go to the rear of their camp and get the white girl, and when I have her I will send word to you and immediately you can return to the village, where, behind the palisade, we shall be safe against attack."

Now this plan well suited the west coast blacks, who had no stomach for the battle looming so imminent, and so they danced and yelled and menaced more vociferously than before, for they felt they were doing it all with perfect impunity, since presently they should retire, after a bloodless victory—to the safety of their palisade.

As Luvini, making a detour, crept through the concealment of the dense jungles to the rear of the camp while the din of the west coast blacks arose to almost deafening proportions, there dropped suddenly to the ground before the two white women from the tree above them, the figure of a white giant, naked except for loin cloth and leopard skin—his godlike contour picked out by the flickering light of the beast fire.

"John!" exclaimed Lady Greystoke. "Thank God it is you."

"Sssh!" cautioned the white giant, placing a forefinger to his lips, and then suddenly he wheeled upon Flora Hawkes. "It is you I want," he cried, and seizing the girl he threw her lightly across his shoulders, and before Lady Greystoke could interfere—before she half-realized what had occurred—he had lightly leaped the protecting boma in the rear of the camp and disappeared into the jungle beyond. For a moment Jane Clayton stood reeling as one stunned by an unexpected blow, and then, with a stifled moan, she sank sobbing to the ground, her face buried in her arms.

It was thus that Luvini and his warriors found her as they crept stealthily over the boma and into the camp in the rear of the defenders upon the opposite side of the beast fire. They had come for a white woman and they had found one, and roughly dragging her to her feet, smothering her cries with rough and filthy palms, they bore her out into the jungle toward the palisaded village of the ivory raiders.

Ten minutes later the white men and the Waziri saw the west coast blacks retire slowly into the jungle, still yelling and threatening, as though bent on the total annihilation of their enemies—the battle was over without a shot fired or a spear hurled.

"Blime," said Throck, "what was all the bloomin' fuss about anyhow?"

"Hi thought they was goin' to heat hus hup, an' the blighters never done nothin' but yell, an' 'ere we are, 'n that's that."

The Jew swelled out his chest. "It takes more as a bunch of niggers to bluff Adolph Bluber," he said pompously.

Kraski looked after the departing blacks, and then, scratching his head, turned back toward the camp-fire. "I can't understand it," he said, and then, suddenly, "Where are Flora and Lady Greystoke?"

It was then that they discovered that the women were missing.

The Waziri were frantic. They called the name of their mistress aloud, but there was no reply. "Come!" cried Usula, "we, the Waziri shall fight, after all," and running to the boma he leaped it, and, followed by his fifty blacks, set out in pursuit of the west coast boys.

It was but a moment or two before they overtook them, and that which ensued resembled more a rout than a battle. Fleeing in terror toward their palisade with the Waziri at their heels, the west coast blacks threw away their rifles that they might run the faster, but Luvini and his party had had sufficient start so that they were able to reach the village and gain the safety of the palisade before pursued and pursuers reached it. Once inside the gate the defenders made a stand for they realized that if the Waziri entered they should all be massacred, and so they fought as a cornered rat will fight, with the result that they managed to hold off the attackers until they could close and bar the gate. Built as it had been as a defense against far greater numbers the village was easy to defend, for there were less than fifty Waziri now, and nearly two hundred fighting men within the village to defend it against them.

Realizing the futility of blind attack Usula withdrew his forces a short distance from the palisade, and there they squatted, their fierce, scowling faces glaring at the gateway while Usula pondered schemes for outwitting the enemy, which he realized he could not overcome by force alone.

"It is only Lady Greystoke that we want," he said; "vengeance can wait until another day."

"But we do not even know that she is within the village," reminded one of his men.

"Where else could she be, then?" asked Usula.

"It is true that you may be right—she may not be within the village, but that I intend to find out. I have a plan. See; the wind is from the opposite side of the village. Ten of you will accompany me, the others will advance again before the gate and make much noise, and pretend that you are about to attack. After awhile the gate will open they will come out. That I promise you. I will try to be here before that happens, but if I am not, divide into two parties and stand upon either side of the gateway and let the west coast blacks escape; we do not care for them. Watch only for Lady Greystoke, and when you see her take her away from those who guard her. Do you understand?" His companions nodded. "Then come", he said, and selecting ten men disappeared into the jungle.

Luvini had carried Jane Clayton to a hut not far from the gateway to the village. Here he had bound her securely and tied her to a stake, still believing that she was Flora Hawkes, and then he had left her to hurry back toward the gate that he might take command of his forces in defense of the village.

So rapidly had the events of the past hour transpired that Jane Clayton was still half dazed from the series of shocks that she had been called upon to endure. Dwarfing to nothingness the menace of her present position was the remembrance that her Tarzan had deserted her in her hour of need, and carried off into the jungle another woman. Not even the remembrance of what Usula had told her concerning the accident that Tarzan had sustained, and which had supposedly again affected his memory, could reconcile her to the brutality of his desertion, and now she lay, face down, in the filth of the Arab hut, sobbing as she had not for many years.

As she lay there torn by grief, Usula and his ten crept stealthily and silently around the outside of the palisade to the rear of the village. Here they found great quantities of dead brush left from the clearing which the Arabs had made when constructing their village. This they brought and piled along the palisade, close against it, until nearly three-quarters of the palisade upon that side of the village was banked high with it. Finding that it was difficult to prosecute their work in silence, Usula despatched one of his men to the main body upon the opposite side of the village, with instructions that they were to keep up a continuous din of shouting to drown the sound of the operations of their fellows. The plan worked to perfection, yet even though it permitted Usula and his companions to labor with redoubled efforts, it was more than an hour before the brush pile was disposed to his satisfaction.

Luvini, from an aperture in the palisade, watched the main body of the Waziri who were now revealed by the rising of the moon, and finally he came to the conclusion that they did not intend to attack that night, and therefore he might relax his watchfulness and utilize the time in another and more agreeable manner. Instructing the bulk of his warriors to remain near the gate and ever upon the alert, with orders that he be summoned the moment that the Waziri showed any change in attitude, Luvini repaired to the hut in which he had left Lady Greystoke.

The black was a huge fellow, with low, receding forehead and prognathous jaw—a type of the lowest form of African negro. As he entered the hut with a lighted torch which he stuck in the floor, his bloodshot eyes gazed greedily at the still form of the woman lying prone before him. He licked his thick lips and, coming closer, reached out and touched her. Jane Clayton looked up, and recoiling in revulsion, shrunk away. At sight of the woman's face the black looked his surprise.

"Who are you?" he demanded in the pigdin English of the coast.

"I am Lady Greystoke, wife of Tarzan of the Apes," replied Jane Clayton. "If you are wise you will release me at once."

Surprise and terror showed in the eyes of Luvini, and another emotion as well, but which would dominate the muddy brain it was difficult, then, to tell. For a long time he sat gazing at her, and slowly the greedy, gloating expression upon face dominated and expunged the fear that had at; first been written there, and in the change Jane Clayton read her doom.

With fumbling fingers Luvini untied the knots of the bonds that held Jane Clayton's wrists and ankles. She felt his hot breath upon her and his bloodshot eyes and the red tongue that momentarily licked the thick lips. The instant that she felt the last thong with which she was tied fall away she leaped to her feet and sprang for the entrance to the hut, but a great hand reached forth and seized her, and as Luvini dragged her back toward him, she wheeled like a mad tigress and struck repeatedly at his grinning, ugly face. By brute force, ruthless and indomitable, he beat down her weak resistance and slowly and surely dragged her closer to him. Oblivious to aught else, deaf to the cries of the Waziri before the gate and to the sudden new commotion that arose in the village, the two struggled on, the woman, from the first, foredoomed to defeat.

Against the rear palisade Usula had already put burning torches to his brush pile at half-a-dozen different places. The flames, fanned by a gentle jungle breeze, had leaped almost immediately into a roaring conflagration, before which the dry wood of the palisade crumbled in a shower of ruddy sparks which the wind carried to the thatched roofs the huts beyond, until in an incredibly short period of time the village was a roaring inferno of flames. And even as Usula had predicted the gate swung open and the west coast blacks swarmed forth in terror toward the jungle. Upon either side of the gateway the Waziri stood, looking for their mistress, but though they waited and watched silence until no more came from the gateway of village, and until the interior of the palisade a seething hell of fire, they saw nothing of her.

Long after they were convinced that no human being could remain alive in the village they still waited and hoped; but at last Usula gave up the vigil.

"She was never there," he said, "and now we pursue the blacks and capture some of them, from whom we may learn the whereabouts of Lady Greystoke."

It was daylight before they came upon a small of stragglers, who were in camp a few miles of the west. These they quickly surrounded, winning their immediate surrender by promises of immunity in the event that they would answer truthfully the questions that Usula should propound.

"Where is Luvini?" demanded Usula, who had learned the name of the leader of the west coast boys from the Europeans the evening before.

"We do not know; we have not seen him since we left the village," replied one of the blacks. "We were some of the slaves of the Arabs, and when we escaped the palisade last night we ran away from the others, for we thought that we should be safer alone than with Luvini, who is even crueller than the Arabs."

"Did you see the white women that he brought to the camp last night?" demanded Usula.

"He brought but one white woman," replied the other.

"What did he do with her? Where is she now?" asked Usula.

"I do not know. When he brought her he bound her hand and foot and put her in the hut which he occupied near the village gate. We have not seen her since."

Usula turned and looked at his companions. A great fear was in his eyes, a fear that was reflected in the countenances of the others.

"Come!" he said, "we shall return to the village. And you will go with us," he added, addressing the west coast blacks, "and if you have lied to us—" he made a significant movement with his forefinger across his throat.

"We have not lied to you," replied the others. Quickly they retraced their steps toward the ruins of the Arab village, nothing of which was left save a few piles of smoldering embers.

"Where was the hut in which the white woman was confined?" demanded Usula, as they entered the smoking ruins.

"Here," said one of the blacks, and walked quickly a few paces beyond what had been the village gateway. Suddenly he halted and pointed at something which lay upon the ground. "There," he said, "is the white woman you seek."

Usula and the others pressed forward. Rage and grief contended for mastery of them as they beheld, lying before them, the charred remnants of a human body.

"It is she," said Usula, turning away to hide his grief as the tears rolled down his ebon cheeks. The other Waziri were equally affected, for they all had loved the mate of the Big Bwana.

"Perhaps it is not she," suggested one of them; "perhaps it is another."

"We can tell quickly," cried a third. "If her rings are among the ashes it is indeed she," and he knelt and searched for the rings which Lady Greystoke habitually wore.

Usula shook his head despairingly. "It is she," he said, "there is the very stake to which she was fastened"—he pointed to the blackened stub of a stake close beside the body—"and as for the rings, even if they are not there it will mean nothing, for Luvini would have taken them away from her as soon as he captured her. There was time for everyone else to leave the village except she, who was bound and could not leave—no, it cannot be another."

The Waziri scooped a shallow grave and reverently deposited the ashes there, marking the spot with a little cairn of stones.

CHAPTER XVIII—THE SPOOR OF REVENGE

As Tarzan of the Apes, adapting his speed to that of Jad-bal-ja, made his comparatively slow way toward home, he reviewed with varying emotions the experiences of the past week. While he had been unsuccessful in raiding the treasure vaults of Opar, the sack of diamonds which he carried compensated several-fold for this miscarriage of his plans. His only concern now was for the safety of his Waziri, and, perhaps, a troublesome desire to seek out the whites who had drugged him and mete out to them the punishment they deserved. In view, however, of his greater desire to return home he decided to make no effort at apprehending them for the time being at least.

Hunting together, feeding together, and sleeping together, the man and the great lion trod the savage jungle trails toward home. Yesterday they shared the meat of Bara, the deer, today they feasted upon the carcass of Horta, the boar, and between them there was little chance that either would go hungry.

They had come within a day's march of the bungalow when Tarzan discovered the spoor of a considerable body of warriors. As some men devour the latest stock-market quotations as though their very existence depended upon an accurate knowledge of them, so Tarzan of the Apes devoured every scrap of information that the jungle held for him, for, in truth, an accurate knowledge of all that this information could impart to him had been during his lifetime a sine qua non to his existence. So now he carefully examined the spoor that lay before him, several days old though it was and partially obliterated by the passage of beasts since it had been made, but yet legible enough to the keen eyes and nostrils of the ape-man. His partial indifference suddenly gave way to keen interest, for among the footprints of the great warriors he saw now and again the smaller one of a white woman—a loved footprint that he knew as well as you know your mother's face.

"The Waziri returned and told her that I was missing," he soliloquized, "and now she has set out with them to search for me." He turned to the lion. "Well, Jad-bal-ja, once again we turn away from home—but no, where she is is home."

The direction that the trail led rather mystified Tarzan of the Apes, as it was not along the direct route toward Opar, but in a rather more southerly direction. On the sixth day his keen ears caught the sound of approaching men, and presently there was wafted to his nostrils the spoor of blacks. Sending Jad-bal-ja into a thicket to hide, Tarzan took to the trees and moved rapidly in the direction of the approaching negroes. As the distance between them lessened the scent became stronger, until, even before he saw them, Tarzan knew that they were Waziri, but the one effluvium that would have filled his soul with happiness was lacking.

It was a surprised Usula who, at the head of the sad and dejected Waziri, came at the turning of the trail suddenly face to face with his master.

"Tarzan of the Apes!" cried Usula. "Is it indeed you?"

"It is none other," replied the ape-man, "but where is Lady Greystoke?"

"Ah, master, how can we tell you!" cried Usula.

"You do not mean—" cried Tarzan. "It cannot be. Nothing could happen to her while she was guarded by my Waziri!"

The warriors hung their heads in shame and sorrow. "We offer our lives for hers," said Usula, simply. He threw down his spear and shield and, stretching his arms wide apart, bared his great breast to Tarzan. "Strike, Bwana," he said.

The ape-man turned away with bowed head. Presently he looked at Usula again. "Tell me how it happened," he said, "and forget your foolish speech as I have forgotten the suggestion which prompted it."

Briefly Usula narrated the events which had led up to the death of Jane, and when he was done Tarzan of the Apes spoke but three words, voicing a question which was typical of him.

"Where is Luvini?" he asked.

"Ah, that we do not know," replied Usula.

"But I shall know," said Tarzan of the Apes. "Go upon your way, my children, back to your huts, and your women and your children, and when next you see Tarzan of the Apes you will know that Luvini is dead."

They begged permission to accompany him, but he would not listen to them.

"You are needed at home at this time of year," he said. "Already have you been gone too long from the herds and fields. Return, then, and carry word to Korak, but tell him that it is my wish that he, too, remains at home—if I fail, then may he come and take up my unfinished work if he wishes to do so." As he ceased speaking he turned back in the direction from which he had come, and whistled once a single, low, long-drawn note, and a moment later Jad-bal-ja, the golden lion, bounded into view along the jungle trail.

"The golden lion!" cried Usula. "When he escaped from Keewazi, it was to search for his beloved Bwana."

Tarzan nodded. "He followed many marches to a strange country until he found me," he said, and then he bid the Waziri good-bye and bent his steps once more away from home in search of Luvini and revenge.

John Peebles, wedged in the crotch of a tree, greeted the coming dawn with weary eyes. Near him was Dick Throck, similarly braced another crotch, while Kraski, more intelligent or therefore possessing more inventive genius, rigged a small platform of branches across two parallel boughs, upon which he lay in comparative comfort. Ten feet above him Bluber swung, half exhausted and wholly terrified, to a smaller branch, supported in something that approximated safety by a fork of the branch to which he clung.

"Gord," groaned Peebles, "hi'll let the bloody lions 'ave me before hi'll spend another such a night as this, an' 'ere we are, 'n that's that!"

"And blime, too," said Throck, "hi sleeps on the ground hafter this, lions or no lions."

"If the combined intelligence of the three of you was equal to that of a walrus," remarked Kraski, "we might have slept in comparative safety and comfort last night on the ground."

"Hey there, Bluber, Mister Kraski is spikin' to yer," called Peebles in fine sarcasm, accenting the Mister.

"Oi! Oi! I don't care vot nobody says," moaned Bluber.

"'E wants us to build a 'ouse for 'im hevery night," continued Peebles, "while 'e stands abaht and tells us bloomin' well 'ow to do it, and 'im, bein' a fine gentleman, don't do no work."

"Why should I do any work with my hands when you two big beasts haven't got anything else work with?" asked Kraski. "You would all have starved by this time if I hadn't found food for you. And you'll be lion meat in the end, or die of exhaustion if you don't listen to me—not that it would be much loss."

The others paid no attention to his last sally. As a matter of fact they had all been quarreling much for such a long time that they really paid little attention to one another. With the exception of Peebles and Throck they all hated one another cordially, and only clung together because they were afraid to separate. Slowly Peebles lowered his bulk to the ground. Throck followed and then came Kraski, and then, finally, Bluber who stood for a moment in silence, looking down at his disreputable clothing.

"Mein Gott!" he exclaimed at last. "Look at me! Dis suit, vot it cost me tventy guineas, look at it. Ruined. Ruined. It vouldn't bring vun penny in der pound."

"The hell with your clothes!" exclaimed Kraski. "Here we are, lost, half starved, constantly menaced by wild animals, and maybe, for all we know, by cannibals, with Flora missing in the jungle, and you can stand there and talk about your 'tventy guinea' suit. You make me tired, Bluber. But come on, we might as well be moving."

"Which way?" asked Throck.

"Why, to the west, of course," replied Kraski. "The coast is there, and there is nothing else for us to do but try to reach it."

"We can't reach it by goin' east," roared Peebles, "an' ere we are, 'n that's that."

"Who said we could?" demanded Kraski.

"Well, we was travelin' east all day yesterday," said Peebles. "I knew all the time that there was somethin' wrong, and I just got it figured out."

Throck looked at his partner in stupid surprise. "What do you mean?" he growled. "What makes you think we was travelin' east?"

"It's easy enough," replied Peebles, "and I can prove it to you. Because this party here knows so much more than the rest of us we have been travelin' straight toward the interior ever since the niggers deserted us." He nodded toward the Russian, who stood with his hands on his hips, eyeing the other quizzically.

"If you think I'm taking you in the wrong direction, Peebles," said Kraski, "you just turn around and go the other way; but I'm going to keep on the way we've been going, which is the right way."

"It ain't the right way," retorted Peebles, "and I'll show yer. Listen here. When you travel west the sun is at your left side, isn't it—that is, all durin' the middle of the day. Well, ever since we ve been travelin' without the niggers the sun has been on our right. I thought all the time there was somethin' wrong, but I could never figure it out until just now. It's plain as the face on your nose. We've been travelin' due east right along."

"Blime," cried Throck, "that we have, due east, and this blighter thinks as 'ow 'e knows it all."

"Oi!" groaned Bluber, "und ve got to valk it all back again yet, once more?"

Kraski laughed and turned away to resume the march in the direction he had chosen. "You fellows go on your own way if you want to," he said, "and while you're traveling, just ponder the fact that you're south of the equator and that therefore the sun is always in the north, which, however, doesn't change its old-fashioned habit of setting in the west."

Bluber was the first to grasp the truth of Kraski's statement. "Come on, boys," he said, "Carl vas right," and he turned and followed the Russian.

Peebles stood scratching his head, entirely baffled by the puzzling problem, which Throck, also, was pondering deeply. Presently the latter turned after Bluber and Kraski. "Come on, John," he said to Peebles, "hi don't hunderstand it, but hi guess they're right. They are headin' right toward where the sun set last night, and that sure must be west."

His theory tottering, Peebles followed Throck, though he remained unconvinced.

The four men, hungry and footsore, had dragged their weary way along the jungle trail toward the west for several hours in vain search for game. Unschooled in jungle craft they blundered on. There might have been on every hand fierce carnivore or savage warriors, but so dull are the perceptive faculties of civilized man, the most blatant foe might have stalked them unperceived.

And so it was that shortly after noon, as they were crossing a small clearing, the zip of an arrow that barely missed Bluber's head, brought them to a sudden, terrified halt. With a shrill scream of terror the Jew crumpled to the ground. Kraski threw his rifle to his shoulder and fired.

"There!" he cried, "behind those bushes," and then another arrow, from another direction, pierced his forearm. Peebles and Throck, beefy and cumbersome, got into action with less celerity than the Russian, but, like him, they showed no indication of fear.

"Down," cried Kraski, suiting the action to the word. "Lie down and let them have it."

Scarcely had the three men dropped among the long grass when a score of pigmy hunters came into the open, and a volley of arrows whizzed above the prone men, while from a nearby tree two steel-gray eyes looked down upon the ambush.

Bluber lay upon his belly with his face buried in his arms, his useless rifle lying at his side, but Kraski, Peebles, and Throck, fighting for their lives, pumped lead into the band of yelling pigmies.

Kraski and Peebles each dropped a native with his rifle and then the foe withdrew into the concealing safety of the surrounding jungle. For a moment there was a cessation of hostilities. Bitter silence reigned, and then a voice broke the quiet from the verdure of a nearby forest giant.

"Do not fire until I tell you to," it said, in English, "and I will save you."

Bluber raised his head. "Come qvick! Come qvick!" he cried, "ve vill not shoot. Safe me, safe me, und I giff you five pounds."

From the tree from which the voice had issued there came a single, low, long-drawn, whistled note, and then silence for a time.

The pigmies, momentarily surprised by the mysterious voice emanating from the foliage of a tree, ceased their activities, but presently, hearing nothing to arouse their fear, they emerged from the cover of the bushes and launched another volley of arrows toward the four men lying among the grasses in the clearing. Simultaneously the figure of a giant white leaped from the lower branches of a patriarch of the jungle, as a great black-maned lion sprang from the thicket below.

"Oi!" shrieked Bluber, and again buried his face in his arms.

For an instant the pigmies stood terrified, and then their leader cried: "It is Tarzan!" and turned and fled into the jungle.

"Yes, it is Tarzan—Tarzan of the Apes," cried Lord Greystoke. "It is Tarzan and the golden lion," but he spoke in the dialect of the pigmies, and the whites understood no word of what he said. Then he turned to them. "The Gomangani have gone," he said; "get up."

The four men crawled to their feet. "Who are you, and what are you doing here?" demanded Tarzan of the Apes. "But I do not need to ask who you are. You are the men who drugged me, and left me helpless in your camp, a prey to the first passing lion or savage native."

Bluber stumbled forward, rubbing his palms together and cringing and smiling. "Oi! Oi! Mr. Tarzan, ve did not know you. Neffer vould ve did vat ve done, had ve known it vas Tarzan of the Apes. Safe me! Ten pounds—twenty pounds —anyt'ing. Name your own price. Safe me, und it is yours."

Tarzan ignored the Jew and turned toward the others. "I am looking for one of your men," he said; "a black named Luvini. He killed my wife. Where is he?"

"We know nothing of that," said Kraski. "Luvini betrayed us and deserted us. Your wife and another white woman were in our camp at the time. None of us knows what became of them. They were behind us when we took our post to defend the camp from our men and the slaves of the Arabs. Your Waziri were there. After the enemy had withdrawn we found that the two women had disappeared. We do not know what became of them. We are looking for them now."

"My Waziri told me as much," said Tarzan, "but have you seen aught of Luvini since?"

"No, we have not," replied Kraski.

"What are you doing here?" demanded Tarzan.

"We came with Mr. Bluber on a scientific expedition," replied the Russian. "We have had a great deal of trouble. Our head-men, askari, and porters have mutinied and deserted. We are absolutely alone and helpless."

"Oi! Oi!" cried Bluber. "Safe us! Safe us! But keep dot lion avay. He makes me nerfous."

"He will not hurt you—unless I tell him to," said Tarzan.

"Den please don't tell him to," cried Bluber.

"Where do you want to go?" asked Tarzan.

"We are trying to get back to the coast," replied Kraski, "and from there to London."

"Come with me," said Tarzan, "possibly I can help you. You do not deserve it, but I cannot see white men perish here in the jungle."

They followed him toward the west, and that night they made camp beside a small jungle stream. It was difficult for the four Londoners to accustom themselves to the presence of the great lion, and Bluber was in a state of palpable terror.

As they squatted around the fire after the evening meal, which Tarzan had provided, Kraski suggested that they set to and build some sort of a shelter against the wild beasts.

"It will not be necessary," said Tarzan. "Jad-bal-ja will guard you. He will sleep here beside Tarzan of the Apes, and what one of us does not hear the other will."

Bluber sighed. "Mein Gott!" he cried. "I should giff ten pounds for vun night's sleep."

"You may have it tonight for less than that," replied Tarzan, "for nothing shall befall you while Jad-bal-ja and I are here."

"Vell, den I t'ink I say good night," said the Jew, and moving a few paces away from the fire he curled up and was soon asleep. Throck and Peebles followed suit, and shortly after Kraski, too.

As the Russian lay, half dozing, his eyes partially open, he saw the ape-man rise from the squatting position he had maintained before the fire, and turn toward a nearby tree. As he did so something fell from beneath his loin cloth—a little sack made of hides—a little sack, bulging with its contents.

Kraski, thoroughly awakened now, watched it as the ape-man moved off a short distance, accompanied by Jad-bal-ja, and lay down to sleep.

The great lion curled beside the prostrate man, and presently the Russian was assured that both slept. Immediately he commenced crawling, stealthily and slowly toward the little package lying beside the fire. With each forward move that he made he paused and looked at the recumbent figures of the two ferocious beasts before him, but both slept on peacefully. At last the Russian could reach out and grasp the sack, and drawing it toward him he stuffed it quickly inside his shirt. Then he turned and crawled slowly and carefully back to his place beyond the fire. There, lying with his head upon one arm as though in profound slumber, he felt carefully of the sack with the fingers of his left hand.

"They feel like pebbles," he muttered to himself, "and doubtless that is what they are, for the barbaric ornamentation of this savage barbarian who is a peer of England. It does not seem possible that this wild beast has sat in the House of Lords."

Noiselessly Kraski undid the knot which held the mouth of the sack closed, and a moment later he let a portion of the contents trickle forth into his open palm.

"My God!" he cried, "diamonds!"

Greedily he poured them all out and gloated over them— great scintillating stones of the first water—five pounds of pure, white diamonds, representing so fabulous a fortune that the very contemplation of it staggered the Russian.

"My God!" he repeated, "the wealth of Croesus in my own hand."

Quickly he gathered up the stones and replaced them in the sack, always with one eye upon Tarzan and Jad-bal-ja; but neither stirred, and presently he had returned them all to the pouch and slipped the package inside his shirt.

"Tomorrow," he muttered, "tomorrow—would to God that I had the nerve to attempt it tonight."

In the middle of the following morning Tarzan, with the four Londoners, approached a good-sized, stockaded village, containing many huts. He was received not only graciously, but with the deference due an emperor.

The whites were awed by the attitude of the black chief and his warriors as Tarzan was conducted into their presence.

After the usual ceremony had been gone through, Tarzan turned and waved his hand toward the four Europeans. "These are my friends," he said to the black chief, "and they wish to reach the coast in safety. Send with them, then, sufficient warriors to feed and guard them during the journey. It is I, Tarzan of the Apes, who requests this favor."

"Tarzan of the Apes, the great chief, Lord of the Jungle, has but to command," replied the black.

"Good!" exclaimed Tarzan, "feed them well and treat them well. I have other business to attend to and may not remain."

"Their bellies shall be filled, and they shall reach the coast unscathed," replied the chief.

Without a word of farewell, without even a sign that he realized their existence, Tarzan of the Apes passed from the sight of the four Europeans, while at his heels paced Jad-bal-ja, the golden lion.

CHAPTER XIX—A BARBED SHAFT KILLS

Kraski spent a sleepless night. He could not help but realize that sooner or later Tarzan would discover the loss of his pouch of diamonds, and that he would return and demand an accounting of the four Londoners he had befriended. And so it was that as the first streak of dawn lighted the eastern horizon, the Russian arose from his pallet of dried grasses within the hut that had been assigned him and Bluber by the chief, and crept stealthily out into the village street.

"God!" he muttered to himself. "There is only one chance in a thousand that I can reach the coast alone, but this," and he pressed his hand over the bag of diamonds that lay within his shirt— " but this, this is worth every effort, even to the sacrifice of life—the fortune of a thousand kings— my God, what could I not do with it in London, and Paris, and New York!"

Stealthily he slunk from the village, and presently the verdure of the jungle beyond closed about Carl Kraski, the Russian, as he disappeared forever from the lives of his companions.

Bluber was the first to discover the absence of Kraski, for although there was no love between the two, they had been thrown together owing to the friendship of Peebles and Throck.

"Have you seen Carl this morning?" he asked Peebles as the three men gathered around the pot containing the unsavory stew that had been brought to them for their breakfast.

"No," said Peebles. "He must be asleep yet."

"He is not in the hut," replied Bluber. "He vas not dere ven I woke up."

"He can take care of himself," growled Throck, resuming his breakfast. "You'll likely find him with some of the ladies," and he grinned in appreciation of his little joke on Kraski's well-known weakness.

They had finished their breakfast and were attempting to communicate with some of the warriors, in an effort to learn when the chief proposed that they should set forth for the coast, and still Kraski had not made an appearance. By this time Bluber was considerably concerned, not at all for Kraski's safety, but for his own, since, if something could happen to Kraski in this friendly village in the still watches of the night, a similar fate might overtake him, and when he made this suggestion to the others it gave them food for thought, too, so that there were three rather apprehensive men who sought an audience with the chief.

By means of signs and pidgin English, and distorted native dialect, a word or two of which each of the three understood, they managed to convey to the chief the information that Kraski had disappeared, and that they wanted to know what had become of him.

The chief was, of course, as much puzzled as they, and immediately instituted a thorough search of the village, with the result that it was soon found that Kraski was not within the palisade, and shortly afterward footprints were discovered leading through the village gateway into the jungle.

"Mein Gott!" exclaimed Bluber, "he vent out dere, und he vent alone, in der middle of der night. He must have been crazy."

"Gord!" cried Trock, "what did he want to do that for?"

"You ain't missed nothin', have you?" asked Peebles of the other two. "'E might 'ave stolen somethin'."

"Oi! Oi! Vot have ve got to steal?" cried Bluber. "Our guns, our ammunition—dey are here beside us. He did not take them. Beside dose ve have nothing of value except my tventy guinea suit."

"But what did 'e do it for?" demanded Peebles.

"'E must 'ave been walkin' in 'is bloomin' sleep," said Throck. And that was as near to an explanation of Kraski's mysterious disappearance as the three could reach. An hour later they set out toward the coast under the protection of a company of the chief's warriors.

Kraski, his rifle slung over his shoulder, moved doggedly along the jungle trail, a heavy automatic pistol grasped in his right hand. His ears constantly strained for the first intimation of pursuit as well as for whatever other dangers lurk before or upon either side. Alone in the mysterious jungle he was experiencing a nightmare of terror, and with each mile that he traveled the value of the diamonds became less and less by comparison with the frightful ordeal that realized he must pass through before he could hope to reach the coast.

Once Histah, the snake, swinging from a hung branch across the trail, barred his way, and the man dared not fire at him for fear of attracting the attention of possible pursuers to his position. He was forced, therefore, to make a detour through the tangled mass of underbrush which grew closely upon either side of the narrow trail. When he reached it again, beyond the snake, his clothing was more torn and tattered than before and his flesh was scratched and cut and bleeding from the innumerable thorns past which he had been compelled to force his way. He was soaked with perspiration and panting from exhaustion and his clothing was filled with ants whose vicious attacks upon his flesh rendered him half mad with pain.

Once again in the clear he tore his clothing from him and sought frantically to rid himself of the torturing pests.

So thick were the myriad ants upon his clothing that he dared not attempt to reclaim it. Only the sack of diamonds, his ammunition and his weapons did he snatch from the ravening horde whose numbers were rapidly increasing, apparently by the millions, as they sought to again lay hold upon him and devour him.

Shaking the bulk of the ants from the articles he had retrieved, Kraski dashed madly along the trail as naked as the day he was born, and when, hour later, stumbling and at last falling exhausted, he lay panting upon the damp jungle earth, he realized the utter futility of his mad attempt to reach the coast alone, even more fully than he ever could have under any other circumstances, since there is nothing that so paralyzes the courage and self-confidence of a civilized man as to be deprived of his clothing.

However scant the protection that might have been afforded by the torn and tattered garments he discarded, he could not have felt more helpless had he lost his weapons and ammunition instead, for, to such an extent are we the creatures of habit and environment. It was, therefore, a terrified Kraski, already foredoomed to failure, who crawled fearfully along the jungle trail.

That night, hungry and cold, he slept in the crotch of a great tree while the hunting carnivore roared, and coughed, and growled through the blackness of the jungle about him. Shivering with terror he started momentarily to fearful wakefulness, and when, from exhaustion, he would doze again it was not to rest but to dream of horrors that a sudden roar would merge into reality. Thus the long hours of a frightful night dragged out their tedious length, until it seemed that dawn would never come. But come it did, and once again he took up his stumbling way toward the west.

Reduced by fear and fatigue and pain to a state bordering upon half consciousness, he blundered on, with each passing hour becoming perceptibly weaker, for he had been without food or water since he had deserted his companions more than thirty hours before.

Noon was approaching. Kraski was moving but slowly now with frequent rests, and it was during one of these that there came to his numbed sensibilities an insistent suggestion of the voices of human beings not far distant. Quickly he shook himself and attempted to concentrate his waning faculties. He listened intently, and presently with a renewal of strength he arose to his feet.

There was no doubt about it. He heard voices but a short distance away and they sounded not like the tones of natives, but rather those of Europeans. Yet he was still careful, and so he crawled cautiously forward, until at a turning of the trail he saw before him a clearing dotted with trees which bordered the banks of a muddy stream. Near the edge of the river was a small hut thatched with grasses and surrounded by a rude palisade and further protected by an outer boma of thorn bushes.

It was from the direction of the hut that the voices were coming, and now he clearly discerned a woman's voice raised in protest and in anger, and replying to it the deep voice of a man.

Slowly the eyes of Carl Kraski went wide in incredulity, not unmixed with terror, for the tones of the voice of the man he heard were the tones of the dead Esteban Miranda, and the voice of the woman was that of the missing Flora Hawkes, whom he had long since given up as dead also. But Carl Kraski was no great believer in the supernatural. Disembodied spirits need no huts or palisades, or bomas of thorns. The owners of those voices were as live—as material—as he.

He started forward toward the hut, his hatred of Esteban and his jealousy almost forgotten in the relief he felt in the realization that he was to again have the companionship of creatures of his own kind. He had moved, however, but a few steps from the edge of the jungle when the woman's voice came again to his ear, and with it the sudden realization of his nakedness. He paused in thought, looking about him, and presently he was busily engaged gathering the long, broadleaved jungle grasses, from which he fabricated a rude but serviceable skirt, which he fastened about his waist with a twisted rope of the same material. Then with a feeling of renewed confidence he moved forward toward the hut. Fearing that they might not recognize him at first, and, taking him for an enemy, attack him, Kraski, before he reached the entrance to the palisade, called Esteban by name. Immediately the Spaniard came from the hut, followed by the girl. Had Kraski not heard his voice and recognized him by it, he would have thought him Tarzan of the Apes, so close was the remarkable resemblance.

For a moment the two stood looking at the strange apparition before them.

"Don't you know me?" asked Kraski. "I am Carl—Carl Kraski. You know me, Flora."

"Carl!" exclaimed the girl, and started to leap forward, but Esteban grasped her by the wrist and held her back.

"What are you doing here, Kraski?" asked the Spaniard in a surly tone.

"I am trying to make my way to the coast," replied the Russian. "I am nearly dead from starvation and exposure."

"The way to the coast is there," said the Spaniard, and pointed down the trail toward the west. "Keep moving, Kraski, it is not healthy for you here."

"You mean to say that you will send me on without food or water?" demanded the Russian.

"There is water," said Esteban, pointing at the river, "and the jungle is full of food for one with sufficient courage and intelligence to gather it."

"You cannot send him away," cried the girl. "I did not think it possible that even you could be so cruel," and then, turning to the Russian, "O Carl," she cried, "do not go. Save me! Save me from this beast!"

"Then stand aside," cried Kraski, and as the girl wrenched herself free from the grasp of Miranda the Russian leveled his automatic and fired point-blank at the Spaniard. The bullet missed its target; the empty shell jammed in the breech and as Kraski pulled the trigger again with no result he glanced at his weapon and, discovering its uselessness, hurled it from him with an oath. As he strove frantically to bring his rifle into action Esteban drew back his spear hand with the short, heavy spear that he had learned by now so well to use, and before the other could press the trigger of his rifle the barbed shaft tore through his chest and heart. Without a sound Carl Kraski sank dead at the foot of his enemy and his rival, while the woman both had loved, each in his own selfish or brutal way, sank sobbing to the ground in the last and deepest depths of despair.

Seeing that the other was dead, Esteban stepped forward and wrenched his spear from Kraski's body and also relieved his dead enemy of his ammunition and weapons. As he did so his eyes fell upon a little bag made of skins which Kraski had fastened to his waist by the grass rope he had recently fashioned to uphold his primitive skirt.

The Spaniard felt of the bag and tried to figure out the nature of its contents, coming to the conclusion that it was ammunition, but he did not examine it closely until he had carried the dead man's weapons into his hut, where he had also taken the girl, who crouched in a corner, sobbing.

"Poor Carl! Poor Carl!" she moaned, and then to the man facing her: "You beast!"

"Yes," he cried, with a laugh, "I am a beast. I am Tarzan of the Apes, and that dirty Russian dared to call me Esteban. I am Tarzan! I am Tarzan of the Apes!" he repeated in a loud scream. "Who dares call me otherwise dies. I will show them. I will show them," he mumbled.

The girl looked at him with wide and flaming eyes and shuddered.

"Mad," she muttered. "Mad! My God—alone in the jungle with a maniac!" And, in truth, in one respect was Esteban Miranda mad—mad with the madness of the artist who lives the part he plays. And for so long, now, had Esteban Miranda played the part, and so really proficient had he become in his interpretation of the noble character, that he believed himself Tarzan, and in outward appearance he might have deceived the ape-man's best friend. But within that godlike form was the heart of a cur and the soul of a craven.

"He would have stolen Tarzan's mate," muttered Esteban. "Tarzan, Lord of the Jungle! Did you see how I slew him, with a single shaft? You could love a weakling, could you, when you could have the love of the great Tarzan!"

"I loathe you," said the girl. "You are indeed a beast. You are lower than the beasts."

"You are mine, though," said the Spaniard, "and you shall never be another's—first I would kill you—but let us see what the Russian had in his little bag of hides, it feels like ammunition enough to kill a regiment," and he untied the thongs that held the mouth of the bag closed and let some of the contents spill out upon the floor of the hut. As the sparkling stones rolled scintillant before their astonished eyes, the girl gasped in incredulity.

"Holy Mary!" exclaimed the Spaniard, "they are diamonds."

"Hundreds of them," murmured the girl.

"Where could he have gotten them?"

"I do not know and I do not care," said Esteban. "They are mine. They are all mine—I am rich, Flora. I am rich, and if you are a good girl you shall share my wealth with me."

Flora Hawkes's eyes narrowed. Awakened within her breast was the always-present greed that dominated her being, and beside it, and equally as powerful now to dominate her, her hatred for the Spaniard. Could he have known it, possession of those gleaming baubles had crystallized at last in the mind of the woman a determination she had long fostered to slay the Spaniard while he slept. Heretofore she had been afraid of being left alone in the jungle, but now the desire to possess this great wealth overcame her terror.

Tarzan, ranging the jungle, picked up the trail of the various bands of west coast boys and the fleeing slaves of the dead Arabs, and overhauling each in turn he prosecuted his search for Luvini, awing the blacks into truthfulness and leaving them in a state of terror when he departed. Each and every one, they told him the same story. There was none who had seen Luvini since the night of the battle and the fire, and each was positive that he must have escaped with some other band.

So thoroughly occupied had the ape-man's mind been during the past few days with his sorrow and his search that lesser considerations had gone neglected, with the result that he had not noted that the bag containing the diamonds was missing. In fact, he had practically forgotten the diamonds when, by the merest vagary of chance his mind happened to revert to them, and then it was that he suddenly realized that they were missing, but when he had lost them, or the circumstances surrounding the loss, he could not recall.

"Those rascally Europeans," he muttered to Jad-bal-ja, "they must have taken them," and suddenly with the thought the scarlet scar flamed brilliantly upon his forehead, as just anger welled within him against the perfidy and ingratitude of the men he had succored. "Come," he said to Jad-bal-ja, "as we search for Luvini we shall search for these others also." And so it was that Peebles and Throck and Bluber had traveled but a short distance toward the coast when, during a noon-day halt, they were surprised to see the figure of the ape-man moving majestically toward them while, at his side, paced the great, black-maned lion.

Tarzan made no acknowledgment of their exuberant greeting, but came forward in silence to stand at last with folded arms before them. There was a grim, accusing expression upon his countenance that brought the chill of fear to Bluber's cowardly heart, and blanched the faces of the two hardened English pugs.

"What is it?" they chorused. "What is wrong? What has happened?"

"I have come for the bag of stones you took from me," said Tarzan simply.

Each of the three eyed his companion suspiciously.

"I do not understand vot you mean, Mr. Tarzan," purred Bluber, rubbing his palms together. "I am sure dere is some mistake, unless——" he cast a furtive and suspicious glance in the direction of Peebles and Throck.

"I don't know nothin' about no bag of stones," said Peebles, "but I will say as 'ow you can't trust no Jew."

"I don't trust any of you," said Tarzan. "I will give you five seconds to hand over the bag of stones, and if you don't produce it in that time I shall have you thoroughly searched."

"Sure," cried Bluber, "search me, search me, by all means. Vy, Mr. Tarzan, I vouldn't take notting from you for notting."

"There's something wrong here," growled Throck. "I ain't got nothin' of yours and I'm sure these two haven't neither."

"Where is the other?" asked Tarzan.

"Oh, Kraski? He disappeared the same night you brought us to that village. We hain't seen him since—that's it; I got it now—we wondered why he left, and now I see it as plain as the face on me nose. It was him that stole that bag of stones. That's what he done. We've been tryin' to figure out ever since he left what he stole, and now I see it plain enough."

"Sure," exclaimed Peebles. "That's it, and 'ere we are, 'n that's that."

"Ve might have knowed it, ve might have knowed it," agreed Bluber.

"But nevertheless I'm going to have you all searched," said Tarzan, and when the head-man came and Tarzan had explained what he desired, the three whites were quickly stripped and searched. Even their few belongings were thoroughly gone through, but no bag of stones was revealed.

Without a word Tarzan turned back toward the jungle, and in another moment the blacks and the three Europeans saw the leafy sea of foliage swallow the ape-man and the golden lion.

"Gord help Kraski!" exclaimed Peebles.

"Wot do yer suppose he wants with a bag o' stones?" inquired Throck. "'E must be a bit balmy, I'll say."

"Balmy nudding," exclaimed Bluber. "Dere is but vun kind of stones in Africa vot Kraski would steal and run off into der jungle alone mit—diamonds."

Peebles and Throck opened their eyes in surprise. "The damned Russian!" exclaimed the former. "He double-crossed us, that's what e' did."

"He likely as not saved our lives, says hi," said Throck. "If this ape feller had found Kraski and the diamonds with us we'd of all suffered alike—you couldn't 'a' made 'im believe we didn't 'ave a 'and in it. And Kraski wouldn't 'a' done nothin' to help us out."

"I 'opes 'e catches the beggar!" exclaimed Peebles, fervently.

They were startled into silence a moment later by the sight of Tarzan returning to the camp, but he paid no attention to the whites, going instead directly to the head-man, with whom he conferred for several minutes. Then, once more, he turned and left.

Acting on information gained from the head-man, Tarzan struck off through the jungle in the general direction of the village where he had left the four whites in charge of the chief, and from which Kraski had later escaped alone. He moved rapidly, leaving Jad-bal-ja to follow behind, covering the distance to the village in a comparatively short time, since he moved almost in an air line through the trees, where there was no matted undergrowth to impede his progress.

Outside the village gate he took up Kraski's spoor, now almost obliterated, it is true, but still legible to the keen perceptive faculties of the ape-man. This he followed swiftly, since Kraski had hung tenaciously to the open trail that wound in a general westward direction.

The sun had dropped almost to the western tree-tops, when Tarzan came suddenly upon a clearing beside a sluggish stream, near the banks of which stood a small, rude hut, surrounded by a palisade and a thorn boma.

The ape-man paused and listened, sniffing the air with his sensitive nostrils, and then on noiseless feet he crossed the clearing toward the hut. In the grass outside the palisade lay the dead body of a white man, and a single glance told the ape-man that it was the fugitive whom he sought. Instantly he realized the futility of searching the corpse for the bag of diamonds, since it was a foregone conclusion that they were now in the possession of whoever had slain the Russian. A perfunctory examination revealed the fact that he was right in so far as the absence of the diamonds was concerned.

Both inside the hut and outside the palisade were indications of the recent presence of a man and woman, the spoor of the former tallying with that of the creature who had killed Gobu, the great ape, and hunted Bara, the deer, upon the preserves of the ape-man. But the woman—who was she? It was evident that she had been walking upon sore, tired feet, and that in lieu of shoes she wore bandages of cloth.

Tarzan followed the spoor of the man and the woman where it led from the hut into the jungle.

As it progressed it became apparent that the woman had been lagging behind, and that she had commenced to limp more and more painfully. Her progress was very slow, and Tarzan could see that the man had not waited for her, but that he had been, in some places, a considerable distance ahead of her.

And so it was that Esteban had forged far ahead of Flora Hawkes, whose bruised and bleeding feet would scarce support her.

"Wait for me, Esteban," she had pleaded. "Do not desert me. Do not leave me alone here in this terrible jungle."

"Then keep up with me," growled the Spaniard. "Do you think that with this fortune in my possession I am going to wait here forever in the middle of the jungle for someone to come and take it away from me? No, I am going on to the coast as fast as I can. If you can keep up, well and good. If you cannot, that is your own lookout."

"But you could not desert me. Even you, Esteban, could not be such a beast after all that you have forced me to do for you."

The Spaniard laughed. "You are nothing more to me," he said, "than an old glove. With this," and he held the sack of diamonds before him, "I can purchase the finest gloves in the capitals of the world—new gloves," and he laughed grimly at his little joke.

"Esteban, Esteban," she cried, "come back; come back. I can go no farther. Do not leave me. Please come back and save me." But he only laughed at her, and as a turn of the trail shut him from her sight, she sank helpless and exhausted to the ground.

CHAPTER XX—THE DEAD RETURN

That night Esteban made his lonely camp beside a jungle trail that wound through the dry wash of an old river bed, along which a tiny rivulet still trickled, according the Spaniard the water which he craved.

The obsession which possessed him that he was in truth Tarzan of the Apes, imparted to him a false courage, so that he could camp alone upon the ground without recourse to artificial protection of any kind, and fortune had favored him in this respect in that it had sent no prowling beasts of prey to find him upon those occasions that he had dared too much. During the period that Flora Hawkes had been with him he had built shelters for her, but now that he had deserted her and was again alone, he could not, in the role that he had assumed, consider so effeminate an act as the building of even a thorn boma for protection during the darkness of the night.

He did, however, build a fire, for he had made a kill and had not yet reached a point of primitive savagery which permitted him even to imagine that he enjoyed raw meat.

Having devoured what meat he wanted and filled himself at the little rivulet, Esteban came back and squatted before his fire, where he drew the pouch of diamonds from his loin cloth and, opening it, spilled a handful of the precious gems into his palm. The flickering firelight playing upon them sent scintillant gleams shooting into the dark of the surrounding jungle night as the Spaniard let a tiny stream of the sparkling stones trickle from one hand to the other, and in the pretty play of light the Spaniard saw visions of the future—power, luxury, beautiful women—all that great wealth might purchase for a man. With half closed eyes he dreamed of the ideal that he should search the world over to obtain—the dream-woman for whom he had always searched—the dream-woman he had never found, the fit companion for such as Esteban Miranda imagined himself to be. Presently through the dark lashes that veiled his narrowed lids the Spaniard seemed to see before him in the flickering light of his camp fire a vague materialization of the figure of his dream—a woman's figure, clothed in flowing diaphanous white which appeared to hover just above him at the outer rim of his firelight at the summit of the ancient river bank.

It was strange how the vision persisted. Esteban closed his eyes tightly, and then opened them ever so little, and there, as it had been before he closed them, the vision remained. And then he opened his eyes wide, and still the figure of the woman in white floated above him.

Esteban Miranda went suddenly pale. "Mother of God!" he cried. "It is Flora. She is dead and has come back to haunt me."

With staring eyes he slowly rose to his feet to confront the apparition, when in soft and gentle tones it spoke.

"Heart of my heart," it cried, "it is really you!"

Instantly Esteban realized that this was no disembodied spirit, nor was it Flora—but who was it? Who was this vision of beauty, alone in the savage African wilderness?

Very slowly now it was descending the embankment and coming toward him. Esteban returned the diamonds to the pouch and replaced it inside his loin cloth.

With outstretched arms the girl came toward him. "My love, my love," she cried, "do not tell me that you do not know me." She was close enough now for the Spaniard to see her rapidly rising and falling breasts and her lips trembling with love and passion. A sudden wave of hot desire swept over him, so with outstretched arms he sprang forward to meet her and crush her to his breast.

Tarzan, following the spoor of the man and the woman, moved in a leisurely manner along the jungle trail, for he realized that no haste was essential to overtake these two. Nor was he at all surprised when he came suddenly upon the huddled figure of a woman, lying in the center of the pathway. He knelt beside her and laid a hand upon her shoulder, eliciting a startled scream.

"God!" she cried, "this is the end!"

"You are in no danger," said the ape-man. "I will not harm you."

She turned her eyes and looked up at him. At first she thought he was Esteban. "You have come back to save me, Esteban?" she asked.

"Esteban!" he exclaimed. "I am not Esteban. That is not my name." And then she recognized him.

"Lord Greystoke!" she cried. "It is really you?"

"Yes," he said, "and who are you?"

"I am Flora Hawkes. I was Lady Greystoke's maid."

"I remember you," he said. "What are you doing here?"

"I am afraid to tell you," she said. "I am afraid of your anger."

"Tell me," he commanded. "You should know, Flora, that I do not harm women."

"We came to get gold from the vaults of Opar," she said. "But that you know."

"I know nothing of it," he replied. "Do you mean that you were with those Europeans who drugged me and left me in their camp?"

"Yes," she said, "we got the gold, but you came with your Waziri and took it from us."

"I came with no Waziri and took nothing from you," said Tarzan. "I do not understand you."

She raised her eyebrows in surprise, for she knew that Tarzan of the Apes did not lie.

"We became separated," she said, "after our men turned against us. Esteban stole me from the others, and then, after a while Kraski found us. He was the Russian. He came with a bagful of diamonds and then Esteban killed him and took the diamonds."

It was now Tarzan's turn to experience surprise.

"And Esteban is the man who is with you?" he asked.

"Yes," she said, "but he has deserted me. I could not walk farther on my sore feet. He has gone and left me here to die and he has taken the diamonds with him."

"We shall find him," said the ape-man. "Come."

"But I cannot walk," said the girl.

"That is a small matter," he said, and, stooping, lifted her to his shoulder.

Easily the ape-man bore the exhausted girl along the trail. "It is not far to water," he said, "and water is what you need. It will help to revive you and give you strength, and perhaps I shall be able to find food for you soon."

"Why are you so good to me?" asked the girl.

"You are a woman. I could not leave you alone in the jungle to die, no matter what you may have done," replied the ape-man. And Flora Hawkes could only sob a broken plea for forgiveness for the wrong she had done him.

It grew quite dark, but still they moved along the silent trail until presently Tarzan caught in the distance the reflection of firelight.

"I think we shall soon find your friend," he whispered. "Make no noise."

A moment later his keen ears caught the sound of voices. He halted and lowered the girl to her feet.

"If you cannot follow," he said, "wait here. I do not wish him to escape. I will return for you. If you can follow on slowly, do so." And then he left her and made his way cautiously forward toward the light and the voices. He heard Flora Hawkes moving directly behind him. It was evident that she could not bear the thought of being left alone again in the dark jungle. Almost simultaneously Tarzan heard a low whine a few paces to his right. "Jad-bal-ja," he whispered in a low voice, "heel," and the great black-maned lion crept close to him, and Flora Hawkes, stifling a scream, rushed to his side and grasped his arms.

"Silence," he whispered; "Jad-bal-ja will not harm you."

An instant later the three came to the edge of the ancient river bank, and through the tall grasses growing there looked down upon the little camp beneath.

Tarzan, to his consternation, saw a counterpart of himself standing before a little fire, while slowly approaching the man, with outstretched arms, was a woman, draped in flowing white. He heard her words; soft words of love and endearment, and at the sound of the voice and the scent spoor that a vagrant wind carried suddenly to his nostrils, strange complex of emotion overwhelmed him—happiness, despair, rage, love, and hate.

He saw the man at the fire step forward with open arms to take the woman to his breast, and then Tarzan separated the grasses and stepped to the very edge of the embankment, his voice shattering the jungle with a single word.

"Jane!" he cried, and instantly the man and woman turned and looked up at him, where his figure was dimly revealed in the light of the campfire. At sight of him the man wheeled and raced for the jungle on the opposite side of the river, and then Tarzan leaped to the bottom of the wash below and ran toward the woman.

"Jane," he cried, "it is you, it is you!"

The woman showed her bewilderment. She looked first at the retreating figure of the man she had been about to embrace and then turned her eyes toward Tarzan. She drew her fingers across her brow and looked back toward Esteban, but Esteban was no longer in sight. Then she took a faltering step toward the ape-man.

"My God," she cried, "what does it mean? Who are you, and if you are Tarzan who was he?"

"I am Tarzan, Jane," said the ape-man.

She looked back and saw Flora Hawkes approaching. "Yes," she said, "you are Tarzan. I saw you when you ran off into the jungle with Flora Hawkes. I cannot understand, John. I could not believe that you, even had you suffered an accident to your head, could have done such a thing."

"I, run off into the jungle with Flora Hawkes?" he asked, in unfeigned surprise.

"I saw you," said Jane.

The ape-man turned toward Flora. "I do not understand it," he said.

"It was Esteban who ran off into the jungle with me, Lady Greystoke," said the girl. "It was Esteban who was about to deceive you again. This is indeed Lord Greystoke. The other was an impostor, who only just deserted me and left me to die in the jungle. Had not Lord Greystoke come when he did I should be dead by now."

Lady Greystoke took a faltering step toward her husband. "Ah, John," she said, "I knew it could not have been you. My heart told me, but my eyes deceived me. Quick," she cried, "that impostor must be captured. Hurry, John, before he escapes."

"Let him go," said the ape-man. "As much as I want him, as much as I want that which he has stolen from me, I will not leave you alone again in the jungle, Jane, even to catch him."

"But Jad-bal-ja," she cried. "What of him?"

"Ah", cried the ape-man, "I had forgotten," and turning to the lion he pointed toward the direction that the Spaniard had escaped. "Fetch him, Jad-bal-ja," he cried; and, with a bound, the tawny beast was off upon the spoor of his quarry.

"He will kill him?" asked Flora Hawkes, shuddering. And yet at heart she was glad of the just fate that was overtaking the Spaniard.

"No, he will not kill him," said Tarzan of the Apes. "He may maul him a bit, but he will bring him back alive if it is possible." And then, as though the fate of the fugitive was already forgotten, he turned toward his mate.

"Jane," he said, "Usula told me that you were dead. He said that they found your burned body in the Arab village and that they buried it there. How is it, then, that you are here alive and unharmed? I have been searching the jungles for Luvini to avenge your death. Perhaps it is well that I did not find him."

"You would never have found him," replied Jane Clayton, "but I cannot understand why Usula should have told you that he had found my body and buried it."

"Some prisoners that he took," replied Tarzan, "told him that Luvini had taken you bound hand and foot into one of the Arab huts near the village gateway, and that there he had further secured you to a stake driven into the floor of the hut. After the village had been destroyed by fire Usula and the other Waziri returned to search for you with some of the prisoners they had taken who pointed out the location of the hut, where the charred remains of a human body were found beside a burned stake to which it had apparently been tied."

"Ah!" exclaimed the girl, "I see. Luvini did bind me hand and foot and tie me to the stake but later he came back into the hut and removed the bonds. He attempted to attack me— long we fought I do not know, but so engrosses were we in our struggle that neither one of us was aware of the burning of the village about us. As I persistently fought him off I caught a glimpse of a knife in his belt, and then I let him seize me and as his arms encircled me I grasped the knife and, drawing it from its sheath, plunged it into his back, below his left shoulder—that was the end. Luvini sank lifeless to the floor of the hut. Almost simultaneously the rear and roof of the structure burst into flames.

"I was almost naked, for he had torn nearly all my clothing from me in our struggles. Hanging upon the wall of the hut was this white burnoose, the property, doubtless, of one of murdered Arabs. I seized it, and throwing about me ran into the village street. The huts were now all aflame, and the last of the natives was disappearing through the gateway. To my right was a section of palisade that had not been attacked by the flames. To escape into jungle by the gateway would have meant into the arms of my enemies, and so, somehow, I managed to scale the palisade and drop into the jungle unseen by any.

"I have had considerable difficulty eluding the various bands of blacks who escaped the village. A part of the time I have been hunting for the Waziri and the balance I have had to remain in hiding. I was resting in the crotch of a tree, about half a mile from here, when I saw the light of this man's fire, and when I came to investigate I was almost stunned by joy to discover that I had, as I imagined, stumbled upon my Tarzan."

"It was Luvini's body, then, and not yours that they buried," said Tarzan.

"Yes," said Jane, "and it was this man who just escaped whom I saw run off into the jungle with Flora, and not you, as I believed."

Flora Hawkes looked up suddenly. "And it must have been Esteban who came with the Waziri and stole the gold from us. He fooled our men he must have fooled the Waziri, too."

"He might have fooled anyone if he could have me," said Jane Clayton. "I should have discovered the deception in a few minutes I have no doubt, but in the flickering light of the campfire, and influenced as I was by the great joy of seeing Lord Greystoke again, I believed quickly that which I wanted to believe."

The ape-man ran his fingers through his thick shock of hair in a characteristic gesture of meditation. "I cannot understand how he fooled Usula in broad daylight," he said with a shake of his head.

"I can," said Jane. "He told him that he had suffered an injury to his head which caused him to lose his memory partially—an explanation which accounted for many lapses in the man's interpretation of your personality."

"He was a clever devil," commented the ape-man.

"He was a devil, all right," said Flora.

It was more than an hour later that the grasses at the river bank suddenly parted and Jad-bal-ja emerged silently into their presence. Grasped in his jaws was a torn and bloody leopard skin which he brought and laid at the feet of his master.

The ape-man picked the thing up and examined it, and then he scowled. "I believe Jad-bal-ja killed him after all," he said.

"He probably resisted," said Jane Clayton, "in which event Jad-bal-ja could do nothing else in self-defense but slay him."

"Do you suppose he ate him?" cried Flora Hawkes, drawing fearfully away from the beast.

"No," said Tarzan, "he has not had time. In the morning we will follow the spoor and find his body. I should like to have the diamonds again." And then he told Jane the strange story connected with his acquisition of the great wealth represented by the little bag of stones.

The following morning they set out in search of Esteban's corpse. The trail led through dense brush and thorns to the edge of the river farther down stream, and there it disappeared, and though the ape-man searched both sides of the river for a couple of miles above and below the point at which he had lost the spoor, he found no further sign of the Spaniard. There was blood along the tracks that Esteban had made and blood upon the grasses at the river's brim.

At last the ape-man returned to the two women. "That is the end of the man who would be Tarzan," he said.

"Do you think he is dead?" asked Jane.

"Yes, I am sure of it," said the ape-man. "From the blood I imagine that Jad-bal-ja mauled him, but that he managed to break away and get into the river. The fact that I can find no indication of his having reached the bank within a reasonable distance of this spot leads me to believe that he has been devoured by crocodiles."

Again Flora Hawkes shuddered. "He was a wicked man," she said, "but I would not wish even the wickedest such a fate as that."

The ape-man shrugged. "He brought it upon himself, and, doubtless, the world is better off without him."

"It was my fault," said Flora. "It was my wickedness that brought him and the others here. I told them of what I had heard of the gold in the treasure vaults of Opar—it was my idea to come here and steal it and to find a man who could impersonate Lord Greystoke. Because of my wickedness many men have died, and you, Lord Greystoke, and your lady, have almost met your death—I do not dare to ask for forgiveness."

Jane Clayton put her arm about the girl's shoulder. "Avarice has been the cause of many crimes since the world began," she said, "and when crime is invoked in its aid it assumes its most repulsive aspect and brings most often its own punishment, as you, Flora, may well testify. For my part I forgive you. I imagine that you have learned your lesson."

"You have paid a heavy price for your folly," said the ape-man. "You have been punished enough. We will take you to your friends who are on their way to the coast under escort of a friendly tribe. They cannot be far distant, for, from the condition of the men when I saw them, long marches are beyond their physical powers."

The girl dropped to her knees at his feet. "How can I thank you for your kindness?" she said. "But I would rather remain here in Africa with you and Lady Greystoke, and work for you and show by my loyalty that I can redeem the wrong I did you."

Tarzan glanced at his wife questioningly, and Jane Clayton signified her assent to the girl's request.

"Very well, then," said the ape-man, "you may remain with us, Flora."

"You will never regret it," said the girl. "I will work my fingers off for you."

The three, and Jad-bal-ja, had been three days upon the march toward home when Tarzan, who was in the lead, paused, and, raising his head, sniffed the jungle air. Then he turned to them with a smile. "My Waziri are disobedient," he said. "I sent them home and yet here they are, coming toward us, directly away from home."

A few minutes later they met the van of the Waziri, and great was the rejoicing of the blacks when they found both their master and mistress alive and unscathed.

"And now that we have found you," said Tarzan, after the greetings were over, and innumerable questions had been asked and answered, "tell me what you did with the gold that you took from the camp of the Europeans."

"We hid it, O Bwana, where you told us to hide it," replied Usula.

"I was not with you, Usula," said the ape-man. "It was another, who deceived Lady Greystoke even as he deceived you —a bad man—who impersonated Tarzan of the Apes so cleverly that it is no wonder that you were imposed upon."

"Then it was not you who told us that your head had been injured and that you could not remember the language of the Waziri?" demanded Usula.

"It was not I," said Tarzan, "for my head has not been injured, and I remember well the language of my children."

"Ah," cried Usula, "then it was not our Big Bwana who ran from Buto, the rhinoceros?"

Tarzan laughed. "Did the other run from Buto?"

"That he did," cried Usula; "he ran in great terror."

"I do not know that I blame him," said Tarzan, "for Buto is no pleasant playfellow."

"But our Big Bwana would not run from him," said Usula, proudly.

"Even if another than I hid the gold it was you who dug the hole. Lead me to the spot then, Usula."

The Waziri constructed rude yet comfortable litters for the two white women, though Jane Clayton laughed at the idea that it was necessary that she be carried and insisted upon walking beside her bearers more often than she rode. Flora Hawkes, however, weak and exhausted as she was, could not have proceeded far without being carried, and was glad of the presence of the brawny Waziri who bore her along the jungle trail so easily.

It was a happy company that marched in buoyant spirits toward the spot where the Waziri had cached the gold for Esteban. The blacks were overflowing with good nature because they had found their master and their mistress, while the relief and joy of Tarzan and Jane were too deep for expression.

When at last they came to the place beside the river where they had buried the gold the Waziri, singing and laughing, commenced to dig for the treasure, but presently their singing ceased and their laughter was replaced by expressions of puzzled concern.

For a while Tarzan watched them in silence and then a slow smile overspread his countenance.

"You must have buried it deep, Usula," he said.

The black scratched his head. "No, not so deep as this, Bwana," he cried. "I cannot understand it. We should have found the gold before this."

"Are you sure you are looking in the right place?" asked Tarzan.

"This is the exact spot, Bwana," the black assured him, "but the gold is not here. Someone has removed it since we buried it."

"The Spaniard again," commented Tarzan. "He was a slick customer."

"But he could not have taken it alone," said Usula. "There were many ingots of it."

"No," said Tarzan, "he could not, and yet it is not here."

The Waziri and Tarzan searched carefully about the spot where the gold had been buried, but so clever had been the woodcraft of Owaza that he had obliterated even from the keen senses of the ape-man every vestige of the spoor that he and the Spaniard had made in carrying the gold from the old hiding place to the new.

"It is gone," said the ape-man, "but I shall see that it does not get out of Africa," and he despatched runners in various directions to notify the chiefs of the friendly tribes surrounding his domain to watch carefully every safari crossing their territory, and to let none pass who carried gold.

"That will stop them," he said after the runners had departed.

That night as they made their camp upon the trail toward home, the three whites were seated about a small fire with Jad-bal-ja lying just behind the ape-man, who was examining the leopard skin that the golden lion had retrieved in his pursuit of the Spaniard, when Tarzan turned toward his wife.

You were right, Jane," he said. "The treasure vaults of Opar are not for me. This time I have lost not only the gold but a fabulous fortune in diamonds as well, beside risking that greatest of all treasures—yourself."

"Let the gold and the diamonds go, John," she said; "we have one another, and Korak."

"And a bloody leopard skin," he supplemented, "with a mystery map painted upon it in blood."

Jad-bal-ja sniffed the hide and licked his chops in anticipation or retrospection—which?

CHAPTER XXI—AN ESCAPE AND A CAPTURE

At sight of the true Tarzan, Esteban Miranda turned and fled blindly into the jungle.

His heart was cold with terror as he rushed on in blind fear. He had no objective in mind. He did not know in what direction he was going. His only thought—the thought which dominated him—was based solely upon a desire to put as much distance as possible between himself and the ape-man, and so he blundered on, forcing his way through dense thickets of thorns that tore and lacerated his flesh until, at every step he left a trail of blood behind him.

At the river's edge the thorns reached out and seized again, as they had several times before, the precious leopard skin to which he clung with almost the same tenacity as he clung to life itself. But this time the thorns would not leave go their hold, and as he struggled to tear it away from them his eyes turned back in the direction from which he had come. He heard the sound of a great body, moving rapidly through the thicket toward him, and an instant later saw the baleful glare of two gleaming, yellow-green spots of flame. With a stifled cry of terror the Spaniard relinquished his hold upon the leopard skin and, wheeling, dived into the river.

As the black waters closed above his head Jad-bal-ja came to the edge of the bank and looked down upon the widening circles which marked the spot of his quarry's disappearance, for Esteban, who was a strong swimmer, struck boldly for the opposite side of the stream, keeping himself well submerged.

For a moment the golden lion scanned the surface of the river, and then he turned and sniffed at the hide the Spaniard had been forced to leave behind, and grasping it in his jaws tore it from the thorns that held it and carried it back to lay it at the feet of his master.

Forced at last to come to the surface for air the Spaniard arose amid a mass of tangled foliage and branches. For a moment he thought that he was lost, so tightly held was he by the entangling boughs, but presently he forced his way upward, and as his head appeared above the surface of the water amidst the foliage he discovered that he had arisen directly beneath a fallen tree that was floating down the center of the stream. After considerable effort he managed to draw himself up to the boughs and find a place astride the great bole, and thus he floated down stream in comparative safety.

He breathed a deep sigh of relief as he realized with what comparative ease he had escaped the just vengeance of the ape-man. It is true that he bemoaned the loss of the hide which carried the map to the location of the hidden gold, but he still retained in his possession a far greater treasure, and as he thought of it his hands gloatingly fondled the bag of diamonds fastened to his loin cloth. Yet, even though he possessed this great fortune in diamonds, his avaricious mind constantly returned to the golden ingots by the waterfall.

"Owaza will get it," he muttered to himself. "I never trusted the black dog, and when he deserted me I knew well enough what his plans were."

All night long Esteban Miranda floated down stream upon the fallen tree, seeing no sign of life, until shortly after daybreak, he passed a native village upon the shore.

It was the village of Obebe, the cannibal, and at sight of the strange figure of the white giant floating down the stream upon the bole of a tree, the young woman who espied him raised a great hue and cry until the population of the village lined the shore watching him pass.

"It is a strange god," cried one.

"It is the river devil," said the witch doctor. "He is a friend of mine. Now, indeed, shall we catch many fish if for each ten that you catch you give one to me."

"It is not the river devil," rumbled the deep voice of Obebe, the cannibal. "You are getting old," he said to the witch doctor, "and of late your medicine has been poor medicine, and now you tell me that Obebe's greatest enemy is the river devil. That is Tarzan of the Apes. Obebe knows him well, and in truth every cannibal chief in the vicinity knew Tarzan of the Apes well and feared and hated him, for relentless had been the ape-man's war against them.

"It is Tarzan of the Apes," repeated Obebe, "and he is in trouble. Perhaps it is our chance to capture him."

He called his warriors about him, and presently half a hundred brawny young bucks started at a jog trot down the trail that paralleled the river. For miles they followed the slowly moving tree which carried Esteban Miranda until at last at a bend in the river the tree was caught in the outer circle of a slow-moving eddy, which carried it beneath the overhanging limbs of trees growing close to the river's edge.

Cramped and chilled and hungry as he was, Esteban was glad of the opportunity to desert his craft and gain the shore. And so, laboriously, he drew himself up among the branches of the tree that momentarily offered him a haven of retreat from the river, and crawling to its stem lowered himself to the ground beneath, unconscious of the fact that in the grasses around him squatted half a hundred cannibal warriors.

Leaning against the bole of the tree the Spaniard rested for a moment. He felt for the diamonds and found that they were safe.

"I am a lucky devil, after all," he said aloud and almost simultaneously the fifty blacks arose about him and leaped upon him. So sudden was the attack, so overwhelming the force, that the Spaniard had no opportunity to defend himself against them, with the result that he was down and securely bound almost before he could realize what was happening to him.

"Ah, Tarzan of the Apes, I have you at last," gloated Obebe, the cannibal, but Esteban did not understand a word the man said, and so he could make no reply. He talked to Obebe in English, but that language the latter did not understand. Of only one thing was Esteban certain; that he was a prisoner and that he was being taken back toward the interior. When they reached Obebe's village there was great rejoicing on the part of the women and the children and the warriors who had remained behind. But the witch doctor shook his head and made wry faces and dire prophecies.

"You have seized the river devil," he said. "We shall catch no more fish, and presently a great sickness will fall upon Obebe's people and they will all die like flies." But Obebe only laughed at the witch doctor for, being an old man and a great king, he had accumulated much wisdom and, with the acquisition of wisdom man is more inclined to be skeptical in matters of religion.

"You may laugh now, Obebe," said the witch doctor, "but later you will not laugh. Wait and see."

"When, with my own hands, I kill Tarzan of the Apes, then indeed shall I laugh," replied the chief, "and when I and my warriors have eaten his heart and his flesh, then, indeed, shall we no longer fear any of your devils."

"Wait," cried the witch doctor angrily, "and you shall see."

They took the Spaniard, securely bound, and threw him into a filthy hut, through the doorway of which he could see the women of the village preparing cooking fires and pots for the feast of the coming night. A cold sweat stood out upon the brow of Esteban Miranda as he watched these grewsome preparations, the significance of which he could not misinterpret, when coupled with the gestures and the glances that were directed toward the hut where he lay, by the inhabitants of the village.

The afternoon was almost spent and the Spaniard felt that he could count the hours of life remaining to him upon possibly two fingers of one hand, when there came from the direction of the river a series of piercing screams which shattered the quiet of the jungle, and brought the inhabitants of the village to startled attention, and an instant later sent them in a mad rush in the direction of the fear-laden shrieks. But they were too late and reached the river only just in time to see a woman dragged beneath the surface by a huge crocodile.

"Ah, Obebe, what did I tell you?" demanded the witch doctor, exultantly. "Already has the devil god commenced his revenge upon your people."

The ignorant villagers, steeped in superstition, looked fearfully from their witch doctor to their chief. Obebe scowled. "He is Tarzan of the Apes," he insisted.

"He is the river devil who has taken the shape of Tarzan of the Apes," insisted the witch doctor.

"We shall see," replied Obebe. "If he is the river devil he can escape our bonds. If he is Tarzan of the Apes he cannot. If he is the river devil he will not die a natural death, like men die, but will live on forever. If he is Tarzan of the Apes some day he will die. We will keep him, then, and see, and that will prove whether or not he is Tarzan of the Apes or the river devil."

"How?" asked the witch doctor.

"It is very simple," replied Obebe. "If some morning we find that he has escaped we will know that he is the river devil, and because we have not harmed him but have fed him well while he has been here in our village, he will befriend us and no harm will come of it. But if he does not escape we will know that he is Tarzan of the Apes, provided he dies a natural death. And so, if he does not escape, we shall keep him until he dies and then we shall know that he was, indeed, Tarzan of the Apes."

"But suppose he does not die?" asked the witch doctor, scratching his woolly head.

"Then," exclaimed Obebe triumphantly, "we will know that you are right, and that he was indeed, the river devil."

Obebe went and ordered women to take food to the Spaniard while the witch doctor stood, where Obebe had left him, in the middle of the street, still scratching his head in thought.

And thus was Esteban Miranda, possessor of the most fabulous fortune in diamonds that the world had ever known, condemned to life imprisonment in the village of Obebe, the cannibal.

While he had been lying in the hut his traitorous confederate, Owaza, from the opposite bank of the river from the spot where he and Esteban had hidden the golden ingots, saw Tarzan and his Waziri come and search for the gold and go away again, and the following morning Owaza came with fifty men whom he had recruited from a neighboring village and dug up the gold and started with it toward the coast.

That night Owaza made camp just outside a tiny village of a minor chief, who was weak in warriors. The old fellow invited Owaza into his compound, and there he fed him and gave him native beer, while the chief's people circulated among Owaza's boys plying them with innumerable questions until at last the truth leaked out and the chief knew that Owaza's porters were carrying a great store of yellow gold.

When the chief learned this for certain he was much perturbed, but finally a smile crossed his face as he talked with the half-drunken Owaza.

"You have much gold with you"' said the Old chief, and it is very heavy. It will be hard to get your boys to carry it all the way back to the coast."

"Yes," said Owaza, "but I shall pay them well."

"If they did not have to carry it so far from home you would not have to pay them so much, would you?" asked the chief.

"No," said Owaza, "but I cannot dispose of it this side of the coast."

"I know where you can dispose of it within two days' march," replied the old chief.

"Where?" demanded Owaza. "And who here in the interior will buy it?"

"There is a white man who will give you a little piece of paper for it and you can take that paper to the coast and get the full value of your gold."

"Who is this white man?" demanded Owaza, "and where is he?"

"He is a friend of mine," said the chief, "and if you wish I will take you to him on the morrow, and you can bring with you all your gold and get the little piece of paper."

"Good," said Owaza, "and then I shall not have to pay the carriers but a very small amount."

The carriers were glad, indeed, to learn the next day that they were not to go all the way to the coast, for even the lure of payment was not sufficient to overcome their dislike to so long a journey, and their fear of being at so great a distance from home. They were very happy, therefore, as they set forth on a two days' march toward the northeast. And Owaza was happy and so was the old chief, who accompanied them himself, though why he was happy about it Owaza could not guess.

They had marched for almost two days when the chief sent one of his own men forward with a message.

"It is to my friend," he said, "to tell him to come and meet us and lead us to his village." And a few hours later, as the little caravan emerged from the jungle onto a broad, grassy plain, they saw not far from them, and approaching rapidly, a large band of warriors. Owaza halted.

"Who are those?" he demanded.

"Those are the warriors of my friend," replied the chief, "and he is with them. See?" and he pointed toward a figure at the head of the blacks, who were approaching at a trot, their spears and white plumes gleaming in the sunshine.

"They come for war and not for peace," said Owaza fearfully.

"That depends upon you, Owaza," replied the chief.

"I do not understand you," said Owaza.

"But you will in a few minutes after my friend has come."

As the advancing warriors approached more closely Owaza saw a giant white at their head— a white whom he mistook for Esteban—the confederate he had so traitorously deserted. He turned upon the chief. "You have betrayed me," he cried.

"Wait," said the old chief; "nothing that belongs to you shall be taken from you."

"The gold is not his," cried Owaza. "He stole it," and he pointed at Tarzan who had approached and halted before him, but who ignored him entirely and turned to the chief.

"Your runner came," he said to the old man, "and brought your message, and Tarzan and his Waziri have come to see what they could do for their old friend."

The chief smiled. "Your runner came to me, O Tarzan, four days since, and two days later came this man with his carriers, bearing golden ingots toward the coast. I told him that I had a friend who would buy them, giving him a little piece of paper for them, but that, of course, only in case the gold belonged to Owaza."

The ape-man smiled. "You have done well, my friend," he said. "The gold does not belong to Owaza."

"It does not belong to you, either," cried Owaza. "You are not Tarzan of the Apes. I know you. You came with the four white men and the white woman to steal the gold from Tarzan's country, and then you stole it from your own friends."

The chief and the Waziri laughed. The ape-man smiled one of his slow smiles.

"The other was an impostor, Owaza," he said, "but I am Tarzan of the Apes, and I thank you for bringing my gold to me. Come," he said. "It is but a few more miles to my home," and the ape-man compelled Owaza to direct his carriers to bear the golden ingots to the Greystoke bungalow. There Tarzan fed the carriers and paid them, and the next morning sent them back toward their own country, and he sent Owaza with them, but not without a gift of value, accompanied with an admonition that the black never again return to Tarzan's country.

When they had all departed, and Tarzan and Jane and Korak were standing upon the veranda of the bungalow with Jad-bal-ja lying at their feet, the ape-man threw an arm about his mate's shoulders.

"I shall have to retract what I said about the gold of Opar not being for me, for you see before you a new fortune that has come all the way from the treasure vaults of Opar without any effort on my part."

"Now, if someone would only bring your diamonds back," laughed Jane.

"No chance of that," said Tarzan. "They are unquestionably at the bottom of the Ugogo River," and far away, upon the banks of the Ugogo, in the village of Obebe, the cannibal, Esteban Miranda lay in the filth of the hut that had been assigned to him, gloating over the fortune that he could never utilize as he entered upon a life of captivity that the stubbornness and superstition of Obebe had doomed him to undergo.

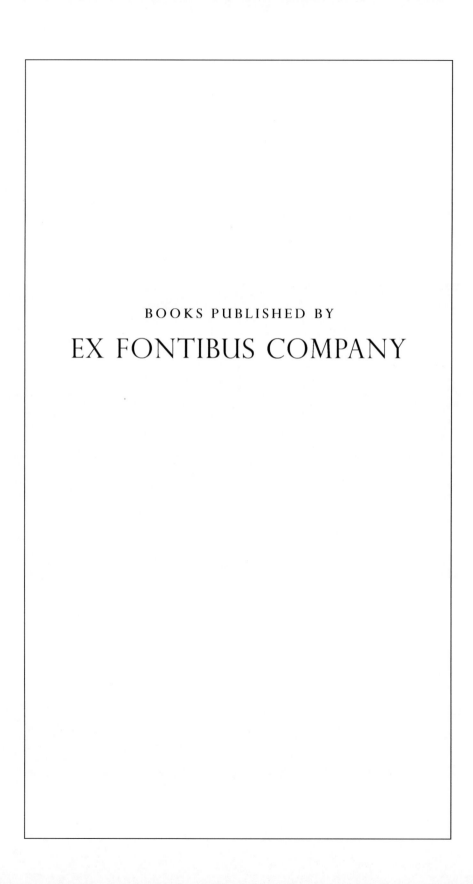

BOOKS PUBLISHED BY

EX FONTIBUS COMPANY

CONTENTS

CATALOGUE LISTING AS OF APRIL 16, 2020

BOOKS PUBLISHED BY

EX FONTIBUS COMPANY

http://www.exfontibus.com
contact@exfontibus.com
http://www.facebook.com/exfont
exfontibuscompany@gmail.com

*Our books are sold on our own website, at Amazon.com,
& through other retailers*

Get the latest news on our page!

SACRED TEXTS—SCRIPTURE, LITURGICAL TEXTS, AND PRAYER

Biblia Sacra—The Holy Bible in Latin and English [3 vols.]
A beautiful parallel Latin/English edition of the Bible of the medieval Catholic Church, using the Latin of the Clementine Vulgate and the English of Douay-Rheims Challoner Revision. **Vol. 1** includes the Pentateuch (Genesis, Exodus, Leviticus, Numbers, Deuteronomy) and the Historical Books (Joshua, Judges, Ruth, Samuel/Kings, Paralipomenon/Chronicles, Ezra/Nehemiah, Tobit, Judith, Esther). **Vol. 2** contains Job, Psalms, Proverbs, Ecclesiastes, the Song of Songs, Wisdom, Ecclesiasticus (Ben-Sirah), Isaiah, Jeremiah, Lamentations, Baruch, Ezechiel, Daniel, Hosea, Joel, Amos, Obadiah, Jonah, Micah, Nahum, Habakkuk, Zephaniah, Haggai, Zechariah, Malachi, Machabees. **Vol. 3** contains the entirety of the New Testament.

Biblia Sacra–New Testament and Psalms in Latin and English
An elegant smaller volume containing only the New Testament and the Psalms. [This third edition enlarges the formerly-cramped font.]

The Septuagint, with Apocrypha, in English (Second Edition)
The Septuagint (LXX), the ancient Greek translation of Jewish sacred writings, is of great importance in the history of both Judaism and Christianity. Translated from Hebrew and other originals in the two centuries before Jesus, the Septuagint

provides important information about the history of biblical text. It captures a moment in time, illuminating for us how Greek-speaking Jews of that time read and interpreted the Hebrew Scriptures that they translated. In its time, it made the Jewish Scriptures accessible to peoples and cultures outside of Judaism through *koine* Greek, the common language of the Mediterranean world. The Septuagint was the Bible of Greek speaking Jews; it was the Bible of the first Christians. It is cited in the New Testament and by the great luminaries of early Christianity. In this edition of the famed translation by Lancelot C. Brenton, many archaisms have been removed and personal pronouns rendered consistent with modern English—yet without sacrificing any of the accuracy, power, or beauty of the original translation. [This second edition corrects several errors from the first edition.]

Kyriale Romanum

Gregorian chant has long transmitted the mystery and majesty of the Catholic liturgical tradition. Newly republished, the Kyriale Romanum of 1961, preserves between its covers an invaluable patrimony of ancient and medieval chants for the Ordinary of the Mass that can be used with both the extraordinary (1962) and the ordinary (post-1970) forms of the Roman Missal. It collects from the Graduale the most frequently-used chant settings throughout the liturgical year, with eighteen mass settings, six credos, and numerous settings for feasts and holy days, including the solemn procession on the feast of Corpus Christi. This beautiful and affordably-priced volume is of great value to all who wish to encounter this venerable musical tradition of the Roman Rite.

The Prayerbook of Ælfwine of Hyde

Decades before the Norman conquest of England in A.D. 1066, a Benedictine monk at Hyde Abbey named assembled a small prayer book from the tradition of early Saxon Christianity. That monk, who later became Abbot of Hyde, passed to his heavenly reward but fifteen years before the influx of Norman culture from France would reshape the prayer and liturgical tradition of English Christianity. The prayers that are preserved in his book bear witness to the zeal and vigor of early English Christianity, with a poetry that stirs the soul over ten centuries since first they were prayed.

THEOLOGY—PATRISTIC AND MEDIEVAL*

ST. IRENÆUS OF LYONS
Against Heresies and Other Writings
The complete text of *Against the Heresies*, with fragments of other writings. Available nowhere else as a standalone volume. Bishop St. Irenaeus of Lyons wrote his *Against Heresies* ca. A.D. 180 to preserve the Christian rule of faith against the Gnostic heresy. To vindicate the Incarnation against the Gnostics, he described and attacked their principal doctrine: the evil origin of the natural world. Affirming the unity of Old and New Testaments, the goodness of the Creator and the created world, and finally the mystery of divinization whereby human beings are elevated into the divine life, the saint produced an outstanding example of early Christian biblical theology. For the early Fathers, doctrines were taught to safeguard the confession of God's saving love revealed through His Incarnation as Jesus Christ. Of such work there is no better example than Irenaeus, disciple of Polycarp, disciple of John the Evangelist.

ORIGEN OF ALEXANDRIA
Against Celsus (Contra Celsum)
This is Origen's great apologetical work, undertaken in answer to the attack on Christianity by the pagan philosopher Celsus. The text that Origen composed to refute Celsus's self-styled   (*True Discourse*) consists of eight books, and belongs to the latest years of his life. It has always been regarded as the great apologetic work of antiquity; and no one can peruse it without being struck by the multifarious reading, wonderful acuteness, and rare subtlety of mind that it displays. A great work, well-deserving the notice of the students of Apologetics and of Early Christianity in general.

ST. ATHANASIUS OF AELXANDRIA
Essential Writings on the Incarnation [Forthcoming]
In collaboration with Christian Classics, an imprint of Ave Maria Press of Notre Dame, Indiana.

ST. AMBROSE OF MILAN
Theological and Dogmatic Works
These works present the thought of St. Ambrose, the bishop whose preaching first renewed St. Augustine's interest in Christianity. Included in this volume are several of Ambrose's works on the chief doctrines of the faith: "The Mysteries," "The Holy Spirit," "The Sacrament of the Incarnation of Our Lord," and "The

---

* Chronological listing.

Sacraments," including his famous teaching on the transformation of bread and wine into the Body and Blood of Christ.

ST. BASIL OF CÆSAREA

Exegetic Homilies

Basil the Great, of Caesarea, here offers homilies on the creation of the cosmos (the Hexameron, or the Six Days), God's providential ordering of the world, and on selected Psalms. A great work of early Christian biblical exegesis and a monument of patristic theology, now available in an attractive and affordable edition.

ST. JOHN CASSIAN

On the Incarnation of the Lord, Against Nestorius

Near the end of his writing career, Cassian the monk was commissioned by an archdeacon—the future Pope Leo the Great—to write a reply to the Christological positions of Nestorius, who saw in Christ two subjects, that of the Word and that of the man Jesus. Cassian's foray into ecclesiastical controversy, a cannonade of arguments from the Scriptures and the early Fathers, offers a blusteringly-effective representation of the general Christological views of East and West. Unsurprisingly, for one such as Cassian who was so concerned with the heights of Christian sanctity, it places special emphasis on the distinction between Christ's divinity and the indwelling of the Word in the saints—for the full divinity of Christ is what indeed makes it possible for *Christ* to be said to dwell within those saints who tread the heights of union with God. What he lacks in the precision of an Athanasius or a Maximus the Confessor, Cassian more than makes up for in the passion of his argumentation.

ST. GREGORY THE GREAT

Dialogues

In the series of dialogues that he patiently holds with his deacon Peter, St. Gregory describes a vision of sacred stability in an unstable world; this stability is to be found in the saint's life, lived in the love of Christ and anchored in the power of God. Through tales of miracles and examples of charity, including a famous dialogue on heaven, hell, purgatory, and the power of the Mass, Gregory illustrates the guiding hand of providence in the life of the saint and in the divine power manifest in that saint's deeds and words. Through these stories he aims to teach his readers to offer themselves on the "altar of the heart" as a living sacrifice of love in union with the sacrifice of Christ on the Cross.

Moralia in Job (Morals on the Book of Job) [3 vols.]
Pope Gregory the Great (r. 590–604) wrote his *Moralia*, or moral homilies on Job, one of his greatest works, before his accession to the See of Peter. Seeking a life of contemplation, Gregory had retired to a house on Rome's Caelian Hill, forming the monastic community of St. Andrew's. Shortly thereafter, however, he was sent obediently but unhappily to Constantinople as papal nuncio (*apocrisarius*) at the court of the Byzantine emperor. There too he gathered a small community to whom he delivered his famed homilies on Job. For Gregory, Job is a figure of Christ, who suffered innocently—not for his sins but for the increase of his merits and the salvation of others by love. These homilies span Christian doctrine, from Creation to final Judgment, from the height of angelic hierarchies to the innermost depths of the human soul. Confident that the Holy Spirit has not idly chosen the words of Scripture, Gregory finds a depth of allegory out of which he draws a brilliant picture of Christ, whose humanity must mark our own and whose Cross is our path to eternal rest. A beautiful meditation on suffering, on the path from fear to love, and on the healing and glorification of the individual soul which, as a member of Christ's body, comes to participate in the life of the holy Trinity. When Gregory was elected bishop of Rome just a few years later, he would continue to draw on and to develop the teaching herein, to guide the spiritual lives of his flock amidst the terror-filled final dissolution of the Western Empire. The teaching of the *Moralia* became a source for the doctors of the middle ages, including Hugh of St. Victor, St. Thomas Aquinas, St. Bonaventure, and many others. Western Christianity today owes an incalculable debt to the homilies that Gregory preached to his small circle of ascetics so many years ago.

ST. JOHN OF DAMASCUS

Writings
St. John Damascene, among the greatest of the Eastern fathers during the patristic age, produced his work *The Fount of Knowledge* as a summary of Christian philosophy and theology. It is one of the most important works of the Greek patristic age. Included are "The Philosophical Chapters," "On Heresies," and the justly-famous "Exact Exposition of the Orthodox Faith"—a veritable *Summa* of the doctrine of the Eastern fathers. Now available in an attractive and affordable edition.

ST. ANSELM OF CANTERBURY

Complete Philosophical and Theological Treatises
We are proud to re-print Jasper Hopkins' philosophically sensitive translations of the complete treatises of Anselm of Canterbury, the "Father of Scholasticism." The present volume contains, in English translation, all of St. Anselm's treatises, as

well as his important Meditation on Human Redemption and four of his didactic letters. Collectively, these constitute his intellectual writings. Included are: *Monologion*; *Proslogion*; *Debate with Gaunilo*; *De Grammatico*; *On Truth (De Veritate)*; *Freedom of Choice (De Libertate Arbitrii)*; *The Fall of the Devil (De Casu Diaboli)*; *Two Letters concerning Roscelin*; *The Incarnation of the Word (De Incarnatione Verbi)*; *Why God Became a [God-]man (Cur Deus Homo)*; *Philosophical Fragments*; *A Meditation on Human Redemption (Meditatio)*; *The Virgin Conception and Original Sin (De Conceptu)*; *The Procession of the Holy Spirit (De Processione)*; *Letters on the Sacraments (De Sacramentis)*; *Foreknowledge, Predestination, Grace, and Free Choice (De Concordia)*. In an appendix is included a scholarly bibliography of resources on Anselm.

Cur Deus Homo

Available here in an attractive paperback edition, Anselm's famous treatise *Cur Deus Homo* (Why the God-Man?) attempts to show believers that, far from being an unfitting and irrational act, God's incarnation as man was a suitable, even (contingently-speaking) a *necessary* act by which to restore balance to a cosmos afflicted by sin. Anselm's "satisfaction" theory of atonement formalized a tradition with its seeds in the patristic period and set the context for much reflection on the Cross in the Middle Ages and throughout the Reformation period.

Cur Deus Homo and Other Works on Christ [Forthcoming]

This selection focuses on Anselm's treatises, meditations, and prayers that address the Incarnation, the Cross, the Resurrection, and the role of Christ in the spiritual life. Among other works are included his *Epistle on the Incarnation of the Word*, the famous *Cur Deus Homo*, his *Meditation on the Humanity of Christ*, *Meditation on the Passion of Christ*, *Meditation on Human Redemption*, his *On the Dignity and Woe of Humanity's Estate*, and others.

HUGH OF BALMA

On Mystical Theology [Forthcoming]

Translated by Jasper Hopkins.

HUGH OF ST. VICTOR

On the Sacraments of the Christian Faith (De Sacramentis).

Hugh of St. Victor (1096–1141) was a renowned medieval philosopher, theologian, and mystical writer. Because of his great familiarity with the works of St. Augustine, he is sometimes called "the Second Augustine." His work *On the Sacraments of the Christian Faith (De Sacramentis Christianae Fidei)*, composed about 1134, is his masterpiece as well as his most extensive work. It is a veritable *Summa*, a dogmatic synthesis unrivaled in Hugh's time.

By "sacrament," Hugh means not only grace-giving ceremonial signs and actions but also all "mysteries" of the Scriptures, the natural world, and the Church by which God elevates humankind into His life. Hugh's theology draws on Augustine, Gregory the Great, Anselm, and Abelard; and Hugh was also in contact with Bernard of Clairvaux. In the *De Sacramentis*, Hugh separates all of history into the "work of creation" and the "work of restoration." The work of Creation is the triune God's creative activity, the natures of created things, and the original state and destiny of humanity. Hugh's description of the Six Days of Creation is heavily influenced by Augustine's exegesis of Genesis. Divine Wisdom is the archetypal form of creation. The creation of the world in six days is a "sacrament," that is, a spiritually-illuminating mystery for man to contemplate. God's forming order from chaos to make the world is an instruction that guides human beings to rise in love from their own chaos of ignorance to become creatures of Wisdom and therefore beauty. This kind of mystical-ethical interpretation is typical for Hugh, who finds Wisdom's instruction everywhere in creation and in the Scriptures.

The work of Restoration includes the Incarnation of God the Son "with all its sacraments." Here the word "sacrament" refers to the means of salvation that flow from the Incarnation itself, including what are now called the traditional "seven sacraments." Hugh reflects on the mystery of God's freedom—why the Son came into the world even though this was not strictly necessary. Over all, Hugh's work is both an exegetical treatise and a work of spiritual instruction—an example of the inseparability of doctrinal reflection and spiritual growth as understood by this great twelfth-century theologian.

NICHOLAS OF CUSA

Speculative Theology [Forthcoming]
Translated by Jasper Hopkins.

Early Sermons [Forthcoming]
Translated by Jasper Hopkins.

Didactic Sermons [Forthcoming]
Translated by Jasper Hopkins.

Last Sermons: 1457–1463 [Forthcoming]
Translated by Jasper Hopkins.

ST. CATHERINE OF GENOA

The Treatise on Purgatory

St. Catherine of Genoa's treatise gives her teaching on the repentant soul's purification by the fire of God's divine love. A beautiful meditation on both the love of God and Christian perseverance.

THEOLOGY—MODERN AND HISTORICAL*

JEAN DANIÉLOU, S.J.

From Shadows to Reality: Studies in the Biblical Typology of the Fathers

From the first centuries of its existence, the Church has interpreted the historical events recounted in the Old Testament as being "types" or "figures" of the events of the New Testament and of the sacraments instituted by Jesus Christ. Jean Cardinal Daniélou, one of the foremost Catholic scholars of the twentieth century, and a theologian especially concerned with the relationship between history and the Christian revelation, examines in this book the typological interpretation of the Fathers of the Church and their contemporaries during the first three centuries of the Christian era. Among examples he discusses are the crossing of the Jordan by the Israelites as a type of baptism, Rahab as a type of the Church, and the fall of Jericho as a figure of the end of the world. The complex interpretations of Adam, the flood, and the sacrifice and marriage of Isaac are also described in full and commented on. The work is divided into five books entitled "Adam in Paradise," "Noah and the Flood," "The Sacrifice of Isaac," "Moses and the Exodus," and "The Cycle of Joshua". Each book is divided into chapters discussing the various types and the interpretations of Irenaeus, Clement, Gregory of Nyssa and their contemporaries, including Philo.

ÉTIENNE GILSON

The Philosophy of Saint Bonaventure [Forthcoming]

ARTHUR F. KRUEGER

Synthesis of Sacrifice According to Saint Augustine: A Study of the Sacramentality of Sacrifice

Sacrifice is, for Augustine, simply that life of love that is both the perfect worship of God and the core of participation in His divine life. Arthur Krueger's is the only book-length study of this central theme of Augustine's theology. Krueger considers the bishop of Hippo on sacrifice and priesthood, both in the abstract

---

* Alphabetical listing.

and in the concrete sacrifices of the Old and New Testaments. He particularly investigates these themes in their relation to Augustine's notion of sacrament, which Krueger presents as a "binding and synthesizing concept" at the heart of the great theologian's sacrificial teaching.

EMILE MERSCH, S.J.

The Whole Christ

In the Scriptures, both the Savior in heaven, alive without suffering as victor over death, and the suffering Christians dragged to prison by Saul, are depicted as constituting together one man, who is, therefore, as Augustine called it, the "Whole Christ." In that mystic unity, Christ, the Incarnate Word, is the Head. We are the members. As for His sake the members suffer persecution He suffers in them, and on the contrary, as He is the Incarnate God they in turn are divinized through their union with Him. Through this same union they are, as co-members, most intimately united also with each other; and finally through their union with Christ as the second Person of the Triune God they are united with the Godhead, with the Most Blessed Trinity. This, Emile Mersch tells us, is the mountain peak of revealed religion, a teaching that pierces into the heavens far beyond our earthly ken. To seek understanding thereof is to ascend into fuller life with Christ. He unfolds this teaching by recourse to Scripture, to the early Church fathers, and to the great doctors of the Catholic tradition.

The Theology of the Mystical Body

As a sequel or companion to *The Whole Christ*, this doctrinal, speculative study endeavors to investigate how and in what measure all dogmas can be seen as discoursing of the "whole Christ"—to ascertain whether dogma is always and everywhere Christ. Emile Mersch writes: "*We would see Jesus* (John 12:21). We are setting out in search of the truth which Christ has brought. Our aim is to see Christ who is the truth, to see Him in it and it in Him. For the truth is like a great panorama that shows forth what He is, depicting Him in His divinity, in all mankind, and in Himself, and nothing but Him. Is He not light and life?"

JOHN HENRY NEWMAN

Oxford University Sermons

Newman's fifteen sermons on faith and reason, sanctity, and the development of doctrine; preached before the University of Oxford between A.D. 1826 and 1843 by John Henry Newman.

AIDAN NICHOLS, O.P.

Epiphany: A Theological Introduction to Catholicism
(Second Edition)

Now in its second edition. Renowned Dominican theologian Aidan Nichols presents the Catholic faith as a unique source of illumination for the good, the true, and the beautiful. That faith, he argues, is destined to be, and humbly offered as, light for all peoples. It was as "light" that that the babe Jesus Christ was hailed by the aged prophet Symeon when he was presented in the Jerusalem Temple. The Church, too, has applied the term "epiphany"—shining forth—to his first, pre-verbal contact with the Gentiles, as his mother held him out to the "magi," the representatives of the non-Jewish nations. Thus the title of this book.

The book is a theological "Introduction" because one could hardly encapsulate all the illuminating richness Catholic Christianity can offer. Still, Nichols skillfully weaves into his own work a truly-catholic gathering of other great lights from the tradition.

This is a traditional theology and, as Nichols writes, "a consciously non-liberal theology, but not, I think, an illiberal one, for its subject is the generosity of God in his revealing Word and sanctifying Spirit. . . It is not a neutral work, since it aims to arouse a 'Christian maximalism' and the boldness to seek in Catholicism's theological tradition inspiration for present and future."

This second edition corrects some errors in the original.

EDWARD DENNIS O'CONNOR, C.S.C.

The Dogma of the Immaculate Conception [Forthcoming]

A history of the dogma of the immaculate conception, given in a series of scholarly papers published half a century after the dogma's promulgation. Long out of print but useful to the novice and the specialist alike, this volume takes the long view of Church history and tradition, showing a doctrine's development in action.

MATTHIAS SCHEEBEN

Mariology (complete in one volume)

Writing in the nineteenth century, Matthias Scheeben forged a new creative synthesis of the teaching of the Fathers and of the scholastics. Scheeben's work had a decisive influence on later Catholic theologians such as Hans Urs von Balthasar. His primary theme is the nuptial union of God and the created order through the Incarnation, a marriage of heaven and earth that begins in the conception of Christ in the womb of the virgin Mary. Mary, therefore, is the temple in which God and humankind are reconciled. This and all that flows from it and preceded it by way of preparation is the subject-matter of his work Mariology. He draws together the teaching on the Incarnation, on deification, on the Marian dogmas, sacramental theology, and ecclesiology in a truly beautiful work. Originally published in two volumes, the entire work is gathered here in a single volume for the first time. It has been out of print for decades, now made available once more.

THOMAS G. WEINANDY

Jesus the Christ

Father Thomas G. Weinandy—sometime Oxford tutor and later head of the Secretariat of Doctrine for the United States Conference of Catholic Bishops—opens the fascinating world of Christian theology to all readers. In clear language, he begins in Scripture to draw out the plan of salvation, leading the reader through the development of the Church's grappling with the glorious and paradoxical conviction: That no-one less than God Himself has lived nothing less than a human life. From within the life of the Trinity, to the womb of a young woman, to the Cross upon Calvary, the empty tomb, and the ascension into heaven, Fr. Weinandy unfolds the theological consequences of the Incarnation as the central belief of Christian faith in an understandable Catholic introduction to the theological wisdom of the ages. He hopes that it may be of use to every Christian who wants to understand Jesus and His work of Salvation better.

HISTORY AND CONTROVERSIES

DOM JOHN CHAPMAN

Studies on the Early Papacy

Dom John Chapman, fourth abbot of Downside Abbey, was a renowned scholar of early Christianity. On the question of the papacy in the early Church, he eschews selective apologetics in favor of a reasoned study of textual sources in the context of historical events. At these pivotal moments, he argues, the bishop of Rome both took and was expected to take a prominent and indeed authoritative role. This volume offers much substance to those who wish to take up the question of papal prerogatives. Chapman argues in favor of the Catholic claims, but does so with such care as a historian that his work has received high approval even from such an eminence as the famed Anglican historian Henry Chadwick who, in his own book on the history of the early Church, saw fit to recommend Chapman's work to readers interested in the question. There have been many successors to

Chapman but few, if any, have engaged precisely with the matters that he discusses with such detail and clarity. His book, therefore, remains an important voice in the modern conversation.

EMILY HICKEY

Our Catholic Heritage in English Literature of the First Millennium

(Originally entitled *Our Catholic Heritage in Pre-Conquest English Literature*). Ms. Hickey's reflections sweep us into a magical world of ancient epic, poetry, and allegory--by the verses of Cædmon and Bede; in stories of the Phoenix, the Cross, and King Alfred; in old runes and lost loves--in all of which one again and again discovers that Christ has been the narrative's subject all along. She writes: "This little book makes no claim to be a history of pre-Conquest British Literature. It is an attempt to increase Catholics' interest in this part of the 'inheritance of their fathers.' It is not a formal course, but a sort of talk, as it were, about beautiful things said and sung in old days: things which to have learned to love is to have incurred a great and living debt. I have tried to clothe them in the nearest approach I could find to their original speech, with the humblest acknowledgement that nothing matches that speech itself. If this little book in any way fulfils the wishes of those who have asked me for some thoughts on English Literature, I shall be glad indeed."

LITERATURE—GREAT BOOKS AND GOOD BOOKS

Ex Fontibus Company is proud to present reprints of some difficult-to-find literary texts, such as Alexander Pope's translation of the *Iliad* and the *Odyssey*. However, our offerings are not limited to only the great books. We have also chosen to reprint some that are merely "good" books—yet not for that unworthy of our attention. Indeed, in his book *The Death of Christian Culture*, Dr. John Senior (1923–1999), founder of the once famed Integrated Humanities Program at the University of Kansas, offered a list of 1,0000 "good books" that prepare one to read the "great books." Among the "good" he includes such volumes as the Tarzan novels by Edgar Rice Burroughs:

> Taking all that was best in the Greco-Roman world into itself, Western tradition has given us the thousand good books as preparation for the great ones. . . . For us today, the [useful] cutoff point is World War I, before which cars and the electric light had not yet come to dominate our lives and the experience of nature had not been distorted by speed and the destruction of shadows....[These books are] part of the ordinary cultural matter essential for an English-speaking person to grow in.

Ex Fontibus offers the following—both good books and great—as points of entry into that heritage.

ROBERT HUGH BENSON

Lord of the World

> Interesting it must be to all to whom the deepest convictions of a man's heart are of moment. And in the artistic balance and taste of Father Benson's literary power every reader will find delight.
>
> —*The New York Times*

> Mr. Benson sees the world, . . . generations hence, free at last from all minor quarrels, and ranged against itself in two camps, Humanitarianism for those who believe in no divinity but that of man, Catholicism for those who believe in no divinity but that of God.
>
> —*The London Times*

> "The book as art is beautiful, delicately balanced, deeply inspired, intelligently executed.
>
> —*Putnam's*

One of Pope Francis's favorite novels, Benson's 1907 apocalyptic tale of the Antichrist is one of the first modern dystopias. Humanism has eliminated world conflict but practices a subtle barbarism upon the human mind. Religion is either suppressed or ignored. The Catholic Church, confined to ghettos, occupies an increasingly perilous position in the public square. The populace turns toward euthanasia as the solution to bodily pain and spiritual crisis. Meanwhile, a mysterious figure of apparent hope, Julian Felsenburgh, rises to become the head of a single world government. The plot follows a priest, Father Percy Franklin, who finds himself caught up in the final and increasingly open struggle between Antichrist and Christ. *Completely re-typeset with Latin phrases translated in footnotes.*

ROBERT HUGH BENSON

The Dawn of All

Benson's alternative to *Lord of the World*, this later novel vividly imagines the final peace of the world in the triumph of Christianity and the re-establishment of the Church at the center of daily life. A mysterious priest who cannot remember his own name, nor even anything of the past, must make his way as a Monsignor in a world undergoing a dramatic transformation in preparation for the return of Christ. The world itself becomes an image of the priest's soul. Benson himself writes: "In a former book, called *Lord of the World*, I attempted to sketch the kind of developments a hundred years hence which, I thought, might reasonably be expected if the present lines of what is called "modern thought" were only prolonged far enough; and I was informed repeatedly that the effect of the book was exceedingly depressing and discouraging to optimistic Christians. In the present book I am attempting — also in parable form — not in the least to withdraw anything that I said in the former, but to follow up the other lines instead, and to sketch — again in parable — the kind of developments about sixty years hence which, I think, may reasonably be expected should the opposite process begin, and ancient thought (which has stood the test of centuries, and is, in a very remarkable manner, being "rediscovered" by persons even more modern than modernists) be prolonged instead." As always, the story is rendered with suitable dramatic tension and—as is characteristic of Benson—a spiritual conflict of individual souls that matches the large-scale conflicts in the wider world. *Completely re-typeset with Latin phrases translated in footnotes.*

CHARLOTTE BRONTË

Jane Eyre

Jane Eyre (originally *Jane Eyre: An Autobiography*) was published in 1847 under the pen name "Currer Bell." The novel follows the emotions and experiences of its title character, including her growth to adulthood and her love for Mr. Rochester, the byronic master of fictitious Thornfield Hall. In its internalization of the action — the focus is on the gradual unfolding of Jane's moral and spiritual sensibility and all the events are colored by a heightened intensity that was previously the domain of poetry — Jane Eyre revolutionized the art of fiction. Charlotte Brontë has been called the 'first historian of the private consciousness' and the literary ancestor of writers like Joyce and Proust. The novel both reflects and heralds the literary movements of its day, containing elements of social criticism, with a strong sense of morality at its core, an individualistic protagonist, and explorations of class, romantic attraction, religion, and the social position of women.

EDGAR RICE BURROUGHS

The Tarzan Novels, Vol. 1 (Five Novels), Second Edition
The Tarzan novels initiate the young person or the adult into the thrilling and sometimes terrifying world of nature, a world in which one can glimpse something of the eternal Beauty—undimmed even by the savage violence of man and beast. Welcome to the "primeval forest." This omnibus collection presents the first four complete novels of the thrilling adventures of Tarzan of the Apes, along with the collected *Jungle Tales* of Tarzan's early life. Son of an English Lord, raised by the savage apes that killed his father, found again by a civilization that he would never quite come to call his own, he was at home in the jungle in which he was reared. Swinging through the treetops, bane of lions, tamer of elephants, terror of cannibals, finder of lost cities, and beloved of the American woman Jane Porter, this knight of the forest, never trained in chivalry, was known to the outside world as John Clayton, Lord Greystoke—but to himself and the denizens of the jungle in which he grew up, he would be forever Tarzan, King of the Apes. Included in this volume: *Tarzan of the Apes*; *The Return of Tarzan*; *The Son of Tarzan*; *The Beasts of Tarzan*; *Jungle Tales of Tarzan*. A new introduction gives the history of Burroughs' novels and addresses certain points that later writers have rightfully questioned. [This second edition enlarges the previously-cramped font, for a more enjoyable reading experience.]

The Tarzan Novels, Vol. 2 (Four Novels), Second Edition
This omnibus collection, second in a series, presents the next four novels of Edgar Rice Burroughs' enthralling Tarzan of the Apes. In *Tarzan and the Jewels of Opar*, the ape-man engages in a battle of wits and strength with a corrupt Belgian soldier, as they struggle to lay claim to the treasures of a long-lost colony of Atlantis—a struggle made more difficult by Tarzan having lost his memory! In *Tarzan the Untamed*, World War I disrupts the peaceful life of Tarzan with his wife Jane on their East African estate. Taking up once more the way of the savage ape-man, Tarzan vows vengeance against the German soldiers that he believes to have murdered his wife. His adventures take him through and across a deadly desert, fighting enemies all the way. In *Tarzan the Terrible*, Tarzan finds himself in the

mysterious country of Paul-ul-don, an evolutionary island in the African jungle interior. Here dinosaur descendants and intelligent tailed ape-men live amidst fabulous lost cities. In *Tarzan and the Golden Lion*, our hero rebuilds his life in Africa, only to be abducted and held prisoner in the lost city of Opar, whose priestess would have him as her mate. Trekking through the legendary Valley of Diamonds, Tarzan finds himself followed by a mysterious man—who is Tarzan's own double! From his stirring descriptions of the jungle itself to his adept conjuring of scenes of action and mystery, Burroughs does not fail to deliver the thrilling narratives that have made Tarzan so very famous. [This second edition enlarges the previously-cramped font, for a more enjoyable reading experience.]

JAMES FENIMORE COOPER
The Complete Leatherstocking Tales (2 volumes)
Cooper's epic historical romances of frontier and Indian life in the early American days created a unique form of American literature. In two volumes five novels are collected, following the order of the stories' internal chronology (rather than historical publication order).
Volume I—*The Deerslayer*; *The Last of the Mohicans*.
Volume II—*The Pathfinder*; *The Pioneers*; *The Prairie*.

HOMER

The Iliad, translated by Alexander Pope

> The thing that best distinguishes this from all other translations of Homer is that it alone equals the original in its ceaseless pour of verbal music. . . . Pope worked miracles in highlighting the play of vowels through his lines. . . . Every word is weighted, with a pressure of mind behind it. This is a poem you can live your way into, over the years, since it yields more at every encounter.
>
> —"On Reading Pope's Homer," *The New York Times*, 6/1/1997

> Many consider [this translation] the greatest English Iliad, and one of the greatest translations of any work into English. It manages to convey not only the stateliness and grandeur of Homer's lines, but their speed and wit and vividness.
>
> —Daniel Mendelsohn, "Englishing the Iliad: Grading Four Rival Translations," *The New Yorker* Blog, 11/1/2011

> For Homer to take his place among our classics it must be the case that a rendering could exercise the same spell over the collective ear as English-language poets. You could not memorize Fagles, or Lattimore—or Hobbes, a few phrases apart—while Pope, even at his least Homeric, is memorable. . . . Pope is not superseded.
>
> —David Ricks, Kings College, London, *Classics Ireland*, vol. 4, 1997

When Alexander Pope's majestic translation of Homer's Iliad appeared between 1715 and 1720, it was acclaimed by Samuel Johnson as "a performance which no age or nation could hope to equal." Pope himself was only 25 years old. While other translations have since claimed distinction in this or that respect, Pope's translation remains unrivaled in its melodious beauty. This is the Iliad that has formed generations of British and American culture through a beauteous poetics that lends itself to easy recollection. With a clean and crisp text illustrated by the inimitable line drawings of Flaxman, this edition finally gives to audiences a fitting rendering of this monument of English verse which captures uniquely the song of Homer himself.

The Odyssey, translated by Alexander Pope

The tale of Odysseus's return from the war at Troy, seeking Ithaca his home and Penelope his wife. Along the way he encounters the murderous Cyclops, the treacherous Circe, and the nymphs, gods, and goddesses who variously assist and impede his homeward journey. Many are his travails and dramatic his final homecoming wherein he joins battle with Penelope's erstwhile suitors. As with the Iliad, Pope, who had two collaborators on this project, renders Homer into a muscular and euphonious English poetry worthy of reading aloud. This volume is likewise illustrated by Flaxman.

J.-K. HUYSMANS
The Durtal Trilogy

Joris-Karl Huysmans's trilogy of novels charting the religious and life journey of Monsieur Durtal, who once investigated a satanic order in decadent late nineteenth century Paris (*Lá-bas*, "The Depths" or "The Damned"), and now, turning toward God and becoming a Catholic, undertakes a mystical journey of sorts through a monastery (*En Route*; "On the Way"), the cathedral of Chartres (*La Cathédrale*, "The Cathedral"), and finally enters life as a Benedictine oblate (*L'Oblat*, "The Oblate"). This trilogy is intensely autobiographical, following the pattern of Huysmans's own life. Huysmans was an art critic as well as a novelist and thus the exquisitely constructed *Cathedral* has been used by generations of visitors as a guidebook to Chartres Cathedral. This edition offers the flowing translations that brought the original to an English-speaking audience, but with footnoted annotations explaining many of the erudite Huysmans's more obscure references to the artists, saints, and plant-life that populate the unfolding epic of Durtal's journey. Huysmans and his character Durtal are central to French author Michel Houellebecq's best-selling and controversial novel *Submission* (2015).

JOHN HENRY NEWMAN
Callista: A Tale of the Third Century

Callista, a young and beautiful Greek girl, has just arrived with her brother in North African Carthage. Though she is a gifted young woman, she is unhappy with her life. Wooed by a troubled and lovesick young man named Agellius, Callista is drawn into his own struggle between a newfound Christian faith and the traditional pagan beliefs of his mother, a witch. After a terrible plague of locusts, a popular rage breaks out into persecution against the Christians and both Agellius and Callista must face for themselves the question of what indeed is the truth. Written by Newman after his reception into the Catholic Church, this novel of the early Church is surely a bright light in a flourishing nineteenth century genre that produced few classics and many mediocrities. Indeed, Charles Kingsley, whose later attacks prompted Newman's own *Apologia Pro Vita Sua*, had essayed an earlier effort at early Church fiction with the novel *Hypatia*. To Kingley's dismay, Newman's *Callista* had been received as the better work. *Callista* is rich in prose and vivid in its imagining of Christian life in the early Church.